Orname

1971 – 2021

Chris Fogg is a creative producer, writer, director and dramaturg, who has written and directed for the theatre for many years, as well as collaborating artistically with choreographers and contemporary dance companies.

Ornaments of Grace is a chronicle of twelve novels. *A Crown of Glory* is the last in the sequence.

He has previously written more than thirty works for the stage as well as four collections of poems, stories and essays. These are: *Special Relationships, Northern Songs, Painting by Numbers* and *Dawn Chorus* (with woodcut illustrations by Chris Waters), all published by Mudlark Press.

Several of Chris's poems have appeared in International Psychoanalysis (IP), a US online journal, as well as in *Climate of Opinion*, a selection of verse in response to the work of Sigmund Freud edited by Irene Willis, and *What They Bring: The Poetry of Migration & Immigration*, co-edited by Irene Willis and Jim Haba, each published by IP, in 2017 and 2020.

Ornaments of Grace

(or *Unhistoric Acts*)

12

Moth

Vol. 2: A Crown of Glory

by

Chris Fogg

flaxbooks

First published 2021
© Chris Fogg 2021

Chris Fogg has asserted his rights under Copyright Designs & Patents Act 1988 to be identified as the author of this book

ISBN Number: 9798736282630

Cover and design by: Kama Glover

Cover Image: The Romans Building a Fort at Mancenion, one of the Manchester Murals by Ford Madox Brown, reprinted by kind permission of Manchester Libraries, Information & Archives.

This book is sold subject to the condition that it shall not, by way of trade or otherwise be lent, resold, hired out, or otherwise circulated without the publisher's prior consent in any form of binding or cover other than that in which it is published and without a similar condition, including this condition, being imposed upon the subsequent purchaser.

Printed by Amazon

Although some of the people featured in this book are real, and several of the events depicted actually happened, *Ornaments of Grace* remains a work of fiction. Some dates and names may have been changed.

For Amanda and Tim

dedicated to the memory

of my parents and grandparents

Ornaments of Grace (*or Unhistoric Acts*) is a sequence of twelve novels set in Manchester between 1761 and 2021. Collectively they tell the story of a city in four elements.

A Crown of Glory is the final book in the sequence.

The full list of titles is:

1. Pomona (Water)

2. Tulip (Earth)
    Vol 1: Enclave
    Vol 2: Nymphs & Shepherds
    Vol 3: The Spindle Tree
    Vol 4: Return

3. Laurel (Air)
    Vol 1: Kettle
    Vol 2: Victor
    Vol 3: Victrix
    part 1: A Grain of Mustard Seed
    part 2: The Waxing of a Great Tree
    part 3: All the Fowls of the Air

4. Moth (Fire)
    Vol 1: The Principal Thing
    Vol 2: A Crown of Glory

Each book can be read independently or as part of the sequence.

"It's always too soon to go home. And it's always too soon to calculate effect... Cause-and-effect assumes that history marches forward, but history is not an army. It is a crab scuttling sideways, a drip of soft water wearing away stone, an earthquake breaking centuries of tension."

                        Rebecca Solnit: Hope in the Dark
                        (*Untold Histories, Wild Possibilities*)

Contents

"The peppered moth story is easy to understand, because it involves things that we are familiar with: vision and predation and birds and moths and pollution and camouflage and lunch and death. That is why the anti-evolution lobby attacks the peppered moth story. They are frightened that too many people will be able to understand. If the rise and fall of the peppered moth is one of the most visually impacting and easily understood examples of Darwinian theory in action, it should be taught. After all, it provides the proof of evolution."

Mike Majerus: Professor of Evolution, Cambridge University

ONE

Larvae (p17)

Chapter 1: 2013
Day 1	19
Day 2	75
Day 3	112
Day 4	131

Chapter 2: 2017
Day 1401	159
Day 1402	172
Day 1403	188
Day 1404	212
Day 1410	213
Day 1417	226

Chapter 3: 2019
Day 2251	230
Day 2252	235
Day 2253	249
Day 2260	263

TWO

Pupae (p265)

Chapter 4: 1986	267
Chapter 5: 1973	284
Chapter 6: 1971	302
Chapter 7: 1981	390
Chapter 8: 1983	410
Chapter 9: 1986	452

THREE

Imagines (p475)

Chapter 10: 2017
　　Day 1, Day 2, Day 8, Day 4, Day 8
　　Day 1 minus 7, Days 8/1/8/1/8, Day 11, Day 14　　475

Chapter 11: 2020 – 2011 – 2015 – 2020
　　　　1995 – 1996 – 2020　　525

Chapter 12: 2021　　581
Epilogue　　682

Postscript　　690
The Story of a Coin　　694

Life Cycle of the Manchester Moth	*15*
Moss Side: 2nd night of the riots, 1981	*18*
Map of Chat Moss	*266*
Adshead's Map of River Medlock, circa 1850	*476*
Languages Spoken in Manchester	*698*
Other Manchesters	*702*
Illustrated Variants of the Manchester Moth	*704*
Current Map of Greater Manchester	*705*
Dramatis Personae	*706*
Acknowledgements	*725*
Biography	*728*

Ornaments of Grace

"Wisdom is the principal thing. Therefore get wisdom and within all thy getting get understanding. Exalt her and she shall promote thee. She shall bring thee to honour when thou dost embrace her. She shall give to thine head an ornament of grace. A crown of glory shall she deliver to thee."

Proverbs: 4, verses 7 – 9

written around the domed ceiling of the Great Hall Reading Room
Central Reference Library, St Peter's Square, Manchester

"Fecisti patriam diversis de gentibus unam..."
"From differing peoples you have made one homeland..."

Rutilius Claudius Namatianus:
De Redito Suo, verse 63

"To be hopeful in bad times is not just foolishly romantic. It is based on the fact that human history is a history not only of cruelty, but also of compassion, sacrifice, courage, kindness. What we choose to emphasise in this complex history will determine our lives. If we see only the worst, it destroys our capacity to do something. If we remember those times and places—and there are so many—where people have behaved magnificently, this gives us the energy to act, and at least the possibility of sending this spinning top of a world in a different direction. And if we do act, in however small a way, we don't have to wait for some grand utopian future. The future is an infinite succession of presents, and to live now as we think human beings should live, in defiance of all that is bad around us, is itself a marvellous victory."

Howard Zinn: A Power Governments Cannot Suppress

Moth (ii)

*"Between our birth and death we may touch understanding,
As a moth brushes a window with its wing ..."*

> Christopher Fry: The Boy with a Cart

"The moth settled onto the curtain and sat still. It was an astonishing creature. So much detail goes unnoticed in the world...."

> Barbara Kingsolver: The Prodigal Summer

*"The desire of the moth for the star
Of the night for the morrow
The devotion to something afar
From the sphere of our sorrow..."*

> Percy Bysshe Shelley: One Word Is Too Often Profaned

*"Only a dark cocoon before I get my gorgeous wings
And fly away..."*

> Joni Mitchell: The Last Time I Saw Richard

Fire (ii)

*"There's a fire down below, fire down below
Fire in the heaven above me..."*

> Graham Nash

"It is not light that we need, but fire; it is not the gentle shower, but thunder. We need the storm, the whirlwind, and the earthquake. ..."

> Frederick Douglas: Address to the Ladies' Anti-Slavery Society
> Rochester, New York

"Set your life on fire. Seek those who fan your flames ..."

> Rumi

A Brief Introduction to the Life Cycle of the Manchester Moth

The peppered moth, or *biston betularia*, is a temperate, mostly night-flying species, widely distributed across the world. Evolutionary polymorphism has produced variant phenotypes, more commonly called *morphs*. In Britain there are three such morphs of the peppered moth: the white morph – *typica*; the black – *carbonaria*, and the intermediate – *medionigra*.

The evolution of the peppered moth over the last two hundred years has been studied in detail. At the start of this period, the vast majority of peppered moths had light-coloured wing patterns, which effectively camouflaged them against the light-coloured trees and lichens upon which they rested. However, due to widespread pollution during the Industrial Revolution in England, many of the lichens died out, and the trees which peppered moths rested on became blackened by soot, causing most of the light-coloured moths, or *typica*, to die off due to predation. At the same time, the dark-coloured, or melanic, moths, *carbonaria*, flourished because they could hide on the darkened trees. This led to the black peppered moth being given the name of the *Manchester Moth*.

The improved environmental measures introduced into cities, including Manchester, have resulted in a rise in the number of *medionigra* variants, with a gradual return of the *typica*. Examples of all three are now quite common, with inter-breeding occurring successfully between each.

The peppered moth is *univoltine*. That is to say, it has just one generation per year, one chance to make sure the species survives.

The lepidopteran life cycle consists of four stages: *ova*, the eggs; *larvae*, the caterpillars; *pupae*, the cocoons, which over-winter in the soil, and *imagines*, the adult moths.

ONE

Larvae

The larvae of the moth are fitted with two sharp mouth parts called mandibles. Working them from side to side they use these to eat their way through the membranous lining of the egg sac. Immediately after hatching, the caterpillars separate from one another, for resources are scarce, and each must consume what they can in as short a time as possible.

They move rapidly from one place to another, hiding among the leaves and branches of trees. They are instinctive twig mimics, varying their colour to match their surroundings, though sometimes they are known to announce their presence more boldly.

Not all will survive…

Moss Side Riots, 1981

1

2013

Day 1

Jenna looks out of the window of the Airbus A340 that is taking her from Dubai to Sana'a, the capital city of Yemen. It has just commenced its long, slow descent over the Rub al Khali, the empty quarter of the Saudi desert, before crossing the border. Below her to the right she can clearly see the long chain of the Asir, Sarawat and Hejaz mountains, which stretch along the eastern edge of the Red Sea. They take her breath away. Not simply because of their majestic beauty, but because she has seen them before. The shock of recognition is overwhelming, all the more so because she has never been to this part of the world in her life, and yet the outline of the mountains is as familiar to her as the pattern on the palm of her hand. She has known it for as long as she can remember.

Her father.

Sol.

He came here more than half a century ago, while he was barely more than a boy, on National Service. He drew these mountains – after whom his father was named – and sent them back to his grandfather, Yasser, who had been born here, but who later lived (and died) in Patricroft, beside the Ship Canal he had helped to build. He pinned them up in the front room, above the fireplace, where they have remained ever since, where Jenna looked at them every day as a child, to the point where she no longer saw them. They became just another part of the furniture, along with the curtains and the sofa and the armchair and the sideboard, the backdrop to her growing up, constant, unchanging, so that, in the end, she could not wait to get out of it, to leave it as quickly as she could.

And yet...

It isn't easy to cast aside an entire home. It endures. Like the colour of her skin. So that now, as she flies over the land of her ancestors, she must, she realises, look just like any other Yemeni, returning after a business trip abroad perhaps, with a husband to meet her at the airport.

She smiles.

There *will* be someone to meet her. But not her husband. Jenna has no husband. She never has had. Nor does she imagine she ever will. She turned fifty earlier this year, a landmark she finds she is entirely comfortable with. She has a successful career, with a portfolio of high profile clients. She and her daughter, who is shortly to begin a degree in Fine Art, see eye to eye on most things. She has a relationship – with Séydou, French Senegalese and several years younger than she is, who will be meeting her when she lands – which suits both of them very well, and the situation with her father is currently in a good place too. This has not always been the case with any of these aspects of her life, and never before with all of them simultaneously. Fingers crossed. She won't be counting any chickens just yet. It does not do to look too far ahead. Enjoy the good times while they last – that has always been her motto. It is something she has had to learn the hard way.

Right now she wants to believe that things between herself and her father are finally fixed for good. She fervently hopes so. Her mother, Nadia, has told her, privately, that he is not well, and Jenna can see this for herself. His skin is sallow, his forehead permanently beaded with drops of perspiration, and he has that dreadful, racking cough. "He's been having tests," Nadia tells her, when she's certain Sol can't hear her. "We're waiting on results…"

She'd phoned her the previous evening. Jenna had presumed it was about what the doctors had said, and so she braced herself, but it wasn't.

"I'm just checking you're all set for tomorrow?"

"Yes," Jenna had said distractedly. "My flight leaves from Manchester at some ungodly hour."

"Your flight?"

"Yes. Didn't I tell you?"

Evidently she had not. Jenna wonders what her mother had meant therefore by asking her about tomorrow.

"The Exhibition," says Nadia pointedly.

Jenna smacks her forehead with the flat of her hand. Shit. She had forgotten all about it.

"At Manchester Metropolitan? Don't say you can't come? The George Wright retrospective? They've asked to borrow his photographs of your father's mural. It will be the first time anyone will have seen it outside of the family since he painted it all those years ago. It means a great deal to Sol. He particularly wanted you to be there. You helped him finish it after all…"

Jenna holds the phone to her chest and closes her eyes, guiltily blinking back the tears. Shit, shit, shit, shit, shit…

She is fifteen. It's a freezing cold Sunday morning. She stands shivering in the wasteland of the former Pomona Docks on Trafford Park. The whole family have gathered there for 'the grand unveiling'. It's all anyone has been able to talk about for weeks. Jenna can't see what all the fuss is about, why it's such a big deal. It's only a mural. It's all going to be torn down by the developers in a matter of weeks. She can't see the point of it. All she knows for certain is that it has obsessed her father for the past ten years. Ten years! Every evening and every weekend, squirreled away in some basement boiler room with George at *The Mechanics' Institute* as he puts it all together. She's hardly seen him during all that time. Not that that has bothered her too much. She didn't see him at all until she was nearly five. While he'd been in prison. Which nobody ever talks about.

She shoves her hands deep into her pockets and furiously turns away, while George, and then her father, make stupid speeches. A ship's siren from the nearby canal wails mournfully through the mist that rises up from the scum-encrusted surface. She wonders where it has come from, where it might go next, and whether it might take her with it. A wedge of white birds that she thinks might be egrets skewer through the mist. Their dry nasal croak sounds like the back of her own throat after a hangover.

Then the tarpaulin is pulled back to reveal the completed mural. It's much bigger than Jenna had expected, not that she'd thought about it much, more than fifty yards long, half a football pitch. Everyone exclaims with amazement. They make a bee-line straight for it, poring over every last detail. But Jenna hangs back. There's no rush. She'll take a closer look later. Maybe. Maybe not. Right now, though, she has to admit that the scale of it is impressive. From a distance it appears to resemble nothing less than the history of the world, a teeming throng of people, permanently on the move, a mass migration, not unlike the battery of birds she has just seen, with all of them headed here, to this city, this corner of it, this very spot where she herself now stands, at the centre of something much bigger than she is, yet somehow she is a part of it. It's hard to connect all that with her father, with something he has created, out of nothing seemingly, that she has grown up with all these years, yet kept herself separate from.

But now he is approaching her. He is standing beside her. He is opening his mouth. The words float out of his mouth like paper cut-outs. He takes her by the hand and leads her towards the bottom right hand corner of the mural, away from everyone else. He points to a small child, who is offering something to a figure that might represent Sol himself, carrying a rucksack and stepping out of a front door, onto a quiet street, with a view of the Barton Aqueduct in the distance.

"Do you recognise this?" he asks her.

She nods. "There's something missing."

"I know," he says. "You gave it to me. But I lost it, remember?"

Despite herself, Jenna smiles.

"But I think I've found it now."

"What do you mean?"

"Here." And he hands her a small paint brush. "Fill it in for me."

Jenna's face breaks into the broadest of grins. "Really?"

"Really."

She frowns in concentration, and, with the brush her father has handed to her, paints in the missing black umbrella…

She frowns again now, remembering.

She hears her mother speaking far away down the line on the phone, which Jenna is still holding to her chest.

"What was that?" she says.

"You mentioned a flight," says Nadia. "Where are you going?"

"Yemen," says Jenna.

She can hear the gasp from her mother. Then a long silence.

"What shall I tell him?" she says eventually. "Your father."

"Nothing," says Jenna. "I'll tell him myself."

"Make sure that you do."

"I will."

"Really?"

"Yes."

"Promise?"

"Promise."

She hears another long-drawn-out sigh empty down the phone.

"I've got to go now, Ma. Or I'll be late. Bye."

She takes a deep breath. Then she taps out a rapid text.

"Hi, Dad. Good luck with the Exhibition. Will definitely catch it when I get back. xxx"

The next day, while waiting to board the flight from Dubai to Sana'a, on the last leg of what has already been a mammoth journey, an angry text arrives from her daughter. Molly.

"Why didn't you tell me you were going to Yemen? Didn't it occur to you that I might want to know? That I might be interested? That I might have wanted to come with you? In case you're wondering, Granddad's mural drew big crowds at the Exhibition with people poring over every last detail – including the little girl handing him the umbrella – which I only found out today was actually painted by you!!! Naturally I was the last to know!!! Honestly, Mum, what is it with you…? Off to see The Stone Roses now at Heaton Park with some new friends I've made at Uni. More your era than mine. No doubt you saw them at *The Haçienda*? Call me when you get back. I want to know all about the land of my ancestors."

Jenna smiles when she reads this. She's secretly delighted that Molly is so pissed off with her. That the fruit has not landed too far from the tree.

"Yes I did see The Stone Roses at *The Haçienda*. 1985, I think. Can't really remember. Either *I* was too much off my face, or *they* were. Probably both. Have fun. Will call when I get back…"

Three hours later she is gazing from the window of her plane down towards the Hejaz Mountains. The sight of them continues to astonish her. Not so much the way they rise up so dramatically out of the desert, though that is spectacular enough, but in the way her father managed to capture them so perfectly in just a few lines, hastily sketched from the back of an army jeep. It was nothing short of miraculous really, especially considering that he was always at risk of being caught up in an ambush by one of the various rebel factions operating out of the desert. Like the one which caused him to lose two of his fingers.

He still draws now. More so since he retired – laid off early when Turners Asbestos on Trafford Park went into administration – and she's seen him nursing his wounded hand from time to time, as if he still experiences pain in his fingers, even though they are no longer there. Like a phantom memory. These days he mostly sketches Nadia. In the evenings after she's finished her chores. He never tires of drawing her. When Jenna asks him why, he tells her quite simply that he can always see something new, something he hasn't quite caught yet. He smiles when he says this. "I don't suppose I ever will," he says, before another bout of coughing overtakes him.

Jenna presumes that it is from Sol that Molly has inherited her own talent at drawing. He has always been so patient with her, even when she was little. Far more than she, Jenna, ever was.

She asked him once, when she was a teenager and angry all the time, if he still bore a grudge towards the people responsible for the explosion which cost him his fingers.

"No," he told her, "I never did. They were just boys. Not as old as you are. All they wanted was their independence, a land they could call home."

It's what they still want today. That's partly why Jenna is making this trip. Since taking up her current position with the Manchester headquarters of the Refugee Council, she's been monitoring the situation in Yemen closely. It's a powder keg that could ignite at any moment. That's what Séydou has told her, and he should know. He is much closer to the situation than she is. He works for *Médecins Sans Frontières*. He has arranged for her to visit several key locations and organised her flight from London with a lay-over at Dubai. There is civil unrest growing at an alarming rate in the area surrounding Sana'a. Molly has decided she needs to take a look at how things are for herself, on the ground, which is gradually looming closer as the plane continues its descent. She can see the mountains much closer now. This ancestral homeland that Molly has asked her to tell her about...

She has a childhood memory, of creeping downstairs late at night, when she is meant to be asleep, drawn by a piece of music. It's the night of her mother's fortieth birthday. She peeps through the railings of the banister and sees her father go quietly towards the record player in the corner of the living room. First he places his hands across her mother's eyes, requesting her not to look. "Make a wish," he says. Then he takes from the rack a record he has inserted while Nadia isn't looking, removes it from its sleeve, and places it on the turntable. Finally he turns back towards her as it begins to play.

"Remember this?" he says.

And out of the silence Nadia hears again, for the first time in over twenty years, the crackling sound of Johnny Ray, played as a request for her from Sol on the radio, on *Two Way Family Favourites*, for when she was eighteen, while he was away in Aden...

"What did you wish for?" he whispers into her ear.

Nadia smiles. "This," she says, and kisses him.

Jenna watches her parents dance slow and close. Although she is trying hard not to make a sound, so that they won't know she's there, a part of her wants them to hear her, to see her looking at them from the stairs, and then invite her over to dance with them. She hears the song once more, drifting down the years.

'Look homeward, Angel
Tell me what you see
Do the folks I used to know
Remember me...?'

But before she can continue to imagine this, she is interrupted by an announcement from the Captain.

"We are just being informed that there is some kind of trouble at Sana'a Airport, and so we are being advised to divert to Aden further south. There is nothing to worry about, I can assure you, but for your safety we would advise you to please fasten your seat belts. We should reach our new destination in just under fifty minutes' time. Please accept our sincere apologies for the disruption to your journey. There will be further information upon our arrival in Aden on how you may be able to make any necessary onward journeys."

For 'trouble', thinks Jenna, read 'rebel activity'.

Damn. How will she get from Aden to Sana'a? Will Séydou still be there to meet her?

Her thoughts turn back to her father, who must have had to face far greater uncertainty on a daily basis. This is a minor inconvenience by comparison. The plane banks steeply to the left and begins to climb once more, leaving the Hejaz Mountains behind her.

A message pings in to her phone. It's Séydou.

> Just heard the news. When you get to Aden go to Hotel Al Amer. I'll meet you there as soon as I can.

She looks down at his photo on her phone and smiles. He has a look of Lance. All of her boyfriends have a look of Lance...

She first meets Lance when she's just left school. She has 'A's in all her exams, her place at Manchester to study Politics is confirmed. All she needs now is a place to live...

"You've got a place to live," says Nadia. "*This* place."

"No way, Ma." She breezily slams the front door behind her as she runs off to catch the first of the three buses she needs to get her to the campus.

Nadia sighs heavily.

"Let her go," says a voice from behind her. It is Esther, Nadia's mother-in-law, known to all now as Ishtar. As she has been for twenty years. Ever since Yasser died and she converted fully to Islam. "She'll only resent you if you make her stay."

"I suppose."

"Believe me. I know what I'm talking about. I speak from experience."

Nadia knows she is referring to the rift that grew between her and Sol, a rift that was only healed when he recreated his own father's journey – Jaz, named for the Hejaz Mountains, which Jenna flies over now – to reclaim a lost heritage.

"I know you're right," says Nadia. "But I worry, that's all."

"Of course you do," says Ishtar. "That is a mother's lot. But we have to let our children make their own mistakes, and hope they learn from them." She looks at Nadia meaningfully. "Like Sol had to."

Nadia nods. "It's just that Jenna is so…"

"Impatient?"

Nadia smiles. "I was going to say 'wilful'."

"She knows her own mind, that's for sure. She always has done. But she's always managed to land on her feet."

"So far."

"She's a survivor. You'll see…"

A dozen years later, when Jenna reveals that she is pregnant and that Lance is the father of the yet-to-be-born child, she insists that everyone comes together to discuss the situation like grown-ups.

"It's not as if as I'm a kid any more," she says. "I'm thirty now." She looks from one to the other of those gathered in her mid-terraced house on Slate Lane, overlooking the Ashton

Canal, with the tow-path running just outside the back yard, close by Audenshaw Bridge, not far from the Moravian Settlement in nearby Fairfield. She'd purchased it when she got her job with the northern branch of the Institute for Public Policy & Research, less than a year ago, when she'd returned from one of her stints of working in London. "I'm selling out," she'd gleefully reported at the time. "First foot on the property ladder. I'm New Labour now," she'd joked.

They're all of them there, all that can be – Sol and Nadia, Lance and his mother Anita, and Jenna. Nadia and Anita greet each other like sisters-in-arms, which in a way they are, have always been. They had met while working as shop-window dressers at Kendal Milne Department Store in the run-up to Christmas back in 1964. Lance was only four at the time, and Jenna just one. Two lone mothers, each with an absent husband, struggling to make ends meet. They've kept in touch sporadically ever since, their paths occasionally intersecting, Nadia working in Adult Literacy, Anita in Citizens Advice, each becoming more prominent as the years rolled by, Nadia taking an increasingly city-wide role, Anita becoming a linchpin of the Moss Side community. They would at times refer clients between each other. When Lance and Jenna first started seeing each other, back in the eighties, Nadia and Anita shared a smile between them. "Who would've thought it...?" they joked. "We could never have imagined..." "Do you remember Miss Gresty...? Those rats..." "It's a small world..." But they're neither of them smiling now. Not in the face of Jenna's steely resolve.

She and Lance had got back together shortly after she'd moved into Slate Lane. Not that they'd ever really *been* together. Jenna had never considered herself half of a couple. She still doesn't. But they'd never quite been apart, either. Somehow they always seemed to drift back towards each other. Like an itch that they needed to scratch...

Jenna has a list of approved bed-sits from the University's Accommodation Officer. "There are still a few places available in the Halls of Residence," she'd been told. "Owens, Dalton-Ellis, Ashburne…" But she doesn't fancy any of those. What she wants is something grittier, more real, more independent. The Accommodation Officer sighs and hands her a list of approved digs.

Jenna heads off down Moss Lane East, just the other side of Whitworth Park, beyond the Student Union building. She reaches Number 242, where the first address on her list is situated, and rings the bell. While she waits, she scans through the details once more. One room, shared bath and kitchen. Not ideal, but cheap, which is her main criterion.

When nobody answers, she rings the bell a second time. Two doors down – at 246 – she sees a group of who she assumes to be students sitting on the steps, smoking, drinking beer, listening to music. This looks more like it, she decides, and heads towards them. One of them, a tall young man deliciously easy in his body, calls out to her.

"Ain't nobody dere, man. Never is durin' di day. Cum on over."

His smile is irresistible.

"Wah gwaan?" he drawls.

"Mi de yah," she replies, grinning.

How goes it?

I'm fine.

He whoops with delight, flicks his fingers, takes her through an elaborate, ritualised high-five, which she matches move for move.

"Wah yuh name, gyal?" he asks.

Jenna looks him squarely in the face, which bears an undeniably roguish charm. His eyes glow mischievously. Very well, she thinks. Two can play at this game.

"My name is a bird that's always in flight," she says. "See if you can catch it aright."

"Now yuh talkin'," he says, flicking his fingers once more, his whole body dancing with pleasure. "Where mi cum from, wi 'ave all kinda exotic birds."

"Where's that then?"

"Di Leeward Isles. St Kitts & Nevis."

"Don't listen to him," pipes a voice from behind them. A girl with a striped Mohican is sitting on the step, rolling a cigarette. "He grew up just a couple of streets from here, round the corner on Upper Lloyd Street."

"Mi talkin' 'bout mi roots, gyal. Mi sweet Carib grackle, mi black-faced grassquit..." He slowly circles around Jenna, throwing out more and more bird names as he does so. "Mi brown trembler... Mi Antillean euphonia... Mi purple-throated Carib... Mi pearly-eyed elaenia... Mi scaly-breasted thrasher..."

The girl with the Mohican striped hair rams the cigarette she's been rolling into his mouth to shut him up. But he's unstoppable.

"Mi white-eyed golden oriole... Mi New World warbler... Mi northern water thrush..."

"OK," says Jenna at last. "Northern water thrush – *that* I can live with..."

There is much laughter all round as Jenna is introduced to the rest of the crew who live at number 246...

But there's no laughter twelve years later in the house on Slate Lane. The sparkle has gone from Lance's eyes. This is no longer a game they're playing. This is for real.

"I've made up my mind," says Jenna. "I intend to keep the baby, but I don't want you to feel you have to marry me, Lance. In fact, if you asked me, I'd say no. I'm not the marrying type. And nor are you. Commitment's never been your strong point, so I don't expect anything from you at all by way of child support, or shared custody, or even basic parenting. I don't want to live with you. We tried that once before. It didn't work back then, and it wouldn't work right now. Especially with a baby. We both know that we'd be climbing the walls and throwing things at each other before you could say…"

"Mi New World warbler," he says, finishing the sentence for her, spooling back the years, but Jenna is not to be swayed.

"You can see her after she's born as often or as little as you like. Just don't make any promises you can't keep, that's all I ask…"

"It a girl den?"

"Yes. It's a girl."

They hold each other's gaze a long time, both of them not so much remembering, as imagining future scenarios…

He comes bearing presents. Balloons and bubbles, which dance around the living room. Whenever he comes he brings colour and laughter along with him. Molly adores him. He lifts her high into the air, above his head, circling her round and round, until she is giddy with happiness.

Jenna knows the feeling well.

But then he will disappear for months at a time. Molly comes to understand that her father is not a man she can rely on. She bears him no malice for this. She learns to accept that it is better to take him on his own terms, to enjoy his increasingly infrequent and all-too-brief visits, when he will descend upon her like Dionysus from Olympus, his words and promises tumbling from his lips like grapes, then evaporating into the air like the bubbles he still brings with him each time he comes, before leaving her again with the tattered shreds of a burst balloon.

The last time she sees him is when she is sixteen and about to take her GCSEs. He arrives with plane tickets for St Kitts & Nevis, where mostly he lives these days. "Mi run into a bit o' luck," he tells her. He's in a party mood. He wants to celebrate. Then he wants to take her back to show her "weh yuh cum from, gyal, weh yuh roots are." The old familiar spiel.

But Molly is firm. She is not so easily beguiled by his honeyed tongue as her mother was.

"No," she says, putting her hands on her hips. "I've got exams coming up."

"Yuh can do dem any time, gyal," he says.

But she is not to be persuaded. "No," she says again, and Lance can see in her eyes that her mind is made up, so he doesn't persist.

"Yuh got yuh madda's strent, gyal," he says admiringly.

She doesn't see him again for years. Though occasionally postcards will arrive for her, wishing her 'Happy Birthday', even if the date doesn't coincide, depicting different beauty spots. Palmetto Point. Gingerland. St Mary Cayon. St John Figtree. He appears to spend his time working in festivals around the two islands. Green Valley. Easterama. Carnival and Capisterre. What he does exactly at these festivals is less clear. A bit of this, a bit of that. "He deals," says Jenna to Molly, in a voice that brooks no disagreement.

Molly religiously keeps all of Lance's photographs in a special folder, which she decorates with drawings of the brown pelican, the islands' national bird, but, as the months go by and fewer and fewer postcards arrive, she rarely looks at them. Though when she does, it is without any bitterness or regret.

She suspects that her father, like the brown pelican she has sketched, is a survivor, breeding successfully all along the Atlantic sea board, nesting in secluded colonies, living quite happily on a plentiful diet of amphibians and crustaceans. In spite of its unprepossessing name, the bird has a rather rakish plumage of olive, ochre, yellow and maroon...

Jenna and Lance both smile, each of them imagining their

yet-to-be-born, independent-minded daughter neatly closing her folder of postcards and sketches...

Anita and Nadia exchange an anxious look between them. Both of them are thinking how different it was for them when they each found out they were pregnant before they were married, with men neither of whom were ready to settle down.

Leroy never was. 'Beauregard' was the perfect name for him, for he regarded himself more finely than anyone else. Anita hasn't seen or heard from him in years. He could be dead for all she knows. But when he played that trumpet of his, and when he looked at her in a certain way, she could never resist him, even though she knew she should. She glances across to Lance. He is nervously chewing his bottom lip, reminding her of how he used to be sometimes as a child if she ever caught him doing something he knew he shouldn't. But such expressions would never last for long. He would turn that smile he had inherited from his father upon her, trusting that she wouldn't stay angry with him for long. And she never did. Like father, like son. Now he tries that same smile on Jenna.

"Mi sweet Carib grackle," he croons, "Mi sure wi can work sumtin' out."

"No," says Jenna decisively. "Those are my terms. Take them or leave them."

Nadia watches her daughter, hardly able to breathe. She reminds her so much of how she had had to be with Sol when he was sent to prison, when Jenna was just a few weeks old. She looks across to him now – what must *he* be making of all this? – and smiles. He smiles thinly back. At least Sol was able to reflect on what he had done and learn to change. Since when he has really tried his best. Particularly with Jenna, who has still not quite forgiven him for not being around until she was five, and he returned to their house a stranger, a shadow, for ever apologising, for ever trying to make it up. Perhaps this will be his second chance? It's all very well for Jenna to proclaim that she doesn't need Lance to support her, doesn't *want* him to, in fact, but a child needs a father, and Jenna will find out soon enough that it isn't easy to bring up a baby by herself. Anita and Nadia both knew this, but at least they had help from older women – Merle and Ishtar. Perhaps Jenna will allow Sol a foothold back into her life by letting him have a role to play in helping her to bring up his granddaughter...

But the twinkle in Lance's eye a dozen years before, on that hot afternoon in the summer of 1981, when Jenna first challenges him to 'catch her name aright', gives no clue as to where that particular bird in flight will finally come home to roost...

The Airbus A340 lands without further incident at Aden. The check-in is surprisingly smooth. She has letters of introduction from both the Refugee Council and *Médecins Sans Frontières*, together with approval from the Yemeni Government for her to travel along the corridor between Sana'a and Aden, except that now she will be travelling along this in the opposite direction from which she had originally planned.

Once through Customs she spots a sign with her name on it. Holding it up is a young woman who looks around the same age as her daughter. In fact she reminds her of Molly in other ways too. The way she dresses. That contemporary mix of western and Arabic. She wears a knee-length bottle-green tunic over denim jeans, hidden beneath a quilted parka, her head covered by a white *qurqash*. Her name is Zafirah. "Séydou has been in contact," she says. "He's making his way to Aden as we speak," she adds. "He should be here by around midnight. If all goes well. *Inshallah*."

Zafirah has a car waiting to take Jenna to the *Hotel Al Amer*. "It's only two kilometres away," she tells her. "It shouldn't take us long. But," she pauses, "the traffic in Aden these days is a nightmare."

Jenna takes this to mean the military. Everywhere she looks there are army trucks patrolling the streets. Nobody seems in the least perturbed. Except for Jenna. They freak her out. She supposes she would get used to them. Given time, you can get used to anything.

On the way to the hotel Zafirah briefs her.

"Two years ago," she says, weaving between the various road blocks, "as part of the Arab Spring, a popular uprising managed to force President Ali Abdullah Saleh, who had led Yemen in a dictatorship for more than two decades, to hand over power to his former Deputy, Abd Rabbuh Mansoor Hadi, before fleeing to neighbouring Saudi. But over the next twelve months Hadi failed to unite the various factions within the country, allowing both Al Qaeda and Houthi militants to establish local power bases. Meanwhile Saleh's son, Ahmed, continued to exercise control over Yemen's military."

Now an uneasy truce hangs over the country like a fog from the annual summer monsoon, the *khareef*, which shows no sign of lifting.

"Each of the factions is consolidating," continues Zafirah, by which she means building up funds from their various overseas supporters. "Al Qaeda from the wider Caliphate; the Houthis, allegedly, from Iran, and Hadi, bolstered by Ahmed, from Saudi." And, by extension, though Zafirah does not say this explicitly, Britain and America. "Al Qaeda," she says, "will probably be squeezed out, for the Caliphate is stretched too thinly in other theatres across the Middle East, so the war, when it comes," and Zafirah feels it is only a matter of time before it does, for the entire country is a tinderbox right now, "will be a predictable one, between Sunni and Shia."

The Houthi, who are Shia, are based in the north, while the Saudi-led Sunni hold sway in the south. It is rumoured that the

Houthi are slowly advancing on the capital, Sana'a.

"Which is probably why your plane was diverted," says Zafirah. "While here in Aden, the people mostly stay loyal to Hadi."

"Mostly?" asks Jenna.

"There are further tribal splits and divisions," explains Zafirah. "Some want a breakaway country of South Yemen, while others want a return to smaller tribal enclaves."

But Jenna knows that Saudi will never allow either of those things to happen. The prospect of an Iranian-led Shia stronghold on the tip of the Arabian peninsula is not something they can contemplate...

Jenna is reminded briefly of the in-fighting which bedevilled the Labour Party in Manchester during the eighties and nineties, when she twice attempted to gain selection as the prospective Parliamentary candidate for Openshaw, and failed on both occasions. The constant battles between the pragmatists and the idealists, between New Labour and Militant Tendency, the Blairites and the Bennites. In the eighties these differences could be temporarily set aside in pursuit of the one cause that united them all. They may not have been able to agree on what they were *for*, but they were unanimous in what they were *against*. Or rather *who*. Margaret Thatcher and all that she carried with her in those handbags with which she reputedly would bash the more lily-livered members of her Cabinet.

The issues for Jenna are simple and straightforward – a fairer, more just, more compassionate society, equal shares for all. But how to achieve those goals is less simple and far from straightforward. Many argue for direct action – not to instigate any violence that may ensue as a consequence, but neither to shrink from it if retaliation proves necessary – while others favour a more subtle approach – the darker arts of entryism, the infiltration of like-minded, left-leaning activists into the corridors and committee rooms of the mainstream, whereby they might influence policy from within, elect their own leaders, create their own agenda.

The Graham Stringers, John Nicholsons and Pat Karneys.
The Arnold Spencers, Bernard Suttons and Roy Graingers.
Big fish in small ponds.

The Zookeeper, in a royal blue tailored suit with pleated skirt, bouffant hair a lacquered helmet, wielding a matching armour-plated pocket-book, will toss them a few scraps from time to time, then stand back and watch them fight in a feeding frenzy, until all that remains is for them to devour each other.

At different times Jenna finds herself pursuing both courses of action – taking part in riots on the streets – first against the Police, next against the Poll Tax – and later when she tries to become an MP. Neither ends well, and in both she learns the hard way that, whatever divisions may arise over tactics and strategy, the one thing above all that unites the warring factions is the desire for power, a power that exists only for the boys, who must wrestle with the scourges of Compulsory Competitive Tendering imposed by the Zookeeper, leaving the less-headline-grabbing Equal Opportunities agenda as a sop for the girls to sort out, the setting up of Community & Neighbourhood Services, like *Sure Start*, offering much-needed support for children and families. Jenna throws herself heart and mind, body and soul into this fray. But to no avail. When the boys lose their wrestling match with the Government on a technical knock-out, *Sure Start* is tossed out of the ring with them. Immediately Jenna throws her own hat back in, but by then the bell has rung for the end of the bout.

"Sorry," they say, after her second failure to secure selection. "It's nothing personal."

But politics *is* personal, thinks Jenna bitterly. They are two strands of the same thread and they cannot be separated. Not without becoming weaker as a consequence. Very well, she decides. *Ita fiat esto*. Let it be so. I will advocate for the voiceless, the nameless, the dispossessed. I will seek to influence opinion on every side, persuade politicians of every colour. And so she joins a series of think tanks and policy groups...

Whichever way it pans out here in Yemen, she reflects now, there are going to be hundreds of thousands of displaced people – women and children mostly – refugees seeking safe havens and sanctuary right across the world.

"Which is where *we* come in," says Jenna.

"Yes," says Zafirah. "That's why Séydou wants you to see for yourself the situation on the ground before it's too late, to help establish the humanitarian corridors that will be needed to bring aid in. "

Yes, thinks Jenna, and get people out. She has some experience with the concept of sanctuary...

She is standing outside the Church of the Ascension on Stretford Road in Hulme. It is exactly one mile from the Squat. She is with a tight knot of people protesting against the Home Office's decision to deport the human rights activist, Viraj Mendis, back to Sri Lanka. Viraj is well known among those on the left in Manchester. He arrived more than a dozen years ago to study Engineering at UMIST, the city's university for science and technology.

But when his visa runs out, he decides to stay.

"I'm Sinhalese," he explains, in his characteristically soft-spoken way. "But before I came to this country, I actively campaigned for justice for the Tamil people, a persecuted and repressed minority. I have continued to speak out against their attempted genocide by the Sinhalese ever since I arrived here. If I return to my country, where there is currently a civil war raging, I am almost certain to arrested. Probably tortured.

Possibly executed. That's why I choose to stay. But also to try and mobilise international support for the Tamils before it is too late…"

In the years that he stays he puts down roots. He becomes well known, well liked. He gets involved in all manner of local community projects. He develops a relationship with a fellow campaigner from England, Karen Roberts.

When the Home Office instructs the Police to arrest him, he flees. He rushes to the Church of the Ascension, where he is known, where the rector, Father John Methuen, is a keen supporter. He requests, and is granted, sanctuary.

Sanctuary. A sacred retreat, or shrine. A safe haven. A refuge. A place of protection for those fleeing persecution, where the fugitive is immune to arrest. legally recognised from ancient times.

But no longer.

Karen leads the vigil, alongside Father Methuen. Jenna stands shoulder to shoulder with them. As do others from the Squat. Even Lance sometimes…

It's December, and bitterly cold. The protesters light a fire, which they stand around to keep warm. They sing songs. Freedom songs. With Christmas approaching, they appropriate the traditional carol *We Wish You A Merry Christmas* and give it new words.

We don't want to be deported
We don't want to be deported
We'll stay here until it's sorted
That Viraj can stay…

Their numbers grow, and, with them, their conviction. Their voices swell, lifted skywards by the sparks rising from the fire, which are carried by the wind up towards the stars, where, for the last few months, the eyes of the world have been trained, watching for the arrival of Halley's Comet, which visits the

Earth once every seventy-five years. Always it is a sign, an omen, a signifier of portents.

We don't want to be deported
We don't want to be deported
We won't let our will be thwarted
The world is our home...

Jenna feels her own path will be even more brightly illuminated by its appearance.

But she is disappointed. The positioning of the comet and the Earth, on opposite sides of the sun, creates the worst viewing circumstances for more than two millennia. She and Lance will look up and squint, and point and wonder. The only time they feel sure they have seen it is when it is leaving, when its tail is dropping below the horizon, as its orbit takes it to the outer reaches of the solar system.

Like all comets it is an unstable mixture of volatile compounds, mostly poisonous gases and polluted ice. As it nears the sun, these compounds begin to sublimate from the surface of its nucleus. This causes it to develop what's called a coma, an atmosphere more than sixty thousand miles across. Evaporation of the dirty ice releases particles of dust, which travel with the gases away from the nucleus. The gas molecules in the coma *absorb* solar light, which they then re-radiate at different wavelengths – a phenomenon known as fluorescence – whereas the dust particles *scatter* the solar light. Together they combine to make the coma visible. Ultraviolet rays, caused by pressure from the solar wind, stretch the coma out into a tail, which extends a hundred million miles into space.

It is this that Jenna sees, just as it finally disappears. Poisonous gas, polluted ice, particles of dust, a coma...

They keep up the vigil for just over two years. A rota is drawn up so that there are always people guarding the doors to the Church.

But Douglas Hurd, the Home Secretary, will not be moved.

In the January of 1989 the Police storm the Church. They break down the doors. They arrest Viraj on the steps of the altar. In a matter of days he is deported and flown back to Sri Lanka. But once there he is neither tortured nor executed. Nor is he arrested. He has attracted too much attention internationally while he has been in sanctuary – that is what his supporters claim – from the likes of Amnesty and the UN. Sri Lanka will not risk further isolation on the world stage, or sanctions, so they too promptly deport him. He relocates to Germany, who grant him asylum in Bremen, where he is joined by Karen, and where he becomes Chair of the International Human Rights Association.

Father Methuen claims it as a victory, albeit a Pyrrhic one, for they have lost a friend, and the community has lost *him*. But in the end a kind of justice has prevailed. He lights a candle in the Church, which he pledges to keep burning to remind them, that in a dark world there can still be light.

Jenna pictures the last faint traces of the comet before it finally disappears. It may have burned dimly this time, but it will be back again, once it has completed another orbit of the sun…

A sun which is just now beginning to set in Yemen, as Jenna is being driven from the airport towards her hotel.

Zafirah switches on the car radio. Her face lights up like a flower.

"Oh," she says, "you should listen to this," and she turns up the volume.

"She's a beautiful girl, such a beautiful girl
She's awake every day just a-helpin' her mom…"

"It's Amani Yayha," says Zafirah. Yemen's first female

rapper. She's only twenty but she already has a huge following, both here and abroad, in spite of attempts made to prevent her, for a girl to sing in public is *haram* – forbidden – even though the tradition stretches back centuries. But she won't be silenced.

"Listen," says Zafirah.

And Jenna does.

The song is called *Mery*. It's based on a true story, about a girl called Meryam, who is murdered for refusing to be a child bride. She's eleven years old.

"They put a gun to her head
The tears fall from the sky..."

What affects Jenna the most is the simple, unadorned manner in which Amani Yayha tells the story. It's a quiet song, sung with quiet dignity. The rage is there, but suppressed beneath the sorrow. A hymn to lost innocence that is infused somehow with hope.

She has simple dreams
Books inside her playground are all what she needs...

Jenna is deeply moved by it. She wants to know more about this Amani Yayha. Zafirah doesn't know where she lives. In Sana'a, she thinks. She sings in English because she wants the world to know about what's going on here. She has had no formal training. She taught herself English by listening to western music and watching movies. She tried to perform in the UK but she was refused a visa.

"Don't tell me," says Jenna. "They thought she would try to seek asylum once she got there?"

"But she's a Yemeni girl," says Zafirah. "She wants to reform from within. She hopes her songs will bring about change. Especially for girls and young women."

"And you?" asks Jenna. "Do you share this hope?"

"I do," says Zafirah. "There are twenty-eight million people living in Yemen. Nearly half of this number are aged fifteen years or younger. This is why I hope…"

Later, after she's checked in, Jenna looks up Amani Yayha on YouTube. She sends a text to Molly.

"Check out this link", she says. "It's important."
https://www.girltalkhq.com/yemens-first-female-rapper-amani-yahya-using-music-highlight-womens-rights-arab-world/"

A few seconds later she receives a ping on her phone. That was quick, she thinks. Molly must have checked it out immediately. But a quick look shows her that the incoming text is not from Molly. It couldn't be. Given the time difference, she's probably at that Stone Roses gig in Heaton Park. She wonders if any of the songs she's been listening to will resonate as strongly as the one about Meryam has with her. *Where Angels Play* perhaps…

'Come with me to a place no eyes have ever seen
A million miles from here where no one's ever been
God-given grace and a holy heaven face
I'm on the edge of something shattering
I'm coming through…'

The text that's coming through to Jenna now is from Séydou.

"I'm about four hours away. Maybe less. With God's grace. Don't wait up."

By which, of course, he means *do* wait up, which she has every intention of doing.

While she waits, she checks out her immediate surroundings. Next door to the hotel is what appears to be an empty apartment block built of whitewashed breeze-block.

Empty while it awaits repairs and renovations perhaps. But closer scrutiny reveals it to be occupied.

"Illegally," Zafirah tells her. "Squatters. Students. Harmless, most likely, but," she explains, "all students are regarded with suspicion here, especially by the Police and the Army."

Tell me about it, thinks Jenna.

"In all probability they have just spotted a vacant building and taken advantage of it," says Zafirah. "Rents have sky-rocketed in Aden," she continues, "especially since Hadi took control last year. Someone's making a killing. Meanwhile the local people are forced further and further away from the centre. There've been protests, but only random ones, nothing organised. Nevertheless, whenever squatters show up – like here – the authorities keep a close eye on them."

"What does that mean?"

"Basically a form of house arrest. Nobody leaves without being followed. Nobody goes in without being photographed. Then, when the developers finally move in, the squatters move out."

"And go somewhere else?"

"Maybe. Maybe not. There are always new alliances forming."

And old ones breaking up, thinks Jenna. It sounds familiar.

Jenna remembers the pattern well from her own time in the Squat. Or Squats. They were never in one place for long. But there was never a shortage of boarded-up, empty properties either. Not back then. In the eighties. In Moss Side...

She moves into 246 Moss Lane East within half an hour of meeting Lance and the Girl with the Mohican, who she learns is called Bex. There's about a dozen living there – give or take. Most don't stay very long. Some, only a few days, while they are 'getting themselves together'. But a hard core of five remain. Lance, Bex, Spike, who looks like Malcolm X, Dougie and Caroline, who come as a couple and who dress identically and who Jenna can't always tell apart – white skinheads in ripped black T-shirts and jeans, black DMs, safety-pin nose-rings, the words 'love' and 'hate' tattooed across the backs of the knuckles of each hand.

"Now wi six," says Lance as he introduces Jenna to the rest.

The others join in, one at a time, reading from the verses Bex has written round the walls.

"When I was One
I had just begun

When I was Two
I was nearly new

When I was Three
I was hardly me

When I was Four
I was not much more

When I was Five
I was just alive

But now I am Six, I'm as clever as clever
So I think I'll be six now for ever and ever....

Just begun, nearly new, hardly me, not much more, just alive, clever as clever...

Jenna rolls this litany round and round in her memory, looking up at the occupied apartment building next to her hotel in Aden, on the Al Aqba Road, what used to be known as the Esplanade Road, which once her father must have patrolled, as part of his National Service.

Other quotes from A.A. Milne come back to her now. These

too were copied by Bex in her meandering, spider's-web scrawl, down the hallway, up the stairs, along the landing.

'Here I am in the dark alone...'

'I can think whatever I like to think...'

'What would I do if it wasn't for you...?'

'No one can tell me, nobody knows
Where the wind comes from, where the wind goes...'

'That was just a dream some of us had.' Joni Mitchell playing on an endless loop, Jenna's walking with her man, lost in a dream. A.A. Milne again...

"If it wasn't for you..."
"True," says Lance, "it ain't much fun, jus' bein' one..."
"But two...?"
"Two can stick together."
"I'm never afraid," she says, "never afraid with you."
"Raz, gyal – dat jus' how it lie..."

'Songs are like tattoos,' sings Joni. *'Ink on a pin. Underneath the skin. An empty space to fill in...'*

But with Lance there are just too many blanks.

'He has his little ways
Sometimes he disappears on her
For days and days and days...'

But when he comes back, Joni sings for both of them. He loves her so naughty, makes her weak at the knees...

She can't get enough of him. His hands, his tongue, his cock. She wants him everywhere inside her simultaneously, coming again and again...

On that first night he takes her to *The Factory* in Hulme – Tony Wilson's place before *The Haçienda.* New Order are playing. It's their first gig since Ian Curtis hanged himself. They've changed their name from Joy Division. But joy is what they're still providing. Bernard Sumner's singing now. Gillian Gilbert's playing keyboards. Lance knows her. Lance knows everyone. People come to him with hugs and high-fives. He introduces Jenna to them all. They tell her that she looks like Gillian Gilbert, only darker. The same eye make-up, the same hair. "No," Lance corrects them. "It di oddah way around. Gillian Gilbert look like *she*." Jenna feels more alive than she's ever known. The music and the lyrics pound through the soles of her feet, coursing through her veins, till she feels she is going to explode with the pure, unadulterated joy of it. The blank canvas 'New Order' of it.

They play through the set that will form the main body of their first album. *Movement.* A movement Jenna feels a fully signed-up member of, especially when they launch into *Closer*, and Lance draws her tightly to him, so tightly they couldn't be much closer, not even when, while kissing her deeply on the dance floor, he lets an 'e' slide deliciously from his tongue onto hers, and the walls and floor and ceiling of *The Factory* dissolve around her, and the two of them are outside, beneath the railway arches that straddle the old Hulme Locks Junction Canal, a stretch of muddy water that once linked the Irwell, Medlock and Bridgewater, now disused and overgrown, their hands greedily all over each other, the moon rippling from the surface of the Canal across their fused skin in shards of jagged light, till they are spent and gasping, the water sloshing and lapping beneath them, while the boom of the music from *The Factory* a quarter of a mile away still surges through them, till they are ready to begin again, with New Order, singing to the world that dreams never end.

"Now we know what those hands can do
No looking back now, we're pushing through..."

When *did* the dreams end?

Jenna asks herself that question from time to time. But each time she comes up with a different answer. Perhaps they never end. Perhaps they simply transform into different dreams. Or do they? Perhaps it's not the dreams that change, but the canvas on which she tries to picture them. Like the most up-to-date computer technology, which can now accommodate a hundred million transistors within a single pinhead, with eight and a half billion of them combining to create the chip inside her mobile phone, which has sufficient capacity to store ten thousand photos and five thousand songs comfortably within its sixty-four gigabytes of memory. That's more than two million times greater than that used by the computer on board Apollo 11, which took Neil Armstrong to the Moon and back. But even her phone's sixty-four gigabytes pale into insignificance alongside the two and a half million that reside inside her brain. There's no limit to her imagination. Only that which she imposes on it herself.

Maybe the dreams have just got smaller, that's all, as the world has shrunk to fit inside a single microprocessor, less than forty-five nanometres in width, a million of which are needed to make up a single millimetre.

Maybe it's not the dreams that have changed, but she, Jenna, who has?

What *are* her dreams these days?

The same they have always been, she likes to think, since her days as a student. A fairer, more just, more compassionate society. But whereas before, in the Squat, her canvas had been local, now she operates on a global scale.

It was the Scottish town planner, Patrick Geddes, who first coined the phrase, 'Think global, act local.'

It was Spike who first told her that, during her first week at 246 Moss Lane East. She can hear his voice now in her head, like a call to arms, so that when she and Bex and Dougie and Caroline stand on street corners distributing leaflets, or chanting on marches, they feel that though they are most definitely acting locally, they are part of some wider global struggle for that better world that is certain to come. But now that that world can be fitted inside her mobile phone, it is no longer so easy to distinguish between what's local and what's global. The tribal factions here in Yemen jealously guard their borders with invisible lines drawn in the desert sands, while simultaneously mobilising their forces a thousand miles away via a communication satellite in space...

If Lance is her lover in the Squat, and Dougie and Caroline are her comrades, and Bex is her mate, then Spike is her teacher.

He writes instructional quotes on the walls. Or rather, he gets Bex to.

"For our delectation and delight," he says with a smile.

'Now all these things happened to them as examples, and they were written for our admonition, upon whom the ends of the ages have come...' Corinthians.

'What belongs to you today, belonged to someone else yesterday, and will be someone else's tomorrow. Change is the law of the universe...' Baghavad Gita.

'What we obtain too cheap, we esteem too lightly. It is dearness only that gives everything its value...' Thomas Paine.

'He who fights can lose. He who doesn't fight has already lost...' Bertolt Brecht.

Spike is especially fond of the Brecht quote. He tells them

that when Brecht was developing his theories for an Epic Theatre for the modern age, he devised the notion of a Living Newspaper.

Spike encourages them to go out into the streets. "Observe what happens," he tells them. "The little everyday things. The ordinary people going about their quiet lives. These are the real heroes. Listen to their stories. Collect them like coupons. Save them like string. Store them up like breadcrumbs. Then bring them back here to share."

He exhorts them to recreate them, word for word, deed for deed, without alteration or embellishment, then take them back out on to the streets, to present them back to their originators, so that they might see what they do through different eyes and understand just how heroic they are.

Verfremdungseffekt, he calls it. Alienation technique. Making the familiar strange…

When she and Lance have finally sated themselves beneath the railway arches beside the Canal, they walk the two miles back to Moss Lane East with hands and eyes only for each other. While just four miles in the opposite direction, back in Patricroft beside the Barton Aqueduct, Nadia and Sol worry about how late it is getting, and wonder why she hasn't phoned. They were expecting her home hours ago.

But it never enters Jenna's head to do so. As far as she's concerned, she *is* home, and her new home is a world away from her old one…

Now, five thousand miles away, in a different time zone, she brings up their number on her mobile and taps. Within seconds she's connected, their voices as clear as if they are sitting right beside her in the *Hotel Al Amer*, which, to all intents and purposes, they are…

"Hi. It's me."

"Jenna? Is everything all right?"

"Yes. Why?"

"It's late."

"Is it? Sorry. I was forgetting. It's three hours ahead here in Yemen, not behind."

"So why have you phoned?"

"No reason. Just to let you know I've arrived safely."

Silence, followed by a low, wry chuckle.

"What?"

"Are you *sure* you're all right?"

"Yes."

"Only it's not something you do as a rule."

"What?"

"Phone."

"No. I know. I should have. I must have worried you sick."

"You did. Always. You still do."

"I didn't mean to. I just didn't…"

"Think?"

"No. I suppose not. I was too caught up with everything."

"You always were. Still are, for all I know."

"What the eye doesn't see, the heart can't grieve over."

"Is that what you thought?"

"Something like that."

"When in fact it's the opposite that's true. The not knowing. You always fear the worst."

"When you're young, you think you're invulnerable."

"But you're not."

"No."

Another pause, before Jenna tentatively asks.

"How did you…?"

"What?"

"Find the strength to keep going?"

"When your father was in prison?"

"Yes."

"I had to. For your sake. That's all there was to it."

Jenna closes her eyes.

"Didn't you mind?"

"Of course I bloody minded. But what choice did I have?"

You could have left Sol, thinks Jenna. That's what I'd have done.

As if reading her mind, Nadia intervenes. "I couldn't just abandon your father. He may have committed a crime, but he was a good man – *is* a good man – he just lost his way for a while."

"How is he?" asks Jenna, trying to lighten the mood.

"The same," says Nadia. "No better, no worse. That cough still troubles him."

"How did the Exhibition go?"

"You should ask him yourself."

"Can I?"

"Not now, love. Like I said, it's past midnight. He's fast asleep. Try him another time. Better still, call round when you get back. I'll ask Farida to come too. You've always liked to see her…"

It's true. She has. All through those years in the Squat, it's Farida Jenna turns to – her mother's older sister – who she can say what she likes to, who never judges, whatever she's done, who always tells Nadia that she's seen her, to reassure her that she's OK, but never to betray her confidences. What's said between them, stays between them…

She's nineteen. She's just had an almighty row with Lance. He's been on walkabout again. He has this habit of disappearing on her. Sometimes just for a night, but sometimes for days, weeks even. One time it's for several months, when, on a whim seemingly, he takes himself off to St Kitts & Nevis.

"Mi need to see where mi come from, gyal, weh mi roots are planted..."

But that all lies in the future, after she's left Uni. On this occasion, he's only been absent for a week.

It doesn't do to complain. Exclusivity in relationships is frowned upon in the Squat. It's regarded in much the same way as individual property ownership, something distinctly bourgeois, to be eschewed, part of the great capitalist conspiracy.

Bex writes more slogans on the walls, passages that Spike is frequently quoting.

'Learn from me, if not by my precepts, at least by my example, how dangerous is the acquirement of knowledge, without the necessary responsibility that must accompany it, and how much happier that man is who believes his native town to be the world, than he who aspires to be greater than his nature will allow.' Mary Shelley.

The last part of which Jenna will come to believe applies directly to a summary of Lance's shortcomings.

'Il faut cultiver notre jardin.' Voltaire.

Jenna wonders if, when he first wrote this, Voltaire had in mind the giving over of land to just a single crop, as Bex appears to have taken it to mean, with her obsessive growing of cannabis plants in the attic and cellar, which Lance is only too happy to test for their quality.

'Property is theft.' Pierre-Joseph Proudon.

Which Jenna has come to understand refers specifically to her unspoken claim to Lance and his body.

Even Dougie and Caroline, who are never to be seen more than a couple of feet apart from one another, subscribe to this.

In theory anyway. Though Jenna has never seen either of them making out with anyone else. Not separately. Sometimes Bex has been known to join them. But only to sleep, as far as Jenna can tell. Stepping over them in the middle of the night on her way for a pee, a shaft of moonlight falling upon them through a crack in the threadbare, worn curtains, they remind her of the lost babes in the wood, who are covered with leaves by robins. She instinctively rearranges the blanket that has slipped from them, in the way Farida does sometimes when she crashes at her place...

"Yuh no' own mi, gyal," Lance will tell her if she tries to exert some kind of claim over him, some kind of deed of entitlement. He will sing lasciviously into her ear:

"If yuh can't be wid di one yuh love
Love di one yuh wid..."

Then he will scoop her up in his arms and lay her on one of the mattresses on the floor. She both hates it and loves it when he does this.

She has long had to overcome any sense of shyness or bashfulness when it comes to making love in the Squat, where every space is shared and communal. She no longer hears the shuntings of other couples. Nor does she mind any longer that she and Lance will have sex sometimes where others can see them. Sometimes these others may join in...

One time he comes back with wounds and injuries.
"Badges of honour," says Spike. "Wear them with pride."
A cracked rib, a split lip, a swollen eye, a cut head.
"What've you been up to?" she asks.
"Mischief an' mayhem," he replies. "No worry, gyal. Mi give as good as mi get."
"Spreading the word," declares Spike. "Preaching the truth.

We must expect the occasional brickbat."

"No brickbats, no bouquets," throws in Bex, coming in from outside with a daisy chain, which she proceeds to drape around Lance's neck.

"If yuh grab 'em by di balls," he grins, "di hearts an' minds dem sure to follow."

Jenna loves Lance's balls. She likes to place them one at a time, whole, inside her mouth and suck them, which she proceeds to do right now. It makes him harder, quicker. Bex and Spike decide to leave them to it, and go back outside, laughing.

But Lance uncharacteristically resists.

"Whoa gyal," he is saying, lifting her face from between his legs. "Slow down. Mi a' work all week. Mi bushed. Mi need a little shut-eye first."

Reluctantly smiling, Jenna tiptoes out of the room. Lance is already snoring by the time she reaches the door...

She goes to the library to finish an essay. *Gender and Power: The Shifting Paradigm.* When she returns, it's beginning to get dark. The sky over Whitworth Park looks like spilt paint, streaking her skin with infinite possibilities. Spike has decided to throw a party. "To celebrate Lance's coming home." Not that an excuse is needed. There are always parties in the Squat.

Dougie and Caroline are hanging fairy lights round the front door. Bex is sitting on the front step with her guitar, singing more Joni Mitchell. It's all she knows, but she never tires of playing it, or the rest of them from singing along.

"I met a redneck on some isle
He did the goat dance very well..."

She pauses briefly mid-song and looks meaningfully at Jenna.

"Oh the rogue, the red, red rogue…"

But Jenna's head is still too far stuck in her essay, the shifting paradigm of gender and power, to get the reference, and she breezily steps over her, skipping under the fairy lights, down the hall, then into the front room, where earlier she had left Lance snoring, loud as a linty.

He's not snoring now. He's wide awake. When she bursts in, he's making out with two girls Jenna doesn't know or recognise even. They must be some of the passers-through. There is always a steady stream of them. Most don't stay long. Just till they get themselves together, or find somewhere more permanent, or simply move on. Jenna is furious. She storms across the room, yanks each of them by the hair and drags them away from a complaining Lance.

"Hey gyal," he says, "wah gwaan? Cum on in, di wata's fine."

"How about *this* water?" she says, grabbing a jug and flinging its contents all over him. "Is this 'fine' enough?"

"Yuh too greedy, gyal. Share an' share alike."

She is spitting with fury. "You said you needed to sleep. I said I'd be back."

"Mi woke up," he shrugs. "Yuh wuh no' here."

She flings a book at him, one about gender and power, then flies from the house. Bex is still intensely strumming and singing.

"I know that you've got all those pretty girls coming on
Hanging on your boom-boom-pachyderm
Well, you tell those girls you've got German Measles
Honey, tell them you've got germs…"

It takes Jenna just over two hours to walk the seven miles from Moss Lane East, not to her old home with Sol and Nadia on Stanley Road, but to Farida's in Monton Green. She's always gone there whenever she's been in trouble.

She passes the railway arches beside the remnant of the Hulme Locks Junction Canal, where she and Lance first had sex, without affording them a second glance. She crosses St George's Island, between the Canal, an outflow of the Medlock, and the intersecting waters of the Irwell and the Bridgewater, till she reaches Cornbrook Weir, from where she drops down towards the derelict Pomona Docks, via Brough Bridge, a former paved causeway over the Irwell known as Woden's Ford, where travellers of old would deposit a coin for luck into Woden's Den, a low cave beneath the bridge. Long gone now. Though even if it had still been there, Jeena would not have wasted a penny with it. She believes people make their own luck, which is why the anger she still feels burning in her belly drives her onwards. But this rage is now directed at herself, rather than at Lance. Lance is what he is, what he has always been, what he will always be. She can't control that. But what she can control is the way she feels about him. She can't allow herself to be manipulated by him any longer. She knows he will charm her into bed again at some point. What she needs to learn is to simply enjoy those moments for *what* they are, *when* they are, moments of intense physical pleasure, but nothing more than that. Sometimes that will be enough. But if she is seeking commitment, fidelity even, then she is only consigning herself to certain disappointment.

She turns into Ordsall Lane, passing the Old Hall, a former moated Tudor mansion, where it is rumoured Guy Fawkes and Robert Catesby devised the Gunpowder Plot in the Hall's Star Chamber, before escaping via a tunnel that led to the Hanging Bridge, near the Cathedral. As she passes Guy Fawkes Street, Jenna smiles grimly. Another of Bex's slogans, painted on a wall in the Squat, reads: *'Guy Fawkes Was Right'*.

From there she cuts through Salford Quays, skirts around Weaste Cemetery, where four survivors of the Charge of the

Light Brigade are buried, along with Charles Hallé, the founder of the city's orchestra, and Mark Addy, the celebrated Salford publican and oarsman, who rescued more than fifty people from drowning in the foul and toxic waters of the Irwell, which, according to his obituary, 'laid the foundation of an illness that would eventually gain the mastery of his powerful, well-knit frame'. He died of tuberculosis shortly after saving a small child on Whit Monday in 1890. Jenna remembers doing a project about him when she was at primary school, not far from where she now walks, Godfrey Ermen Primary, named for the local mill owner and partner of Friedrich Engels. She particularly enjoyed the story of one of Addy's most famous rescues, one of his first. He was returning from a funeral in a new black suit, with a valuable gold watch in his pocket, when the cry went up, "A child is in the river!" Mark rushed to the spot and, without divesting himself of a single garment, plunged in and pulled out the child. As he stood dripping before the crowd of excited onlookers, one said to him, "Mark, tha's spoiled tha' clothes." "What o' that?" came the reply. "I reckon it'll also 'ave made a mess o' me watch, but it matters nowt. There was a young life at stake…"

Jenna will have cause to reflect on this twice more in her life…

From the Cemetery, she walks along Eccles New Road, underneath the M602 motorway, which roars above her, before crossing it via the footbridge on Stott Lane, turning left into Half-Edge Lane, then cutting through Ellesmere Park, till she reaches the Linear Walkway of Chorlton Fold, where once a railway ran from Worsley to Eccles, connecting the collieries of The Delph, the Loop Line, linking the Boothstown Basin with the pits of Linneyshaw Common. She passes the Unitarian Chapel where the son of the vicar there, a certain John Henry Poynting, became the first person to understand and measure the transfer of energy from different electrical and magnetic sources. This enabled him to track their pathways as their unique intricacies unravelled when set against something constant. Like gravity. Jenna feels herself unravelling, the further she is propelled away from her own particular electrical, magnetic source. Namely Lance. The crucial difference being that Lance is not constant. With this knowledge Poynting was able to accurately measure the weight of the Earth for the first time.

Thirteen billion trillion tons.

Poynting managed to arrive at that figure by closely observing gravity. By studying the way things fall towards it.

But he also discovered that this weight, the density of its mass, is not evenly distributed. It is far denser towards the core, the red hot molten lava of its heart, than it is at its outer layers, the thin covering of its crust.

Jenna doesn't understand the equations, she can't even begin to comprehend the sheer scale of the numbers involved, but she grasps the principle, feeling the full weight of it as she troops the length of the Loop Line towards Farida's.

'*We explain an event,*' Poynting wrote, '*not when we know why it happened, but when we show that it is like something else happening elsewhere, which has already been described by a Law previously set forth.*'

Jenna, reading this a few days later on a plaque beside the Chapel, when she is feeling less agitated, when she can begin to distance herself more calmly from her own actions and emotions, sees the wisdom in Poynting's conclusions.

'*When we examine Nature's garment,*' he continued, '*we discover just how many, or rather how few, threads of which it is woven. We try to detect a pattern. We observe how each separate thread enters the pattern, and then, from our understanding of these patterns from the past, we try to predict the pattern yet to come.*'

But Jenna is not satisfied by this. She sees potential flaws when it comes to applying this formula to her own behaviour. Poynting's theory suggests laws of immutability, resistant to the possibility of change, a change she feels determined to implement when it comes to succumbing less easily to Lance's charms than she has done in the past.

But Poynting is not yet finished.

'We stand in front of Nature's Loom as we watch the weaving of the garment. While we follow one particular thread in the pattern, it suddenly disappears, and a thread of a different colour takes its place. Is this a new thread? Or is it merely the old thread turning a new and unfamiliar face to us? How can we tell? So, as we watch the weaving of Nature's garment, we resolve it in our imagination into threads of ether spangled over with beads of matter. But should we, or should we not, therefore, conclude from this reasoning a single, irrefutable Law, which can be applied to every case in all instances? Or should we rather regard a Law of Nature as nothing but a formulation of observed correspondences?'

The attraction of this for Jenna is that it offers the possibility of new correspondences not yet observed.

In recognition of his contribution to our understanding of the planet we inhabit, a large impact crater is named after him on the far side of the moon, the dark side, the side still hidden from Jenna as she pounds along its ribboned light, feeling the weight of the world on her shoulders, the length of the Linear Walkway, waiting for its secrets to be revealed to her...

Farida is expecting her.

She lets Jenna cry and curse and complain over mugs of hot chocolate spiced with cinnamon and ginger. Until she is all cried out.

Then she paints her hands with henna, while they listen to Egyptian pop songs – Naghat al-Saghira. Mounira al-Madeyha. – but mostly Leila Mourad, Farida's favourite, *Alba al Dalili*.

"The world is a garden and we are its flowers
Fire is in our hearts, its colour is in our cheeks
Who will make us happy?
We open our eyes to the whispering of birds…"

They sing along with her, right through the night, of the fire in Jenna's heart, until the whispering of the birds brings a new morning.

Jenna will recall this moment thirty years later, when she appears on *Desert Island Discs* and selects this song…

"Let me ask you something," says Farida, when Jenna has finally stopped crying. "This young man of yours – he's feckless and childish and selfish – but when you are with him, is he kind? Is he gentle?"

Jenna smiles fondly. "Mostly," she says. "Unless I ask him not to be."

Farida shakes her head. "But does he try to make you do things you don't want to?"

"No," says Jenna. "Never. Why?"

Farida pauses, as if weighing the cost of any words she might say next.

"I have little experience of sex," she says eventually. "Only with Salim. My husband."

Jenna looks down. Salim died nearly twenty years ago. In this very house. From a fall down the stairs. This same house where now Farida runs a nursery through the week, for the children of parents who must go out to work. *Busy Bees*, she has called it. '*The world is a garden and we are its flowers,*' she has painted on the walls. Jenna remembers helping her aunt to decorate this garden.

"It was such a sterile, arid place before," Nadia tells Jenna one time. "Full of secrets. Farida was always on her hands and knees, keeping it spotless, scrubbing away all traces of what went on there, behind its locked doors, its shuttered windows."

Now it is full of light and noise and laughter.

"My husband was *not* kind," says Farida to Jenna now. "*Not* gentle. If he looked in my eyes, it was only to see himself reflected back. He took particular pleasure in devising newer, more subtle ways of inflicting pain and humiliation upon me."

Jenna feels her cheeks suffuse with colour. The whispering of the birds outside grows to a clamour.

"I have never told this to anyone," continues Farida. "Not even your mother. But she knew, I think. When I used to look after you, when you were a baby, which I had to do behind my husband's back, for he did not want you or Nadia to enter our house, she would catch me sometimes, applying make-up to cover the marks where his hands had been, and I would flinch if she tried to touch me. But I am telling you this tonight because you have some experience now of the way men can be sometimes."

"No," says Jenna. "Nothing like that."

"Then that is good. May you never. *Inshallah.* "

She pauses once more, collects herself, then continues to apply the finishing touches to the henna on Jenna's hands.

"So although this young man of yours is not to be trusted, not to be counted or depended on, at least he is not cruel. Not in that way. Not intentionally so. When you are with him, he gives you pleasure. Fire is in both your hearts then. And when you are not with him, when you don't know where he is, when he is not where he has said he will be, banish him from your thoughts. The world is a garden. There are plenty of flowers to pick."

She turns the volume on the record player up high. Leila Mourad sings out bravely and defiantly. Farida takes Jenna's hennaed hands in her own and lifts her to her feet. The two of them dance together in the morning light. Outside, the whispering of the birds grows into a full-throated chorus…

In her hotel room in Aden Jenna switches on her television, selecting a channel devoted to Egyptian pop songs, and there once more, echoing down the years, are the passionate, quivering tones of Leila Maroud. *Alba al Dalili. Let my love be my guide…*

The sound of a text pinging into her phone shakes her from her reverie. She thinks it's probably an update from Séydou, giving her his latest ETA. But no – it's from Zafirah.

"Call me when you get this."

"What is it?"
"Forgive me if I wake you?"
"No. I'm not tired."
"Séydou rang me to say you will need to be ready to leave early tomorrow."
"Why didn't he call me himself?"
"He probably thought you would be sleeping."
"Yes. I see. Why the urgency?"
"He didn't say. But I can guess. "
"The trouble in Sana'a?"
"It's increasing. I think this might be it."
"The start of a big push by the Houthi?"
"Yes. It's been coming for months."
"Listen – where are you? I'm much too wired to sleep."
"Actually I'm downstairs."
"In the lobby?"
"Yes."
"Have you eaten?"
"It's gone ten o'clock."
"Sorry. My body's all over the place. Let me buy you a drink. I take it the bar's still open?"
"It is. But it has stopped serving alcohol for the night."
"Pity. Sorry. Don't mean to cause offence."

"None taken."

"But I could really do with a drink right now."

"They do a range of halal mocktails. Very nice. I can recommend them."

"Hmm. I think I'll have a coffee. Especially if I've to stay awake. I'll be down in five minutes…"

Over coffee in the bar Jenna plugs Zafirah for more information.

"I'm sorry," she says. "The internet keeps going down."

"Which is suggestive, wouldn't you say?"

"Possibly. Possibly not. Reception is patchy even at the best of times."

"But these aren't the best of times."

"No."

Jenna puts down her cup. "I think I'll have another," she says. "You?"

Zafirah shakes her head. Jenna can see that her fingers are trembling.

"What will happen if the Houthi take Sana'a?"

Zafirah puts her head in her hands. "It doesn't bear thinking about," she says. "In the north, where they're strongest, where they feel most confident, they've already put the cause of women back decades. What we can wear, what we can do. Mostly what we *can't* do. I wouldn't be sitting here talking to you."

"But you're not a supporter of the Saudis, surely?"

"Shh," she says, her eyes widening in panic. "Not so loud. You don't know who might be listening."

"I'll take that as a 'no' then."

"They're just as bad," she whispers, "but in subtler ways. Beneath the trappings of wealth and decadence, with attractively groomed women reading the news on state-controlled television, they still monitor every aspect of our lives. They throw us the occasional tit-bit, like allowing us to study at university, but then they forbid us from applying for any of the jobs we're now qualified for. We still can't drive, and lashes, hangings and even beheadings are still permissible forms of punishment if we are found to have transgressed. Me? I'm one of the lucky ones. Legally women are permitted to drive here in Yemen, even though we are discouraged from doing so. But since the Arab Spring two years ago, more and more of us have taken the wheel..."

"Which part of Yemen are you from?"

"Taiz. You know it?"

"I've heard of it of course. We're scheduled to visit it tomorrow."

"It's very beautiful. Especially the old quarter."

"Do you know Tawakkol Karwan?"

Zafirah's eyes light up. "No," she says. "I have never met her. But I've heard her speak. We're very proud of her. Not just in Taiz. But in all of Yemen."

"Unless you're one of Saleh's supporters."

"In the Arab Spring she was dubbed the Mother of the Revolution."

"But she's not here now."

"No."

"She's accepted Turkish citizenship. Another leader-in-exile. I wonder how long it will be before she begins to speak out against her new protectors."

"If she sees injustice, she will speak out," says Zafirah fervently.

"So I should hope. Now that she's a recipient of the Nobel Peace Prize, she has a moral responsibility, wouldn't you say?"

"Her father was a poet. She will find the words."

"And her mother was a lawyer."

"The first Yemeni woman to study at Harvard."

"Then she knows the legal consequences of those words she

may find. And any actions they may inspire."

Jenna has met Tawakkol Karwan – in Istanbul the previous year – when she first took on her role with the Refugee Council...

Tawakkol is at pains to point out the pitfalls of trying to pigeon-hole the cauldron that is simmering in Yemen as a problem that is predominantly tribal.

"That's a massive over-simplification," she says, "and a typical example of western stereotyping. Yes," she continues, "the tribes are important in Yemen, massively so, but they too are splintered, riven by political divisions of their own, so that alliances form that cross both tribal and geographic borders. Some of these federations can be quite loose, but others can be extremely strong, bound by a particular world view, both in terms of a vision for Yemeni nationhood, and the relationships that nation might then go on to form internationally. Sometimes these visions are driven by ideology, sometimes by economics, sometimes by a combination of both. That's why the Houthis have been so successful recently."

"But you've publicly spoken out against them", says Jenna.

"Yes," she acknowledges, "and I've been denounced for doing so. It's why it's no longer safe for me to be there."

"But you've also denounced the Saudi-led attempts to prop up the former President Saleh, as well as his successor, Hadi?"

"Naturally. Saudi is not interested in Yemen except in ways that guarantee its economic dominance across the whole peninsula. Saleh and Hadi are little more than its puppets."

"Meanwhile Al-Harik, the Southern Separatist Movement, look to secede and restore an independent South Yemen?"

"Like I said, it's complicated."

She checks to see whether Jenna is recording their conversation on her phone.

"You are?"

"Yes. I can switch it off if you prefer."

"No. I want people to hear this," she says, before taking a deep breath.

"In contemporary Yemen," she continues, "the tribe-state relationship is characterised by two elements – a tribal perception that separates national identity from the concept of a sovereign state, and an alienation of tribesmen from their tribal leaders who exercise political power in the centre. Both elements reflect a situation where the tribes and the state are disengaged and function in separate spheres – the state in the centre and the tribes on the periphery. This situation emphasises the core of Yemen's political dilemma. Unlike what many might think, the critical task facing Yemen is not nation-building. If we define a nation as a psychological bond that joins a people together, differentiating it, in the subconscious conviction of its members, from all other people in a most vital way, Yemen stands as a clear example of a nation. Yemeni people, including tribesmen, have hardly any doubt about their national identity. However, when tribesmen state proudly that they are Yemenis, the question that follows is which Yemen are they talking about? That is where they cannot agree, and it remains doubtful whether they ever shall. None of the incarnations of the state that have been attempted since the British left have been able to integrate the tribes into a political system in a manner that generates their acceptance of a single sovereign state. To succeed in this is an extraordinary challenge, but only if it is attained, will a true nation-state of Yemen be born. Until then, the people who live there, the families and their children, Sunni and Shia both, face the terrible prospect of years and years of war, with no end in sight to the suffering that will rain down upon them..."

And where do *I* fit into all of this, thinks Jenna, me a third generation British-born Yemeni? Where do any of us? The pathetic, internal wranglings within the Labour Party, with all of their petty point-scoring, feel shameful by comparison with the task that now faces Yemen. She quails at the sheer Sisyphean enormity of it...

"Then we must focus only on those things we *can* do," Séydou tells her. "Help as many individuals as we can to a place of safety. Even if it is just one."

Even if it is just one...

This is said the last time Jenna saw Séydou. On her return from Istanbul. They had decided to meet up in Paris. In front of the statue of Thomas Paine in Le Parc Montsouris...

"Why there?" asks Séydou.

"Because," says Jenna, "he wrote *Common Sense* and the *Rights of Man*, which have always been a blueprint for action. I remember his words written on a wall in one of the Squats I once lived in. They have always been a call to arms. As they were for the Radicals seeking Reform in Manchester before Peterloo. After the massacre, the writer William Cobbett brought Paine's bones, which had been dug up in America because of objections to his views on religion, to Salford, to be paraded through the streets of Manchester and be ceremonially buried there. But they only made it as far as the New Bailey Bridge. The town's Magistrates, fearful of another riot, refused them entry. Meeting in front of his statue will be like a promise fulfilled. If we do manage to rescue refugees fleeing from the inevitable crisis to come in Yemen, Manchester will not refuse them entry on this occasion..."

She alights from the Métro between the Pantheon and Le Jardin des Plantes, close by the Grand Mosque. From there she walks along the Rue de Saint-Jacques, past the Cemetery of Montparnasse, the Catacombs, the Observatory until she reaches the statue, where Séydou is waiting for her, with a bottle of wine and two glasses, which he solemnly pours.

" '*These are the times that try men's souls*'," he says, as he raises his glass.

" '*The harder the conflict, the more glorious the triumph*'," answers Jenna, raising her own glass in turn.

"You're going to have to tread on a lot of people's toes," he says.

"I've never been afraid to do that," she says.

" '*Moderation in temper is always a virtue*'," he continues, " '*but moderation in principle is always a vice*'."

Jenna nods in agreement. "I've not always managed the former," she says.

" '*But he who dares not offend*' ," he replies, " '*cannot be honest*'."

"Nor she."

"Nor she."

If there must be trouble, she thinks, which it seems certain there will be, let it be so that a child may have peace. Recalling another of Tom Paine's maxims, she drains her glass.

" '*To begin the world over again...*' "

"The Rub al-Khali is the world's largest sand desert", says Zafirah. "There's nothing else there. That's why people call it 'the Empty Quarter'. It stretches into four different countries, Yemen being one of them. But even the sand is not constant. It changes. It shifts. The wind blows it into huge fantastical shapes. Ergs. Sometimes these can reach up to hundreds of metres in height, over time burying entire civilisations, which can lie lost for centuries. But then they can collapse and disappear overnight."

"Everything old is new again," says Jenna.

"The Rub al-Khali doesn't stretch as far as Taiz," says Zafirah. "But sometimes the *Shamal* will blow in from there. A hot desert wind that can last for between thirty and fifty days. It covers everything. Inside and out. Every building, every surface. Even our eyelids. When it finally subsides and retreats, it leaves behind a patina, a trace of where it has been. Nothing escapes it. We open our eyes, and everything looks different somehow. The same, but altered."

"*Verfremdungseffekt,*" says Jenna, more to herself than to Zafirah, who appears not to have heard her...

Sometimes, in the Squat, late at night, Spike likes to read to them. 'Bedtime Stories for Anarchists,' he calls them. These come back to Jenna down the years. They will flit across her mind like a warm wind blowing in from the past. Like this one. A particular favourite of Spike's, from *An Essay on the Art of Lying* by Jonathan Swift...

"Well, boys and girls, are we sitting comfortably?" he asks.
"Yes, Daddy," they chorus back.
"Then I'll begin."
"Ah," they sigh with satisfaction.
"Once upon a time...

" *'The Poets tell us, that after the Giants were overthrown by the Gods, the Earth in revenge produced her last offspring – the Political Lie. A Political Lie is sometimes born out of a discarded statesman's Head, and thence delivered to be nursed and dandled by the Rabble. Sometimes it is produced by a Monster, and licked into shape. At other times it comes into the world completely formed, and is spoiled in the licking. It is often born an infant in the regular way, and requires time to mature it; and often it sees the light in its full growth, but dwindles away by degrees. Sometimes it is of noble birth, and sometimes the spawn of a stock-jobber. Here it screams aloud at the opening of the womb; and there it is delivered with a whisper. I know a Lie that now disturbs half the Kingdom with its noise, which, although too proud and great at present to own its parents, I can remember its whisperhood. To conclude, the nativity of this Monster, when it comes into the world without a sting, it is still-born, and whenever it loses its sting, it dies. But if it should survive, it will take upon itself the false appearance of a Goddess.*

" 'This Goddess flies with a huge looking-glass in her hands, to dazzle the crowds, and make them see, according as she turns it, their ruin in their interest, and their interest in their ruin. In this glass you will behold your best friends and your worst enemies. Her large wings, like those of a Giant Moth, are of no use but while they are moist. She therefore dips them in mud, and, soaring aloft, scatters it in the eyes of the multitude, flying with great swiftness; but at every turn is forced to stoop in dirty ways for new supplies.

" 'I have been sometimes thinking, if we had the art of the second sight for seeing lies, as they have in some parts for seeing spirits, how admirably we might entertain ourselves in this town, by observing the different shapes, sizes, and colours of those swarms of lies which buzz about the heads of some people, like flies about a horse's ears in summer; or those legions hovering every afternoon in Exchange Alley, enough to darken the air, or over a club of discontented grandees, and thence sent down in cargoes to be scattered at elections.

" 'So it is that the Political Lie is the last relief of a routed, earth-born, rebellious Party in a State. But here the Moderns have made great additions, applying this art to the gaining of Power and preserving it, as well as revenging themselves after they have lost it; as the same instruments are made use of by animals to feed themselves when they are hungry, and to bite those that tread upon them...' "

"We stand at the cross-roads in Taiz," says Zafirah, rousing Jenna from her reverie. "We always have. Right now we're on the front line, the exact meeting point between Houthi and

Saudi, where the boundaries of their spheres of influence intersect. It's a powder keg."

Jenna can see just how frightened Zafirah is. She can already see the monster in her mind's eye, hear the heavy beat of its wings beyond the horizon. It's coming. Soon it will swoop down and pluck her out of her car with its huge mandibles. There'll be no escape. Zafirah's fingers tremble as she continues.

"The government just about tolerates *Médecins Sans Frontières*, and one of two other NGOs, but they still try to limit what we can do. Or rather, they *will* do, once the civil war kicks off for real – which it's just about to, if the reports coming out of Sana'a are true."

Jenna nods, then tries to steer her back towards a safer haven.

"How did you meet Séydou?" she asks

Zafirah immediately relaxes. The tension leaves her face and she smiles. It is like water trickling down a *wadi* after a long drought.

"He appointed me," she says. "He needed someone to set up local networks of contacts, so that if we have to start evacuating people quickly, we can be ready to do so. *He* sees to the official channels, liaising with local Government personnel, while *I*, and others like me, try to mobilise people on the ground, making them aware of the potential dangers of any upcoming insurgency – not that they need any reminding, we've all of us learned to be in a state of permanent readiness and expectation – so that they can be quickly moved if necessary…"

In the Squat Spike urges them to rid themselves of their worldly possessions. Like a snake shedding its skin. "Then we shall be unencumbered by any goods or chattels." As impoverished students this is no great sacrifice. But they grasp the principle – to be ready to move on at a moment's notice if they have to, which they do, often...

"I'm going to try and get some sleep," says Jenna finally. She takes Zafirah's hands in both of hers. "*Shukraan*," she says.
"*As-salaamu alaikum.*"
"*Va-alaikum as-salaam.*"
She falls asleep the instant her head touches the pillow. She hears again Bex channelling Joni.

"I was driving across the burning desert
When I spotted six jet planes
Leaving six white vapour trails across the bleak terrain
It was the hexagram of the heavens, the strings of my guitar
Dreams – dreams and false alarms..."

She wakes suddenly, her senses on high alert. A shadow is padding silently across the room. She bolts upright.
"Sorry," says a voice. "I didn't mean to startle you."
It's Séydou, his face grey in the monochrome dark.
"No," she says, with relief. "I'm glad you did – wake me, I mean." She opens her arms wide to enfold him to her...

Sex with Séydou is a different country from Lance.
Not beak and claw, but fur and feather.
Instead of the slash and burn of forest fires, the gentle tilt and bend of a candle flame.
The slow drip of melted honey poured from a spoon.
The brush of fingertips along the neck's nape.
The nuzzling of earlobes.
The grazing of lips upon closed eyelids...

Afterwards, when they have finished, Jenna adjusts the rhythm of her breathing to the gentle rise and fall of Séydou's as he rests, his head nestled between her breasts. She drifts in and out of sleep till morning, hearing Bex, hearing Joni, dreaming of seven-forty-sevens over geometric farms...

> *"The drone of flying engines is a song so wild and true*
> *It scrambles time and seasons till it gets through to you*
> *Then your life becomes a travelogue of picture-postcard charms*
> *Dreams – dreams and false alarms..."*

The song becomes caught up in other sounds. Helicopters circling overhead, soldiers marching through the streets, the muezzin's dawn call to prayer. Like Icarus ascending...

> *"Some have found their Paradise, while others just come to harm...*
> *And looking down on everything I crashed into his arms...*
> *Dreams – dreams and false alarms..."*

*

Day 2

Jenna feels Séydou's hand on her shoulder, gently shaking her.

"Wake up," he says. "We need to make a start. If we're to reach Sana'a before nightfall."

"What time is it?"

"Early. Can you be ready in five minutes?"

Jenna nods. Life in the Squats has prepared her for the quick getaway.

As soon as they step outside they are aware of a tension in the air, like the hum of telegraph wires.

An Army Jeep screeches to a halt. Half a dozen soldiers, armed with Kalashnikovs and carrying battering rams, leap from the back. In a well-practised drill they silently converge in battle formation on the apartment block adjacent to the hotel, the one Zafirah has told Jenna probably contains students. The Army Commander holds up a gloved hand. He has three fingers pointing. Then two, then one. At his signal the rest of the soldiers proceed to break down the door, before charging in, all of them shouting at the tops of their voices. The students, with arms raised above their heads, blinking in the strong lights being shone directly into their faces, stumble into the street, plainly terrified. They look, to Jenna's eyes, like children...

She remembers the same fear and panic when she first experienced a similar bust...

The Police charge in through the door while it is still dark. They fan out in all directions. There are enough of them to search every room of the house simultaneously. This is while she is still at 246 Moss Lane East. The Police drag the sheets off all of the mattresses, shining their torches on Jenna's and Lance's nakedness. One of them, a white Policewoman, points hers directly between Lance's legs. "Oh," she says, sneering, "it's not true then, what they say?"

Jenna tries to grab a blanket to cover herself, before being ushered none too gently out into the street, where a crowd has started to gather, despite the lateness – or earliness – of the hour. They're all of them on the side of the squatters, and they give the Police a hard time.

"Leave 'em be," they shout. "They ain't doin' no 'arm."

"I'd keep quiet if I were you," the Police shout back. "Unless you want to keep this lot company in the cells."

Spike demands to know on what grounds they are being arrested, what charges are being brought against them?

"How about this for starters?" says one of the Officers. And he waves a plastic bag filled with what look like dried brown herbs.

"You planted those," Spike protests, before being bundled

into the back of the van.

It's true. They none of them need to resort to the bought variety, not when they've got Bex's fresh supplies in the cellar and the attic. The Police mustn't have bothered to check either of those, not once they'd rounded up most of the squatters, those who, unlike the temporary passers-through, have not managed to slip out the back and shin over the brick wall, to escape down the labyrinth of cobbled alleys without getting caught. It's just the six regulars who are taken down to Moss Side Police Station on Platt Lane – Spike, Bex, Dougie, Caroline, Lance and Jenna.

After a couple of hours, Bex, Dougie and Caroline are released without further charge.

"Mi wonder why," says Lance to the white Desk Sergeant.

In solidarity Bex, Dougie and Caroline at first refuse to leave, but in the end they are persuaded to by Spike.

"Go back to 246," he says. "Salvage what you can."

"And bring us back some clothes," pleads Jenna, still wrapped only in a blanket and shivering…

But, twelve hours later, it is not Bex or Dougie or Caroline who arrive – though later Jenna learns that they tried repeatedly to, but were refused entry – but Farida, who the Police have called after Jenna has given them her phone number as a point of contact. She's my Auntie, she tells them truthfully, and, when they decide they can hold her no longer, they call Farida to come and collect her.

"Don't tell my mum," says Jenna the moment she sees her aunt.

"Don't worry," says Farida, shaking her head, "I shan't. But next time…"

"There won't be a next time," says Jenna, hastily interrupting her.

"There'd better not be," says Farida, before bestowing a

stern, old-fashioned look upon her wayward niece...

Jenna and Séydou steal away from the *Hotel Al Amer* almost guiltily, as soon as the Army Jeep has driven away with a squeal of tyres and a burst of gunfire.

The first part of their journey is fairly routine and uneventful. Séydou has arranged a series of meetings with local Government Officials – in Crater, Ma'alla and Tawahi – the three ports along the Aden isthmus, to confirm access for humanitarian aid from outside the country, should the need arise. Séydou has already formulated contingency plans on behalf of *Médecins Sans Frontières*, which it will be up to these Officials to implement. Jenna asks whether, in the event of hostilities escalating to the point where local services may be threatened with being overrun, any casualties may be ferried across the Bab-el-Mandeb Strait the hundred and fifty miles to Djibouti, where they might receive the necessary medical treatment. They assure her that this will indeed be the case, but they hope it will not come to that. Jenna agrees and thanks them.

Afterwards Seydou reminds her that these assurances she has just received are in fact meaningless. Well-intentioned but without foundation. "It won't be them making the decisions," he explains. "It won't even be Army Generals or local leaders. In the end it will come down to the rulers of Saudi and Iran, who will not of course speak directly to one another, but only through the mediation of the UN, while responding to whatever pressures are put on them by US and EU Governments. That is why *we* are so important," he adds, "the international NGOs. We're neutral. We help everyone. At least we try to. If they let us..."

Jenna finds it hard to equate neutrality with passion. She always has done. As far as she's concerned, you're either *for* something, or *against* it. She has no time for the equivocators, the fence-sitters...

"Which side are you on?
Which side are you on?
Are you on the side who loves to hunt?
Are you on the side of the National Front?
Are you on the side who call women a cunt?
Which side are you on...?"

She and Bex and Caroline hitch-hike to Newbury to join the thirty thousand women who 'embrace the base' at Greenham Common by circling hands around the nine-mile perimeter fence. Many of the women attach photographs of their children to the wire mesh, threaded with pieces of coloured wool, to signify that this protest is for *them*, their futures. They begin a low keening as they rock the fence, forward and back, which turns into wilder ululations as some of the women, Jenna, Bex and Caroline among them, use bolt cutters to take down sections of it, enabling them to enter the base and dance around the silos that have been erected to house the Cruise Missiles.

"Are you on the side of suicide?
Are you on the side of homicide?
Are you on the side of genocide...?"

She's always known exactly which side she's on.

As she and Séydou drive along the Express Highway from Aden to Taiz, they sing verse after verse, buoyed by their shared conviction.

"Are you on the side of atrocity?
Are you on the side of poverty?
Or are you on the side of humanity?
Which side are you on...?

At first their progress is smooth. They pass through Lahij and Al-Awdhali. They stop off at a roadside supermarket for bottled water at Al-Anad. But then they face more and more hold-ups. The frequency of the road-blocks increases. The time it takes for their papers to be checked and approved becomes longer. Through Sarhan, Aqan, Kirsh and Asher. But at Ar-Rahidah, where they must cross from the Lahij to the Taiz Governorate, they are detained for over an hour. Séydou must use all of his diplomatic skills to gain permission for them to continue. Then, just before they reach the village of Najd Sabri, they are forced to leave the Highway altogether and take a rockier, narrower, local road, as they climb towards the summit of the plateau where Taiz will await them.

Immediately the atmosphere changes. They are now travelling *through* the landscape, not hovering above it. They feel a part of it, instead of screened off from it. The centuries slip by. A thousand years before, all of the land here belonged to Saladin. Two hundred years later, when Ibn Battutah, the Muslim Berber scholar, who travelled the world even more extensively than Marco Polo, visited Taiz, he declared it the largest and most beautiful city in all of the Levant. As they drive towards it now, along a dried-up river-bed, it dominates the horizon at every turning, sheltering beneath the summit of Jabal Sabir, one of the highest mountains in the country. On its slopes grapes are grown for raisins, as well as coffee and *qat*, the narcotic which unites all Yemenis, whichever branch of Islam they might follow. They pass an old man, leading a small straggle of black goats, his jaw grinding away as he chews the plant's leaves. A part of Jenna is curious to try some, the old part, the part she casts aside when she is pregnant with Molly, when she stops smoking cannabis, and which she has not resumed since. Though she still succumbs to tobacco more frequently than she cares to admit. A small boy follows them, pedalling furiously on a beat-up bike, bouncing through the pot-holes. He is soon joined by a posse of other curious children.

"You got dollar?" they ask them. "You got pen? Dollar? Pen?"

Jenna wants to give to them all, but Séydou warns her not to. "You'll cause a stampede," he tells her, "then dozens more will come. What will you do then?"

"Dollar, dollar, dollar, dollar?"

Jenna knows he's right, but she'd gladly tip out the entire contents of her wallet if he'd let her. She knows such a gesture is futile, that it achieves nothing in the longer term, except the worst kind of dependency. But the power of guilt exerts a strong pull. She can't just drive past. The people of Taiz earn an average of eight thousand rials a month. That's around twenty-five dollars. And this goatherd substantially less. By comparison Jenna is awash with money. She winds down the window and tosses out all the small change she has, plus a dozen dollar bills. The children chase after them like desert skylarks, their voices tiny stones, skittering down the hillside, stones that can start an avalanche...

It's a hot summer's night. About one in the morning. Jenna and Lance are just leaving *The Reno Club* on the corner of Princess Road and Moss Lane East. It's less than five minutes away from the Squat and a favourite hang-out. One of the few places in the city where the races mix freely, together with its sister club, *The Nile*, directly above. Where *The Nile* specialises in punk, *The Reno* plays a fusion of reggae, ska and soul, the music presided over by DJ Persian, a local celebrity and mate of Lance's, who he fills in for sometimes, an hour here, an hour there, when Persian needs to take a break.

This has been one such night. Lance has his sights set on a career in the music business, a promoter maybe. He's tried his hand a few times already. He helped out at the *Rock Against*

Racism festival at Alexandra Park a couple of years back – when Steel Pulse and The Buzzcocks headlined. Jenna had attended that gig. She's always been a fan of The Buzzcocks. She still is. She didn't know Lance then. But already, it seems to both of them now, their separate threads were being drawn together even then.

They're remembering that now as they step out of *The Reno* into the thick muggy air of the night. Local band Harlem Spirit have been playing, and the club has been rammed. Lance first heard them as support on the same bill as The Buzzcocks, and he's been pressing Persian to give them a spot ever since. Tonight it's finally happened. They've gone down a storm, as Lance has known all along they would, and Persian is delighted. Tony Wilson has been there, as he is frequently, scouting for talent for Factory Records, and has brought along his usual entourage. It's not quite the heady days of the seventies, when Persian remembers playing host to the likes of Muhammad Ali and Bob Marley, who each dropped in unannounced on separate occasions, but a good night nevertheless. He's promised Lance more gigs in the future, and Lance is on a high.

He and Jenna are still singing the songs of Harlem Spirit as people spill out onto the streets. Especially one, *Dem a Sus*, a real crowd-pleaser, and timely, too, in its attack on the recently introduced 'sus' laws, which entitle the police to stop and search anyone they please, anyone who they think might be posing some kind of threat to public order, which in reality means a licence to arrest young black men. Harlem Spirit know what they're singing about. They're from Moss Side themselves and have fallen foul of the 'sus' laws on more than one occasion – only to be released afterwards without charge, but with several bruises – as has Lance.

The track begins with the ominous sound of police sirens, followed by lead vocalist Rikki Rogers dedicating the song "to the people of the ghettoes, especially in Moss Side..."

*"We all live together
We flock like birds o' one feather..."*

Then the music starts to find its groove.

*"Dem a sus, dem a sus
Right here in di Moss*

*Dem a sus, dem a sus
Don't let dem pressure us..."*

... before Max Thompson's sax really gets the party moving. Lance and Jenna grind their bodies slow and close in time to its rock-steady beat.

But the moment they leave the club, the mood changes. The sound of real live police sirens is now all around them. A cluster of black youths is being taunted by a smaller knot of white men, who Lance recognises as off-duty Policemen.

"There'll never be a riot in Manchester," calls out one of them.

"They've not got the bottle," says another.

"Wi shud go," says Lance. He knows what they're referring to. He's only recently got back from visiting contacts in Brixton and Toxteth, at Spike's instigation, to suss out the lie of the land and report back.

"Dem be local trigger," says Lance on his return. "But di root cause is di same. "

*"Do you hear me now about di law dem call sus...?
Cos it's happenin' now right here in di Moss..."*

Spike nods grimly.

"*Unity*," cry Harlem Spirit. "*Flock together*."

Out on the street the tension simmers. Like a kettle boiling. Another white man emerges from a parked van on the corner of Raby Street and throws a brick through the window of a Pawnbroker's.

Then the kettle whistles. The force of it blows off the lid.

Shop windows the entire length of Princess Road begin to be smashed by the cluster of black youths, whose numbers are growing. Fires are lit along the hard shoulder.

Lance takes Jenna by the wrist and runs her back to the Squat, their footsteps skittering like those same tiny stones she will hear more than thirty years later. The avalanche is beginning...

Jenna and Séydou drive through rocky fields of millet, gorged on by flocks of finches, the golden-winged grosbeak, Yemen's national bird. A pair of buzzards circle overhead, their high-pitched mewing cry the only sound to be heard. The finches seem unconcerned. A murder of ravens appears, seemingly out of nowhere, and remorselessly sets about mobbing the buzzards. The finches momentarily look up, then return to their feasting. The sight of them trilling, waving their long white tails in the air fills Jenna with unease...

She is remembering a time back in Slate Lane, shortly after Molly is born. She is hanging nuts and fat-balls in a feeder at the back of the house, close to the tow-path beside the Canal...

Flocks of finches swoop at the feeding station, gorging on the nuts and fat-balls, nudging aside the native sparrows, restoring the fat of their bodies, after half a year's desperate travel from the east, forty percent of them always on the move, crossing oceans and continents, mountains and rivers, desert and forest, to alight here, this pocket-sized Manchester garden, just as the tulips are budding, caught in the hard glint of a winter sun, at the tail-end of the year's storms.

Pausing for breath they lift their eyes from the feasting. The crows are already circling, jackboot black, their close-cropped jack-hammer heads primed and ready, beaks like batons, wings raised like riot shields. The finches tsirrup and trill. They wave their undulating tails like flags of welcome or surrender – cower, retreat, move on – back to their make-shift nests of cobwebbed hair and feathers.

Two-year-old Molly claps her hands in delight at the sight of them. She only succeeds in scaring them away.

Tomorrow more will come...

And here they are, pouring out of the edge of Taiz.
And this is just the beginning of them...

Jenna and Séydou loop back onto the Express Highway and are immediately brought to a halt. More road blocks have been set up. Soldiers are stopping and checking each individual vehicle approaching the city. There are not many wanting to enter, but still it is taking an eternity for the line to inch forward, while in the opposite direction a flood of people are trying to leave. It is more than a flood. It is a tidal wave, an exodus of biblical proportions. Whole families, with all their pitiful possessions piled high on shopping trolleys, pour out of the city.

It's started then, thinks Jenna. Zafirah is right. Taiz has become the front line.

It takes an hour for them to pass through the checkpoint to enter the city. In all that time there is no let-up in the line of those leaving. Séydou manages to find the General in charge of the evacuation. He's part of the Saudi-backed Coalition's forces under President Hadi. The road south, he tells them, remains under Government protection. But all the other routes into Taiz are falling under Houthi control as their armies march down from the north. There's no fighting yet. But it's only a matter of time. He advises them to get out of the country as fast as they can.

"That's all very well," argues Séydou. "But we're protected under international agreements."

"For now," warns the General darkly.

"But the people here in Taiz are not," persists Jenna. "What happens to *them*? Not all will want to head south."

The General regards her with suspicion. "We are offering a safe passage for all who wish to leave," he says, indicating the stumbling exodus.

"But what about those who choose to stay?"

"Those we shall not be able to protect."

Séydou hurries Jenna away, before she can say anything further.

"We have to deal with all sides equally," he reminds her, and she scowls. "There will be enclaves set up," he says, "for each of the different communities."

"Where they will be sitting ducks for each other's forces," she rasps back. "There have to be ways out in every direction, not just south."

"And somewhere for them to return to when all this is finally over." Jenna falls silent in the face of Séydou's candour.

They are in the old quarter. The white minarets of the city's two main mosques – the Ashrafiyar and the Mudhaffar – straddle either side of the square they now find themselves in. Soldiers are erecting two sets of barricades in a direct line from one to the other, creating a demarcation zone between the different sectors of the city, which is rapidly being carved up. Séydou and Jenna wave their *Médecins Sans Frontières* papers in front of the soldiers, who hastily hurry them through.

Just as they are midway between the barricades, the no-man's-land where neither side has overall control, two fighter planes roar overhead from opposite directions. They circle, clockwise and counter-clockwise, their vapour trails intermingling. A MiG-21 and an Su-22. Out of the belly of each, dozens of small, cylindrical bombs are disgorged. The people in the city, looking up, at first begin to panic. Jenna and Seydou find themselves caught up in the melée, jostled and buffeted and spun like tops. But then the bombs explode in mid-air and release their cargo, not of explosives, but leaflets, propaganda, each blaming the other side for the current crisis, some urging the people to stay, some warning them to leave. They shower down upon them, like confetti, like ticker-tape. But there are no weddings taking place this day. Nor trophies being won. Or heroes being welcomed home. Their messages, though directly contradicting one another, are identical in their unequivocation.

"Read me," they shriek, "for I am in sole possession of the truth. Thou shalt have no other gods but me..."

Jenna is sixteen. She has gone into school early, before anyone else has arrived. She sneaks into the Reprographics Room. She is on a mission. She takes from her bag a single sheet of paper, onto which she has written, in bold block capitals, the words to her own creed, taken from a song by The Buzzcocks, *I Believe...*

She switches on the photocopier. The room is filled with the sound of its deep, satisfying hum. She waits the ninety seconds it takes for the machine to warm up in an agony of anticipation, hopping from one foot to the other, darting to and from the door to check that no one is coming down the corridor. Eventually the machine is ready. She places the sheet of paper face down on the glass plate and closes the lid. Then she takes out a full, unopened ream from the stationery cupboard, which she opens and inserts into the paper tray. She selects '500' for the quantity, then presses 'Copy'. Immediately each one in turn begins to shoot through to the receiving tray on the other side, where they quickly accumulate. She continues to check the corridor in case one of the teachers might be wanting to prepare material for a morning class, but she's in luck. The machine finishes copying just as Mrs Martin, the Head of Resources, walks through the door.

Morning, Miss, says Jenna cheerfully, as she dodges past her. "I was just collecting something I need for our Year Group Assembly."

Mrs Martin frowns, but says nothing. What Jenna has said sounds quite plausible.

Jenna dives down the corridor, but then, instead of heading back to the Sixth Form Common Room, which is where she is meant to be before school officially starts, and instead of ducking behind the bike sheds for a quick cigarette with some of her girl friends, which is what she does most mornings, she takes the stairs to the classrooms at the top of the building two at a time. Her target is the Geography Room, which has a window that opens onto a flat roof, overhanging the main entrance to the school. By the teacher's desk is a globe, which Jenna spins, just for the hell of it, then stops with a jab of her index finger. When the world stops turning, she looks to see on which country her finger has landed. It's Yemen – the country where her mother's parents and her father's grandfather were born, before they came to Manchester. She smiles. It's a good omen, she thinks. It must be.

She opens one of the windows, using a long wooden pole, then carefully climbs through it, to step out onto the flat roof, where she waits.

She waits till the electric bell for the start of school rings. A rush of people – staff and pupils – converge on the double doors directly beneath where she is standing. Just when she feels the crowd below her is at its densest, she jumps up and hurls the photocopied sheets of her creed – *I Believe* – onto the unsuspecting masses, who watch the leaflets fall upon them like a gift, a blessing, manna from heaven, which, to Jenna's eyes, is exactly what they are...

*STOP. GO. WAIT HERE. GO THERE. COME IN. STAY OUT.
LIVE. DIE.
BE A MAN. BE A WOMAN. BE WHITE. BE BLACK. YES. NO.
DO IT NOW. DO IT LATER.
BE YOUR REAL SELF. BE SOMEBODY ELSE. FIGHT. SUBMIT.
RIGHT. WRONG.
MAKE A SPLENDID IMPRESSION.
MAKE AN AWFUL IMPRESSION.
SIT DOWN. STAND UP.
TAKE YOUR HAT OFF. PUT YOUR HAT ON.
CREATE. DESTROY. REACT. IGNORE.
LIVE IN THE PAST. LIVE IN THE FUTURE. LIVE NOW.
BE AMBITIOUS. BE MODEST. ACCEPT. REJECT.
DO MORE. DO LESS. PLAN AHEAD. BE SPONTANEOUS.
DECIDE FOR YOURSELF. LISTEN TO OTHERS.
TALK. BE SILENT.
SAVE MONEY. SPEND MONEY. SPEED UP. SLOW DOWN.
THIS WAY. THAT WAY. RIGHT. LEFT.
PRESENT. ABSENT. OPEN. CLOSED.
UP. DOWN. ENTER. EXIT.
IN. OUT.*

She doesn't pretend she isn't responsible. She stands above them, up on the roof, her fist raised in triumph, defiant and proud.

When the Deputy Head suspends her, she is unrepentant...

Now, as she recalls that moment, with the leaflets from the opposing forces in Taiz cascading all around her, she feels her actions at school, even allowing for the hubris of youth, were ridiculous and naïve. What kind of manifesto is it that tries to play both sides against the middle, to have it both ways, without coming down firmly either way? She supposes that it could be regarded as a plea for tolerance – live and let live, the total acceptance of otherness, the acknowledgement that everyone's entitled to their opinion, whatever rocks your boat or turns you on – but really, who was she kidding? She was just posturing. It was fashion, nothing more. Fence-sitting of the worst kind. But the more she thinks about those words by The Buzzcocks, with their in-built contradictions, the more she comes to see the wisdom of them. There are no easy answers. There are always two sides to a coin. But here, with people fleeing in every direction at once, the choice is a stark one. The top line of her own creed could not be more apposite.

STOP. GO. WAIT HERE. GO THERE. COME IN. STAY OUT. LIVE. DIE.

Whatever the people decide, there are no guarantees. Whether they choose to stay or leave, there is no knowing the outcome, whichever decision they take, whether they will live or die.

Jenna wonders what she would do in their position. She has no idea. It's a binary choice – off, on, on, off – with seemingly random consequences.

She flails. She flounders. She wants to take them all back home with her. Just as she wanted to give a dollar to every one of those children earlier. But she knows that that is merely fanciful, unrealistic. She understands, possibly for the first time in her life, that, however hard an outer shell she presents to the world, she is a hopeless romantic, which is an utterly untenable position. It's simply a luxury she cannot afford. No more than can any of the citizens of Taiz, as they ponder what they must do next.

LIVE IN THE PAST. LIVE IN THE FUTURE. LIVE NOW.

And what of she and Séydou? Should they continue on up to the Citadel at the summit of the city, where they have an appointment with a Government official? Or should they retrace their steps and return back down to Aden?

Just when she feels she will bore a hole into the ground with her endless turning around and around, Séydou takes charge.

"We've got to leave," he says. "We've got to get you out of the country as quickly as we can. With my MSF credentials I can stay longer if I have to. But your visa is only for a week. If we don't leave here today, who knows how long we might be forced to stay?"

Jenna sees the sense in what he is saying. The *common* sense. But she needs to speak to the Government official first. She needs to get some guarantees – if she can – that, should the need arise, safe passage will be granted to all those fleeing the fighting, whichever side they're on.

"There can be no such guarantees," says Séydou. "You know that."

"At least let's try," she says. "Then we'll go…"

UP. DOWN. ENTER. EXIT. IN. OUT.

When they finally reach the Citadel, the chaos is, if anything, even worse. The Officials are packing up to leave themselves.

"We've been recalled to Sana'a," says one harassed Administrator.

"But we can't go there," says another. "The Houthis have more or less taken control."

"So we're heading for Aden," says the first.

"We've been told to take only what's essential," says the second, "and destroy the rest."

Already there are several small fires burning in the compound outside, onto which more office workers are emptying the contents of filing cabinets.

Meanwhile hundreds of frightened civilians are trying to force their way in. They need papers stamped if they are to be able to leave and pass safely through the road blocks they will encounter beyond the city walls, whichever direction they take.

Already a small task force of Houthi troops have entered the compound and are beginning to impose themselves. They appear to have met with little resistance on their way in. What few of the Coalition soldiers remain are too busy making safe their own sector of the city south of the line between the two mosques.

Jenna manages to catch up with the Government official they have an appointment with, while Séydou goes to speak to the Major in charge of the Houthis.

They both ask the same question.

"Can you guarantee a humanitarian corridor and a temporary cease of hostilities while aid is brought in and casualties taken out?"

They each receive the same answer.

"There will be no casualties. There will be no need for aid."

"But if there is?"

"In that case, then of course we can guarantee this corridor. For humanitarian purposes only of course. But we cannot speak for the other side. If we get a whiff of suspicion that such a corridor might be used for military purposes, then of course, we should have to close it. With immediate effect. We take it that you understand our answer?"

Oh yes. There isn't space for a scintilla of doubt.

"And we recommend that you yourselves leave at the earliest opportunity. There are still flights running from Taiz International Airport *today*. *Inshallah.* But tomorrow? Who knows…?"

Their meaning could not be clearer. The underlying threat is palpable…

Just as they are about to attempt to leave, a violent commotion erupts in a corner of the compound.

Crowds of local people, many still desperate to get their papers stamped to provide them with the necessary authority to move freely from district to district across the country, with even more seeking sanctuary and protection from the growing chaos outside on the streets, press towards the Main Admin Building, while at the same time the Government officials trapped inside desperately try to make their way out. The ensuing gridlock creates panic and fear. The small deployment of Houthi troops outside, in an attempt to re-establish order and seize control of the compound for themselves, begin firing weapons into the air, above the heads of the surging crowds. But the effect of the gunfire is to cause yet further panic. Then the panic turns to anger. Fights break out between the people and the officials, as well as between rival factions within the crowds. Windows are smashed. Doors are forced open. The offices are looted. More fires are started. The Houthi soldiers begin deploying tear gas. Local youths hurl stones and homemade missiles. Within minutes the entire compound is under siege, with nobody really knowing who is attacking who.

Séydou grabs Jenna by the wrist and races her through the crowds towards the square outside the compound. He puts his jacket over both of their heads to offer at least some kind of shield against the hail of small stones that are raining through the air.

Through the blur of bodies, the sting of smoke, the sounds of shattering glass and bullets, Jenna feels the force of the years, like a hand on her collar at the back of her neck, roughly dragging her back, squeezing her through a barbed wire fence...

It's the summer of 1981. The second night of the Moss Side riots...

"We can't stay indoors," says Spike. "We need to be showing solidarity with our brothers and sisters."

"Right on," say Dougie and Caroline together.

"But we've got to be careful," insists Spike...

He has been at a meeting all afternoon at Platt Lane. The Police have invited community leaders to discuss the events of the previous night and discuss what to do in case there's a repeat tonight, which everyone is fearful of. As well as Spike, a lot of young black people have turned up. But then the Police keep them all waiting. They don't show up for more than an hour. In the end most of the young people drift away, disillusioned. But not Spike. He stays. When the police do eventually appear, they are led by the Chief Constable for Greater Manchester, James Anderton.

"What kind of Police presence will there be this evening?" asks Spike.

"Whatever is required," replies the Chief Constable.

"I think it's important that every effort should be directed at lowering the temperature, not raising it," says Spike.

The Chief Constable says he agrees.

"A large Police presence on the streets is more likely to provoke than to prevent trouble."

At no point does Chief Constable Anderton argue with this opinion, or indicate that he is contemplating a different strategy. "But should any trouble arise," he says before leaving, "you can be assured that we shall take all the necessary steps to deal with it…"

"I don't trust him," says Spike now to the others. "That's why we need to be out there tonight, trying to keep a lid on things, making sure the people stay calm."

"Mi not so sure," says Lance. "Mi bound tuh get arrested."

"Not if you keep your head down," says Bex. "Do nothing to draw attention to yourself."

"Yeah right," says Lance witheringly, pointing to the colour of his skin.

"I'll look after you," says Jenna fiercely.

"Now yuh talkin', gyal," he grins…

Jenna's not feeling as brave as she sounds. She's not at all sure what her position is regarding the riots up and down the country. She completely gets Spike's insistence that private property is theft. But that doesn't excuse looting. Or condone violence. She thinks the 'sus' laws are a disgrace, a dangerous threat to individual liberty, which disproportionately target young black men – like Lance – especially those whose appearance makes them stand out from the crowd, with their tams and dreads – again, like Lance – so she understands his misgivings. But on the other hand, this feels like one of those key moments in history, when freedom and democracy are really on the line. There's no way she's not going out onto the streets this night.

And if *she* does, she knows Lance will too. He'll feel he has to.

"Let's go," she says.

The others rally around her determination.

"Right," they shout, raising their clenched fists. "Power to the People."

" '*Get up, stand up*'," sings Lance. " '*Stand up for yuh right*'."

"And if any of those nice young men in blue ask us what we're doing," says Jenna, "we'll tell them, sweetly and politely, that we're simply exercising our democratic right to engage in peaceful protest."

The others laugh and applaud.

"Protest 'gainst wah, gyal?"

"Whatta you got…?"

"Mi sweet Carib grackle," he croons…

Jenna doubts, though, that the protest will remain peaceful. She deplores violence – in all its forms – but she doesn't rule out her own capacity to lash out in defence of herself or her comrades…

By the time they hit the streets, there are several hundreds of others already there. More and more fires have been lit. They form a chain of beacons lighting their way, which they all of them follow. All roads, it seems, lead inevitably to Platt Lane, where the Moss Side Police Station sits like a fortress...

People later will say that it is a well-planned operation, that outside agitators from Liverpool and London, as well as local ringleaders, are responsible for a callous and calculated attack against authority, with a total lack of regard for law and order. But that is not how Jenna remembers it at all. It feels more random and spontaneous to her. Not unlike the way Amani Yayha taught herself English. By listening to western pop music and watching American movies. The Siege, as some newspapers will describe it, of the Platt Lane Police Station, bears many of the hallmarks of John Carpenter's film *Escape from New York*, starring Kurt Russell, a dystopian nightmare in which all of Manhattan has been turned into a maximum level prison for violent offenders, who attempt to break free by first besieging the high security Police Headquarters at the centre.

But Moss Side Police Station is far from high security. When the protesters first arrive, a little after half-past ten, there are only fourteen Officers inside. Whether they are luring the youths into a trap, or are simply unprepared, is unclear. But what *is* clear is that, after less than half an hour, during which time bricks and stones are hurled indiscriminately through the windows, accompanied by angry anti-Fascist chanting, eight black Marias screech into the yard, disgorging ten Officers each, who proceed to bang the sides of the vehicles with their truncheons in a menacing rhythm, before bringing them crashing down upon the heads of the now-trapped young people...

Jenna does not witness this. She only hears about it

afterwards. Before she reaches Platt Lane, she is met by a panicked rabble of beaten and bloodied protesters fleeing the scene, heading straight towards her, threatening to flatten her, so that she has no option but to turn tail and join the stampede.

By now it is nearly midnight. Rival gangs of local black and white youths are rampaging out of control, sometimes fighting the Police, sometimes each other. The air is thick with smoke from petrol bombs and small fires. The whole of Moss Lane East and Princess Road is in flames.

Jenna runs full tilt into Raby Street, around the corner from the Squat, thinking it might be quieter there, only to collide head-on with a fully deployed Riot Squad, who charge with batons and shields.

She dives into an open doorway to escape their path, then follows them back out into Princess Road, where the main body of protesters have gathered on a piece of waste ground not far from the Harp Lager Brewery known locally as 'The Meadow'.

Jenna is now separated from her friends – Lance, Bex, Dougie and Caroline – but she sees Spike, speaking through a loud hailer, appealing for calm on both sides. She tries to make her way towards him, when she realises that this is what the Police have been planning for all along. Convoys of vans and pandas have circled The Meadow, the beams of their headlights directed towards the protesters, kettling them into the centre.

The protesters, sensing the trap, begin to build barricades out of anything they can lay their hands on. Railings, fences, gate-posts. Crates, beer kegs, packing cases. Items of looted furniture, rusting fridges, burnt-out cars.

Someone tries to wrench Spike's loud hailer from him, and an unseemly tussle ensues, resulting in it being flung high into the air. Jenna watches its slow arc through the night sky, briefly illuminated by the rising flames, as it passes from light into shadow. It lands with a resounding crack a few feet away from her, before emitting a loud, complaining wail of feedback, until one of the Officers from the Riot Squad smashes it hard, once, with his truncheon, silencing it in an instant.

There then follows a full-blooded, deep-throated roar from the rest of the Squad, once more banging their shields with their batons in a rising crescendo, followed by an even louder, guttural cry from the protesters.

The Riot Squad charges, only to be met with a fire storm of petrol bombs and other missiles.

For over an hour the battle rages.

Fortunes ebb and flow. The tide turns first one way, then the other.

Jenna watches, powerless and paralysed. She continues to search frantically for her friends, calling out their names, but to no avail.

Inch by brutal inch the Police relentlessly advance.

Then Jenna catches sight of Dougie and Caroline. One of the Riot Squad has knocked Dougie to the ground and is beating him with his truncheon. Caroline is desperately trying to stop him. She grabs his elbow to pull him away, only for a second to wrestle her to the ground and punch her in the stomach. Jenna runs towards her, but she is caught in the path of more charging Police Officers, who brush her aside with no more thought than they would a buzzing fly. She curls herself tightly into a ball until the rest of the Squad have passed over her. When she finally lifts her head, she can no longer see Dougie or Caroline. But she hears a voice calling out her name.

"Dis way, gyal!"

It's Lance. He's been doing what Bex suggested earlier, keeping his head down, trying not to attract attention. But not any more. Jenna sees him, attempting to make his way towards her from the far side of Princess Road, remonstrating with Police Officers who try to prevent him, beckoning her away from The Meadow. She lifts a hand in greeting, scrambles painfully to her feet, opens her mouth to answer him, to tell him that she's all right, when she feels something strike the back of her head, hard, then nothing.

The final things she sees before the blackness takes her are the sparks and embers of the last of the fires dancing above her in the night sky...

Jenna opens her eyes. She's not sure how long she's been out. She raises a hand to the side of her head. Blood is weeping from a small cut.

"It's nothing serious," says a voice. Séydou. "A stone. "

It was thrown just as they were leaving the compound, Séydou tells her. She wasn't the target. She was just unlucky. Right now she feels she couldn't be luckier. She's alive.

Séydou is driving extremely fast.

"Where are we going?" she asks.

"The airport. Once we get there, we'll be able to fix you up properly."

If we get there, she thinks, but doesn't say.

"How far is it?" she asks.

"Twelve miles out of the city," he says, "north, along the road to Ibb. We're more than halfway there. It shouldn't be long now. Try to rest if you can. "

Easier said than done.

She turns her head to look back towards the city. Columns of smoke hang in the air above it. A feeling of *déjà vu* overwhelms her. She closes her eyes...

When she opens them, she can't at first remember where she is. She's not sure how long she's been out. She raises a hand to the side of her head. Blood is weeping from a small cut.

"It's nothing serious," says a voice. A man's. But one she does not recognise.

"What happened...?"

"A stone. A truncheon. It's impossible to tell."

She turns her head to see who might be speaking to her. She squints her eyes to try and focus. Smoke and ash from the fires cloud her vision. The face of the man with the voice looms into view. The expression in his eyes is kind and concerned. Then she realises. Her jaw drops. It's a Policeman...

At the turn-off for the airport, less than a mile from the terminal, they encounter the final road block. It's manned by Houthis. They confirm that Sana'a Airport is still closed, until their forces can make it secure.

After the riots in Moss Side Princess Road remains shut for three days...

But the airport at Taiz stays open. For now. "If you hurry," say the soldiers, "you might make one of the last flights out."
Jenna's mouth goes dry. Tears prick the back of her eyes. As they always do when she is confronted by the kindness of strangers...

When she recovers from the shock, she tries to look more closely at her rescuer. The Policeman is older than she'd have expected. Late thirties. Forty possibly. The same age as her father...

As the last soldier waves them through, Jenna mouths a silent *shukraan*. Thank you. He smiles and salutes. He's only a boy, she thinks. Probably no older than her daughter. Molly. The thought of it breaks her heart...

"What's your name?" asks the kind Policeman.
"Jenna. What's yours?"
"Nigel."
"I've never known a Nigel."

"Well – now you do. P.C. Nigel Taylor, at your service."

He puts a plaster over her cut.

"You'll need to wash an' dress that properly when you get home. But it should hold for now."

"Aren't you going to arrest me?"

"Does it look like I am?"

"No," she says, then looks down. "Thank you."

He shakes his head.

"What're you doin' out here anyway?"

"I could ask the same of you."

"Me? I'm just doing my job."

"Really? What job's that?"

"Trying to keep the peace."

"Me too."

"Is that what this is," he says, looking around at the debris and the devastation, the fires still smouldering, "keepin' the peace?"

"And how is charging at kids with riot shields and batons helping to keep the peace?"

"Not me, love," he says, turning away. "I'm just an honest copper."

The Riot Squad have mostly gone now. Jenna can still see one or two of them in the distance, standing beside police vans, removing their gear, laughing and joking with one another, like it's all been some kind of game to them. The streets are quieter. A few paramedics are tending to the more seriously injured. She looks around further. There's no sign of Lance, or Spike, or Dougie and Caroline, or Bex. She hopes they've made it back to the Squat in one piece.

She tries to stand but immediately feels whoozy, as if she might faint.

"Steady does it, lass," says Nigel. "Best sit down a bit longer, eh?"

She allows herself to be guided gently back to the

pavement.

"How long was I out?" she asks.

"Couldn't say," he answers. "You were just startin' to come round when I found you. Nearly tripped over you. An' I've been here with you – let me see..." He checks his watch. "Fifteen minutes. You kept calling for Lance. Is he your boyfriend?"

Jenna nods.

"Not much of a boyfriend if he's not around when you need him, is he?"

Jenna feels her cheeks going red.

"We got separated," she says. "He's probably gone back to our flat."

"Far, is it?"

She shakes her head.

"Five minutes," she says.

"Right. I'll walk you there. As soon as you can stand wi'out fallin' over again. Let's give it a bit longer, shall we, before we try that again?"

Jenna nods again.

He looks around. "It's a terrible mess," he says. "It's goin' to take a long time to clean all this up. An' even longer for things to get back to normal again."

"But we don't want them to go back to 'normal', as you put it. We want things to change."

"Fair enough. But there has to be a better way than this, surely? Look around you."

Jenna scans the vicinity. There's not a house that hasn't had its windows smashed. Not a shop that's not been looted. Although several have been put out, there are still dozens of small fires burning. The acrid smell of the smoke stings the back of her eyes. She has to swallow hard.

"You're right," she says. "But what *is* that better way? My boyfriend would say, 'Let wi trow a party, gyal. Yuh canna' be fightin' if yuh dancin'...' "

"He's got a point."

The two of them smile wearily at one another.

"Well," says Nigel, "do you think you might be strong enough to stand now?"

Jenna nods and scrambles to her feet, using his arm for support.

Just at that moment a small group of protesters skitter towards them. There are six of them, a mixture of black and white, four men, two women.

"What're you doin'?" yells one of them.

"Which side are you on?" says another.

"Are you some copper's bitch now?"

"Why don't you give 'im a blow job then?"

At which point one of them hurls a brick aimed directly at Jenna. Nigel instinctively throws himself in front of her, and the brick hits him full square on the side of his head, knocking off his helmet, felling him like a tree.

The protesters run off, laughing and swearing, while Jenna immediately kneels beside him to check he's OK. She takes off her sweater and folds it like a pillow, placing it directly underneath his head, which she lays gently on the kerb.

In the moment that she does this, she is dimly aware of someone with a camera close by, stepping out of the shadows, to capture this act of tenderness for all time. She is certain she hears the click of the shutter. She turns, but no one is there...

Years later, when she returns from Yemen, her daughter will text her to tell her that she has just seen this photograph, in the same Exhibition in which the picture of her father's lost mural is hanging. She will take herself to see it, on a quiet afternoon when nobody else is in the gallery, and look at it for a long time, remembering...

As soon as she is certain that Nigel is comfortable, she stands up and looks around for someone to call for help. A hundred yards away, on The Meadow, she sees an ambulance. A couple of paramedics are carrying one of the more seriously wounded casualties on a stretcher towards the back of it. She calls them over, tells them what's happened.

"Right," they say grimly. "We'll come straight back as soon as we've taken this one to the Infirmary. Can you stay with him till then?"

Jenna replies that she can – she will – then she hurries back to Nigel.

The cut on the side of his head is bleeding quite freely, which at first sight looks alarming, but when she examines it more closely, she decides that it's not as bad as it appears. "Head cuts always bleed a lot, don't they?" she says as cheerfully as she can. Nigel coughs and agrees that they do.

"Do you think you can sit?" she asks.

Without waiting for him to reply, she gently raises him to a sitting position.

"Better to be upright, I think," she says, trying to dredge up what little first aid she can remember from watching MASH.

She takes off her T-shirt, quickly replacing it with the sweater that has been acting as the pillow for Nigel, then proceeds to tear her T-shirt into strips, which she fashions into a make-shift bandage.

While she winds it tightly round his head, as they wait for the ambulance to return, he slowly starts to speak.

"I want to tell you a story," he says.

"OK then," she says, frowning in concentration as she continues to wrap the torn strips of cotton around his wound. "I'm listening...."

"My Dad were a miner. At Bradford Colliery. Before they closed the pit. He were livid when they did that. 'There's enough coal down there for another century,' he said. 'Mebbe more. But it costs too much to dig it out. It's uneconomic, that's what they reckon. Meaning they don't mek as much profit as they'd like. So they're shuttin' us down. Greedy bastards.' That was the way 'e talked. It were always 'us' against 'them'. Everythin' were black an' white, no grey areas in between. It would get 'im into a lot o' trouble. You know, strikes an' that? Secretly I were glad when they shut down t' pit. It meant I wouldn't 'ave to go down meself. I'd've 'ated it. But I'd've done it, rather than disappoint me Dad. I got the biggest surprise o' me life when 'e told me 'e were not sorry that I wouldn't 'ave to go through what 'e'd ad to. That gave me the courage to tell 'im that I wanted to become a copper. 'Whatever dost tha' want to do that for, lad,?' 'e said. 'Tha'll get nowt but grief.' So I tried to explain it to 'im. Like I'm tryin' to explain it to you now, lass. 'I want to mek a difference,' I said. 'I'm fed up wi' all the fightin' an' quarellin'. I want people to work together. We all want t' same thing, when it comes down to it. Enough money to pay t' rent an' put food on t' table, wi' a bit left over for th' odd pint on a Friday, football on a Sat'day, two weeks' holiday somewhere warm, an' for our kids, if we 'ave any, to 'ave a better time of it than *we* did.' 'Ay', 'e said, 'I reckon tha's in t' right of it, but 'ow's bein' a copper goin' to 'elp wi' all that?' 'Because,' I said, 'a copper's at the heart o' things. Like the parson, or the teacher, the postman or the publican. The Bobby on 'is beat. Everyone knows 'im, an' *'e* knows everyone. They trust 'im. They come to 'im if they've a problem. An' 'e can try an' sort things out for 'em.' But the way me Dad reacted it were like I'd punched im in t' stomach. 'I'm not sorry tha' won't be goin' down t' pit, son,' he said, 'but joinin' t' Police? Them who's been t' bane o' me life? It's as if tha'd said tha' were goin' to vote Tory.' I were really mad when 'e said that. 'I'm done wi' all that talk of 'us' an' 'them', Dad,' I said. 'I want to be in t' middle, in t' thick o' things, bringin' people together, not drivin' 'em apart. I know it won't be easy. An' I'll probably mek loads o' mistakes, an' mebbe I'll get it wrong more often than I get it right, but at least I'll 'ave given it a go. I want to be able to look meself in t' mirror each night an' know that I've done me best. I've tried'."

He winces as Jenna finishes tightening the home-made bandage.

"Well," continues Nigel, "I did. I joined t' Police, did all me trainin' an' got a job down t' local nick in Clayton. Nobbut a mile from where I still lived wi' me Mam. Me Dad 'ad passed away by then. We never did set things right between us, an' I'm still reet sorry about that…"

He pauses briefly, remembering.

"I wa'n't married then, I were still in me early twenties. Then – wouldn't you know it? – me very first task turned out to be on patrol at Bradford Pit, *after* it were closed but *before* it were pulled down." He breathes deeply, conjuring up the scene in his mind's eye. "It were like a ghost town. The Management'd just upped an' left, leavin' loads o' stuff behind, not to mention huge mountains o' coal – slag 'eaps an' that. It were a real adventure playground for t' kiddies, but it weren't safe. So – if I caught anyone trespassin', it were my job to tell 'em to 'op it, like. Mostly it were all reet. I'd turn a blind eye to t' women fillin' up prams wi' lumps o coal – I mean, their 'usbands'd dug 'em up in t' first place, so I reckoned they were entitled to their share, so long as they didn't take the piss. An' if any kids showed up, which they did every single day, I only 'ad to 'oller, an' they'd be off an' away, like rats up a drainpipe."

He laughs at the memory, then grimaces again.

Jenna wonders why he's telling her this, where it's all leading.

"Then, one day – a Sunday afternoon it were – just before t' site were going to be completely sealed up, I caught this feller shinnin' over t' wire fence an' rummagin' through th' offices. Now they was strictly out of bounds, so I blew me whistle an' called 'im over to me. I thought 'e'd leg it, but no – 'e just stood there, as docile as a lamb, as though butter wouldn't melt. I asked 'im what 'e were doin', an' 'e told me the strangest thing…"

Jenna can feel the hairs on the back of her neck start to prickle and rise. She knows what's coming next in Nigel's story…

Sol has been walking the tow-paths of four canals for two days. The Bridgewater, Rochdale, Ashton and Ship. He finally reaches his destination just as the sun dips below the clouds, before disappearing again, painting flickering stripes on the surface of the water – Beswick Locks 4 to 6 – where he can still make out what once must have been a landing station, and a flight of stone steps, which he climbs, slowly and with relief, to reach the entrance to Bradford Colliery.

Unlike when his father, Hejaz, climbed these steps forty years before, there are no cheering crowds, no brass bands playing *God Save the King*, no line of dignitaries with chains of office waiting in line to greet him, no soldiers in dress uniform. Instead the rain has begun to fall again, clattering on the tin roofs of the deserted sheds and outbuildings. Rooks caw on the telephone wires. Water from the canal slaps against the steps. The abandoned winding gear creaks and groans in the wind. A high fence bars his entry, with a sign saying "*Danger. Keep Out*". But he has not walked all this way to fail at the last. He straps his rucksack tighter onto his back and climbs the gate, landing heavily on the other side. He picks himself up, dusts himself down and walks towards the pithead. The mine is full of ghosts.

The shafts are partly sealed up, with most of their entrances blocked, but coal wagons still wait on the rusting rail tracks. The wash house, where the men could take showers after each shift, lies silent. Sol pushes against one of the doors and it opens beneath him. He wanders through it, reminded of a similar set-up back in Walton Gaol, and hears again the jokes and songs, the thwack of wet towels against bare backsides, imagines the slip of a soap bar falling from his fingers, feels the rush of water against his skin. Now all that remains is the drip, drip, drip from a broken tap.

Back outside he stops to look around and tries to get some sense of where things must have been. He sees the metal chutes circling the site like a big dipper towards the store houses, where tons of coal would have been deposited each day to be graded and sorted and then carted off for delivery by trucks to the train station, or transported by wagons down rails to the Canal steps where the barges would have pulled up by the dozen, morning, noon and night. He locates where the Administrative Centre once was, a low brick building with a flag pole on the top, though no flag flies today, and heads towards it. The doors are locked, but all the windows are smashed, so he climbs inside, where a snowstorm of paper – memos, notices, invoices, reports – lifts in the breeze, blowing through the offices. He walks on broken glass through this gently cascading drift.

What he is looking for is nowhere to be found, and in truth he hasn't expected it to be. Anything of value or importance must surely have been packed away before everyone left and the building was locked, but given how closely the whole scene resembles that of the *Marie Celeste*, with unwatered plants still in their pots, a scarf hanging on a hook by the door, it might have been possible to find it after all. He picks up a framed photograph from the floor, its glass mount cracked and in pieces, and studies the faces from a bygone age. Men in frock coats and top hats, an elegant lady cutting a ribbon, but nothing resembling a royal visit, and certainly no mounted lump of coal with accompanying brass plaque.

He wanders back outside. The rain is falling stronger now. In the distance he sees children running up and down the slag heaps, shrieking as they slide down the tumbling scree. On the far side of the yard he sees a pair of older men emerging from behind one of the sheds, pushing a pram into which they are piling everything they can lay their hands on, and beneath the coal chutes he notices women, whom he must have missed when he first climbed over the gate, crawling like crabs across the ground, bent low to the earth, trawling for pieces of coal, which they are putting into baskets strapped to their backs.

Suddenly a loud whistle pierces the air. Everyone freezes, and then simply vanishes into holes in the ground, all, that is, except for Sol, who turns about him, bewildered. Running towards him he spies a young Policeman, still whistling and shouting.

"Oi, you! Stay where you are! Don't move!" His helmet falls from his head in his haste and Sol wonders whether he should make a dash for it. But where would he go? And if he were caught, having been warned, that would only make matters worse. The thought of having to return to prison floods through his veins like ice, so he remains where he is, rooted to the spot, until the young Constable reaches him, fixing his helmet back on as he speaks.

"Can't you bloody read?" he says. "Property of the National Coal Board. No trespassing. Danger. Keep Out."

"Sorry," says Sol. "I'd read about the closure of the pit and I was just curious."

"Arms out," says the Policeman, and he proceeds to tap beneath Sol's arms, down the front and side of his coat, then down the outside of both his legs. "OK. What's in the rucksack?"

"Nothing. Just a flask and…"

"What's this?" He holds up Sol's father's drawing between the finger and thumb of one hand suspiciously, as if it might blow up.

"Please," urges Sol, "don't tear it. My father drew it. Before he died. He came here once, forty years ago, to please his own father…"

"What happened?"

"It's a long story."

"And why are *you* here?"

"To try and make amends, I suppose."

The Officer nods, as if he understands, then hands the drawing back to Sol, who folds it carefully and puts it back inside his rucksack. "Thanks."

"My dad used to work here too. Till he got the black lung."

"I'm sorry."

"It's all wrong, closing this place. There's at least a hundred years' worth of coal still waiting to be dug up right underneath where we're standing. Vast reserves. Premium quality too."

"I don't understand."

"Subsidence. Houses nearby. Walls started to crack. Whole streets threatened with collapse or demolition. It's just too expensive to keep mining it, they say. Uneconomic. So people lose their jobs, a whole community ends up on the scrap heap, and I end up having to chase off trespassers. Like you."

Sol nods.

"So hop it."

Sol heads back towards the direction of the Canal.

"Not that way. Over there." And the Policeman points towards a different gate, open, where his blue and white panda car is parked, engine still running.

Sol turns around, thanks the Officer once again, and walks away from the pit. As he reaches the gate, he sees a large lump of coal, lying among the dust of smaller pieces, and bends to pick it up. He looks back towards the Policeman and raises his hand. "Souvenir," he says, then moves on...

"That were nearly fourteen year ago," says Nigel to Jenna now. "But I've never forgotten it. Like 'e were tryin' to atone for summat 'e'd done. Or mebbe not done. An' mek things reet again. Like I were never able to wi' me own Dad."

Jenna finds that she cannot speak. Sol has never spoken about this incident. At least, not to her.

"It made me even more determined to try an' bring folk together. But then summat like all this," he says, gesturing vaguely at the wreckage all around him, "makes me realise I've just been pissin' into t' wind."

He grips Jenna's wrist tightly.

"We all of us want change," he says. "But not like this. There's got to be a better way."

Jenna looks into his eyes. She sees the intensity of their expression, the way the flames from the fires still burning flicker there, her own reflection very small staring back.

A better way.

An ambulance approaches them, its blue revolving light flashing. Two paramedics jump out. "All right," says one of them, gently releasing Nigel's grip from Jenna's wrist, "we'll take it from here."

She watches them lift Nigel into the back, then drive away into the night, its blue light still flashing.

She suddenly feels cold and shivers. Hunching her shoulders, she picks her way through the debris back towards Moss Lane East, and the Squat at 246. It's a route she's walked a thousand times. But tonight it looks different. Not just the damaged buildings from the riot, but how she feels about it. She's in this for the long haul, she realises. Maybe she needs a change of plan. And not just her, all of them. Maybe Nigel is right after all. Work *with* people, not *against* them. Change the system from within, rather than knock it down altogether. That doesn't have to make her any less angry, any less passionate, or committed to the cause, the fight against unfairness, she'll just go about it differently. She doubts if Spike will agree with her. He'll accuse her of selling out. But he'll not ask her to leave. No, he'll say, we listen to all opinions here, even those we disagree with. Besides, he'll add with a grin, you can be our undercover mole…

But tonight, when she finally steps through the door, they are simply all relieved to see that she's safe.

"Tank God," says Lance. "Mi bin worried sick 'bout yuh, gyal."

"Let's take a look at that cut," says Spike.

Dougie and Caroline lie slumped on a mattress in the corner, exhausted. They've not long come back from the hospital. Dougie has three cracked ribs, Caroline a dislocated jaw that's been bandaged up. Bex is playing her guitar.

Yesterday a child came out to wander
Caught a dragonfly inside a jar
Fearful when the sky was full of thunder
And tearful at the falling of a star…

Outside the night is filled with the sounds of sirens wailing, like lost and frightened children, a constellation of blue revolving lights trying to find them…

*

Day 3

The inside of the terminal resembles, to Jenna's mind, an egg. The plate glass windows let in the light from the world outside but only dimly. The air-conditioning, which is, surprisingly perhaps, still working, further screens her from the intensity of the heat beyond this egg's shell, which, temporarily, protects her from its glare and danger. But like all eggshells it is fragile. It might crack at any second.

Outside the egg, soldiers scan the skies for signs of imminent danger, beaks and talons primed and ready. Like anxious parents who fear for their charges' safety if they were to leave the nest too early.

Jenna surveys her fellow fledglings. There are perhaps two hundred of them, huddled together, strangers but confederates, in this agony of waiting, for they are just as desperate to take wing as those who watch over them. The majority refrain from exchanging glances, as if avoiding any kind of scrutiny that might get too close, hunched over their mobile phones, tapping furiously, hoping to make contact with whoever might be waiting for them somewhere else. Except the few children who are there, who guilelessly wander up to perfect strangers, subjecting them to a hard, unblinking stare, daring them to look back, and perhaps exchange a smile, however fleeting, before scampering back to their parents.

Like this one in particular. A toddler, perhaps two years old, with a cheeky smile. Jenna plays peek-a-boo with her, covering her eyes with her fingers, then opening them wide. It's a game the child never tires of, buzzing around like a dragonfly in a jar, until her mother calls her back to her.

"Maleek," she says. Her name is Maleek.

'Yesterday a child came out in wonder
Caught a dragonfly inside a jar...'

Jenna smiles, as if to say, she's no trouble, the opposite in fact, a delight, please don't think she's bothering me. But she returns to her anyway, without fuss.

The mother is not, Jenna now realises, one of her fellow fledglings, but part of that invisible army of ghosts who glide silently around the terminal concourse, picking up litter, putting it into plastic bags, which will later be dumped in the desert somewhere, or incinerated out of sight.

In fact, the closer Jenna looks, the more she comes to understand that none of the children here are passengers. They are all of them attached to young Yemeni women, working in the terminal as cleaners or caterers. The only people travelling are foreigners, who can't get out fast enough, but who are for the moment forced to endure this excruciating uncertainty. Their plane has already been delayed twice…

Jenna is no longer at Taiz.

The night before she and Séydou manage to board the last remaining flight out of there in an unseemly scramble, with people elbowing each other out of the way in an undignified charge across the runway in the blistering late afternoon heat.

Once they are airborne they are informed that the flight will only be going as far as Hodeidah, a hundred and eighty miles to the north-west on the Red Sea coast, where they will be able to pick up a connecting flight to Cairo, which will be waiting for them on arrival. Hodeidah is the principal port serving Sana'a. It will play a key role in any humanitarian efforts that might be needed to bring overseas aid into the country, and it is where Jenna and Séydou had planned to visit after Taiz.

But not like this. Now there will have to be a drastic rethink.

"You must take the flight to Cairo," Séydou tells Jenna. He insists upon it. "You heard what the soldiers said. There may not be another. It's your only chance."

"But what about you?"

"Don't worry about me. I have my MSF papers. I'll speak to the relevant people here in Hodeidah, then catch a ferry to Massawa."

"Where's that?" asks Jenna, feeling annoyed at her ignorance.

"Eritrea," says Séydou calmly. "Three hundred miles across

the Red Sea. From there it's just an hour and half's drive to Asmara, the capital, and from there I can catch a flight back to Senegal."

"And see your family?"

"Yes."

Jenna feels her mouth go dry. Séydou has a wife back in Dakar – separated but not divorced – and two children, a son and a daughter, Omar and Awa, both at university, UCAD – Université Cheik Anta Diop – named after the Senegalese historian and anthropologist, who pioneered pre-colonial studies in Africa, specialising in the origins of *homo sapiens*. Omar studies Chemistry, Awa Medicine.

The spoken question is always when. When will he divorce his wife?

To which the spoken reply is always the same. When they have finished school. When they've obtained their degrees.

But the *un*spoken question is *why*. Why do you keep asking me this? Why do you need to know? What is it you want from me? What is it you are saying about how you view the future between us? If indeed you *do* see a future? *Do* you?

To which the unspoken answer signifies – what? Uncertainty? Hope? Fear?

All three of these possibilities haunt Jenna now as she tries to persuade Séydou to let her stay on with him in Hodeidah, particularly if the port is to be as pivotal to their plans as they both believe it will be.

But Séydou is adamant. "If no more flights leave Taiz after tonight, there's a chance of you outstaying your visa," he says. "In which case you risk being held here indefinitely, which in turn imperils *me*, for I will stay too to try and get you released, any delay to which will put both our organisations in jeopardy."

He's right. She knows this. The logic is unarguable. Reluctantly she agrees. As the plane takes off steeply, the roar of the engines sounds like distant thunder, making further conversation between them impossible.

> *'Fearful when the sky was full of thunder*
> *And tearful at the falling of a star…'*

She finds herself for the second time in just forty-eight hours looking down upon the Hejaz Mountains, sketched with such sharp and rapid clarity by her father that she will always recognise them…

> *'And the seasons, they go round and round*
> *And the painted ponies go up and down*
> *We're captive on the carousel of time…'*

Halfway through the one hour flight Jenna reaches across her hand towards Séydou's. Their fingers seek each other out and intertwine…

> *'We can't return, we can only look*
> *Behind from where we came*
> *And go round and round and round in the circle game…'*

As they land, those wishing to continue on to Cairo are told to wait on board while the plane refuels. Everyone else is made to disembark. Jenna and Séydou exchange a hurried farewell, with promises to text regularly…

But after an hour of just sitting there on the runway, they are informed that there has been an unforeseen delay, and they need to go to the terminal, where they must wait for further instructions…

Four hours later, during which time the tension has ratcheted and tempers have frayed, they are requested once more to approach the Departure Gate. "Quickly please. The flight to Cairo is ready to leave immediately." Only for them to be hastily turned back once more when halfway across the tarmac...

A further four hours have passed since then, so that it is now the middle of the night. Two in the morning, to be precise. Tempers have given way to tiredness, frustration to a growing sense of unease, fear almost. People gather together in twos and threes, whispering.

"What's the delay? Why won't they tell us anything...?"

The rumours are rife. In the absence of hard facts, speculation prospers, conspiracy theories thrive. A situation not helped by the internet being down.

"Power surges," they are told. But nobody believes this.

"It's a third world country," says someone, "what do you expect?"

Jenna quickly puts him in his place. "Power cuts happen back home too," she says. Doesn't he remember? Or has he conveniently forgotten?

But others posit far wilder theories.

"It's deliberate," they say. "The Coalition Government don't want it known just how much of the country they've lost to the Houthis already, who've taken Sana'a, and who are now advancing closer to Hodeidah with every hour that passes."

"In which case all the more reason why we should leave now."

"But if we leave now, that's a sure sign to the rest of the world that President Hadi's days are numbered. This way, they're keeping calm and carrying on."

"Except that they're not calm and they're not carrying on anywhere."

"We're simply stuck here, going nowhere, and if we ask them what's happening, they bark at us to stop asking questions."

"Everything will become clear," they say. "All in good time. Trust us. *Inshallah*."

Except that nobody knows who or what to trust.

Jenna thinks there might be some currency in the possibility that the internet is being deliberately shut down by the Saudi-backed Coalition to prevent the spread of misinformation. They learned a hard lesson two years ago during the Arab Spring, the success of which was largely down to social media. Rebels were able to keep in touch, spread messages, disseminate hope via Facebook and Twitter. Zafirah has talked about this. Jenna hopes that Séydou will hold to his promise to look out for her. She has already predicted correctly that Taiz would be the tinder box. And she has warned Jenna about the shifting sands of power in the country. It's no coincidence, then, that when a military coup takes place the first thing the new rulers do is take control of the media – who controls the message controls the masses – which tells her that this might mean the Houthis have not made the kind of advancements they had hoped for. Yet. For surely, if they had, they'd be broadcasting it to the world? This, she feels certain, is what Zafirah would say. More likely, then, that the Coalition forces still hold here in Hodeidah. Just. For it's a flimsy coalition, as Zafirah has explained, with many factions. The sands have much more shifting left to do before they will settle.

Jenna believes the problem may be even more basic – though no less easy to resolve. She wonders if the airport simply doesn't have sufficient fuel for the plane to take off and carry them all the way to Cairo. But that supplying that fuel is not so simple. The way the country is splitting is not clear cut. From what she can gather, the Houthis may have captured Yemen's heart, at Sana'a, while Hadi may still control the gut at Aden and to the south, but the country's face is erupting like a disease, plukes of tribal enclaves, which pock-mark the desert irregularly, with empty, as yet uninfected spaces in between, whose loyalties may shift with the sands blown through by the dust-laden *Shamal*. As a result, the transporting of goods from one part of the country to another is hazardous, not knowing which pock-marks to avoid and which plukes to risk puncturing, letting the pus explode.

A wilder rumour spreading through the terminal is that the Saudis have switched off the oil pipelines for fear of offering too tempting a target for Houthi war-planes, while others fear an even more apocalyptic scenario. That the Saudis are planning a night-time raid on the airport here at Hodeidah to make the runway unusable for years to come, in order to prevent a Houthi-controlled Sana'a from having a link to the outside world for its necessary imports. But this makes no sense to Jenna. It would be to admit that the Coalition has already conceded defeat. If that were the case, the soldiers still guarding the terminal would have departed long ago.

Unless they don't know what's happening either. And that when they ask us to trust them, it's their way of trying to convince themselves that all will be well eventually. *Inshallah.*

Inshallah.

The answer to any insoluble problem.

But that's what comes from placing all of society's utilities in the hands of the state, thinks Jenna ruefully.

What goes around, comes around. You reap what you sow.

It's not just Hindus, Buddhists and Christians who trot that out. It's in the Quran too. *'If you do good, you do good to yourself. But if you do evil, likewise do you do evil to yourself.'*

She shakes her head, recalling with a grim irony her own words when she is invited to make a short speech on the day of her graduation nearly thirty years before…

"And this year's Sir Bernard Crick Award for Outstanding Achievement by a Graduating Student for Best Journal Article of the Year goes to…."

The Vice-Chancellor fumbles with the envelope. Eventually he succeeds in tearing it open somewhat indecorously.

"... Jenna Ward, for her article *The Beating Heart* in the latest edition of *The Political Quarterly*. Ms Ward is also the recipient of this year's Rothschild Future Leaders Award. Congratulations."

Jenna strides to the front of the Whitworth Hall confidently relishing her moment in the spotlight. She accepts her certificate from the Vice-Chancellor, then turns to face the audience of several hundred capped-and-gowned students and their families looking up at her. She's not sure what the usual protocols are for such occasions, but surely some form of acceptance speech is the order of the day, isn't it? Jenna decides that it is. Before anyone can stop her, she launches her tirade...

"Thank you. I'm delighted to be receiving this award today. In my article I argued that the best measure of a democracy's well-being is to be found in how it responds to criticism aimed against the government of the day. The right to peaceful protest – taking to the streets if necessary – is its beating heart. Sometimes the results can be messy – chaotic even – but they are essential to the health of this beating heart. But is chaos necessarily a bad thing? Physicists tell us that it is the natural order of things, and, as such, we should embrace it. I know *I* do. Chaos theory is defined by mathematicians as the apparently random or unpredictable behaviour in systems thought to be governed by more deterministic laws. The inherent paradox in this is what many people find so disturbing. But I believe that its attempts to find connections between opposing ideas that are commonly held to be incompatible to be truly inspiring. I find such attempts to wrestle with these seemingly irreconcilable contradictions to be nothing short of heroic. In chaos theory, the butterfly effect is the sensitive dependence on initial conditions in which a small change in one state of a deterministic nonlinear system can result in large differences in a later state. The term 'butterfly effect' is closely associated with the work of Edward Lorenz, an American meteorologist. It is derived from the metaphorical example of the details of a tornado – the exact time of formation, the precise path taken – being influenced by minor perturbations such as a distant butterfly flapping its wings several weeks earlier. I prefer to draw parallels with the moth, rather than its more delicate cousin. For it is stronger, more resilient, more resistant to change. Something we're used to here in Manchester, where we have always agitated for it, when we have needed to do so in order to survive. Like the Manchester Moth, which famously evolved into a new variant to avoid detection by its more powerful predators. Not only did this behaviour enable it to survive, but in fact to thrive. To keep striving towards the light. When I was a child, I used to be fascinated by the way moths did that. I later learned that, being mostly nocturnal, they use the moon to orientate themselves in the dark – a process known as positive phototaxis – and that they constantly adjust their direction – their flight path, if you will – to keep the light source at the required angle to the eye. Their desperate, sometimes self-destructive efforts to reach the light have lessons for us all – especially today – when Mrs Thatcher has announced her decision to privatise British Telecom. This will be, she tells us, with that zealot's steely gleam in her eye, an expression we have all of us learned to recognise in recent years and regard with a certain foreboding, just the beginning. For she intends to follow this up by privatising all of the nation's utilities. Gas, electricity, water, coal. And where will she set her sights after those? Transport, health, education? Will nothing be spared? It reminds me of the *Parable of the Pearl Beyond Price*, which appears in the Bible, in Matthew's Gospel. The Kingdom of Heaven, it says, is like unto a Merchant, seeking goodly pearls. When he sees one pearl of great price, he sells all that he has in order to possess it.

It is directly preceded by another. *The Parable of the Hidden Treasure*. In this the Kingdom of Heaven is compared to a treasure hidden in a field, which a man finds and then hides. But he is prevented from digging it up again because he is only a poor labourer. He does not own the field. It belongs instead to the rich merchant, who is unaware of the treasure's existence but is now entitled to it nevertheless. My parents brought me up to believe that the real Pearl Beyond Price is my education, which no one can take from me, and which I have been fortunate enough to have had bestowed upon me as a gift, offered freely to me, with no expectations or obligations being placed upon me after I have received it as to what I should do with it. It is one of the essential freedoms granted to all of us living in a democracy. Like these other essential utilities that Mrs Thatcher wishes to sell off to the highest bidder, like the Crown Jewels, which are for Public Good not Private Profit. For the benefit of us all, not just the privileged few. And so I am taking this opportunity to exercise another of my basic freedoms – that of free speech – to express my fundamental right to use this platform to protest in the strongest way possible against this violent seizure of what is ours, of what belongs to all of us, and I urge you to join me. And if that leads to what some people may condemn as an incitement to chaos, then I make no apology. For our actions here today may lead to a moth somewhere else at last finding its way towards that treasure which is no longer hidden, that pearl beyond price, that elusive silver light of the moon..."

That moon is a huge silver disc now, shining above her in the ominous Yemeni sky, outside the terminal where still she waits, along with her other anxious fellow travellers. The desert sky at night, for the most part unpolluted by extraneous light sources, is like nothing Jenna has ever experienced before. Its blackness is so intense it is like a glove, pressed close and hard to the eye, blocking everything else out, except for the sense of her own insignificance.

The child Maleek toddles across to her once more. She is blowing bubbles from a tube of soapy water with a small plastic wand. They delight and entrance her. She offers the tube to Jenna, who duly obliges by blowing her a bubble large enough to frame her entire shining face, bathed in its myriad rainbow colours. Her small pudgy hands poke starfish fingers towards it, waiting for it to pop and burst…

Jenna remembers how her own daughter, Molly, when she was Maleek's age, loved to blow bubbles…

Maleek's mother calls her child towards her. But she is too entranced by the flotilla of translucent globes, tiny worlds, ascending to the roof, to hear her. Jenna scoops her up in her arms and carries her wriggling back towards her mother. Jenna sees at once how young she is, younger than Molly is now. The mother thanks Jenna, shyly pulling the cloth of her *qurqash* across her face. Jenna notes the name tag looped around her neck, signifying that she is an employee of the terminal. *S. El-Harazy*. For some reason it lodges in her brain and sticks…

After her outburst at the Degree Ceremony, which does not go down well, she is politely requested not to attend the reception afterwards. Sol and Nadia are mortified with embarrassment.

"Why do you always have to make such a fuss?" asks Nadia.

"Those things needed saying."

"But there's time and a place."

"I thought this was exactly both."

Nadia shakes her head. "In that case why is everyone avoiding you? Why are you not surrounded by people congratulating you?"

"Prophets in their own land," says Jenna.

"Really?" says Nadia? She is furious. "Then it's time you grew up."

Sol, who has been silent all this time, speaks softly in Jenna's ear while Nadia is not looking.

"Your grandmother would have been proud of you," he says.

Ishtar. Yes, thinks Jenna. She's missed her more and more these past three years.

"Let's go," says Nadia. "I can't bear all these whispers and glances. She suddenly catches sight of Sol, who is smiling ruefully. "What?" she asks crossly.

"I was just thinking what my mother might have said."

"Your mother was a saint."

"What," asks Jenna, "might she have said?"

"You can't make an omelette without breaking a few eggs."

"That's all very well," says Nadia to Sol, "but that doesn't mean you have to fling the contents back in people's faces."

She turns back to Jenna, who is appalled to discover that her mother is crying.

"Why don't you learn to change things from within…?"

Jenna bites her bottom lip. Her mother is expressing the same disappointments as Nigel, the Police Constable who had placed himself directly in harm's way at the Moss Side Riots three years before, instinctively taking the brick that had been thrown at her to his own head, whose wound she had afterwards bandaged.

Find a better way…

A few days after the riots have ended, she returns to her parents' home in Patricroft for a brief visit. She doesn't tell them about her encounter with Nigel, the story he told her about the chance meeting with her father, or about her involvement in the riots.

She only stays one night. She leaves early the following morning. Before she goes, she takes a closer look at the joined collage of photographs taken by George Wright of Sol's mural. She's not looked at it properly for years. Over time it has simply become a part of the furniture, taken for granted. She scrutinises it minutely. The detail takes her breath away. This is more than just her father's story. Or her grandfather's – Hejaz's. More than just Nadia's and Ishtar's, Rose's and Yasser's. It feels like nothing less than the history of the world. But through the prism of one family. Hers. And that somehow she has her own part to play in it still. Perhaps her father understood this. Perhaps that's why he gave her the paint brush to complete it, by filling in the detail of the child – herself aged five – giving the umbrella to her father. She finds that section of it now and smiles at the memory.

She examines it further until she finds what she is sure she has spotted before but never really taken note of properly. Yes. There it is. In a corner near the bottom. A view of Bradford Colliery through a wire fence. The headstocks are no longer turning. A Policeman with a helmet is pointing to them. He's talking to a figure who appears to be her father. Surely it is Nigel – it has to be, doesn't it? – telling her father, then telling *her* a dozen years later, to find a better way...

She is just about to turn away from the mural, when something else catches her eye. Right in the centre of it. Another pair of figures. A different man in a long wet overcoat standing with his back to the viewer. A woman in old-fashioned clothes is standing beside him. She appears undecided as to whether to speak to this man or not. Jenna knows who these figures are of course. She's heard the story many times. But now, looking at them again in the early morning light, she fancies she hears it for the first time, on the day the mural was first unveiled in the disused Pomona Dock…

Ishtar and Nadia are walking towards it, to inspect it more closely.

"Oh look," they say. "See," they point. "Do you recognise this?" they wonder. "And that?" they ask. "And isn't this…?"

Ishtar clings to Nadia with such pride and joy. "He's done it," she says, her eyes shining. "He's captured it all. Every last detail."

Nadia links her arm through hers and leads her gently towards the centre of the mural.

"Isn't that you, standing at the top of the colliery steps, about to go and speak to Hejaz for the very first time?"

Ishtar brings her eyes right up to the painting. "Was I really so certain he would turn back when I called?"

Nadia laughs warmly. "I'm so glad that he did…"

Jenna hears her mother's laughter falling through the cracks of the years. Like motes of dust dancing in a shaft of light. A moth stubbornly trying to angle its gaze back towards the moon, imperceptibly fading as tiny streaks of grey begin to filter through the black Yemeni night…

What goes around, comes around, Jenna reminds herself. Be careful what you wish for…

Here in Yemen there has been no privatisation of utilities. Everything is strictly state-controlled. Exactly what she'd been advocating for in her impassioned, ungracious call to arms when accepting the Bernard Crick Award. Why, then, does this manifestation of her *cri de coeur* back then not fill her with more satisfaction today? Nadia would say that perhaps it's a sign that she's grown up at last. But Jenna knows there's more to it than that. Yes, things are more complicated than how she saw them back then. The black-and-white certainties she held onto then have since become diluted with ever more shades of grey. Like the lightening sky above her now. For one thing, Yemen is not a democracy. When Saleh is overthrown in the Arab Spring, presidential elections are held to replace him, but there is only one candidate – Hadi, Saleh's former deputy. She likes to think that if she doesn't agree with a government policy back in England, despite the inadequacies of the country's electoral system, she can, in theory, still vote for a different government, who might introduce a different policy.

A better way...

Change from within...

When she leaves Uni, she also leaves the Squat, which also means that she leaves Lance. But they remain on friendly terms, hooking up from time to time, stoking the old flames of desire, but as quickly as they spark, they fade, burning too brightly and too briefly.

"Wah gwaan, gyal?"

"Mi de yah..."

She works as an aide in Graham Stringer's office in Manchester Town Hall, while he is Leader of the City Council, but all that her duties appear to consist of are making tea for his various cronies, who only seem interested in staring at her tits...

For a brief period she takes her *Change from Within* mantra literally and gets a job with the Adam Smith Institute, whose papers on privatisation become Thatcher's Bible. The Gospel According to Douglas Mason, Chief Policy Writer at the Institute, advocates the breaking up of the Royal Mail – *The Last Post*; the introduction of charges in public libraries – *Ex Libris*; and the complete removal of subsidies for culture –

Expounding the Arts. This is all too dispiriting for Jenna, whose own minor triumphs – *Operation Underclass*, aimed at creating jobs for the long-term unemployed without risking a loss of benefits in the short term, and *Let Your Voice Be Heard*, a collaboration with Ipsos MORI to create opinion polls tracking the goals of students and young people, at the same time measuring public attitudes to state services – seem small fry by comparison, though both will be taken up after she has left the Institute, when Blair comes to power...

Then, in the early nineties, after another rush of blood sees her almost get arrested for an over-exuberant participation in the Poll Tax protests, she sees an advert for a position in the newly-opened Manchester office of the recently formed IPPR, the Institute for Public Policy Research, which offers a refreshing alternative to the dogma of free market fundamentalism she has been unsuccessfully trying to infiltrate at Adam Smith, applies and is successful. She is happy on several fronts. At last she can stop pretending and be part of something she actually believes in, something which might conceivably make a difference. She can return to Manchester, which she's been missing. London just doesn't cut it to her mind. And she has a three-year contract, which means she can secure a mortgage. She pauses to think what Spike would make of this sudden *volte face* on her part, but only briefly. She's coming up to thirty. She's had her fill of squats and kipping down on friends' sofas. She wants a roof over her head. Her own roof.

She hits the ground running. She contributes several articles to their quarterly journal, first on devolution – *State of the North*; next on globalisation – *Home and the World*; and then on immigration – *Let Them All Come*. Outspoken, provocative, radical, she finds her opinions being listened to and taken seriously. At last.

In 1993 she closes the deal on the house on Slate Lane. She's in the mood to celebrate. So too is Lance. He's slowly but surely finding his niche as a DJ and music promoter, appearing in a range of underground venues and festivals. He's just back from another trip to St Kitts & Nevis, where he's beginning to develop something of a following. He's also on a high because Manchester United have won their first League Title since 1967. Lance is a huge fan. Even more so since Eric Cantona joined the team. Or *King* Eric, as Lance has dubbed him.

"Him more dan a footballer," he enthuses. "Him a poet, him a dancer, him an artist…"

When, a mere eighteen months later, King Eric will be dethroned, as he leaps into the crowd after an opposition supporter has hurled a xenophobic slur towards him and assaults him with a flying kung-fu kick, he will perplex the world still further with his inscrutable appearance at a press conference, at which all he will say to the baffled and bewildered reporters is the riddle with which he will be forever synonymous.

"When the seagulls follow the trawler, it is because they think sardines will be thrown into the sea…"

But Lance will be delighted.

"Yuh shud listen to I. See what mi tell yuh. Him a poet. Him a philosopher too."

And he will sample recordings of it into his sets as a DJ…

But on this night such thoughts are far away. It's a hot and sultry midsummer's eve. They make love under the stars, which shimmer and sparkle on the surface of the nearby Canal, casting liquid patterns of shadows and light upon their entwined bodies…

Eight weeks later Jenna knows for certain that she's pregnant. It's not part of any life-plan she might have had, but she finds she is delighted, astounded by the randomness of it, that so many separate circumstances have had to combine to produce this miracle, currently the size of her thumb nail. What are the chances? Of the forty million sperm cells released by Lance when he comes inside her, less than two million manage to swim their way like tiny tadpoles towards her cervix. Half of these at most will reach her uterus. Of which a mere ten thousand will make it to the top. But half of these will head off in the wrong direction. Of the half that will find their way to the utero-tubal junction, perhaps a thousand will arrive at the entrance to the fallopian tube, and only a fifth of these – just two hundred – will reach the waiting egg. And then just one – *one* – will succeed in penetrating and fertilising it. One out of forty million...

The same number of displaced people on the move across the world at any given moment in time. That is according to the latest figures collected by Jenna on behalf of the Refugee Council. All of them in search of a home. Lost and wandering. If she can help just one of them, it will be worth it...

Maleek totters towards her once more, her arms outstretched for balance, like a seagull hoping for a sardine, waiting for her to catch her and gather her up into her trawler...

Jenna decides she will raise her baby by herself. Why shouldn't she? Countless millions have done so before her. Her own mother had to for the first four years of Jenna's life. She will be fine. She will cope, she is sure. And she will have help. She will not be alone. There will be Nadia and Farida if she needs them. But not Lance. He is not part of the equation. Oh, he can see the baby whenever he wants to, which she's sure he will, but Lance isn't someone for the long haul. It would be like pinning the wings of a moth to a board. Or confining him to a sealed jar. He would simply wither away and die. Better to unscrew the lid, unfasten the case, and let him fly free. He'll be a better part-time father than a bitter full-time one.

When she tells him of her decision, it is like watching the sun break through after a dark cloud has passed…

When a female moth lays her eggs, she stays close by to watch over them till they are ready to hatch. Sometimes the male stays with her to ensure paternity. But not always. Sometimes he simply flies away…

*

Day 4

A red sun rises, dipping the peaks of the Hejaz Mountains in flame.

Jenna watches in awe. She tries to take a picture of them with her phone. But even with the aid of its 1.4 micrometre active-pixel image sensors, its 16 millimetre wide-angled aspheric lens and digital zoom capability, she fails miserably to capture even a fraction of their essence, which her father caught so effortlessly with just a few strokes of a pencil.

She rubs her eyes and stretches. It's been a long night. Her fellow passengers are doing likewise. Some have rolled out a prayer mat and are unselfconsciously performing their morning prayers. Some are going through a series of well-practised yoga exercises. But most simply stand and try to shake off the stiffness in their legs. As Jenna does. Then she ferrets in her carry-on bag for her toothbrush with the intention of plodding towards the terminal wash-room to freshen up.

Before she has got halfway there she is stopped in her tracks by a high piercing wail of feedback over the PA system, followed by a too-loud announcement, first in Arabic, then in English, ordering them all to proceed at once to the Departure Gate. Their plane for Cairo has been cleared for immediate take-off.

Everyone stops whatever it is they have been doing, scoops up their bags and runs *en masse*, fumbling for their passports, papers and boarding passes. But these are not required apparently, and they are frantically waived through by frightened-looking airport staff, watched over by jumpy, armed soldiers.

Out on the tarmac the day is already becoming blisteringly hot. The plane sits in the centre of the runway with its engines running. The air-stair is being hastily fitted into the clamshell door on the side of the Yemenia Airways Airbus 310, an old plane that has clearly seen better days. More soldiers urge them to hurry. "*Yalla, yalla,*" they shout. "Quickly. Let's go."

From the corner of her eye Jenna catches sight of an empty army jeep parked on the tarmac close to the terminal. She thinks she sees a soldier emerging from underneath it before rejoining his unit, but she isn't sure.

Then she hears a voice, a child's voice, shouting her name. "Jenna! Jenna!"

She turns. It's Maleek. She is stumbling towards her as fast as her tiny legs can carry her. Jenna has taught her her name, and what it means in Arabic. A bird in flight. Maleek flaps her hands in front of her, thumbs locked together, like wings.

"*Mumtaz,*" she shouts. "*Muta'anaq. Sayida.*"

Beautiful classy lady.

"*Nazra.*" Look at me.

Behind her, her mother tries to call her back. She shouts her name. She starts to run towards her, but is held back by one of the soldiers. A second soldier races across the tarmac. Like an eagle swooping down from the mountains, he scoops up Maleek one-handed and tucks her under his arm.

"*Mama!*" screams the terrified child.

At precisely that moment, almost as if the child's voice has been the detonator, the bomb beneath the jeep explodes.

Everything at once turns into slow motion.

The air appears to buckle and fold in on itself.

The force of the blast throws Jenna backwards, off her feet, towards the foot of the air-stair. Those passengers already halfway up it cling onto the hand-rail and somehow manage to save themselves. But the plate-glass windows of the terminal shatter, firing thousands of shards of glass into the still-quivering air. Anyone standing in the vicinity is speared and shredded by them. Jenna is aware of body parts scattering on the tarmac.

Her ears are ringing. She can no longer make out sounds properly. As if she is underwater. Then, one by one, they return. Sirens. Gunfire. Shouts. Screams. Then Maleek's voice again, high-pitched, insistent, piercing her ear like a needle.

"*Mama... Mama...*"

And Jenna is flung back still further. Seventeen years. To another bomb. In Manchester's city centre. She wheels around, frantic, searching, her feet crunching on broken glass, hearing another voice, Molly's, her daughter's.

"*Mama... Mama...*"

"*Mama... Mama...*"

She reaches out towards the sound...

But then a soldier has grabbed her round the waist. He is turning her round, forcing her back in the direction of the air-stair.

"*Yalla, yalla.*"

She tries to keep looking back over her shoulder. She catches a last lunging look at Maleek, retreating further from her, back towards the smouldering terminal, still tucked under the other soldier's eagle wing, her tiny arms and legs thrashing and flailing, squirming and wriggling like a tadpole, trying to swim against the current. In one of her hands she carries the tube with soapy water. She dips the wand into it with her other hand and tries to blow a bubble, a bubble so big she can hide inside it.

Mama... Mama...

And then Maleek is gone. Jenna can see her no longer. The soldier thrusts her through the clamshell door at the top of the air-stair, which is then rapidly wheeled away.

Inside the plane a deathly silence has fallen. They are all of them in shock, their eyes shuttered, their bodies trembling, their minds numb, Jenna among them, as if she is trapped somehow inside Maleek's giant bubble. The light above her flashes a sign instructing her to fasten her seat belt. Like an automaton, she obeys.

The plane accelerates along the runway. The inside of the fuselage shakes. It rattles and vibrates noisily. Like old bones. The pitch of the engines rises to a scream as the Airbus 310 heaves itself into the air. It flies towards the Hejaz Mountains, ablaze now beneath a fully risen sun, then, just when it seems certain it will crash directly into them, it banks steeply away, tilting towards the coastal plain and the Red Sea beyond. At the same moment two Saudi MiG 21s tear out of the sky and position themselves either side of the A310, where they stay, hovering like giant insects, until they have safely escorted it out of Yemeni air space, before peeling off and away from them in each direction, leaving behind nothing but two matching vapour trails, a pair of moth's wings, which the airbus flies between, before they evaporate and disappear...

*

Four hours later.

Jenna staggers from the plane into the air-conditioned concourse of *Maṭār El Qāhira El Dawly*, Cairo International Airport. She's finally been ushered into the Departure Lounge after a long, and at times tetchy vetting process. But she's through the worst of it. Now it's just a matter of more waiting. Her flight back to Manchester, via Charles de Gaulle in Paris, leaves in another two hours.

She finds a place to sit and texts Séydou immediately.

"I've arrived. Safe, but numb. Just waiting on connections. You?"

She hears back within seconds.

'*Dieu merci. Tout va bien ici. Aussi bien que peut. Pardon.* Sorry. I've been speaking French all day. Both sides agree the need for a corridor. In principle at least. *Attendons le crunch, n'est-ce pas?* "

"Oui." She takes a deep breath before continuing. "I need you to do something for me. It's important. Call me please…. xx"

He phones her back at once. She tells him as calmly as she can all about the explosion at Hodeidah airport. He already knows. A Houthi insurgent apparently. But the who and why are not what now concern her. She needs to know what has happened to Maleek. And her mother.

"Can you do that?" she asks.

Something about the urgency in her voice disturbs Séydou. "Of course," he says. "I'll try. Do you have a name?"

The sight of the mother's name tag flashes before her eyes, the way she so shyly pulled the piece of cotton cloth across her face.

She screws her eyes tightly shut, trying to conjure it in front of her. For a moment there is nothing, then, suddenly, there it is, floating in space in front of her.

"El-Harazy," she says in triumph. "Plus an initial. S." She lets out a long held-in breath.

"I'll see what I can do," says Séydou. "Call me when you get back to Manchester."

"Will do. When do you leave for Massawi?"

Another couple of days.

He had been hoping to leave sooner than that. He was already picturing the gruelling eighteen-hour flight back to Dakar across the entire width of Africa. But that will have to wait now that he has promised to try and find this child and her mother, who seem to matter so enormously to Jenna. It will be like searching for a needle in a haystack. But at least he has a name…

The birth is fairly straightforward. Not for Jenna, obviously. For her it is a time like no other. A time when she loses all sense of it. From when her waters break to when Molly is born, twelve hours elapse. But for Jenna it feels more like twelve days. Afterwards, when it is all over, it feels like twelve minutes. It's as if she's been engaged in some strange kind of time warp, enclosed in her own private world, a bubble, which only bursts once Molly is born, when the outside world of nurses, midwives and doctors, family, friends and well-wishers come crashing in on her once more.

But for the hospital there is nothing unusual about it at all. A fairly routine delivery, with no complications. The baby – a girl – is born as the sun comes up. She cries lustily and loud, weighs a healthy seven pounds, six ounces, and latches onto the breast without difficulty. Another twelve hours later mother and daughter are pronounced fit and ready to go home…

It is afterwards when the difficulties start.

After the adrenalin rush of the birth, the crash which follows is intense. Jenna finds herself crying for no apparent reason. She feels unfathomably low and permanently anxious. The midwife tells her not to worry. "It's quite normal," she says. "The baby blues," she calls them. "They're common. Many new mothers experience them. They'll pass, you'll see."

But they don't pass. Not in a fortnight. Not in a month. If anything, they grow worse. She feels listless and sad – and unutterably tired – all the time. But not just because of the lack of sleep, the broken nights – in fact Molly is what they call 'very good', in that she soon begins to sleep right through, a phrase Jenna loathes, as if, by not sleeping, a baby is being somehow deliberately 'bad' or wilfully vindictive. The tiredness goes much deeper. It's a mind-deadening, bone-wearying exhaustion, which empties her, leaving her feeling... what?

Actually, nothing at all. She has no interest in anything around her. She doesn't venture outside, unless she absolutely has to. She doesn't bother to keep her home, or herself, particularly tidy or clean. Most worryingly of all, she appears to feel nothing towards Molly. She's developed no real bond with her. Apart from feeding and changing her, she largely ignores her.

It's Farida who notices it first.

One Saturday morning she decides to drop by with some flowers for a surprise. If the weather's nice, maybe they'll take Molly out in her pram and walk along the tow-path beside the canal. It's been three months now since the birth, and Farida hasn't seen Molly for about four weeks.

When she arrives and knocks on the door, she hears Molly crying, so she's not surprised when Jenna doesn't answer at first. But when, after a few minutes, Jenna still hasn't come to the door and Molly is crying louder than ever, Farida becomes suspicious. She peers in through the front window and sees Molly lying there in her carry-cot, her legs kicking furiously, and her face purple with the effort of crying. Jenna is nowhere to be seen. Farida rushes down the ginnel at the side of the house, round to the gate, which she forces open, not caring if she breaks the latch, then runs to the back door, which luckily is not locked. She hurries into the kitchen, where she finds Jenna sitting at the table, not moving, but staring out of the window, seeing nothing.

Ignoring her for the moment, and dumping the flowers beside her, she heads for the front room, where she picks up the now nearly hysterical Molly, holds her against her shoulder, gently rocking her back and forth, speaking soothingly, kissing the top of her head, her hair damp with sweat, and drying the tears on her hot cheeks. Farida, who has run a nursery for more than twenty-five years, is quite familiar with the ways of crying babies. She soon calms Molly down, and within a few minutes, she has her giggling again.

She cleans her up, changes her, then carries her back upstairs and lays her gently down in her cot. Molly is so exhausted she is asleep before her head touches the pillow. Then, making sure the baby alarm is switched on, Farida creeps back downstairs and goes to the kitchen to see to Jenna, who has not moved from where she left her. She doesn't believe she has even registered her arrival.

She takes Jenna by the hand and gently leads her upstairs to the bathroom. She removes all of her clothes, then stands her under the shower. Jenna passively lets her do all these things. She herself is absent, somewhere else, though quite where she is, she cannot say, for she does not know.

Afterwards, while Molly continues to nap, Farida brushes her niece's hair, then paints her hands with henna. Like she used to do when she was a teenager, when Jenna would come to her house, rather than her parents', hung over from some party or other. Back then Farida would make light of it all, sparing her sister Nadia from most of the details. But this is not something that can be kept from her.

Slowly Jenna begins to return from the dark corner she has crept into. The tiniest flicker of an eyelid, the slightest twitch of a cheek, the merest suggestion of a smile upon her lips. Farida turns her face towards her and speaks very quietly to her.

"You're not well," she says. "It's not your fault. It can happen to anyone. It doesn't mean you're going mad. It doesn't mean you're a bad parent. I've seen it many times before. No one knows why some people feel like this while others don't. It's just the way it is. But there are things we can do. You can speak to your doctor. You can get help. A healthy diet. Regular exercise…"

"And work," says Jenna suddenly. These are the first words she has spoken.

"Yes," says Farida carefully. "Work. If that is what you think you need."

"I must work," says Jenna. "If I don't work, I disappear…"

Farida nods. She knows what she means. Work has been her salvation too…

As it has been for Nadia.

And Anita too, Lance's mother.

She and Nadia have stayed in touch ever since they first met, when they were each young mothers themselves, struggling to manage alone, picking up whatever scraps of work they could find in order to get by. Including a week of working nights at the Kendal Milne Department Store, preparing the window displays for Christmas, when each of them was at their lowest point…

They watch from the rooftop as tens of thousands of rats are herded the length of Deansgate by huge Council trucks with enormous snow ploughs driving them from one sewer to another. Like displaced refugees…

Afterwards, on her way home, Anita is confronted by a

homeless woman in a shop doorway, with a tattoo of an angel on her shoulder, who grips her wrist and demands of her: *"Who's minding the store...?"*

Farida takes Jenna and Molly back with her to Patricroft, so that they might stay with Nadia and Sol for a few days. The following evening she, Nadia and Anita meet to discuss a plan of action, while Jenna sleeps upstairs.

Farida's nursery – *Busy Bees* – is full to bursting, she says. "I simply can't take in any more. I wish I could, but I'll lose my licence if I do. I'll put Molly on a waiting list for when someone leaves, so till then I'm happy to look after her at weekends."

For an hour they toss ideas back and forth between them, until at last a plan emerges, a plan that all of them think can work. When they put it to Jenna the next morning, she bursts into tears of gratitude…

Jenna will work three days each week – Tuesdays, Wednesdays and Thursdays. A job share is agreed for her at IPPR. Another recent mother is looking to return to part-time work – Amreen Qureshi – and the arrangement suits both of them perfectly.

During those three days Anita will take Molly to the West Indian Sports & Social Club in Moss Side, where there is a morning crêche. In the afternoons she will look after her in her own home on Raby Street, until Jenna can collect her when she has finished work.

They can spend Saturdays with Nadia and Sol in Patricroft, then Sundays with Farida's in Monton.

The problem has been what to do about Mondays and Fridays. None of the women think Jenna is strong enough to risk leaving her entirely alone with Molly for two whole days. It is Nadia who comes up with the solution. Her mother, Salwa, lives just around the corner. She's seventy-four now, but still active and spry. Since her husband, Jamal, died a dozen years ago, she has got into the habit of meeting up with some of the other Yemeni widows for a weekly gossip over coffee and honey cake – *binth al sahn* – every Friday.

"This is perfect," agrees Farida, clapping her hands. "The 'Aunties' will adore having Molly to fuss over."

"Then afterwards," chips in Nadia, "I can pick her up on my way home – I finish early on Fridays. Then she can stay the night with us, and Jenna can join us in time for lunch on Saturday."

"Excellent."

This leaves only Mondays to arrange. Now it is Farida who has the idea.

"Through *Busy Bees*," she says, "I am connected with a wider network of other playgroups and nurseries. There's one in Fairfield, not five minutes from Slate Lane. It's held in the Moravian Church. I know the woman who runs it. Barbara. Jenna can take Molly there. I'll ask Barbara to keep an eye on them. Just in case. But I think it will be good for Jenna to have one whole day by herself with Molly. To ease her way back in."

Jenna agrees readily to the arrangements these three strong women have put in place for her. She also agrees to see her GP, who sympathetically confirms that she has post-natal depression. She also prescribes a dose of mild anti-depressants to help readjust the chemical imbalance in her system, as well as recommending a twelve-week course of therapeutic counselling. "Then let's see where we are, shall we?" she adds kindly…

She finds the counselling both helpful and instructive, on many levels. Jenna has always felt a sense of certainty – in her opinions, her actions, the choices she has taken, the decisions she has made – until Molly, since when she has experienced, for the first time, doubt, a doubt so crippling that she has been floored by it utterly. Now she questions everything – her past as well as her present – while the future is something she can scarcely contemplate.

But her therapist – whose name is Dr Warner, but who insists on being called Ruth – encourages her to embrace this doubt. "Ultimately it makes us stronger," she maintains, "not weaker. It makes us see things more whole, more rounded. It helps us to understand that we are fallible. That we all of us make mistakes. But it is through these mistakes that we are able to learn, to grow, to understand ourselves better."

"That all sounds too pat," says Jenna, "too easy. Like it's from some kind of manual. 'How To Change A Light Bulb.' 'How To Fix A Kettle.' But I'm not an appliance. I'm more complicated than that."

"Good," says Ruth.

"What do you mean, 'good'?"

"You're sounding more like your old self."

"You never knew my old self."

"The light bulb's flashing back on. The kettle's coming to the boil."

"Fuck off."

"There – that's better. You say I never knew your old self. I think I just met her."

"Sorry."

"No. Don't apologise. From what I can tell, you're someone who feels passionately about things. Hold on to that. It's what defines you."

"No – that's work which does that."

"I'm tending to think they're one and the same thing. You say that it is work that defines you, and the work you choose to do is directly linked to the political causes you espouse."

"Yes."

"But...?"

"What?"

"I sensed a 'but' in your previous answer."

"Well..."

"Yes?"

"When Molly was born it felt as though my mind just went to mush. I was unable to concentrate at work. I resented the way my body and my brain were no longer functioning the way they used to. They were letting me down, and in turn I felt I was letting my work down."

"In what way?"

"The people whose lives depend on me."

"That's quite a claim."

"Well, not *me* exactly, but the changes in government policy I hope to bring about, which will lead to better lives for those people in the future."

"But it's not just you, is it? You have colleagues, I presume? You're part of a team?"

"Yes. A good one."

"Then it's not all down to you, is it? "

"No, but I wasn't pulling my weight."

"Like you said – you've just become a mother. Cut yourself some slack. I'm sure your colleagues do."

"Perhaps."

"Have they said anything? Complained in any way?"

"No. But they wouldn't."

"Wouldn't they? Why not? If, as you say, people's lives depend on what you do."

"Theoretically. And not just me."

"Exactly."

Jenna pauses, trying to take this in.

"Then I'd get home and Molly would be gurgling contentedly away, seemingly without a care in the world."

"Why would she have?"

"And then my mother would leave, or my auntie, or whoever had been looking after her, and she'd start crying, and I'd just think..."

"What?"

"Here was something else I was failing at..."

Jenna looks away, out of the window of Ruth's consulting room, picking at her fingers, which are red and sore. Outside, on a patch of bare grass, a blackbird dispassionately tugs at a worm. Ruth says nothing. She slides a box of tissues towards her. Crossly Jenna takes one and blows her nose.

"I hate this," she says, so quietly that Ruth barely hears her.

"What? These sessions?"

"Yes. Well, no. Not really."

"What then?"

"This feeling of inadequacy. Of not being good enough. Of..."

"Yes?"

Jenna is having to drag the words out of herself, from deep within the pit of her stomach. Each one has to be painfully wrenched from her.

"Of... being... found... out..."

The blackbird at last extracts the worm from the ground, which it then proceeds to swallow whole.

Ruth leans forward in her seat and makes sure that Jenna is looking directly back at her, before she speaks.

"I want you to give me your full attention, Jenna, to what I'm going to say next. OK?"

Jenna nods tremulously.

"Cognitive behavioural therapy – which is what I practice – is based on the idea that unhelpful and unrealistic thinking leads to negative behaviour. You weren't altogether wrong before when you referred so disparagingly to my using a manual. There are patterns we fall into sometimes – all of us, myself included – that can bring about this negative behaviour if we're not careful, and it's my job to work with you to help you begin to recognise these triggers for yourself, and then do something about them. It sounds simple when put like that, but the reality is much more difficult, and it's different for each individual. But some of these patterns are quite common, particularly where post-natal depression occurs. For example, some women – especially so-called high achievers like yourself – have unrealistic expectations about what being a mother is meant to be like. They feel they should never make mistakes. But of course they *do*. Everyone does. But for people like this – like *you* – this is not acceptable. Such thoughts are not helpful. *Your* task now, Jenna, is to turn those thoughts into positive ones. And *my* task is to try and help you do that. OK?"

Jenna nods again. "OK." Then, after a further pause, she asks, "How long will it take?"

"You're booked in for twelve sessions. You should expect to start feeling better well before then. Make sure you eat healthily. Cut down on caffeine. Avoid alcohol. Plenty of fresh vegetables. And take regular exercise."

Jenna smiles thinly. It's exactly what Farida had said. It's a long way from her life in the Squat, which was fuelled by coffee, booze, weed and cigarettes, and the only regular exercise was sex with Lance...

Ruth's prognosis proves accurate. After twelve sessions Jenna has indeed made positive progress, and she is signed off from Ruth. They agree that from now on Jenna will come to see Ruth less frequently, once a month to begin with, then once a quarter, then only if she needs to.

For two years all goes well. Molly is a happy, contented baby. She is delighted by all her grandmothers and aunties, and the attention they bestow on her.

Gradually Jenna gets better. She grows stronger, clearer,

more balanced. Above all, she feels relieved. Relieved to see the progress Molly is making. And though she may not be the one to observe those early landmarks – the first smile, the first step, the first word – she experiences all of them soon enough. Yes. Relief floods through her.

It's Lance who is the cause of some of Molly's earliest words. He breezes in one week from wherever he's been. Jenna finds him happily installed at Anita's, his mother's, one afternoon when she comes to collect Molly after work. She's taken to running from the IPPR office in the city centre back to Moss Side each day, as part of her new exercise regime, and she's hot and sweaty when she bursts in to find Lance swinging Molly high above his head, throwing her up in the air and catching her, much to her delight. When he sees Jenna, he grins, then sheepishly hands Molly to her.

"Wah gwaan gyal?" he says in his customary twang.

Before Jenna can reply, Molly pipes back. "Mi de yah…"

Jenna particularly enjoys her Monday mornings at the Moravian Church. She finds the simplicity of its design soothingly pleasing. She becomes interested in its history. She is particularly impressed by some of its achievements – its emphasis on self-help and self-sufficiency, its focus on providing education for girls at a time when this was not common, its sense of continuity. There is still a girls' school in the community now, though open to pupils from outside as well. Even the Burial Ground, she finds, provides solace and calm. She likes the way wild flowers push their way up through the earth between the graves in the spring. Snowdrops, crocuses, daffodils. They seem to mirror her own return to life…

One afternoon, when she is coming back from the Burial Ground, a thin sun splinters the low cloud. She passes between these bars of light as she walks along the tow-path. She thinks she sees a figure, hunkered low against the brick wall beside the gate that leads into the back yard of her house. But she's not sure. It slips in and out of the shifting shadows. As she gets nearer, she becomes more certain. Yes. There's definitely someone there, squatting cross-legged on the ground, wearing an old, dark overcoat, her hair hanging low across her face in long, matted coils. She has a guitar slung around her neck. She starts to sing, haltingly at first, but gradually growing in conviction...

*"There's a sorrow in your eyes
Like an angel made of tin..."*

She makes Jenna think of Bex, who she's not seen in years, singing Joni Mitchell again. For one fleeting moment she thinks perhaps it might be her. But when she gets nearer, she sees it can't be. This woman is much older...

*"What will happen if you try
To place another heart within...?"*

She stops. Jenna is standing right beside her now. She looks directly down on her from above, casting a shadow so that she cannot make out her face. The overcoat coat slips off her shoulder. Jenna is briefly aware of a tattoo etched into the weathered skin, but she's not sure what it is. She has a vague impression of a pair of wings. The hand that was strumming the guitar suddenly thrusts out and clutches Jenna round her ankle. Her voice, when she speaks, is quite different from when she sings – lower, hoarser, more urgent, demanding to be heard.

" '*For every one of us there is a succession of angels, before and behind us, who protect us. Inshallah...*' "

Jenna tries to free her leg from the woman's grasp, to step

over her and reach the sanctuary of her home.

" 'But they cannot change a single hair of your head, nor any thought in your heart, until you make the change within yourself...' "

On the last leg of her long journey home, shortly after take-off from Charles de Gaulle, Jenna googles the name Maleek on her phone. 'Angel,' it says. 'Messenger...'

It is her final session with Ruth.

Jenna wonders whether to mention the woman with the guitar, the tattoo, the message. But she decides not to. It's altogether too weird, probably just another homeless person, of which there are now more and more across the city, stoned and wasted, raving, most of them, and who can blame them? They're the real children of Thatcher, thinks Jenna, more than the 'loads-a-money' traders on the Stock Exchange floor, all of them screaming in each other's faces across the great divide – a gulf that's growing wider and wider, rich and poor, haves and have-nots, North and South.

She and Amreen are working on a new report: *Creating A Level Playing Field*. With the increasingly likely prospect of a Labour Government at the next election, there may at last be an audience ready to listen – as she was made to by the woman with the angel tattoo.

What she said has not disturbed her. But the fact of her existence has. It makes her furious. That *she*, Jenna, has a roof over her head while this woman does not. Nor thousands more like her. Her own years in the Squat have made her highly tuned to just how slippery the so-called property ladder is, how easy it is to fall through the cracks and become invisible. A statistic...

Flying over the English Channel, Jenna is googling more statistics. Two years ago, in the Arab Spring of 2011, more than two thousand people were killed in a single day. She tries to find the figures for this morning's attack at Hodeidah. Reuters, Associated Press, the BBC have barely mentioned it. She's not surprised by this. Neither British nor American participation in Yemen is acknowledged by either government, although both are deeply involved in a covert capacity. But it still infuriates her. Old habits. Ruth would be pleased, she thinks, that she has lost none of her moral outrage. Only Al-Jazheera reports on it in any detail. But even they have few hard facts. Forty dead. Possibly more. Over a hundred injured.

And this is only the start. Once the war begins in earnest...

Jenna turns off her phone and rubs her eyes with the back of her hands.

The Captain makes a short announcement that they will soon be making their descent into Manchester. "Will passengers please fasten their seat belts...?"

In the end Jenna *does* mention the incident with the tattooed woman to Ruth, but only briefly, in passing, to underline her sense of indignation that such basic human rights as food and shelter are being denied to so many people. Ruth nods in agreement.

Jenna tells her about a performance she has been to at Contact Theatre recently by *Cardboard Citizens*, a theatre company made up entirely of actors with experience of homelessness. She likes how they engage the audience directly, using what they call 'Forum Theatre', where live, unscripted discussions take place, based on the scenarios offered up by the actors, scenarios with multiple possible endings, which the audience has to debate and decide on. It reminds her of her days in the Squat, with Spike and his use of Brecht's 'Living Newspaper'. She tells Ruth about some of the things she got up to back then, causing her to smile.

When Jenna leaves for the last time, Ruth feels cautiously hopeful.

"You've made great strides," she tells her. "You should be proud. It's important to acknowledge the positives," she says.

Smiling, Jenna thanks her and shakes her hand.

Privately Ruth still has her doubts. Yes, Jenna has made remarkable progress. But this new-found energy feels perhaps a little too forced, too bright, too brittle. A bubble about to burst. She hopes her fears are unfounded.

"Well," she says, as she opens the door, "you've got my card, you know where to reach me. Call me any time…"

Jenna steps off the plane at Manchester and is immediately struck by the contrast in temperature. How cold it is compared to the searing heat of the desert that she left behind just fourteen hours before.

While she's waiting in line for her passport to be checked one last time, she turns her mobile back on. She intends to call her parents, to let them know she's landed, and to ask if she can stay at theirs for the night. She's so much she wants to share with them. She especially wants to stand in front of her father's drawings of the Hejaz Mountains again, in the front room, where they have hung for more than half a century, and to tell Sol that she has actually seen them, twice in forty-eight hours, how she's sorry she's never really taken notice of them before, how she's never been any good at seeing what's right in front of her.

But just as she's about to bring up their number, a text pings in.

It's from Séydou.

"Call me when you get this," it reads. "I've news…"

It's a perfect Saturday morning in June. A hot yellow sun in a cloudless blue sky.

Jenna is making a change to her usual routine. Molly has just turned two. For a birthday treat Jenna decides to take her into the city centre, to Piccadilly Gardens, to see who Molly calls 'The Bubble Man'. He blows giant bubbles from an extra long wand, bubbles that expand to several feet in diameter, so large that Molly wants to jump right inside them and float high into the air – if only they didn't keep bursting just as she reaches them.

Sometimes there are so many that they surround her in a sea of them. She is so excited she doesn't know which way to turn next. She spins herself round and round until she gets so dizzy she falls down, and Jenna has to scoop her up in her arms, squirming and wriggling like a tadpole...

It is not a planned outing, more a spur-of-the-moment thing. Jenna wakes up early alone in Slate Lane. Molly has been at her Great Grandmother Salwa's house the day before. She spends every Friday there, being thoroughly spoiled by all of the Aunties, who hand her between them like a game of *Pass the Parcel*, in which she is always the prize. Normally she will stay the whole of Saturday with Nadia and Sol. Sometimes Jenna will arrive around lunch time, having had a lie-in, or sometimes she will have the day to herself. It varies. But today is such a glorious morning that she decides she will dispense with routine. She will act spontaneously. She will accede to Molly's much-repeated request and take her to see the Bubble Man...

They catch the Number 67 bus from Patricroft to Manchester. They sit on the top deck, which Molly always enjoys. She loves looking down on the people below and at the birds flying past. She is fascinated by birds. From before she starts talking properly she will copy the sounds they make.

Even now she likes to hook her thumbs together and flap her hands like birds' wings...

Through the Crescent in Salford she delights in the flocks of pigeons alighting on the head of the statue of The Shouting Lancashire Fusilier, a memorial from the Boer War. Then again on Queen Victoria in Piccadilly Gardens.

But the Bubble Man isn't there.

"Perhaps he's not arrived yet," says Jenna. "Shall we come back later?"

Meanwhile there is much to distract Molly among the Saturday morning shoppers along Market Street. Jenna decides they will head towards St Ann's Square. The Bubble Man has been known to visit there too. But she doesn't mention it to Molly. She doesn't want to risk disappointing her a second time.

They walk past the entrance to the Arndale Centre. They are just reaching Marks & Spencer, opposite the turning for the Square, when people suddenly begin to run. Among them is a young couple just about to get married. The bride has hitched up her long white wedding dress and is running for her life.

"Look, Mummy," laughs Molly. "She's like Cinderella."

Yes, thinks Jenna, trying to escape before the clock strikes twelve..."

A Policeman with a loud hailer is instructing everyone to clear the area as quickly as possible. Something in the tone of his voice makes Jenna scoop Molly under one arm and join the stampeding throng. Molly giggles. She still thinks it's a game. She flaps her arms and legs. A tadpole swimming in mid air...

They have just passed the Royal Exchange when the explosion happens. The force of the blast flings Jenna to the ground. Molly slips from her grasp. A storm of broken glass, brick and cement dust rains down upon her. Instinctively she covers her head with her arms.

When it is over, Jenna scrambles to her feet. She looks around her wildly. But Molly is nowhere to be seen. There are people running in every direction, shouting and screaming. They buffet Jenna this way and that, as she frantically searches for her daughter. She calls her name. "Molly! Molly!" Over and over. Her voice sounds far away, drowned by the ringing in her ears.

"Molly...! Molly...!"

"Maleek...! Maleek...!"

"I have news," says Séydou.

"Mama...! Mama...!"

"Mama...! Mama...!"

Jenna *hears* her first. Then *sees* her. She's safe. She's in the arms of an older woman who leans against the door of St Ann's Church in the far corner of the Square. Jenna hurtles towards her, heedless of the glass and debris she must run across to reach her.

"She's quite safe," says the older woman, handing her across. "Barely a scratch. It's miraculous."

It's true. Jenna checks her minutely. The tiniest cut on her left cheek is the only mark she can find. That and a light sheen of grey dust upon her skin and hair, which Jenna delicately brushes away, as if her daughter is a rare archaeological find she has tumbled across.

A man hurries past them, muttering loudly. "Bloody IRA," he is saying.

"You don't know that," hisses Jenna. She is like a feral cat. She holds Molly closer to her.

"I'm afraid it is, my dear," says the older woman, who

Jenna has learned is called Grace. "It bears all the hallmarks..."

"A Houthi bomb," explains Séydou. "They've claimed responsibility on Al-Jazheera..."

Jenna reels. She feels the earth beneath her tilt a second time...

"I've been on marches," she says, "in support of them."
"You're not responsible," says Grace kindly.
"No," agrees Jenna bitterly, taking a quite different meaning. "I'm not..."

"I've done some checking," says Seydou. "The girl – Maleek – she's safe. She's been taken to the Al-Salaam Hospital on Jamal Street in Hodeidah."
"You're sure?"
"Yes. She's suffered serious lacerations and burns to her arms, legs, face and torso."
Jenna howls.
"But the doctors are treating her. They're confident she'll recover. The burns are mostly superficial.
"Mostly?"
"It's still early days..."

Jenna decides she will wait with Grace until the paramedics come for her. She is disabled, Jenna realises. She wears a calliper on her left leg, while her right leg is splayed beneath her at an awkward-looking angle. Grace catches sight of Jenna glancing at it.

"It's broken, I fear," she says. "But it will mend..."

"What of the girl's mother?" asks Jenna. "Mrs El-Harazy...?"
There's a silence on the other end of the phone. Jenna hears Séydou sigh. An audible exhalation of air.

"With the initial 'S'?" he says eventually.

"Yes."

"You're sure it was 'S'?"

"I am, yes."

Another pause. Séydou clears his throat.

"In that case, I've managed to trace a *Saba* El-Harazy from the list of airport employees."

"And?"

"She died, I'm afraid. She was much closer to the bomb when it exploded. All those in and around the Departure Gate appear to be dead. The latest reports list seventy-three fatalities. But the figures are still rising. They were able to identify Mrs El-Harazy by the same name tag that *you* saw…"

Jenna's mouth goes dry.

"There's more," says Séydou.

More, thinks Jenna? What more could there possibly be?

"Mrs El-Harazy is listed as a widow. Her husband died during the uprising of two years ago."

Jenna feels the weight of this sink in.

"So Maleek is now an orphan?"

"Yes. I'm afraid so."

Jenna tries to project some kind of future. But fails.

"What will happen to her?" she asks eventually. "After they've released her from hospital?"

"I don't know," says Séydou simply. "I don't know…"

While they wait for the paramedics to arrive for Grace, Jenna checks Molly for the umpteenth time. But she appears to be fine. Oblivious of the carnage around her, she points instead to a small flock of starlings wheeling across the Square. She points with a pudgy finger at the direction of their flight as they come in to land upon a ledge in the Church tower above them. Jenna follows her daughter's gaze. There's a curious set of marks carved into the sandstone beyond the top of the door.

Grace observes her studying them.

"It's a benchmark," she says. "The tower marks what used to be the centre of the old town. Surveyors would use it to calibrate heights and distances in relation to other locations."

Jenna shakes her head. She feels as though she has not only lost her own benchmark, but her entire compass...

"Can we keep a track of Maleek somehow?" she asks Séydou.

"I don't know," he replies. "We can try, I suppose."

"Please," she says. "Can we...?"

After the paramedics have arrived and confirmed that Molly is completely unscathed, but that Grace's leg is indeed broken, Jenna accompanies them as they transfer Grace to an ambulance that is waiting for her back at Piccadilly Gardens. She is mumbling to herself darkly under her breath.

" *'What goes around, comes around. What you reap so shall you sow. If you do good to others, you do good to yourself. But if you do evil to others, likewise do you do evil to yourself...'* "

"You need to calm down, Miss," says one of the paramedics, a woman younger than Jenna. "You don't want to upset your little girl now, do you?"

"No," says Jenna unhappily.

"It's not as if you planted the bomb yourself, is it?" adds the young paramedic.

"Of course she didn't," says Grace, stepping in firmly. "It's been a terrible day," she adds more kindly. "Nothing can prepare us for something like this." She turns to speak directly to Jenna once more. "Try not to be so hard on yourself. Rejoice in your daughter."

"Yes," says Jenna. "I will. Thank you..."

The doors to the ambulance close. Jenna watches it drive

away from her. She looks about her. She is standing beside the statue of Queen Victoria again. She hardly knows where she is. The city looks so altered.

She feels a tug at her sleeve. She looks down. Molly is pointing. Jenna follows the direction of her outstretched arm. It's the Bubble Man. He's there after all. He is dipping his wand into a bucket of soapy water. He is catching rainbows. He scoops them up into the ring at the end of the wand and blows a bubble large enough to encircle Molly completely, a globe so enticingly perfect yet fragile, that Jenna is afraid to get too close to it, in case she should burst it...

She hoists Molly on to her hip.

"Shall we go and see Grandma and Granddad?" she says.

Molly's face beams with delight.

"Let's go and see when the next bus to Eccles leaves then, shall we?"

She carries her daughter towards the Bus Station on the far side of the Gardens. Together they walk through a chimera of bubbles. Jenna's mind is made up. She will ask her mother and father, Nadia and Sol, if they will look after Molly instead of her.

"I'm not up to it," she mutters miserably under her breath. "I can't do this any more. Not on my own."

The clusters of bubbles bump against each other, until they become one single joined-up giant, shepherding Jenna along the path she must take. The closer she looks, the more she comes to understand that it is she, Jenna, who is the chimera. Body of a woman, tail of a serpent, head of a dragon, breathing fire. A monster, conjured up to frighten children...

Molly never lives with Jenna again.

She sees her. Often. Most weeks, though not all. Not for a while if she's working away, which she does sometimes.

Sometimes she stays with her at Slate Lane. Then later, when she moves, to the converted waterfront apartment of the Grade II-listed former *Daily Express* building on Great Ancoats Street in the centre of the city, overlooking the *Rochdale* Canal now, instead of the *Ashton*, she stays with her there. At other times Jenna stays with Molly at Sol and Nadia's, close by the *Ship* Canal. All of Molly's growing feels circumscribed by water. Whereas Jenna's is more by fire. Molly is not at all disturbed by this difference in their temperaments...

The week after the bomb, after she has returned from dropping off Molly at her parents, not knowing at the time that this is to be a permanent arrangement, Jenna calls Ruth to see if she might see her again for some more sessions. It's been just over two years since she last saw her.

"I don't know what to do," she says. Her voice sounds small and far away, frightened and lost.

"Then I'll tell you," says Ruth. "We start again. Do you understand?"

"Yes," says Jenna. "I think so."

"We start again..."

2

2017

Day 1401

Starting again, for both Jenna and Ruth, takes a series of surprising twists and turns, which neither of them anticipates when their sessions together recommence...

Jenna is visiting Yemen a second time. After that first occasion, four years before, she has had to wait until it is deemed safe for her to return. But in fact it is not safe. Not safe at all...

She nearly returned two years ago.

As Zafirah had predicted, Taiz proved the touchstone for serious, prolonged fighting. The country is now in a state of brutal and complicated civil war.

Territories have changed hands several times over.

Jenna has tried to keep abreast of what has been happening, but the changes are just too rapid.

After capturing Sana'a, the Houthis advance first to Taiz, next to Lahij, finally reaching the outskirts of Aden, before the Saudi-backed Coalition forces drive them back. Saudi warplanes bomb the port and airport at Hodeidah repeatedly, pushing the Houthis back into their northern heartland, where they are further harried by ISIS forces in the desert proclaiming an Islamic Caliphate there. Meanwhile, the Coalition forces themselves split, with the formation of the Southern Movement, which aims to create a separate breakaway state. Fierce fighting rages for control of Socotra and the other off-shore islands in the Red Sea, which are highly-prized strategic targets. With casualties on both sides reaching the tens of thousands, the situation is made even more desperate by the onset of famine and disease. MSF claims that almost a half of the population – nearly fourrteen million people – is faced with starvation, while cholera is rife in the hospitals and camps.

Oman, the only country in the region not in any way militarily involved, brokers a temporary truce and ceasefire to allow food and other aid to be brought in and distributed where it is most urgently needed. Which is everywhere.

The window will last just five days.

But after less than twenty-four hours the truce is broken. Each side blames the other. It is no longer possible for the aid agencies to travel there, and Jenna's trip is cancelled...

She has to wait a further two years for another opportunity.

On this occasion the ceasefire is brokered by the UN, who place troops along the agreed corridor, which both sides pledge to evacuate for the week of the visit.

The emergency is made even more acute by the timing. It is just a week since President Trump's inauguration in January. While Obama had consistently cut back on support for the Saudis in response to their repeated attacks on civilians, Trump has pledged not only to restore it, but to increase it, in his determination to repel the Iranian-backed Houthis. Although the Senate has blocked his efforts so far, Trump is determined to override them. The agencies must therefore act quickly...

Jenna and Séydou fly in on an MSF-chartered plane from Djibouti. He tries to brief her about the current state of play. During the previous twelve months Jenna has been focusing almost entirely on the seemingly unstoppable flow of migrants escaping from Syria right across Europe, particularly on trying to assist as many of those who have made it as far as Le Jungle de Calais as she can, a situation made even more desperate by the recent Brexit vote, so that thousands of refugees cling and huddle on the edge of the port, while the French authorities bulldoze the makeshift camp. Hundreds of those left stranded are unaccompanied children. It is these who occupy Jenna's attention the most.

She has some success in placing a number of them in temporary foster care in Manchester, where more than sixty percent of voters choose to remain in the EU, but there is only space for so many, and this visit to Yemen is bound to throw up thousands more. Manchester cannot take them all.

"But the example we set," she tells Radio 4's Mishal Husain on the *Today* programme, "can serve as a beacon to the rest of the world. Yemen has become a forgotten war," she says. "Let's shine a light on it so that we all of us become more aware and do what we can – together – to bring it to an end..."

"That was good," Mishal tells her afterwards, in the thirty-second break she has before introducing her next item.

"Really?"

"Absolutely. We're getting all manner of tweets and responses in favour."

Possibly, thinks Jenna. But not as much as if she had been given an earlier slot, instead of this brief one just five minutes before the programme finishes, squeezed in ahead of the obligatory feel-good item at the end, which this morning is about the return of the corncrake to northern England after an absence of more than half a century. Its rasping 'crek crek' call is played just before the Greenwich pips. A half-forgotten, creaking gate demanding to be opened, to push through the rust of absent years, and, having once been heard, be re-admitted...

"You need a celebrity."

"I beg your pardon?"

"If you want to be heard more loudly." It's Mishal Husain again, catching up with Jenna after the programme has gone off air. "Preferably a rock singer. But a film star is an acceptable consolation prize."

Jenna knows this to be true. Lily Allen's comments on the situation she has witnessed personally in Calais have received far wider coverage than anything Jenna has been able to generate through the more formal channels afforded her by the Refugee Council. But even Lily Allen's comments, though irreproachably heart-felt, have been pale in comparison with the more florid and feisty tone she adopts in her pop songs. Likewise Benedict Cumberbatch, who has also spoken out against the appalling conditions to be found in Le Jungle, especially for lone, unaccompanied children, but who subsequently apologises for his outburst, admitting that he doesn't really know what he's talking about, and that he gets carried away sometimes.

That's exactly what we need more of, thinks Jenna. Much more. What's happened to that good, old-fashioned, undiluted, foul-mouthed rage and fury more usually associated with rock stars? Why can't the Gallagher brothers get involved, she asks herself, instead of merely trading insults with each other…?

She recalls the time forty years before, back in '85, when the Live Aid Concert was in full swing, and the whole world was watching it on TV in bars, and Bob Geldof was interrupting the BBC presenter David Hepworth, who was attempting to provide a list of addresses to where donations might be sent, by famously saying, "Fuck the addresses, just get the phone numbers." Immediately the donations went from zero to three hundred pounds per second.

Jenna loves the way Geldof cuts through the crap, goes straight for the jugular, not caring if he offends, because he knows that with each second that passes more lives might be lost.

She and Lance organise an impromptu party at *The Reno* to raise more funds. In between each of the acts performing at Wembley, local bands play live at the club. In one glorious moment, the two fuse together. On screen Elvis Costello announces that he will sing what he calls 'a northern folk song', before launching into an acoustic, semi-reggae version of *All You Need is Love*, while inside *The Reno* Harlem Shuffle immediately join in, and the whole joint is jumping...

Over the years Jenna comes to realise the truth of these words. In the end love is all you need. It transcends politics, whichever side you're on. But even then, it frequently requires a helping hand from someone with a higher profile than she has. Three years from now she will remember again Mishal Husain's advice when the Manchester United footballer Marcus Rashford will lend his voice and support for the organisation FairShare in their campaign to eradicate child food poverty during the Covid pandemic, which will tear through Yemen like a time bomb, with more than two million cases being reported in a matter of weeks. And these are only the official figures. She will watch in admiration at the way Marcus, by the sheer force of his will, combined with the power of being simply who he is, will persuade Prime Minister Johnson to change his mind, to do a publicly humiliating U-turn, and provide free school meals for all those children who need them. In Yemen, where there is no such high profile figure to embarrass them, the Coalition Government at first denies that the virus has reached the country at all. The reality is much, much worse....

But in 2017 Covid is not on the horizon, not even a blip on the farthest edge of the solar system, where a previously unseen comet might herald its appearance.

The last of the Greenwich pips sounds in the BBC recording studio. The newsreader clears his throat, like a returning corncrake, before delivering the latest figures on the number of refugees seeking asylum across Europe, so many of them heading for Calais, from there to England, and, once arrived, spreading like much-needed new blood through her arteries criss-crossing the body of her map, not that this view is shared by all. The newsreader goes on to give details of a leaked memo sent by the Home Secretary Amber Rudd privately to the Prime Minister outlining her plans to 'arrest, detain and ruthlessly deport' all illegal immigrants, no matter where they are from, or whatever horrors they are fleeing...

Zafirah is there to meet them at Hodeidah. Jenna no longer recognises it. Yemen has become a country with no known maps. The people are lost, while they try to make new ones.

The terminal building, which to Jenna before had seemed like an egg, is now little more than a shattered shell, having been bombed by both sides repeatedly. Even parts of the runway have been damaged, so that the pilot has to manoeuvre their landing between pot-holes and craters. All civilian flights have long since ceased to operate. Soldiers patrol the perimeter. Jenna cannot make out which side they are on. Both, Zafirah tells her...

While Séydou liaises with other government and UN aid agencies about the immediate distribution of food and medical supplies, Zafirah drives Jenna to the refugee camps of Kharaz and Mishqafa. Although she is now well-briefed and has been following the situation in both on a weekly basis, she is still not prepared for the shock of actually being there. The visceral reality is overwhelming, a physical and emotional assault so intense that she has to ask Zafirah to stop the car for her to lurch away from it and be sick...

When she has emptied out her insides, the acidic bile at the back of her throat burns and makes her retch once more. This is human suffering on a biblical, apocalyptic scale. Thousands of children press against the wire fences. Shrivelled, skeletal fingers poke through the mesh. But even worse are the blank expressions on their faces, dead already, all hope fled. Flies crawl across their swollen lips and eyelids unchecked...

Jenna tries to force herself not to look away.

A tidal wave of emotions surge through her like a virus. They invade every part of her. Séydou has told her that a close symbiotic connection exists between humans and viruses. Geneticists now believe, he tells her, that as many as half of all human DNA may have originated from viruses that infected and embedded their nucleic acid in our ancestors' egg and sperm cells. They occupy every one of our bodies' surfaces – the skin, the gut, the mucous membranes. In fact, he explains, we are made up of ten times more microbial than human cells, blurring the line between where viruses end and humans begin. Most of them thrive, establishing themselves as persistent colonists, in closely clustered communities, within and on our bodies. In this way they derive benefits from being with us. Sometimes, as hosts, we also experience the same benefits. But sometimes they can make us sick, even kill us. In the most catastrophic of cases they can spread through whole families, villages, cities, countries, even continents, wiping out all in their path. But rarely. For in the long run they have a shared interest in our survival.

This is what Jenna clings to. She looks back through the wire mesh of the fence around the perimeter of the refugee camp at Mishqafa, registering each separate emotion as it courses through her.

Shock. Horror. Revulsion. Guilt.

Fear. Rage. Helplessness. Guilt.

Defiance. Determination. Love. Guilt.

Then Loss. Grief. Recovery. Persistence.

And more guilt.

And finally love again.

Rising up through all the boils and blisters, scabs and scars, wounds and sores, broken bones and bloated bellies, that old northern folk song.

There's nowhere she can be that isn't where she's meant to be. Nothing she can say, but she can learn how to feel in time…

"We need to learn how you might channel this guilt you're carrying around with you," says Ruth to her, "instead of bottling it up. It will only spread through your system like poison otherwise. We must try to flush out as much of it as we can. Just leave the tiniest amount in there. As an early warning alarm system to alert you when it threatens to rear its head again. Which it will do. But when it does, you'll know what to do about it. You'll be able to recognise it, acknowledge it, confront it, then utilise it."

This is all said at their first session back together again, after the IRA bomb attack on Manchester, and Jenna's reaction to it. After she's handed Molly over to her parents.

"Abandoned her, more like," says Jenna.

"There you go again," says Ruth. "Guilt, guilt, guilt…"

Jenna is back at the Squat. Bex is writing up another of Spike's quotes on the peeling wallpaper.

'Guilt is to danger what fire is to gunpowder. A man need not fear to walk among it if he have no fire about him…'

"A man called John Flavin wrote this," says Spike. "A 17th century Dissenting preacher in response to the Five Mile Act."

"What was that?" asks Jenna.

"To give it its long title," he says, taking the marker pen from Bex and writing as he speaks.

"An Act for Restraining Nonconformists from Inhabiting in Corporations." He hands the pen back to Bex.

"It forbade clergymen from living within five miles of any parish from which they might have been expelled for expressing views that were contrary to the Establishment, unless they swore an oath never to resist the authority of the King, or attempt to overthrow the Government of the Church or State."

He smiles down benignly on his followers, who are hanging on his every word.

"I like to think that *we* are Nonconformists, whatever our background, but the Corporations will not restrain us from speaking out against their falsehoods or wrongdoings. For it is not we who are guilty, but those who try to silence us. Think what fire we carry with us."

Then he asks Bex to write up another of his quotes. This one is by Voltaire.

'Every man is guilty of all the good he did not do…'

"That's a honey," agrees Ruth.

Bex picks up her guitar again and starts to sing.

"Anima rising
Uprising in me tonight
She's a vengeful little goddess
With an ancient crown to fight…"

"What are you telling me here?" asks Ruth.

Jenna hears her voice echoing down the years as she enters the camp at Mishqafa, feeling the soldiers' eyes upon her, in spite of her modest clothes, the respectful veil…

Bex is singing a different song.

"Caught in the middle
We're middle class, middle-aged
We were wild in the old days
Birth of rock & roll days…"

Ruth likes the fire in Jenna's belly. She doesn't want in any way to douse those flames, but to help her to learn instead how to put them to more constructive use. Cleanse and purify, instead of slash and burn...

"My child's a stranger
I bore her
But I could not raise her..."

"But she's not a stranger," interrupts Ruth. "You get to see her whenever you want."

"No," says Jenna vehemently. "She's better off without me..."

Sol has taken early retirement from his work as a draughtsman at Turner's on Trafford Park to look after Molly. They were making cuts in any case, so Sol offers to be one of the first to go. Molly lives with him and Nadia full time from then on, though she still spends lots of time with Farida and Anita, and Salwa and the Aunties. It's completely normal to her. Seeing Jenna, her mother, is just another part of this colourful mosaic.

"She's happy," Ruth reminds Jenna. "Rejoice in that. It's your 'get-out-of-jail-free' card..."

When she's older, when she describes to Michael what her childhood was like, in those early days when they are still getting to know each other, Molly tells him she feels lucky to have been part of such a wide extended family. Michael will smile. He understands. His own upbringing in Nigeria bears similar traits...

Afterwards, when she is feeling better, Jenna will laugh and say that in developing countries a child will often be raised by a whole village. That it's better for the child to have the love and support of many, rather than just the one...

Molly knows that Jenna believes this. Ruth knows it too. A mantra Jenna repeats to herself to lessen the guilt...

"There are two kinds of guilt," says Molly when she turns twenty-one, "the kind that drowns you until you are useless, and the kind that fires your soul to purpose."

"When did you get so wise?" says Jenna, arching an eyebrow.

"I didn't," smiles Molly. "I read it. Here." She takes out a book from her bag. *The Ember and the Ashes* by Sabaa Tahir. "I bought it with some of the money you sent for my birthday."

Jenna picks it up. She flicks through it cursorily. She doesn't read fiction as a rule. She doesn't see the point. And besides, she doesn't have the time. The writer's a young woman, she notices, born in Pakistan, grew up in England, now living in America. The blurb reveals it's a fantasy novel. She hands it back, shaking her head.

"Not your thing, I realise," smiles Molly again. "But you shouldn't be so dismissive. A young woman fights to save a small child from prison. A soldier battles to be free from an oppressive regime..."

"Child with a child's pretending," sings Bex as Joni...
"Weary of lies you are sending home
So you sign all the papers in the family name
You're sad and you're sorry but you're not ashamed..."

"Aren't you?" asks Ruth...

"Little Green – have a happy ending..."

"By the way," asks Molly, "my Final Year show opens next week. Can you come?"

"Oh, "says Jenna, "does it? I'm not sure. I'll try."

"No worries," says Molly. "It's on for a month..."

In the end Jenna does make it to Molly's show. Not to the opening – she's presenting the annual Eleanor Rathbone Lecture in Liverpool on that evening – but a few days later, when the gallery is quiet, and Jenna has the exhibition all to herself, apart from a tall young man from Nigeria, who introduces himself to her somewhat formally as Michael Chidi Promise Adebayo, and who is clearly much taken with Molly's drawings.

As is she.

Sketch after sketch of birds – starlings mostly – in restless murmuration. Jenna is mesmerised by them. The effortless way her daughter has captured their questing motion. A passage that is simultaneously graceful yet desperate, harnessed by some unseen choreographer. Instinct? Desire? Need? Or is the impulse the artist's? Molly's? Or perhaps it is just something she has sensed within herself. This primeval yearning to find a home, sanctuary, a safe haven. A connection.

Whatever the source, Jenna herself experiences something of this same connection. It chimes with aspects of the lecture she delivered in Liverpool. She is deeply touched by Molly's dedication in the catalogue accompanying the exhibition, a single sheet of A4 listing the title of each drawing.

'In memory of my grandfather, Solomon Ward – Sol – who died earlier this year. He was a wonderful artist himself. It was he who first encouraged me to pick up a pencil. He would take me into Manchester to watch the starlings soar above the city at twilight, and he taught me to ask questions of everything I saw. How do they stay together? How do they know the exact moment when they are to change direction, faster than a heartbeat, when to come home to roost, and when to take to the skies once more...?'

"These are wonderful," says the tall, young Nigerian.

"Yes," agrees Jenna. "They are." But she says nothing

more. She is on the edge of tears and fears betraying her emotions if she speaks further.

Michael appears to understand this. Sensitively he withdraws, allowing her to be alone.

She feels a double sense of guilt begin to leave her, a tight band loosening around her head, the weight of the years slipping from her shoulders. If Molly hadn't been raised by Sol, she might never have discovered this talent she undoubtedly has, a talent it would appear she has inherited from him. Jenna thinks of the drawings her father made of the Hejaz Mountains during his time in Aden, conjuring a whole world with just a few bold pencil strokes, just as Molly has evoked that heart-stopping moment between movement and stillness, between take-off and landing, flight and fall, when all outcomes are still possible, before any decisions have been taken. Somehow her mark-making depicts these contradictions, offering surprising patterns within their seemingly chance collisions.

Perhaps Molly would have drawn anyway, without Sol's influence. Who knows? Nature, nurture? Jenna remembers him handing her the paint brush to paint that last missing section of the mural, that lost umbrella, a time of rare connection between them when she was young…

She is weeping quite openly now as she stands before her daughter's drawings alone in the gallery, grateful that her father has had this second chance at raising a child, a chance that her own failings as a mother had made possible, in recompense for the chance she had denied him as a daughter.

Molly's starlings fill the gallery. Jenna is surrounded by them. They wheel above, around and through her, screeching in a wild but unified chorus, demanding to be heard…

As they do now above the camp at Mishqafa – the Socotran starlings, cousins of the European species, endemic to Yemen, passerines all.

The sun is slipping below the ridge of the crater of the wakening volcano, which sits in the heart of the Hejaz Mountains. The black silhouettes of the starlings are blocking out the light.

"Let's come back tomorrow," says Zafirah. "Make a fresh start."

Jenna feels a sudden shiver despite the heat...

*

Day 1402

The Annual Eleanor Rathbone Lecture is a prestigious affair. It is a rare honour to be invited to deliver it. As Jenna is, five years after being appointed to head up the Refugee Council's Manchester office.

She begins by paying tribute to Miss Rathbone on the seventieth anniversary of her death. She lists her many achievements – her early life in Liverpool, where her father, William, was the sitting MP and a pioneering social reformer; her succeeding Millicent Fawcett in 1919 as President of the National Union of Women's Suffrage Societies, a position she held until equal voting rights were granted to all women as well as men a decade later, when she herself was elected as MP for the Combined English Universities; her courageous maiden speech in Parliament against the hitherto taboo subject of female genital mutilation; her tireless campaigns in support of human rights, even when she was a lone voice advocating support for those opposing Franco in the Spanish Civil War – she even tried to hire a ship to run the blockade of Spain and help remove Republicans at risk from reprisals – or condemning Italian atrocities in what was then Abyssinia; her signed letter to the *Manchester Guardian* in support of granting Trotsky political asylum; her prophetic warnings against Nazi incursions into Czechoslovakia; her pressure on the Government to grant entry for dissident Germans, Austrians and Jews, and, arguably her most enduring legacy, her championing of the Family Allowances Act. Jenna is particularly fond of one particular anecdote. Such was her tenacity, apparently, that ministers and civil servants at the Foreign Office would reputedly duck behind pillars if ever they saw her coming. Her lifelong companion was her fellow suffragist Elizabeth Macadam, with whom she shared a house from just after the end of the First World War until Eleanor's sudden death in 1946, the seventieth anniversary of which coincides with Jenna's lecture.

But it is on Eleanor's unending work on behalf of refugees and the dispossessed that Jenna focuses for the main body of her talk, which she gives not just in her capacity as Regional Director with responsibility for the Middle East at the Refugee Council, but also as a member of the Board of the European Council for Refugees and Exiles, and as the recently appointed Chair of CARE International UK, which works to find long-term solutions to poverty in more than a hundred countries world-wide.

"There are currently more than forty million people around the world," she concludes, "who have been forcibly displaced as a result of persecution, conflict, or violence, the vast majority of whom become refugees. They have no choice, for their homes have been taken from them. Many of these are currently making headlines right now, because of the wars going on in Syria, Iraq, Afghanistan and Yemen, but although our television screens show so many of them knocking at our borders, most never reach us here in Europe. Oughtn't we, therefore, do all that we can to help those who do? I'm sure that's what Eleanor would think. It's what she tried to do all her life, especially here in Liverpool. While thirty miles down the East Lancashire Road in Manchester, we too have a tradition of welcoming the strangers at our gates. But just at a time when providing protection and support to those forced to leave everything behind is more needed than ever, Governments across Europe have introduced policies to prevent, or at least try to deter, entry into their countries. Alongside this deliberately hostile strategy, the treatment of those who do make it here is daily deteriorating. Thereby, as both the Bible and Quran tell us, we entertain angels unawares. Let us instead build bridges, not walls..."

A year later Zafirah tells her that her parents are among that forty million...

When, four years earlier, the fighting really breaks out in Taiz, the day after Jenna and Seydou make their night-time dash from there to Hodeidah, the fierce, brutal hand-to-hand variety that sees opposing forces slug it out street by street, she manages to reach them just in time. She bundles them into the back of her car and drives them the sixty miles to Mocha, an abandoned port on the Red Sea, now little more than a fishing village, where she is able to put them on a boat to Djibouti, which is currently a safe haven for refugees, with Somalis going to the Ali-Addeh camp in the south, Ethiopians to the Holl-Holl camp in the centre, and Yemenis, like Zafirah's parents, to the Markazi camp in the north.

After a few months, through Séydou's contacts, she is able to find a room for them above a cobbler's in Les Caisses, the large, sprawling market along the Boulevard de Bendère in Djibouti City, where she joins them whenever she can, in between assignments such as these, which are becoming increasingly rare as Yemen spirals out of control.

"Poor country," her father says, a retired teacher and lover of Shakespeare, "almost afraid to know itself..."

There have been times when Jenna has felt the same about

Manchester...

Jenna and Lance are walking back home. Home. It's a word that sits awkwardly on both their lips. The Squat has been shut down for a year now. After Moss Lane East they had moved to Raby Street. From there to Upper Lloyd Street. From there to Great Western Street. And from there back to Moss Lane East. In the end they decide to split. There's just too much hassle from the Police these days, and there are only so many times they can keep moving on, only so many boarded-up houses that can become available. The writing's been on the wall for some time. Or rather, it hasn't. They've not been able to stay anywhere for long enough of late for Bex to write up any of Spike's slogans or watchwords. Instead she writes her own.

'Last Chance Saloon.'
'End of the Line.'
'Last Exit to...'
'It's life, Jim, but not as we know it...'

Even so, Spike insists they must vote on it.

Bex picks up her guitar and starts to sing – The Clash song they all of them know. One by one they join in.

"Darlin' you got to let me know
Should I stay or should I go?
If you say that you are mine
I'll be here 'til the end of time
So you got to let me know
Should I stay or should I go...?"

"One person, one vote," says Spike.

But Dougie and Caroline insist they should only have one vote between them. "We're joined at the hip anyway," they argue. "It wouldn't be fair otherwise."

"If you're sure," says Spike.

"We're sure," they say together.

So the voting begins.

Bex votes to go. Spike votes to stay.

Dougie and Caroline vote to go. Lance votes to stay.

That's two votes each. All eyes turn towards Jenna, for her vote will decide the fate of them all.

She looks at each of them in turn. Finally her eyes light upon Lance.

"I vote we go," she says.

"So be it," says Spike.

Without another word Jenna leaves.

"Wah yuh aw say, woman?" cries Lance. Then storms out after her…

He catches up with her in Whitworth Park. She's standing in its centre, by the broken remnants of a marble plinth, now overgrown with weeds. When she senses him coming, she sits in the grass, her back leaning against one of the blocks of weathered stone.

"There used to be a statue here once," she says. "Christ blessing the little children."

"Wah happen tuh it?"

She shrugs. "They took it down. Along with everything else that was here. A bandstand. A pavilion. A boating lake. Fountains. Flower beds. A War Memorial. All gone. No one knows where any of them are now."

"Wi still here, gyal."

She smiles thinly. "There was even something called a Soldier's Room."

"Wah duh that?"

"Where old soldiers returning from the War could sit and smoke."

"Mi reckon wi old soldias."

"Not so old."

He sits beside her and starts to roll them each a cigarette.

"And the War's not over."

"Den wah mek yuh vote leave?"

She looks at him steadily. "Because we've got to fight this one by ourselves..."

They spend the next few nights in DJ Persian's store room at the back of *The Reno*. It's not much more than a cupboard, but there's a stained mattress wedged between old decks, turntables, cables and cassette tapes, where they can just about squeeze themselves in.

"It be ok till mi find sum place betta," says Lance...

But after a week they have to leave anyway, for *The Reno* is closing down. It's losing money fast. Especially when it becomes the target for the rival gangs from Moss Side and Cheetham Hill in their escalating turf wars, territories changing sides like shifting sands. A month later the bulldozers move in. adding their own percussive beats to Persian's final playlist. *Money's Too Tight To Mention*. The Valentine Brothers. But it's no Valentine for Jenna and Lance. They can't get that 'unemployment extension...'

Lance arranges for them to go back to his mother's place for a few nights. Anita's.

"Jus' tuh tide wi ova."

But Anita is good friends with Nadia. There's no way Jenna wants the truth about her current homeless situation getting back to her mother. Besides, she's due to start her internship with Graham Stringer in less than a month. She needs a base – somewhere that's safe, secure, where she can cook, have a shower, keep her clothes clean – so, using her Social Security, she rents a bed-sit on Claremont Road.

"You can come too," she tells Lance. "But you have to pull

your weight, pay something towards your keep."

"Yuh no' worry bout a ting, gyal. Mi get a job."

Jenna's eyebrows shoot up. "Really? Where?"

"Mi got contacts..."

The bed-sit doesn't become available for another two weeks. Till then they can doss down on Dougie and Caroline's floor in Fallowfield. To Jenna's surprise Lance does indeed land himself a job.

He comes back one evening brandishing a leaflet, a broad grin on his face.

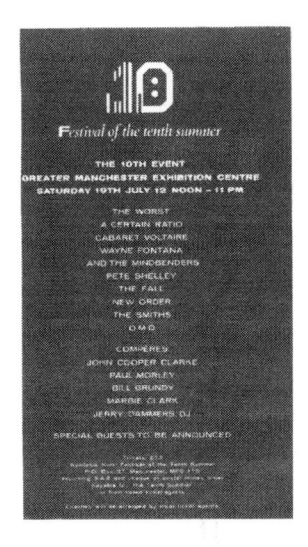

Festival of the tenth summer

THE 10TH EVENT
GREATER MANCHESTER EXHIBITION CENTRE
SATURDAY 19TH JULY 12 NOON – 11 PM

THE WORST
A CERTAIN RATIO
CABARET VOLTAIRE
WAYNE FONTANA
AND THE MINDBENDERS
PETE SHELLEY
THE FALL
NEW ORDER
THE SMITHS
O M D

COMPÈRES
JOHN COOPER CLARKE
PAUL MORLEY
BILL GRUNDY
MARGIE CLARK
JERRY DAMMERS DJ

SPECIAL GUESTS TO BE ANNOUNCED

It's advertising Tony Wilson's latest extravaganza. A ten-day Festival to celebrate ten years of Factory Records. Ten years since the Sex Pistols played at the Lesser Free Trade Hall. Ten years since their infamous interview on Granada TV, when they swore at Bill Grundy, who, in a sly nod to that notorious incident, Tony Wilson has invited to co-host the Festival, and who, seeing the joke, has, to everyone's surprise, agreed, a role he will share with John Cooper Clarke, The Bard of Salford, The Poet Laureate of Punk, to be held at *G-Mex*, the former Central Station, tucked behind *The Midland Hotel*, now a multi-purpose venue. It's a stellar line-up, including The Smiths, The Fall, and New Order – just three of the luminaries scheduled to appear. Lance has managed to get himself hired as a DJ to play music between each of the acts.

He comes to Jenna singing. He's cock-a-hoop.

"Mi told yuh no' tuh worry, gyal," he crows. Then he starts to sing Bob Marley and dance a little jig, twirling Jenna round under his arm, coiling his fingers through his dreads.

"Ev'ry little ting gonna be alright..."

His mood is infectious. Jenna can't help herself from smiling and joining in.

"Mi got yuh sumtin', darlin'," he says, producing a small piece of paper from his jacket pocket like a rabbit from a hat.

"What is it?" she asks.

"Dat fi mi tuh kno' an' yuh tuh learn," he grins, keeping it just out of Jenna's reach, only relenting when she agrees to a kiss.

With a final flourish he goes down on one knee and presents her with it.

It's a Guest Pass backstage for the last night. The night The Smiths are playing.

"Woo-hoo!"

She returns his kiss with interest...

Later she arranges to meet Lance after the gig. He'll be too busy till then...

She steps out of Dougie and Caroline's one-roomed basement flat on Cadogan Street, crosses the Princess Parkway by the Harp Lager Brewery, close to The Meadow, which still bears the scars from the night of the Riot, the scorched earth, where the grass has not grown back properly, then plunges into the warren of Hulme Crescents – John Nash, William Kent, Robert Adam, Charles Barry – emerging at the entrance to the underpass which takes her beneath the Mancunian Way, through to Knott Mill Station, tucked beneath the Bridgewater Viaduct at the foot of Deansgate, where the last dregs of the River Medlock drain into the Castlefield Basin. She can just make out the twinkling reflection of the tail of Halley's Comet, coming to the end of its once-in-a-seventy-five-year cycle of visiting the Earth, before departing once more...

Throughout the one-and-a-half-mile walk she listens to The Smiths' latest album on her Walkman, *The Queen is Dead*, Morrissey's mournful voice a clarion call for urban renewal. *There's A Light That Never Goes Out.*

'Take me out tonight
Where there's music and there's people
And they're young and alive...'

While all around her the city rots, the buildings black with soot and pigeon-droppings. She sings along, trying to shut out the incessant roar of demolition and destruction, the pneumatic jackhammer drills pounding the concrete.

It's more than forty years since the Second World War has ended, but they've still not finished clearing the bomb sites. And where they have, they've bulldozed whole streets, entire communities, razing them to the ground – more scorched earth

– replacing them with... what? Are these rat-infested crescents really the best they can offer? Or the yellow-brick rabbit hutches by Alexandra Park? With tiny windows that look like gun emplacements?

She passes by the turning to *The Haçienda*. Little wonder the young of Manchester go there to lose themselves in the music...

She will recall this moment, thirty years later on *Desert Island Discs*, when she asks for this track to be played as one of her choices. When Kirsty Young asks her why, she starts up on another of her rants...

"Because Manchester is a light that never goes out," she will say. "One of the reasons that *The Haçienda* was so successful was that it was a place you could go to really let off steam, have a party, and forget about just how crap Manchester had become in those years. All the things that had made Manchester what it was – the mills, the mines, the factories – they were all closing down, and nothing was replacing them. I used to walk to lectures from my student flat in Moss Side and it was like a ghost town. Whole streets were boarded up, there were squats everywhere, huge numbers of homeless sleeping rough, blocks of flats going up that nobody wanted to live in, that were riddled with damp, and no jobs. Unemployment topping three million, and this song just spoke to us, all of us, at the time..."

'Take me out tonight
Take me anywhere
I don't care, I don't care, I don't care...'

But she does not say what really happened. Like the rest of the programme, it's selective. A carefully crafted version of events, not allowing the listeners to get too close, deliberately keeping them at arm's length, editing out anything too personal.

"It's for their own good," she would joke if challenged. When really it was for her own protection.

"You can choose," says Ruth to her in one of their sessions, "what to include and what to leave out, what to tell people and what to keep to yourself…"

In the darkened auditorium of the *G-Mex* the anticipation grows. The Smiths are fashionably late. Their gig should have started half an hour ago, so that when, at last, Johnny Marr launches into one of his signature jangly arpeggios on his Fender Stratocaster guitar, the crowd is ecstatic, surging forward, to be as near to the stage as they can. Morrissey, with a scrubby bush of eucalyptus leaves hanging from his jeans' back pocket, looking like something he might have just picked from one of the city's waste grounds, or maybe Whitworth Park, near to where Jenna and Lance had had their heart-to-heart, turns in ever-decreasing circles in a spotlight in the centre of the stage, waving his arms above his head, delicately revolving his wrists, as if he is performing some kind of arcane, invisible poi, which only he can see. Everyone knows what's coming. When he finally starts to sing, the entire audience joins in, Jenna included. All of them part of the same huge, shared, private joke.

"I was happy in the haze of a drunken hour
But heaven knows I'm miserable now…"

Projected onto a screen behind the band are looped, repeated clips from Rita Tushingham movies. *A Taste of Honey, A Place to Go, A Smashing Time, The Leather Boys, The Bed-Sitting Room, The Knack & How to Get It…*

Jenna catches a glimpse of Lance standing in the wings – or

thinks she does, she can't be certain – next to Tony Wilson and a coterie of fans, young girls mostly, several of whom hang on Lance's arm. They look more than casual acquaintances. From what she can tell they're on fairly intimate terms. Or appear to be...

Or maybe it's *not* Lance. With the flashing lights it's difficult to be sure. Whoever it is retreats further into the wings and she loses sight of him.

Morrissey is seemingly singing directly to her.

"Girlfriend in a coma – I know, I know, it's serious...
Do you really think that she will pull through...?"

Jenna's not sure if she will. How long has she been sleepwalking like this?

"Stop me if you think you've heard this before..."

She evades the security guards, leaps up onto the stage, then hurls herself back towards the heaving sea of fans below, who catch her, passing her along from one to another as she surfs the wave of them, lying on her back, staring up towards the vanishing point of the *G-Mex*'s domed glass roof, beyond which she can see the stars and constellations wheeling, and the last of Halley's Comet, before its orbital path takes if far away from Earth.

"There is a light that never goes out...
There is a light that never goes out..."

Until she shuts her eyes and it disappears...

She remains there for several minutes. When the gig is over and the audience begins to leave, they are forced to step over her. Most shake their heads or shrug indulgently, assuming she must be tripping. One or two bend down to ask if she's OK.

She assures them that she is, smiling beatifically. They leave her where she is.

Eventually one of the security guards shakes her by the shoulder.

"Time you were on your way, love," he says, not unkindly.

She shows him her Guest Pass.

"You're too late," he says. "They all went off with Tony a while back."

"Where?"

"No idea. He said he knew a place to go. You know Tony? He always knows where there's a place to go."

Lance does too, she thinks, slowly standing up. The knack, and how to get it. It seems that she hasn't managed that yet.

She starts to walk away, unsteadily at first, until she finds her balance.

"Will you be OK?" he calls after her.

"I'm fine," she says, spreading out her arms. "I've had a smashing time."

Outside the roadies are packing up the van. A flotilla of bikers escort it out of the old station yard. The leather boys.

A gentle rain begins to fall. Jenna hangs out her tongue to catch the first few drops, to take away that bitter taste of honey.

She hears herself humming the final song from the set as she starts to walk away. *I Know It's Over*. Morrissey has taken the small bush from his back pocket and is plucking the leaves one by one. Jenna realises they're not faded eucalyptus, but dried pods of honesty.

"I can feel the soil falling over my head
And as I climb into an empty bed
Oh well – enough said
I know it's over…"

She retraces her footsteps back the way she first came – towards the River Medlock, the Castlefield Basin, the

Bridgewater Viaduct, Knott Mill Station – with no trailing comet to guide her this time.

"I know it's over
But in my heart it was so real
You even spoke to me, you said
If you're so clever
Then why are you on your own tonight...?"

She doesn't have any answers. The rain is coming on harder now, in bitter squalls. She's not dressed for it, just a T-shirt and jeans. In no time at all she's soaked to the skin.

She reaches the railway arches. She decides she'll take shelter. At least till the rain eases off. One of them especially looks inviting. It's low and goes a long way back. Stooping, she enters into it. It's like a fox's lair, a bear's cave. The blackened bricks are dry to the touch. She crawls in as far as she can, then crouches in a corner. Little by little the shivering stops. Her eyes slowly become accustomed to the darkness. Her fingers seek out the cracks and crevices between each brick until they alight on something deeper, something carved and notched. Not looking, she traces their shape.

She stops, holds her breath, eyes wide open.
She fingers their outline a second time, just to make sure.
Yes. There's no mistaking them.
'S-W...'

Surely, she thinks, it must be a coincidence?
But must it? Why shouldn't they be the same...?

Sol is following the same route that his father did, despite the prospect of a night beneath these arches.

He walks beside them, hoping perhaps one of them may be open, not locked or shuttered, accessible. He passes garages where men are still working in pits beneath broken cars being patched and mended. He reaches a lock-up just as an acned youth is pulling down a metal shutter, who looks at Sol suspiciously. He is drawn to where he sees the light of what might be a fire burning inside and stumbles into a forge, a bare-chested blacksmith hammering horse shoes at an anvil with one hand, while pumping a large pair of bellows with another. He hears the distant whinny of a horse rising from behind an adjoining bricked up builder's yard, until eventually he reaches an arch with a cobbled recess stretching back and in, several yards away from the street, before tapering down to the ground.

This will do, he thinks, as he curls up in the farthest corner, his back against the stone, and places his rucksack behind his head to use as a kind of pillow. He takes a firm grip of the umbrella and looks about him, his eyes adjusting to the shadows. Others have used this spot before him, he can see, from the evidence of discarded cigarette stubs and a few beer cans. He does not expect to get much sleep this night, but at least it will be dry and away from the wind and rain, and it will not be too many hours before daylight streaks the sky once more.

But he is wrong. The exertions of the day have taken their toll. More than ten hours of walking, some of it more like clambering and slithering, have exhausted him. Now that he has allowed himself to stop, he finds his eyes drooping almost at once, and, before he can start to contemplate the rest of the journey that awaits him tomorrow, he is almost asleep. Some long-buried instinct impels him to pick up a small sharp stone and carve his initials, 'S-W', into the farthest corner of the recess, before he curls up in a foetal position for the rest of the night...

Jenna rests her fingers within the carved grooves of these letters, which she dares to dream were made by her father. It's possible, she thinks. It's not too long ago for them to have survived and not been overlain by others. Less than twenty years.

And still Morrissey sings to her inside her head.

"And in the darkened underpass
Oh God, my chance has come at last
But then a strange fear gripped me
And I just couldn't ask..."

The rain is driving down in stair rods. But here beneath the arch it's dry. She'll not go back to Dougie and Caroline's basement tonight. It's too humiliating. She'll stay here instead. At least until daybreak. She curls herself up into a tight foetal position and waits, waits till the fear that has gripped her begins to subside, to try and formulate the question she should have asked herself before. But the words won't come. She stares at the street light opposite, on Deansgate, at its junction with Constance Street. The light that never goes out...

She is woken with a start just before daybreak. Crazed, bloodshot eyes are staring at her right up close, caught in the flare of a recently struck match. Jenna can just make out a mass of matted hair and a pair of hands reaching towards her. She can smell the man's sour breath as the blackened fingers of one of these hands slowly caterpillar the air above her face. The other hand carries an old broken, black umbrella, which jabs and pokes into Jenna's ribs. She makes a grab for it. A brief tussle ensues between them, tugging the umbrella back and forth, until the man wrenches it free and darts backwards out from underneath the arch. Jenna follows him. There is something about the umbrella that is familiar. Even though little of it remains but its skeletal frame and a few strips of black cloth, torn and flapping in the wind...

Could it be, she wonders? But before she has time to

consider it further, the man is gone. A rat scampering down a drain. She must be hallucinating, she thinks, It's hours since she last ate or drank anything. She needs to get herself together. She looks around to find her bearings. The familiar street names anchor her.

Constance Street.
Alpha Place.
Albion Court.
Jordan Way.
The light still burns...

*

Day 1403

Jenna feels a hand shaking her shoulder. It's Zafirah.

"Wake up," she says. "We need to make an early start."

After the *muezzin*'s dawn call to prayer, an uneasy silence hangs over the city. Following years of daily bombardments, the air trembling with gunfire, the sudden ceasefire seems strangely surreal, other-worldly almost.

"It's remarkable what you can get used to," says Zafirah bitterly. The stillness that has descended on them feels acutely threatening, the knowledge that it will not last, that it's only a matter of time before the hostilities resume...

She and Jenna return to the camp at Mishqafa.

The listless children barely stir. Jenna recalls the mischief of the young boys and girls who besieged the car as she and Séydou drove on country roads through villages not yet touched by the fighting, excitedly jostling them, asking for pens and dollars. That was four years ago. Now not a single part of Yemen has not been blighted by the war. These children lie in the sand like dry and brittle stalks of millet, wilting in the fierce heat, all their seeds long since raided by the Socotra starlings shrieking overhead.

There are more than two and a half thousand of them here at Mishqafa, Jenna learns, of whom at least half are orphans. Probably. "It's not possible to give exact figures," says one exhausted aid worker. "More arrive each day," she explains, "but at the same time many die. Cholera is sweeping through the camp. We have little food, fresh water is increasingly scarce, and we ran out of medical supplies a fortnight ago."

"What about the hospitals?" asks Jenna naïvely.

The aid worker looks at her witheringly. "They are overrun with war casualties. They patch them up as best they can, then tip them back out onto the streets again, to make room for the next wave. Many of those find their way here. Now – if you'll excuse me – I have patients to attend to…"

Jenna feels angry and ashamed. But it's the sense of utter powerlessness that threatens to overwhelm her most. There must be something she can do.

"That is why you're here," Zafirah reassures her, "isn't it? A fact-finding mission. So that you can return to Britain and tell people what it's truly like here. So the politicians might change their minds and stop selling arms to the Saudis?"

If only, thinks Jenna. The Government has just pledged £180 million pounds' worth of aid to Yemen. At the same time it has sold £4 *billion* pounds' worth of arms to the Saudis. The sheer bloody-minded hypocrisy of it all infuriates Jenna. She is heartened by news of a letter to *The Guardian*, signed by the likes of Bill Nighy, Simon Pegg, Ian McEwan and Chris Martin of Coldplay, deploring the double standards, but this barely makes a ripple elsewhere in the media. Nothing in comparison to when William Hague manages to persuade Angelina Jolie to share a platform with him at the London Docklands summit to launch an international protocol for the future investigation into the use of rape as a weapon in armed conflicts. Jolie's star presence persuades a hundred and seventeen countries to sign up to the protocol, though significantly it does not hold any of them to account.

It's a major breakthrough nevertheless, and Jenna is once again reminded of the wisdom of Mishal Husain's advice on the *Today* programme. Find a celebrity. Jolie has recently been made a Special Envoy for the UNHCR, the United Nations Refugees Agency. Jenna makes a mental note to contact her again on her return.

But in the meantime she has to do *some*thing – something practical, however small or insignificant – a symbolic gesture if nothing else. She has met Ms Jolie once before. At the opening two years ago of a new Centre for Study at the London School of Economics, whose sole mission is to combat the brutalities faced by women in war zones around the world. She made a short, but memorable speech.

"We need the empowerment of women," she said, her voice rising above the constant clicking of cameras and the raucous clamour from the crowds for selfies with her, "to be the highest priority for the finest minds in the best academic institutions. This new Centre marks an important first step. Students who come here will have the chance to change the world. And isn't that what we all want? But if you were to ask me who I think this Course is for first and foremost, I picture someone who is not here today. I think of a young girl I met in Iraq three weeks ago. She is only thirteen years old. But instead of going to school, she sits on the floor of a makeshift tent, a victim of rape and violence against her..."

Jenna repeats these words to Zafirah.

"For Iraq, read Yemen," says Zafirah. "For rape and violence, read child brides and branding."

For the thirteen-year-old girl, read Maleek, who will, by Jenna's reckoning, be just six now...

Zafirah counsels caution.

"I know what you mean," she says. "Statistics alone can be just too mind-numbingly appalling to take in. You need a face to bring them home to people. Something people can relate to. Like an individual child. But you've got to be careful. You can't manipulate a person's suffering like that. However well intentioned. It might backfire on you. People might accuse you of opportunism. Or even exploitation."

But Zafirah doesn't understand. Jenna has no intention of manipulating Maleek like that. Or anyone. She simply wants to find out what has happened to her in the four years since she last saw her. To make sure she's still alive, to check that she's recovered from her injuries. And if she hasn't, to try and do what she can to help her. Just one small act that will make her feel that she is at least doing something. Even if that something is so small as to more or less pass unnoticed. To atone for her own guilt. To make amends.

What is it that Ruth had said to her when they resumed their sessions together after Jenna had left Molly with her parents?

"We start again."

Yes. That was it.

We start again...

*

Ruth closes the curtains in the front room of her house on Lapwing Lane in Didsbury. This same front room which also now serves as her consulting room. She catches a final glimpse of Jenna, standing beneath the street light at the end of the driveway. She is lighting a cigarette, a habit she has resumed again recently, which she thinks Ruth is not aware of. But, however hard she may try to disguise the fact, she cannot conceal the smell of the tobacco from her clothes or hair, especially if she has had one just before her session, which she normally does, then again afterwards, when it is finished. Ruth smiles. She finds it rather touching that so many of her patients try to hide things from her, so desperate are they for her approval. In fact she doesn't care a jot if Jenna has taken up smoking again. Not if it helps her get through her current crisis. She is so consumed with guilt about her failure – as she sees it – to raise her daughter that her self-esteem has plummeted. What does it matter therefore if the occasional cigarette helps to calm her anxiety and soothe her nerves? Ruth believes these cigarettes *are* only occasional. And temporary. When Jenna finally comes to accept that Molly is quite unaffected by the arrangement, is actually thriving as a result of being brought up by two grandmothers, one grandfather, one great-grandmother and several aunties – in addition to her mother – that in fact she is benefiting from Jenna's decision, she will begin to feel better again, and the need for the confidence-boosting, stress-relieving cigarettes will diminish. In time, Ruth believes, it will disappear entirely.

Jenna has been coming to see her once a week for almost six months now, and the improvement is palpable. That's not just Ruth's considered professional opinion, but the response from others too – particularly Nadia, who telephones Ruth regularly to report on Molly's progress – excellent – and Jenna's mood – encouraging, and Barbara, the person in charge of the playgroup at the Moravian Church in Fairfield, who has become a good friend to Jenna, who has invited her to bring Molly along with her to the playgroup on those occasions she might have her to herself for a day, or even if she doesn't. "We can always use an extra pair of hands", she tells her. Yes, all in all things are progressing nicely with Jenna. It will soon be time to suggest to her that they might consider reducing the frequency of sessions from weekly to fortnightly, then to monthly, and finally to bring them to a gradual conclusion, with the option that she can always ring to make a fresh appointment if she thinks it necessary.

Ruth pours herself a glass of wine, her own particular indulgence at the end of a busy week, and looks around. With a slight rearrangement of the furniture she is quickly able to transform this room from a professional to a domestic setting. She has no choice. When her mother, Lily, died ten years ago, the house became hers. Her father, Roland, had died not long before, and that had seemed to knock from Lily the last of any fight she might have possessed. That and her decade-long battle with cancer. Lily's adoptive brother, George, who died not long afterwards, was her only other relative, so the house fell to her to do with what she liked.

It was a large house. Too large for just one person. It had been too large when both her parents had still been alive. Lily had some time before ceased to foster children there. Once she started to become ill, she was no longer able to manage it, and so *Blossoms*, her safe haven for orphans, so-named from the film *Blossoms in the Dust*, starring Greer Garson, which Lily had first seen at the *Levenshulme Palace* during the Second World War, when she was an ack-ack girl, and which had given her the idea in the first place, was no more. Ruth had qualified as a psychotherapist by this time and saw patients through the NHS at the local GP's surgery less than a mile away on Wilmslow Road. As her practice increased, it was Lily who had suggested they convert the lounge at the front of the house into a consulting room for her. The arrangement worked very well, and Ruth was able to combine her practice with looking after her mother, whose needs increased as the disease took greater hold over her.

But when she finally, mercifully, passed away, the house seemed suddenly cavernous. Ruth found the solitude unnatural. For this had been a house that had, until comparatively recently, been filled with the noise of an ever-changing gallery of children, whose high, piping, frequently-laughing, occasionally-crying voices had formed the soundtrack to Ruth's growing-up. It needed to be put to use. But it took a further ten years before Ruth came up with a solution, during which time her practice and her reputation steadily grew.

And then it came to her, an idea so fully formed that she wondered why it had taken so long to surface. She would convert all but one room of the house, which she would keep for her own bedroom, into a series of consulting rooms for a range of different health practitioners. She would retain the front room for her psychotherapy, while the dining room and three other bedrooms would be offered up on a first come-first served basis. They were snapped up within weeks.

And so now Ruth shares the daylight hours of the house with an acupuncturist, an osteopath, a reflexologist and a chiropractor, who each pay her a monthly rent for their customised room, while between them they share the cost of employing a receptionist, Meera, who greets clients as they arrive in the spacious hallway of what has now been renamed *Tulip House*, after the model yacht, *The Tulip*, built by Ruth's great-grandfather while he was interned on the Isle of Man during World War 1, and which now holds pride of place in a mounted glass case behind Meera's desk, from where she coordinates everyone's appointments with a military precision.

A satisfactory arrangement all round.

Ruth is quite content using just the front room, kitchen, bathroom and bedroom of what had hitherto been a large family house. She feels happily self-contained.

She is not married, has never been, nor is this something she feels she is missing out on. By the time of her second series of sessions with Jenna, Ruth is forty-two years old. She is single, independent and, to all outward appearances, completely self-sufficient. She loves her work. She finds it challenging but rewarding. She has a small but close circle of friends, with whom she goes regularly to the theatre, to concerts – both classical and jazz – and for meals to celebrate each other's birthdays. Currently there is no significant 'other' in her life.

Every Saturday morning, without fail, she arrives at the wonderfully eccentric Didsbury Library just as it is opening its doors, with its ornate, octagonal tower and crenellated roof gables, a gift to the town from the philanthropist Andrew Carnegie, who donated a number of libraries to Manchester, such as this one, which was ceremonially opened in 1915 with a golden key, from where she takes out three books each week. She is a particular admirer of the novels of Elizabeth Taylor, Rosamund Lehmann, Dorothy Whipple and Lettice Cooper. She is a subscriber to the Winter Season of Sunday night proms at the Hallé, and she is not infrequently to be found haunting late-night weekend sessions at *The Band on the Wall* on Swan Street. She is a particular admirer of Florence Blundell, a young jazz trumpeter and vocalist.

She almost always finds her clients grateful and appreciative. Some elect to stay in touch, not as friends – that would not feel professional, she prefers to keep her work and her social life quite separate – but as acquaintances, so that it is rarely awkward if she happens to bump into any of them after their course of treatment has finished. A much smaller number have become people with whom she is in contact by correspondence. One or two she has occasionally agreed to meet for a coffee in one of Didsbury's plentiful supply of independent bistro cafés. She hopes that Jenna might become one of this select group, for in Barbara from Fairfield they have a mutual friend. In fact, she has an idea that she plans to put to Jenna – once her treatment is complete, though this will not be for a month or two yet – the timing for which will be perfect. If Jenna agrees...

*

Outside the camp the stench of unwashed bodies is overpowering. Zafirah and Jenna have arrived early, before the rest of the delegations from the UN, Amnesty International, the Red Cross, Save the Children, Oxfam, MSF. Séydou will be joining them later. Jenna covers her mouth and nose with the scarf she wears on her head at all times here out of respect, though it makes little difference to the smell. A smell of dirt and disease, overcrowding and fear. But mostly it is a smell of resignation and despair. It breaks Jenna's heart.

She longs for a cigarette. Just as she used to after her sessions with Ruth. But she's given up now. Though this does not stop her from craving one sometimes. Like she does now. She looks across towards Zafirah, who must have had the same thought, for she is in the process of lighting one for herself. Jenna is surprised when she learns that Zafirah is a smoker.

"You shouldn't be," says Zafirah. "Yemen has the second highest percentage of women smokers of any Muslim country in the world," she tells her. "Only Turkey has more. Before the war it was a sign of our growing confidence. We would go into *shisha* cafés for a coffee and a smoke. Now we just do it to reduce the stress and suppress our hunger. Want one?"

Jenna hesitates, then accepts gratefully. Zafirah lights it for her with her own, then passes it across. Jenna draws on it deeply. The instant hit of the tobacco is reassuringly familiar, a simultaneous balm and jolt to the senses. It is exactly what she needs right now...

The rest of the convoy arrives, ready to begin their tour, which has been coordinated by Naveed Khan, a retired Army Major. Born in Pakistan, educated in England, he was part of the UN Relief Force in Bosnia, after which he was assigned to Somalia, and subsequently here to Yemen. They are shown around the camp by a team of doctors and aid workers with shocking candour. Nothing is hidden from them, however distressing, however appalling. They see hundreds of children still suffering the after-effects of burns and other injuries.

"They can't remain in the hospitals," explains the harassed and exhausted aid worker from the previous day. "There isn't the room. New casualties – far more serious than these you are seeing here – arrive each day. We simply have to prioritise."

She shrugs, then leads them further into the camp. Jenna admires how she makes no apology for a situation not of her making. They steer a wide berth around one enormous tent that is for cholera victims only.

"Actually it's everywhere," says the aid worker. "These are just the worst cases."

"What are their chances of recovery?" asks Jenna.

She shrugs again, as if to imply, 'What do you think?'

"We do what we can," she says. "*Inshallah*."

"And those that get better," persists Jenna, "what happens to them?"

"Look around you. They stay."

"Why? Why don't they leave?"

She looks at Jenna as if she has just landed from another planet, which, to all intents and purposes, she has.

"Where would they go?" she says.

But Jenna is not satisfied. "I take your point, but some do, even so?"

"I suppose."

"You suppose?"

"We don't keep registers," she replies, her patience wearing thin.

"No. I'm sorry. I'm just trying to get a sense of the whole picture here."

"It's true," Major Khan intervenes. "Several do leave. I don't know how many. Most will try to find a fishing boat to take them to Djibouti."

"Like my parents," Zafirah reminds Jenna.

"Or Eritrea. Ethiopia even. From there, some will try to make it to Europe."

Jenna nods. This is what she had surmised...

They move on to a different part of the camp, where those with less easy to diagnose conditions are temporarily housed. These are mostly victims of trauma, locked deep within their memories. There are others with cancers, some with both.

"There's no long-term provision for patients like these," explains Major Khan, who insists they call him Naveed. "I'm not in the Army now," he says. "The Al-Amal Hospital, where Aden's only psychiatric ward is housed, has been bombed. Al-Saber, Aden's General Hospital, is overrun, and the Basuhaib is for military personnel only."

Jenna asks, as gently as she can, if they keep records. Names. Charts.

"We try to," says Naveed, "but inevitably we miss some. There are those who slip through the net."

"I'd like to ask about one patient in particular, if I may?"

Séydou looks at her sharply. She returns this with an imploring one of her own. Séydou takes Naveed to one side and speaks quietly to him for a few moments.

"I'll see what I can do," he says. He moves directly across to Jenna. "Wait here please." Then he explains the request in Arabic to another of the aid workers, who nods, before scrolling through columns of data on a battered tablet.

"If the rest of you will follow me please," says Naveed, and all but Jenna move on to their next port of call, the makeshift field hospital, where urgent procedures can be carried out if the camp itself is hit by shells from mortar attacks...

Jenna waits.

"What name was it again?" asks this new aid worker. Her name is Zainab, a young Lebanese woman, a Druze, whose family moved to England when she was a girl, to Leigh near Manchester, where she qualified as a psychiatric nurse, and who is now volunteering here in Yemen as part of an accelerated programme of further specialist training.

"Maleek El-Harazy."

Zainab nods and continues scrolling down.

She reminds Jenna of Awa, Séydou's daughter, who also studied Medicine, back in Senegal, and who is now similarly volunteering, at the Za'atari Camp in Jordan, which houses eighty thousand Syrian refugees. More than twenty times the size of Mishqafa, with its own market and school and clinic, where Awa works, Za'atari is just one of five such camps for Syrians, as well as a further ten for Palestinians, housing between them more than three and a half million people. Conditions are dire, well below what might be considered acceptable, but at least the residents are safe. No civil war rages in Jordan – yet – so plans can be put in place for the gradual integration of the camps' inhabitants back into the general populations of those countries who will agree to house them. But who *will* take them, when the political overrides the humanitarian? There lies the rub indeed. And it is wrestling with this seemingly intractable problem that takes up ninety percent of Jenna's time in her endless rounds of meetings and conferences with charities, NGOs, government departments, and international agencies, with no solution yet in sight.

It is another reason why the fate of Maleek El-Harazy is assuming more and more importance to her. If she might personally intervene to help just one person, that would at least be something...

She is frequently asked to give talks to local schools and groups around Manchester, which she agrees to do whenever she can. After a meeting of the Ladies Group at the Moravian Church in Fairfield, which she first began attending when she lived on Slate Lane, and which she has continued to go to after she moved to her apartment in the former *Daily Express* building in Ancoats, her friend Barbara asks her if she might consider speaking to a group of Year 11 students at Fairfield High School, where Barbara is a teacher. Jenna agrees gladly.

The school, originally set up by the founders of the first Moravian Community to be established in Fairfield in 1796, was the first non-private school for girls anywhere in England. It is still for girls only, open to pupils of all faiths and cultures. In 1996, the year of the IRA bomb attack on Manchester and the second and most profound of Jenna's breakdowns, it celebrated its bicentenary with the installation of a stained glass window, designed with input from many of the girls themselves, the school motto inscribed within it –

Vicit agnus noster, eum sequamur. Let us follow the lamb who has conquered.

– with its emphasis on service and sacrifice in pursuit of peace.

On the day she arrives to give her talk she is treated to a short performance of *New Beginnings* by the Manchester poet Tony Walsh, who, having a sister who attended the school, while he himself went to the neighbouring boys' school at Audenshaw, wrote the poem especially to welcome each new intake of eleven-year-olds on their first day in their new school, the latest of whom present it to Jenna now.

"Welcome to your new school
Welcome to your futures
New beginnings here and new rules
New classrooms, new computers

New timetables, new faces, new names
New corridors, new signs

Some things change, some stay the same
But some truths last for all time

You'll take out just what you put in
You'll reap just what you sow
So face each test, do your best
Work hard, play hard, and grow

Remember that you're different
There's no one quite like you
Make good friends, the ones who'll lend
A hand to get you through

For people just like you and me
Can do most special things
Aim higher, be high-flyers
Be bold, unfold your wings

Because our town has a history
Of producing boys and girls
Who, from humble roots, pull up their boots
And go on to change the world..."

Jenna finds herself having to blink back the tears when she hears these words, delivered with such high piping intensity by these eager, shining eleven-year-old girls, and she is reminded of them again now, in Yemen, as she thinks of Molly, and Awa, while watching Zainab painstakingly search for evidence that Maleek is still alive, among all the many thousands of children here in Mishqafa, and in Za'arata, and all the other camps across the world, who all deserve their chance to unfold their wings...

While she is waiting, a ladybird alights on her finger. Jenna gasps in surprise and wonder.

"Look," she says, showing it to Zainab.

"*Colleoptera coccinellidae*," she replies automatically. "A recent study found that there are eighty-five sub-species of ladybirds here in Yemen alone, seventy-seven on the mainland, eight on the island of Socotra. Seventeen of these are new to the country in the last ten years, and two are completely new to science. There's hope in that, I find," she says, then adds, "The children here like them, those that are able to see them."

Jenna nods, taking this in. She thinks back to the previous summer, when her flat was teeming with them. She can't remember seeing any for years, not since she was a small child. She had assumed they were becoming rarer, that probably pollution was to blame. Yet here they were, proliferating again...

The sight of them brings her such simple, unalloyed joy. They creep through every crook and crevice, flop on window-sill and work-top. Such exotic splash of colour in these dark, damp days.

But it seems they're not universally welcome. She hears people talking on the radio. They're the wrong type. Foreign interlopers, voracious harlequin invaders, marauding Ghengis Khan hordes, hammering the window panes. There's no stopping them. They resist all forms of pest control, carried on the wind, washed up by the tide. Not tunnels, not fences can hold them back. Vampire swarm, they suck our native species dry...

Like bluebells. The English flower too has become diluted, it would seem. Under threat, in danger of extinction, a last century relic, subject to all manner of unwelcome incomers...

But Jenna disagrees. Diversity brings strength. The air teems with the new arrivals' thrumming wing beats. She opens her windows wide, looks out towards imagined woods where next spring clouds of paint box blues will carpet the paths...

She looks back down on the ladybird on her finger, here at Mishqafa Camp, relishing its unique, unreplicable pattern of black spots on a red back...

"Let them all come," she says at the end of her talk to the Year 11 students at Fairfield High School, who all applaud her enthusiastically, and later reward her with personalised drawings of ladybirds, which she pins up on her notice board in the kitchen of her flat in Manchester...

"Here we are," says Zainab at last. "Maleek El-Harazy."

Jenna holds her breath as Zainab brings her tablet across for her to see.

"The case notes are rather sketchy, I'm afraid. She was initially treated in Al-Salaam Hospital in Hodeidah for injuries received following a car bomb explosion."

"I know. I was there."

Zanaib looks up briefly, then returns her gaze to the screen, scanning through the notes. "Minor burns. Superficial cuts. She was lucky."

"Hardly."

"No. Of course not. In the circumstances, I mean."

"What else does it say?"

"Er..." She checks once more. "Discharged after a week. Transferred first to the camp at Kharaz. Then to here. No family to go back to, I assume?"

"No. Her mother was killed in the same explosion. Where is she now?"

"I'm sorry," says Zainab. "I'm relatively new here. I only arrived a month ago. According to her notes, she should be in the adjoining tent."

"The one we just left?"

"Yes. "

"For patients with longer term injuries?"

Zainab nods. "Trauma victims in the main. It wouldn't be surprising, would it? Come on. Follow me. Let's try and find her, shall we?"

Zainab hurries on ahead of Jenna, who almost has to run to keep up. Zainab quickly makes enquiries in Arabic of other aid workers and volunteers, and is eventually directed towards a length of tarpaulin stretched out across the floor in a far corner, weighted down with stones, on which half a dozen small children are lying squashed together, staring up at the roof of the tent with listless, dead eyes.

"Which one of you is Maleek?" asks Zainab kindly.

One of the sick children points a skeletal finger at a small girl lying on her side. When Zainab and Jenna reach her and bend down to be able to look at her more closely, she appears not to register them. Patchy tufts of newly-grown hair lie close against her scalp, which has been crudely shaved. A fly crawls across her cracked lips, which Zainab brushes away. She gently lifts a stick-thin arm, circling her wrist too easily with her thumb and middle finger. But as soon as she applies the slightest pressure to her skin, the child winces, then cries out in pain. Zainab repeats the same procedure with Maleek's other arm. Then she tries to touch her chest, her hip, her neck. Each time, as soon as she makes the slightest of contacts with the surface of her skin, Maleek cries out.

"This girl's in a lot of pain," says Zainab in a low, concerned voice.

"What do you think it is?"

Zainab breathes deeply. "I've still not finished my training," she says, "so I'll have to ask one of the more senior doctors, but if I were to hazard a guess – an educated guess..."

"Yes?"

"I'd say she was suffering from shrapnel sickness."

"What's that?"

"Sometimes tiny fragments of shrapnel can embed

themselves deep inside the body. They're so small they're easy to miss, especially if there are many pieces, and the hospital is treating lots of injured patients as quickly as they can..."

"Which I imagine they were..."

"A person can carry them around inside them for years without anyone realising, and without apparently suffering any harm. But sometimes the metal may disintegrate and enter the blood stream, from where it can reach vital organs."

Jenna covers her mouth in shock.

"Penetrating injuries to the soft tissue are particularly hard to find," continues Zainab. "Sometimes the fragments might enter the body through inhalation. The patient simply breathes them in. This is a particular problem in places where desert conditions prevail. The dust from the rocks and sand gets mixed in with them, making them even more difficult to detect. Metal particulates in smoke from destroyed vehicles in such an environment present additional problems. Often these present psychologically, as much as physically. The patient might simply withdraw into their own private world of pain. Given the cause of the injuries to Maleek, this would appear to be what is happening here."

"But why has no one picked it up before?"

"Because the shrapnel migrates so slowly to other parts of the body, and this takes even more time before it manifests itself in the kind of acute pain we are witnessing here. Given Maleek's near catatonic state, it's understandable that she's been diagnosed as a trauma patient, which she almost certainly is as well, so that a doctor simply hasn't been called. They're all too busy anyway, dealing with more obvious injuries, and besides, there are simply nowhere near enough of them to go round."

Jenna nods. The truth of what Zainab is saying is self-evident.

"You stay with her," says Zainab. "I'll try and find someone else to look at her..."

It is late afternoon. A Friday. Ruth has deliberately arranged this last appointment of her week to coincide with what has been agreed will be Jenna's final session. For now. But Jenna knows that Ruth's door will always be open to her, should she need to return.

The session goes well. It is light, positive, forward-facing. When it has finished, Ruth wishes Jenna good luck. Jenna thanks her warmly. They shake hands. Jenna, who is by nature an effusively physical person, impulsively turns the hand shake into a hug. Ruth, who by contrast is usually stiff and rather formal, accepts this transgression nevertheless for the spontaneous gesture it is. Nothing more.

Just as Jenna is about to put on her coat, Ruth asks her if she wouldn't mind staying an extra five minutes. "There's something I'd like to ask you," she says. Intrigued, Jenna puts down her coat once more and waits.

"I think we might risk a glass of wine, don't you?" says Ruth brightly. "It is a Friday after all, and I have no more clients till Monday."

Jenna, never one to turn down a free glass of wine, readily accepts.

"Cheers," says Ruth.

"Cheers," responds Jenna. What is going on here, she wonders to herself?

"Do you like the theatre?" asks Ruth, suddenly, out of the blue.

Actually Jenna doesn't care for it that much. She's never seen the point of it. Dressing up and pretending to be someone else. It's a distraction from the more important business of real life. The only time she has ever had any time for it was when she was in the Squat, and Spike had inculcated them into the ways of Bertolt Brecht. Theatre as Living Newspaper. Theatre as Propaganda. But that was different. That was for a cause. Agitation. Direct Action. An attempt to change people's hearts and minds. 'Make the familiar strange,' had been Spike's rallying cry, she recalls. *Verfremdungseffekt*.

But it strikes Jenna now that it would be rather churlish and ungrateful of her to respond so aggressively to what she is certain is nothing more than an innocent question on Ruth's part, a conversational ice-breaker, so she answers her more simply.

"I don't know," she says. "I don't get time to go."

"Oh you should," enthuses Ruth. "I go as often as I can. And I was wondering...?"

"Yes...?"

Ruth puts down her glass and composes herself. If she's not careful, what she is about to propose might be misinterpreted as the clumsiest of pick-ups – which could not be further from her intentions.

"Would you like to go to the theatre with *me*?"

"Oh."

"Not *just* me, let me add, before you get the wrong idea. Barbara too." Early in their sessions it became evident that Barbara was a mutual friend they each of them had in common. "She and I go together quite often" continues Ruth hastily. "Her husband has his rugby, so *she* has her theatre."

"Yes. I see," says Jenna, her curiosity piqued still further. Where's this all leading?

"The timing," says Ruth, more expansively now, "could not be more fortuitous. It's at The Royal Exchange," she adds meaningfully. But when Jenna appears not to pick up on this, she is forced to elaborate further. "In St Ann's Square. Where you and Molly found yourselves after the IRA bomb went off." Jenna nods seriously. "Well," says Ruth, after a suitable pause, "the theatre was so badly damaged in the aftermath of the explosion that it's been shut for more than two years. But now, the repairs have been finished at last. It's all been beautifully restored – they say it looks even better than it did before – and they're opening again in three weeks' time."

"Oh…"

"Quite…"

"What's the play?"

"That's just it. They've decided to open with the same production that was due to be presented at the time of the bomb. As a kind of message. That things will carry on just as before. That we will not be intimidated by any kind of external threat. That nothing will stop us from living our lives, freely and without fear. And I thought it offered the perfect opportunity for us to celebrate your own renaissance too. That you, like the city, are back on the road to recovery. All of us coming back to the light."

"Wow."

"Sorry. I get carried away sometimes."

"No. It's great that you're so passionate about it."

"It's just that this particular production has a special significance for me personally."

"How so?"

"It's *Hindle Wakes*."

"Sorry. I haven't heard of it, I'm afraid. "

"By Stanley Houghton."

Jenna shrugs. "Nor him either."

"That's hardly surprising. It was written a long time ago. Barbara could tell you more – being an English teacher – but it was first performed in 1912. At Miss Horniman's *Gaiety Theatre* on Peter Street. It was something of a *cause célèbre* in its day. Extremely controversial."

"In what way?"

"To begin with it had a distinctly northern setting, written in a truly authentic voice, and it made no apologies for doing so. It placed a single working-class woman centre stage – Fanny

Hawthorne, a mill worker. During the Annual Wakes Week she goes on holiday to the seaside, where she sleeps with the son of the mill owner. When this all comes to light, rather than feeling embarrassed or awkward, she admits to it freely. If it's socially acceptable for a man to sow his wild oats before he gets married, why not for a woman also? This was pretty inflammatory stuff back in 1912 as you can well imagine, but when the young man offers to marry her, to avoid any scandal that might fall on his family, she turns him down. Flat. Even though she would be dramatically improving her social and economic standing. She admits they had a good time together, but it was only sex, not love. She insists on staying true to who she is."

"Good for her."

"And it still has something relevant to say to audiences today."

"So it's a period piece that's also contemporary?"

"Exactly so."

Jenna wonders what precisely it is about the play that holds such personal significance for Ruth, and whether she's about to explain it to her now, so she waits, taking another sip of her wine.

"Why it's important to me," says Ruth, correctly interpreting Jenna's silence for interest, "is that my grandmother – who I'm named after – attended that very first performance back in 1912."

Jenna's eyes widen. She puts down her glass and listens more intently.

"I never knew my grandmother. She died giving birth to my mother, Lily, who was subsequently raised in an orphanage – a convent – till she was fourteen, after which she had to make her own way in the world. She had to endure an extremely tough few years. Homeless. Sleeping rough. Living off the streets. Until eventually she was rescued. Which is a whole other story.

But then, many years later, when I was about six, she met by chance a woman who had known her mother, who'd looked after her when she was pregnant, and who'd been with her on the night she died. This woman's name was Mary, and she and Lily became great friends. Mary told Lily all she could remember of Ruth. How brave she was, how independent, how passionate when it came to calling out injustice or inequality. Sound familiar?"

Jenna looks down and smiles.

"When she went to see *Hindle Wakes*, it was to celebrate her engagement to a young man who was himself the son of a wealthy mill owner. Afterwards her fiancé's parents were disgusted by the play's message and appalled by the outspoken Fanny Hawthorne. But Ruth stood up for her and defended her, even when her fiancé failed to support her against his parents. That took a lot of courage, I think."

"Yes. It did. What happened? To the engagement, I mean?"

"A story for another time, I think. The short version is that her fiancé was killed in the First World War."

"Oh. I'm sorry."

"Yes. So many wasted lives. But I don't believe they would have married had he survived. Or if they had, they would not have been happy. Fanny Hawthorne spoke more prophetically than she knew."

Both women fall quiet for a while, each in their own separate thoughts.

Wars, separations, orphans.

Children left to fend for themselves.

Casualties, victims, survivors…

An hour later Zainab's initial diagnosis is deemed "distinctly possible" following a brief examination by one of the visiting doctors from the International Red Cross delegation, Dr Nina Müller from Geneva.

"But I can't be certain till we've carried out a comprehensive set of tests – tox screen, X-rays, bloods, urine samples."

"None of which are possible here," says Zainab.

"I know," says Dr Müller. "Not any more. Both sides have been ruthless in their attacks on hospitals. Five years ago the Al-Saber was as good as any hospital in the region. Now…?"

She spreads her hands in a gesture of hopelessness.

"Nevertheless," she continues, "it is my belief that this girl needs to receive immediate attention. The lasting damage to her soft tissue if the shrapnel is not removed is potentially life-threatening."

Jenna involuntarily gasps.

"May I make a suggestion?" says Séydou He has quickly rejoined them, following an earlier anxious text from Jenna. "MSF has established good relations with Jordan, particularly the Al-Khalidi Medical Centre in Amman. As part of this brief window afforded us by the five-day ceasefire, they have offered a humanitarian corridor to allow us to fly a small number of patients there for emergency treatment. I'm speaking to them right now." He holds up his phone.

"How many?" asks Major Khan, who has accompanied Séydou back to the tent.

"Just a moment please…"

Séydou urgently consults with his colleague in Amman.

"Nine."

A further gasp greets this announcement.

"Is that all?" says Naveed.

"We mustn't forget," says Séydou patiently, "that Jordan currently has more than three and a half million refugees within its borders."

"In which case," intervenes Dr Müller, "may I request we send children, this girl among them?" She gestures towards the barely conscious Maleek, whose fingers agitatedly pluck at imaginary terrors only she can see, threatening her from the air…

"So," says Ruth eventually, "will you accept?"
"Yes," says Jenna. "I will. Thank you…"

*

Day 1404

The mercy mission for flying out nine seriously sick and wounded children to Jordan is arranged for a week's time. This is after the current ceasefire expires, but both sides agree to permit a further two-hour window to coincide with the medically-fitted transport plane's departure from Aden International to Queen Alia Airport in Amman.

Jenna insists she will stay on in Yemen until Maleek has been safely transferred. Séydou manages to arrange for her to remain under the protection of the UNHCR on the understanding that she does so at her own risk, that there can be no guarantees for her security. He himself must return with Zafirah via Hodeidah back to his other MSF duties in Djibouti, from where they can continue to work towards the establishment of a more permanent humanitarian corridor, while the shaky international peace negotiations stumble and falter.

Jenna meanwhile contacts Mishal Husain back at the BBC.

Might they, she wonders, be interested in her observations of what life is like on a day-to-day basis for the ordinary Yemeni people, trying to go about their lives under a permanent state of siege?

Mishal replies that they most definitely would be. "What did you have in mind?" she asks.

"A series of audio diaries," suggests Jenna, "recorded on my phone, then sent as separate sound files…?"

"Sorting out the contract, though, might take a little time," says Mishal. "The BBC doesn't currently have a correspondent in Yemen."

"Don't bother with the formalities," urges Jenna. "It's not like I want paying or anything. But the world needs to know what's happening here. Just refer to me as an eye-witness source, then present the diaries in whatever format, on whatever platform, works best for you. I'm only here for another week…"

*

Day 1410

Extracts from Jenna Ward's audio diaries broadcast by BBC Radio 4 variously on the *Today* programme, *From Our Own Correspondent* and *Woman's Hour*.

"In the Book of Genesis, chapter 2, verse 11, the Bible states: 'The name of the first is Pishon; that is it which compasseth the whole of the Land of Havilah, where there is gold to be found…'

"Pishon is one of the four lost rivers of the Garden of Eden. The other three are the Gihon, the Hiddekel and the Euphrates. There have been countless attempts to identify these rivers over the centuries, but nothing conclusive has ever been proved. Scholars cannot even agree for certain that the Euphrates that flows through modern-day Iraq is the same as the one mentioned in the Bible.

"But there is a growing belief, based on recent geological surveys carried out across the entire Arabian peninsula, that the Pishon flowed through what we now call Yemen. Not that there is much evidence of it today. In his article 'The River Runs Dry', the Harvard archaeologist James Sauer describes how satellite images have detected an underground river bed

beneath the Wadi al-Batin, a dry creek running close to the Hejaz Mountains in the country's arid western region.

"But Yemen is no Garden of Eden today. The Wadi al-Batin, all that remains of the fabled lost River Pishon, is more likely to flow with blood than with water in this, the world's forgotten war, in a country ravaged by years of bitter civil conflict, now made even worse by famine and disease, in which the only Biblical figures are the apocalyptic numbers of the wounded and the dead, the hundreds of thousands of innocent people killed, the tens of millions of children starving.

"Nor is there any gold to be found here now. Except in the gleam of the eyes of the generals and politicians on all sides as they lust for the power that eludes them.

"And yet sometimes I will see traces of this gold – in a child's eyes still clinging on to life despite having to endure unimaginable pain and suffering, taking pleasure in such simple things, like catching a ball, or spinning a top, or blowing bubbles...

"Two days ago, less than twenty-four hours after the lifting of the temporary truce to allow much-needed humanitarian aid to enter this forsaken land, new atrocities were committed by all parties.

"In central Hodeidah hundreds of medical workers and patients, including a malnourished woman carrying her daughter in a surgical robe and a man still hooked up to a catheter, fled in terror as a series of large explosions rocked the Al-Thawra hospital there in an attack reportedly carried out by Coalition war-planes and helicopters on Houthi positions in the city. A medical worker, who was inside the Al-Thawra hospital at the time, told me how hundreds of patients and staff desperately tried to dodge a hail of shrapnel as they fled in panic. The sustained bombardment near the hospital lasted for more than an hour.

"In armed conflict, hospitals are supposed to be places of

sanctuary. But as the battle for control of Yemen's major cities intensifies, both sides seem intent on eviscerating the laws of war and disregarding the protected status of even the most vulnerable civilians.

"The following day a Houthi drone missile bombed the Badr and Al-Hashoosh mosques in Yemen's capital city, Sana'a, at a time when they were most likely to be filled with worshippers for Friday prayers. Which they were. A hundred and twenty-six people are reported dead, with many more injured.

"Then yesterday, in the village of Al-Raqa, in the Bani Qais district some fifty-five miles north-west of the capital, a Saudi-led air-strike deliberately targeted a wedding party, killing thirty-three and seriously wounding more than forty other guests. The top provincial health official, Khaled al-Nadhri told Al-Masirah, the local TV station, that most of the dead were women and children, including the bride..."

Jenna remembers Molly's wedding day.

That Molly is choosing to marry at all baffles her. What is it with young people today who seem to feel the need to conform to such outmoded traditions? She herself would never have consented to such an antiquated notion, even if anyone had asked her – which they haven't. It's barely one step up from slavery. As if becoming a wife is little more than being a chattel. In Yemen child brides are still alarmingly common. She doesn't know how old the bride who was killed in Al-Raqa was, but she suspects she was very young. Since the escalation of the war, girls have been getting married younger and younger there. It's a harsh economic reality. Packing off a daughter to be married represents one less mouth to feed for starving families, who, in a country where there is a desperate water shortage, can no longer afford bottled water, which has more than trebled in price.

What kind of fate would have awaited Maleek had her mother survived the explosion? Jenna has heard first hand of many disturbing accounts of a recent rise in the ancient use of branding as a last desperate throw of the dice to deal with the psychological injuries caused by shrapnel wounds in children. One of her last audio diaries attempts to tackle the issue...

"Hana Absi was walking back home from school on the 14th of October when an air strike targeted a motorcycle near her on 7 July Street in Hodeidah.

"Shrapnel exploded around the 12-year-old girl. Dead bodies lay all about her, the vision seared in her memory. Overcome by the scene, Hana fainted.

" 'I saw a man and his child covered in blood near the school,' she told me. 'Shrapnel nearly killed me. It reached all the way to the fence of the school.'

"Following the incident, the young girl from the Ghulail neighbourhood of Hodeidah began exhibiting symptoms of psychological trauma, and remained too afraid to go back to school, so close to where she had witnessed the deadly strike.

"Walaa Absi, Hana's mother, felt helpless faced with her daughter's anguish. Her husband, a teacher in Hodeidah, had not been paid in two years, and the family could barely afford to put food on the table – let alone move to a safer area or give Hana access to therapy.

"Finally, Walaa said, she felt no choice but to go for 'the last resort', and mark her daughter with a hot iron.

"An old Arab saying goes: 'The last cure is branding.'

"Now, many needy Yemeni families are turning to branding with an iron in a desperate attempt to cure their children of physical illness and psychological trauma, marking the resurgence of a dangerous folk remedy, as proper medical care has become increasingly inaccessible after four years of war.

"Following the air strike, Hana began to suffer from

dizziness, insomnia, exhaustion and a lack of appetite. At night, the girl lay awake in her bed, fearing that the battles she could hear raging some five kilometres away would soon reach her home.

" 'I stay up all night listening to the bombs falling,' she said. 'I feel they might kill us like the man and his child.'

"Walaa was desperate to find a solution for Hana.

" 'I tried to take my daughter to a hospital, but that had been bombed,' Walaa told me. 'After a week, I took my daughter to an old woman to get her branded. The old woman heated up a piece of iron until it became red, and then she put it on the belly of my daughter. Hana cried and I felt sinful. Then the old woman put toothpaste on the burning belly of my daughter to reduce the pain.'

"Walaa paid the old woman 1,000 Yemeni rials (roughly £1.50), but Hana's suffering had now become twofold – the psychological wounds left by the air strike, and the new, physical and mental pain of having been branded.

"I wish I could say that this was an isolated incident, but I can't. Yet while this deadly proxy war continues, more and more people are turning in desperation towards these old folk remedies, while the forces on all sides of the conflict continue to deliberately target schools and hospitals, while the outside world looks on – no, turns a blind eye in fact, knowing full well what is going on, for the western powers are all of them covertly to blame..."

In spite of Jenna's misgivings, Molly's wedding day is a happy occasion.

When Molly first introduces them to each other, Jenna and Michael do a double-take.

"Haven't we met before...?"

"I'm sure I recognise you...?"

"Molly's Exhibition," they both declare simultaneously,

each of them remembering their shared silent contemplation of Molly's sketches of starlings. Like a communion. Neither wanting to intrude upon the other's private thoughts.

"I think I fell in love with her as soon as I saw those drawings," he says.

"And there was I, thinking it was my dazzling conversational skills that had won you over," jokes Molly.

"Those too," laughs Michael, putting a huge arm around her tiny shoulders.

They make an odd couple, thinks Jenna, he so tall, her daughter so petite, but clearly a happy one. They have eyes only for each other. So that Jenna is only slightly dismayed that Molly is taking Michael's surname – Adebayo – but is at least retaining her own – Ward – professionally, and has in fact elected to revert to the original Yemeni., 'Wahid', meaning 'unique', 'peerless'. A name to live up to. Jenna applauds the ambition in that…

It's a wedding for all cultures.

Michael is Christian, and so there is a traditional service held at Christ Church on Liverpool Road in Patricroft. In her memory Jenna hears Bex singing as Joni once more, her voice rising up through the years.

"She showed me first you get the kisses
And then you get the tears
But the ceremony of the bells and lace
Still veils this reckless fool here…"

Jenna feels the incipient threat of unexpected tears. Sol's presence hangs over all of them, having died less than a year before. Nadia is walking Molly up the aisle in his place.

Jenna is pleased that Molly has decided not to get married in white. That would have been too much. Instead she wears a simple, full length dress in a dramatic red with a matching *qurqash*. She looks fabulous.

Afterwards all the guests transfer the half-mile to the Assembly Room of Eccles Town Hall, with its distinctive clock tower, cupola and mansard roof, where Farida and Salwa, together with all of the 'Aunties', have arranged a traditional Yemeni supper of *mihshi*, stuffed vegetables with meat, followed by nuts and fruit, washed down with copious amounts of sweet tea, flavoured with mint, ginger and lemon.

Older relatives sing traditional songs accompanied by the *oud*, but these then give way to something altogether different. Ngozia, Michael's mother from Lagos, has flown in with her two sisters, Nnenne and Ndidi, and together they have persuaded Molly, Nadia, Farida and Anita to join them in a traditional female Yoruban dance, the *nkwa umu agbogho*. Jenna is invited too, but for some reason she baulks at the idea. Watching them now, she wishes she had said yes. Ngozia, a textile artist, has brought with her bolts of cloth for each of them, *aso oké*, wood-block-printed with her own designs in bold geometric patterns of black on purple and yellow on blue, which the women drape around their bodies and wrap around their heads in an elaborate *gele*. After they have entered, they form a circle within which they perform a series of stooping, low-to-the-ground movements, with rhythmic stamping of the feet and graceful swaying of the hips. The older women especially are quite magnificent in the way they own the space. Jenna can't now wait to join in, which she is soon encouraged to do, along with everyone else, by Ngozia and her sisters.

No sooner has this finished when Molly, together with all the younger women, sashay and strut to Beyoncé's *All the Single Ladies*, before Molly hurls her bouquet of flowers over her shoulder, high into the air, leading to the inevitable scrum by the girls to catch it.

"If you like it then you should've put a ring on it," they shriek in chorus, raising their ring fingers provocatively, before

saucily slapping the side of their hips with the flat of their hands.

All this clamour to be the next one up the aisle, tuts Jenna, shaking her head. But she is smiling in spite of herself, caught up in the infectiously joyous atmosphere of celebration.

Even Lance is behaving himself. He's flown in specially from St Kitts, much to Molly's delight, for – typically – he had not told her beforehand he would be coming.

"Mi sweet Carib grackle, mi black-faced grassquit," he says, opening his arms to greet her. "Mi purple-throated Carib... Mi pearly-eyed eleania... Mi white-eyed golden oriole... Mi New World warbler... Mi northern water thrush..."

"Honestly, Mum," laughs Molly, disentangling herself from Lance, "were you really taken in by all this crap?"

"I'm afraid I was," says Jenna, playfully ruffling Lance's still impressive dreads.

"Thank heavens you were," declares Michael, beaming happily at Molly. He holds out his hand towards Lance. "Pleased to meet you, sir."

"Mi like dis man, dawta. Wen di laas time dem call mi sah?"

Lance DJs the night away, playing his favourite mix of reggae and ska, ending with a Bob Marley medley.

'Old pirates, yes dey rob I
Sold I tuh di merchant ships
Minutes after dey took I
From di bottomless pits...'

Everyone raises their arms aloft and sings with one voice.

"Won't yuh help tuh sing dese songs o' freedom
'Cause all wi ever have is redemption songs..."

Jenna sings loudest of all.

"Redemption songs..."

Outside the Town Hall, just before Molly and Michael are driven away to spend their wedding night in the Kimpton Clock Tower Hotel, the former terracotta Refuge Assurance Building, next to the Palace Theatre in the heart of Manchester, overlooking a recently renovated stretch of the River Medlock, all the guests gather to watch Lorrie, one of Molly's student friends, perform fire poi on the steps.

She delicately revolves her wrists, spinning on sinewy lengths of cord the tethered weights of Kevlar, which she dips in fuel, then sets alight, creating abstract, rhythmic patterns of tracer fire that orbit around her head and body.

Everyone watches in breathless, awed silence as Lorrie weaves her constantly shifting web of flame mesmerizingly around them. The spell is only broken as the exhaust from Farida's vintage mini, in which she has agreed to drive Molly and Michael the five miles to their hotel, backfires and recoils, as it boomerangs down the road...

A year later, Jenna passes another tense and sleepless night in Aden. The pounding of mortar shells, like a thousand cars backfiring, reverberate around her. Flashes of tracer fire illuminate the night sky like poi. A redemption that deafens and blinds in equal measure...

Jenna arrives at the theatre a full half-hour before she needs to. There is something she has to do before she meets up with Ruth and Barbara in the foyer. They have agreed to go to the Saturday matinee performance. Ruth has deliberately chosen this time, and Jenna understands why. It was a Saturday when the IRA detonated their bomb in Manchester two and a half years ago. They both believe it will act as a more powerful exorcism for her of the traumatic events of that day if her revisiting the site of where it happened is as close to the actual time as it can be.

The damage wrought to the theatre by the bomb has proved more extensive than at first thought, and so the date of its reopening has kept on being pushed further and further back. But now it has arrived. The second Saturday in December.

She stops. She looks about her, trying to get her bearings.

It is as cold today as it was hot back then on that Saturday morning in June. But the sky is the same cloudless, crystalline blue. Jenna steels herself. It's not that she hasn't been into the city centre since that time – she has done so many times, it would be impossible to avoid – but she has not ventured into St Ann's Square, where the theatre is situated and where she was when the bomb exploded.

She remembers little by way of detail. Mostly it is impressions. The initial deep-throated roar of the explosion. The rumble of thunder vibrating through the soles of her feet from under the earth. The way the concrete tipped and heaved and buckled beneath her. The sensation of flying through the air, almost as if she were in slow motion, noticing the individual shards of shattered glass, frozen, suspended, reflecting a thousand broken images of herself as they revolved together in a kind of dance. The juddering thud as she hit the ground again, all the breath knocked out of her. The deafness which followed. The ringing in her ears. Seeing the panic on the faces of the people, knowing that they were screaming, but hearing nothing. Like being underwater in a swimming pool. Then all of it clamouring back. The loudest sound of all her own voice, howling her daughter's name. "Molly! Molly!" Over and over, wheeling round frantically, trying to find her in all the mayhem and madness…

And there she is.

Happily waving and smiling when she catches sight of her.

Safe in the eye of the storm. Buffeted from the slings and arrows raining down all around her by the warm, strong arms of an older woman.

Dr Chadwick, Grace, the archaeologist, who, ignoring her own injuries, her awkwardly twisted, broken leg, protects Molly from harm till Jenna can reach her...

How afterwards, as the three of them lean against the door of St Ann's Church in the corner of the Square, while they wait for the paramedics to come, Molly miraculously unscathed, Grace tells Jenna about the benchmark scored into the stone lintel above them. When it was first carved, in 1712, it represented the highest point at the time in all of Manchester. They could use it to gauge the heights of all the new buildings that were mushrooming into the air. Grace explains how the first surveyors put their faith in trigonometry, the measured calculations of sines and cosines, to give them the accuracy of distances and angles. She marvels at the precision of compass and theodolite, which has made the building of this tower possible, so that it can withstand the very worst the bomb could fling at it. Jenna doesn't really take in what Grace is saying. She simply marvels at the way the light bounces off the still-intact windows above her, creating new isosceles triangles of their own, which no amount of measuring could have predicted, and which now dance upon her daughter's peerless, unspoiled face among all this carnage, almost as if the tower has been designed specifically to cradle and enfold, shelter and protect her in this way, at this moment, the living embodiment of one of the stained glass angels caught in the shimmering glass...

Now Jenna stands alone. She looks across the Square towards the Church tower. The sun bounces off those same windows today slicing the air with sharp daggers of light.

She walks towards it and looks up, shielding her eyes from

the glare till she locates the benchmark. Yes. There it is, tethering her to both then and now, centering her. She breathes in deeply. Then out. Again. Again. Till she feels herself finally letting go.

She is ready to enter the theatre...

She climbs the stone steps towards the entrance, walks through the set of revolving doors at the top, then stops in her tracks. Nothing has prepared her for the surprise of seeing the theatre itself, which, with its tubular structure of alloyed steel and darkened glass, resembles nothing less than a giant spacecraft. A lunar module that has somehow landed from another galaxy in the vast empty universe of the Royal Exchange, the former cotton trading market floor that straddled the world, buying and selling cloth from all corners of the Empire, including textiles from Yemen, with its pink marble pillars holding up a cycloramic glass-domed ceiling decorated with stars and planets. The module, which weighs a hundred and fifty tons, is suspended from the columns that support this domed ceiling, so that it appears to hover and float, as if it might take off again at any moment. The audience sits in a circle enclosing the space on which the actors will perform. It is the largest theatre-in-the-round in the world, wrapping itself around the eight hundred people it can contain, rising up in a steep rake, so that no one is more than thirty feet away from the action. When it was first opened, by Sir Laurence Olivier just twenty years before the IRA attack, he famously stood in the centre to welcome people, slowly rotating on the spot, as he spoke to them in that distinctive, dulcet yet declamatory tone he was famous for. "Good...good... good... evening..."

Jenna finds its intimacy simultaneously familiar but unsettling, like being trapped inside a giant bubble, which she is afraid might at any moment pop and burst, and she will be somewhere else. Another time, another place...

When, at the end of the play, the heroine Fanny defies convention and refuses the proposal of marriage from the mill owner's son after their week's dalliance together, she stands in the centre of the space and passionately declares her intention, confident in her skills as a weaver.

"I shan't starve," she says. "I'm not without a trade at my fingertips. I'm a Lancashire lass, and so long as there's weaving sheds in Lancashire, I shall earn enough brass to keep me going."

She then appears to speak to the audience directly, to confide in them, so that Jenna feels the words are aimed solely at her.

"I'm going to be on my own in future. There's no call to be afraid. So long as I've to live my own life, I don't see why I shouldn't choose what it's to be..."

Afterwards Ruth looks enquiringly at Jenna.

"Well...?"

Jenna nods. "You were right," she says. "This was exactly the right thing to do. Like you said. A kind of exorcism."

She is remembering the final words Grace said to her as she was driven away in the ambulance in the aftermath of the explosion. "Stay true to who you are." And her own response at the time. "You reap what you sow..."

Ruth too has reached a decision. Nothing so radically life-altering as Jenna, but a shift in direction even so. She has decided to pursue a part time post-graduate course at Salford University. An MSc/PgDip in Housing Practice, with modules in Policy, Context, Society and Sustainability. So many of the clients she sees have at some point in their lives suffered periods of homelessness. Every day she sees more and more rough sleepers on the city's streets, and more and more will come, as the global refugee crisis worsens. She knows this. She feels a moral obligation to do more than offer just talking therapy. In this she is at one with Jenna. Some kind of direct action is what is needed. She'll continue to take in patients at *Tulip House*, but she wants a seat at the table where the important decisions are taken, so that she's not merely called on as the last resort, to pick up the pieces, to try and apply a sticking plaster, which will do nothing to address the root societal causes that create the collateral damage she is currently called on to fix…

Like leaving a piece of shrapnel to embed itself and migrate…

*

Day 1417

A week later a specially converted C295 Airbus is hastily preparing for take-off from Aden International for its three-and-a-half hour flight to Aqaba Airport in Amman. The airbus has been chartered by MSF from Cairo, thanks to the bilateral agreement that exists between Egypt and Jordan, strengthened by both countries being members of the Arab League, as is Yemen also, though currently not a fully functioning one. Aden is currently under the control of the breakaway STC, the Southern Transitional Council, who have agreed to provide military protection while the C295 is on the runway. Surveillance drones are circling the airport, which can also act as a temporary defensive and interceptive strike force if either Coalition or Houthi forces attempt to mount a raid to prevent the Airbus from taking off.

The MSF has fitted out the plane with the barest minimum in terms of medical equipment to enable the nine seriously ill patients to be transported safely. There are insufficient endotracheal tubes for airway management, IV lines, or portable oxygen concentrators to go round, and so a lower-than-usual flight path has been agreed to reduce the risks of hypoxia, epistaxis, pneumothorax and tachycardia.

Dr Nina Müller has liaised with colleagues at the Queen Alia Hospital in Amman to meet them at the airport with all the necessary equipment not available to them here in Aden, before they complete the transfer to the Al-Khalidi Medical Centre, where the children are to be treated, while Major Naveed Khan has coordinated all the necessary paperwork and documentation for the patients and medical personnel accompanying them. Including Jenna, who has insisted on travelling with Maleek.

After a further agonising delay, while Naveed has to negotiate an eleventh hour bribe demanded by the STC to clear the runway, the C295 Airbus lumbers reluctantly into the skies above Yemen, heading out directly towards the Red Sea and the relative safety of international air space, before ascending as gradually as possible to its agreed flight height of just eight thousand feet, in order to minimise the rate of increase of pressure inside the cabin.

As well as Dr Müller, Zainab is also travelling with them. Séydou has arranged for his daughter Awa to meet them when they arrive, whose current internship is with the Al-Khalidi, and who will be Jenna's first point of contact.

They make it out just in time. Later that same day President Trump orders a lightning strike on a suspected Al-Qaeda enclave in Al-Ghayil, a remote village in the Yakla region of Central Yemen. Ostensibly an intelligence-gathering operation, its main target is the group's leader, Qasim-al-Raymi. Not bothering to go through the usual National Security Council channels, nor any other formal protocols, Trump impulsively orders the attack over a Big Mac in the White House. Not properly planned, the operation is completely botched. US helicopter gunships and fighter planes become unnecessarily involved in a fire fight with Al-Qaeda forces, inflicting scores of civilian casualties as the local clinic, school and mosque are all bombed and destroyed in an already impoverished village, and al-Raymi escapes unhurt to release an online audio message taunting Trump's failure. Unsurprisingly this brings about an immediate backlash, with ferocious fighting breaking out in tit-for-tat retaliations right across the country.

A day later, the C295 Airbus from Egypt would not have been permitted to land at Aden, nor pick up the critically sick children, or then transport them to the safe haven of Amman. Jenna would have been trapped, any hope of a future for Maleek snuffed out...

Halfway through the flight, Jenna looks down on Maleek. She's been sedated. Her breathing is shallow but regular. She appears calm. The pain has lessened. Jenna glances out of the window to her right. She can clearly make out the distinctive outline of the Hejaz Mountains running along the edge of the coastal plain. She thinks about the drawings her father had made of them. The way he captured their very essence with just a few strokes of a pencil, a gift he appears to have passed on to Molly. Holding Maleek's hand very gently in one of her own, she delicately traces the lines in the palm, an emerging landscape of their own.

At the precise moment Jenna is thinking these thoughts, a text pings in from Molly. It's an image that almost stops her heart.

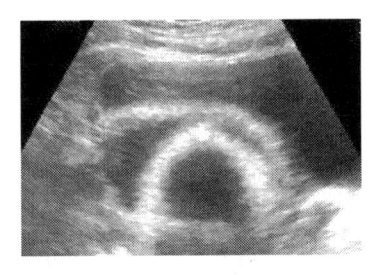

Then underneath a brief message.

> Hi Mum,
> It looks like you're going to be a grandmother...
> xxx

Jenna's eyes pore over every detail of it, trying to make sense of every line and pixel. It reminds her of the tracer lights of poi danced at Molly's wedding, sparking into life...

An hour later, when her eyes are dazzled by it, she texts back.

> I can't be a grandmother. Grandmothers knit and talk about the Blitz. I danced in the mud in a field in Glastonbury. I sang at Greenham Common for fuck's sake...
> Congratulations. How are you feeling?
> xxx

To which she receives an immediate reply.

> I'm fine.
> Thanks for not going all gooey over it. I don't think I could take that. I wouldn't know it was you.
> When will you be back...?
> xxx

Jenna looks back down on the sleeping Maleek.
When indeed...?

She feels the slightest of pressure from Maleek's fingers as they try to squeeze her own...

3

2019

Day 2275

Jenna is making another flight to the Middle East. Not to Yemen this time. But to Jordan. To Amman. To Maleek.

Awa has been sending her regular reports. She has extended her internship at the Al-Khalidi Medical Centre by a further year in order to be able to furnish Jenna with comprehensive updates. But these are no substitute for seeing her. And so Jenna has taken to visiting Amman as often as she can. A dozen times in the last two years.

Maleek's shrapnel sickness has been confirmed. Traces of many different metals have been found throughout her body. Lead, iron, copper, nickel. Even arsenic. Each with their own potentially disastrous consequences. Lead for the kidneys, iron for the intestines, copper for the liver, nickel for the blood and arsenic for the nervous system. In the past the health risks of embedded fragments were considered low, for it was believed they were rendered inert once they entered the body. But as doctors have become more experienced in treating the victims of roadside bombs in the recent conflicts in Iraq, Syria and Afghanistan, so their understanding of the subtler, less easily detectable symptoms caused by ingestion of metals and other particles into the blood stream has grown. This is particularly important if the foreign bodies contain radioactive elements. The accurate identification and localisation of such elements becomes crucial in the subsequent surgical management of the injury. More and more case reports have uncovered incidents of longer-term adverse health effects in victims arising when no interventions have taken place. IEDs – improvised explosive devices, of the sort used in the car bomb which has caused Maleek's injuries – present additional problems in that a range of novel and unusual combinations of material are frequently incorporated into the making of them, so that the embedded fragments may contain properties whose specific toxicological and even carcinogenic capabilities are not fully known or understood.

The bacterial cellulitis uncovered in Maleek's case is found in the deeper layers of skin. The doctors in Amman are able to diagnose nephrosis, indicated by severe proteinuria, with dangerously high levels of albumin in her urine, acute edema around her eyes, together with her extreme lethargy and listlessness. She is immediately prescribed a strong dose of prednisone. By stabilising the nephrosis, the doctors are then able to tackle the more worrying cellulitis. To begin with, her internal wounds are carefully and thoroughly debrided. All hyperkeratotic skin is scraped away, followed by the removal of the infected, dead or necrotic tissue, as well as any foreign debris that has not dissolved entirely into the blood. Ideally the doctors prefer to do this non-surgically, autolytically using the patient's own enzymes to re-hydrate, soften and liquefy non-viable tissue, but it is too late for this in Maleek's case. Her debridement has to be administered surgically, with a scalpel to excise the remaining, minute fragments of metal. Simultaneously, chemical enzymes, derived from micro-organisms including clostridium, histolyticum, collagenase and varidase, are used to slough off further necrotic tissue, followed by a course of hydrotherapy in which a syringe and catheter are used to irrigate the last remaining traces.

Although no neurovascular damage is noted pre-operatively, the metal fragments extracted are worryingly close to the median nerve, whose motor functions stimulate the flexor and pronator muscles in the forearm, as well as the thenar muscles and lateral lumbricals in the hand. Following closure after surgery, the doctors note some transient cutaneous sensory deficit at the wrist. The same results are observed in Maleek's legs as well as her arms and hands

Dr Müller – Nina, as she now is to Jenna – diagnoses extensive peripheral nerve injury, distressingly common among survivors of IED attacks. She has tried to explain the complexities of Maleek's condition to her in numerous emails and satellite calls.

"Normal wound-healing," she tells her, "is a dynamic and complex process, part of an acute inflammatory response to the initial injury. This involves a series of coordinated events, including bleeding, coagulation, the regeneration, migration and proliferation of connective tissue and parenchyma cells, the subsequent repair and remodeling of these, alongside the synthesis of extracellular matrix proteins and collagen deposition, thereby enabling the healing to take place in a measured and controlled manner."

But this is not what has happened with Maleek.

Nina elaborates further. "Some wounds," she says, "do not heal in a timely or orderly manner. Multiple systemic and local factors may slow the course of wound healing by causing disturbances in the finely balanced repair processes, resulting in chronic, non-healing wounds. This is further exacerbated if the wounds are internal."

As they are with Maleek.

A complicated wound is a special entity and is defined as a combination of an infection and a tissue defect. Infection poses a constant threat to the wound. Every wound is contaminated, irrespective of the cause, size, location and management. Whether or not a manifest infection develops depends on the virulence, number and type of micro-organisms, as well as on the local blood supply and the patient's inherent resistance. Typical characteristics of infection are the five signs and symptoms that have been well documented – redness, heat, pain, edema and loss of limited function in the affected part.

"Maleek," says Nina, "suffers with all of these."

Immediately after injury, coagulation and haemostasis take place in the wound. The principal aim of these mechanisms is to prevent exsanguination. It is a way to protect the vascular system, keeping it intact, so that the function of the vital organs remains unharmed despite the injury. This is where complications arising from so-called shrapnel migration may occur if not detected quickly.

"Which, by definition," says Nina, "is what almost always occurs. The impact of the initial injury migrates, via the blood stream, elsewhere in the body."

In Maleek's case this has had significant consequences for her vascular system.

Further X-rays reveal that minute traces of shrapnel still remain in Maleek's right arm and left leg. "In each case," Nina explains, "the fragment is less than a millimetre away from a nerve. The condition is irritated each time Maleek tries to move either limb, causing her acute pain. The movement in turn continues to wear away the nerve sheath, resulting in a neuroma."

Nina proposes two separate nerve transfers. The procedure will involve harvesting nerves from Maleek's left arm and right leg respectively. She will then graft each piece of harvested nerve into the infected area of each limb, while simultaneously preserving the damaged, but still functioning part of the injured nerve. At the same time she will remove the offending fragment of shrapnel. This will require two separate operations, with a period of recovery time in between of several weeks.

Nina, acting *in loco parentis*, assumes responsibility for taking this decision, but as a courtesy asks Jenna for permission to proceed, which Jenna grants unequivocally.

After each operation, progress is painfully slow. Maleek appears to have lost all movement in the treated limb. "This is to be expected," explains Nina, but it is discouraging even so. Then, over the next eighteen months, Maleek begins to improve. With the aid of extensive physiotherapy she relearns how to use her muscles. At first this is just the barest, discernible flicker, in her toes, in her fingers, until gradually she is able to regain almost full mobility. She can manipulate objects with her right hand once more, use a fork, a spoon, pick up a pencil and draw, operate a mobile phone. Eventually she can stand, then walk, then run. Most importantly of all, she is at last free from pain...

Awa has been invaluable every step of the way in Maleek's rehabilitation. She is someone who Maleek can recognise, can trust, and who both Nina and Jenna have come to rely on. Unfairly so. She cannot be expected to put her own career on hold indefinitely. It has been made clear to her that her internship with UNHCR will not be extended a further year...

So, too, with Zainab. Another familiar, friendly face. Someone else Maleek has come to depend on. But she too has had to return to Manchester to continue her training, which has necessitated Jenna travelling to Jordan as often as she can...

Next begins the even harder task of treating Maleek's psychological and emotional injuries.
"This will take a long time," explains Nina.
"How long?" asks Jenna.
"Longer than she will be able to stay here at Al-Khalidi," says Nina, as delicately as she can...

The implications of this are left unspoken. They hang in the air between them, each on their satellite phone, the silence spanning the more than three thousand miles that separate them across the ether....

*

Day 2252

A lot has changed for Jenna in the last two years.

Following the broadcast of her audio diaries from Yemen she is awarded one of the prestigious *Women of the Year* Awards.

WOMEN OF THE YEAR

In 2017 this annual event is held at The Inter-Continental Hotel in Mayfair. Over lunch *Women of the Year* President Sandi Toksvig reminds the assembled gathering of the history of the awards.

"For over sixty years," she says, "*Women of the Year* has proudly acknowledged the achievements of some of the world's most incredible and bravest women. Begun in 1955, as the brainchild of Lady Antonella Lothian, a journalist and mother of six, it honoured, equally, five hundred remarkable women. It took place at a time when Britain was radically changing as a result of the War and the Labour Government that followed, and was the first of its kind. Today this lunch remains unique in championing those women who fall into no other category than the sometimes silent work they do within their community and for the greater good, who, as George Eliot so memorably remarked, 'have spent their lives in channels which have no great name on the earth. But the effect of their being on those around them has been incalculably diffusive. For the growing good of the world is partly dependent on unhistoric acts.' And that things are not so ill with us as they might have been is half owing to women like these who we celebrate today, who faithfully live their hidden lives, seeking no reward other than the deeds they do for the benefit of others.

"These women are the unsung heroines who are the

backbones of charities, emergency and medical services, industries, and indeed every profession possible. The remarkable women who make up the attendees and winners at this year's lunch are being recognised for their work in making the world a better place."

Jenna can scarcely believe she is being included within such a pantheon, to the extent that she tells nobody. But the news leaks out, and Nadia is able to accompany her.

"You're not expected to make a speech today, are you?"

"No. Why?"

"I was remembering that time when they gave you the Bernard Crick Prize."

Jenna, blushing, looks across at her mother, but Nadia is smiling.

"I shan't embarrass you today, I promise."

Nadia shakes her head. "You didn't embarrass me then. I was upset, but I was proud of you. I was just worried that that tongue of yours might get you into trouble."

"It has. Many times."

"I know, love. Believe me, I know…"

After the lunch Jenna is presented her award by Camilla, Duchess of Cornwall. When she sits down at their table again after collecting it, having said nothing other than 'thank you', she insists on handing it to Nadia.

"If anyone's an unsung heroine, she says, it's you…"

Hot on the heels of the *Women of the Year* comes an appearance on *Desert Island Discs*. One of the last interviews carried out by Kirsty Young before she hands over the reins to Lauren Laverne.

This is a carefully stage-managed affair. Jenna consciously constructs a narrative of her life that presents the person she would like to be, rather than who she actually is. She self-deprecatingly charts a romanticised, rose-tinted version of her younger self as the student radical, making no mention of Lance, deliberately choosing music that paints her as a true daughter of Manchester – which she is of course – though not so crudely as this mask she puts on to deflect more forensic scrutiny might indicate. The Buzzcocks, The Smiths, Oasis, New Order. With deft asides to Tony Wilson, Danny Boyle and Tony Walsh, together with seemingly spontaneous references to the Moss Side Riots, the IRA Bomb, the Northern Powerhouse, the terrorist attack after the Ariana Grande concert.

But there is nothing spontaneous about her performance at all. Except when she is singing the praises of her mother and aunt, Nadia and Farida, which are unequivocally heart-felt. But she is holding on by her fingernails. Right at the end she is almost tripped up when Kirsty asks her to name her luxury item. Jenna chooses a simple black umbrella. She hopes this will come across as modest, unassuming, a little enigmatic perhaps, possibly a jokey allusion to Manchester's reputation for rain, and that it will pass off unchallenged.

But Kirsty questions it. "It sounds too practical to be considered a luxury," she quips. "Why is it so special?"

That is when Jenna lets her guard slip, just for a moment. "It reminds me of my father," she confesses.

Kirsty seizes upon this at once and probes for further revelations, but, fortunately for Jenna, runs out of time. Jenna manages to rescue the situation by describing the moment she chanced upon her parents dancing close and slow to Johnny Ray's *Look Homeward, Angel*, which she saves for the final piece of music…

Afterwards, when the recording has finished, Kirsty and Jenna reflect separately on the disappointment each of them feels about how it went…

Kirsty watches Jenna leave the studio and thinks what an unsatisfactory edition this has been, apart from that one instance when, for a brief moment, she caught a fleeting glimpse of a more vulnerable, more complex and, as a result, more interesting person than the one she presented for the rest of the programme, which she'd turned into a kind of platform for her various hobby horses, and Jenna had insisted that that section had to be cut. Oh well, you win some, you lose some... Pity, she thinks. She likes Jenna, especially her feisty 'take-no-prisoners' combativeness, and feels people would warm to her far more if she'd let them get a little closer, but this armour-plating she's encased herself in makes her just seem cold-hearted and not a little manipulative. That chink she'd almost revealed, that last minute reference to her father, the choice of the black umbrella for her luxury item. What was that all about? Hmm...

While Jenna hurries out of the studio without once looking back. As soon as she steps outside, onto the concourse of Salford's Media City, she pauses, lights up a cigarette and inhales deeply. She is almost shaking.

That was close, she thinks. She's not ready to tell the world her full story. Not yet. That will have to wait, she tells herself, till another time, till later...

She stubs out her cigarette and strides purposefully towards the nearby Metro Link station to catch the tram back to New Islington. She goes over what she has said minutely as she walks. It has not been an entirely unmitigated disaster. The worst she can be accused of is an economy with the truth. Nothing she has said has been a lie. Yes, there have been omissions. But isn't that what everyone does...?

When she is first invited to take part in the programme, she is astonished, flabbergasted. Why *her*? Then she becomes excited. It's a game that everyone secretly plays, isn't it? Choosing the eight discs they would include? And then, as the date draws nearer, she grows increasingly nervous, anxious, agitated, and finally terrified. The thought of having to trawl back through memories she thought she had buried, of incidents she had no desire to revisit, fills her with a deep dread. It's been twenty years since she finished her sessions with Ruth, sessions which were enormously beneficial – more than that, they had saved her, from herself – but at least they had been private, confidential, not shared between the three million listeners *Desert Island Discs* gets each week.

She contemplates cancelling, but knows that's not an option. It would be bound to come out, and that would only lead to yet more awkward questions. So she accepts, providing Kirsty Young, in her opening introduction, will make a reference to Jenna's current work with the Refugee Council and CARE – which of course Kirsty agrees to do. Why wouldn't she? It's her work with those organisations which has brought her more widely to the public's attention, which has led to her *Women of the Year* Award, which is why she's been invited to appear in the first place.

But this does nothing to alleviate Jenna's fears.

In desperation, with less than a month to go before the date for the recording, Jenna contacts Ruth and asks for advice. The two women are now friends. They see each other three or four times a year and keep in regular contact via WhatsApp in between. It is Ruth who suggests the strategy she eventually adopts.

"It's *your* programme," Ruth reminds her. "Control the agenda through the music you select. Let each piece dictate what you say. Which stories and anecdotes you feel able to share, and which ones you don't. Then steer the conversation towards those you feel comfortable with, and away from those you want to avoid…"

It's a strategy that proves successful. By and large. Until that slip about Sol near the end. But even that she manages to dance deftly around. In between she has spoken passionately about the things that matter to her, while simultaneously poking fun at herself for getting carried away sometimes. She has made some surprising musical choices, which will have wrong-footed her listeners, who will find it difficult to pigeon-hole her. Her comments about Oasis are a particular case in point.

"I love the way they just stick two fingers up to the rest of the world," she says, "yet at the same time can be tender and insightful. Like here."

Don't Look Back In Anger.

"I take it that's a sentiment you agree with?" Kirsty asks her.

Jenna agrees. "I try if I can, she says, always to look forward."

Which she does.

But when she does recall the past, she does so with warmth and affection. She speaks with genuine pride about Nadia and Farida and Ishtar.

"I've been very lucky," she says, "to have grown up among such strong, remarkable women."

And when Kirsty presses her – gently but firmly – about Molly, specifically about why Jenna chose not to raise her own daughter – a matter that is already in the public domain – she is only momentarily thrown. She asks for the recording to be halted while she composes herself. The last thing she wants to do is cry on national radio. Then she gives the answer she has prepared.

"I could, I suppose, cite post-natal depression," she says, "and there would be some truth in that, but the real reason is I simply wasn't very good at being a mother, not at first. My own mother and grandmother were so much better, so much more patient than I was. And then there was my job. It was better for Molly that way. In so-called developing countries a child is often raised by a whole village. That seems a much healthier approach to me..."

She breathes in deeply once more as she goes back over this. Just because an answer is prepared doesn't of itself invalidate it. Or make it any less true.

"Time for your next piece of music," says Kirsty respectfully...

Why, then, this reluctance to speak about her relationship with Sol, her father? It's simply too painful, she supposes, and difficult, wrapped up in complex, contradictory feelings of guilt and forgiveness. On both sides. She believes they made their peace eventually...

Jenna boards the tram back to her newly-converted waterfront apartment at the Grade II-listed former *Daily Express* Building on Great Ancoats Street with a sense of gratitude and relief...

... where she is due to meet Molly. More significantly, where she is due to meet Blessing, Molly's new-born daughter, for the first time, which partly explains her distraction during the recording...

Michael Adebayo added 8 new photos.
26 September 2017·
Molly and I would like introduce you to our newest addition, Blessing Dawn Wahid Adebayo, born yesterday at 06:18 at home as planned, weighing 8lbs. We are over the moon and Blessing is already living up to her name. Molly never ceases to amaze me!

Only Ruth can guess just how much this performance has cost Jenna…

But when the programme is aired, a few weeks later, everyone declares themselves delighted.

Farida is thrilled by the inclusion of the song by Leila Mourad. Nadia laughs out loud at the story of how Jenna showered her teachers with photocopies of those lyrics by The Buzzcocks from the roof of her school. Molly teases her about how she has chosen only music from the last century. "It's time you moved with the times, Mum," she says. "Here…"

And she hands across a mewling Blessing for her to hold.

"She's been grizzling all day," she says. "I've been up two nights straight. I'm knackered. See if *you* have any better luck with her…"

She says this like it's the most natural thing in the world, then flops on the sofa exhausted. Jenna holds her granddaughter in her arms, awkwardly at first, delicately, fearfully. As if she is made of porcelain. As if she might break…

Blessing pauses in her crying. She opens her eyes, which up until now have been tightly scrunched up, and gazes at Jenna, her milky vision swimming in and out of focus.

Jenna gazes back.

They each look intently at the other. As if both are entering unknown territory. Each trying to comprehend the lie of the land, the whole map of it, which, just when they think they have begun to grasp the shape and outline of every contour, every feature, will alter and change and reveal a new tract of country as yet undiscovered…

*

There have been other changes too.

Who we are   Countries   News, Stories   Media   Policy   Contact Us   Donate

News

Jenna Ward, who has been Chair of the Board of CARE UK for the past 5 years, is stepping down for personal and family reasons.

"An unexpected change in my personal circumstances means that I can no longer commit the amount of time necessary to the ever-increasing demands required by the role of Chair as our organisation continues to work in more and more countries across the world. I intend to remain as a trustee for as long as the Board wishes, and I will offer my successor whatever support I can. Let me take this opportunity to thank each and every one of our dedicated team working tirelessly to Defend Dignity and Fight Poverty wherever it is needed."

Jenna and Séydou marry in the Pankhurst Suite of Heron House on Lloyd Street, less than a quarter of a mile away from Manchester's Central Library.

It is the 1st of May, a Thursday morning. Only a few guests are there to witness it. Omar and Awa. Nadia and Farida. Molly, Michael and Blessing. Ruth, Barbara. All of whom are taken by surprise by the suddenness of the announcement, when they first hear about it four weeks earlier...

.

"Jenna? Married? I thought she didn't believe in it," they say.

"I don't," she says. "Not really."

"Then why?"

"I can't tell you," she says. "Not yet. I will. Soon."

"When?"

"As soon as I can."

"This is uncharacteristically mysterious of you, Mum," says Molly.

"But characteristically impulsive," remarks Nadia, eyeing her daughter squarely.

"That's a bit harsh, Gran," says Molly, trying to persuade Blessing to eat some yoghurt, pretending the spoon is an aeroplane, while Blessing is having none of it, keeping her lips firmly shut.

"At least at your age you can't be pregnant," continues Nadia.

"Hardly," says Jenna.

"Not that that persuaded you before."

"Gran!"

"I've told you," says Jenna firmly. "I can't say right now. But as soon as I can, you'll be the first to know…"

The wedding takes place less than a month later.

Jenna wears a black soft crepe blazer and trousers, white tie-neck blouse, black leather ankle boots, and a black jersey *hijab*, of the kind she has taken to wearing since her second trip to Yemen two years before. An ensemble she has worn before for professional meetings. A far cry from the cropped T-shirts and ripped jeans of her days in the Squat.

The Registrar smiles at Jenna and Séydou with genuine warmth. Marriages between more mature couples – finding love unexpectedly at last, or grasping at an unlooked-for second chance, or simply seizing the day while they still can – always give her a deep satisfaction to perform. She wonders what the story behind this particular couple might be.

This is precisely what everyone else is wondering. The small gathering of close family and friends are still collectively pinching themselves, trying to understand what has happened to prompt this sudden and uncharacteristic *volte face* on the part of Jenna.

Just at the moment when the Registrar – Sybil, as she prefers to be called – is asking whether anyone knows of any legal reason, any just cause or impediment, why the couple should not be joined in marriage, a mobile phone cuts into the question before she can finish it, or before anyone can begin to answer. Its ring tone is set to the chorus of Patti Smith's *Because the Night*. Everyone looks round to see whose it is, embarrassed and awkward while the ringing continues, insistent and loud.

'Because the night belongs to lovers
Because the night belongs to lust...'

Belatedly Jenna owns up to it being hers. She fumbles in her bag until she has found it, looks to see who the call might be from, then, holding it to her chest, raises an apologetic finger.

"Excuse me," she says, "I have to take this," and she tiptoes away to a far corner of the Pankhurst Suite.

Desire is hunger is the fire I breathe
Love is a banquet on which we feed...

The others can hardly take in what they're witnessing. Their collective jaws drop, aghast. Nadia is furious. She wants to storm over to Jenna and really give her a peace of mind, but is prevented from doing so at the last moment by Farida, who places a restraining hand on her sister's arm. How dare Jenna do this? On today of all days? At least Sol is not here to see it, be thankful for small mercies. Barbara puts her head in her hands, Ruth looks anxiously towards Jenna, wondering if perhaps she is having another breakdown and that maybe she should intervene, while Blessing begins to wail, which conveniently saves Molly from the embarrassment of having to hide her own initial reaction, which is to laugh. How typical of her Mum to contrive to do something like this. Sybil looks from one to another of them in open-mouthed disbelief.

Only Séydou seems unperturbed. He watches Jenna intently. His eyes never leave hers for a moment.

After what seems a lifetime, she hangs up. She continues to look intently at Séydou. Her eyes are shining.

"*Alors?*" he says.

She nods, once, then hurtles towards him, flinging her arms about his neck.

Sybil, with alacrity and relief, takes this opportunity to wrest back control. She speaks as loudly and as quickly as she can.

"I now pronounce you husband and wife."

'Because the night belongs to us...'

*

Jenna has moved.

When she and Séydou decide they will marry, she looks for somewhere larger than her apartment in the former *Daily Express* building. Somewhere that Awa and Omar can use as a base too if they would like...

Awa is now a Junior Doctor at the Royal Manchester Children's Hospital on Oxford Road. A new facility, less than ten years old, but with a history going back two hundred and thirty, it has always been a pioneer of new technologies and new ways of treating patients, specialising in trauma, in which she is already experienced from her time in the field in Amman..

Omar, having completed his PhD in Biochemistry at UCAD in Dakar, has secured a Research Fellowship at the Manchester Institute of Biotechnology under the leadership of Dr

Konstantina Drosou, a principal investigator into ancient DNA. Her research focuses on the investigation of the origins, lifestyle and evolution of infections, using modern discovery omics from minimally invasive biopsies. These analyses predict evolutionary data for both humans and organisms, bring understanding of the developmental timeframe of genetic diseases, and, combined with archaeological data, inform a cultural understanding of sickness-management, alongside long-term care for individuals with chronic conditions, population characteristics, kinship analysis and ancestry identification.

In other words – who we are, where we have come from, and where we might go next. Jenna finds it fascinating.

Séydou is shifting focus, cutting back. He is fifty-two now. MSF is encouraging him to consider taking more of a backroom, strategic role, rather than heading up Field Operations, as he has been doing for almost twenty years. The idea of a change suits him. He would like to spend more time with Omar and Awa, having missed so much of their growing up…

Jenna, now fifty-six, discusses the situation with Barbara, who she sees most weeks. Over the years she has become her closest friend. Barbara, too, is contemplating change. She has been Head of English at Fairfield High School for Girls for more than a decade, but, at fifty-five herself, she feels the time has come to hand on the mantle to a younger, equally capable colleague. She will continue to teach, but on a part-time basis only, allowing herself more time for her work across the Moravian Settlement as a whole, where she has recently become one of its Elders.

In its early days the Settlement adhered strictly to a policy known as the Lot. This was the method by which all major decisions were made. If an important matter needed to be settled – such as allowing somebody new to join them in their community, or whether a couple should be permitted to marry – three slips of paper were placed in a wooden box. On these were written respectively: 'Yes', 'No', with the third left blank. The Elders would then pray for guidance before drawing one of the slips. The belief was that only God can decide these matters, and so His advice was sought in this manner. His judgement was deemed to be true and wise, and the congregation dutifully abided by whichever verdict was delivered. Yes or no. If the blank slip was drawn out, this signalled that the matter was uncertain and so should be submitted again at a later date for a further judgement by the Lot...

Gradually, though, over time, the Lot has been abandoned. A question was put to it in 1820 asking whether men and women might be trusted to decide for themselves whether or not they might marry, and the Lot pronounced in the affirmative.

But there is still a Committee of Elders, who manage the affairs of the Settlement, the appointment of Ministers for the Church, the maintenance of the Burial Ground. They retain a close connection with the school, with representation on the Board of Governors. They have converted what had formerly been the Single Brethren's Residence into a Museum. And it is they who decide who might come to live in the Settlement if ever a property there should become vacant. There is a long waiting list, for such properties come on to the market rarely, and, when they do, they are in high demand, for the houses are extremely well-built and pleasingly designed, each of them unique, a mix of one-, two-, three-, and four-bedroom dwellings. Prospective buyers do not need to follow the Moravian faith, but they do have to be able to offer something positive they can bring to the Settlement – a skill, a craft, a commitment to become involved. They must face an interview with the Elders, who will then assess their suitability. If the property that becomes available contains only one bedroom, it will hardly be appropriate for a family, while a single person is unlikely to be considered for one with four bedrooms.

It is one of these four-bedroom properties that has just become available. Jenna, who has maintained her membership of the Ladies Group, and who has recently been invited to join the Governing Body of the School, applies for it. Her case is considered. Her skills and experience, together with those of Séydou, Awa and Omar, are deemed to be exactly what the Settlement needs just now, and her application is successful.

Jenna and Seydou will occupy one bedroom, Awa and Omar will occupy the second and the third. Leaving the fourth still to be filled...

*

Day 2253

Jenna rubs her eyes, then checks the time on her phone. 05.46. She raises the blind by her seat and looks through the ovoid window of the Royal Jordanian Airlines Boeing 787, which will be landing at Amman's Queen Alia Airport in just over an hour.

The sun is just rising. A blazing disc of red fire.

Even though Jenna has made this trip many times in the last two years, dawn over the desert never fails to astonish her. It is an elemental, heart-stopping sight.

Below her the Wadi Rum stretches endlessly in every direction. The Valley of the Moon. Its mountains, plateaus and plains etched clearly. Even from this height, it is a magical landscape. Like a scene from *Scheherazade*. She has visited it once. When her return flight was delayed for a couple of days...

She takes a camel ride along the Khaz'ali Canyon, skirting

the edge of the shadow cast by the twin peaks of Jabal Ram and Jabal Umm ad Dhami, the highest mountains in the desert, on whose rock faces are carved ancient petroglyphs depicting the interplay of humans and animals. They date back to Thamudic times, an earlier Bedouin settlement from ten thousand years before. There are Bedouins here still. Jenna passes tents made from goat-skin, with camels tethered close by. There are also four-wheeled jeeps parked alongside, plus two modern buildings that are only half-finished. These will be schools, she is told. One for boys and one for girls. The settlement is evolving. Just as Fairfield has had to, to accommodate the modern world…

Then there's a windowless concrete bunker which houses *Dawriat Alhasa'*, the Desert Patrol, a paramilitary border force, monitoring for signs of ISIS…

Now, through the window of the Boeing, she can see the outskirts of Amman rising up through the haze. It won't be long now.

She wakes her two companions.

"Nearly there," she says. "Best get all our papers ready."

Entering Jordan is a complicated business. Visas are required but cannot be obtained beforehand. They must join a series of long lines in the airport once they've disembarked. But some of these lines can be avoided by filling out certain forms in advance, which the stewards are now handing out to passengers. Jenna's Refugee Council status, together with official letters of introduction from MSF arranged by Séydou, mean that they will be fast-tracked. Not waived through like diplomats, but the next best thing.

Her two companions stretch and yawn. It has been a long flight. Almost twelve hours including the change at Frankfurt.

Awa and Zainab.

Each accompanying Jenna on this, her final mission.

Neither wanting to miss it.

"Wild horses," they say...

They join the queue for the loo straggling along the aisle, emerging afterwards groomed and immaculate, these three head-scarved women from different countries – Senegal, Lebanon, Britain, by way of Yemen – now Mancunian all...

Nina, having flown in from Switzerland a few days before, is waiting for them in Arrivals, brisk and business-like as usual.

"I have a car standing by," she says. "Hurry. Maleek is waiting."

Maleek.

The reason why these four women have crossed continents to be here.

Jenna looks at the others with immense warmth and gratitude. She could not be doing this without them...

An hour later, having survived the trial and torment of Amman's rush-hour traffic – mostly they shut their eyes and pray for a safe deliverance, *inshallah* – they enter the comparative calm of Al-Khalidi Medical Centre.

Maleek sees them before they see her and runs – yes, runs – to greet them. Each of them lifts her high into the air in turn and swings her round and round...

The paperwork is checked and double-checked, then checked again. Thankfully it is all in order. Every 'i' dotted and 't' crossed.

Jenna has ACS to thank for this. *Active Care Solutions*. A multi-faith, culturally-diverse, inter-governmental agency, which seeks to place orphaned refugee children from war zones around the world into long-term fostering care in the UK, regardless of age, ethnicity, gender or sexuality. Jenna has come across them through her work with both the Refugee

Council and CARE. She knows their reputation and she trusts them. They offer support, guidance, training and the all-important legal advice. They're in it for the long haul. Long-term fostering means until the child reaches the age of eighteen. Maleek is eight. She will be nine in July. Jenna is fully committed to being there for her for the next ten years. For longer. For always. For however long she is needed...

Among the dotted 'i's and crossed 't's is the question of Jenna's status. ACS adopt a rigorously non-discriminatory policy. 'Regardless of age, ethnicity, gender or sexuality' is more than mere window-dressing. They abide by it fundamentally and will call out prejudice whenever they come across it.

However.

They are also pragmatists.

Legally speaking, according to strict *Sharia* law, it is not possible for the biological parents of a child to ever be replaced by adoptive parents. In order to look after a child, the would-be adoptive parents would have to become the child's guardians or *de facto* foster carers, but can never usurp the legal rights of the parents. This is known as the *kafala* system and essentially enables the biological parents to request the return of their child to them in law, whenever they choose, even if the child is happily settled with its new family. Crucially this right can extend to wider members of the child's birth family if both parents are deceased. As is the case with Maleek. Would-be adopters of children from non-*Sharia* countries are therefore required to sign a proviso before the child is handed over confirming that they will do nothing to extinguish the rights of the biological parents, or legitimate members of their wider family. In order to get permission for the child to enter the UK, they have to inform the Local Authority, as well as the Immigration Entry Clearance Officer, that the child is being brought into the country by virtue of a private fostering arrangement, or as a *kafala* child. Once in British jurisdiction the guardians then need to apply for a special order under the *Children Act 1989* so that they can acquire formal parental responsibility for the child, which enables them to make all the day-to-day decisions in relation to the child's care and upbringing that an actual parent would make. This can be exercised to the exclusion of any other person, apart from the named special guardian. It does not, however, extinguish the legal relationship between the child and his or her birth parents, or their family. In Maleek's case, the prospect of this clause ever being activated is extremely remote, with both parents having died and no record existing of any wider family.

ACS judiciously attend to all of this paperwork. But they hit a snag when the question of Jenna's status comes up. 'Single, unmarried mother' does not sit well with the Jordanian authorities. ACS assure Jenna that they can – and will, if need be – challenge this ruling, and the inevitable delay that will ensue.

But.

If Jenna is able to be more flexible, more accommodating to a more conventional domestic arrangement, it would unquestionably expedite matters greatly...

Jenna understands that ACS are only trying to help. The Jenna of old would have held true to her principles, would have instructed ACS to proceed strictly according to the letter of the Law, that her rights as a single, older, mixed-race woman were inviolable and must be upheld.

But she is no longer that same Jenna.

The new Jenna knows only too well that the clock is ticking. The sands are running out fast on how much longer Maleek will be permitted to remain at Al-Khalidi Medical Centre. Her injuries have all been treated. She has made a good recovery – as far as her physical wounds are concerned. Her bed at the Centre is needed for other, more critical patients.

Unless arrangements can be made for her transfer to the UK quickly, she will be sent to the camp at Za'atari, which houses more than two million other refugees, where she will be lost for ever...

"Let me make a phone call," says Jenna to ACS...

When Jenna calls him, Séydou is not surprised. He knows how the system works. But he wants to be clear. "Where do *I* fit into all this?" he asks. "What *am* I to you?"

Jenna understands. Séydou does not wish to be some kind of flag of convenience, whereby a ship may be registered in a country different from that of her owners, so that she may be subject to laws that are more favourable and advantageous to her than they would otherwise be. "That is a smokescreen," he says. "Is that all I am to you?"

Jenna understands that she is about to cross the Rubicon. She and Séydou have been lovers for ten years. But they are not, in the conventional sense, a couple. *She* lives in Manchester, *he* lives in Dakar. When they meet, it tends to be through their work. In Paris, Djibouti, Yemen, and now Jordan. Only occasionally have they spent time in the other's domain. But when they have, it has been easy. Jenna gets on well with Awa and Omar. Molly approves of Séydou. Jenna has even met Ndeyou, Séydou's wife, who she finds she really likes.

"*Oui,*" says Ndeyou, "*tu as bien aidée mon mari. Merci.* "

This made Séydou's divorce from her easier than it might have been, so much more civilised, which he did as he promised he would, as soon as Awa and Omar had graduated from UCAD. The possibility of their relationship shifting to something else since has continued to hover, unspoken, before them.

Now, Jenna realises, it can remain unspoken no longer. Maleek is a catalyst, not an excuse. Not a flagship of convenience, but a safe harbour, a refuge...

They meet as a matter of urgency in Paris. This is a conversation that needs to be conducted face to face, not over the phone.

"The arrangement we have had these past ten years has worked very well," she says.

"Yes," he agrees. "It has suited us both."

"We each lead busy lives."

"We each have our professional duties to carry out."

"Which sometimes overlap."

"But which sometimes force us apart."

"And you have your responsibilities to your family."

"As do you."

"Less so than you."

Séydou spreads his hands. He knows of the particular, nuanced relationship that exists between Jenna and Molly, and some of the reasons behind it.

"It's more complicated for you," he acknowledges. "I understand that."

"Thank you," she says. "But I wouldn't say so. You have had your wife's feelings to consider."

"*C'est vrai.*"

"Anyway, Molly is married now. She has Michael. And Blessing."

"*Oui.*"

"And..."

"*Oui?*"

Jenna feels her mouth go dry.

"Meeting Maleek has changed me. "

"I know this."

"I feel as if I'm being given a second chance."

"*C'est une rédemption.*"

"More than that."

"*Qu'est-ce que tu veux dire?* "

She pauses. She looks up at Séydou.

"I love you," she says simply. "I've not said that before. Not to you. Not to anyone. But it's true. I do. Completely. I can't imagine a life without you…"

One month later, in the foyer of Al-Khalidi, all the paperwork completed, a wedding band upon her finger, Jenna kneels down in front of Maleek. She holds both her hands in her own.

"*Hal 'ant jahiz?*" she asks. "Are you ready?"
"*Nem*," answers Maleek solemnly. "Yes…"
Each sees the other as a raft they can cling to.
"*Linadhab 'iilaa almanzil*," says Jenna. "Let's go home…"

*

After the surprise success of her visit to see *Hindle Wakes* in the *Royal Exchange*, Jenna discovers that she is not as averse to theatre as she had thought. She goes four or five times a year, sometimes with Ruth and Barbara, sometimes by herself.

There are three main theatres in the city. As well as the *Royal Exchange*, there is *Contact*, in Moss Side, less than a stone's throw from where the Squat once was, and Danny Boyle's *Home*, opposite where *The Haçienda* had been. The synchronicity of each of these theatres having such strong connections to some of the key events in her life chimes powerfully with her. An exchange of ideas between people trying to make contact with each other, all of them in search of a home, proves irresistible.

She sees plays from around the world – from China, Somalia, Israel and Georgia – all of them taking root here in Manchester…

At the turn of the year she sees a flyer for *Mother Courage* at the *Royal Exchange*. The first time it has ever presented a play by Brecht. She is intrigued. She realises, for all the talk by Spike of Living Newspapers and *Verfremdungseffekt*, she has never actually seen one of his plays. Nor read any. Yet somehow they have entered into her bloodstream. They form part of who she is.

Neither Ruth nor Barbara can make it, so she decides to go alone.

Mother Courage is a play set in the endless Thirty Years' War, which devastated Europe between 1618 and 1648, largely fought in the lawless, tribal lands of the Holy Roman Empire, a loose, fragmented confederation of assorted territories that now make up modern Germany, but which then belonged to no one, a patchwork mosaic, with different tiny princely states forging and breaking alliances seemingly at will, as fortunes vacillated this way, then that. It was nominally a religious war, waged not just between Catholic and Protestant armies, but between different factions within both. It was also a proxy war, with the principal players being the richer empire nations of France and Spain, Sweden and Denmark, the Netherlands and Austria. When peace was finally restored, with the signing of the Treaty of Westphalia, there were no winners. Only losers. An exhausted, ravaged Europe lay in ruins. Estimates of the total number of deaths, some military but mostly civilian, were reckoned to number eight million. Sixty percent of the entire continent's population had died, mostly from disease and starvation.

It feels chillingly familiar to Jenna, still scarred from her experiences in Yemen.

Mother Courage herself, the play's eponymous heroine, together with her three children, pulls her cart across a land laid waste by war and strewn with corpses, from which she scavenges what she can to sell in order to survive. She's a battle-hardened, unapologetic profiteer, who nevertheless takes in various waifs and strays she meets along the way, soldiers, deserters, cooks and beggars, including Yvette, a child prostitute brutalised by the war. Brecht does not invite his audience to sympathise with Courage, for she is a character who continually defies sentiment and subverts what might be expected of her by a series of contradictory actions. Instead he wants them to view the bigger picture – that virtue is not rewarded in corrupt times – against which the lives of his characters unfold. They arrive and then depart, mostly without explanation, so that in the end Courage loses all three of her children and must hitch herself to her cart and pull it alone, as the war drags inexorably on. Brecht further interrupts the narrative with a series of songs, which invite further considered reflection on the part of the audience. He uses a whole gamut of theatrical devices designed to prevent them from becoming too emotionally involved and thereby losing their objectivity. His characters speak directly to them, so that they can never forget that they are watching a play. The settings are emblematic rather than representational. Harsh, rather than atmospheric lighting is deployed, and, most tellingly of all, each scene is introduced before it begins in which the audience is told what is going to happen within it, removing at a stroke any remaining element of surprise.

Yet, for all of Brecht's explicit instructions, whenever the play is performed, something altogether different happens. The actor portraying Mother Courage will bring her own unique humanity to the role, as does the former *Coronation Street* star Julie Hesmondhalgh in this particular version, so that audiences may not approve of what she does, or like her, they may even be appalled by her sometimes, but they understand her. They sympathise with the terrible choices she is faced with. They admire her tenacity, her refusal to give up, her determination to keep going no matter what fate throws at her. Courage is as Courage does…

'Now spring awakes and winter dies
The dead stay dead, the living rise
Cos if your breath and pulse ain't gone
You stagger up and carry on...'

The production at the Royal Exchange has translocated the play to the future. The year is 2080. Europe is ravaged by a war that nobody remembers the causes of any more. It simply exists. Refugees roam the land. In a constant state of flight, but with no safe haven to shelter them. The normal rules of society have broken down. Only trade continues to mean anything. But there are no goods left to buy or sell, just people, who are trafficked as commodities. Money has lost all value. The world's currencies have collapsed. People must shift how they can to survive. Mother Courage's cart is a mash-up of scrap metal and broken parts. Like something out of *Mad Max*. Yet still she endures. She holds up a mirror as if to say, 'Who dares cast the first stone...?'

Jenna, sitting on the front row, less than six feet away from the action, feels like she has been kicked in the gut by it, her face smeared in the viscera of it. But it is not revulsion she feels, but vindication. She has known for some time that she can no longer stand by and do nothing. She cannot stop the war in Yemen. She can't prevent the constant rise of casualties from the bombing by all sides, the victims of cholera and disease, the growing numbers of displaced people there. No more than she can hold back the tide. She can tell people about what's happening there – as she *has* done – but that is not enough. Yet she can still do one thing. Mother Courage may lose all her children. But she, Jenna, can do what she can to save *one* of them...

Maleek...

When the play has finished, she remains seated. She is too

stunned by what she has seen to leave at once. She thinks instead about all that will need to be done if she is to make her idea a reality.

After a few minutes she begins to come back to herself. She breathes in deeply, stands, steadies herself, and looks around.

Standing opposite her, on the far side of the circle, but still within the lunar module that hovers inside this former Cotton Exchange, floating above the old trading floor, as if it might take off at any moment and transport her to a different place, where virtue may be rewarded, she sees two faces from the past that nearly send her reeling, spinning in a different orbit altogether, familiar but strange and altered. A true *Verfremdungseffekt*.

It is Spike and Bex.

Jenna blinks just in case she is seeing things, to check she isn't dreaming.

No. She's not. They're still there. They see each other at the same moment. They wave and smile, then walk across to meet halfway, in the centre of the circle.

After the high fives and hugs the three of them stand there, staring at one another, not knowing quite what to say next. Jenna has not seen either of them for more than twenty years.

"What are you up to these days?" she asks, somewhat lamely.

It seems they are both very active in the *Extinction Rebellion* movement. This doesn't surprise her. In fact she is delighted that they are still so deeply engaged in radical underground politics. They believe in the community ownership of shared public spaces, a collective resistance opposed to the disproportionate influence of major corporations in homogenous globalisation.

"Otherwise we get a situation like the one depicted in the play," says Spike.

"What did you think of it?" asks Bex.

"I was reminded of our times in the Squat," says Jenna. "Wasn't one of the things Mother Courage said a quote we had scrawled up there?"

"The writing on the wall," smiles Bex. "It still is."

" '*What happens to the hole once the cheese has been eaten?*' " says Spike, remembering, holding up the first two fingers of each hand in imaginary quotation marks.

"Yes, that was it," says Jenna, smiling. "I never really understood it. I still don't."

"It can mean many things," says Spike sagely.

"I suppose so."

"That's why it's such a good jumping-off point for discussion and debate."

"Maybe. These days I prefer solutions to questions. I'm too impatient."

"You always were," he says kindly. "It's one of your strengths."

"My mother would disagree with you," laughs Jenna.

There is another pause.

"So," says Jenna, awkwardly, "what do you do at these *Extinction Rebellion* events?"

"We reclaim the streets," says Bex. "Have a party. Play music. Dole out free food. Dance. You should come along."

"Maybe I will," says Jenna. "It sounds like something Lance would enjoy."

"He does. He came to the one we held last summer. He arrived like Mother Courage, pulling all of his gear on a cart. Spike and I took it in turns to cycle a fixed bike to generate the electricity he needed to play his music."

Jenna smiles. She can imagine Lance enjoying that. She hears him calling out to all the people gathered there.

"Wah gwaan?" he cries.

"Mi de yah," they shout back.

"Cum wi dance di night away. Tek I tuh di limit…"

"How is he? she asks,

"Good," says Bex. "He's in St Kitts mostly. I expect you know that. Running festivals. He's found his niche."

That's what we all need to do, thinks Jenna.

Yet another pause. She should be going. But somehow none of them wants to make the first move.

"We heard you on *Desert Island Discs*," says Bex out of the blue.

"Oh? What did you think?"

"It was good. "

"Really?"

"Yeah. Though I was sorry you didn't play any Joni Mitchell."

"Oh," says Jenna, "I couldn't imagine them not being sung by you."

Bex grins sheepishly. For a moment Jenna can see the twenty-year-old student with the striped Mohican beneath Bex's current persona, which has not changed all that much. The army great-coat, the DMs, the tight jeans, the baggy jumper. The piercings, the tattoos, the short steel-grey hair shot through with rainbow stripes. Not unlike Mother Courage.

Spike looks no different. The same Rasta scholar.

"What d'you think of this place then?" asks Bex, looking around.

"I like it," says Jenna at once. "It makes me think of a space ship."

Bex immediately launches into Bowie. *Major Tom*.

"Here am I floating in my tin can
Far above the moon…"

Jenna cannot help herself joining in.

"Planet Earth is blue
And there's nothing I can do…"

"Except there is," says Spike, interrupting the song. "We can all of us do something. Each in our own way."

"Can we?" asks Jenna, suddenly serious. "Are you sure…?"

They say their goodbyes.

Jenna watches Spike and Bex walk away from her, swallowed up by the night and the city, till she can see them no longer.

She takes a last look back at the lunar module of the theatre. She remembers another of Mother Courage's maxims.

"Sometimes I see myself driving through hell with this wagon, selling brimstone. And sometimes I see myself driving through heaven, handing out provisions to wandering souls. If only we could find a place where there's no shooting, me and my children – what's left of 'em – we might rest a while…"

She is resolved…

*

Day 2260

Jenna takes off from the barren lunar landscape of the desert. She circles half the earth, floating in her tin can. When she comes back down to land, she is back where she started from. The same but not the same.

This time she is not on her own.

Walking across the tarmac beside her is a small child, tightly holding her hand.

Maleek.

"*'Ayn 'ana,*" she says in a voice so quiet she can barely be heard? "Where am I? *'Ayn tadhhab alan?* Where are we going?"

"*Alsafhat alrayiysia,*" replies Jenna. "Home."

When they finally arrive at what is to be her new home, the house in Fairfield Square in the heart of the Moravian Settlement, a small welcoming party is waiting to greet her.

Nadia, Farida, Molly, Blessing.

Ruth, Barbara, Zainab, Awa.

The women speak in low, hushed tones so as not to frighten or overwhelm her.

"*Marhabaan*," they say. "Hello. *'Alaan bik*. Welcome."

"*Shukraan*," she says. "Thank you."

"*As-Salaam-Alaikum.*"

"*Wa-Alaikum-As-Salaam.*"

And then they simply smile.

She smiles back.

They sigh.

She laughs.

Molly approaches her slowly and carefully. She is holding something in her hand, which she stretches out towards Maleek.

Maleek looks with wide eyes up to Jenna, who nods. "Yes," she says. "It's all right."

Maleek turns back to Molly, who is still holding out her hand towards her.

Resting in her open palm is a tube of bubbles. She shakes it, takes out the small wand, places it to her lips, and softly blows.

The bubble slowly expands and grows until it is the size of Maleek's face. It captures her reflection and holds it there. It floats above them, orbiting the room. Fragile, translucent, it wears an expression of pure rapture, of undiluted, joy. It is a transfiguration.

TWO

Pupae

When they are ready to pupate caterpillars seek out a suitable place to complete this part of their life cycle. It may be on a plant or tree, buried under leaf and other litter on the ground, or, in many cases, burrowed beneath the earth.

Before transformation each caterpillar spins threads of silk, by which they may float downwind. In spite of evidence of intelligence of design, where they land is often the result of chance.

Safe within the pupa, the latent moth undergoes a transformation. Clusters of cells, known as the imaginal discs, are released as blueprints for the emerging adult. As the larval tissues are broken down, the discs repurpose them, forming the legs, eyes and wings of the soon-to-be imagine.

Other key structures, however, do not break down, such as the trachea, so that it may continue to breathe through the membranous cocoon, as well as, significantly, some key neural connections. Through these the emerging imagine remembers the experiences of the caterpillar and what threats to watch out for…

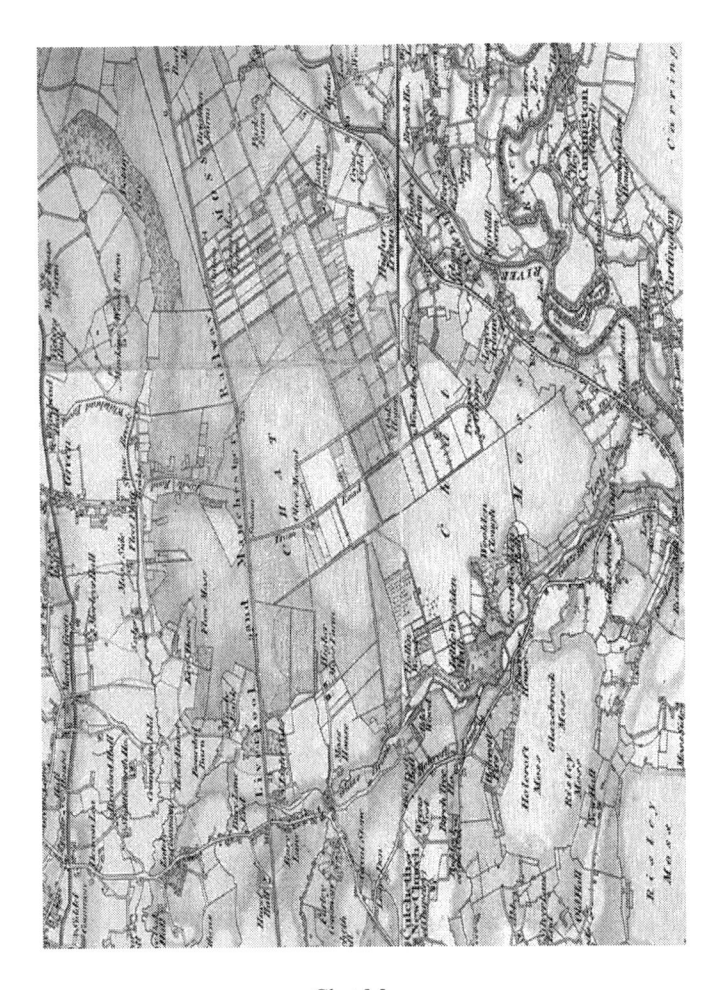

Chat Moss

4

1986

Ruth sees the letter as soon as she steps through the front door, lying on the mat, her name staring up at her in immaculate copper plate. She picks it up, turns it over. On the back is a red wax seal beneath the sender's address.

Sleigh, Son & Booth Solicitors
1 Market Street
Denton
M34 2BN

Why would a firm of solicitors from Denton be writing to her?

Then it dawns on her. Francis. Of course…

She had read of his death in a brief notice in *The Guardian* nearly six months ago…

Suddenly, at his home, aged 88 years.
Son of August Halsinger, founder of A Grain in a World of Sand, the former Glass Emporium in Manchester, and Caitlin Mallone, the renowned glass artist.

This was followed a few days later by a more appreciative obituary…

Francis will be remembered for his many breakthroughs in the fields of photography, sound recording and astronomy. Using his own specially commissioned equipment he successfully transmitted one of Henry Wood's Promenade Concerts in London live as it happened to the people of

Manchester from the summit of Heaton Park, converting the Rotunda of the Greek Temple there into a natural amplifier, treating his astonished audience to Beethoven's 'Prometheus', the Bringer of Fire.

He worked with the BBC in its early days of radio, when, in no small measure due to his input, the Manchester Studio 2ZY was at the forefront of technological and programming innovation for almost a decade during the 1920s.. He was a pioneer of the Kinamo, an early home movie camera, which allowed him to make on-the-spot records of key historical local events, such as The Kings Cup Air Race in 1930, famously won by the Manchester aviatrix 'Winsome' Winnie Brown, and the opening of Manchester Central Library by King George V in 1934.

During the War he worked on the highly secret propaganda project Radio Aspidistra, headed up by Sefton Delmer, broadcasting fake light entertainment programmes in a successful effort to lower German morale. This required him to evade enemy detection by bouncing sound waves across the ether at speeds of less than two thousandths of a second ahead of his pursuers, which he managed to achieve with his customary elan.

After the War he played a crucial role in the early development of radio telescopes alongside Sir Bernard Lovell at Jodrell Bank.

A modest man and a single man, he managed all of these remarkable achievements while at the same time running an Optometry and Photographic business in Denton, which, in later years, served as The Spectacle Gallery, housing a regular programme of exhibitions by local, emerging artists. He was a sociable man with many friends and was often to be seen at The Queen's Hotel, listening to Chamomile Catch, the much-missed Manchester Songbird…

Ruth wondered who had written this. It was accurate enough, as far as the basic facts were concerned, but it failed to do justice to the many other facets of his personality – his wit, his bonhomie, his wicked sense of humour, his kindness, his loyalty to his friends...

Nor any mention of George...

Francis was the last connection to Ruth's family and their close circle of friends. All of them had gone – Lily, Roland, Delphine, Ishtar, Cam, George, and now Francis.

This last decade had been a continuous, unbroken procession of funerals...

She looks once more at the envelope, hesitates, then nervously breaks the seal to open it. The letter is handwritten on a fine, high-quality linen paper, seemingly with a fountain pen, in the same flowing copper plate that was evident on the address.

Dear Ms Warner,

I write to you on behalf of my colleague, Mr Lester Sleigh, whose task it has been to administer probate on the estate of Mr Francis Hall, formerly Halsinger, deceased.

Having no issue, Mr Hall died without heirs, but in his Will he has left instructions for the distribution of his assets, among them a series of individually identified items, to a number of named beneficiaries.

I am advised by Mr Sleigh to invite you to present yourself in person at our office in Denton two weeks hence at 10.30am, where, providing that you can satisfactorily demonstrate that you are indeed Miss Ruth Warner of Lapwing Lane, Didsbury, niece of the late Mr George Wright, he will be delighted to hand over to you the particular item left to you by Mr Hall.

To that end we will be most obliged if you would bring with you two separate documents to verify your identity, namely a passport or driver's licence, plus a household bill containing your name and address.

We look forward to meeting you on the aforesaid date and time.

Yours faithfully,

Lorna Woods, Ms
pp L. Sleigh Esq, LLB, LLM, MLS

Ruth is intrigued. What can Francis have possibly left for her? She did not know him that well. On the outer ring of orbiting satellites only. She only ever met him through her mother, or George. And hardly at all since they had both passed. The last occasion she saw him was just before he died as it turned out. Though he looked as fit as a fiddle at the time. It had been at the Gay Pride March. He wasn't marching himself. He was being wheeled along in some kind of Roman chariot by a pair of very fetching gladiators and was clearly having the time of his life. She had been walking just behind him, wearing a rainbow-coloured, feathered Native American head-dress as part of the group Village People Barbara had insisted she wore.

Francis had died later that night.

A friend of his had tried to phone him the following morning – Giulia Lockhart, the fashion designer with the shop on King Street. When she got no reply, she decided to call round in person. She rang his bell but he didn't come down. A light was still on in an upstairs window. She opened the letter box and called out his name. Again, nothing. Giulia was puzzled. Her puzzlement turned to concern, so she called for an ambulance. When they arrived, they had to break down the front door to gain entry. They found Francis sitting in a chair, close to the lamp that Giulia had seen from below. He had evidently been reading.

"Heart attack," said one of the paramedics. "It would have been very quick."

Giulia herself had died not long afterwards. Another to add to Ruth's dolorous roll call of the dead...

Accordingly Ruth presents herself at *Sleigh, Son & Booth* at the appointed hour the following week.

"Please sit down, Ms Warner," says the avuncular Lester Sleigh after Ms Woods has shown her in. "Can we get you a coffee? Excellent. Lorna usually has a pot on the go. And perhaps we might run to a biscuit?"

"No thank you, Mr Sleigh."

"Are you sure? We have an excellent selection. Fig rolls, Garibaldis, Bourbons? You're sure you can't be tempted?"

Ruth politely declines and sits in the chair offered to her in Lester Sleigh's tastefully furnished office, with its framed photographs of Denton's Market Street over the years, depicting a constantly shifting array of shop fronts, modes of transport, and changing fashions. Only the building in which they now sit appears to have remained unaltered.

Lester catches Ruth looking at them.

"There's been a 'Sleigh's Solicitors' here for more than a century," he declares proudly. "A reassuring constant in ever-changing times. We find our clients are comforted by that sense of continuity," he adds.

"I'm sure," replies Ruth, taking a sip of her coffee, which is rather weak and tepid for her liking. She puts it down upon the table beside her.

"To business then," says Lester. He presses the buzzer on the intercom on his desk. "Could you bring in the package for Ms Warner please, Lorna? Thank you."

Lorna returns almost immediately. She carries a large cylindrical object wrapped expertly in brown paper, which she balances in front of her across the palms of both hands. She duly presents it to Lester, who, rising to receive it, then offers it to Ruth with due ceremony. He is evidently enjoying himself hugely.

Ruth looks down at the package with a bemused frown.

"Am I to open this now?" she asks.

"That is entirely up to you, Ms Warner. Such a sad business. Mr Hall was with us for more than fifty years."

"Yes," says Ruth. "Indeed." It takes her a moment to register who he is talking about. Mr Hall? Francis has never been that. He has always been just Francis. Just as he has always been a part of the fabric of her life. She still can't believe he is gone. At least her final memory of him is a happy one. After the Gay Pride Parade had finished, they had all of them gathered outside *Bookbinder's*, a jazz club on Minshull Street belonging to the Salford-born singer Elkie Brooks, where they had listened to the trumpeter Florence Blundell, who coaxed Francis to join her on stage – not that he needed much persuading – to accompany her in a glorious rendition of Noel Coward's *Mad About The Boy*. Francis had been in his element...

"Ms Warner...?"

Ruth is roused from her reverie by the discreetest of coughs from Lester Sleigh.

"I'm sorry. I was just..."

"Quite."

"I think I'll wait till I get back home before opening it. If that's all right...?"

"Of course," says Lester, inclining his head propitiously to one side. "I completely understand your wish for privacy. But before you leave, I am instructed also to give you this." With a deft flourish he pulls back the drawer in his desk, which slides open with that pleasingly quiet hum of furniture that is expertly crafted and always expensive, and produces from inside it another envelope, which he holds up circumspectly between the first two fingers of his left hand.

Ruth takes it from him. On it she sees her own name, written with characteristic boldness in Francis's instantly recognisable hand.

"Mr Hall wished you to read this first, before you open the package."

"I see. Thank you."

Juggling with the package and the envelope, she picks up her bag, collects her coat and heads for the door.

"May we arrange a taxi for you, Ms Warner?"

"No. I have my car outside."

"In that case, we wish you good day. Lorna?"

Lorna holds open the door for Ruth. Just as she is about to step outside, Lorna whispers quietly to her.

"We're so sorry for your loss. We all adored Francis..."

Half an hour later, having driven the twelve miles back to Didsbury, Ruth lays the package and the letter down upon the table in her kitchen in the house on Lapwing Lane, the house which was her adoptive grandmother's – Mrs Wright, Annie, who she never knew – then her mother Lily's, and now hers. She pauses, then picks up the envelope with Francis's flamboyant curlicued calligraphy filling every available inch. She opens it and greedily reads the letter it contains, hearing his voice in every syllable, not noticing that there is another piece of paper, yellow and faded, folded with careful precision, tucked inside the envelope...

Darling Ruth,

If you are reading this hastily scribbled missive, it can mean only one thing – that I have at last shuffled off this mortal coil for that undiscovered bourne from which no traveller returns...

Do not be sad or grieve for me. All's well that ends well, they say. Life is a shuttle. The web of it is of a mingled yarn, good and ill together. And, for the most part, mine has been good...

I have few regrets. I should like to have known my mother for longer, I should like to have spent more of my life with George, and I should like to have heard Cam sing again...

So now, before the final curtain falls, I intend to act on the instant, stand not upon the order of my going, nor feed contention in a lingering act...

How much do you know of your mother's life, Ruth? Knowing Lily as I did, I imagine she has told you all. Like the best of plays it contained five acts. The first took place within the cloistered shadows of the convent. The second in the stifling, airless doll's house of Globe Lane. The third in the hellish underworld of Angel Meadow. The fourth, her road to recovery, rescued by St George from the dragons of her dreams, her keeping of promises made but not forgotten, her life alone, as a plotter, a dispatch rider, an ack-ack girl. And the fifth, her journey back into the light – her meeting with Roland, the nurturing of her 'blossoms', the saved souls of lost children, and their final flowering with you...

When I finally returned from those four wasted years of internment on the Isle of Man, and I walked my way back to Manchester by following the line of telegraph poles marching across the land, I knew as soon as I saw it that this would be my new home. After three days of walking, I stopped beneath the sign of the giant spectacles which jutted from the wall above me. They seemed to look towards a future of unimagined possibilities. And so it has proved.

The very next day I made the necessary enquiries and purchased the premises right there and then. I have lived here ever since. The previous owner was a Mr Friedrich Kaufmann –

born a German, like me, but, also like me, someone who had lived all of his life in Manchester. For me it was from the age of one. For him, from the age of five. I know this because we were both dispatched to the Isle of Man on the same boat. We both felt the same injustice keenly. He died on the island. But not before he had carved a model yacht for his daughter, which he called 'The Tulip', because that was her favourite flower. His daughter was called Ruth. She was your grandmother. You are named after her. I expect you know this. But you may not know about the circumstances surrounding your mother's birth. For I am not sure Lily knew them herself...

Before you continue reading my letter further, you might care now to look at the newspaper clipping I have enclosed...

Ruth, her hands shaking, lays the letter to one side, and picks up the envelope once more, from where she delicately extracts the faded newspaper clipping, which she unfolds with the utmost care, fearful she might tear it where it has creased with the years...

The Manchester Union

8th May 1915

LUSITANIA SUNK!

NUMBER OF DEAD ESTIMATED AT 1000

NOT MORE THAN 600 KNOWN TO BE SAVED FROM WRECK

The Great Cunarder, *RMS Lusitania*, lies at the bottom of the ocean off the southern coast of Ireland, having been attacked at sea by a German submarine. As the dead and wounded are brought ashore, the casualty list grows...

Disturbing Scenes Follow in City Centre

Riots erupted across Manchester within minutes of the

news breaking. Angry crowds targeted shops and businesses owned and run by German families, smashing windows and setting fire to properties.

In one particularly distressing incident in Denton, a young woman, not yet twenty-one, who for the sake of her further protection this newspaper will not name, was violently attacked by a mob while trying to defend her father, a hitherto well-respected and highly-regarded optician. She was subjected to gross incivilities to her person, and, as a result, suffered a broken arm and several fractured ribs. She is now being treated in Manchester Royal Infirmary.

In the wake of this and other attacks, Mr Robin Peacock, Chief Constable for Manchester, has issued warrants for the arrest of all German shopkeepers resident in the city.

"In the interests of public safety and for the sake of the Germans themselves," his statement read, "prompt action is now required. Otherwise attacks on property might easily develop, through the natural transition of mob law, into further attacks on the person. Accordingly I am ordering the immediate impounding of all German males between the ages of seventeen and fifty-five years in readiness for their deportation in due course, as soon as His Majesty's Government has put the necessary measures in place..."

Ruth picks up Francis's letter once more. Her whole body is now trembling...

I found this clipping tucked away in a drawer in a desk in one of the rooms once I had taken possession of the property. The brave young woman referred to in the report, trying to protect her father, was of course your grandmother. Such wicked, wicked times...

Something else I found shortly after my arrival is the subject of the package, which I shall ask you now to open...

Ruth unties the string with which the package is secured and slowly unwraps the neatly folded brown paper. As she reveals what it contains, Ruth involuntarily gasps. It is a telescope. It feels quite old, not that she knows anything about such matters, but it remains in pristine condition.

She returns to the letter...

I found this telescope still on its stand on a window sill in what I presumed had formerly been used as a bedroom. Later I learned that it had in fact been Ruth's, your namesake's, the very room where your mother was born, and where your grandmother died.

The telescope, as I say, was still on its stand and pointing towards the night skies, directly through the framed outline of the sign of the spectacles, which hung just outside the window. When I looked through it on my first evening there, I discovered it was trained upon the four Galilean moons of Jupiter – Io, Europa, Callisto and Ganymede – which were all in perfect alignment. I took this to be some kind of sign. But of what I had yet to discover.

As you know, lenses are my stock-in-trade. Cameras, microscopes, binoculars, telescopes. I know a great deal about them. And I could tell at once that this was an exquisite example. A Dollond & Aitchison from around 1900. A powerful, three-draw instrument, leather-clad, with a pancreatic tube offering four levels of magnification from 35 to 50 times in finely calibrated, equal increments. The eyepiece cup was protected by an integral swivel dust protector, a most desirable embellishment.

But what made – makes – this telescope even more special – unique in fact – are two additional customisations that would have been added after purchase. The original lenses have been replaced by ones that offer even greater magnification and crystal clear vision. I believe these to be the work of Mr Kaufmann himself, who had a reputation for the excellence and precision of his lens grinding. The second addition is an inscription to be found on the bronzed brass of the tube, which is only revealed when drawn to its fullest extent. I believe Mr Kaufmann to have been responsible for this too, for he was also a highly skilled engraver. The inscription contains just two words:

'For Ruth...'

As soon as I read these words I knew the telescope had been a gift from a father to a daughter, and that here was evidence that the daughter was in the habit of observing the night skies – more precisely the four Galilean moons of Jupiter – right up until she died.

I have used this room as my own bedroom ever since. Many a night I too have chosen to observe these moons through this telescope, even though I now have much more powerful instruments at my disposal. I have been looking through it again recently, noting the course of Halley's Comet as it has once more bestowed upon us the favour of allowing us to look upon the path of its seventy-six year trajectory that brings its orbit so tantalisingly close to our own.

It is fading from us now. I shall not live to see it again. And nor, I suspect, will you. Unless you live to be a hundred and eight – which of course you might. But between now and then there will be many more miracles to witness...

I would like you to accept this telescope as a gift, not from me so much – I have merely been its temporary custodian – but from your grandmother, for it bears both your names...

'Remember me when I am gone away
Gone far away into the silent land...

Yet if you should forget me for a while
And afterwards remember, do not grieve:
For if the darkness and corruption leave
A vestige of the thoughts that once I had,
Better by far you should forget and smile
Than that you should remember and be sad...'

Francis x

Ruth props the letter against the carriage clock upon the mantelpiece in the sitting room at the front of the house. The clock had belonged to her adoptive grandfather, Hubert, whom she never knew. It has ticked steadily and reassuringly down the years, and it will continue to do so, as long as Ruth remembers to wind it each week, which she fully intends to.

She places the telescope on its stand on a table beside the French windows at the back of the room, directing its gaze back towards the sky. Tonight, when it grows darker, she will look through it herself and see what she may find there.

She gazes round the rest of the room, adorned now as it is with souvenirs from all those who have died in the past ten years. It is a *memento mori*.

As well as the clock and the telescope, there is the toy yacht made by Friedrich while he was in the Isle of Man, the only thing that tethered Lily to her lost family through her years of wandering; a series of collagraphs, collages made from bark, twigs, leaves and berries, mixed in with paint and charcoal, depicting a spindle tree in each of the four seasons, made by Lily after she'd been adopted by Annie; an early example of a Computer Logic Board from the Manchester Baby, looking like a piece of modern art, complete with its three transformers and forty-two valves all in place, which Roland had helped to design and develop; a copy of one of the first photographs ever taken by George, on the day of *The Kings Cup Air Race*, a snapshot of the sixteen-year-old Giulia Lockhart, the newly-crowned 'Miss Manchester Ice Creams', swatting with her tiara at a small dog snapping at her ankles; a recording by Cam; a dry, brittle bird's nest that had once belonged to Delphine; a crude drawing on a square of hardboard of Halley's Comet, when it last appeared in 1910, made by Eve, Delphine's mother, from a mixture of mosses and plant dyes, the tail-end of whose current visitation Ruth hopes to catch a last glimpse of through the telescope left to her by Francis later that night; and finally a framed sampler, with yellow tulips embroidered in running stitch around its borders, with a verse from Deuteronomy in its centre, stitched by Annie on the night that George stumbled over Lily in Angel Meadow...

'That which was lost is found...'

All of these objects, which are only indirectly linked to Ruth for the most part, weigh oppressively on her. They have become a heavy responsibility. Almost as if she has become the curator of a museum devoted to preserving the memories of her dead family and their friends – *their* friends, not her own, though she was fond of them all. Freighted with such significance and meaning, they threaten to drag her down, like the locks and chains of Marley's Ghost, which she must carry around with her always, wherever she goes. And yet...

And yet...

Precisely because they are connected so closely to the people who have combined to shape her into the person she now is, she feels a duty – and also a desire – to maintain these links. To preserve them. To make sure that none of them become lost again, as so many of them have been at one time or another. They represent an unbroken line, so finely spun as to be almost invisible, but strong for all that, connecting her, not only to her ancestors stretching back through the generations, but to Manchester itself, the way, not unlike a spider's web, it has spread over the centuries to cover almost the entire globe. Producing silk from the spinneret glands at the tip of her abdomen, the spider will typically start in a modest way, to protect her body and her eggs, as a means of basic survival. Then, once she is confident of her safety, she will cautiously begin to extend her range, for hunting purposes, to feed her eggs when they hatch. First she will send out guide lines to ensure she can always find her way back home. Next, signal lines, in order to be able to communicate with other spiders, either as a plea for help, or as a warning to unwelcome intruders. These are usually earthbound. Finally, when she is in her full pomp, she will spin aerial webs, constructions so delicate, yet of such extraordinary tensile strength, greater than their equivalent weight in steel but far more elastic, so that they appear to float, to defy gravity, tubular webs, funnel webs, tangle webs, sheet webs, and the spectacular spiral orb webs, architectural wonders that can, in some instances, when spun cooperatively, cover vast distances.

Ruth feels, if she is not careful, that she might get caught up in such a web, a web that she herself has helped to build, wrapping up these precious inherited objects in sticky cocoons, when what they really want is to be dusted clean, taken out into the light, where they can be seen by others, appreciated for what they represent, not just as part of their own individual stories, but for everyone. She understands that she needs to stop looking into the past, as if she needs permission somehow from all these objects, but instead to forge her own path, create her own objects, which she might pass on to those who come after her.

She looks around at them all once again. These sticky cocoons are not so much caught up in a spider's web, as buried beneath the earth, like the pupae of a whisper of moths, the Manchester moths, the *biston betularia*, the *medionigra* version, the more recently evolved stronger, more resilient hybrid of the original *typica* and the later *carbonaria*, who are simply biding their time underground, waiting for the right moment when they can emerge in their full glory as the adult imagines. Ruth knows that she must press her ear close to the ground, to listen to that whisper as it grows into a roar...

She lifts the telescope left to her by Francis, with her own name eerily inscribed upon it. She realises that when she looks through it, deep into space, to try and identify if she can those four Galilean moons of Jupiter – Io, Europa, Callisto and Ganymede – she will in fact be looking back into the past. The light those moons are sending back to her is already an hour old by the time it reaches her. An hour ago she had not known of the existence of the telescope. The light from Sirius, the brightest star in the night sky, is nearly nine years away. Nine years ago George, Francis, Giulia and Delphine were all still alive. While the light from Orion's Belt takes an unimaginable fifteen hundred years to reach her. Round about the same time the Romans were leaving Manchester...

She needs somehow to find a way of training that telescope towards what matters *now*, in the present, and in her more immediate future. But how? Without disrespecting the trust and faith placed in her by all who have made her the keeper of the keys to her own museum...?

She picks up the record by Cam and places it on the turntable. She will listen to this once more as the start of a kind of exorcism, a necessary shedding of the exoskeleton of the pupa, before she hardens, then stretches her wings...

Following the familiar warmth of the crackle and hiss as Ruth carefully places the stylus onto the disc, Cam's rich, mellifluous, honeyed tones fill the quiet of the room...

"How do you measure a life
Beyond the investment of years

Daughter and mother and wife
Each with their suitcase of fears?

And how do you balance the worth
When the losses outnumber the gains
And the marks your feet make on the earth
Are washed away by the spring rains?

One bushel, two pecks
The balance and checks
Tournant en l'air, port de bras

Accepting our fates
In the measures and weights
En unités avoirdupois...

The Song of the Weights & Measures. Cam's voice instantly transports her back through the years, to a morning in 1973, when an army of bulldozers moved in to demolish *The Queen's Hotel*, and she, Ruth, had been there, aged just nineteen, with Lily, with George, with Francis, and others who *they* all knew but *she* didn't, standing outside in the cold, beside the statue of Queen Victoria, on the edge of Piccadilly Gardens, witnessing the end of an era...

5

1973

Manchester Evening News

24th May 1973

DEMOLITION MARKS END OF AN ERA

Special Souvenir Edition

Photo by George Wright

Yesterday, on an appropriately unseasonable chilly morning in May, *The Queen's Hotel*, one of Manchester's most loved landmarks, was demolished, after having lain empty for almost three years.

On a day which also happened to coincide with the birthday of Queen Victoria, after whom the hotel was named when it first opened in the summer of 1848, a small crowd of friends, supporters and well-wishers gathered to pay their respects and say their last goodbyes. Standing alongside the Onslow Ford statue of the old Queen on the corner of Portland Street and Piccadilly Gardens, who was clearly looking 'not amused' to witness the demolition of her namesake, this was the closest the hotel's loyal followers could get to their favourite old haunt, on this, her final outing.

A far cry from her former glory days...

Here she is just five years ago, with a Rolls Royce pulling up alongside her colourful, striped awning, with another of her many illustrious guests.

In her hey-day, the hotel was described as being *'known not only over the whole breadth of the United Kingdom but throughout the entire world, its patrons comprising the élite of all nationalities visiting the city of Manchester, the Empire's premier cosmopolis.'*

Hotel records show that this was no exaggerated claim, for that élite included the Kings of Belgium, Portugal and Romania, the Emperor of Brazil, Prince Napoleon, President Grant, General Gordon of Khartoum, Dickens, Thackeray, and countless others.

Here's an almost identical view of *The Queen's* shortly after she first opened. The two photographs have been taken a hundred and twenty years apart, but apart from the fashions of the clothes and the modes of transport being used, little else has changed...

Originally the home of wealthy textile tycoon William Houldsworth, in 1845 the house was left to his nephew, Mr Thomas Houldsworth, a keen racehorse breeder and owner of the Houldsworth Cotton Factory on Little Lever Street, just off Piccadilly. It was he who transformed this fine town house into an elegant hotel.

An advertisement from the time gives a flavour of its ambition:

'Mr T. Houldswourth has the honour to inform the Nobility, Gentry, and Public in general, that a new hotel is to be opened to his friends and patrons on the 20th of March, within most eligible and spacious premises occupying a site of approximately 810 square yards of land, which are about to be converted into a first-rate Family and Commercial Hotel, situate in Piccadilly, Manchester; convenient to the railway stations and intended to be called The Queen's Hotel. The establishment is furnished in an elegant style, and with every comfort that can be suggested. It is a large building in the Italian style. The porch is projecting, with a broken pediment. The capitals of the pilasters are original and in very good taste, and this is equally true of some other ornamental parts. The Smoking Room is ventilated on an improved plan. The Billiard Room is complete with every modern improvement. Hot, cold and shower baths are available on the premises. An ordinary 'every day' at half past one. Dinners, routes and balls provided. Raw ice constantly on sale...'

In the 20th century *The Queen's* continued to establish its reputation for its fine cuisine. It was particularly renowned for its turtle soup. Live turtles were kept in tanks in the hotel's cellars, not only for use within the hotel, but for wider export. *'Turtles sent to any part of the kingdom,'* was their promise, and they became the hotel's emblem.

The 1920s saw the arrival of the first New Orleans Jazz Band in Manchester, when Louis Mitchell's Dixie Kings became the hotel's first live resident musicians. They were soon joined by a young singer by the name of Chamomile Catch, the Manchester Songbird, who quickly gained an ardent following.

Mlle Chamomile Catch
The Manchester Songbird

Cam, as she was affectionately known, stayed at *The Queen's* for the next thirty years, the one becoming completely synonymous with the other. So that when the Manchester Songbird sang for the final time in 1958, some say that the fortunes of the hotel began to fade from that moment on. She was irreplaceable and so was simply never replaced. Other hotels have opened in the city, other bars play live music, and gradually the owners of *The Queen's* have had to bow to the inevitable and bring her long and glorious reign to an end.

It is a sad day for all who remember her in her prime, and so, fittingly, let us leave the final words to Cam. Born the daughter of a Louisiana freed slave and a Native American escapee from a Wild West Show in Belle Vue, the very first song Cam sang at *The Queen's* was a Creole song her mother, Clémence Audubon Lafitte, taught her.

> "J'ai passé devant ta porte
> J'ai crié bye bye à la belle
> Y'a personne qui m'a pas répondu
> Oh-Yé-Yaille mon cœur fais mal..."

Photo by George Wright

*

They have agreed to meet by the statue of Queen Victoria. Or as near to it as they can get. George, Francis, Lily and Ruth.

Ruth is running late. Lily has been having a bad morning. A week ago she began her second round of chemo, and she has been feeling rough ever since. She seems to be running the entire gamut of possible side effects. Tiredness, fatigue, anaemia, difficulty sleeping, loss of appetite, dry skin, broken nails, nausea, mouth ulcers, nose bleeds, hair loss. She has a card on the notice board in her kitchen, which says, 'Cancer's not for cissies.' "Hear, hear to that", she says.

When she first detected the lump in her breast, it was already well advanced. The treatment has had to be aggressive as a consequence. She goes to Christie's, the oldest and largest cancer hospital in Europe, on Wilmslow Road in Withington.

"Just down the road," she'd joked when her first appointment came through, then winced with the pain. "What's the prognosis?" she'd asked the consultant before he could say a word. When he had replied with the usual platitude – "it's too early to tell," – she had immediately countered, "Don't fuck with me, Doctor. I want the truth."

"It *is* the truth," he replied, apparently unphased by her directness. "Nothing you say can shock me. I've heard it all before. So please don't feel you have to in any way censor yourself."

"Don't worry. I shan't."

"Good," he said. "Then I think we understand one another. You have a better chance of beating it if you are prepared to fight it. Your determination and spirit are your best weapons."

"I hope you've got something stronger," she said.

"We'll do our best," he said.

And they had. The first round of chemo pole-axed her. Now the second round is threatening to outdo even that.

But in the face of everything the disease and the treatment can throw at her, Lily's determination remains undaunted, her spirit unbowed.

Even so, it has been a struggle for Ruth to get her ready to leave the house this morning.

"Do you have to go?" she asks her mother, who looks as white as a sheet.

"No," says Lily. "I don't have to. But I want to. I made a promise. And I never break a promise…"

It's true. She doesn't. She never has. Ruth knows this to be so. It always has been. Ever since she promised to return to St Bridget's Orphanage for Jenny and Pearl on the day she was being secretly removed herself against her will in the middle of the night. Against all the odds, she was as good as her word. Just as she was when George found her half-naked and sick in the mud of Angel Meadow and offered to take her to a place of safety, only for her to try and wriggle away from his grasp in order to salvage a tattered, threadbare bundle of rags lying drenched and forlorn in a puddle.

"What's to stop you from just running away?" a worried George had asked her, before letting go of her wrist.

"I won't," she had said. "I promise. And I never break a promise."

And she hadn't. She had returned to him meekly clutching

the pathetic bundle closely to her, as the rain continued to pour in torrents.

That bundle had turned out to be the toy yacht, made for her by her grandfather, who she never knew, and passed on to her by her mother, who she also never knew.

The yacht now sits on a shelf in Lily's bedroom, in the house where she now lives out the last of her days, the same house that George had taken her to for sanctuary on the night he had quite literally stumbled upon her…

"We'd best get a move on," says Ruth, "if we're to get there on time…"

Reluctantly Lily has allowed Ruth to push her the last hundred yards from where they have parked the car in the wheel chair provided by Christie's. Lily hates it, the confinement and dependency of it. But Ruth tries to persuade her to see it otherwise.

"Think of it as your friend," she says, "enabling you to get to places you wouldn't be able to by yourself. Like today."

Lily is stubborn – she has always been – but she recognises the sense in her daughter's words.

"When did you get so smart all of a sudden?"

"I can't imagine," grins Ruth. "It can't have been from you."

Mother and daughter regard each other with a raised eyebrow.

"University must be teaching you something after all," says Lily eventually.

"That must be it," agrees Ruth ruefully.

Ruth is almost twenty. She's coming to the end of her second year studying for a degree in Psychology. She started it at Leeds, but when Lily became ill, she arranged a transfer to Manchester, so that she can be on hand to take care of her if the disease worsens. Not so much if, as when.

"It's OK," she tells George, when she first comes back. "With Dad dying a couple of years back, there's no one else."

"There's me," replies George. "I only live up the road."

"Six and a half miles," Ruth reminds him. "No. It's fine. Well – not fine obviously, but it is what it is. I'll manage. *We'll* manage. If I need any help, I'll be sure to ask you for it."

"See that you do. Please."

"I'll give you a copy of my timetable. If you could pop in on those days when I might have to stay late? Or when I've got an assignment to finish?"

George nods. "We'll work it out," he says.

And by and large, they have...

By the time Ruth and Lily reach the statue of Queen Victoria, quite a crowd has gathered. It takes them a while to spot anyone they know. Or rather, anyone Lily knows. Apart from George and Francis, Ruth doesn't know anyone. This was all before her time. *The Queen's Hotel.*

Francis catches sight of them first and hurries to join them. Giulia Lockhart is by his side. After each of them has kissed Lily, they appraise the wheel chair with a professional eye.

"I could decorate this for you," says Giulia, "if you would like? Some ribbon here, some feathers there – *abracadabra, alakazam* – in no time at all I could transform it into..."

"What? A tart's boudoir?" laughs Lily.

"A carriage fit for a queen," corrects Giulia.

"Really?" interrupts Francis, striking a pose. "You'd do all that *pour moi*?"

Giulia playfully pinches his cheek. "No wonder you used to like this place so much," she says, pointing to the hotel's name.

"My home from home."

"Not for much longer," says George, who now joins them. He carries his camera as usual and stoops to take a quick snap of Lily. "Hi, Sis," he says.

"Hi," she replies quietly, then wheels herself away a few yards.

She has positioned herself behind the statue of Queen Victoria, from where she can get a better view of the other sculpture, carved on the opposite side of the plinth on which Victoria sits. *Maternity*. A bronze mother with her children, one on each arm, and above them, St George, rearing up on his horse as he triumphantly slays the dragon.

"I used to come here when I lived on the streets," she says. "This was one of my regular pitches. Cam found me here one evening and tried to offer me some food, but I ran away."

"You came back, though," says George, gently placing his hand upon her shoulder.

"Yes," says Lily, turning to look back up at her adoptive brother. "I was waiting for St George to come and rescue me. And he did. But not on a horse. A DOT Racer motor bike."

"A most reliable steed," declares George, smiling. He points to where it is parked further down Portland Street.

Lily smiles, then shivers.

Ruth is immediately at her side – Giulia, too, who wraps her own shawl around Lily's painfully thin shoulders.

Allowing a moment's pause, Francis again steps forward.

"How fitting therefore that I should now present you with this!"

He places a portable cassette player on the marble steps leading up to the statue.

"This is no ordinary machine," he declares, launching into his old familiar sales patter. He may no longer have a shop, having converted the optician's in Denton to a gallery more than a decade ago, where he now regularly exhibits George's photographs, but he has lost none of his former gifts.

"The Manchester Songbird may be seventy-five," he says, "or would have been, had she not been taken away from us before her time, but age cannot wither her, nor custom stale her infinite variety, and today, through the wonders of modern technology, she will sing for us once again. Ladies and Gentlemen," he continues, holding up the cassette player for all to see, "I give you the Tandberg TCD 3014, known in the trade as the 'Dragon Slayer'. A beast of a machine designed and manufactured in Norway in a direct response to Nakamichi's earlier standard-bearer, the 'Dragon'. Hence her name. The gold standard in state-of-the-art, high-end performance cassette decks. With four separate motors incorporating dual flywheels to stabilise speed and achieve superior tape alignment across an electro-magnetic reed-head no bigger than a sugar cube, I can promise you, Cam will never have sounded better..."

"Except when she sang live of course," quips a woman in her thirties, who has just arrived.

"Naturally," admits Francis. "But the next best thing."

"Anita?" says Lily to the recent arrival. "Is it you?"

"I couldn't miss this," she says. "This is where so many things began for me."

Lily nods and takes Anita's offered hand in her own. She is so grateful for the human contact. Normally, when people discover that she has cancer, they keep their distance, as if they fear they might somehow catch it from her by touch or proximity. But not today. Today she is among friends. Everyone is a friend today.

"Me too," she says, in answer to Anita.

"Not all of them good, mind," continues Anita. "But important."

"Yes," says Lily.

Actually, she thinks, with the exception of that first encounter with Cam, when fear and embarrassment had got the better of her, all her memories of *The Queen's* have been positive ones.

"This is where Roland and I spent our wedding night," she says.

She hears Cam's voice, echoing down the years. *"Long ago and far away..."*

While Lily is drifting away on her memories, Ruth takes the opportunity to take Anita to one side, out of her mother's earshot. "Before you ask," she says in a low voice, "Roland died. Two years ago. Bronchial pneumonia."

"Oh." Anita puts her hand to her mouth. "I didn't know," she whispers. "Thank you for telling me..."

Francis has now finished assembling his sound equipment. He claps his hands and calls for quiet.

"*Mesdames et Messieurs,*" he says, "*meine Damen und Herren*, Ladies and Gentlemen, I give you once again The Manchester Songbird, Mademoiselle Chamomile Catch."

He presses 'play' and Cam's unforgettably husky tones drift across Piccadilly on this cold May morning. Everyone pauses to listen to her. Even the traffic temporarily stops. Her voice touches them all uniquely, evoking particular memories for each.

"And how can you count the true cost
Of everything you leave behind
Or retrieve all those things that were lost
Out of sight but yet not out of mind?

And how do you weigh in the scales
The minuses 'gainst every plus
When you step from the usual trails
To find a new journey for us?

So how to contain
Two links in a chain
Accroché dans la balançoire?

Let's meet at the gates
In the measures and weights
Listé dans l'avoirdupois..."

Lily looks around as she listens. As well as George and Francis, Giulia and Anita, there are other faces she begins to pick out from the crowd gathered by the statue, listening to the song with the kind of reverence more usually associated with being in a church, faces she has not seen for many years, not since she last came here, on the day of Cam's funeral, after which the hotel no longer played live music.

Isn't that Giancarlo, she wonders, the young desk clerk who brought me Roland's coat one winter's night, after I had stepped out for some fresh air and had been joined by Cam? The night I learned that the young boy who had saved Roland's life when his parachute became caught in the canopy of a tree in Salford's Buile Hill Park was none other than Cam's own son, Richie, who had become a pilot because of the words Roland spoke to him that night, of seeing angels among the stars, when the Northern Lights danced above them, turning the buckling sky inside out...?

And who is that standing beside Giancarlo? Elderly and frail, but still determinedly upright, as if listening to Cam singing is akin to an old soldier remembering the fallen on Armistice Day? Could it be Luigi? Giancarlo's Uncle? Surely not? He must be a hundred if he's a day...

Ninety-eight, she learns later. He was recalling the train of events that began with the explosion more than eighty years before, that destroyed *The Royal Pomona Hotel*, where he had just started work as a bell-hop, that subsequently led him to spend almost three quarters of his life behind the desk here at *The Queen's*, then afterwards silently patrolling the corridors and staircases of the hotel, long after the guests had left or retired to their rooms for the night. To him every grain of polished wood along the banister rails held a special story, known only to him. What secrets he could tell, had he a mind to. But he does not have a mind to, has never had. It is his discretion which has won him the life-long trust and gratitude of his customers down the years. Now those secrets will be lost, plundered by the wrecking ball. They will never be prised from Luigi's lips...

Lily scans more faces. So many of them familiar, even if she can no longer put a name to them all. Wait, though. One face in particular troubles her. She feels she really should know him. His hair flops down upon his forehead in a somewhat dilettante fashion. He tries to light a cigarette but struggles as a gust of wind blows out match after match. His face darkens as he turns away and borrows a stranger's to light his own at last. The way his mouth pouts so sulkily, then transforms with the relief he experiences from that first inhalation of tobacco. Now she remembers him. It is Arnold Murray, Alan Turing's tormentor. The years have not been kind to him. He was such a pretty boy back then, she remembers. It was no wonder he had so many admirers. They circled around him like gulls. Poor Alan never stood a chance. He was completely gulled, failing his own Turing test. Lily has heard that Arnold was filled with remorse afterwards for what he had done. So he bloody well should have been, she thinks. He went to London for a while, she understands, playing the guitar in the coffee bar scene there, but that after a couple of years he came back. Last she knew he was working as a mental health nurse at the nearby Prestwich Hospital. She wonders if that is what he still does, whether he took it up as some form of redemption. She shakes her head. She learned long ago that, unless and until you forgive yourself, it doesn't matter how many other people do. You'll never be able to move on...

Her eyes now alight upon Anita. She is someone who has moved on, and no mistake. A pillar of the Moss Side community now. A highly respected, indispensable administrator at the Medical Centre there. She has been mouthing the words as Cam has sung them. *Accroché dans la balançoire*. The weights and measures, hanging in the balance.

Anita appears to have the scales in perfect parity and equipoise these days. Lily looks at her more closely. Her eyes are gazing at a single fixed point. Lily follows their direction, until she reaches what, or rather who, their sights are trained upon. It is Roy – Beau – Leroy Beauregard King, who once upon a time Anita's eyes would feast upon with such hunger that she would starve herself of every other sustenance just to get an extra morsel of him. She could simply never satisfy her insatiable thirst for every last drop of him. Nor could she ever have imagined that there would come a time when she would grow tired of him, that the taste of him would turn bitter in her mouth. But it did. And all too quickly. But now, more than a decade later, she can look at him with tolerant affection once more and smile with fondness at her own foolishness. She does not now regret those few fiery tempestuous years she spent with him, but is happy that she now occupies much calmer waters. There have been other men since Roy, and there is a good chance there will be more, though there is no one special just now. She has her hands full with her son – *their* son – Lance, who Roy never sees, but who is turning out to be a chip off the old block. Not yet fourteen he has inherited his father's fine looks and easy tongue. He can charm the birds out of the trees with his talk. Already, she has noticed, the local girls are beginning to gather in flocks around him.

She links her arm through Roy's, who practically leaps out of his skin in surprise. He raises his pork-pie hat from his head, giving Anita a mock bow, then quickly replaces it. But not before Lily has had chance to notice how that luxurious crop of close black curls has begun to grow thin on top, with flecks of grey in between.

Lily smiles. At her heels she always senses time's wingèd chariot hurrying near these days. She is particularly susceptible to signs of it in people's hair. Especially since her own has started to fall out in handfuls. She adjusts the knitted rainbow-coloured hat that Giulia has given her, pulling it more firmly down so that it covers her ears. Not out of vanity – she doesn't care a jot if people see her how she truly is – but to keep out the cold. The wind has picked up more. It blows through the police tape that has been put up all around the hotel to keep people at a safe distance, which flaps like a lost bird trapped inside an empty room, fluttering against a dusty window-pane, trying to stave off those deserts of vast eternity that lie before it.

Roy has his trumpet tucked under one arm. Cam has finished the second verse and chorus of the song on Francis's recording of her. Lily can picture the way she would step away from the microphone at such moments, leaving centre stage for the band for a while, though somehow everyone's eyes would remain fixed upon her, even in the shadows, like today, years after she has stepped away for good. Roy lifts the trumpet to his lips, tips back his head and adds a new solo within the instrumental break. The notes soar into the sky, aching but true, improvised but sure, unpredictable but inevitable, tumbling one into another, gathering in pace and momentum, until they can go no further, and they break, faltering but pure, yearning to begin again.

Just when Lily thinks she can take such bitter sweetness no more, he pauses, at exactly the moment when Cam returns to sing the final verse.

"So how do you measure a life
Beyond the investment of years?
Take heart from the storms and the strife
That nobody quite disappears

A cast in the colour of eyes
An expression that crosses the face
For nobody ever quite dies
In all of us part of you stays..."

And she does, in all of them, gathered here to witness her last rites. Her voice sings for them all.

"Eight furlongs one mile
The ghost of a smile
Not goodbye, but only au revoir

We'll end the debates
In the measures and weights
C'est la chanson de l'avoirdupois..."

The last note hangs in the air, reverberating with memory. The people hold their collective breath. But the moment does not last for long. Before they can exhale, the giant wrecking ball swings high above their heads. Their eyes as one trace its pre-determined arc as it smashes into the metre-tall letters that spell out the hotel's name in the once-proud sign above the now ripped and tattered striped awning, leading to the padlocked front door. It lands with a sickening crunch, splintering through the glass and metal, like the baying cry of a once-great beast, a Maharajah elephant, chained and shackled, now being torn apart, limb from limb.

The crowd stands firm in the face of such dispassionate desecration. As one, they burst into defiant applause. Lily, Ruth. Francis, George. Anita, Roy. Luigi, Giancarlo. Giulia, Arnold. All of them. They clap till their hands are sore. But they do not stop until the demolition is complete, and all that remains of *The Queen's Hotel* is a shell, a husk, a skeleton. But while they applaud, something of the old girl lingers, her last bow.

When the clapping finally stops, its pulse remains, like a heartbeat...

A heartbeat that continues for Lily for one year more.

She manages to make it to Ruth's graduation.

Just.

Then the heartbeat stops.

She is not yet fifty-nine...

The same players who had gathered to say their last farewell to *The Queen's* the previous year now come together again in St Paul's Methodist Church in Didsbury for Lily's funeral, the same location that had served for her wedding to Roland twenty-five years before.

There are others there too, of course – Delphine, as upright and commanding as ever; Anita's brothers, Christopher and Clive; Pearl and Lamarr, together with their five children, Lamarr Jr, Candice, Dwight, Kendra and LaShawne. Lamarr Jr and Candice have children of their own too now, and the extended family fills two pews between them. Many of the 'blossoms' have come too, the orphaned children Lily had fostered in the years immediately following the end of the War, as many as Ruth has been able to track down.

Also there is Jenny, who Lily promised she would come back for, a promise she had faithfully kept, as she had with all her promises. Jenny stands before the entire congregation.

"I sang this hymn in this very spot when Lily got married here," she says through a sheen of tears. "It feels right to sing it again today."

Everyone sits spellbound as Jenny now sings, with her companion, the ageing Gertrude Riall still accompanying her, Mendelssohn's *Hear My Prayer*.

"The enemy shouteth, the godless come fast
Iniquity, hatred, upon me they cast

The wicked oppress me, ah where shall I fly?
Perplexed and bewildered, O God hear my cry..."

Her voice soars up through the vaulted nave of Henry Hill Vale's Victorian Gothic chapel.

"O for the wings, for the wings of a dove
Far away, far away would I rove
In the wilderness build me a nest
And remain there for ever at rest..."

It rises past the lancet windows, the gleaming colonnades and marble columns with their carved capitals towards the painted barrel roof depicting flights of birds, where the notes hang miraculous and unbowed.

Their two voices could not be more different, Jenny's and Cam's. Jenny's is as light as air itself, as ethereal as Cam's is rooted deep in the earth. Together they run through the years like water, each combining with the other to create a spark, whose flames may yet ignite a hard-struck future.

6

1971

Cadishead & Irlam Guardian

Wednesday 15th April 1971

BOB'S LANE FERRY DISASTER

5 Die As Ship Canal Self-Ignites?

Tragedy struck our small town yesterday when the Manchester Ship Canal suddenly, and without warning, self-ignited. The explosion destroyed the ferry boat conveying factory workers from nearby Partington and Warburton, on their way to the Steel, Tar, Soap and Margarine Works at Irlam, killing up to five men.

The historic ferry has been carrying passengers over the Canal for almost 80 years, the short crossing from Our Lady of Lourdes School on Lock Lane in Warburton to Bob's Lane in Cadishead taking less than five minutes. It has been estimated that for each of those years the ferry has carried more than 35,000 people.

The first ferry began in 1894, immediately after the Ship Canal, linking Manchester to Liverpool, was opened by Queen Victoria. It was set up by Mr Sammy Fish, a Native American who had helped to dig the Canal, having previously worked as a starvationer on the underground waterways of The Delph. He and his wife Eve successfully ran the ferry until 1919, when sadly both succumbed to the ravages of Spanish Flu. Their daughter, Delphine, worked as a teacher for the deaf before going on to become Professor of Audiology at Manchester University.

The Tragedy Unfolds

Yesterday dawned bright and fair, a lovely spring morning filled with promise. The early bird catches the worm, they say, and the current ferryman, Mr Bernard Carroll, aged 27 years of Lock Lane, Warburton, began his shift as usual at 5.30am. Normally he would continue right through until 11pm at night, with trips every 15 minutes.

But on this particular morning Mr Carroll was worried.

Strange Smell...

During the first couple of crossings, he had noticed an unpleasant and unusual smell. Several of his passengers had complained of feeling unwell during the short trip, so Bernard decided to suspend the service until he had sought further advice. As he was phoning the Police, several passengers, waiting on the jetty, were worried that they would be late for work and decided to row themselves over to the opposite bank.

On his return Bernard could see the boat in the middle of the Canal with the passengers obviously affected by a 4-foot-high mist that had started to rise from the surface of the water. He jumped into another boat and immediately began to row towards them.

Eyewitnesses later told the Police that when Mr Carroll was about 20 yards from the other boat the Canal suddenly exploded into a sea of flames, and both boats were engulfed in fire. This was followed by a series of explosions which shook houses up to a quarter of a mile away. A one-mile length of the Canal became a river of fire 60 feet high and nearby houses in Lock Lane had to be evacuated. Nothing could be done until the flames had died down, then both boats were brought to the bank.

The Ferryman had died and five people in the other boat were badly burned.

A Community Stunned...

The injured were taken to Hope Hospital in Salford,

where one died on arrival. The others were later moved to the Burns Unit at Withington Hospital, where they are currently still being treated. Some time later it was discovered that three other passengers from the boat were missing, having either jumped or fallen into the blazing water. The Canal was too polluted for Police frogmen to be used and too deep to be dragged, and so the whereabouts of the three missing persons are still not known, but it must be presumed that they have not survived, bringing the likely death toll to five.

The whole community is stunned by the disaster, which has devastated the lives of nine local families...

Delphine does not read this report when it first comes out. She has not taken the *Cadishead & Irlam Guardian* in over half a century. There has been no need for her to do so. She learns of the news instead through a letter from her good friend, Esther. Or Ishtar, as she now describes herself. Though this, too, is delayed in reaching her, for Delphine has very recently moved and has not yet got around to letting everyone in her address book know of her current change in circumstances.

She now lives in a ground floor flat in Newbury House on Daisy Bank Road in leafy Victoria Park, which offers sheltered housing for the retired. It is completely independent – Delphine would not wish it to be anything other. She has her own front door and separate entrance, but there is a communal lounge, should she desire company, and an on-site warden, offering twenty-four hour emergency support, if she should need it.

'Not that I do,' writes Delphine, 'yet. But it is well to be prepared.'

Newbury House was, half a century before, the home of Sir Henry Platt, the eminent orthopaedic surgeon from the Manchester Royal Infirmary, later becoming a nursing home for wounded soldiers during the Second World War. It was converted for its current use in the 1950s.

Delphine had been sorry to leave her flat on Upper Brook Street, where she had been happy for more than forty years. It had been so convenient for her while working at the University, and she enjoyed being at the heart of things. However, with the loss of the green square she overlooked, which she especially enjoyed in the spring when the cherry trees were in full blossom, the enlargement and expansion of the hospital, and the development of new roads, she had become increasingly isolated and cut off there. The year before she finally moved she had been nearly knocked down on two occasions, once by a car and once by a speeding bicycle.

This will not do, she had thought. I am becoming a liability. The thought of becoming dependent on others in any way whatsoever was repugnant to her. When a former colleague told her of the sheltered accommodation in Victoria Park, she seized the opportunity.

"Perfect for retired folk like you and me," he had said.

She could have kicked him. Retired? How she hated that word. She may have no longer been lecturing in the Audiology Department, but she still kept herself busily occupied with the various committees and boards she sat upon. And as for 'sheltered', well... that was possibly worse. While she supposes that for some the notion of a university professor might conjure thoughts of ivory towers, rarefied academic seclusion from the world, she herself saw it quite differently. She always thrust herself full-tilt-pell-mell into whatever came her way. As a child she had loved that line from the three witches in *Macbeth*, 'When the hurly burly's done, when the battle's lost and won.' She has been in the hurly burly for as long as she can remember, and she has loved it. She has fought plenty of battles too. She's never been afraid of taking on what others might have considered a lost cause. Especially if she has caught a whiff of injustice or unfairness in the air. Yes, she's waged her fair share of battles. Lost a few, but won plenty more. It feels fitting to have come to what was once a home for wounded soldiers. Not that she regards herself in any way as wounded. Far from it. But here, in this mistakenly named 'retirement' home. she feels secure – secure that she can now continue much as she was before, far from retired and further still from retiring, but safe in the knowledge that, should anything unforeseen waylay her, help is on hand, and she will not be beholden to anyone.

She is not far from the University, there is a bus stop round the corner, and there is room in her ground floor flat – she shan't miss the stairs of Upper Brook Street – for the things that matter to her. Her books, her music, her few possessions. The brittle bird's nest that she had rescued from her parents' burnt wooden cabin in the woods above the ferry at Bob's Lane still occupies pride of place on a small table by the window, which catches the early sun, where she likes to sit and read her *Manchester Guardian* each morning, and attend to her correspondence.

It is on just such a morning, when she is enjoying reading about the absurdity brought on by the *Law Reform (Miscellaneous Provisions) Act*, that she first learns of the incident at Bob's Lane Ferry. The Act, which was passed the previous day, sets out to provide for any party entering an agreement to marry, who in turn makes a gift of property to the other party on the basis that it shall be returned should the agreement be ended, the right to be able to seek the recovery of that property if the decision to marry is reversed. What, therefore, asks Alastair Hetherington in his Leader column that day, is the legal status of an engagement ring? It turns out that any such ring is presumed to be what is termed an *absolute* gift, meaning that the recipient of it is entitled to keep it, *unless* it can be proved that the ring was only given on the condition that, if the marriage does not take place, it should be duly returned to the giver.

The problem identified by Hetherington is when do you have that tricky conversation with your betrothed? The cartoonist Les Gibbard has great fun with this, depicting a young suitor down on one knee, proffering an ostentatious ring to a suitably blushing fiancée-to-be, saying, "By the way, darling, if we end up separating before we get married, you will give me the ring back, won't you...?"

More seriously, the newly-passed Act remains ambiguous on the legality of any party seeking to recover property if the agreement has been to co-habit rather than marry, especially as far as the woman is concerned.

Delphine crossly throws the newspaper onto the floor. She thanks her lucky stars for the umpteenth time that she has never been tempted to enter into such an agreement – either to marry or co-habit – despite having been pressed to do so on more than one occasion.

She is thinking particularly of Charles, who asked her to marry him more than once. He was always baffled, as well as rather put out, each time that Delphine turned him down. He simply couldn't – or wouldn't – bring himself to try and understand the situation from her perspective. She was more than happy to go out with Charles, for dinner, or to a lecture or a concert, even to sleep with him and go away on holiday with him. But she valued her own independence far too much to compromise it by marrying him. Or anyone. It was as if he regarded their entire relationship as a series of transactions – legal and financial – each of which must be negotiated in a journey towards the inevitable destination of the altar – or the Registry Office – which made her feel more like a commodity than a person. When she tried to explain this to Charles he claimed not to understand her, which was a pity, for when he was not pursuing her solely for marriage, like a quarry he could never quite capture within his sights, he was good company. Witty, well-educated, informed and, in every other aspect of his life, modern, in both his thinking and his actions. He was particularly keen on making sure that the hospital where he worked as a surgeon was always equipped with the latest technical innovations.

In the end his insistence on continually trying to woo her caused her to have to end their relationship completely. For a while she missed his intellect, the sparks that would fly between them, particularly whenever they disagreed with one another, which they did quite frequently, but always amicably, like a game of chess or a duel with swords that bend rather than penetrate, but as the years passed, they saw less and less of one another. Charles did not take well to retirement. He became irascible and withdrawn, preferring to look back, rather than forward, the antithesis to her own outlook on life, so that if by chance their paths should ever cross, which they did increasingly rarely, she did not know what to say to him. Small talk had never been a strong point for either of them.

When he died, nearly ten years ago now, she had only known when his solicitor, in tying up his affairs, had sent her some letters she had written to him decades before, which evidently he had kept. Sadly they were none of them love letters. They were either rejections of his proposals, or trifling matters, such as an invitation to a drinks reception, or a suggestion for a play or exhibition. When they arrived, she saw little point in keeping them. They were, after all, *her* notes to *him*, not the other way round. Not that she had kept any of his many letters to her. They did not survive the move to Newbury House. She has kept one photograph, however, taken on a rare picnic they had enjoyed at Heaton Park. They are in a boat on the lake. She is rowing, something he is perfectly content to allow her to do, for it is an unarguable fact, having been born the daughter of such an accomplished waterman as her father, that she is, when all is said and done, simply better than he is at it…

And so, when she opens Esther/Ishtar's letter to her, containing the clipping from the *Cadishead & Irlam Guardian* about the Bob's Lane Ferry Disaster, she finds herself looking backwards, something she so rarely does, to her days as a child and then a young woman, when she lived an almost feral existence in the wild, untamed Rixton Moss beside the Canal, trapping birds in Coroner's Wood and catching fish in Glaze Brook....

Dear Delphine,

I thought you might be interested to read the enclosed. Apologies for its somewhat creased and stained appearance, but I was using it to wrap potato peelings in when the headline caught my eye.

All is well here. Sol has fully settled back into 'normal' life now and seems happier and more at peace with himself than I can ever remember. He has a secret project he is working on in the evenings, which he is being very mysterious about, but which he is also very driven by. A good thing, I think. He is drawing again, which I am delighted by. His tutor at night school, George Wright, is most encouraging. He is very good for Sol.

Nadia goes from strength to strength. As well as continuing to teach English to new arrivals in the city, she has recently been promoted to Course Manager. Jenna meanwhile keeps us all on our toes. She is ferociously bright but extremely challenging. The two often go together, I imagine? You would know best with all your experience. She is especially hard on her father, who she has still not forgiven, I don't think.

I hope all is well with you? I'm sorry to be the bearer of such sad tidings. I know from our conversations of old how happy you were at Bob's Lane as a child.

Your friend, Ishtar

Six weeks later Delphine receives a second clipping.

Cadishead & Irlam Guardian

Wednesday 1st July 1971

BOB'S LANE FERRY VICTIMS – CORONER DECIDES

Investigation

What really happened at the Bob's Lane Ferry six weeks ago when the surface of the Manchester Ship Canal apparently self-ignited and exploded, causing the instant death of ferryman Bernard Collier and the serious injury of four other passengers, one of whom died in hospital? A further three people were missing at the time, with attempts to rescue them having to be abandoned by the Emergency Services on account of the extremely polluted state of the Canal.

Following weeks of exhaustive investigations by the North-West Forensic Laboratory, who tested multiple samples from the polluted water, and by teams of officers patrolling the Canal banks in an effort to discover the true cause of the fire, the delayed inquest has at last been able to take place to hear all of these findings in an attempt to finally solve the mystery behind the tragic events that unfolded on that fateful morning.

On April 30th, three days after the explosion, the bodies of the three other missing persons were all found. None had survived. A fund has been set up to help dependants, to which the local Bucklow Council, the Manchester Ship Canal Company, together with neighbours and friends, have already donated the sum of £2300. In the days immediately following the incident, residents have been understandably nervous, and the Fire Brigade has been called out several times since, whenever unexplained smells have once more emanated from the still fog-bound Canal.

On May 21st Shell Chemicals, whose company abuts the Canal in nearby Partington, announced they had carried out their own internal enquiry, as a result of which two workers have been suspended from duty, pending the further findings of the Inquest.

Inquest

On June 26th the inquest took place at Eccles Town Hall, where the Coroner, Mr. Leonard Gorodkin, heard the evidence.

It was revealed that several hours before the disaster the Dutch-owned vessel *Tacoma* was being loaded with 1800 tons of petrol at Partington Coaling Basin. It was normal practice to have two men observing this operation as a safety precaution to ensure that petrol did not overflow into the Canal. The two men admitted that, instead of being on the quayside, they had gone to the canteen, and had been there from 2.00am until almost 6.00am, drinking coffee and talking. During this period it was estimated that as much as 14,000 gallons of petrol had leaked into the Canal.

The Coroner stated: "We will never know just what caused the petrol to ignite in this most horrifying incident." He continued: "As a result of this inquest I hope people will realise that safety regulations are not just bits of paper to be filled in and then ignored."

There was a suggestion that the fire started when one of the ferry passengers lit a cigarette, but this has not been proved.

A verdict of Death by Misadventure was thus recorded on the five who died in the accident: Albert Wimbleton, aged 56, of Yew Walk; Brian Hillier, aged 18, of Wood Lane; Roy Platt, 29, of Daniel Adamson Avenue; Alan Cliff, aged 17, of Birch Road, and the ferryman, Bernard Carroll, aged 27, of Lock Lane, all of Partington. The following were injured: Daniel MacAlister of Wood Lane,

George Morrell of Lime Walk, Robert Kilgour of Camomile Walk and Stephen Hunter of Wood Lane.

Aftermath

The ferry re-opened two weeks after the fire but has not done well. Too many passengers have been afraid of another disaster taking place. Jim and Dorothy Fogarty ran the service during that time, but passenger numbers continued to fall, and the service has now ceased.

Due to the closure of the ferry, local workers now face an eight-mile detour over the High Level M63 Motorway Bridge, in order to reach Cadishead's Soap, Tar, Margarine and Steel Works...

Delphine puts down the clipping. She is shocked to feel the incipient prick of tears at the back of her eyes. She decides she must be tired, for it is not in her nature to be sentimental. It is not that she feels no sympathy for the losses so keenly felt by the families of the bereaved, but normally she would respond less emotionally, focusing instead on how, if proper procedures had been followed as they should have been, such a tragedy might have been avoided. She has a keenly analytical mind that is able to separate fact from speculation, discern truth from innuendo. But today such powers are eluding her, and the tears which threatened have now become realised, shockingly so, for she finds she is weeping copiously.

She allows herself to give in to them completely and let them have free rein until she has at last cried herself out. Exhausted, she pours herself a stiff drink. Such moments call for the Napoleon brandy she keeps at the back of her cupboard, normally reserved for those occasions when she has guests for supper, more rarely these days since she finished at the University, and she sips it satisfyingly, feeling its restorative warmth spread comfortingly through her body, bringing with it an immediate, soothing balm.

With this, too, comes a return of her customary equilibrium, so that she can examine her reaction more closely. It does not take her long to recognise that what has happened has been a sudden and violent rising to the surface of feelings she had thought were long buried. The article evidently triggered some synapse deep within her brain, firing the neurotransmitter at the junction between two nerve cells, causing them to pass a series of electro-chemical signals between each other, which had not been exercised for many years and had lapsed into a semi-dormant state. Delphine understands that these synapses play an important role in both the creation and retrieval of memories. As the neurotransmitters activate receptors across the synaptic cleft, the connection between the two nerve cells is strengthened when both are active simultaneously, dependent upon the effectiveness of their signalling mechanisms. But, like any muscle, they need to be taken care of, with regular use and exercise. The plasticity of these synapses can be controlled in the presynaptic cell, a process known as long-term potentiation. Its opposite, long-term depression, can occur when there is an imbalance within the electro-chemical signals. This imbalance can be caused by the neglect, wilful or accidental, of a specific memory.

Delphine recognises that she has never properly grieved for the loss of her mother and father. The discovery of their bodies more than fifty years before, locked in a tender embrace as they succumbed to the H1N1 influenza virus, was so horrifyingly traumatic, followed as it was by all that she had to do as a consequence – the digging of a pit on the edge of a wood, the dragging and then burying of their bodies, the burning of their log cabin, her rowing of her father's starvationer canoe along a stretch of the Manchester Ship Canal, to its junction with the Bridgewater, and from there its deliverance into the depths of The Delph – it is little wonder that she has buried it so deeply in her brain. Nor, having been so unexpectedly awakened by the incident of the Bob's Lane Ferry Disaster, taking place as it did on the very stretch of water where her parents had first begun that same crossing, is it any surprise that her reaction has been so emotional and so extreme.

Delphine was assisted at the time by a chance meeting with a complete stranger, who just happened to arrive at the ferry at the same moment that she did. He was on one side, she the other. She untethered the wooden boat that she had found so surprisingly untended and rowed him across. It was then, together, that they made the shocking discovery, and it was this stranger who had helped her perform much of the grisly task.

Francis.

Their paths have crossed from time to time over the years since, but not often. Francis was friendly with Charles for a time, which brought them into occasional contact. Then later, when Delphine had taken a special interest in the case of Roland, while he was still a prisoner-of-war, she was introduced to Lily, who by that time had already formed a deep attachment to Roland. Lily was the adoptive sister of George, and George and Francis were friends. More than that. Much more. Their relationship had been forged by the chance intervention of Esther, after a collision between George's motor cycle and a heron had resulted in Francis breaking his leg in several places, an injury that was complicated by their being abandoned in the wilds of Chat Moss, while Esther raised the alarm.

And so this tangled web of accident and coincidence has bound them down the years, so that when circumstance contrives to bring them together, they are able to acknowledge each other more deeply than if their acquaintance had been born out of something more trivial. Their strange encounter at the Bob's Lane Ferry hung always in the air between them, known but never spoken of.

Perhaps it is time that it was, thinks Delphine?

Perhaps she needs to lay the ghosts of her parents to rest once and for all?

But to do so, she will need the assistance of Francis once more.

She sips the last of her brandy, rises from her chair, and goes to the telephone in the hall...

Francis is coming to the end of what has been an extremely busy day. He has spent the entire time supervising the hang of his next exhibition. They change every four weeks. The first Monday of each month sees a new opening, a private view for the artist and invited guests, which is always hosted by Francis. He adores these openings. His friend Giulia picks out a special gown for him for each one, something in keeping with the theme and mood of the particular artist's work. Tomorrow's opening is for an up-and-coming engraver, an Irish girl, Saoirse Kineen, who works with sea glass. She reminds him of his mother, Caitlin Mallone – not in her appearance, for Francis never knew her, she died when he was less than a year old – but in her work, examples of which he's seen in The Whitworth Museum & Art Gallery. He loves the way it uses light, capturing abstract shapes of differently coloured glass that appear to float. Saoirse displays similar traits. All of the pieces for her current exhibition are blue, tipped with flecks of orange and red. Like water catching fire. Francis loves them. Giulia has designed a dress for him, which is similarly ambiguous. Oh, how he loves to tease! He will greet his guests like a shimmering ocean, out of which a golden sun is rising...

But right now, in overalls that have definitely seen better days, he resembles more a mud flat than an ocean. The hang has not been easy. Saoirse is proving temperamental and Francis can feel a storm is threatening. Thank heavens for Giulia. She's had more openings than hot dinners and brooks no nonsense from the artists, all of whom, in awe of her reputation, are as meek as lambs before her. All she has to do, if ever any of them veer towards a tantrum, is to arch an immaculately pencilled eyebrow, and they back down immediately. Then, when the hang is complete, and Francis pops open a bottle of red, they will all stand back and survey the gallery with quiet pride and satisfaction at a job well done.

"You were right," they will say to Giulia, as Saoirse does now, "the large piece looks much better on its own," and Giulia will say nothing, merely raise her glass, accompanied by that characteristic cat-like smile of hers.

The Gallery had been George's idea originally, suggested during a quarrel between them on the last ever Tulip Sunday at Philips Park, more than a decade ago now. Francis had grown fretful about the future of his Audio-Visual establishment, with its range of cameras, telescopes and binoculars, mixed in with hi-fi sound equipment, plus an optician's service that had become increasingly outdated and uninteresting to him. Then, when his *Passepartout* of thirty years – Winifred – had announced that she was planning to retire in order to spend more time with her partner, Victor, and her grandchildren, he was both panic-stricken and bereft. He had come to depend on Winifred utterly and he knew he would flounder without her. He had already begun to run down his stock, and frequently he could hardly be motivated to open at all. That was when George had suggested the Gallery, and it had worked like a dream. He had never worked harder, but he loved every second of it.

In return for her help with each new hang, Francis allows Giulia to open her Spring and Autumn collections there each year, and these have become a much-anticipated fixture in the Manchester calendar, as have George's own frequent exhibitions, of which there is always one each year. George has a national reputation now, as well as a loyal local following, and so his shows are always booked up well in advance.

George himself hates openings, disliking any kind of fuss, but he recognises that they are a necessary part of being an artist – a term he would never choose to apply to himself, preferring something more industrial instead. When the artists' collective known as The Welfare State – a name George wholly approved of, for that is how he liked to view his own work, as a contribution to the health of the nation – published their manifesto, they described themselves as 'Engineers of the Imagination'. George liked that very much. He wished he'd thought of it first.

In deference to his dear friend's modest sensibility, Francis would dress more soberly for George's openings. Not in one of Giulia's romantic gowns, but in a dignified dinner jacket and bow tie, his only nod towards ornamentation coming in the form of his *boutonnière*. He eschewed the lily of Oscar Wilde – too obvious – in favour of something subtler – a dainty gypsohilia and waxflower, for example, with a hardy foliage surround, eucalyptus perhaps, soft ruscus, or ivy. Francis would always be especially pleased if George took time to comment on his choice, which he invariably did. Dear George...

They were no longer lovers. Not for a decade. Even though homosexuality had been legal for five years now, having been so gaily steered through the Lords by Arthur Kattendyke Strange David Archibald Gore, 8th Earl of Arran. Now there was a name to conjure with. No wonder he preferred the diminutive 'Archie', which he had insisted Francis call him at a party to celebrate the eventual passing of the Bill. But for all that, as far as Francis was concerned, George remained, and would always be, the great love of his life. Achilles to his Patroclus...

"Penny for them," says Giulia, topping up his glass.
"Sorry," he replies. "I was miles away."

"Not so many, I don't think. Let me guess. Adelphi Street?" Francis smiles. "My slip must be showing."

Adelphi – Greek for brothers – where George lives, and has done since the War.

And at once Francis bursts into song to cover his feelings – Lerner and Loewe. *My Fair Lady* – which Saoirse picks out on the piano in the corner of the Gallery.

> *"I have often walked down this street before*
> *But the pavement always stayed beneath my feet before*
> *All at once am I*
> *Several storeys high*
> *Knowing I'm on the street where you live…"*

Giulia joins in with him, and together they foxtrot their way around the floor.

> *"Are there lilac trees in the heart of town?*
> *Can you hear a lark in any other part of town?*
> *Does enchantment pour*
> *Out of every door?*
> *No it's just on the street where you live…"*

As always Giulia knows how to pick him up whenever he threatens to become maudlin or sentimental.

"Why don't you invite him to Saoirse's show tomorrow night?" she says.

"I think I shall," says Francis with a spring in his step. "Better still, why don't *you* invite him? He can never say 'no' to you. Unless he's working on that young man's mural he's become so obsessed about lately."

"Never mind. He can always come another night."

"You're right," he says, his mood now considerably lighter. He immediately conjures the spirit of Scarlett O'Hara. "After all, tomorrow *is* another day…"

The sudden ring of the telephone cuts into their laughter, causing them to joke even more.

"Perhaps that's him?" suggests Saoirse.

"Or maybe Rhett Butler?" offers Giulia.

"I should be so lucky," quips Francis. He picks up the phone. "Hello? *Spectacle Gallery*. How may I help you?" There is a brief pause. "Oh…"

The atmosphere is at once serious, puncturing the levity of just a moment ago, like air escaping from a slowly deflating balloon…

On the other end of the line Delphine is speaking urgently.

"Francis? I need to ask you a favour…"

Francis, his eyes growing ever wider, listens intently. He sits down on a chair beside the phone. He waits till Delphine has finished speaking.

"Yes," he says simply. "Of course… When…? The day after tomorrow…? What time…? I'll be there… You can count on it…"

He puts down the receiver and remains sitting on the chair. His face has grown visibly paler.

"What is it?" asks Giulia gently, kneeling by his side. "You look like you've seen a ghost…"

"Thank you for coming," says Delphine, as Francis arrives promptly at the appointed hour, dressed with sober restraint befitting the purpose of their meeting. "Lily has offered to drive us there," she continues. "She should be here at any moment. Would you like to come in till she arrives?"

Francis is just about to step inside when a car pulls up behind him, a bottle green Vauxhall Viva, built thirty-five miles to the south-west in Ellesmere Port on the Wirral peninsula in Cheshire. Lily had bought the car two years earlier, on George's advice, who always advised to buy as local as possible. "Though why you should want to exchange two wheels for four defeats me," he had said, shaking his head.

"My motor bike days are behind me," Lily had replied. "You forget, George, that I'm not footloose and fancy-free as you are. I have a husband and a teenage daughter now. Two can fit on a DOT Racer, but not three."

"You could always attach a sidecar," George had suggested, but Lily could see he was joking. And so she had ridden pillion on the back of his bike for the last time, as he had taken her to the Vauxhall car factory at Ellesmere Port to pick up the bottle-green Viva.

But it is not Lily who is driving the Viva today, but Ruth, who hops out from behind the wheel, smiling brightly as she opens all four doors.

"Sir, Madam – your carriage awaits."

"What's happened to Lily?" asks an anxious Delphine.

"Oh," says Ruth, her expression immediately clouding over. "It's Dad. He's really not well. They've had to call the doctor out."

"Is it his chest again?"

Ruth nods. Roland's years as a prisoner-of-war have taken their toll on his health. He's only fifty-two but looks considerably older. When Ruth left home half an hour before, his skin had assumed a sickly grey pallor.

"Wouldn't you rather be with him?" says Delphine.

"To be honest, no," says Ruth. "I'd rather be busy, and besides, Mum said this was important."

"Yes, but it can wait. Really."

"No. It's fine."

"Are you sure you're old enough to drive this thing?" asks Francis, looking rather doubtful.

"I'm seventeen," says Ruth indignantly. "I passed my test over a month ago."

"Well, in that case, what are we waiting for? he says, allowing himself to be helped into the back. "Why, thank you, my dear. I have always depended upon the kindness of strangers."

Delphine winces.

"Not today, Francis, if you don't mind. I'm not in the mood for your jokes."

Francis turns away, his cheeks colouring with embarrassment.

"I'm sorry, Francis," relents Delphine. "That was uncalled for. I'm not myself this morning, I fear."

"Will someone please explain what's going on?" says a perplexed Ruth. "Where are we going?"

"Do you have a road atlas?" asks Delphine.

"An A to Z," replies Ruth. "Why?"

"Hand it across to me, will you please? I'll give you directions, It will provide me with something else to focus on as we go. Francis will explain, won't you, Francis?"

"I'll do my best."

Ruth pulls away from Newbury House along Daisy Bank Road until they reach the junction with Upper Brook Street, where she turns left, then right into Dickenson Road, passing the BBC TV Studios there.

"That's where Giulia worked for a time," says Francis, pointing it out. "When it was still *Mancunian Films*. She was in some tacky picture with Sandy Powell – *Cup Tie Honeymoon*. Not cinema's finest hour, but Giulia of course was marvellous. Hammer made a lot of their Horror films there. Diana Dors in *Man Bait*. So deliciously camp. *The Glass Tomb* with Honor Blackman, before she was a Bond girl. Stanley Baker all gritty and butch in *Hell is a City*. None of the Dracula films sadly. Giulia had looked forward to being bitten on the neck by Christopher Lee. Then the BBC took it over."

"I know," says Ruth. "I went to a recording of *Top of the*

Pops there once. I saw The Bee Gees."

"Who?"

"Ha, ha," sneers Ruth. "I know you know who they are. They used to live in Manchester. In Chorlton…"

"…which is the direction we should be heading in," interrupts Delphine. "Left here please, Ruth."

Ruth turns onto Wilmslow Road, then quickly right onto Wilbraham Road towards Chorlton, then bears right again onto Edge Lane, past Longford Park until they reach Stretford, where they must wait for the traffic lights. On their right is the wonderfully ornate Art Deco *Essoldo* cinema, now sadly a rather forlorn-looking Bingo Hall.

"I remember when this cinema was first built," recalls Francis. "There was a much smaller cinema on the corner opposite – where that circular pub is now, *The Bass Drum* – *The Picturedrome*, it was called. At the height of the cinema boom, the owners, Jackson and Newport, wanted to extend it, but there wasn't the room, so they built what they called a 'Super Cinema' across the road."

"*The Essoldo?*"

"That's right. Only it was called *The Longford* at first. After the Park.

"How do you know all this?"

"Because the architect – Henry Elder – was a friend of mine. We used to meet at *The Queen's* from time to time. He brought me in to advise with the sound system he wanted to install there."

"And was it?"

"What?"

"A 'Super Cinema'?"

"It was certainly big. It seated fourteen hundred. A great barn of a place. But warm. The first cinema in the country to be heated by electric storage heaters."

"Another first for Manchester?"

"There's been plenty of them."

"What's that curved frontage meant to represent? It looks like a Mohican haircut."

"At the time people called it 'the Cash Register'."

"Oh yes – I can see that. Why?"

"Henry said it was meant to symbolise the business aspect of cinema."

"And did it do good business?"

"For a while. People flocked to it. It was the last word in luxury. Lush deep-pile carpets in a dark apricot sheen. Wide seats with velour coverings and plush, padded arms. Double seats for courting couples at the end of each row. Art Deco panels on either side of the screen, which would glow in different colours as the lights changed in time with the music being played. The audience would gasp as they saw it."

"Thanks to your sound system?"

"I like to think so. The curtains in front of the screen were of ruched satin. Just before the picture started, these would be a deep red at the top and a rich green at the bottom."

"Like a forest fire."

"Exactly."

The traffic lights also now change from red to green as the car inches forward in the heavy traffic. But, just as they reach the front of the queue, they change again.

"What was the first film they showed?" asks Ruth.

"*Tudor Rose*. A costume drama about the life of Lady Jane Grey."

"The Nine-Day Queen?"

"The same."

"Who played her?"

"Nova Pilbeam."

"Who?"

"You might well ask. She was quite a star in the thirties and forties. She was in Hitchcock's *The Man Who Knew Too Much* with Peter Lorre, and she was the original choice for *Rebecca* before Joan Fontaine."

Ruth shakes her head, unsure whether to believe Francis or not. He's such a convincing storyteller.

"What about the last film then?"

"Ah," says Francis, "rising to his theme, "that has a Manchester connection. *Quatermass & The Pit*, part of which was filmed in Mancunian Studios on Dickenson Road. Hammer's Queen of Horror, Barbara Shelley, played a palaeontologist's glamorous assistant, who uncovers a five million-year-old skull in the London Underground, which turns out to have telekinetic powers derived from Mars."

"You're making this up."

"I kid you not. Giulia helped with some of Barbara's costumes and they became good friends for the duration of the shoot. Barbara spent a lot of time in Rome and so spoke fluent Italian. Together, she and Giulia were able to say whatever they felt like without worrying about being overheard. According to Giulia, Barbara was deliciously indiscreet about everyone and everything."

"I don't believe a word of it," laughs Ruth.

"Nor do I," says Delphine.

The lights change once more and they are at last able to be on their way again.

"One last thing," says Ruth, "how did it get to be called *The Essoldo*?"

"Twenty years ago, Newport and Jackson sold the cinema to the impresario Solomon Sheckman, his wife Esther and their daughter Dorothy. He took the first letters of each of their names to come up with the new name for the cinema. Es-Sol-Do. He liked the sound of it so much that he bought a whole chain of cinemas right across the country, calling each one of them the same."

"I don't think I believe that either," says Ruth,

concentrating on the road ahead.

"Well," retorts Francis, leaning back in his seat with his arms folded, "wait till you hear the story behind the next cinema we pass in about another half-mile. Look – there it is on your right. *The Pyramid*."

"Eyes on the road if you don't mind please," interrupts Delphine. "Honestly, Francis. What is it Nietzsche says in *Also Sprach Zarathustra*?"

"I have no idea, Delphine. But I've a feeling you're going to tell me."

"In the Prologue to the Richard Strauss opera. 'You have made danger your vocation'." And she immediately begins to hum it to herself.

"I shall take that as a compliment," replies Francis. "I *think*…"

"Tell me about *The Pyramid*," asks Ruth.

"An early Egyptian theme park with usherettes dressed as Nefertiti." Francis is enjoying himself hugely, as he always does with a captive audience. "With its own in-house telephone reception…" He mimes picking up a receiver, while adopting a posh female telephonist's voice. "This is PYR 123…" Encouraged by Ruth's giggles, which now even Delphine cannot resist, he continues. "… as the Pyramid Orchestra played live *The Entrance of Cleopatra* – portrayed by Manchester's Mary Thornley, All England's première senior danseuse. And the Lido Singers – Winnie & Hilda: *A Song, A Smile & A See-Saw* – sang on stage three times nightly before *Movietone News* and *Mickey Mouse*."

"Bravo!" cries Delphine.

"I don't believe a word of any of it," declares Ruth, laughing all the while.

"Why let the truth get in the way of a good story?" says Francis.

"But we don't need to today, do we, Francis?" says

Delphine, suddenly serious, catching his eye in the mirror above the dashboard.

"No indeed," says Francis, becoming at once more appropriately sober and restrained."

"I think perhaps it's time that Ruth learned the reason behind our journey this morning, don't you?"

"If you say so, Delphine."

"I do."

The two of them hold each other's gaze a long time. Ruth feels the temperature inside the car drop several degrees.

"Right here please," says Delphine.

Ruth manoeuvres her way through the oncoming traffic and heads into Harboro Road.

"They say, do they not," continues Delphine, "that the truth can be stranger than fiction at times? Listen to what Francis is about to tell you, then see if you think the same."

Intrigued, Ruth waits for Francis to begin, as they now begin to leave behind the suburbs of Sale and Ashton-on-Mersey, and head out across the bleak expanse of Carrington Moss...

"It was 1919," begins Francis. "July. The War had ended more than eight months before, but the Government still refused to release us from internment. Even though most of us – including myself – had British passports. I may have been born in Germany, but that was by accident because my mother became ill while on a trip there. She died shortly after I was born, from the Asian flu epidemic that swept across Europe at the time. This was 1898, and I was back in England before I was a year old. But... my mother had Irish antecedents, and my father's were Jewish – hardly the most popular combination at the time – though in Manchester we were welcomed with open arms. I knew nothing but happiness and acceptance as a boy. My future seemed clearly mapped out for me. Until *The Lusitania* was sunk. Then all hell was let loose. There were riots right across the country. Including Manchester, I'm afraid. You know all about this, Ruth, from Lily of course, and from what her own mother had to endure as a result. I suffered only a minor inconvenience by contrast. But it did not feel like that at the time. I was just seventeen when I was rounded up along with everyone else who had a vaguely German-sounding name. The four years I was held against my will I bitterly regarded as wasted years, lost years. I still do...."

He pauses, remembering the anger and frustration he had felt so keenly, no trace of which now remained. Such is the great healing capacity of time. " '*The great doctor*', as the Roman playwright Menander is reputed to have said," muses Francis out loud. "Along with so many other wise words. My father was always quoting him. '*We live not as we would wish to, but as we can.*' That was a particular favourite. As was, '*Art is man's refuge from society.*' I've always remembered that, and tried to live by it..."

He falls quiet. A rare occurrence for Francis, Delphine allows herself to rest in the oasis of it. She recalls another of Menander's aphorisms, a reminder of her days at Our Lady of Lourdes School, where it was much impressed upon her by the nuns there. *'Nothing is more useful than silence.'* It hung on a wall in the chapel.

Delphine is familiar with silence. "As a child I grew up with it," she says, *à propos* of nothing. "Silence," she explains, in response to Ruth's puzzled expression. "My mother was both deaf and dumb. Profoundly so."

"I didn't know that," says Ruth.

"There's no reason why you should. She couldn't speak, but she could write. Unfortunately, my father couldn't read, and so they developed their own secret, private world of sign language, through which they would communicate with one another. But mostly they didn't need to. They existed in perfect contentment in absolute silence for most of the time. While I chattered around them non-stop from dawn till dusk, like the birds in the trees in Coroner's Wood."

"Is that where you lived?"

Delphine nods.

"And is that where we're heading now?"

Delphine nods a second time.

"But why? What happened there?

Delphine and Francis look at each other. The car continues to move across the bog of Carrington Moss like a dark green caterpillar hugging the contours of the land. Ruth's eyes widen as, between them, Francis and Delphine relate their story...

"It took two trains to reach there then," begins Delphine, "both on lines that no longer exist, having fallen to the swingeing blows of Dr Beeching's cruel axe. But as I alighted at Cadishead Station, my spirits were as high as the sun on that cloudless Saturday morning. It was 1919, as Francis has said. I was about to begin my work at the University – at the first Audiology Department to be opened anywhere in the country – and I was coming to share the news with my parents, who I had not seen since Christmas..."

Delphine skipped down the steps from the Cadishead Viaduct. It was then just a short walk along the Liverpool Road, past the bandstand in the park, where a gaggle of ragged children could be heard screeching as they rode the lethal Witch's Hat, until she turned into Bob's Lane and dropped down towards the Canal. It was a walk she could have made blindfolded.

But as soon as she reached the ferry, she sensed that something was different. It was more than six months since her last visit home, but as a rule very little ever changed. It was this constancy that she clung to, almost like a faith. The first thing she noticed was the boat itself. It was tied up against the bank, where it bobbed forlornly. Usually her father would have been there too, waiting to carry passengers across, or fetch them from the opposite bank. On the rare occasion he might be called away somewhere else, her mother would have been there in his stead. They operated the ferry seven days a week from seven in the morning till eleven at night. Week in, week out. Autumn, winter, spring and summer. Today neither of them was there, yet standing on the opposite shore, clearly needing to come across, stood a young man, looking up and down the Canal, as if he might summon assistance from thin air.

"Hello?" he called out. "I'm looking for the boatman. Do you know where he might be found?"

"Yes," shouted back Delphine. "I'll just..." The rest of what she said was abruptly drowned out by a piercing blast from the siren of one of the Manchester Liners' ocean-going ships, which hove into view on its way to the city from Liverpool. She had to wait several minutes until the vessel, a tanker from Aden, had passed between them.

"Yes," she began again. "I know where they live," she explained. "I'll just go and see what's keeping them. I shan't be long."

And with that, she hitched up the hem of her skirt and ran diagonally up from the water's edge towards a small copse of trees on the brow of a low hill, through which the young man thought he detected the outlines of a small settlement of wooden cottages. He took off his jacket and sat on the iron capstan to which the ferry's rope would be tethered while its customers stepped aboard, had it been operating as normal.

She had not gone more than fifty yards, however, when she suddenly stopped, turned around, and ran as adroitly down the slope as a mountain goat – almost as if she had been born on such terrain, the young man mused.

"I'll fetch you first," she called, untying the rope as she

spoke, "and then go and investigate why they're not here afterwards. You've been waiting long enough."

"Thank you. That is most kind of you, Miss – er...?"

"Fish," she called back.

The young man smiled. For a moment he was sure she had said 'Fish'.

"But please call me Delphine." She felt oddly exhilarated. It must be the sun, she thought, and smiled too.

"Delphine?"

"Yes."

"Are you French?"

"No."

By now she was already rowing across the Canal and was answering his questions in between strokes.

What an extraordinary young woman, he thought. Why, she handles this boat like a sailor. Or perhaps *matelot* would be more appropriate, and he chuckled to himself at his own joke.

"And what," she began, still rowing, "might I..." Another pull on the oars. "...call you?"

"Oh," he said, somewhat taken by surprise. "That's rather a difficult question to answer." Heavens, he thought. What kind of fellow will she think I am? Only rogues and vagabonds are evasive about their names.

"Are you," she asked, "an actor?"

He burst out laughing. "No," he said. "Not the sort you mean anyway."

"I see," she rowed. "What sort... of actor... are you...?"

"I haven't quite decided," he said, a little less loudly, for now she had almost reached him.

"Names are complicated," she agreed, leaping lightly out of the boat. She gestured with the rope towards the capstan, on top of which the young man had placed one foot. "Excuse me."

He stepped out of her way as she deftly looped the rope around it with a single throw. She was evidently much at home here, and he felt oddly wrong-footed.

"Take mine," she said.

"Miss?"

"My name. My father is a Sioux Indian." The young man's pale eyebrows shot up. "It's not every day you hear that now, is it? And they don't have names, not in the sense we understand them. His father called him 'Leaps Like A Fish', because he loved to swim in the stream near their camp, and when he tried to explain that here, someone thought he was describing a salmon. So – 'Sammy' he became. Sammy Fish. And my mother, well – she doesn't have a last name. She can't speak. She's a mute. So she couldn't tell us anyway, even if she had one."

She paused for breath. She'd never told this to anyone. Yet here she was, confiding in a perfect stranger.

"And Delphine?" he asked, his eyebrows returning to their more usual position.

"Ah," she said, and stopped. No, she thought. I shan't explain that. "It's personal," she said. "Private."

He nodded. "I can respect that."

"Thank you." She looked at him squarely...

"I can tell you now," says Delphine in the car, interrupting her story. "For a time my father worked in The Delph, the underground canals that serviced the coal mines near Worsley. He first met my mother one night when rowing his starvationer canoe out of The Delph back to the camp on the Irwell by the Bittern Wood, where he lived with three other Native American friends, who had escaped together from the Wild West Show at Belle Vue. One of these – a blacksmith known as Catch – had taken up with a runaway Louisiana slave called Clem who he had met in the heart of Chat Moss. She spoke a kind of Creole French. It was she who suggested my name, after the place where my father worked."

"I never knew that," says Francis.

"And Clem," continues Delphine, "was Cam's mother."

Francis sits back in wonder, hearing Cam's voice singing once more in his memory.

"Them that's got shall have
Them that's not shall lose
So the Bible said and it still is news
Mama may have, Papa may have
But God bless the child that's got his own
That's got his own..."

Delphine returns to her narrative...

She looked at him squarely. "Have you decided what your own name is yet?"

"Well..."

"Hop aboard," she said, "then you can tell me while I ferry us back across. It's hard to row and speak at the same time."

He stepped into the flat-bottomed boat and perched along the stern, while Delphine, facing him from the prow, began to pull on the oars. Her hair had become unpinned and, from time to time as she rowed, she tried to blow stray wisps away from her face.

"I'm thinking of changing it," the young man said eventually. "My name, that is."

"Why? Are you on the run?"

"No," he said, more forcibly than he intended, "but it feels as though I may as well be."

He was silent for a while and then, as if having taken a decision, he began once more to speak.

"My name is Franz Halsinger," he said. "As you can no doubt discern, that is a German name. After the sinking of *The Lusitania*, I was interned. On the Isle of Man."

"Oh, I'm sorry," interrupted Delphine. "I thought that was

such a wicked and unjust thing to do. It made me feel ashamed to be English."

"That's just it. I didn't. Not at first. At the time, although I was angry, I could sort of understand why it was being done."

"I don't agree. I hate the idea of labelling people like that. We're each of us individuals, regardless of geography. Unique. Special. That's what I tell my children."

"Your children?"

"I'm a teacher."

"I see."

"Or I was."

"Was?"

"Never mind. You were telling me your story."

"My father was quite an old man. At least that's how he seemed when I was a boy. I always had to be quiet around him. So he was not taken away, like I was. He was considered too frail. I was put on a ship with hundreds of others, all of us frightened, confused, not understanding what was happening. As soon as we arrived in Douglas, we were taken across the island to a camp, where we were to be held for the duration of the War."

"It must have been terrible."

"Actually it wasn't that bad. Once we got there. It was fairly relaxed. The Camp was large so it didn't feel hemmed in. We worked on a farm close by. Those that wanted could play sports…"

Not you, though, thought Delphine. She had never seen anyone quite like him before. With his white hair, fair skin, pink eyes. She supposed he must have some form of albinism. Yet it did not appear in any way to incapacitate him. Any more than her mother's inability to speak or hear had.

"… or make music, read books," he continued. "It was…"

"What?"

"Not so much the loss of liberty as the loss of years. More

than four years of my life taken from me. It's the waste as much as the injustice that still rankles with me."

"Yes. I can see that."

"Can you?"

" 'As tyme him hurt, so tyme doth him cure'."

"I beg your pardon?"

"Chaucer. *Troilus & Criseyde.*"

"Oh…"

They had almost reached the other side of the Canal now. He had fallen silent. He felt continually wrong-footed by her. Delphine regarded him, the way he sat there, hunched up, facing, but not looking at her. He reminded her of a snail who had just pulled in his horns, who was carrying a heavy burden upon his back, like a shell he had constructed around himself, and which had now formed a second skin – this extraordinarily pale skin, which Delphine looked at more closely, like something that has been deprived of sunlight for too long, that you might come across if you turned over a dead branch in the wood, with translucent, blinking eyes.

"What have you been doing since the War ended?"

He looked up, startled, when she said that. "That's just it. Didn't you know? No, I suppose not. They won't have reported this in the newspapers. I'm only just on my way home now. They wouldn't let us leave till a week ago. They wanted to deport me back to Germany. 'But I'm not from Germany,' I kept telling them. 'I'm English. I've lived here since before I was one.' Eventually they agreed. The ship docked in Liverpool yesterday. We had to make our own arrangements once we got there. There was a telegram. It was sent to the ship's captain, who handed it to one of the stewards, who gave it to me just as we neared shore…"

"What did it say?"

"It was from my father's solicitor, informing me that my father had died a week ago…"

"Oh, I'm so sorry."

"...and that he'd left everything to me when I turn twenty-one."

"And when's that?"

He looked directly at her for the first time in a while. "Today."

She said nothing.

They had now crossed the Canal. Delphine automatically threw the rope around the windlass and jumped ashore, steadying the boat while Franz got to his feet. She stretched out a hand which, after a brief pause, he took and stepped onto the waiting jetty.

"What will you do now?" she asked.

"I'm sorry. I hadn't known I was going to say any of this. You've been most kind, allowing me to. So – to answer your question, I think the first thing I'm going to do is to change my name."

Now it was Delphine's turn to raise her eyebrows in surprise.

"Why?"

"I feel like a fresh start. I have no family. But I'm lucky. For I have money. My father was a wealthy man. I want to put these last four wasted years behind me and never speak of them again."

Delphine nodded. "What to?"

He smiled. "Franz Halsinger will become Francis Hall. Very English, don't you think?" he added wryly.

"What happened to 'singer'?"

"I haven't quite decided yet. But I will not lose him altogether."

"Well – good luck," she said, and held out her hand towards him. He considered it a moment, then shook it, quite formally.

"Thank you."

"Do you know where you will go first?"

"To Manchester, that is all. I have been following the line of telegraph poles all the way from Liverpool." He pointed towards a long line of them stretching beside the Canal, before departing from it again as the Canal, following the course of the Mersey at this point, took a bend in the river. They looked like sentries standing in a row, to attention, on guard.

"Whatever for?" she said, laughing.

"That is another story, and too long in the telling…"

Now it is Francis's turn to interrupt the story.

"I don't know why I said that. It's not that long. While I was on the ship, waiting for the telegram about my father to be fully received, I was enthralled by the sound of the operator, tapping out the message on his machine. It sounded like…"

"What?" asks Ruth.

"The future," says Francis. "During my internment on the island, time had moved so slowly. The years had dragged by. I thought they would never end. Yet here, in a matter of seconds, this message was being transmitted more than fifty miles across the sea. This was a world in which time seemed to move at a different speed. The world of the future. And I wanted to be a part of it…"

"I have detained you enough," he said as he alighted from the boat.

"In that case," said Delphine, "I'll go and see if I can find out what's been detaining my parents. Goodbye."

He watched her hitch up her skirts once more and run off up the slope towards the copse of alder trees at the top of the hill. When he could no longer see her, he turned back towards the line of telegraph poles marching across the land and lit up a cigarette. He would smoke it and then be on his way…

Delphine was nearing the crest of the hill. The copse was

strangely quiet as she entered it. Even the rooks seemed to be taking a siesta in the heat of the afternoon and were snoozing dustily in the sun, which made dappled patterns on the ground as she approached her parents' settlement. Flecks of light fell onto her hands and arms where she had rolled up the sleeves of her blouse. Motes of dust danced in the air, which hummed with the low drone of insects.

The fire which was always kept alight, whatever the season, for it was still her parents' only source of heat for cooking, had been left to go out – quite recently, from the faint glow Delphine could still see in the ashes – and the wooden porch was littered with their usual detritus – ends of rope, a box of tools, empty eel traps stacked in a heap. It was as if they had suddenly decided, on a whim, to take themselves off on a trip. They did this sometimes. But Sammy's narrow, wooden starvationer canoe lay upturned a little way off from the huts.

Puzzled, Delphine called out their names.

A pair of rooks cawed back desultorily. Otherwise nothing.

Perhaps they'd gone for a walk. It was a beautiful day after all, and her mother liked to pick wild herbs and flowers from the tangled carpet of undergrowth beneath the alders for use as medicines if needed.

Delphine called again.

Frowning, she decided to look indoors. The door was not locked – it never was – and she swung it open before stepping inside to its shaded cool.

The smell hit her at once. That overpoweringly sweet, sickly smell, which, even though she had never encountered it before, instinct told her at once signified death. She covered her mouth and nose with her arm and made her way towards the room at the back where they slept.

They were lying facing one another, arms wrapped around their bodies in a tender embrace, lips touching, eyes closed.

They had not been dead long – perhaps a day – for there

was no decay, no indignity. A few flies buzzed around, but not too many yet. *Rigor mortis* had begun to wear off and there were no signs of bloating or extending. But for the lack of any rise or fall of breathing, they could almost have been asleep.

Delphine backed slowly out of the room. She could not bear to see them like this. It felt like an intrusion into that most private and intimate of moments. Which one of them, she wondered, had died first? Which one had watched the other slip away, before patiently waiting for their own turn? She supposed it must have been the Spanish flu, which was on everyone's lips these days.

Once she had finally left the room, she suddenly turned and ran, out of the hut, through the copse, and down the hill towards the jetty, where she could see the young man was still standing, smoking a cigarette.

"Franz," she shouted. "Francis…"

He was just finishing his cigarette and gathering himself to set off once more, when he heard her shouting his name, his names. He turned and saw her hurtling down the slope towards him like a hare attempting to outrun a pack of hounds…

Four hours later the two of them were sitting on the rickety steps leading up to the front porch of the wooden hut that had once been Delphine's home. Francis, as Delphine was now quite used to calling him, had lit two more cigarettes, one for himself and one, now, for Delphine. They sat side by side, smoking in silence, each in their own private thoughts. Their hands, arms, faces and clothes were smeared with dust and earth, but so dry had been the summer this would quickly brush away.

"Thank you," she said at last.

He smiled thinly.

"I don't know what I should have done if you'd not been

still here."

"Someone would have come."

"Perhaps."

They became quiet once more. Delphine drew deeply on her cigarette. She was not a routine smoker, but appreciated the sense of calm the tobacco spread through her, though her hands, she noticed, were still shaking.

"I could have managed to dig the graves," she said, "but not to carry the bodies."

Francis said nothing. The nightmarish unreality of what she had told him, and then asked him to do to help her, was already starting to evaporate in the wreaths of smoke drifting above their heads.

She had torn two strips of cloth she had found lying about. "Tie this around your face," she'd said, and he'd obeyed without a second thought. These were not the first dead bodies, he'd seen. An old man had died while he had been interned at Knockaloe. Someone had found him sitting on a rock overlooking the Irish Sea, holding a carved toy wooden boat in his hands. They'd thought at first he was sleeping and had tried to wake him. Then they'd realised. Francis had been commandeered by one of the guards to help carry the old man back to the Camp on a stretcher. But he'd been covered with a blanket, and so Francis had seen very little of him...

"Your great-grandfather, Ruth," says Francis, as comfortingly as he can.

Ruth nods. "Yes," she says, blinking back the threat of tears. "I realised..."

This had been very different. There was no mistaking the irrefutable deadness of Delphine's parents, their bodies so delicately but irredeemably locked together. His first thought, he was ashamed to confess, had been whether they were still infectious. Delphine assured him that she did not think so. She was extraordinarily calm, he noted, given what had happened. She was, and had always been, a practical person. She knew what had to be done, but physically she could not manage to carry this out without the helping hand of a second person.

She had stood at the foot of the bed, looking down on where her parents lay, turned back to Francis and said, "Don't worry. I'm not asking you to lift the bodies. Or touch them even. I don't want to separate them."

"Do you want me to fetch an undertaker? Or a priest? Or stay here while you do so?" He was looking distinctly nonplussed and not a little green. Suddenly, he clutched the piece of cloth even closer to his mouth. "Forgive me," he had said, and then rushed from the room.

Delphine heard him retching outside and waited while he composed himself before joining him on the porch.

"I'm sorry to ask this of you. I'm not thinking straight."

"Please. I understand. This must have been an enormous shock."

"Thank you. Let's sit here for a while, and let me try to explain what needs to be done."

They sat on the step and he waited for her to begin.

"I told you on the ferry that my father is – or, rather, was – a Sioux Indian."

"Yes. I remember."

"Lakota tradition instructs that when a person dies, he must be left untouched for a day…"

"But…?

"…to give his spirit time to leave the body."

Francis nodded.

"Then he must be buried, as close to where his body was found as possible, unless that was within a further day's journey from his home. I don't believe they've been dead for more than two days, judging from the…" Her voice was beginning to tremble. "...lack of decomposition."

Francis looked away.

"He would want them to be buried according to tradition, and so what I'm proposing is... that we bury them just there," she said, and pointed towards a tree about ten yards away from the hut.

Francis again said nothing. He found that his mouth was terribly dry.

"What I'd like you to do please," Delphine continued, "is help me to drag the bed they're lying on over to that spot." She spoke slowly, deliberately, as if by naming each separate task dispassionately, she might lessen the enormity of what she was suggesting. "Then we shall need to dig a hole deep enough and wide enough for them to be lowered into. And then cover them over with the freshly dug earth." She looked at him directly, her face devoid of all ornamentation. "Please."

Francis stood up. "Yes," he said. "But I suggest we dig the grave first. I assume they had spades?"

Delphine fetched them one each, and for the next two hours they dug wordlessly. The alder tree beneath which the bodies were to be laid offered a welcome shade, and they worked as quickly as the dry, baked earth allowed them to.

Eventually, when they decided they had dug deeply enough, Delphine handed her spade to Francis. "Wait here," she said and walked off in the direction of one of the many small outbuildings clustered around the main hut. A few moments later she came back with two thick coils of rope.

Francis nodded and followed her back towards the house, re-tying the cloth around his face. They found three old railway sleepers, which they lay across the steps leading from the porch down to the ground below. They tied a length of rope to each of the legs of the bed, and then, with agonising slowness, they proceeded to drag it, inch by painful inch. They slid it precariously down the three sleepers, then hauled it across the hard earth towards the open grave. Once there, they transferred the three sleepers to form a shallow ramp for the bed to slide down into it.

They then stood side by side looking down. Francis delicately retreated back towards the hut, leaving Delphine some time to be alone. She looked for the last time upon them. Their locked embrace had survived this last journey, and this is how she would remember them for ever afterwards, the two of them as one in death, as they had been in life.

At last she turned away, walked briskly back towards the hut, stepping past Francis and going inside, from where she returned with a thick blanket, which she delicately placed over the bodies of her parents.

"I can manage by myself now," she said, beginning to shovel the earth back into the grave. "Thank you."

Francis walked back towards her, picked up the second spade and, without saying a word, loaded it with more earth...

Now they had finished. They sat back on the rickety steps and smoked their cigarettes.

"Will you be all right?" he said after several minutes.

She nodded.

"What will you do?"

"I'll stay the night," she said, "sort out the house."

"Do you want me to stay and help?"

She shook her head. "No. I'd rather do it by myself. Thank you. You've done so much. But I'd like some time alone now, I think."

"Yes," he said. "I can understand that." He stood up and began dusting himself down.

"Where will you go?"

"I'll just keep following those telegraph poles," he said, then tapped the side of his nose. "I have a plan."

She stood up and faced him. "I've shaken your hand and

wished you luck once already today. May I do so again?"

"Of course," he said, as he took her offered hand.

They held each other's gaze a moment longer, and then he put his jacket back on, turned and walked quickly away. When he reached the bottom of the slope, he stopped, looked back towards her, gave a short wave, before setting off once more in the direction of Manchester, whose distant factories and smoking chimneys added an even redder glow to the evening sunset...

The car has completed its crossing of Carrington Moss. Ruth is now driving past the vast array of cooling towers, factory chimneys and power stations of the Shell Chemical Works on the approach to Partington. She is speechless. A pall of thick smoke hangs in a sulphurous yellow above them. At night, when the chimneys belch out huge pillars of fire, a pulsing crimson glow illuminates the sky for miles around...

Delphine sat for a long time on the steps after Francis had gone, looking down the short hill towards the Ship Canal, watching the light dancing on the water. It reminded her keenly of so many similar nights she'd spent there as a child. In the past ten years she'd not been back more than once or twice a year, and after this night she would not, she realised, be returning again.

She felt suddenly exhausted. Her arms and legs were stiff and heavy with all the exertions of the day, and the realisation that both her parents were dead, at a single stroke, was just finally beginning to dawn. She was shivering. Delayed shock, she supposed, and she began to cry.

She had been so happy when she set off to see them at the start of the day, excited to be sharing her news with them of her new position at the University. They may not have fully understood the nature of what she did, but they were always so pleased and proud of her achievements, especially her mother, who knew that what her daughter now did for her work had been influenced by her own condition.

Inspired is how Delphine would have described it.

Her mother's isolation had been so acute but, as far as she had been able to tell, had not appeared to distress her at all. It was a fact she simply accepted, along with being orphaned from when she was still only a child. Communication was never easy for her, especially when it came to relating things that may have happened in the past, even with the unique system of signing which she and her father had developed between them, and which Delphine had picked up before she had learned to talk herself, and so she knew next to nothing about her life before she met Sammy, only what her father had told her, and he was not a man for talking.

What he did say was how she visited him and the others in the Camp beside the Bittern Wood when they were near to starving their first winter there, how she would come in the nights and leave tiny gifts – a pair of rabbits, an eel and some fish, a pigeon – but that they never saw her. They thought she must be a spirit, some kind of angel sent to watch over them, and then, just at dawn one morning, Sammy saw her carefully carrying a nest of eggs, creeping barefoot in the snow, before she seemed to disappear right in front of him, and so he had been convinced that, yes indeed, she truly must be a spirit.

Her mother would smile secretly at her when Sammy told this story, widening her eyes, but when Sammy told her how they met a second time, her expression would grow serious, and her gaze would be fixed entirely upon him.

He was paddling out of The Delph, he would say. It was still dark, and the moon was shining on the water, lighting his way back to the Camp. He went to check the nets, as he did every night when he got back, and on this particular night, caught in the mouth of one of them, was an otter.

"Her eyes were your mother's," he'd say to Delphine, and Eve would shake her head.

She leapt into the river pulling Sammy in after her. He almost drowned trying to keep hold of her, as she dived deep beneath the surface of the river, until finally, gasping for air, he leapt against the current over the weir – "like a salmon," Eve signed, laughing – and landed on the shore, his arms flapping, more like a beached trout. When Sammy opened his eyes, it was no longer the otter, but Eve, who knelt over him, watching his every movement intently.

"Your mother's a selkie," he would say, "she brought me back to life…"

And now they were both dead.

Delphine had never really believed that tale, not even when she was a child, but she never tired of hearing it. Hers had been a childhood like no other when she compared it to those of the other children in her school at Our Lady of Lourdes. She and Sammy and Eve had lived out of time, like lost babes in the wood. She had thought little of it, growing up as she did, having known nothing else. Now, she understood it had been special, unique, priceless beyond measure, but now, it was over, and she missed it. The pain she felt was so strong she thought it might never leave her. She did not think she wanted it to.

"But I buried it," says Delphine now to Ruth. "I never allowed myself to grieve."

"Is that why we're making this journey?" asks Ruth.

Delphine nods.

"But why now? What has happened?"

"In a moment," she says. "Once we get there. But I must finish my story first…"

She knew what she would do. She wiped her face with the back of her hand, not at all caring how she must look, stood up and tried to shake the stiffness from her limbs. She would light a fire, and she began collecting twigs to get it started. She knew there would be a stack of cut logs piled in one of the outbuildings, and sure enough there was.

Soon the fire had taken hold and flames rose up to the darkening sky overhead. She listened to all those remembered childhood sounds of rooks settling in the alders, of foxes barking in the copse, of wood cracking in the heat, and closed her eyes. Mixed in with these familiar, comforting noises drifted the lonely wail of a ship's siren, passing along the Canal below. It reminded her of another sound, one she thought she had forgotten, the haunting, eerie boom from the secretive bird which had given Bittern Wood its name. They were all of them, she felt, singing farewell to her parents. She tried to conjure up the rest of the Camp as she sat there, searching for those old ancestral words. Not just Sammy and Eve, but the rest of them. Catch and Clem. Tommy Thunder and Old Moon...

"E-a-kah-di-wah-da-ho
E-lo-hi-wakan-ho
E-ah-kah-di-wah-da-ho
E-lo-hi-wakan-ho..."

She woke with a jolt while it was still dark. The eastern sky was just beginning to show the faintest traces of white against the black. The moon was waning and the stars arched clear and bright...

She was gripped with a sudden certainty of what she must now do. She found an unlit branch, plucked a handful of dry grass, which she attached to the branch with a mixture of sap from dandelion leaves and her own spit. Then she walked through every room of the hut, followed by all of the different outbuildings that made up the settlement, searching for any keepsakes. As she suspected, there was very little to be salvaged – the net which had captured the otter, the starvationer canoe, the nest which had carried the eggs – and nothing else. She looked everywhere for the board on which Eve had painted Halley's Comet with plant dyes and mosses the night it first appeared in the sky in 1910, the night Delphine had turned twenty-one. But she could not find it...

Another Lakota funeral rite, one which she had not described to Francis, was that, after the bodies had been buried, it was the custom to burn the place where the person had last lived, together with all their belongings, to help them on their journey to the spirit world. It was not that Delphine believed any of this. She definitively didn't. The War had banished any faith she might once have had. But she knew it was what Tommy Thunder and Old Moon would have done quite naturally, and she felt instinctively it was what her parents would have wished.

She lit another branch and carried it across to the main hut. It did not take long for the fire to catch. Her parents' home had been a tinder box, and within a matter of minutes the conflagration was huge, with flames rising high into the sky, consuming the buildings like greedy snakes. And just as quickly it died away again. By the time dawn crept across the sky, all that remained of the settlement was a smouldering skeleton of charred and bleached bones, which would soon be sucked back into the earth and reclaimed...

Ruth drives past the half-timbered *King William IV* pub, which marks where Partington ends and Warburton begins.

"Not far now," says Delphine...

Francis followed the line of telegraph poles which tramped across the land for the next two hours after he had said goodbye to Delphine. He did not look back, Except for once, when he thought he saw pillars of flame licking the night sky.

It had been a shattering experience, and the walk was helping to settle his nerves once more. There was no doubt that an unexpected encounter with death threw things into perspective. He was now more determined than ever to make up for the lost years of his internment.

As he walked across the fields between the various towns and villages strung together by the telegraph wires and the remorseless spread of the city, he speculated over the relativity of distance, speed and time. When his father had been the age Francis was now, the fastest one could travel was contingent upon the speed of a horse on land, or a ship across water. But the last few years had brought automobiles, aeroplanes and now these telegraph wires. The world was getting smaller. Louis Bleriot flew across the Channel in just fifty minutes, and Francis could, if he chose, send a message by telegraph from Manchester, which could be received in Glasgow less than fifteen minutes later.

The ship's captain, when he handed Francis the telegram with the news that his father had died, talked to him enthusiastically about Guglielmo Marconi, the electrical engineer who had sent the first long-distance telegram when he alerted the world about the sinking of the *Titanic*.

"Radio," said the ship's captain, "that's the coming thing. You mark my words…"

This made an immediate impression upon Franz Halsinger, and he decided then and there to change his own name, reinvent himself, look to the future, not to the past. Franz Halsinger would become Francis Hall, and he would open premises which specialised in the latest technical innovations – photography, telegraphy, radio – which he would call Hall & Singer. When people asked him who or where Mr Singer was, he'd narrow his eyes cryptically and drop a casual remark about "a sleeping partner".

The thought of this made Francis smile as he continued his journey. A sleeping partner indeed, a nod to his relinquished ancestry, which had unjustly led to the loss of these last four years, the bitterness of which would now spur him forwards into the future, singing in the humming wires overhead.

"He who owns the air waves, owns the message," he repeated to himself as he placed one foot in front of the other, a phrase that would become his mantra, guiding him as surely as the evening star, towards an as yet unknown destination.

When he reached a junction at the small town of Flixton, where the telegraph poles divided, following two directions, he reached inside his jacket pocket, pulled out a coin and tossed it. Heads or tails. If heads, he'd go left; if tails, right. Tails. He turned at once to the right, whistling as he marched along.

He walked all night.

By dawn, just as Delphine was dousing the final flames of the funeral fire, Francis arrived in Denton. He strode down Hyde Road past a row of shops, which were all still closed. Above them, grocers and bakers, ironmongers and pawnbrokers lay fast asleep. Only he, Francis Hall, was wide awake. Opposite him stood a jeweller's – or, to be more precise, a jeweller's, optician's and engraver's. It was, he noticed, with timely satisfaction, for sale. He smiled. He recognised a kindred spirit, someone who had seen the need for diversification, for moving with the times, for responding to the changing tastes of customers' needs. He, Francis – how he liked the sound of this new name as he continued to roll it around his tongue – he also would diversify, but he would not merely move with the times, he would shape them. He would not simply respond to changes in taste and need, he would define them.

He looked up. Above the shop's Gothic-scripted sign was a large pair of round, rimless spectacles, which jutted at a right angle away from the wall. He was delighted by them. Their all-seeing eyes stared out across the city towards the future. He would keep them...

"And you have," says Ruth.

"I have indeed," says Francis.

"Here we are," says Delphine. "Just keep driving along this track till you can go no further."

Ruth cautiously obeys. The track is unpaved and rutted with pot-holes. Bob's Lane. She proceeds with the utmost care. It drops quite steeply down towards a wide expanse of water, the Manchester Ship Canal, its dull grey sheen reflecting the even darker grey of the sky above, which appears to be holding its breath, that preternatural calm that descends just before a storm is about to break...

Delphine stands by the water's edge. Francis hangs back a little. The events of the day they have just described are vividly returning to him. So little has changed in the fifty years since then. The iron capstan where he sat and smoked a cigarette. The windlass round which Delphine had so expertly tied the rope after rowing him across from the other side. Only the boat is missing.

Delphine is remembering that day too, but many other days before it. She was just four years old when her father first began to operate the ferry here, and she was eighteen when she left to go to Sedgley Park for her teacher training. Although she visited many times after that, she never lived here again. But for fourteen years this was her whole world. More than five thousand days of climbing every tree, exploring every blade of grass. And although she, too, has not been back here for fifty years, she knows it so deeply that, unlike Francis, she notices all the myriad changes that have taken place during her absence. The trees are taller of course, except for those which have been cut down, or coppiced. She recognises every one of them. They all of them had individual names, given to them by Old Moon, kept alive by Sammy and Eve, and then by herself, had she stayed. But she hadn't. Nor was she expected to. And now she has forgotten those ancient, secret names.

Despite its attractions – and she can see there were many, the simplicity, the self-sufficiency, the closeness to nature – this was no place for a life of the mind, for the life of a professional woman, which she identified as what she wanted from a very early age, almost as soon as she could read, when books opened up whole other worlds to her, which Sammy and Eve both knew instinctively she needed to discover for herself. If water was the natural element for both her parents, hers was the air. And although she could handle a boat as well as any waterman, it was in the loftier spheres of the intellect, where she truly found her mooring.

She looks down at the water's edge. Bunches of flowers have been ceremonially laid there in memory of those who lost their lives in the recent explosion. Otherwise there is nothing to signify the disaster that happened here less than two months before, when the entire surface of the Canal ignited into a mile-long river of fire. She sees the flames rising above her in her mind's eye. They merge with her memory of those she herself hurled into the night sky when she set light to the wooden huts her parents had built, lived and, in the end, died in.

She turns to look over her shoulder, back up to the rim of Coroner's Wood, where Francis helped her bury them. She remembers exactly the spot where it was. Whatever changes have altered the land since, she knows she will be able walk unfailingly to it, which is what she decides she must do next. She passes Francis, who instinctively understands what it is she is about to do and rises to follow her. She passes Ruth, who is still looking around her, wondering what it is that has happened to have brought them here today.

"Why now?" she asks Delphine again as she passes her. "Why today?"

Delphine pauses. She opens the small bag she is carrying and takes from it the folded newspaper clipping sent to her by Ishtar.

"Read this," she says. "Then you'll understand."

Ruth perches on the capstan vacated by Francis, as he and Delphine climb back up the hill towards Coroner's Wood. She hears Delphine call over her shoulder, "Did you bring a camera, Francis?"

"I did," he answers. "I've got it right here."

Ruth watches them till they disappear among the trees, then reads the clipping.

When she has finished, she looks out across the eerily still Canal. It's impossible for her to imagine on a day as still as this such a conflagration, such an inferno. The slightest of breezes riffles the surface of the water. Ruth wrinkles her nose. The scene described in the report may be beyond her imagining, but the cause is immediately apparent. The stench of the pollution, which coats the Canal in a thick, crusted sludge is noxiously overpowering.

She turns away, just as the rain begins to fall. Great, fat, heavy drops of it, splashing slowly on her face and arms. She follows where Delphine and Francis went before her, slithering up the slope, trying to gain traction in the mud. Delphine, she notices, for all her eighty-two years, navigates it effortlessly. Her body retains a deep muscle memory of the place, as unerringly she makes her way to a particular alder tree, under whose canopy she now stands. She gestures to Francis to take a photograph of it, but to make sure he does not include her in the picture. Just the tree, and the earth beside it. The site of the grave, now grown over with sorrel and groundsel, but stitched with wild flowers – sweet woodruff, hart's tongue ferns, Solomon's seal, white anemones and wood sage – all of them threaded through with violet ground ivy. Up above, rooks circle noisily. An old raven perches in the alder tree and caws hoarsely, as if it has been a while since last it had cause to use its voice.

Having taken the photograph, Francis retreats further down the slope to afford Delphine some privacy. The rain begins to fall harder. Here in the heart of the wood it makes a gentle, soothing sound, like gloved fingers tapping lightly on newly-washed leaves. Beyond the wood, it is louder, more akin to the striking of stones to try and spark a fire.

Ruth takes herself away. She has no wish to intrude upon Delphine's grief, which, having read the article, she now understands has been buried here for half a century, too long, and that it has taken this terrible explosion to wrench it back to the surface. She wanders deeper into Coroner's Wood, trying to imagine what it must have been like to live here as a child, as Delphine did, but the effort is beyond her. She cannot make the necessary leap. She knows that a world of experience lies between a simple game of make-believe and the hard, grinding reality of what life here must have been like, day after day, year after year, trapping eels, catching fish, shooting birds, gathering nuts, harvesting berries, just to be able to survive. It feels impossible to conceive of it, that such a hand-to-mouth existence was still being eked out here in the 20th century, less than eight miles from the heart of one of the world's most modern cities. She simply cannot equate the sophisticated, intellectual professional woman that is the Delphine she knows with this child of the forest she must have been.

The rain is becoming torrential. With no wind to disturb it, it is falling like arrows, harder and harder, penetrating her clothes, hurting her skin. It is time they were heading back. She decides she must rejoin Delphine and Francis, and urge them to leave. She cannot believe Francis will need much persuading. He may already be taking shelter in the car. She hopes so. She hopes, too, he has managed to convince Delphine to accompany him.

Just as she turns to go, her foot snags on a piece of ivy and becomes caught. The more she tugs on it, the more tangled she becomes, so that she is forced to stoop down to the earth to unravel it.

It is then when she finds it.

A small rectangular piece of wood, no more than eighteen inches by twelve, partly grown over with grass.

Curious, she gently extracts it, brushes away the soil and lichen, and brings it closer to her face so that she might examine it.

She knows at once what it is. From the way Delphine described it, she is certain that this is the painting her mother made more than sixty years ago – the lost painting – with mosses and plant dyes. The marks are crudely made, and the colours have faded with time, but there is no mistaking what it represents. A hut. A fire. Three figures around it. One of them, a child, looking up to the sky and pointing, and there, arching above them, the tail of the comet.

At the exact moment that the truth of this hits Ruth, a bolt of lightning strikes overhead. She sees its twin forks split the sky and spear directly towards the wood. Less than a heartbeat later, the sound of it cracking the air, almost as if it is tearing the fabric of the sky, rips through her. It is followed by another sound. A cry like a bird in pain.

Clutching Eve's painting tightly to her, Ruth runs back down the slope, skittering and sliding as her feet slip in the mud. She reaches the place where she left Delphine earlier, the grave beside the alder tree, to discover her lying prostrate among the wild flowers. She instinctively tries to rush to her side, but Francis holds out a hand to restrain her. Delphine hauls herself up from the earth, remaining on her knees, and proceeds to smear the juices of the leaves and flowers of the plants across her face and arms. She then digs her fingers deep into the soil and daubs streaks of it between the marks she has already made. Like war paint. All the while she is singing, the old Lakota chant she last sang half a century ago, her voice a rasping croak, like a raven's.

"E-a- kah-di-wah-da-ho
E-lo-hi-wakan-ho
E-ah-kah-di-wah-da-ho
E-lo-hi-wakan-ho..."

The rain continues to hammer down. The thunder rumbles round and through them. In the air. Under the earth. The lightning spits and sizzles. And still Delphine beats her chest with her fists, and sings. Till the lightning fades, the thunder quietens, the rain retreats, and Delphine can sing no more...

Afterwards, when Francis and Ruth have between them managed to half-walk, half-carry her back to the car, Delphine begins to recover herself. Luckily, having naïvely thought they might have been going on a picnic, Ruth had brought travel rugs, a thermos and sandwiches, which she has unpacked from the boot, and the three of them now sit inside the car, wrapped in the rugs, shivering less as they each sip their mugs of reviving sweet tea.

"Thank you," says Delphine eventually. "For your indulgence, and for not saying anything. I must have cut an alarming sight. I expect I still do. But I am quite myself now, I assure you."

Ruth and Francis exchange a look, but say nothing.

Ruth decides the time might now be right to show Delphine

the painting she has found. She places it carefully into her hands. The moment Delphine sees it, she involuntarily gasps. She raises a hand to her mouth, which she then rests just below her throat on her chest. She looks at the painting a long time in silence. Eventually she speaks, in a voice so low she can scarcely be heard.

"I thought this was lost," she says. "Irretrievably…"

They finish their picnic. The rain eases. A weak sun bleeds through the leaden sky.

"Time we were going," says Francis.

"I agree," says Delphine. "But I wish to return via a different route. Before you can protest, Francis, it will take us no longer, I promise you."

Once they have driven back up Bob's Lane towards the road again, Delphine directs Ruth away from Partington, towards the Warburton Toll Bridge. Originally constructed in 1863 to cross the River Mersey by the Earl of Ellesmere, it was rebuilt to span the Manchester Ship Canal just thirty years later, when the course of the river was diverted to incorporate it, and a toll of two shillings and sixpence was introduced for all vehicles crossing it. An exorbitant sum back then, but written into the legislation was the proviso that this levy could never be raised. Now, as the bottle-green Vauxhall Viva approaches the toll gate, Francis fishes around for the twelve new pence they need, still flummoxed by the decimalised currency introduced by Edward Heath's government just four months before. Confusingly the old money can still be used alongside the new, but with different values applying.

"Everything old is new again," he says as they approach the barrier. "That's what Giulia always says at any rate."

Eventually, after something of a flurry, they are permitted to cross. They look down through the fretted iron work of the cantilever bridge onto the Canal below them. It looks so benign from this height. It is impossible to conceive of the wall of flame that leapt up from it so recently.

They then follow the Liverpool Road back through Rixton, into Cadishead, past the Steel Works, beyond Irlam, towards Barton. Just five miles. But redolent with memory for both Francis and Delphine. Ruth senses this and remains quiet. She wonders what new revelations are about to emerge.

On their left they skirt the string of Mosses that stretch between Manchester and Warrington – Rixton, Glazebrook, Cadishead, Chat, Irlam and Barton. On their right the Canal tracks them. Mostly it is out of sight. But not out of mind for Delphine, who recalls how, the morning fifty years ago after she had burned down her parents' dwelling and outbuildings, she rowed her father's starvationer canoe all the way along it, till its junction with the Bridgewater Canal, beneath the Barton Aqueduct...

It was still early. The first rays of the sun were already beginning to warm the day. Delphine placed the net and the carefully wrapped nest into the prow of the starvationer. She sat inside it and pushed off from the shore with the oar and began to row.

She caught a glimpse of herself reflected in the surface of the water and hardly recognised who she saw. What a difference a single day had made. The extreme physical and emotional exertions of the previous twenty-four hours, coupled with the fires, had turned her into something resembling a pirate, an outlaw, a highwaywoman, or, perhaps, a Sioux warrior, for that is how she felt, rather than someone who was about to join a new academic team at the University of Manchester. Her clothes, which had been one of her best outfits, were now dishevelled and torn. She had ripped the hem of her skirt to stop it from trailing further in the dirt and, to risk the chance of it tripping her up, she had looped it between her legs and tucked it into her waist band. She had discarded her jacket, now rolled up and stowed at the back of the canoe, and she had undone the top two buttons of her blouse, as well as rolling up the sleeves, so that it was now more like a man's work shirt. Her hair, which had become completely unpinned and fallen loosely onto her shoulders, she had tied back in a kind of turban with the strip of cloth she had used to cover her face the previous day when in close proximity to the bodies of her parents. She had cast off her shoes and stockings, so that she could enjoy the feeling of the warm air over her bare legs and feet, which, like her arms, bore the marks of the events of the last day. But these were superficial compared to the deeply etched lines of sorrow smeared across her cheeks and brow, like war paint.

She had grown up by water, and, although it had been several years since she had last rowed a canoe, her muscles retained the memory of what she must do. She passed a heron at the Canal's edge, which took off in that slow, uncertain, cumbersome way they had, before gaining height with sure, strong wing beats, while she too found her rhythm and began to plough the water with increased confidence, each long pull-through of the oar recalling a remembrance of times past, propelling her towards where she knew she must go next.

She reckoned it was approximately five miles to her first port of call, the Barton Swing Aqueduct, where the wide sluggish waters of the Manchester Ship Canal passed beneath the older, narrower passage of the Bridgewater. At her current rate of progress, she thought she should reach that in a little over two hours.

She rowed through the centre of the channel when she could, enjoying the freedom of the open water. It being a Sunday, there was less traffic than would have been the case on a week day, but she still had to be watchful to steer clear of the coal barges plying up and down, and the occasional large liner making its unstoppable way towards the Port of Manchester. She would hug the shoreline whenever one of these leviathans approached, careful not to be tipped by the surge of their wake, for the starvationer was a narrow vessel, not designed for such open water and easily capsized. The effort and concentration required to reach the Barton Bridges took her mind temporarily away from her grief.

She passed beneath the Cadishead Railway Viaduct, where just yesterday she had skipped down in such high spirits, before navigating her way through the cross currents where the Canal stopped sharing its course with the Mersey, which flowed off towards the meadows of Flixton, until she reached the Irlam Locks. These were manually operated by a series of stone sluices, which powered mechanically-driven vertical sets of steel roller-gates, supported by masonry piers, designed to maintain a continuous water-flow along the Canal's length. Delphine was anxious that the increased turbulence caused by the sluices might sink her, and so she was forced to lift the canoe onto the bank and drag it along the tow path until she had passed the locks completely. One of the gate keepers saw her struggling with it and offered his assistance, which she gratefully accepted, relieved that, while he may have looked at her curiously, he asked her no questions. He must have seen far stranger sights than me, she thought, as she resumed rowing, once she was clear of the locks.

But in less than half a mile, she had to repeat the entire process again in order to negotiate the Barton Locks system. It was more crowded here, and she was attracting more attention. She could sense the eyes of the men upon her bare legs, but there was nothing for it. She had reached her first port of call. If she was to achieve the mission she had set herself, she would have to withstand their stares. She untucked her skirt from its waist band and let its folds unfurl and fall back towards her feet, covering her calves at least. She put on her shoes and walked towards them...

Francis, too, is remembering times past. Though not as far back as Delphine. His thoughts turn to an event some eleven years later, almost forty years ago to the day. But where today has been wild and stormy, the day back then was glorious and warm. It was the Manchester Festival of Speed, held here, just where they are now passing, at Barton Aerodrome, for the occasion of the annual *Kings Cup Air Race*. It is their first outing together, he and George, who is using his first-ever camera, the *Foth Derby* recommended to him by Francis on the day that they met, just a fortnight before, when George had arrived on his DOT Racer, looking heroically handsome in his leather jacket and helmet, removing his goggles to reveal that heart-stopping smile. They had ridden to the aerodrome together. Francis had been forced to loop his arms around George's waist and lean into his back, his face pressed close to the leather jacket, the smell of which had been intoxicating...

Francis is now busy positioning himself with his *Kinamo*, his experimental hand-held cine-camera, with which he hopes to capture footage of all the aircraft and pilots as they land. He will then send this off to Pathé and Movietone, both of whom have expressed interest in inserting edited extracts of any footage he might obtain into the Newsreel Film depicting *The Kings Cup* each aims to present in cinemas by the end of the month.

Looking at him now, through the viewfinder of his *Foth Derby*, George thinks Francis looks like a pioneer, recording as it happens the Race of the Age, portraying these daredevils of the skies as latter day Christopher Columbuses, Vasco de Gamas, Amerigo Vespuccis, which they truly are, conquering new worlds, pushing the boundaries of human endeavour to the absolute limit, at exactly this moment, on this very day, in this very spot, placing Manchester right at the heart of this new spirit of adventure, and then communicating it to the rest of the world.

George waits until he sees that Francis is ready, framing him so that he stands in the centre of the composition, then calls out.

"Francis – look this way."

Francis turns, frowning as he seeks out the voice who has called him, then smiling as his pale eyes pick out George.

George clicks the shutter and takes the photograph.

"My first one," he shouts, his voice raised above the general hubbub. "I wanted it to be of you. Here in the present, about to capture for all time a moment that has yet to take place, but that will soon be consigned to history, using technology that is not yet available. I shall call it 'Future Perfect'."

"I don't know what you're talking about," Francis shouts back, smiling even more broadly…

Delphine has come to a decision.

The synchronicity between the events of fifty years ago and today continues to escalate. The two time zones are almost completely conjoined in her imagination.

"Back then," she says, "I rowed my way to Barton. I needed to find Yasser to help me complete my mission. Sammy had saved Yasser's life while they worked alongside one another to dig the Canal. There had been a chemical explosion on the island of Pomona, between the Canal and the Irwell, not unlike the one at Bob's Lane. Yasser was nearly killed. My father, living up to his name, 'leapt like a fish' across the burning water to pull Yasser from the wreckage and back to safety. I knew that in my own hour of need Yasser would come to my aid. And so he did. He helped me complete my journey, returning my father's starvationer canoe to its spiritual home, the underground waterways of The Delph…"

She pauses briefly, as she marshals her thoughts.

"Yasser is dead now of course. But Esther is still alive. His daughter-in-law. My friend, who sent me the newspaper clipping that set me off on this odyssey I am pursuing. Or Ishtar, as I must remember to call her now. She still lives in the same house. I need to see her. Today. Now. It will be the final act of closure for me."

Francis and Ruth have the same thought simultaneously, as they each regard Delphine's somewhat wild and disheveled state with understandable misgiving.

It is Ruth who voices their shared concern first. "Are you sure?" she says.

"Yes," says Delphine determinedly. "I am." She takes in Ruth's anxious, glanced appraisal of her appearance. "Oh, don't worry about that. Esther – Ishtar – won't care a jot what I look like."

"Francis?" asks Ruth, hoping to solicit some support, but she can see at once that none will be forthcoming. Francis is miles away.

"Did you say 'Esther'?" he asks Delphine...

"Fancy a spin?" asks George. "I was talking to one of the organisers earlier, and he was telling me there are some long, straight, quiet roads that cut across Chat Moss, just the other side of the airfield, where you can really work up a bit of speed." He pats the side of the DOT Racer. "It'd be great to put her through her paces a bit. What do you think?"

Francis watches George fasten the strap of his leather cycling cap under his chin and is once again swept away by how handsome he looks, how fearless and strong. He feels himself being borne aloft by the same spirit of optimism and adventure.

"Yes," he says. "Let's."

As soon as they leave the aerodrome and turn off from the

Liverpool Road onto Barton Moss Road, Francis begins to relax. The crowds, which had begun to bother him at the aerodrome, feel far away now. The land opens out around them, wide flat vistas, big skies and a horizon which definitively proves to any old flat-earth doubters that the world is unquestionably round. Dragonflies hover by the edge of the marshes, above which they now glide along a high bank, then swoop and disappear. Swifts skim and dive before them, carving the air in a dark tracery of speed against the blue canvas of the sky. George opens up the throttle on his DOT Racer and allows their speed to increase, past Black Wood, along Twelve Yards Road, down Raspberry Lane, almost as far as Four Lane Ends, deeper and deeper into the watery wilderness of Chat Moss itself, where a few ramshackle huts and houses hunker low against the land, so completely overgrown that they are almost indistinguishable from it. Last Retreat. Hephzibah. Ebenezer Farm. Hope Cottage.

George becomes conscious of Francis tightening his grip around his waist as he continues to pick up speed. Francis experiences the rush of air against his skin and through his hair. He has rarely felt this happy, or this free. He wants to stretch out his arms wide and high, and shout as loud as he can.

This is us. Now. Here. In this moment. Alive.

But all that comes out of his mouth is a wild, wordless, deep-throated cry. George, caught up in the same exuberance, joins in with him, the two of them roaring their pleasure to the sky.

At the same moment, lifting from the Moss in front of them, a few hundred yards away, a great white bird takes to the air. Its neck is retracted deep into its shoulders. Its wing beats are heavy and long. It is gaining height with exaggerated slowness. Its long bill points towards them like an arrow.

Time stretches.

George sees the bird too late. He ducks his head and brakes

as hard as he dare. He has such little margin for manoeuvre along the narrow embankment, whose slides slope steeply down towards the marshes on either side, that the egret smashes into them. Its wings become entangled with the still outstretched arms of Francis, knocking him off the back of the bike, which George finally manages to stop. When he turns his head, Francis is nowhere to be seen. The white egret, freed at last, is gradually gaining height, seemingly uninjured, its great wings lifting it into the air and away over the Moss...

Some time later, when Francis regains consciousness, a young woman is bending over him. She wears a white scarf around her head and shoulders. She looks to Francis like an angel. She has been ministering to his wounds. It seems he has broken his leg. He doesn't remember. He wants to know where George is.

"I'm here," says a voice, reassuring him, squeezing his hand.

Now the angel is standing up, telling him she is going to get help. She has a bicycle instead of wings.

"Wait," says Francis, his voice dry and rasping. "Follow the telegraph poles."

"What?"

"It'll be quicker, I promise. Follow the telegraph poles. Follow the wires that split out from them to the nearest house. There'll be a telephone there. They may let you use it."

"Yes," she says, getting onto her bicycle. "Good idea."

He watches her cycle away into the haze before drifting off to sleep once more...

When he next wakes up, it has started to grow dark. He is feeling suddenly cold and cannot stop shivering. A pair of gynandrous peppered moths are grazing on the underside of buckthorn leaves in the last of the light.

Just as they do so, another, stronger light sweeps across the Moss, catching them in its beam. George looks towards it, shielding his eyes with one hand, while lifting up Francis to a sitting position with his other. It's an ambulance. It pulls up alongside them, spraying up bits of shale and gravel. The driver and an attendant leap out and fetch a stretcher from the back. They are followed by the angel, who hurries towards a dazed George and Francis.

"Where are they taking me?"

"Hope Hospital in Salford," she calls back. "It's not far."

A hospital called 'Hope', he thinks, must be a good omen. He looks up towards the back of the ambulance just as the angel is mounting her bicycle once more.

"What's your name?" he cries. "How can we ever thank you?"

She turns towards him, her face in silhouette, haloed from behind by the headlights of the ambulance. Her head is covered with the white *qurqash*, which reaches down past her shoulders.

"Esther," she says, but her voice is carried away from him by the wind. "Esther," she says again.

To Francis, as she recedes away from him towards the distant vanishing point, it sounds instead like 'Ishtar...'

"Take the next right," says Delphine. "That's it. Peel Green Road."

Ruth does as she is bid. They are heading back down towards the Ship Canal.

"Then a left," adds Delphine. "Here. Into Higher Croft."

The road climbs back towards Patricroft, past Godfrey Ermen School, from where scores of young children are pouring out through the gates to their waiting parents, then left into Stanley Road.

"Here we are," announces Delphine. "Number 64."

The rain has eased completely now. But the angry expression worn by the eight-year-old girl sitting on the front door step as Delphine, supported on either side by Ruth and Francis, approaches is darker than any thundercloud.

"If you're looking for my Grandma," she scowls, "she's not in. She never is. Nor is my Mum, who's always at work, and nor my Auntie Far, who should be."

"I see," replies Delphine, not in the least perturbed. "And who might *you* be?"

"I'm Jenna Ward, of 64 Stanley Road, Patricroft, Eccles, Salford, Manchester, Lancashire, England, Great Britain, Europe, The World, the Solar System, the Universe. Otherwise known as the Latchkey Kid. For no one was there to meet me from school. And no one is here to let me in at home."

"Then you can't be a Latchkey Kid, can you?" says Delphine. "Technically speaking. Not if you have no key?"

"I suppose not," says Jenna crossly, although she is beginning to like this strange-looking old woman, who doesn't talk down to her the way most grown-ups do.

"I expect there's a simple explanation," says Delphine. "There usually is. Let's try and work out what it might be, shall we?" She sits herself down on the step next to Jenna, who companionably makes room for her. "What do you think might have happened?"

"My Grandma might have been knocked off her bike."

"Goodness me, I hope not."

"I'm always telling her to look where she's going, but she doesn't listen. She's in too much of a hurry."

"I see. That must be very vexing for you."

"It *is*."

"What does she say to you when you tell her to be careful?"

" 'The early bird catches the worm'."

"And what do you say to that?"

" 'A cat has nine lives, but *you* only have one'."

"Very wise. I imagine that gives her *paws* for thought?"

"No, it doesn't... Wait a minute – that was a joke, wasn't it? Paws for pause?"

"It was meant to be. It wasn't very funny, I'm afraid."

"No, it wasn't. But it was a good try."

"Thank you."

"*Ahlan wa sahlan*. That's Arabic for 'You're welcome'. My Auntie Far taught me that."

"Did she?"

"Yes. She should be here by now."

"I don't expect she'll be long. Does she ride a bicycle too?"

"No way. She drives a car. Like you. Only hers is a white Mini."

"And here it comes now, I think," interrupts Ruth, catching sight of it roaring around the corner, as she joins them by the doorstep..

"Yes," says Jenna. "That'll be her. She always drives fast."

"Does she?" says Ruth, smiling.

"Yes. Do you?"

"Not as fast as that, no."

"Perhaps you need more practice?"

"Perhaps I do."

"How old are you? I'm eight and three quarters."

"Are you? I'm seventeen and a half."

"Is this lady your grandmother?"

"No. She's..."

"A friend, I hope," interjects Delphine.

"Why are you dressed up?" asks Jenna, looking closely at Delphine, with the patterned travel rug still wrapped around her shoulders. "Are you playing a game?"

"I suppose I have been really."

"With all those marks on your face, you look like Old Nokomis in *The Song of Hiawatha*."

"Do I? Shall I tell you a secret?"

"Yes please," says Jenna seriously.

Delphine leans across and whispers in her ear. Jenna's eyes widen like saucers.

"Have you been reading that at school?" asks Delphine, after she has pulled back.

"Yes," answers Jenna. "I love it." She begins to chant it in rhythm.

> *"By the shores of Gitchee Gumee*
> *By the shining Big-Sea-Water*
> *Stood the wigwam of Nokomis*
> *Daughter of the Moon, Nokomis..."*

"That's where we've been today," says Delphine. "By the shining big-sea-water."

"Have you?" asks Jenna, her eyes on stalks and her mouth opening wide, so that she reminds Delphine of a fledgling bird. "What was it like?"

But before Delphine can even begin to answer, Farida rushes through the gate, storming up a hurricane.

"Where have you been, young lady? I've been worried sick. You know you were supposed to wait for me by the school gates."

"But you weren't there, Auntie Far," replies Jenna with wide-eyed innocence. "I thought you must have forgotten me."

"How dare you suggest such a thing? As if I would..."

"Not that it matters, for I'm perfectly able to walk home all by myself. As you can see, for here I am."

Farida is furious. "Get inside at once, Madam," she says, juggling various shopping bags and a key. "Go upstairs and change out of your school uniform, then come straight back down and help me get the tea ready."

Jenna knows that when Farida is mad – which is extremely rare – it is best to do as she's told, and so she trots off as meekly as a lamb. "It was very nice to meet you," she says to

Delphine before she finally steps inside.

"And it has been most interesting to meet you too, Jenna," replies Delphine, stiffly getting to her feet.

"I'm sorry about that," says Farida. "I was five minutes late, that's all. But one of the mums at the Nursery where I work was late in collecting her own daughter, so what was I supposed to do?"

"It's quite all right," says Delphine. "Your niece has kept us most entertained."

"I'm sure she has. Now – how might I help you?"

"I'm sorry. You must think me frightfully presumptuous, sitting on your front step like this."

"It's not my front step," replies Farida. "It's Ishtar's."

"Yes," says Delphine. "I know. It's Ishtar I have come to see. We're old friends. Will she be long, do you think?"

If Farida is in any way surprised, either by Delphine's apparent sureness that she will be welcome, or by the somewhat bizarre and startling nature of her appearance, she does not show it.

"Then you must come in," she says, "and get yourself dry and warm. I'm sure Ishtar won't be long. She's rarely away for long. I expect it's one of her waifs and strays. She's always helping out someone in need."

"Thank you. I'm Delphine, by the way. Delphine Fish."

"Why didn't you say sooner?" says Farida at once, putting down her various shopping bags and smiling warmly "I've heard your name mentioned on several occasions. I'll make some spiced ginger tea. You look like you could do with it."

"That sounds most restorative."

Delphine turns back towards Francis and Ruth, who are standing as open-mouthed as Jenna was just a few moments before.

"You two get along now, I shall be quite all right. I shall either stay the night, or, if that is not convenient, I shall easily be able to make my own way back home. It's quite straightforward from here. Just two buses. The 100 followed by the 53. Thank you so much for today. Goodbye."

And without another word she has followed Farida into the house and shut the front door behind her. Francis and Ruth are left to continue gaping outside in the drive.

"She's incorrigible," says Ruth.

"She's formidable," counters Francis. "And quite magnificent."

"But will she be all right?" asks Ruth anxiously. "Really?"

"I don't doubt it for a moment," says Francis. "You've been utterly marvellous, my dear, dealing with what has been a quite extraordinary day."

"I shall never forget it. The way she clawed at the ground like she did. I've never seen such…"

"What? Grief?"

"I was going to say 'passion'."

"They're cut from the same cloth, I believe?"

"I suppose. It was just so… searing, so… naked."

Francis says nothing. To him the experience had been like bearing witness to some kind of spiritual cleansing. An atonement, or sanctification.

Instead he simply says, "Time we went home. You'll be wanting to find out how your father's been getting along."

"Yes. You're right."

They get back into the car. But just before Ruth can turn on the ignition, Francis puts out his hand.

"Wait," he says. "Look."

Around the corner cycles Ishtar with a slow, sure grace. In addition to the white *qurqash* on her head and shoulders, she is now dressed completely from head to toe in white. She glides past them in a shimmer of light, which seems to emanate from somewhere within her. Francis is transfixed. Even after she has passed from their sight, he continues to stare at the space she had occupied, which, to his unreliable eyes, appears still to quiver and vibrate with her presence...

They cross over the Ship Canal for the final time by way of the Barton Swing Bridge. But then, in less than half a mile, the car suddenly judders and jolts, lurching forward in a series of kangaroo jumps, before cutting out altogether. Ruth just manages to guide it into a convenient lay-by, where, after emitting a painful crunching noise, the grinding of metal upon metal, it wheezes to a stop with a painful hissing of steam from the radiator. She leans her head against the steering wheel with a groan. The emotions of the day have suddenly caught up with her, and she bursts into tears.

Francis looks around him. Across the road he spies a telephone kiosk, glowing a reassuring red in the gloom. He pats his hand awkwardly on Ruth's back.

"Wait here," he says. "I shan't be long..."

Half an hour later George is emerging from underneath the bonnet of the bottle-green Vauxhall Viva, wiping his hands on a rag.

"Well," he says, "I won't beat about the bush. There's a fair few things wrong with her. But I should be able to patch her up enough to get you home. Then you'll need to contact a local garage tomorrow to have the repairs done properly. Bridge Motors on Burton Road – they're your best bet. Ask for Derek. Say I said to call him. He'll see you right."

"Thank you, George. You're a life-saver."

"I wouldn't say that exactly, but it's always best to know where you stand. Once a problem's diagnosed, you're half way there to fixing it, that's what I say."

"Yes. So – where *do* we stand?"

"You need oil. Obviously. I've brought enough with me to keep you going. That sound of grating metal you described –

that had me worried. Piston rings. If *they* were shot, you'd be looking at a bill so high you'd be better off thinking about a new car. But luckily we've got to them in time." He pauses briefly, then adds more kindly. "You really do need to make sure in future you don't let the oil get so low, love."

"Yes. I'm sorry. It's usually Mum who sees to that sort of thing. I've only just started driving. But she's... well – she's got a lot on her mind just now."

"I know, love. She telephoned me today."

"Oh? Is there any news?"

"Ay, lass. There is. It's not good, I'm afraid. Your Dad's had to go to the hospital on Nell Lane. Your Mum's there with him now."

"What's happened?"

"I don't think anything has, love. They just need to take a proper look at him, carry out more tests, work out exactly what it is, then find the best way to treat him."

"I see."

"Like I said before, once a problem's diagnosed, you're half way there to fixing it."

"But what if it can't be fixed?" Ruth's eyes are brimming with tears.

"Then I reckon it's best to know that too. Forewarned is forearmed."

"Yes. I suppose so."

"But we're getting ahead of ourselves. Let's see what they find first, eh?"

Ruth nods, blinking rapidly.

"Right now," continues George, "we need to focus on what we can definitely put right with this car of yours."

"It's more than just the oil then?"

"Oh yes. First of all, I hope you don't mind me asking, but are you wearing tights today?"

"Yes. Why?"

"In that case, I'll need you to take them off, I'm afraid. To act as a temporary fan belt. Don't worry – Francis and I shall avert our eyes."

They duly turn their backs, while Ruth wriggles awkwardly out of them, while still sitting behind the steering wheel.

"Here," she says, handing them through the open window.

"Thanks. That's the ticket. And I've got some duct tape to wrap around that burst radiator hose. Then, once I've topped you up with oil and water, and cleaned round the spark plugs, you should be ready to go."

By the time he has finished, the street lamps have come on and are beginning to glow. Ruth watches as the one shining directly above them is already attracting a dare of moths, irresistibly drawn towards it. She shudders as their wings recoil in pain each time they come into contact with the light. Yet still they refuse to yield...

Ruth wants to drive straight to the hospital in Withington, so Francis decides he will go back with George on the back of his DOT Racer. It's only six miles to his flat on Adelphi Street from where they are, and it will take less than twenty minutes to get there...

George rustles up a simple supper – baked beans and an omelette, followed by a glass of beer – while Francis looks around. It's been a long time since he was last here. He can't remember when it was. Years probably. When they were a couple, they mostly used to meet somewhere in town – *The Queen's* as like as not – then go back to Francis's in Denton. They still did afterwards from time to time, though less so over the years, but they have always remained close. When homosexuality was made legal, Francis had half-hoped George might be tempted to renew their relationship, but he shook his head.

"I'm too set in my ways now, love," he had said. "I prefer

my own bed at night."

Francis had been inclined to suggest that he understood, but that he was more than willing to share that bed from time to time.

"Ay, from time to time," George replied, "but not every night."

Francis did not press the point. He was just about to turn seventy when they had this conversation, and, much as he hated to admit it, his libido was showing undeniable signs of waning.

Now, he looks about the sitting room of George's flat, revelling in its familiarity and clutter. The table was stacked with old contact sheets mixed in with various motor cycle parts.

"You must take me as you find me," says George as he brings in the beer.

"Don't worry," smiles Francis. "I'll take you…"

After supper they fall easily into their old ways of conversational intimacy.

"You're lucky it's a Tuesday," says George.

"Why so?"

"Tomorrow I'd be teaching night school at the Institute."

"You're a martyr to the cause, George."

"I love it, Francis. I wouldn't miss it for the world."

"How's your protégé?"

"Sol?"

"Is that his name?"

"You know very well it is. You only pretend to feign disinterest."

"I suppose. How well you know me."

The two of them share a look that stretches down the years.

"What you may not know, however," says George, "is that Sol is Ishtar's son."

"No?"

George watches with pleasure the range of emotions

passing across his friend's face like clouds scudding across a summer sky.

"I had no idea. To think... just a couple of hours ago I was standing right outside his door... Delphine never mentioned him..."

"Why should she? I don't think she knows him. She and Ishtar – Esther as she was still then – were friends in the twenties. They go way back."

"Even further than us."

"I love these random connections."

"But *are* they random, do you think?"

"You're such a hopeless romantic, Francis," says George fondly. "Of course they are."

"Maybe..."

"Another beer?"

"Why not? Let's live dangerously."

"You always have. It's me who's been the cautious one."

"The sensible one. Whereas I..."

"What?"

"... have had my head in the clouds half the time."

"A dreamer."

"If you say so."

"I do."

"What's this Sol of yours dreaming about when he comes to your classes?"

"He's not *my* Sol. But he *is* a dreamer. He wants redemption."

"Don't we all?"

"Yes, to a degree. But with Sol, it's something much deeper. He wants to..."

"What?"

"Make his mark. Leave something behind him after he's gone."

"This mural you're helping him with?"

"In part. Though I've warned him that where he wants to install it means that it has no chance whatever of remaining there permanently. The developers'll be bound to clear it all away once they get their planning permission, which they will do eventually. But that doesn't seem to bother him. 'It's not the mural itself that matters in the end,' he says. 'It's the act of making it'."

"A kind of expiation?"

"That's it in a nutshell, Francis. He wants to atone for his past mistakes, and at the same time forge some kind of link between his father and grandfather, out of which he can make something new, something uniquely his, which he can then pass on to his own children and grandchildren."

"A line."

"That's right. One that might twist and turn and sometimes double-back on itself, but will keep on going. Like the rivers in the city. We may bury them under concrete, force them underground in tunnels, but we know they're still there, even though we don't always see them. One day – who knows? – we might uncover them all again, and watch them create new channels in which to flow, but till then, they'll keep popping up when we least expect them and surprise us."

Francis leans across and kisses George lingeringly on the lips.

"I love you," he says.

"I love you too. I always have."

"So," says Francis, a few moments later, "when will Sol finish this great work of his?"

George sighs. "Not for a long time yet. Six, maybe seven years...?"

"Seven years?!"

"What he's attempting is nothing less than the history of the world, as told through the story of one life."

"Isn't that a tad ambitious, George?"

"It's impossible. But just to attempt it, to contemplate it even, is nothing short of heroic."

"Even more so if you say that once it's finished, it risks being torn down."

"I agree. That's why I find myself so personally invested in it, too."

"Then if you are, so am I."

"Really?"

"Absolutely. Just promise me one thing."

"What?"

"That you'll take me along to its grand unveiling. I'll even ride on the back of your DOT Racer."

"It's a deal."

"And make sure you make a photographic record of it. So at least he will have something to show for all of his effort."

"Don't worry, I will. But even that's not guaranteed to last for ever, is it?"

"Does anything?"

"Photographs fade over time. When I first began taking them, I was completely enthralled watching them emerge from seemingly nothing in the dark room. The way the image would gradually materialise right before your eyes was nothing short of miraculous. I still feel like that today. It's like giving birth."

"Only not so painful."

"Bringing something into the world that did not exist before."

"We're being very philosophical this evening."

"But the reverse happens also. They deteriorate and degrade. Sometimes they disappear entirely. Just like the streets I take photographs of. Almost as if they've never been. Except as a memory."

"But is that enough?"

"It has to be. But not if the photographs disappear too. Then there'll be nothing left at all to remind us of who we are, or where we've come from. Unless..."

"Yes?"

"I was thinking about this while I was fixing Ruth's car."

"What?"

"Actually I was thinking about Roland. When he first started, with the Manchester Baby and the Manchester Madam, he had no idea where these computers would lead us. It was all a bit of a joke, do you remember? Machines so large they needed an entire room to house them? But now, not only are they much smaller, with microprocessors integrating millions of separate bits of data into a single circuit, so that in time, much sooner than any of us think, we'll all be able to have one on our desks at home, but they're far more sophisticated. Where Roland used to fantasise about the next generation of computers being able to make a series of mathematical calculations more rapidly than a human, so that eventually one might be able to play a reasonable game of chess, now they are already programming robots to manufacture cars, which will soon contain more digital than mechanical components, and I'd no longer be able to fix his daughter's car. But more seriously, they will put millions of people out of work."

"But won't they simply be used to do the kind of mindless, repetitive tasks on a production line that are more like drudgery than work, that nobody really wants to do, thereby freeing us up to do more interesting things?"

"Such as what? It's a fine line between what you term drudgery and what others might call craft. There's a dignity in labour that's ennobling."

"Now who's being hopelessly romantic?"

"I know. I'm sorry. But there's something in the way a place is shaped and defined by the work it does, by the things it makes. What's going to happen to Manchester when the cotton mills close, which they *will* do? What's going to happen to somewhere like Durham if they shut down the pits, like they've already done here at Bradford Colliery, which plays such a crucial part in Sol's mural? When I talk about the dignity of labour, I'm talking about the respect and recognition for the traditions that come with it. A fair day's wage for a fair day's work. The sense that each of us can make a contribution that has value and worth, and that it's acknowledged. When Ted Heath talks about taking on the miners, I don't think he has any comprehension at all of how work and community and history and tradition are all so inextricably linked."

"Do people make places or do places make people?"

"Exactly. That's why Joe Gormley will chew him up for breakfast and spit out what he can't swallow for the seagulls to scrap over."

"Poor Sailor Ted."

"He gets no sympathy from me. His *Morning Cloud* can go out on the evening tide as far as I'm concerned."

Francis playfully starts to sing.

"All the nice boys love a sailor
All the nice boys love a tar..."

George throws a cushion at him, but Francis is not to be deterred.

"For there's something about a sailor
Well you know what sailors are..."

George is now laughing in spite of himself. "Sorry about that," he says. "I have a tendency to get on my soap box too much these days."

"At least I know what *not* to get you for your birthday."

"Which you missed this year incidentally."

"And there was I, thinking you didn't really count them any more."

"I don't."

"But now I *do* know what to get you for Christmas?"

"What?"

"A digital camera. So your photos will never be lost."

"That's what I was thinking about while fixing Ruth's car. But they're years away, aren't they?"

"They're closer than you think. NASA have used them already in space when Mariner 4 flew alongside Mars. Michael Thompsett, an engineer working with *Marconi* and *English Electric*, has been using charge-coupled sensor technology with linked capacitors to develop digital images, while in America, at Kansas University, the computer scientist Nasir Ahmed has been creating significant advances in data compression to pioneer what he calls the *Cromenco Cyclops*."

"What's that?"

"Only a twinkle in the eye at the moment, but by next year it might be the world's first commercially produced digital camera."

"You've not lost your touch, I see," smiles George.

"One likes to keep up to date," replies Francis, clearly enjoying the compliment.

"It reminds me of when you sold me my very first camera."

"A *Foth Derby*."

"I have it still."

"It remains a perfectly functioning camera. I used one today in fact to take a picture for Delphine."

"After first running me through the whole gamut of what were then cutting-edge new cameras."

"There will always be technical breakthroughs, leading to newer, more capable cameras."

"Even when they go digital?"

"Especially then. I can envisage a time when they'll be so small and compact that people will simply slip them into their pockets along with their wallets. Everyone will have them, and they'll share the pictures they take with them on their mobile computers."

"What about the dark room?"

"Dispatched to the dustbin of history, old boy. Only to be seen in museums."

"Oh – I should miss them. Some of my happiest times have been spent in a dark room."

"I couldn't have put it better myself," laughs Francis, as he reaches across to turn out the light...

In the small spare room at the top of the house on Stanley Road, Delphine is also just about to turn out the light too, but first she decides to take one more look at the painting of Halley's Comet made by her mother, which Ruth had literally stumbled upon earlier that day.

It seems nothing short of miraculous, not only that Ruth should have found it in the first place, but that after more than sixty years it has survived intact and undamaged. Even more remarkable is that the image has not vanished from the board it was so crudely painted on with those plant dyes and mosses that Eve used to like to collect, that the rain has not washed it all way, and that its colours have not overly degraded. She pores over every detail of it, imagining the way her mother would have painted it, quickly, directly, using her fingers, watching the comet above her in the night sky, then transferring what she saw, *how* she saw it, onto this simple piece of wood, which no doubt had just happened to be lying around, and then, just as promptly, discarding it.

Delphine switches off the light and holds the painting tightly to her. When she gets home, she will prop it up on her mantelpiece, next to the bird's nest she saved from the hut before she burned it, so that it is not in direct sunlight, where she can look on it every day, as just another household object, not precious, for it was never intended as such, not a relic of some bygone age, not something to be shut away in a drawer, or stored out of sight in a suitcase, in an attic, or even a museum, but a simple reminder of how things survive, of how they tether us to where we have come from, and point us to where we might go next.

She has very much enjoyed her evening with Ishtar, a name which now trips easily off her lips, for it becomes her friend so perfectly. A firestar.

They have not reminisced at all. Instead Ishtar has talked about her life *now*, the work she does for the different communities where she lives, Muslim and Christian, Yemeni and British, all Mancunian. She sees no distinction. She has introduced her to her son, Sol, and his wife, Nadia, Jenna's parents. Delphine has particularly enjoyed listening to Nadia describe the work she does as a teacher of English as a Second Language to new arrivals in the city, the importance of finding some meeting point from which communication can begin. It reminds her of the way her own parents, Eve and Sammy, had found their own meeting point. She listens to Sol outline his ideas for the mural he is planning and admires the drawings he did of the Hejaz Mountains of Aden, while he was on National Service there as a young man. The way just a few sure strokes of a pencil have conjured up a whole world. Just as Eve had done with her painting. She notices a lump of coal, highly polished, taking pride of place on a shelf, which no one alludes to, and so she makes no mention of it herself, although she is aware of its unspoken power, how, whenever any of them pass it, they touch it, for luck.

Even Jenna, whose talk is all about what she is currently doing at school, which she loves, though sometimes, she says, the work is too easy, but their next topic she is especially looking forward to. 'Design your City of the Future,' her teachers have asked, and already Jenna is full of ideas.

I imagine a city without smoke, where trains run on rails through the streets. Where canals don't explode by themselves. Where the buildings aren't black with soot, but red. Where there are no zoos. Where animals roam wild and birds fly free. And no one tries to stop them. I would like to see special bridges and underpasses being built to help the smaller animals, such as amphibians and rodents, get from place to place without the risk of being run over. I imagine a city where everyone who wants one has a home. I imagine children living like I do, in a house where parents, grandparents and aunties all live together. Or a circle of teepees. Where people sing songs and dance and tell stories. Where they draw pictures and write wise words on the walls. I imagine cafés on pavements, with waitresses on roller-skates. Where everyone pays with plastic instead of coins. Where they carry their own personal TVs around with them, which they can watch while they're on buses or trains. I imagine skyscrapers of glass and steel. I imagine flying above them in a hot air balloon. I imagine blowing a bubble so large that it covers this whole city of the future, which I can step in and out of, without it ever bursting...

"That sounds like the most wonderful city," says Delphine afterwards. "Especially the part where there are teepees."

"Perhaps," suggests Nadia tentatively, "you might like to ask your Daddy to help you draw it?"

"No thank you," says Jenna promptly. "I don't need Daddy's help…"

Delphine feels her eyelids begin to droop. It has been a day of extremes. Of endings and beginnings. Of closure and renewal. Her outpouring of grief at the site of her parents' grave in the Coroner's Wood shocked her deeply in the violence and extremity of its emotion, exhausting and emptying her. But now, having had a long, soothing soak in a hot bath prepared for her by Ishtar, with scented oils and candles, she feels deeply cleansed and revived.

Sleep, when it comes to her, which it does with a rare swiftness, is filled with dreams of shooting stars and lightning bolts, which she reaches out to grasp…

*

Roland never comes home from hospital.

Ruth can't bear to visit him. Not after the first time, when he is only breathing through a mask, his body connected with tubes to machines. She doesn't recognise him. And he never opens his eyes to see her while she is there. So Lily tells her not to come if she doesn't want to, to try instead to remember him as he was. As if he's already gone from them, which in a way he has.

But in another way he never leaves them. Lily describes how once, just before the end, he does open his eyes.

"I can see them," he says.

Lily says he is remembering the angels he thought he could see when he was a pilot, flying high above the clouds in the sky, so high that the blue turned to black.

But then he looked straight at her and said, "I never knew before, but they were you all along. You and Ruth… and the woman who rescued me…"

Ruth now knows he means Esther, who calls herself Ishtar. Firestar.

"She rescued me, so that you would one day find me…"

"Which I did," says Lily "I had a dream, remember…?"

Lily is walking in a maze. Instead of hedges, high walls

surround her. They remind her of the air raid tunnels in Stockport, the largest and deepest ever built, which she has sheltered in during her nights as a dispatch rider. Every inch of them is covered with initials scrawled and then scratched out. These are not survivors, but memorials to those that perished.

She must reach the centre. She knows that something is waiting for her, something she must rescue and retrieve, then help to carry back outside. She is unwinding a ball of cotton behind her so she won't get lost. But the more she twists and turns, the more the cotton gets snagged on shards of rock, splinters of stone. It unspools behind her like memories she can't quite grasp. If the thread snaps, she knows she'll never get out. Slowly she makes her way to the centre, inch by inch, as if she is waiting in a queue for some unspecified, unrationed item. Others have been here before her. She sees their bleached bones poking through the earth.

When she finally makes it, she is surprised, disappointed almost. Instead of the giant or beast or monster she has imagined dwelling there in the centre, she spies someone small, kneeling down, facing away from her. The figure appears to be digging something in the earth with his bare hands. It turns around...

But she wakes up before she can see who it is...

"It was me," says Roland. "I was planting a seed."
"Yes," says Lily. "I know..."

Lily is a binary girl.

She attends the Camp every day. Sometimes she wears her uniform, sometimes a floral patterned dress. She and the prisoner interlock fingers through the wire fence.

"What's your name?" she asks.
"Roland."
"Where are you from?"

"Koblenz."

"What happened to you?"

"I'm a pilot. I was shot down."

"Oh. Is that how...?" She looks down at his foot.

"*Ja.* I was lucky."

"Lucky?"

"A nurse with a white scarf. She saved my foot. It was crushed. I think they would have cut it off if she had not done what she did."

"Yes, I see. Lucky."

"Lucky they send me here. Lucky I meet you."

Lily looks down.

"What did you do? Before you were a pilot?"

"Mathematics. Look."

He begins to draw with a stick in the dirt. A series of circles and straight lines. Ones and zeros.

"What is it?" she asks.

"The future."

She squats low on her haunches to gain a closer look. "I don't understand," she says.

"Instead of ten digits, imagine just two," he says. "Zero and one." His eyes shine in adoration for the sheer elegance and simplicity of it.

"It looks like one of those games you might play as a child," she says. "Find your way from here to there following only the ones…"

"… or zeros, yes."

"A labyrinth."

"Technically, a maze."

"What's the difference?"

"A labyrinth has only a single, non-branching path leading to the centre, then back out again, with only one entry and exit point. With a maze there are many paths, many directions, many possible entrances and exits."

"But also dead ends."

The two of them regard each other through the wire of the fence.

"Think of it this way," he says. "One equals on, zero equals off."

"Like a switch?"

"Like a switch, *ja*."

Lily nods. Roland continues.

"I want to build a machine that can perform calculations much faster than humans can, using this binary code."

"Binary?"

"Two. On, off. One, zero."

"And unlock the most complicated mazes?"

"*Ja.*"

Lily is entranced. "Tell me more," she says. "Paint me a picture of how it might work."

Roland pauses. "Do you know what a pianola is?" he says.

"Yes," says Lily. "A piano that plays by itself."

Roland smiles. "It looks like a piano that is playing all by itself, but what makes it able to do that?"

"A piece of paper," she says, "with a perforated pattern on it."

"*Genau!* Exactly. The pattern uses binary codes to translate the musical notes into a series of on/off instructions, which tell the piano which keys to play."

"And you want to write new codes which will do even more complicated things?"

"Solve many difficult problems, *ja*."

She looks at him closely. But will it stop this War, she wants to say? Will it tear down this fence between us? Instead she says, "I'm a binary girl. Sometimes I'm happy, sometimes I'm sad. One minute I'm up, the next I'm down. Sometimes I know why, but often I have no idea. I only know that whatever mood I might be in at any given moment, it's not going to last for ever. It changes. With time. But I can't just flip from one to the other at the turn of a switch. I'm more complicated than that."

He looks at her. *Ja*, he thinks. Like a maze. A maze I'd like to get lost in.

Where will it all lead, they separately wonder...?

It leads here. To this moment. This place. A ward in a hospital.

A doctor is talking in a low voice to Lily. He is saying something about switching off a machine.

On, off. On, off.

Off...

Two weeks later, back in the house on Lapwing Lane, Lily and Ruth circle around one other, speaking only when they have to, each locked in their own private grief.

Ruth goes into the box room at the top of the house, which served as her father's study. Leaning against the wall is the Computer Logic Board from the Manchester Baby, his first computer, complete with its three transformers and forty-two valves all perfectly in place. She picks it up and carries it downstairs to where Lily is standing in the hallway, her hand raised towards the handle of the front door, as if she is contemplating stepping outside, only to pull back at the last moment, having forgotten what it was she might have needed to go out for.

Ruth holds up the Computer Board.

"I want to hang this here," she says, "in the hall."

"Why?" asks Lily.

"So we can see it every time we come in or go out."

"Why?" asks Lily again.

"Because it reminds me of him," says Ruth.

Lily now looks at it closely.

"Yes," she says, "all right." Her mouth tries to form a thin smile, but fails, for it has been so long since she last exercised those muscles.

"What is it?" asks Ruth, noticing the effort.

"It's like a portrait of him, isn't it?"

Now it is Ruth's turn to look at it closely.

"Yes," she says. "You're right. It is."

She fetches a hammer and nail from the kitchen. Together they hang his portrait on the wall.

1981

Salford Advertiser

2nd **May 1981**

LOCAL LEGEND DIES AS SHE LIVED

It is with great sadness that we report, in this our first edition since the incorporation of the former much-loved *Salford City Reporter*, the passing of another much-loved local legend.

Last week, in a freak accident on Liverpool Road, Mrs Esther Ward, universally known as "Ishtar", was knocked off her bicycle by an oncoming florist's delivery van, while she was swerving to avoid a small child who had unexpectedly run in front of her.

Mrs Ward, who had recently celebrated her 85th birthday, was a well-loved and familiar sight, frequently to be seen cycling the highways and byways of Eccles, Patricroft, Barton, Peel Green and Monton, in all weathers, clad in her distinctive all-white garb, including a long veil upon her head, known as a *qurqash*, as she rode to help those in need, whatever their background or circumstances.

Reverend A.E. Walker of Christ Church, Patricroft, described her as an "Angel of Mercy", while Mr al-Haideri, founder of Salford's first mosque and a long-time family friend, recalled her courage and compassion. She was warmly welcomed into the Yemeni community here in Eccles, which she so fully embraced after her marriage to one of its most well-respected members, Mr Hejaz Wahid, more than fifty years ago.

Mrs Ward, born Esther Blundell, the second of six children, grew up in Gorton in East Manchester, where she was an active member of the Suffragist Movement. After her brothers left, either to war or to get married, Esther stayed at home to look after her ailing father, whom she nursed uncomplainingly for several years, before finding work as a Canteen Supervisor at Bradford Colliery. It was there, shortly after the famous visit by King Amanullah of Afghanistan, that she met the man who was to become her husband and moved to Patricroft to be near his family.

During World War II Ishtar, as she then became known, volunteered as an ARP Warden, where she was widely praised for her quiet heroism, frequently risking her own life, cycling through unlit streets at the height of an air raid, to come to the aid of someone who had lost their home or their loved ones. She continued her charitable work after the War was over and became a pillar of both the Christian and Muslim communities, helping anyone in need, while raising countless hundreds of pounds for a variety of worthy causes.

She was just returning from a local Bring & Buy Sale she had been supporting at the Holy Cross Community Centre in order to help raise much-needed funds for the *Busy Bees* playgroup that meets there every morning, run by her daughter-in-law's sister, Mrs Farida ul-Haq, when the accident occurred.

Mrs Linda Billings, 23, of Peel Green, mother of the toddler who ran out into the road, told the *Advertiser* she "was devastated" by what had happened. "One minute he had hold of my hand, the next he was off. If Mrs Ward hadn't swerved as she did, my little boy would have been knocked flying."

Mr Alan Rees, 32, from nearby Urmston, the driver of the florist's van, was distraught. "She just appeared in front of me, suddenly, out of nowhere. I slammed on the brakes, but I couldn't stop in time."

Afterwards, traffic came to a standstill as ambulancemen tried to revive her, but were unable to do so. Lying surrounded by a sea of tulip flowers that had spilled from the delivery van, Mrs Ward died of the injuries she had sustained.

She leaves behind a son, Sol, 41, a draughtsman on Trafford Park, and a granddaughter, Jenna, 18, who is currently in her first year of study at Manchester University.

Burial will take place next week at Peel Green Cemetery, where she will be laid to rest next to her husband and father-in-law.

*

Three months earlier.

◆ Sanctuary Housing

Adapting to the Needs of the City

27 Houldsworth Street
Manchester
M1 1EB

2nd February 1981

Dear Miss Fish,

We are writing to inform you that as of the 1st of next month, March 1981, we shall have completed the purchase of Newbury House, and from that date thenceforward we shall be de facto your new landlords. A new tenants' agreement will be sent to you forthwith outlining all of the terms and conditions. But we wanted to write before then, both to introduce ourselves, and to reassure you that there will be no increase to your monthly rent, which will remain exactly the same as it has been for the past twelve months.

However, you will have noticed that those tenants who left Newbury House during the last year have not been replaced, so that a number of flats now lie vacant in the property. That is part of a deliberate policy on our part, and we are pleased to have this opportunity to explain our reasons for this to you.

Sanctuary Housing, as I believe you must be aware, having been a generous donor to our various calls for help in recent years, is a Registered Charity dedicated to supporting those who find themselves homeless here in Manchester. It has long been our ambition to open a centre, offering temporary refuge for people seeking to make the transition from shared hostel to more settled accommodation. We believe that Newbury House offers us the chance to be able to realise this.

Accordingly we are planning a major refurbishment of the premises, which we expect to commence in six months' time, in October of this year, and which is scheduled to take a further eighteen months before it is completed. As a sitting tenant you have statutory rights, which of course we intend to honour. Under Section 15 of the Rent Act of 1977, we, as new owners, are obliged to give you 90 days' notice before asking you to vacate the property, but we herewith extend that notice period to twice that amount, 180 days.

We trust that this arrangement will be acceptable to you, and we of course will do all that we can to assist you in finding appropriate alternative accommodation during that time.

If you have any questions, or if there is anything you would like to discuss with us further, then please do not hesitate to contact us. One of our representatives will be delighted to make an appointment to visit you in your flat.

Once again, may we take this opportunity of thanking you for your understanding and for the support you have shown us in the past.

Yours sincerely,

Michael Wooton
Operations Manager

*

Flat 1, Newbury House
80 Daisy Bank Road

9th February 1981

Dear Ruth,

In haste.

Might you consider becoming the Executor of my Will? I am not getting any younger – ninety-two last birthday – and so I thought it time to get my affairs in some sort of order. I will not beat about the bush – I am asking you because all of my contemporaries and peers are either dead or no longer in possession of those faculties they – we, all of us – once took for granted. You have always struck me as an eminently sensible young woman, even more so since your parents died, which has in no way prevented you from fulfilling your professional aspirations. In fact it could be said to have spurred you to even greater heights. I rejoice in your recent appointment as Consulting Psychiatrist at the Didsbury Medical Centre.

As for being Executor to my Will, there's nothing to it really. You would simply assume responsibility for handling my estate – such as it is! – i.e. money, property, possessions, in the event of my death – which does not feel especially imminent, but of course one never knows. As for property, I have none. The flat is rented, and there are no arrears. As for money, I have little. And what little I do have will all be clearly itemised in the Will. As for possessions, I shall leave them entirely for you to dispose of as you see fit.

I hope you do not mind me dropping this on you out of the blue. Please feel free to say 'no'. But you have been so kind to me these past ten years, visiting me and telephoning me, you were the first person I thought to ask.

With sincere thanks,
Delphine

*

Several weeks later Delphine wakes in the middle of the night with the absolute certainty of what she must do.

She had been dreaming of the demijohns she had found

stored at the back of the woodshed next to the hut where her parents had lived and then died. There were more than fifty of them, each one filled to the brim with pennies saved from the fares of passengers they had transported by ferry across the Canal over the twenty-five years they had operated it. It amounted to more than twice what her annual salary had been back then as a teacher.

Money had meant more or less nothing to her parents. They had little use for it. They found what they needed in the woods and the streams. But Delphine had been struck by just what a difference all those pennies might make to the lives of the deaf children she had once taught at *The Manchester Institution for the Deaf* in the grounds of the former *Royal Botanical Gardens* on Pomona Island. And so she had buried them in a pit by moonlight, the night before she rowed her father's starvationer canoe the five miles from Bob's Lane to Barton Dock along the Ship Canal to seek the help of Yasser…

"Leave this with me," said Yasser. "There are bargemen I know, who owe me favours. I meet you at Bob's Lane. Next Saturday at noon."

Yasser was as good as his word. A week later Delphine stood on the jetty at Bob's Lane, having retraced her steps by train to Cadishead that morning, watching a coal barge steam its way towards her, with Yasser waving from the foredeck.

She had wondered how she might react to being back at the scene so soon after she had buried her parents, but she felt surprisingly calm. It was as if the rituals of burning their settlement and returning the starvationer to The Delph in accordance with their traditions had been a kind of cleansing for her. She felt empty, numb, but pleased to be carrying out this final act.

The barge moored up to the jetty. They passed the raised mound of earth, which marked the grave of her parents. Yasser stood by it in silence, head bowed, for several seconds, before rejoining Delphine. She showed him where the demijohns had been buried, and he and the bargemen set to at once with unearthing them and carrying them aboard.

With a minimum of fuss, as soon as this was completed, they turned around and began to chug their way back towards the Pomona Docks, which was the closest landing point to the school. Delphine stood at the stern, looking back, till the jetty at Bob's Lane could no longer be seen, and then joined Yasser further along the deck.

"Asif will be waiting for us with his cart," he said. "He will drive you across the bridge to the school."

"Thank you again."

Yasser nodded. He was quieter than usual, and this quietness grew stronger the closer they got to Pomona. When they arrived, he helped Delphine down onto the dock.

"Come," he said, "I show you something."

He led her quickly to Dock Number 3, where the Pomona Lock connected the Manchester Ship Canal to the Bridgewater, close to the Trafford Park Road Swing Bridge. He pointed.

"This was where your father rescued me," he said. "Before all this was built. The explosion...." He paused, then turned back towards her. "I thought you should see it."

Delphine nodded. She stood quietly, looking out over the scene. Cranes were unloading goods from one of the great ships the Canal had brought here in huge nets, which passed over their heads before being emptied directly into the wagons of goods trains, hissing with steam, ready to be transported across the city. Stevedores from Africa, Arabia and Asia, from Russia, Poland and Italy, as well as England, Wales and Ireland were climbing ladders, wheeling carts, lifting sacks, running up ramps, down in the holds and up on the gantries, shouting in several languages simultaneously. This was Yasser's world. He was at home here, just as surely as she was not, and it was the actions of her father, rescuing him from the rubble all those years ago, which had made that possible. She looked again at the tumult of movement all around her and began to see pattern and order. She listened more closely to the cacophonous babble and began to hear music and concord...

Music and concord.
Yes. She knows what she must do.

In 1956 *The Royal Manchester School for the Deaf*, as it had then been renamed, moved to new premises, in Cheadle Hulme, near Stockport. In 1976 it changed its name again, to *The Seashell Trust*. Delphine had approved this change. It removed any lingering stigma, but more importantly it suggested hope and possibility, the recovery of lost sounds redolent of other worlds, simply by holding a shell to one's ear.

Music and concord.

Although it is still the middle of the night, she feels wide awake. She roots out the file where she keeps her bank statements. She checks and double-checks the most recent. The balance shows she has in excess of seventeen thousand pounds. She quickly makes a series of calculations. If she allows just over two thousand for funeral and legal expenses, this will mean she can write a cheque for ten thousand pounds to *The Seashell Trust*, leaving five thousand for Ruth. Yes, she decides, that will do nicely. She writes the cheque there and then, puts a coat over her pyjamas, and pops it into the post box just across the road from Newbury House.

Excellent, she thinks. One's money *should* go to the young.

When she comes back, she looks around this flat she has lived in for more than ten years. She is happy that Newbury House is being converted for use as a refuge for the homeless. Everyone deserves a second chance. But the thought of having to pack up all of her things and move again is quite beyond her contemplation. Even worse is the prospect of a Care Home, which, she supposes, is probably inevitable, the way her breathing has deteriorated in the past decade. Ever since her pilgrimage to Coroner's Wood after the Bob's Lane Ferry Disaster, when the heavens opened and her grief, which had lain suppressed for so many years, had finally been unleashed, it has grown progressively worse. First she caught a cold that she couldn't seem to shake off. Next she developed a cough which racked her chest so much that she cracked a rib. Finally she had to be given oxygen. ARDS. Acute Respiratory Distress Syndrome. Not a label she cares for. To name a thing is to own it. To render it impotent. So Confucius taught. But Delphine does not find this to be true. Knowledge is power – isn't that what they say? Francis Bacon thought so – but Delphine discovers that just because she knows its name and what it means, that doesn't make ARDS any less determined a foe. Its progress is relentless, a tide that not even Old Moon or Tommy Thunder could have turned back. Certainly it is not something *she* can do. She has her good days. More than she has bad. She supposes she has more of them to come. But not that many. What is to be gained by waiting for the inevitable slow and possibly painful decline?

She picks up a photograph that is propped up on the mantelpiece, next to the bird's nest and her mother's painting of the comet. It is the one that Francis took that day by her parents' grave. The rain is falling like arrows. Two lightning bolts are splitting the sky. Her hands are raised above her head. The lightning appears to be coming directly from her fingers...

Outside the day is just beginning. She can hear birdsong in the trees outside her window. The friendly, reassuring clink of milk bottles being placed on doorsteps. The newspaper being pushed through her letter box. She goes out into the hall to fetch it. She draws back the curtains to let in the early morning light. She puts on a pair of glasses to read what it says.

LOCAL LEGEND DIES AS SHE LIVED

It is with great sadness that we report, in this our first edition since the incorporation of the former much-loved *Salford City Reporter*, the passing of another much loved local legend.

Last week, in a freak accident on Liverpool Road, Mrs Esther Ward, universally known as "Ishtar", was knocked off her bicycle by an oncoming florist's delivery van, while she was swerving to avoid a small child who had unexpectedly run in front of her...

Delphine puts down the paper and sighs. Ishtar – how typically selfless of her...

She goes into the kitchen, where she makes herself a pot of tea and a round of toast, which she brings back into the sitting room. She puts a record on the turntable. It is one of her favourites. Janacek's *Sinfonietta*. To her ears it is fresh and contemporary still, a hymn to what it means to be human, filled with a deep yearning for freedom and home.

She has made her decision.

Music and concord...

*

Manchester Graduate

Magazine of the University of Manchester Alumni Association

June 1981

OBITUARY:
PROFESSOR. DELPHINE FISH: 1889 – 1981

It is with deep sadness that we report the death of Miss Delphine Fish, who died earlier this month at the age of 92.

Miss Fish joined the Audiology Department in 1919, the year it opened, the first such department in a UK university, and remained there until her retirement in 1954, at which point she was the Department's first female Chair.

A formidable presence, with a razor-sharp intellect, who did not suffer fools, she was nevertheless universally popular with both colleagues and students, for whom her door was always open.

Miss Fish was born in a temporary settlement by the banks of the River Irwell on the estate of the 3rd Duke of Bridgewater. She was the daughter of a Native American father and a Lancastrian mother, who was herself orphaned at an early age, and who was a deaf mute. Was it this that drew Miss Fish to a career in audiology? She herself thought it almost certain.

Educated at Our Lady of Lourdes School in Partington, where, between the ages of 13 years and 18 years, she acted as a Teacher's Assistant, she was then part of the inaugural intake of the Teacher Training College at Sedgley Park. After graduation she took up a post as a primary teacher at St Philip's Roman Catholic School on Cavendish Road in Broughton, Salford, where her affinity with deaf children was first noticed by Sister Basil, the school's headmistress, who encouraged her to apply for a vacant post at *The Royal Manchester School for the Deaf*. That was in 1910. She stayed there for nine years before she was invited to join us here at the University.

A fuller account of her many achievements during her time at Manchester will follow in our next edition...

*

MANCHESTER CITY COUNCIL

Court 1 in Manchester Town Hall, reached via the Mount Street entrance, is almost deserted, as Mr Alan Carmichael, LLB, Attorney at Law, the Coroner assigned to this case, sits down at his desk. The Clerk to the Court reads out the various preliminaries – case number, name of the appellants – before handing over to the Coroner himself.

Mr Carmichael flips open the case file in front of him, reviewing the contents of the various documents inside – statements from the attending Police Constable, the Chief Ambulanceman who was first on the scene, the Doctor who had formally pronounced death, the Pathologist, and the Wardenr who had telephoned the emergency services.

He sees nothing to change his mind from when he first read all the reports. Miss Fish was 92 years old. She had been diagnosed some ten years before with Acute Respiratory Distress Syndrome – a condition that, according to her GP... Here Mr Carmichael consults his notes – ah yes, Dr Hamid of the Surrey Lodge Medical Practice on Anson Road – had been gradually deteriorating ever since, for which Miss Fish had been prescribed self-administering Albuteron, in the form of an inhaler, Doxycycline, a common antibiotic, Naproxen, a pain-relieving analgesic, Xanax, a benzodiazepine sedative, and, more recently, Tramadol, an opioid, all in the form of tablets. Traces of all these substances were found in the deceased's bloodstream during a routine post-mortem. Death would have been swift and painless.

In her report Dr Hamid concluded that she thought the most likely scenario was that Miss Fish had mistakenly taken an accidental extra dose of each medication, possibly as a result of becoming confused about when she may have taken her previous ones. Dr Hamid further added that, when she last saw the deceased, during a routine home visit some four weeks before, she found her in good spirits overall, despite the incremental worsening of her condition. There was nothing whatsoever in her demeanour to suggest that she was feeling in any way depressed, and certainly not suicidal.

Mr Carmichael is inclined to agree. He can find nothing in the circumstances surrounding the death of Miss Fish to persuade him to pronounce any other verdict than:

CORONER:
Accidental Death – due to an unintentional overdose of prescribed medication.

*

In the corridor outside afterwards, Mr Carmichael thanks Dr Hamid.

"What was she like?" he asks. "I knew her by reputation of course, but our paths never crossed professionally."

"Redoubtable," replies Dr Hamid. "There was no pulling the wool over her eyes. After an appointment with her, I felt as though I'd just re-sat my viva for my doctorate."

"And did you pass?" jokes Mr Carmichael.

"If I was lucky."

"I wish I'd met her."

"Yes. She was quite remarkable. One of those patients you never forget. Not that I saw her that often. She was as strong as an ox. It was only after she contracted ARDS, having been caught in a storm in the open for more than an hour apparently

– before my time – did her strength begin to fail her. But only physically. Her mind and intellect remained as sharp as ever."

"Really?" Mr Carmichael raises a quizzical eyebrow.

"But she *was* 92. She did complain of increasingly irregular sleep patterns, and her condition, although under control with the medication, was undoubtedly deteriorating. Poor circulation, oxygen not getting through to the brain as it once did, it's hardly surprising if she became a little confused. When I last saw her, I suggested at the time that we would review her medication at our next appointment. If only I'd acted sooner…"

"You are in no way to blame, Dr Hamid. I believe we both know what happened here."

"What do you mean?"

Mr Carmichael allows the briefest of pauses before answering further. "What I said in my judgement. 'Accidental death due to an unintentional overdose'. "

She returns his questioning gaze. A wordless acknowledgement of a shared suspicion, tinged with silent admiration, passes between them…

*

Lapwing Lane
22nd July 1981

Dear Francis,

It's been almost two months since Delphine died. Yesterday I finally finished emptying out her flat. In her Will she asked if I would keep the bird's nest and her mother's painting of Halley's Comet, but get rid of everything else. Not that she had much by way of furniture or clothes, and I have managed to disperse these through various charity shops. But she had lots of books – academic ones mostly – and so many records, it seemed a shame to split them up, and not honour them somehow.

I offered the books to the University, who were delighted to receive them. The Audiology Department has decided to purchase a special commemorative bookcase to accommodate them all, which will be housed in one of the old Reading Rooms of the Main Library.

As for the records I have persuaded the Library at Levenshulme to accept them. They lend out records and video cassettes now, as well as books, and they were happy to accept them. She had more than five hundred LPs, many of them quite rare, nearly all 20th century classical composers, and in immaculate condition. I stacked them in ten boxes of fifty and took them in a series of relays in my car. Not the bottle-green Viva any more, but a red Chevette. It gets me about...

I decided to keep one of the records for myself. It was still on the turntable when I went into to clear up. I believe it must have been the last one she ever listened to. Janacek's Sinfonietta. But on the table next to it was another. I was attracted to it by the title. 'The Unanswered Question' by Charles Ives. Do you know it? I don't. I shall play it after I've finished writing you this letter, for I decided to keep this one too. Judging from the well-thumbed sleeve notes, I believe it was one she played a lot. There was a watermark on them from where perhaps she had knocked over a glass in her final moments. I wonder if she finally answered that question in the end...

Tucked inside it was a photograph, Francis. It was the one you took of her on the day we all went to where the old ferry across the Ship Canal was situated, where the two of you first met after the end of the 1st World War. She'd asked you to take a picture of the site of her parents' grave, which you did, do you remember? She is kneeling in the mud as the rain pours down and the storm rages overhead. She is throwing back her head and howling to the four winds, caught in the flash of lightning, which appears to be coming directly out of her hands and mouth and hair. It's an astonishing photograph, Francis, a disturbing one, the way the entire electrical storm appears to emanating directly out of the centre of her, but I wondered if you might like it? Please let me know. I can always post it to you...

I'd never been to Levenshulme Library before. It's a beautiful old building. It looks and feels and smells just like a library should do to my mind. I have a postcard of it, which I'm enclosing.

CARNEGIE FREE LIBRARY, LEVENSHULME.

See what I mean? It makes you want to go inside, doesn't it?

It was designed by Mr James Jepson, surveyor and architect for the Manchester Corporation, built with money donated by the philanthropist Andrew Carnegie by local contractors Burgess & Gaitt of Ardwick. (I'm copying this from a leaflet I picked up while I was there). It was opened in 1904 by Sir Charles Alfred Cripps, MP, 1st Baron of Parmoor, nearly half a century after the first completely free public library anywhere in the country was opened in Campfield, off Deansgate, a tradition Manchester has continued with a series of smaller borough libraries across the city. Levenshulme was one of them...

I love that sense of continuity, don't you?

Which brings me to why I'm describing all this in such detail.

Two of its most distinguished features are a long outside verandah, reached through a vestibule door, where – and I'm quoting from the leaflet again here – 'people might sit and read during fine weather, plus a small room set aside for newspapers, periodicals, and board games, such as chess, draughts and halma...' Isn't that delightful? Does anyone play halma any more? I'm not sure I know what it is. Is it like Chinese Chequers? Anyway, it's there, in that small side room, where all of Delphine's records will be kept. It's called the 'Nancy Cotton Room', after a librarian who worked there for many years.

Now – here's the thing. While I was bringing them all in, box after box after box, the most extraordinary thing happened. In front of me, waiting at the desk, were two young women – students, punks. One had a striped Mohican, the other had short jet-black hair sharpened into pointy spikes. This second one looked familiar somehow. I felt as if I knew her. But I couldn't put my finger on how or where or when. They were enquiring about listening to a series of old recordings, originally made on wax discs that had recently been copied onto cassettes, of the hundred-year-old Laurel Stone, who was born on the day of the Peterloo Massacre, actually on St Peter's Field itself, and who then went on to take part in many of the major historical events that took place in Manchester in the decades that followed – the coming of the railways, the Cotton Famine, the Suffragist Movement. There was a poster behind the desk advertising that these new cassettes were now available, and at the bottom it said:

'From the original recordings by Francis Hall.'

I'm assuming that was you? Isn't that amazing? That they should have survived all these years and that students should still want to listen to them?

While they were waiting for the first batch to be brought out to them, the one with the spiky black hair said to her friend, "My grandmother told me about these. She remembers seeing Lauren

Stone when she was a child, flying across the city in a hot air balloon, dropping leaflets onto the people below. That must have been amazing."

The librarian, who was returning with the cassettes just at that moment, must have overheard them, because she said, "Yes, it must have been. The person who was with her in the balloon was Nancy Cotton, the librarian who this room is named after. Now – please could you sign here to say that you've received the first tapes, then hand them back in when you've finished? Thank you."

The two young women went over to the table where the cassette player and headphones were all set up. I sneaked a look at where they'd signed their names. Then I knew where I'd seen the dark-haired one before. It said: 'Jenna Ward'. Do you remember her? The eight-year-old girl who was sitting on the doorstep of Ishtar's house the day we dropped off Delphine there? She was so cross, wasn't she? She thought Delphine looked like Old Nokomis. She wasn't far wrong, was she? Now here she was, listening to stories from a woman her grandmother had seen, who'd played a part in shaping the history of not just Manchester, but the lives of women everywhere, recorded by you! Like the handing of a baton in a relay, the passing of a torch. I think Delphine would have approved, don't you?

I think that's what might lie behind that Unanswered Question. What is it that we might leave behind for others to pick up and run with when it's their turn, like those of us who've yet to make our own marks on the land? Like me...

Later that night, when I'd finally finished clearing out Delphine's flat and I closed the door behind me for the last time, I drove back through the city. I was following the first part of the route the three of us took when we went on that pilgrimage to Bob's Lane. Out of Daisy Bank Road, onto Anson Road, down Dickenson Road, towards Wilmslow Road. But just as I reached that final junction, I was turned back. The Police had closed the road. It was the night of the riots in Moss Side. Ahead of me the city was ablaze. There were fires in the streets, in shop windows and doorways. I saw petrol bombs being hurled through the air, exploding into flames, leaving a trail of sparks in the sky. Like a comet...

I don't believe it was an accident, do you, Francis? Delphine's death? I think she knew exactly what she was doing – the notice to quit her flat, the change to her will, the bequest to the charity, the final upbeat appointment with her doctor, the record on the turntable – just as she always did. Not for her the taking to the streets, the manning of the barricades. Hers was a quieter revolution, forged in a different fire, one that burns more slowly, that seeks out meaning in the silence of those who may not have the power to hear, but who still have the yearning to listen, and then to speak, maybe not through words, but more quietly, through gesture and through action...

The last thing I cleared from her flat was a newspaper article. It had evidently arrived on the morning she died. It was a report of the death of her friend Ishtar, who had sacrificed herself to save a young child. At the end of it was a footnote, which could equally apply to Delphine, as it did for Ishtar. I think Delphine recognised this. That's why she left it where she did, I believe, tucked inside the sleeve of 'The Unanswered Question', knowing that I'd find it.

With love,
Ruth x

*

'Certainly those determining acts of her life were not ideally beautiful. They were the mixed result of a young and noble impulse struggling amidst the conditions of an imperfect social state, in which great feelings will often take the aspect of error, and great faith the aspect of illusion. For there is no creature whose inward being is so strong that it is not greatly determined by what lies outside it...

Her full nature spent itself in channels which had no great name on earth. But the effect of her being on those around her was incalculably diffusive: for the growing good of the world is partly dependent on *unhistoric acts*; and that things are not so ill as they might have been, is half owing to the number who lived faithfully a hidden life, and rest in unvisited tombs...'

George Eliot: Middlemarch

8

1983

Two years later, George finds that he too is clearing out a flat. His own. Not that he has any intention of moving. He's been in Adelphi Street for thirty-five years. He likes to think of himself as dug in. He knows every inch of his neighbourhood. Every street, every corner. Every brick, every cobble – those that still remain, and there are a few, if you know where to look – and also every new tower block, flyover and underpass. He's pounded them all. And he's photographed them all.

He likes to think that the neighbourhood knows *him* too. He's witnessed its many changes during the years he's been there, some of them cataclysmic, the demolition of entire streets, the slum clearances, the high-rise towers that have replaced them, the motorways, the shopping precincts, the multi-storey car parks, the closure of the mills, the factories and canals, then the reopening of many, rebranded as leisure facilities, warehouse apartments, waterside restaurants and bars. A convulsive time, a tumultuous time, and still the changes come. There are plans for a complete regeneration of the docks. Salford Quays, they will be known as, a new cultural hub for the city. There's even talk of a network of trams connecting all parts of the city.

George remembers the *old* trams, which shut down just after the War, and the trolley buses that kept on running right through to the middle of the sixties. He especially enjoyed those, the way the sparks would crackle and hiss in the overhead cables, particularly at night.

Everything old is new again. What goes around, comes around.

He knows this to be true. He is not sentimental or nostalgic for the past. He simply hopes that people learn from their mistakes the first time around and do things better the next time. He's still a Fabian idealist at heart, an old time socialist, who genuinely believes that the natural trajectory of things is for them to improve. By and large. More than anything else, he believes in the fundamental goodness of people, that everyone is just trying to make the best fist of things that they can, to leave the world a better place than when they first came into it, to make their mark.

He's tried to make his own mark with the photographs he's taken and the students he's taught, especially the adults, at night school, who come to learn a new skill even after completing a hard day's work in office or factory, who want to give themselves a second chance, to make amends, to start again. He finds himself humbled and awed in the face of such hope.

He's photographed these same streets every single day in all that time. He's captured the same faces, the same families. He's recorded them growing up, growing old. Then he's photographed their children. They've come to regard him as just another part of the fabric of their lives. Like the policeman on his beat, the postman on his round, the doctor making house calls. He likes to think he offers the same reassuring sense of continuity, in return for which they will trust him to be fair in his depiction of them. And by and large they have.

Every year he has held an informal exhibition of the photographs he has taken during the previous twelve months and invited the community to come and take a look at themselves. Up until last year these sociable affairs have taken place in the Upstairs Room of *The Dock & Pulpit*, a small, quiet pub behind St Philip's Church in Encombe Place, just off Chapel Street. The pub has laid on refreshments, and people have gathered as much to meet up with each other, as to look at the photos, which George has always delighted in. They stop him from ever taking himself too seriously. They mean just as much, if not more to him, than the more formal openings and private views of exhibitions of his work in the more recognised galleries and art centres. He tends to hold these annual get-togethers around Shrove Tuesday, just before the start of Lent, each year's offerings of images like shrivings, almost as if he is seeking absolution from the people for allowing him to photograph them. Of the many positive and praiseworthy things that have been said about his work, his favourite is something he overheard an old boy who was a regular at *The Dock & Pulpit* say to one of his cronies one night: "It must be February again, George is bringing his photos round..." As though he were as fixed and regular a part of the life of the community as the Harvest Supper, the Whit Walks, the start of the football season.

But now *The Dock & Pulpit* has closed down and is boarded up. It looks very sorry for itself, but in truth it had been on its last legs for a number of years. There's talk of a new brewery coming in to redevelop it, tart it up, reopen it maybe. George hopes that, if they do, they won't change its name. He rather likes its juxtaposition of chapel and law. He sometimes feels that his pictures are like gentle sermons and that he is their lay-preacher, and that, while they are on show in the pulpit, he is standing trial in the dock.

He's wondering therefore whether to find another venue or not to hold his annual local show at all this year. Would it be missed? He doubts it. Not really. Would it be welcomed back if he missed a year? He hopes so. But what if he were to miss two, or three, or maybe dispense with it altogether? Would there be a clamour for its return? Of course there wouldn't. Perhaps he'll wait to see if *The Dock & Pulpit* reopens. Perhaps he'll bring it back then if it does...

Perhaps this enforced change in routine has been just the kick up the backside he's been needing. For some time now he's felt in something of a rut. Ever since he finished supporting Sol in his great mural at Pomona Docks, which took more than ten years to complete. It was a mammoth undertaking, one that he counts among the most important of his life, even though it was in the service of another man's work, but five years have passed since then, and only now does he feel that he's beginning at last to emerge from its shadow.

And so this morning, when he woke up, he thought, "Take yourself in hand, George. No more beating about the bush. Seize the day. Make some changes. There's no time like the present to get started." And so now, two hours later, he has embarked on a massive sort-out. He has emptied every drawer, tipped out every cupboard. He has made a series of piles – keep, throw out, consider. At first the 'consider' pile was growing higher and higher, and was in danger of toppling over altogether. No, no, no, he chided himself. This will simply not do. Away with the endless prevarication, and make some decisions. If in doubt, chuck it out.

Having made that decision, he is being bolder and bolder. Soon he has filled a whole roll of bin liners with rubbish for the recycling. He is feeling purged, cleansed, light-headed. He is finding the whole exercise more and more satisfying and therapeutic. An excellent way to begin a new year, a new decade. For today is his birthday. Today George is turning seventy.

He has just pulled out a new drawer. He empties the contents of it onto the table and begins to sift through them. They're mostly old exercise books from when he was at William Hulme Grammar School. Why on earth has he kept them all these years? He is just on the point of throwing them all into another bin bag, when a single piece of paper falls to the floor. He stoops to pick it up, and at once a smile passes across his face.

"I remember this," he says out loud, chuckling to himself.

It's a composition he wrote when he was just eleven years

old, in his first week there, for Mr Vogts, the kindly Anglo-German English teacher. If he closes his eyes, he can hear his clipped voice tripping down the years...

"I would like each of you to tell me something about yourself," he is saying, "who you are, where you live, what your hobbies are, what you might like to be when you leave school, so that I can get to know you just a little and learn how I might be of assistance..."

George, always so dutifully eager to please, remembers taking out the new maroon Sheaffer self-filling fountain pen, bought for him from a shop in King Street as a present by his grandfather Frank for passing the entrance examination to the school, and beginning to write. He does not stop until the bell goes for the end of the lesson...

He scans quickly through what he wrote almost sixty years ago. He finds he is extraordinarily moved by this unexpected encounter with his younger self...

My name is George Wright. I am eleven years and four months old. I live at Number Twelve, Cromwell Avenue, Manley Park, Whalley Range, Manchester. I have only been living there a few weeks and so I haven't had a chance to explore much yet. I like exploring. I think that would be a very exciting thing to do when I am older. The other things I should like to do are, riding a motor cycle and becoming an artist. I love to draw and paint. I'm not very good yet but as my mother always says, "Practice makes perfect," and so I practise very hard. What I like to draw best are parts of the engine of my father's motor car. It's a Crossley Phaeton. Made here in Manchester. In Gorton. Every Sunday he strips it down. He takes out the spark plugs, wipes them clean with a rag, polishes them with something from a tin called Brasso, then carefully puts them back. Sometimes he lets me help him. I like using the spanner best. Father says, "I'm a natural." "But a natural what?" says Mother and she laughs. I think this is one of her jokes. I like jokes but I don't understand this one. When my father cleans the engine, he lays out all the pieces separately on his work bench and I try to draw them. I like the way things are made. I like to take them apart and then see how they all fit together again. "Nuts and bolts," says my piano teacher. Her name is Mrs Tiffin. She is very kind and I like her very much, but now that we have moved house, I may not be able to carry on with my lessons. "We shall have to wait and see," my mother says. I am crossing my fingers that I can. In the meantime I will practise my scales on the piano in the front room of our new house. These are what Mrs Tiffin calls the nuts and bolts of the piano. I have lived in three houses now. The first one was quite small but I liked it. It was across the road from the Printing Works owned by my grandfather, where my father went to work each day. But the noise of the machines was so loud, like bombs, it made him ill, so Mother said we had to move. He is better now. Our second house was much bigger. It was near the University on a road called Daisy Bank Road, but it didn't have a bank, and I never saw any daisies. There were rows of trees along each side. Father said it was more like an Avenue. When I was ten, I helped him to make a crystal radio set. We listened to music on it together. I drew lots of pictures of it. Now we have a proper radio. "It's more modern," Mother says. It's called an RCA Westinghouse and we bought it from a shop in Denton. Mother says I am not to try to take this one apart because it cost a lot of money. But I would be very careful. I like the shop where we bought it. It has a large sign above it of a pair of giant spectacles with staring eyes that never close. I drew a picture of those after we got home. Mother says, "Why don't I draw pictures of things people would like to see?" "Like what?" I ask. "Oh, I don't know," she says, "flowers, trees, people, views..." I try to, but it's very hard. The thing is, when I look at a person, sitting on a bench or walking down a street, I can't help thinking about their skeletons, all of their bones and muscles, what we're all of us like under our skins. That's what I want to draw most, what's underneath everything, below the surface, the nuts and bolts of things, like Mrs Tiffin says. I suppose that's a bit like being an explorer too. Father says there are cameras in hospitals that can take photographs like that. They're called X rays. Perhaps cameras are better than pencils for showing what things are really like. "It all depends," my father says, but when I ask him on what, he doesn't answer. He just says, "Try not to be in such a hurry all the time." But I like being in a hurry. That's why I want to ride a motor cycle when I'm older, as fast as I can...

George lays the composition down, smiling with great affection, both for the comments by Mr Vogts underneath it – 'try to remember to use paragraphs in future' – and for this journey back in time to revisit the boy he once was. Much of what that boy had wished for has come to pass. He feels lucky.

'*The child is father to the man...*'

Who was it who wrote that, George wonders? He fetches down *The Oxford Book of Quotations* that had once belonged to his own father. He flicks through it till he finds what he is looking for. He nods. Gerard Manley Hopkins. 'Written in response to an earlier poem by Wordsworth. *The Rainbow*. Sometimes known as *My Heart Leaps Up*. How the things that awakened emotion in him as a child have stayed with him as an adult.'

The things that made George's heart leap up when he wrote that composition still cause it to do so today. He glances out of the window. It's a fine spring morning. He's been so preoccupied with his sorting that he hasn't noticed. He looks down at the sea of paper he's already earmarked for getting rid of. It lies ankle-deep around him. Fuck it – he's made a good start. He can do the rest later. What he wants to do right now is emulate exactly what he wrote in that last sentence all those years before – ride his motor cycle as fast as he can...

While he is putting on his leathers, he wonders where he will go. The sun is shining, the sky is a cloudless blue. The perfect day for a ride.

His first thought, after reading the essay, is to revisit some old haunts. The various houses he lived in as a boy – Portugal Street, Daisy Bank Road, Manley Park – but that would be a slow journey, necessitating too many stops for traffic lights and risking being caught out by speed cameras. What he really wants is to open up the throttle and really put his bike through her paces. It's another DOT. He's only ever ridden DOTs. First a DOT Racer, next a DOT Villiers, then a DOT Bradshaw. Now a DOT RS. All of them manufactured right here in Manchester and all of them first rate. Especially once he has been able to strip them down and customise them precisely to his own tastes and preferences. Each time he does this, it reminds him of his time as a younger man, when he used to work two nights a week at the Speedway track at Belle Vue, where his skill with adjusting the timing of each bike to maximise their performance had made him much sought-after by the top riders of the day. He regularly rubbed shoulders with the likes of Peter Craven, Ivan Mauger, Ove Fundin, Jason Crump and Peter Collins. He hasn't been in years...

But something about that essay still lingers. George's interest has been piqued. He'd like to return to at least one corner of his past. It's not every day one reaches seventy. Although his inclination has always been to look forward, it's only natural, is it not, to want to look back and reflect on reaching such a landmark? Older than either of his parents managed...

If not to school days, then where? Work? He has always defined himself by his work. Though he has always preferred the word 'vocation'. He's been lucky, he knows. Not everyone has had the luxury of regarding their work as a calling in the way that he has. That is why he called his first photographic exhibition, held in the old Blackfriars Street Gallery by St Mary's Parsonage just off Deansgate, *'Nuts & Bolts'*. After the phrase used by his piano teacher, Mrs Tiffin. It celebrated in dozens of portraits of different workers from all walks of life all that he felt about the fundamental importance of labour in the making of just who we are, both individually and collectively, photographed in heroic poses and dramatic lighting, full of youthful idealism, reminiscent of Soviet propaganda posters.

Here were carpenters and, coal merchants; miners, milkmen and milliners; typists and tanners; cotton workers, car mechanics, ice cream vendors; farriers and foundry men, fitters and firemen; French polishers; plumbers and plasterers; welders and window cleaners; women donkey-stoning their door-steps; seamstresses, laundresses, waitresses; tripe boilers, barbers and bargemen; bus conductors and rent collectors; electricians, lab technicians; shop girls and post boys; panel beaters, pattern cutters; railway porters, road menders, rag-and-bone men; butchers, bakers and candlestick makers –

representing every walk of life, so that the viewers found themselves surrounded on all sides, just as they are across the whole of Manchester, by the ceaseless activity of work, work, work, the convulsive upheaval of all this constant change, witnessed through the eyes of everyone George has photographed since, these faces of the city. The gallery pulsed with them. As they do still, whenever he exhibits new work. The air vibrates. The earth shakes…

George himself has never been afraid of hard work. He has always embraced it. He has always enjoyed what he calls 'tinkering'. Taking things apart, then trying to put them back together again. Hopefully better.

It began in his teenage years, helping his father in the Printing Works on Portugal Street. Gone now of course. A landmine in the Blitz had seen to that. But he still gets a buzz from remembering his early days of working there. Those febrile twelve days in May 1926, during the height of the General Strike, when the printers had been called out in sympathy with the miners, but he and his family – his mother, his father and grandfather – had printed and distributed a daily newspaper to counteract the lies being peddled by Lord Beaverbrook and his like in the mainstream press. George's job had been to deliver the newspapers in batches of fifty across the city on his Raleigh two-wheeler. He was only thirteen, but he loved the speed and responsibility of it. Mostly the speed. He came to know every back-alley and cut-through in Manchester. As the wheels rolled across concrete and cobble, tarmac and cinder, he could feel the rhythm of those printing presses back on Portugal Street rolling with him, rumbling through him, from deep within the earth, setting his wheels on fire…

He recalls two particular portraits from that *Nuts & Bolts* exhibition.

Archie Rowe and Freddie Catch.

Sign writer and blacksmith.

Yes, he thinks. They will be the perfect jumping-off point for this celebratory ride.

Both long dead now of course. But they were a kind of beginning for him. Each of them neighbours in a cluster of low brick buildings tucked between Weaste Lane and Buile Hill Park. George was apprenticed with Archie Rowe straight after leaving school. He can remember his first day there as though it were yesterday...

"Watch and learn," says Archie. "Don't try owt that's fancy, just copy what I do, and tha' shan't go far wrong. And unless tha's got summat worth sayin', say nowt. Right, lad?"

"Yes, Mr Rowe."

"And that's enough o' that Mr Rowe malarkey. Everyone calls me Archie, an' I reckon that'll do for thee, youth, an' all."

George nods.

"Now then, have a go at this for starters." He lays out before him a sheet of paper with the familiar sentence *'The quick brown fox jumps over the lazy dog'* written on it.

George regards it with a puzzled frown.

"There's every letter in th'alphabet in that sentence," explains Archie. "Well, lad, what're you waitin' for?"

He shows George where the tins of paint are kept – "you only ever need these five – red, yellow, blue, white an' black – they can give you all t' colours tha'll want" – where the brushes were kept – "sable an' ox hair – make sure tha' keeps 'em clean, lad" – and proceeded to induct him into the mysteries of the mahl stick. "This," he says, holding it up with near mystical reverence, "is the sign writer's greatest friend. It can be made up of owt – a thin metal rod, a piece of dowling, a copper pipe wi' a cork on one end – so long as it's light, an' so long as it's true. Tha' dun't want owt snappin' or bendin' on thee, else tha'll be up salt creek wi'out a paddle."

"What's it for, Archie?"

"It's to keep thy 'and from shakin', that's what. A sign must be written straight an' true, clear an' bold. If tha' takes too long o'er a single letter, it shows. It comes out all uncertain. Canst tha' see?" And he demonstrates, by painting a slow, spidery letter 's', which dribbles down the board before petering out near the bottom. "Now then, youth, what does that look like? No – don't say owt, for I'll tell thee straight. It looks like when tha's a kid an' tha's been tryin' to write tha' name while pissin' up a wall."

George splutters.

"Don't tell me tha' never tried it tha'self as a nipper. Tha'd be a rum sort of youth if tha' didn't."

George says nothing.

"Quite right, lad. Silence is a virtue. Now, wi' this mahl stick, tha' can grip it in tha' left palm, whilst holdin' t' pot o' paint twixt t' thumb an' t' forefinger, rest t' cork end against t' sign board to hold it still, then balance tha' right 'and on t' mahl stick to keep it steady, whilst tha' paints t' sign, using t' stick to help thee swing up high or reach down low in a single sure stroke. Like this, see...?"

And he would demonstrate with a deftness that took George's breath away. Like all great craftsmen, he made a difficult thing look disarmingly simple.

George persevered. He did as he was bid. He watched and he learned. In a few weeks he was able to render *'The quick brown fox jumped over the lazy dog'* in block or italics, in a variety of fonts and in a range of sizes.

"Ay, lad. I reckon tha's gettin' summat like..."

George was a quick study. He spent two days a week with Archie for the next two years, while the rest of his week was parcelled up between nights at the Speedway track, weekends at the Printing Works, and three days at *The Mechanics' Institute*, as an art student, learning to draw under the tutelage of none other than L.S. Lowry himself, whose main advice to George was two-fold…

"First of all, lad, find yourself a proper job." Lowry himself was a rent collector. "And second, make sure you work outside – *en plein air*, as the French call it. You've got to breathe the same air as the people and places you're trying to represent…"

Breathe the same air…

George has never forgotten this advice…

By the time he's completed his apprenticeship as a sign writer, Archie begins to trust him – albeit in a gruff, begrudging kind of way, which George has come to recognise as his way of offering tacit approval – with more and more demanding jobs. Archie's motto remains the same. "If tha's nowt to say, then don't say owt," which more accurately translates as never offering praise, but always being immediately forthcoming if, for any reason, he finds George's work does not come up to scratch. "Tha' closet seat," he'll rail, "tha' big girl's blouse, what dost tha' call this then, youth? I'll not be setting my name to that rubbish."

But these comments issue from his tobacco-stained, moustache-covered lips much less frequently these days, and so the two of them can mostly be found working side by side in companionable silence, punctured by the occasional, "Ay, that'll do, youth," or even, on one unforgettable red letter day, "Not bad, young 'un. In fact I'm minded to say 'reet gradely'."

It is something of a surprise therefore when George arrives one Monday morning at the beginning of April 1934 to find Archie already waiting to intercept him, as he parks his DOT Racer in the yard outside his workshop, thrusting out a sheet of Manchester Corporation headed note-paper.

"What dost tha' make o' this, lad?"

George reads it slowly and carefully twice, then looks back at Archie with eyebrows raised.

"Ay, that's what I thought, an' all."

Archie snatches it back and reads from it aloud.

```
FAO: Mr A. Rowe, Sign Writer

The following order is issued by the Central
Library Sub-Committee, which has been appointed
to consider the most suitable situation for the
creation of a new Reference Library in the Town
Hall Extension Site with responsibility for the
character of the building and for all fittings
and fixtures required to meet with the agreed
architectural designs as approved by the
Corporation.
```

It is hereby resolved:
```
that the following order be placed - see below:
that the Town Clerk be instructed to prepare
the necessary contract, and:
that under the direction of the Lord Mayor the
Corporate Seal be affixed thereto.
```

Particulars:
```
To carry out the required inscription around
the domed ceiling of the Great Hall Reading
Room of the new Central Reference Library.
```

Amount Authorised:
```
According to the Schedule: a figure not
exceeding £100, to include all materials.
```

Signed: A.A. Flitcroft, Town Clerk
```
pp Alderman Joseph Binns, J.P., Lord Mayor
Manchester Corporation
```

Archie scratches his head. "I don't understand it. It's not

like we tendered for it. I know nowt about this Library, do you?"

"It's the large circular building in St Peter's Square," replies George.

"Ay, I reckon," says Archie, still frowning. "I've not seen it. I don't go into Manchester much."

George smiles. From Buile Hill to St Peter's Square is less than three miles.

"We'd best be tekkin' a look at yon library then, youth, an' see what we're lettin' ourselves in for. Is there room for me on t' back o' that bike o' yourn?"

Half an hour later they're standing in St Peter's Square looking up at the new library, still clad in scaffold. Archie shakes his head. "I see what tha' means about t' shape, lad. It's a rum 'un, and no mistake. It looks more like a gasometer than a library. Still, ours is not to reason why. Let's go inside and see this domed ceiling. I'm not sure I like the sound o' that either."

Once inside the scene resembles a great upturned ship, with the sound of hammers and saws, drills and machinery. Great arcs of flame fountain from the welders' torches, showering on the serried ranks of plumbers, electricians, carpenters and stonemasons below. They are directed up a newly finished marble staircase to the first floor, where they are shown into the Great Hall, which will be the library's Central Reading Room. In here, by contrast, all is calm and quiet. The major building work is finished and an army of decorators is painting the walls. Everyone speaks in hushed whispers, the reason for which soon becomes clear as Archie, recognising one of the painters, calls out his name. The echo bounces around the walls and returns to him at the same time as several other voices badger him to be quiet. Loud voices are of no use here, and George notices how many of the men are using a kind of mimed sign language to communicate with each other whenever they need to shift a ladder or require a new paint brush. There's a kind of unified harmony to the work in here, which reminds George of a ballet. He itches to take out his camera and capture some of its orchestrated synchronicity, but that will have to wait. Archie, now standing in the very centre of the room, beckons George towards him, with an exaggerated, slow motion gesture. The choreography of the space is contagious, and already the two of them are part of it, adding their own individual movements to the overall pattern and frieze.

Archie gulps. "There's no way I can go all t' way up there," he whispers, pointing to the domed ceiling where the inscription is to be placed. "It's all I can do to go up two storeys." It's true. Frequently, George is the one these days to attach their signs, once they have been painted, onto the fascia boards of buildings, especially if they're on the second floor. Archie becomes wheezily breathless when climbing stairs and is becoming more and more shaky if required to ascend ladders. "How high dost tha' reckon it is? Sixty foot if it's an inch! Nay, lad, tha'll have to do it."

"But I'm not ready for such an important job."

"Tha'll 'ave to be, there's nowt else for it…"

Archie's estimate turns out to be uncannily close. The ceiling is actually sixty-*one* feet in height, while the perimeter is three hundred and ninety-nine feet all round. The inscription that they are required to write is fifty-two words in length, which, including spaces and punctuation points, adds up to two hundred and ninety-four characters in total, meaning that they must allocate a rectangle of one foot four inches by one foot for each one, allowing an additional two inches in height to compensate for the foreshortening effect caused by the writing having to be applied to the domed surface that slopes inwards at an angle of approximately thirty degrees.

They check and re-check their measurements and calculations. Archie then instructs and supervises George in a series of trial runs, letter by letter, on various surfaces back at the workshop, experimenting with different fonts and colours, until they settle on the Wallau font, designed a decade earlier by Rudolf Koch in Offenbach, Germany, in Antique Gold paint.

"The Germans produce beautiful fonts," enthuses Archie, in a way that reminds George of how Francis had waxed so lyrically about German makes of cameras. "Rudolf Koch started out in Hanau in a metal goods factory, where 'e also started to draw. 'E studied in Nuremburg an' were a great admirer o' William Morris an' th' Arts & Crafts Movement. 'E began to provide type faces for t' Klingspor Factory there, along wi' t' likes o' Paul Renner, Otto Beckmann an' Peter Behrens." George has never heard Archie give such a long speech before. His face has taken on an expression close to rapture. He goes to a desk at the back of the workshop and pulls out a book, in which there are several examples of Koch's work, both his lettering and some woodcut illustrations.

"Ay, lad," he concludes, "I reckon that the Wallau's got the right kind of heft for this job, eh youth?"

George nods in agreement, revising his view of his normally bluff, taciturn employer.

Over the next few weeks, in between their other jobs, Archie and George continue to refine and practise their use of the Wallau, gradually increasing in size, until George feels ready to take on the task *in situ*.

The foreman at the library negotiates with Archie for them to come in during the evenings after the other workers have left for the day. They need to be completely undisturbed for the duration of the task, for if anyone were to distract George while he is working, or accidentally jolt his elbow in mid-stroke, the results would be catastrophic. He needs to allow his arm time and space to discover the rhythm and freedom necessary for the long, bold, uninterrupted brushwork that will be required to complete the inscription in such a way as to render it weightless, soaring free and unencumbered above the heads of those who look up to read it, like a coronet adorning the head, the crown of which is suffused with light falling through the glass in the ceiling's apex.

George climbs the labyrinth of scaffolding, ladders and platforms until he reaches the point where he is to begin, directly above the gilded clock adorning what will be the central, circular information desk, within which the librarians will sit. Archie waits below, ready to offer advice and correction if necessary from below on the as yet unpolished floor, still covered with sheets to protect it until the final phase of the work is completed. He stands surrounded by the sixty-six marble columns which encircle the Great Hall, their mottled, golden colour dappling in the last rays of the sun slanting down upon them through the skylight in the dome above, a colour which will be picked out even more by the Antique Gold paint they have chosen for the inscription, the first tin of which George is about to dip his brush into and make his first mark. He lights a candle, which he places on a platform just to his left above his head. This will illuminate the expanse of ceiling he is to begin. He recalls the descriptions by Vasari of Michelangelo embarking upon the Sistine Chapel, hoisted to a similar height on a precariously swinging cradle, which his Art History lecturer had read to him at *The Mechanics' Institute*. Not that what George is attempting comes anywhere close to such an enterprise, but it encourages him to think of it.

" '*Faith in oneself is the best and safest course*'." That was one of Michelangelo's. " '*It is necessary to keep one's compass in one's eye and not in the hand, for the hand executes, but the eye judges*'." That was another.

427

He closes his eyes, takes a deep breath, picturing the whole inscription revealing itself letter by letter in his mind around the ceiling's span. They have done their calculations, they have measured lightly in pencil the upper and lower reaches of the imagined lines between which he will write.

" '*I saw the angel in the marble and carved until I set her free*'." That was a third.

He's ready.

He opens his eyes, dips the brush into the paint, steadies the mahl stick in his left hand, rests his right arm upon it, and begins...

The light outside fades. The glow of the candle flame intensifies. George works, and Archie watches, in perfect silence. Each can hear the breathing of the other...

The work will take them five nights. They have calculated that each letter will take George ten minutes. There are two hundred and forty words, which means the whole inscription will take forty hours to complete. Five nights of eight hours each...

They begin on Monday 9th July 1934, exactly one week and a day before the library is due to be officially opened by King George, so there's no margin for error. They must finish by Friday to allow the foreman and his team the weekend to take down all the scaffolding and give the whole interior a thorough cleaning in time for any last minute adjustments on the Monday to be ready for their Majesties on the Tuesday.

George completes the first letter. He looks down towards Archie, who nods. And so he proceeds, letter by letter, throughout the night, trying not to think of the enormity of the Great Hall's perimeter, concentrating instead only on keeping his painting hand flowing freely and evenly in long, measured strokes, making sure he is never tentative, but always bold. At the completion of each letter, he lowers both arms, shakes out the stiffness, rolls his shoulders back and forth, takes a swig of water, before calling out the next letter to Archie below, who responds by repeating it back to him, so there can be no room for error.

"W?"
"W – check."
"I?"
"I – check."
"S?"
"S – check."

At the end of each word, George will stand back as far as he dare on the flimsy scaffold, crane his neck and read it back to Archie.

"W-i-s-d-o-m..."
"W-i-s-d-o-m..."

At four in the morning, as the light from the sky begins to seep through the round window in the centre of the dome, George puts down his brush and replaces the lid on the tin of paint. Forty-eight letters done. Another forty-eight tomorrow.

And so the week progresses.

Tuesday night, another forty-eight letters. Wednesday night, forty-eight more. Thursday night, a further forty-eight, until Friday night arrives, and the final forty-eight wait patiently to emerge upon the ceiling wall, floating like ghostly palimpsests from where they have been lying beneath the plaster, waiting to be born, angels about to be set free and take wing.

As the last full stop is painted, doubled with a final flourish by George into a colon, so that the reader, from wherever he or she may stand in the Great Hall, looking up, will quickly be able to orientate themselves as to where to begin, George lets out an audible sigh, which empties him. Archie, permitting himself to speak at last, is content with merely an "Ay, lad, tha's done it. I reckon Rudolf Koch himself could've done no better."

'Wisdom is the principal thing. Therefore get wisdom and within all thy getting get understanding. Exalt her and she shall promote thee. She shall bring thee to honour when thou dost embrace her. She shall give to thine head an ornament of grace. A crown of glory shall she deliver to thee.'

George feels suddenly overwhelmed with dizziness and has to steady himself against an upright scaffold, behind which, lying prostrate along one of the platforms, he spots a window pole. He slowly draws it along towards him, raises it up to the skylight in the dome above his head, where a new dawn is beginning to poke through, and pulls sharply on it. It opens to let in some much-needed, welcome fresh air, which George drinks in deeply.

A few moments later, they both hear a fluttering against the glass. A tiny wren is perched on the roof outside, curiously looking down at them through the glass. It tips its head first one way, then another, before opening its beak, from which pours forth a glorious descending cascade of rapid notes, followed by a series of inquisitive churrs and chitters. Then, no longer able to contain its curiosity any longer, it dips under the skylight and begins to fly around the vast, empty chamber of the Great Hall, swooping through and between the scaffold towers, perching between the great marble columns, before finally alighting on top of the gilt clock, which delicately chimes the half hour. The wren, startled, trills back in response and then takes off for another skittish orbit of the domed ceiling, passing each of the painted letters in turn, until eventually it lands on the floor between Archie's feet.

With aching slowness, he lowers himself towards it, then,

with a sudden lunge, scoops it up in his huge ham hands. George joins him. Together the two men look down on the tiny trembling bird, fluttering against Archie's fingers like a pulse in the blood. He carries it carefully down the marble staircase towards the front door, where the men who are to take down the scaffolding have already started to arrive and are stamping their heavy boots on the stone steps. George puts his finger to his lips, and the men stand back like the parting of the Red Sea to let them pass. As soon as they are outside, Archie opens his hands and the wren flies away, landing a few yards ahead of them on the recently unveiled Cenotaph designed by Sir Edwin Lutyens in St Peter's Square, from where it eyes them dispassionately, its head bobbing up and down and from side to side.

George and Archie wait until it takes off again, and they can no longer see it, before returning inside the Library, where the men have already begun to take down the scaffolding in the Great Hall, revealing the full inscription unencumbered, as if shaking off its iron carapace. The letters glitter in the morning light, as if ready to take wing...

That was fifty years ago, George reflects now with a certain incredulity. Like Archie, he doesn't get to go into the centre of Manchester much these days either. But when he does, he likes to step into the library and climb the marble staircase to the Grand Central Reading Room. Just to check that what he wrote around its ceiling is still there. He knows it will be, but it still causes him a certain frisson to think those words, those 'ornaments of grace', were actually handwritten there by him...

He's ready to begin his ride.

He puts on his goggles and crash helmet. He lets the choke out on his DOT RS just a little, turns the throttle with his right hand, then kick-starts the engine, which sparks instantly into life with a satisfying roar.

He turns out of Adelphi Street into The Crescent, then left onto Eccles Old Road, skirting Buile Hill Park till he reaches Weaste Lane. He locates the cluster of brick buildings immediately, throwing up chips of gravel as he brakes to a stop. It has taken him just eight minutes to get there.

Being a Sunday everywhere is closed up, which means he can take a look around without being interrupted. Archie Rowe's Sign Writing Workshop is long gone of course. It's been converted to a picture framer's. *Art Imaging*. George is quietly impressed. He looks back across the yard. The blacksmith's forge is gone too, but more of that is recognisable than what is left of Archie's old workshop. It's a Car Mechanic's Garage now – Buile Hill Motor Repairs – and the structure looks much as George remembers it. He fetches a rag from one of the panniers on his DOT RS to wipe clean a smeared window in order to peer inside. The frame is worn and weathered, and in need of a lick of paint. George rubs it vigorously, disturbing a peppered moth taking shelter in one of its crevices as he does so. He watches it reluctantly take off in search of somewhere safer, then returns his gaze to the interior of the garage. His eyes gradually grow accustomed to the gloom. Just as they did the first time he dared to look inside. Where the forge once stood is where the inspection pit now resides. But other than that, and the assortment of car parts, bits of engine, old tyres, little else has changed. He can still picture it as it was. Instinctively he raises his eyes towards the rafters in the roof and remembers…

George is standing outside Archie's workshop, which is tucked behind a railway arch, with a low brick roof, which gets ever lower as it stretches towards the gloomy back wall, where Archie keeps a stack of wood for boards. Across the yard from where they are standing, in a ramshackle huddle of buildings tucked up against the embankment, which carries trains out of Salford towards Wigan Wallgate via Walkden, is a smithy. From time to time George has seen a broad-shouldered, stooping figure emerge from within, bare-chested, his skin a deep chestnut brown, his eyes in shadow, his frame silhouetted against the red glow of the forge burning inside. He and Archie will occasionally nod in the other's direction, but as yet George has never heard them exchange even a word. The man crosses the yard now. and then disappears into one of the other buildings, which George takes to be the smith's cottage.

"Who's that?" he asks, before he has time to check himself.

Archie throws him a withering look. "Ask me no questions and I'll tell thee no lies."

Later, when George has finished for the day, he waits while Archie locks up and pretends to be tinkering with something on his DOT Racer until Archie has left. Then George creeps across the yard towards the smithy and peeps inside.

It takes him several moments for his eyes to adjust to the Stygian darkness of the forge after the bright late sun outside. He ventures further in, fascinated, as he is increasingly becoming, by the different specialist tools of any given trade. He walks past a bench laid out with hammers of different shapes and weights. A second bench is lined with row upon row of neatly arranged files and rasps. In the corner is a mountain of discarded nails. Hung on a wall are dozens of horse shoes.

The sun is dipping lower in the evening sky. While George is wandering silently and reverently through the forge, shafts of light begin streaming through the slats in the far wall. Motes of dust, like tiny dancers, circle slowly in each one. Letting his gaze roam, he chances upon an arrangement of iron sculptures hanging from a beam near the roof. At first he cannot make out what they are. Intrigued, he moves a little closer, until he is standing directly beneath them. The way the light catches them, they remind him of a flock of birds caught on a current of air, and then, the more he studies them, he realises that this is exactly what they are, three birds in flight, with long necks and deep, strong wings. He thinks they might be egrets, but he is not sure. His father will know. He must try to remember every last detail of them. A barrel is standing close by. George drags it over and climbs on top of it in order to get an even closer look. The light from the sun is now catching them with greater clarity and sharpness, and George can make out that all three birds have been fashioned from literally hundreds of individual, uniquely-shaped feathers, each one of them separately cast in iron. It is one of the most remarkable things he has ever seen. He reaches up his hand, carefully, tentatively, wondering if he might dare to touch them. His fingers inch towards them, tantalisingly slowly. He stretches to his full height, raising himself onto the tips of his toes, trying to maintain an increasingly precarious balance. Just as he is about at last to touch them, a voice booms from the open doorway.

"Hey! You!"

Immediately George overbalances and falls from the barrel, knocking it over as he crashes to the ground with a painful thud. At the last second his fingers had brushed against the birds, and now they swing above him, swooping in and out of the light, their metal wings beating against one another.

The bare-chested man towers above him. "You," he says again, "stay where you are." A dog growls at George, guarding him so that he won't try to slip away. The man rights the barrel, leaps upon it with surprising grace and agility, reaches up and calms the clattering birds, until they are still and silent once more. When he is finally satisfied, he jumps back down to the ground and picks up George by the lapels of his jacket in a single, sure and threatening movement, the dog shadowing his every move..

"Who are you?" he says again. "Why are you here?"

George can only stammer a mumbled apology.

Catch looks at him closely. "You're still only a boy," he says at last. "Go. Do not come back. Unless you have business here. Do you have business here?"

George shakes his head.

"Then go."

George picks up his cap and runs to the door.

But when he reaches it, he stops. Something makes him turn around. He looks back to the smith, then points towards the iron birds.

"Those?" he asks. "What are they?"

The dog gives a second low warning growl…

Just as another dog does now. It runs menacingly towards George, barking fiercely up at him, followed closely by his owner.

"Oi – don't you know this is private property?"

George, who is not at all intimidated by the dog – a German Shepherd, he sees now – raises his hands in mock surrender.

"Sorry," he says. "I didn't know anyone was about."

"Oh," says the owner now, who George can see is more relieved than angry. "I thought you might be one of those young kids who hang around. We've had a number of break-ins lately. That's why I'm here. Me and Jake," he adds, indicating the dog, who George is now fondling behind his ears, "we keep an eye out most weekends. Just in case. I'm Craig, by the way." He holds out his hand.

"George."

The two men shake hands.

"I used to work round here," explains George. "Many years ago. This used to be a forge. He turns back to face the garage.

"Ay," says the man, "I know. It had lain derelict for years before me and my brother bought it up."

"I used to know the blacksmith," says George. "I was

wondering..." He pauses a moment before continuing.

"Ay?" says Craig.

"Might it be possible for me to take a look inside? There's something that used to be here. I'm wondering if it still might be?"

"I think I know what you're talking about," says Craig, unlocking an iron chain round the handle. "Come on in..." The years roll back with the slow creaking of the door...

"Those," asks George a second time. "What are they?"

Catch, surprised by the young boy's sudden bravery, pauses, deciding whether or not to answer him, or throw one of the hammers at him instead, like he might to a curious rat, to send him on his way.

"Egrets," he says at last. He thinks of how these birds made their long journeys across the plains, across the ocean, thousands of miles, to this place, here, now.

"Why are there three of them?" asks the strange boy.

This is too complicated a question to answer. He shakes his head. "You go now," he says.

"Might I come another time and look at them again?"

Catch walks swiftly towards him. He stops, barely inches from the boy's face, which he scrutinises intently, then nods.

"Thank you," says George...

Back inside the sequestered shade of the workshop half a century later, George is once more aware of the way the light slips between the slats in the far wall. He looks up. Yes. The iron egrets are still there.

"They're quite something, aren't they?" says Craig, standing beside George.

"They are that," says George.

The two men stare admiringly up at the sculptures.

"I were all for takin' 'em down at first," says Craig, "but

Aaron – that's my brother – he said not to. 'I reckon they'll bring us luck', he said. An' they 'ave. We've done all right ever since we come 'ere, so now I think of 'em as a kind of lucky charm."

"They're probably worth quite a lot of money," says George.

"Mebbe. Mebbe not," says Craig. "But I wouldn't sell 'em now, not for all the tea in China."

"Good," says George. "I'm glad. They belong here. It's right they should stay."

"You seem to know quite a bit about 'em," says Craig. "Did you know 'im, like, the blacksmith?"

"Not well," says George. "But then nobody did. He wasn't one for talking. He was an American Indian. Part of a Wild West Show at Belle Vue. But he escaped. Together with three others. From what I can make out, they set up a camp not far from here. Near Worsley. On the banks of the Irwell. Back in the 19th century, this was. He was fascinated by fire. He studied it. He learned the ways of it. He understood its different habits and characters. It was his natural element, you might say. He became prenticed to a smith out on the edge of Chat Moss, but he soon became his own master. He made the most wonderful things out of fire and iron. He specialised in weather vanes. He liked the way they would turn in the wind. You can see examples of his handiwork on church towers right across the Moss. But then the War came. I'm talking about the First one, back in 1914. He was put to making horse shoes. He made thousands and thousands of them. He made so many of them that he felt he was losing his touch, his craft, his mastery. They blunted his art, if you want to call it that. So he set himself a task. Each day, as he walked to the forge, he'd pick up any bird feather he found and kept it. Then, at dusk, just before he went back home, he'd fashion a copy of it out of iron, just to keep his hand in. Over the years he made hundreds. But he didn't know what to do with them. Till one day, his daughter, a bright little thing by the name of Chamomile, told him it was about time he made a start."

"You seem to know a lot about it."

"Only from what I've heard."

"Who from?"

"His daughter, mostly. Chamomile. Or Cam, as she came to be called."

"Was she a sweetheart of yours then?"

"No," smiles George. "Just a friend."

Craig raises his eyebrows. He can't imagine just being friends with a girl. Still, it takes all sorts, he supposes.

"So what happened? How did he come to make these?" He gestures towards the three iron egrets, turning slowly and gracefully above their heads.

George remembers a time much later, after the Second World War, when he'd decided that there was no future in his relationship with Francis any more, not the sort of future he wanted, a permanent one, like any other type of marriage, and he'd poured his heart out to Cam late one night after one of her sets at *The Queen's*, back in her flat on Great Clowes Street, just around the corner from his own...

Catch no longer cast an iron feather on the anvil for every single horse shoe that he made. There were simply too many. But whenever he had a spare moment he would fashion another and toss it into the heavy munitions box, which had accompanied him and Clem throughout their years of wandering, and which now lay in a corner of the forge. There must have been more than a thousand of them...

It was while he was crouching down, trying to sort through them one September evening in 1918, so that he might close the lid of the box, which he'd just that moment hoisted on to his knee so that he might tip it lengthways, then stand on the top of it to reach down a new tin of nails from a shelf high up, when Cam called to him from the doorway. He was so lost in his thoughts that he didn't hear her, and so she was forced to come closer. She tapped him on the shoulder. Startled, he dropped the box, and dozens of the wrought-iron feathers clattered onto the hard earth floor.

"What are these?" she asked, picking them up and holding them to the light.

Her father explained.

"They're like the three in the kitchen."

He nodded.

"One for each of us."

"Yes."

"Why do you keep so many of them?"

"I thought I'd make something with them one day."

"Like what?"

He shook his head.

"A weather vane for the top of the church?"

"No."

"Why not? It'd turn in the wind. I'd like that."

"I don't want to make something useful."

"What then?"

"Something just for its own sake. Something beautiful."

"Like *Maman*?"

"And you."

"You'd better get started then."

She scrunched up her face and wrinkled her nose. He laughed.

"What did you want? Just now, when you came in?"

"Oh, nothing really. Supper's nearly ready, that's all."

He nodded and she wandered off, still holding one of the iron feathers. He managed finally to close the lid on the box, before standing on it to reach down the tin of nails. When he stepped back down, he paused. Cam had been right. It was about time he made a beginning.

Outside he could hear her singing one of her mother's Creole songs.

"Moi j'm'ai mis à l'observer
Moi j'ai vue des lumières allumées
Y'a quelque chose qui m'disait j'devrais pleurer
Oh yé yaille mon cœur il fait mal..."

At nights Catch would sometimes dream he passed by an open door. He would call out, "Hey there, Beautiful?" But no one would answer. He'd pass by again. He'd see candles lit in the window, but still no one was there. When he woke, his heart would be aching and he'd pull Clem closer to him...

When he walked out of the forge into the yard, Cam was still singing. When she saw him, she stopped and pointed up to the sky.

"Look," she called.

Three great white egrets were flying across the moon.

"Make *them*," she said, laughing, and skipped indoors.

Yes, he thought. Why not?

He remembered the song from the Harvest Home. The last time he and Tommy and Sammy were all together, before they left the Earl's land and their Camp beside the Bittern Wood for good.

"There were three men came from the west
Their fortunes for to try..."

For the next eight weeks Catch worked every night to fashion the three birds, using as many of the more than a thousand iron feathers as he could to build up the complex structures of the wings, layer upon layer.

"They look like angels' wings," whispered Cam to him late one evening.

Catch nodded and kissed the top of her brow.

"When will they be finished?" she asked.

"Soon, I think. Tomorrow maybe."

He had used a couple of hundred to create each of the three long necks and outstretched bills, and a couple of hundred more to mould a large, round full moon, pitted with craters and mountains, whose shadows formed the faint outline of a moth.

On the last night he painted the rest of the moon a whitish yellow, so that the black iron feathers of the birds would fly across it as silhouettes.

Dusk.

Catch applied the final finishing touches, attaching the three birds to the backdrop of the moon. His hammer rang upon the anvil loud and clear, echoing across the evening sky, startling a small wren that had nested in the rafters of the forge. It circled once around the iron moon before flying through a slat into the night...

As one is doing now, while George is remembering this final part to the story, told to him by Cam the same night he had talked to her about Francis. It flutters around the rafters of what had once been the forge, before flying out into the yard, then away over towards Buile Hill Park.

"Thanks for letting me see them," says George, as he and Craig wander back outside.

"Thanks for telling me their story," says Craig. "We'll definitely be keeping them now. They're like our Guardian Angels."

Yes, thinks George. That's true. Catch would have liked that.

George approaches his DOT RS.

"Is she yours?" asks Craig, his eyes caressing it approvingly. "Beautiful machine."

"The best," says George.

"Made right here in Manchester."

"Salford, to be exact. Ellesmere Street."

"D-O-T. Devoid-Of-Trouble."

"That's the one."

"And has she been?"

"So long as I treat her right."

"The same is true with life."

George smiles. The mechanic as philosopher. He's long held the view that the two professions are related. The study of the fundamental nature of things and how they fit together.

"Do you mind if I take a photograph?" he asks.

"Be my guest," says Craig, standing to one side.

George takes a small camera from the pannier on the side of his bike. It's a *Foth Derby*. The first camera he ever had, the one recommended by Francis the first time they met. He frames the DOT RS against the open door of the garage, then squats down low to the ground, so that he is looking up at it from below, making it appear larger, more heroic somehow, with space above for the sculpture of the three iron egrets in the background, turning slowly in the wind. As he prepares to take the picture, he notices that there is a minute, crouching reflection of himself caught in the gleaming chrome of the bike. It reminds him of the self-portrait he included of himself in his very first exhibition, *Nuts & Bolts*, in which he also appeared only as a miniature, almost invisible version of himself, similarly caught in the gleaming frame of a speedway bike, and the symmetry of the moment pleases him. He presses the shutter with immense satisfaction. What he does not notice is, at the precise moment he clicks, the peppered moth he disturbed earlier momentarily alights upon the handlebars, opening, then closing its wings…

Having shaken hands with Craig a second time, George departs, the DOT RS kicking up a shower of gravel, as he roars away in a halo of dust.

He doubles back on himself up Weaste Lane, then right onto Eccles Old Road once more, before taking a second right on Broad Street, and a third on Albion Way, which leads him towards the slip road for the motorway, the M602, where he can really open up the throttle and let his beloved machine at last have her head...

He knows, without consciously having thought it, exactly where he is headed.

The M602 is one of the shortest motorways in England, just four miles long, which George completes in less than three minutes. He negotiates the loop of junctions with the M62 and M63, before exiting on the Liverpool Road, close by Barton Aerodrome, the scene of George's first outing with Francis, when he was still not twenty. He's heading for the heart of the Mosses strung together between Eccles and Warrington, where they had ridden together that first time, and where Catch had first sculpted his feathers of iron, before miraculously transforming them into the three egrets flying across the face of the moon...

He turns away from the Liverpool Road as soon as he can, onto Fiddler's Lane, which takes him to the edge of Barton Moss, where he picks up the first of the levees, the raised embankments on which cinder tracks criss-cross the drained marshes. Raspberry Lane, then Twelve Yards Way, past the Black Wood, towards Four Lane Ends, he follows the route that he and Francis took that late summer's afternoon half a century ago. When he reaches the run of desolate shacks and farms that herald the start of Irlam Moss – *Plant, Ebenezer, Hephzibah, Retreat*, and, last of all, *Hope* – he plunges down lanes that have no name, deep into the heart of Chat Moss itself.

Chat Moss. Chatmos. Catemosse. St Chad's Moss.

Named for a seventh century Mercian saint. Chad, sometimes known as Cedd, who preached against the pagan King Penda, frequently seen wandering in the wilds clad only in rags and carrying an axe. He would reputedly stand naked in a storm at night and bring calm with the singing of psalms.

Moss – Anglo-Saxon for bog or marsh.

Daniel Defoe, on his great *'Tour through the Whole Island of Great Britain'*, divided into 'circuits or journies', during which he dubs Manchester 'the greatest mere village in England', traverses the Moss on his way there, which he describes with fear and dread.

'We pass'd through the great bog or waste call'd Chatmos, the first of that kind that we see in England. The surface, at a distance, looks black and dirty, and is indeed frightful to think of, for it will bear neither horse nor man, unless in an exceeding dry season, and then not so as to be passable, for no one should travel over them. What nature meant by such a useless production, 'tis hard to imagine, but the land is entirely waste, except for the poor cottagers' fuel, and the quantity used for that is very small...'

But to George it possesses a wild beauty in its remoteness. Just ten square miles in size, and hemmed in on all sides by coal mines, steel mills, chemical plants, tar, soap and wire works, yet, for those who dare to venture deep into its labyrinth of hidden tracks that will take them safely through the treacherous mire, there are rare rewards – the newts and lizards, snakes and eels, moths and butterflies, cottongrass and orchids – that are waiting to be found by those who take the time to look for them. This is the haunt of the merlin and hen harrier, the long-eared owl and curlew. And in Botany Bay Wood, which rises up directly from the marshes, nests of herons and egrets abound.

This large peat bog, on which all this wild life thrives, first began to form eleven thousand years ago, with the ending of the last ice age. The peat extends to a depth of more than thirty feet, overlaying sediments of Bunter pebble beds of red sandstone, boulder clay and marl, a carbonate-rich silt, packed with nutrients and preservatives. Twenty-five years before George is taking this celebratory ride, workmen, digging peat close by Olive Mount, the highest point on the Moss, towards which George is now headed, discovered the perfectly preserved two-thousand-year-old head of a young man, a Romano-British Celt, with traces of a garrotte still looped about his neck, suggesting a ritual killing in keeping with pagan practices of the time. He was dubbed 'Worsley Man', and he presaged the discovery of further 'bog bodies' elsewhere in the Moss. Lindow Man and Lindow Woman. Evidence that people have been eking out a life here for millennia, despite what doubters like Defoe wrote of the place, or, before him, John Leland, who chronicled the realm at the command of King Henry VIII, and who thought the Moss even more frightful than Defoe did a century and a half after him.

'Chat Moss fetched up within a mile of Mosley Haul, braking much grounde with mosse thereabout. It destroies all fish, corrupting with stinkinge water the Glase Brook, which the Mersey, thus corrupted, doth carrye forth this black mosse to the shores of Wales, part to the Isle of Man, and some even unto Ireland...'

In the middle of the eighteenth century Mother Ann Lee led her band of Shakers across it as she fled persecution for the promised land of the new world. And George remembers Cam telling him about how her mother, Clémence, a freed Louisiana slave, travelling across it in the opposite direction, along the raft of floating pontoons laid upon the surface of the Moss by

George Stephenson when constructing the world's first passenger railway, thought she caught a ghostly glimpse of her, how later she fled from the mansions of cotton merchants in the centre of Manchester to seek sanctuary there, how she met Catch the blacksmith there, when she pulled him out of this same bog into which he was sinking after the explosion at one of the nearby mines at The Delph had rocked the earth beneath him, and how she had first taught Cam the Creole songs of her childhood, which Cam had later sung at *The Queen's Hotel*…

"Moi j'm'ai mis à l'observer
Moi j'ai vue des lumières allumées
Y'a quelque chose qui m'disait j'devrais pleurer
Oh yé yaille mon cœur il fait mal…"

George imagines those flames now, *des lumières allumées*, lost souls flitting like candles from the bodies buried and preserved in the peat, lighting his way as he rides his DOT RS as fast as he dares across the causeways that arrow across the Moss, just as they enticed the enemy bombers during the last War, when George had deployed the false and flickering 'starfish' fires here to tempt and tease the German planes, flame-tipped sirens, luring their pilots, their star-sailors, away from their real targets with these decoys, these illusions of hope, with their silver-tongued promises.

"J'ai passé devant ta porte
J'ai crié bye bye à la belle
Y'a personne qui m'a pas répondu
Oh-Yé-Yaille mon cœur fais mal…"

He hears their voices now, singing in the wind. The air quivers and trembles with them.

Then, just as he begins the two-mile rise up to the summit of Olive Mount, at only three hundred and seventy feet above sea level the highest point of the Moss, but a gradual climb nevertheless, he sees it. Or thinks he does.

A white egret.

It hangs in the air before him, shimmering.

At first George wonders if he might be seeing a mirage.

But no. He is certain of it now. Its slow, heavy wingbeats propel it skywards.

He is reminded once again of that first ride with Francis. When another egret had loomed up out of the Moss and collided with them, flinging them both from the bike and badly breaking Francis's leg. How, while they had waited for Ishtar to summon the ambulance that would take Francis to the hospital called Hope, not far from a farm bearing the same name, here in a hard, sun-baked hollow, they had told each other their life stories, as all around them the Moss had teemed with new beginnings...

George listens with growing incredulity. His own account feels so pallid by comparison with that of his new friend, with his tales of burying bodies and following telegraph poles, but as he relates some of it, the two of them begin to realise just how closely their lives have intersected, how they have nearly collided on so many occasions at different times and at different points across the city. It is as if they have each been riding the same tram for years and years, but hopping on and off at different stops, vaguely aware of a conjoined spark crackling in the cables overhead, until this highly charged evening, when the air positively bristles with electricity between them.

But Francis is now beginning to drift in and out of consciousness. He is becoming increasingly less coherent. George starts to panic. He gently slaps his friend's cheeks. "Don't fall asleep now, love," he says.

Francis's eyelids flutter awake, a look of astonishment on

his face.

George begins to intone in a hushed, lilting, sing-song voice.

"This is the tale of Thomas-à-Tattimus
Who took two T's
To tie two tups to two tall trees
To frighten the terrible Thomas-à-Tattimus
How many T's are there in all that...?"

Francis slips away once more, so that George has to sing it again.

"This is the tale of Thomas-à-Tattimus
Who took two T's
To tie two tups to two tall trees
To frighten the terrible Thomas-à-Tattimus
How many T's are there in all that...?"

"How many, Francis? Answer me. How many T's are there in all that?"

"I don't know what you're talking about," mumbles Francis, his words increasingly slurred.

"How many T's?" George is shouting now at the top of his voice. "Answer me. How many?"

"Two," whispers Francis at last. "Two." His pale eyes open and focus.

"Yes," says George, "that's right. Two." He can feel tears sliding down his cheek, which he wipes with the back of his hand. "There's only ever been two."

"Only ever been two," echoes Francis, patting the back of George's hand.

They smile and hold each other closely, as a pair of gynandrous clouded yellow butterflies graze on the underside of buckthorn leaves in the last of the light...

George sees one of them again now, rising up out of the peat bog as he rides by.

Only one.

Just as there is only one egret.

Not three, as there had been in Catch's forge.

Just one.

And now it is calling to him, a dry, rasping nasal croak, across the years.

The clouded yellow butterfly flutters in front of his face for a moment, and he realises he was mistaken, just as he must have been before, for it is not a butterfly after all, but a white-peppered Manchester moth, like the one he had disturbed at the garage earlier, its mottled wings as pale and parched as the straw-coloured cotton grass where it lays its eggs, and where its pupae wait and overwinter till the warmer days of summer arrive to waken it, into its full imagined glory.

As one did another time, in this same spot, after the end of the 2nd World War, when George and Francis had ridden here a second time. Though not as a beginning. Nor, even, as an ending. But as a transformation. A different phase in the cycle...

The Manchester moth alights on a tuft of white beak sedge below where George and Francis are sitting. It is quickly joined by another, just as it was all those years ago in this same spot, while George waited for the ambulance to take Francis to that hospital called Hope.

"I've come to realise," he says, "that what I want is impossible. What I want, Francis, is to be married, like my parents were, like Victor and Winifred are, like Lily and Roland would like to be. You and me. Like any other normal couple. But we can't be, can we? The law regards us as criminals, society as a whole doesn't accept us, so we have to hide away, meet in secret, pretend that we're just pals whenever we go out together. Oh I know that we have friends who know, good friends who understand. Christ, I'm pretty sure my mother knew but I could never have dared to mention it just in case she didn't, and I'm sick to death of pretending, Francis, that's the nub of it. We both of us spent the whole of the War engaged in deception of one kind or another, you with your faked news broadcasts and me with my false decoy sites, trying to pull the wool over the eyes of the enemy, and in the end deception becomes an end in itself, you start to get less certain about what is and isn't real…"

"But the War's over now, George. Things are getting back to…"

"To what, Francis? Normal? And what exactly is normal? Are *we* normal?"

"God, I should hope not. You and I could never be anything like so dull as 'normal'. We're much more than that."

"But I want to be normal. I want this – us – to be so normal that it's not even remarked on."

As George is speaking, the two Manchester moths are suddenly joined by a flock of perhaps thirty others, which descend in a cloud, fluttering around and between them, alighting fleetingly on their hands, their hair, before taking off again in a golden drift, until the whole of the Moss is alive with them, their fragile wings opening and closing like eyelids, blinking in the autumn sunlight.

The sight of them stops George and Francis in their tracks, lost in the wonder of it, each of them knowing they will probably never witness such a thing again. They sit, entranced. A whole minute stretches between them like a taut, invisible wire, which, if their senses were differently tuned, they might receive and hear their ultrasonic frequency and understand more of what was passing between them, filtering out the white extraneous noise to uncover that simple undiluted message.

Love.

Then, as if in response to the lifting of a conductor's unseen hand, the moths fountain into the air until only the original two are left, mating on the tip of the white beak sedge...

But today, on George's seventieth birthday, there is just a single moth. And now it too has vanished in the impenetrable miasma of Chat Moss...

And still the egret flies before him, its broad, strong wings ploughing through the thick, hazy air in a relentless rhythmical swoop, beckoning George to follow where they lead.

The narrow, nameless causeway slices through the land, parallel lines racing towards that same vanishing point. George bisects them perfectly. The top of the rise of Olive Mount, the exact position which marks the highest point in the Moss, is directly caught in his sights. A red sun is just beginning to set, its molten disc momentously framed where the parallel lines appear to meet. The egret skewers towards it. It flies into the opening mouth of it. George's heart leaps up as he tries to catch all the rainbow colours of it. He opens the throttle of his DOT RS as wide as it will go and accelerates in pursuit. He reaches the summit at exactly the same moment as his wheels leave the ground. The timing is so exquisitely sweet he can almost taste it. The speed of his ascent propels him into a perfect parabolic arc. As he reaches its apogee, he hangs there, suspended. Time slows, stretches, elongates, until finally it stops altogether, preserving him for ever in a single perpetual freeze-frame, flawless, untouchable, consummate, complete...

9

1986

MANCHESTER CITY COUNCIL

Extract from Minutes of the Equal Opportunities Sub-Committee
4th April 1986

A proposal was put forward jointly by Paul Turner and Maggie Fairweather, respectively Gay Men's and Lesbian Officers with the Council, for the Committee to support an inaugural two-day Festival aimed at raising greater awareness of AIDS across the city. The Festival is scheduled to take place during the August Bank Holiday later this year. The Committee unanimously agreed to award *Manchester Pride*, a charitable organisation newly created to champion gay rights, the sum of £1700 as initial seed-funding…

A year into her internship within the Manchester Labour Party, Jenna is seconded to assist Paul and Maggie in the coordination of this fledgling event.

"This is an historic moment," says Paul, when the meeting has broken up. "We should mark it accordingly."

"I agree," says Maggie. "It's hugely symbolic. The first local authority outside London to endorse an openly gay event."

"And then put their money where their mouth is," adds Paul.

"It's less than two thousand pounds," says Jenna. "That's

hardly unequivocal support."

"No," says Maggie. "It's not a lot, I grant you. But it's a significant statement they're making, an important gesture of good will. It's out there now, right in the public domain…"

"… who are not wholly on our side, let's not forget," warns Paul.

"Quite the opposite in some quarters. The right wing press remains increasingly hostile," adds Maggie.

"Stoking further prejudice," says Paul.

"Adding more fuel to the fire," agrees Maggie.

"Providing more ammunition for the Mary Whitehouse brigade."

"Malcolm Muggeridge."

"Bishop Huddleston."

"Lord Longford."

"Cliff Richard."

"They're anti-everything."

"Even Dr Who," chimes Jenna, who has been watching her colleagues batting their concerns back and forth like ping-pong.

"This is not something to joke about," says Paul, turning towards her.

"Indeed it isn't," says Maggie, berating Jenna just as forcibly.

"Sorry," says Jenna, biting her lip. She is quickly learning that there is little room for levity within the Radical Left.

"So we mustn't blow it," says Paul. "The Police are especially hostile towards us just now…"

"And since those terrible government adverts implying that AIDS is a gay epidemic…"

"Not just implying. That iceberg…

"… that monolith…"

"They're nothing short of hate-crime."

"So we need to be ultra-careful."

"Nothing that causes offence…"

"... or alienates the support we have currently..."
"... which has taken us years to build up..."
"... so let's just take things one step at a time...
"... not run before we can walk..."
"... something small..."
"... modest..."
"... but effective..."
"... maximum impact..."
"... minimum risk..."

"Stop!" cries Jenna, stepping in between them. "Will you just listen to yourselves?"

"What?" say Paul and Maggie simultaneously. They have clearly forgotten Jenna is even there.

"What we need to do is simply throw a party" she says. "The biggest street party Manchester's ever seen. Then invite the whole city to join us. The charity's called Manchester *Pride*. Not Manchester *Scared*. The City Council, by giving us this money, however small, and by appointing you two to your jobs, is clearly showing solidarity and commitment. They're saying Manchester supports the gay community. A party is the best way to bring people together, straight or gay, to simply have fun, by dressing up, listening to great music, and dancing. We should have floats with icebergs and monoliths on them painted in rainbow colours, out of which the most fabulous drag queens burst out and entertain us all. A huge banner across Oxford Street proclaiming who we are, that all of us, of whatever persuasion, are proud to be from a city that has always defended the rights of minorities."

She recalls another of Spike's aphorisms scrawled on one of the walls at the Squat.

" '*Be not forgetful to entertain strangers*'," she declares, " '*for thereby some have entertained angels unawares*'."

Paul and Maggie regard her open-mouthed.

After a lengthy pause, they each begin speaking at once.

"You're absolutely right," says Maggie.

"We get so caught up in the politics," says Paul.

"We forget what got us involved in the first place," Maggie finishes off for him.

"A party," smiles Paul.

"A disco," laughs Maggie.

"A parade," insists Jenna. "With floats from local community groups. So that everyone feels welcome."

And immediately all three of them launch into the Tom Robinson anthem.

"Sing if you're glad to be gay
Sing if you're happy that way – hey..."

*

MICHAEL FISH:

Tomorrow looks set to be the start of one of the wettest August Bank Holidays since records began, with the northwest likely to bear the brunt of it. Hurricane Charley, which is heading in from the Atlantic right now, is almost certain to make landfall by midday on Saturday. We can expect high winds with occasional gusts in excess of sixty miles per hour, unseasonably cold temperatures, which will struggle to make it into double figures, just ten degrees Celsius, and up to fifty millimetres of rain around Manchester. So those of you hoping to attend the Manchester Pride Festival there tomorrow, I'd advise you to take an umbrella, except there's a strong chance of it blowing inside out...

At the precise moment that Great Abel, the eight-ton cast-iron bell in the Town Hall tower, named in honour of Abel Heywood, twice Mayor of Manchester in Queen Victoria's reign, whose voice was reputed to be the only thing louder, begins to toll midday, the heavens open, just as Michael Fish had predicted they would. The Grand Parade of Floats, surrounded by the thousands of people who have assembled in Albert Square in a spectacular array of fancy dress, many of them quite scantily clad, all become drenched within seconds. But if anything, the rain, rather than dampening their spirits, only sends them soaring even higher,

The actress Julie Goodyear, better known as the character Bet Lynch from Coronation Street, who has volunteered to declare the festival open, clad in her trademark leopard-skin strapless dress, with her peroxide bee-hive hair-do and a rainbow-coloured cocktail in her hand, croons into her microphone from the Town Hall steps.

"Good afternoon, Manchester! Are we downhearted by a spot of rain? Not bloody likely! Come on, everyone, let's show the rest of the world what we're made of."

To roars of approval and delight, she launches into the Manchester Anthem. Immediately the entire Albert Square is singing along with her.

"Take me back to Manchester when it's raining
I want to wet me feet in Albert Square
I'm all agog for a good thick fog
I do not like the sun, I like it raining cats and dogs
I want to smell the odours of the Irwell
I want to feel the soot get in me hair
I don't want to roam, I want to get back home
To rainy Manchester ..."

As the cheers continue to ring around the square, Julie steps up to the microphone once more.

"I now declare the inaugural Manchester Pride open! May God bless her and all who sail in her!"

A thousand rainbow-coloured balloons soar into the air, and the procession begins to make its way out of Albert Square, down Mount Street, left into Peter Street, towards St Peter's Square. It is led out by Francis, wrapped in a toga, with a laurel wreath upon his brow. He is dressed as the Emperor Decimus Clodius Albinus, proclaimed as such by both Britannia and Hispania in 195 AD, the Year of the Five Emperors, when the Roman Fort at Manchester was at its height. He sits in a golden chariot pulled by two rather dashing gladiators.

Just behind him, on a raised moving platform, Lance, who Jenna has persuaded Paul and Maggie to hire as the DJ, starts his set with a defiant Barbra Streisand belting out *Don't Rain On My Parade*, which he immediately follows up with hit-after-hit of high-voltage gay classics. Within seconds the whole city is dancing. The marchers, the figures on the floats, the thousands lining the streets, even the men and women of the Manchester Constabulary, all come to worship at the glittering altar of disco, presided over by a benignly smiling Francis.

> Donna Summer, Gloria Gaynor, Chaka Khan.
> *I Feel Love, I Will Survive, I'm Every Woman.*
> Village People. Soft Cell. The Weather Girls.
> *YMCA, Tainted Love, It's Raining Men.*

Ruth finds that she is enjoying herself far more than she could have imagined. When her friend Barbara suggested that they should team up with some others to dress up and join the march, she had been reluctant. She would be more than happy, she said, to stand in the crowds and watch the parade pass by, but take part? No way. She's not a joiner, more an observer from the sidelines. It's par for the course, she supposes. Being a therapist she is always on the outside looking in, rather than diving head first herself. "Besides," she says, "don't you have to be gay to be part of the parade?"

Barbara had looked at her pityingly then. "You need to get out more," she had said. "Look at me," she had added. "I'm not gay, am I? I'm married to Matt, who likes to play rugby, but give him half a chance to put on women's dresses, and he's first in the queue. 'I'm a lumberjack and I'm OK...' "

And so she had allowed herself to be cajoled into coming. And here she finds herself, marching down Peter Street, together with Barbara and four other female friends – Shirley, Jacqui, Yasmin and Bez – all dressed up as Village People belting out *YMCA* at the tops of their voices, while elsewhere in the parade Matt and his entire rugby team are all mincing together as pantomime dames, with vivid neon wigs, huge false eyelashes and enormous blow-up bosoms, having the time of their lives.

Barbara is the Cowboy, Shirley is the G.I., Jacqui the Construction Worker, Yasmin the New York Cop, and Bez the Biker, all in leathers. Ruth finds herself in the centre as the Native American, complete with feathered head dress.

"Young man, are you listening to me?
I said, Young man, what do you want to be?
I said, Young man, you can make real your dreams
But you got to know this one thing..."

Ruth doesn't know Shirley, Jacqui, Yasmin or Bez. They're Barbara's friends. She hasn't met them till earlier this day. But already it feels like they've known each other all their lives. Are they gay, she wonders? The original members of Village People apparently, despite their iconic status, were *not*. Except for the Native American – Felipe Rose. She doesn't know if this is true. It may be just one of those urban myths. But now that she finds herself dressed up in that same costume herself, it makes her wonder.

She's thirty-two now, unmarried, without a partner. She's never had a serious relationship with anyone, male or female. She had a couple of boyfriends as a student, but neither of these amounted to anything, and she's had a number of close female friends, but none of these had ever been anything other than platonic, nor had she wished them to be. She's perfectly content being single. It's not that she doesn't enjoy socialising with a few select friends from time to time, but generally speaking she prefers her own company. She wonders why this is the case. It goes with the natural territory of her profession to ask herself these questions, but so far she has singularly failed to come up with any form of satisfactory answer. She laughs at the thought. Physician, heal thyself!

An integral part of her becoming a psychotherapist was to undergo a course of analysis herself, something she continues to this day. She finds it a necessary and helpful release. But somehow the question of her sexuality has remained unexplored...

"Everyone can see we're together
As we walk on by
And we fly just like birds of a feather
I won't tell no lie..."

The parade has now reached St Peter's Square, where it pauses, while the tail of the procession steers itself out of Mount Street and catches up with the rest of the body. The music ratchets up even higher.

Grace Jones, Dead Or Alive, Sister Sledge
Pull Up To The Bumper Baby, You Spin Me Right Round, We Are Family
Madonna, Bowie, Queen
Material Girl, Boys Keep Swinging, I Want To Break Free

During the hiatus Ruth, together with the rest of her Village People look-alikes, runs up and down the lines of people on the pavement with a large plastic bucket, into which she encourages people to throw in any spare change they might have for the main charity the march is supporting, the creation of a new AIDS Ward in Monsall Hospital to the north of the city between Harpurhey and Collyhurst. The crowds, in spite of the rain, are caught up in the mood of celebration and give generously, singing in time with the music. She catches sight of Yasmin, exchanging her New York City Cop's cap for a Manchester Policewoman's helmet, and smiles.

"We are family
I got all my sisters with me
We are family
Get up everybody and dance..."

Ruth looks back towards the DJ on his raised dais, his multi-coloured dreads swinging to the rhythm, enjoying himself hugely. Beside him, Ruth can now see, dancing wildly and extravagantly, is Jenna. She recognises her instantly. Her jet-black hair is now streaked with rainbows and she is dressed as a painted moth, emerging magnificently from her chrysalis, her mirrored wings new-washed in the teeming rain. Ruth is literally dazzled by her...

The procession moves on.
Into Oxford Street, where the crowds are at their thickest, crammed ten deep on either pavement. The huge rainbow-coloured *Manchester Pride* banner is strung across from *The Palace Theatre* on one side to the *Tootal Broadhurst Building* on the other, fluttering defiantly in the face of everything Hurricane Charley can fling at it. All of Oxford Street's pubs and cafes are rammed to the gills, as well as those in the side-streets just off it, each of them united, rather than competing, to

raise further funds for the AIDS Ward at the Monsall.

The Koh-i-Noor, The Ping Hong, Nick the Greek's, The Kardomah, The Dutch Pancake House, The New Oxford, Rotters, Jerome's, The Salisbury, The Circus Tavern, The Board Room, The Molly House.

Lance continues to ramp up the volume.

Frankie Goes To Hollywood, Sylvester, The Cast from La Cage Aux Folles.
Relax, You Make Me Feel, I Am What I Am.

And still the music plays, and still the people party.

Whitney, Kylie, Abba.
I Wanna Dance With Somebody, I Should Be So Lucky, Gimme Gimme Gimme (A Man After Midnight...)

The rain continues to pour. But no one in the crowd even thinks of leaving. Ruth is exhilarated. She doesn't believe she has ever felt happier, lighter, freer. She must do this more often, she thinks. Dancing with like-minded friends in a large gathering with no other agenda than to set the heart racing and experience this same release. The sheer, unadulterated pleasure of simply letting go. The dizzy, dancing way she feels. She catches fleeting glimpses of the ecstatic expression in her eyes prismatically refracted into multiple versions of herself in the revolving glitter ball spinning above Lance and Jenna, bouncing her reflection around the faces of the crowd. She barely recognises who she is. But she no longer cares. She knows she will find out.

"You make me feel mi-i-ghty real..."

Finally the procession turns up Whitworth Street, crosses over Princess Street, then funnels into Sackville Gardens, before dispersing into the burgeoning Gay Quarter of Canal Street, Richmond Street and Bloom Street.

Lance closes his set with a medley of quieter, timeless classics.

Dusty, Nina and Judy.
You Don't Have To Say You Love Me, My Baby Just Cares For Me, Over The Rainbow...

Ruth finds herself dancing next to Yasmin, who loops her arms around the back of Ruth's neck and jokily mimes to the words.

*"You don't have to say you love me
Just be close at hand
You don't have to stay for ever
I will understand..."*

Ruth smiles sheepishly, while at the same time disentangling herself from Yasmin's embrace, turning it into a part of the dance, so as not to appear like an outright rejection. They twirl around one another shyly as the songs meld into one.

"My baby don't care who knows..."

*"If happy little bluebirds fly
Beyond the rainbow why, oh why can't I...?"*

"It's not every day you get to dance with one of the Boys in Blue, is it?" whispers Yasmin teasingly into Ruth's ear...

*

Some time later Ruth catches up with Francis as arranged at *Bookbinders*, Elkie Brooks' jazz club tucked away on Minshull

Street, the other side of Sackville Gardens. He is happily holding court before a group of adoring acolytes.

"Ah," he says, eyeing Ruth still in her Native American head dress of coloured braids and feathers, "come and sit beside me. What shall I call you? Minnehaha? Pocahontas?"

"Ruth will be fine," she says, smiling.

But Francis is unstoppable. "Ruth the Moabite," he proclaims. "Ruth the Gleaner, Ruth the Compassionate, Ruth who will get her reward in the end."

On the tiny stage in the corner of the bar, the Florence Blundell Quintet has just begun to play.

"If you ain't wrong, you're right
If it ain't day, it's night
If you ain't sure, you might –
Gotta be this or that..."

Francis joins in enthusiastically.

"Can't you see, it's gotta be
One way or the other...?"

Florence delivers a characteristically virtuosic trumpet solo, before returning with the final verse.

"If it ain't dry, it's wet
If you ain't got, you get
If it ain't gross, it's net
Gotta be this or that..."

"Does it?" asks Ruth when the song has finished. "Can't it be both?"

"I think someone wants to have her cake and eat it," teases Francis. "A girl after my own heart."

"Can't you ever be serious?" says Ruth.

"My dear, I'm never anything but..."

Florence is now about to close her set, but before she does so, she walks over to Francis and whispers in his ear.

He feigns surprise, appears to resist, but only for a moment.

"Very well," he says. "If you insist."

He gets to his feet, hoists his toga over his shoulder, then leans across to Ruth. "Darling," he says *sotto voce*, "can you walk me towards the stage please? I fear I may be somewhat in my cups, and it would not do for an Emperor to trip or stumble."

Smiling, Ruth links his arm through hers and ensures there are no mishaps.

"If Your Imperial Excellency will walk this way."

The band strikes up a quick burst of Handel's *Arrival of the Queen of Sheba*, led by Florence on her trumpet, as Francis, aided by Ruth, makes his uncertain way across the room, while the audience clap their hands and stamp their feet in time to the music.

"I hope to God my slip's not showing," he hisses through a fixed grin to Ruth.

"You look fine," she replies. "Fabulous, in fact."

Once he reaches the stage, Florence helps him up the last step and signals for quiet.

"One of my greatest influences is the late, great Miss Chamomile Catch," she says.

Whistles of approval and spontaneous ripples of applause greet this remark.

"Cam would have loved to be a part of an event like today's, the first of what I'm certain is going to get bigger and better with each year that passes. Unlike some of you here today, I never saw Cam sing live. I only came to her music through her records, the first of which I was introduced to by my good friend Francis here. He asked me if I might sing one of her songs for you now, so I said yes. On one condition. That he joins me on stage here to help me." She looks at him with a sideways grin. "I have to tell you – he didn't take much persuading…"

"What can I say?" concedes Francis, holding up his hands in mock surrender, and assuming a Mae West accent. "I generally avoid temptation – unless I can't resist it."

He's on fine form today, thinks Ruth happily, which he hasn't been that often since George died.

"The song I'm going to sing," says Florence, "with the help of Emperor Decimus Clodius Albinus here, is something I can imagine Cam might well have sung, had she been here, and it's one that Francis has requested specially."

She nods towards the pianist, who plays a few bars by way of introduction, then slowly begins to sing.

"I'm mad about the boy…"

There is an audible sigh from the audience, followed by a smattering of further appreciative applause, which Florence acknowledges with a smile.

"I know it's stupid but I'm mad about the boy
I'm so ashamed of it but must admit
The sleepless nights I've had about the boy…"

Francis now steps forward and takes his turn by singing the second verse to even warmer applause.

"On the silver screen
He melts my foolish heart in every single scene
Although I'm quite aware that here and there
Are traces of the cad about the boy…"

"Actually," he says while the music continues underneath, "it was always me who was the cad, not him…"

Florence now takes over once more.

"Lord knows I'm not a fool girl

Really I shouldn't care..."

Then Francis returns to the microphone.

*"Lord knows I'm not a school girl
In the flurry of her first affair..."*

He hands back to Florence again, who now sings with growing strength.

*"Will it ever cloy
This odd diversity of misery and joy
I'm feeling quite insane and young again
And all because –
I'm mad about the boy..."*

She picks up her trumpet and plays a haunting, muted solo, which Francis listens to with his eyes closed, enraptured.

*"I'm feeling quite insane and young again
And all because..."*

Florence holds out her hand for Francis to join her, so that they might sing the final reprise together.

"I'm mad about the boy..."

*

Francis cannot get warm. He has been shivering ever since he arrived home. He remonstrates with himself sternly.

"Well, my dear, if you will insist on wearing only a toga on the wettest and coldest August Bank Holiday on record, is it any wonder you feel so damned cold?"

He has had a long soak in a hot bath, polished off a large bowl of chicken broth, wrapped himself up in his warmest dressing gown, placed a hot water bottle at his back, and poured himself a stiff and generous whiskey, which he raises to his lips with a deep sense of satisfaction.

But even after he has finished this not-so-wee dram, he still feels cold. He decides he will reward himself with another. What the hell, why shouldn't he? Hasn't he earned it?

He carries it upstairs to his bedroom, the room that, more than seventy years before, had belonged to Ruth Kaufmann, and sits in the chair by the window, beside her old Dollond & Aitchison telescope, which he has always kept there. For sentimental reasons mostly. He has others of his own that are far more powerful, but this is still serviceable enough, and he likes to look through it from time to time, to remind himself of just how far the technology has come during his lifetime. Hasn't he ventured deep into the farthest reaches of the Universe, scanning the night skies for radio signals emitting from galaxies millions of light years distant through the telescopes of Jodrell Bank? He has, countless times, almost to the point of losing himself. But something would always bring him back?

Usually it was the thought of George, who, even after he decided they could no longer carry on as they had before, had remained the love of his life. Oh, he continued to have other liaisons, lots of them, some with the prettiest of boys, but these were little more than dalliances, flings, flirtations. Affairs of the flesh rather than the heart, they were but whims, caprices, the megrim of a moment, nothing more, a match that would spark, flare brightly but briefly, then putter and go out, leaving him back in the darkness.

He wonders what George would have made of today's parade. He would have liked its title – *Manchester Pride* – of that he was certain. He was always proud of his city. He may even have been persuaded to decorate his DOT RS in rainbow colours, while his natural attire, his biker leathers, would have fitted in perfectly.

Francis smiles at the thought of it. All this is true. But in all probability George would have preferred to have merged with the crowds, rendering himself invisible, so that he might instead take photographs of it, rather than participate fully. He would have enjoyed hearing Florence Blundell sing. Though he'd have hated it when he, Francis, got up to sing about him. But he wouldn't have needed to do that, had George been there with him.

He misses him so profoundly it is like a pain that grips his heart.

He pours himself another whiskey. He puts his eye to the old telescope. It's trained through the giant pair of spectacles that is still affixed to the wall outside, that same pair which had played such a key role in persuading him to purchase these premises when he first chanced upon them, having followed the line of telegraph poles after helping Delphine to bury her parents. Back then they had seemed to stare out across the city towards a limitless future, filled with possibility. Now, as he gazes beyond them through the telescope into the night sky, they appear instead to look back at him from the past.

Which is true.

The light that enters the lens of his imperfectly formed eye, with its curved astigmatism and misshapen cornea, is already several years old.

The telescope is aligned directly with the Galilean moons of Jupiter – Io, Callisto, Europa and Ganymede – which is where it was positioned when Francis first looked through it. He looks at them now. He's in luck. Their orbits are in a natural four-to-two-to-one resonance with each other, so that occasionally they appear in a direct line, as they do tonight. Francis derives enormous satisfaction from knowing that, in all probability, Ruth Kaufmann saw them in this same configuration, Lily's lost mother, grandmother of that other Ruth, her namesake, who has been so steadfast and kind towards him since that strange day fifteen years ago, when she had driven Delphine and him back to the site of their first ever meeting by the banks of the Ship Canal, when there had been a thunderstorm, with even more rain than there had been for the parade this afternoon, and lightning like he had never seen before, which he had somehow captured, almost miraculously, the forks and bolts appearing to emanate directly from Delphine's outstretched hands as she wept for her dead parents. He picks up that photograph now, which has laid beside his bed ever since Delphine had died ten years later, and studies it closely. She was temporarily deranged that day. The way she had thrown herself to the ground, smeared streaks of dirt and soil across her face, like war paint, so that the eight-year-old Jenna had called her Old Nokomis. He pictures Ruth from earlier today, bedecked in braids and feathers like Minnehaha. He doesn't think he has ever seen her happier. Who will be her Hiawatha, he wonders? Will she fall victim to the seductive West Wind as happened to Wenonah? In whatever guise he, or she, adopts? Or will she walk the earth alone? Like Delphine did? Or he now does?

By his bedside lies a well-thumbed copy of *Leviathan* by Thomas Hobbes. It was given to him more than half a century ago by Charles – Delphine's pursuer – the doctor at the Infirmary, who was always asking her to marry him. He and Charles had been friends back then. They'd played chess at their club, St James's on Spring Gardens, and attended the lecture given by Albert Einstein in the Whitworth Hall together, when the great man had expounded his grand theory of relativity, using a microphone supplied by Francis. Shortly afterwards Charles had given Francis the book.

"*Respice ad finem*," he had said when he presented it to him. "Look to your end. That was Hobbes' watchword. Mine too. Live so that your life will be approved of after your death…"

A matter of relativity, surely...?

Francis understands that his own end is near. It's coming fast upon him. He places his eye to the telescope to gaze upon the heavens once more. There have been times when, in scanning the far galaxies, he has observed a supernova, that most powerful and luminous of stellar explosions, a transient astronomical event occurring in the final throes of a star's life, when a white dwarf is triggered into an unstoppable nuclear fusion, either collapsing in on itself to form a black hole, or releasing just enough energy to create a new star, a neutron star, a quark star, compact, exotic, sufficient unto itself, a continuous state of gravity-defying matter, floating free.

So, too, Francis now, in considering his end, looks to his beginning, specifically that golden afternoon in Philips Park, when, at just twelve years old, he assisted Billy Grimshaw, 'The Gramophone King', in playing records by Caruso to thousands of enraptured Italians listening to the great man sing, reminding them of the homes they had left behind in search of a new life here in this cold, wet, but welcoming northern city, and Billy Grimshaw had given him a sixpence for his trouble, a sixpence he still has, as a reminder of that moment's epiphany, when he witnessed for the first time how art, when mixed with technology, can move the hearts of a multitude, and how he had known in an instant that right there, in that confluence of those two apparent opposites, was where he wanted to live out his life. And by and large he has. He has pushed the envelope of that meeting point several times, helped to shape it, folded and buckled the sky as if for an appearance of the Northern Lights, or when a meteor shower has for a moment lit up the dark. Like love. That ultimate transient astronomical event.

He reaches for that silver sixpenny coin now. He tosses it high into the air, watching the light catch it as it spins, not knowing how, or even if, it will fall. The outcome is for ever out of reach, random, binary, and tantalisingly unknowable, but always worth pursuing.

Respice ad finem.

He opens the window wider. A wind is picking up, that seductive caress from the west, right now. The last shake of the tail from Hurricane Charley. Like the final flicker of Halley's Comet as it burns itself out above him. Another burst of rain begins to fall. He hears it rattling on the roof, quietly at first, but gradually intensifying, innumerable scales of chitin vibrating with each pinion beat. A distant thunder rumbles. Pale sheets of lightning illuminate the sky. Little more than a glimmer to begin with. A moth's wing, opening, then closing, edging ever nearer. The storm is coming.

He switches on his cassette player, hoping that Cam, whose tape is always on it, ready to play, will drown the deluge. Her voice pours into the room like sweet honey.

"Somewhere there's music
How faint the tune
Somewhere there's heaven
How high the moon..."

The lightning is closer now. Its proboscis splits the sky with flame. It sizzles and expectorates, the moth uncoils its tongue, thrusting deep into the heart of the flower to extract every last ounce of its juices. Francis feels his ribs begin to tighten and constrict.

"Somewhere there's music
It's where you are
Does it touch the stars, reach out to Mars...?"

Or maybe even to Jupiter, whose moons his gaze now strays across and is lost among? A last meteor shower slices through his field of vision, bursting from its radiant like explosive flecks of colour in the iris of his eye, melanocytes collecting in a nevus.

> *"There is no moon above*
> *When love is far away too*
> *Till it comes true*
> *That you love me as I love you..."*

The storm is now directly overhead. There is no longer a gap between the lightning's flash and the thunder's crack. Sparks of flame as the hammer hits the anvil. Francis reels. A vice-like fist clenches his heart. The pain is so sharp it is almost exquisite. A firebolt strikes the giant pair of spectacles beyond the window. They frame his face for the final time, caught in a moment of pure bliss, the rapturous joy of release, as the spinning coin topples first one way, then the other, before finally coming to rest.

"The darkest night would shine
If you would come to me soon
Until you will, how still my heart
How high the moon..."

*

Ruth sees the letter as soon as she steps through the front door, lying on the mat, her name staring up at her in immaculate copper plate. She picks it up, turns it over. On the back is a red wax seal beneath the sender's address.

> *Sleigh, Son & Booth Solicitors*
> *1 Market Street*
> *Denton*
> *M34 2BN*

Why would a firm of solicitors from Denton be writing to her?

Then it dawns on her. Francis. Of course...

She places the telescope Francis has left her on its stand on a table beside the French windows at the back of room, directing its gaze back towards the sky. Tonight, when it grows darker, she will look through it herself and see what she may find there.

She looks around the rest of the room, adorned as it now is with souvenirs from all those who have died in the past ten years, and some longer ago than that. This room which has become a shrine. A *memento mori*.

The toy yacht, the collagraph, the sampler.

The photograph, the bird's nest, the painting of the comet.

The Computer Board built by her father.

The telescope, the clock.

*

Ruth recognises that this is not healthy. It is as if she needs their permission before she can begin to move on. If she is not careful, she might get caught up in the web of them, a web that she herself has helped to build, wrapping up these precious inherited objects in sticky cocoons, when what they really want is to be dusted clean, taken out into the light, where they can be seen by others, appreciated for what they represent, not just as part of her own individual story, but for everyone. She understands that she needs to stop looking into the past, but instead to forge her own path, create objects of her own.

But until then she is in danger of becoming buried by them, deep within the earth, like the pupae of a whisper of moths. She knows she must press her ear close to the ground, to listen to that whisper as it grows into a roar...

*

The telephone suddenly rings. It sounds unnaturally loud and shrill in the stillness of the room.

As if waking from a long dream, she picks it up.

"Hello...?"

"Hi. Is that Ruth? It's Yasmin here. I don't know if you remember me. We met at *Manchester Pride*..."

"Yes. Of course. How are you?"

"Fine, thank you. I was wondering..."

"Yes?"

"Are you doing anything this Saturday?" Then before Ruth can say that she is, Yasmin continues in a breathless rush. "Only it's my birthday, the big three-o, I'm having a party, more of a *soirée* really, just a few friends, would you like to come?"

Ruth answers quickly, decisively, before she has time to think about it and come up with possible excuses.

"Yes," she says. "I'd love to."

She hears the audible sigh of relief coming down the phone, before Yasmin launches into further details of time and place, and directions on how to find her.

When Ruth puts the phone down at last, she discovers she is blushing. She is beginning the act of breaking through the hard outer layer of the pupa's casement. Her wings are not yet fully formed. They need flexing first before she can come out fully.

THREE

Imagines

Having spent the winter burrowed under the earth for safety, the adult moths – the *imagines* – emerge in the spring, usually at dusk, under the cover of darkness. This is known as *eclosing*.

In order to eclose, the moth secretes a liquid enzyme, called cocoonase, which softens the hard, outer shell of the pupa. Additionally, it uses two sharp claws, located on the thick joints at the base of the forewings, to force its way out.

Once eclosed, it will rapidly expand its wings by pumping haemolymph, a circulatory fluid akin to blood, into the veins. It will then rest on the empty shell, the shed exoskeleton, while the wings harden. It is during this final stage that it is at its most vulnerable. Until it is able to fly.

The male imagine then flies every night in search of a female, whereas the female flies only on the first night she emerges from her cocoon, when she releases pheromones to attract the male. These pheromones are carried by the wind, so the male flies along what is called the 'concentration gradient', the diffusion of all molecular particles with temperatures above absolute zero, in order to find their source. This is a treacherous journey, for the male must fly the gauntlet of many predators, particularly bats and birds. Once he reaches his target, the male will guard the female from all other interested rivals, until she lays her eggs.

The male usually stays with the female to ensure paternity. But not always. Sometimes he will perish. Sometimes he simply flies away. A mating pair, or a lone female, will spend the day hiding from danger, protecting the eggs till they are ready to hatch.

Then the cycle begins again…

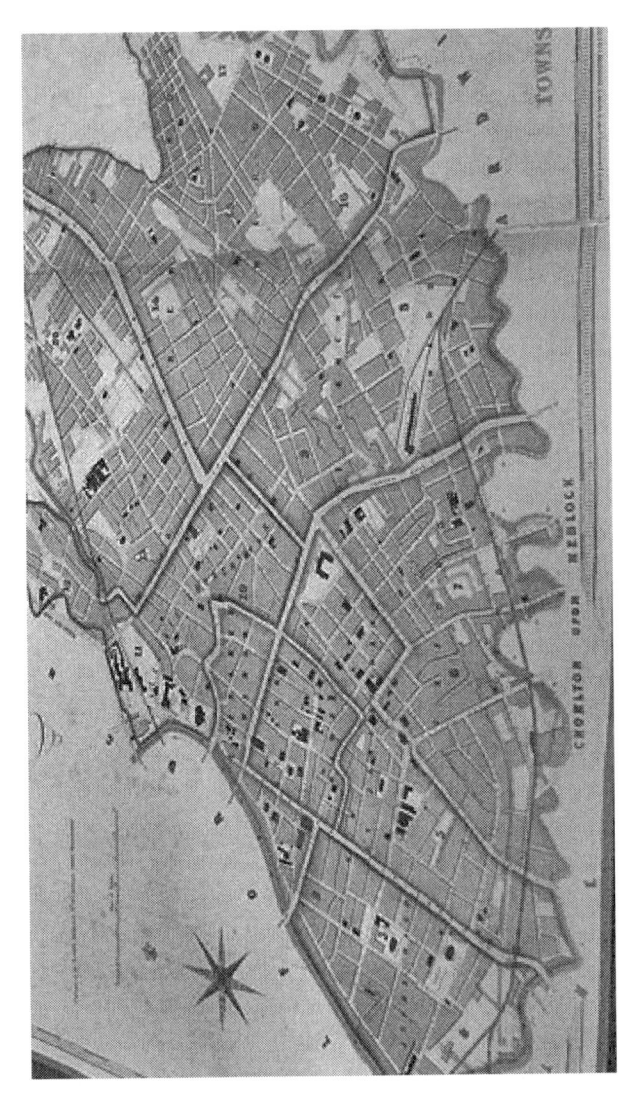

Adshead's Map, showing the River Medlock, circa 1850
forming the southern boundary between the city & the outer suburbs

10

2017

Day 1

BBC BREAKING NEWS

We're just receiving reports of a serious explosion at the Manchester Arena following an Ariana Grande concert attended by more than 20,000 adoring young fans. We understand that 22 people have been killed and more than 100 injured, many of them children and teenagers, in what the Police are describing as a suicide bombing...

TV5MONDE

On vient de recevoir des informations faisant état d'une grave explosion à la Manchester Arena à la suite d'un concert d'Ariana Grande auquel ont assisté plus de 20 000 jeunes fans adorés...

NBC NEWS

Panic and mayhem seized the crowd as the blast reverberated through the building, which is adjacent to Victoria Station, one of the city's busiest interchanges. The attack occurred just as the show was ending, Hundreds of pink balloons were dropping from the rafters in a signature flourish by Ms Grande...

Deutsche Welle

Panik und Chaos ergriffen die Menge, als die Explosion durch das Gebäude hallte... Der Angriff ereignete sich gerade als die Show endete, als Hunderte von rosa Luftballons von den Sparren fielen, in einer charakteristischen Geste von Fräulein Grande...

ALJAZEERA CHANNEL

Traumatised concertgoers, including children separated from parents, screamed and fled what appeared to be the deadliest episode of terrorism in Britain since the 2005 London Underground bombings...

صرخ رواد الحفل المصابون بصدمات نفسية ، بما في ذلك الأطفال المنفصلون عن والديهم ، وفروا مما بدا أنه أكثر الأحداث دموية في الإرهاب في بريطانيا منذ تفجيرات العبور في لندن عام

深圳卫视 SHENZHEN TV

Speaking to reporters early Tuesday, Manchester's Chief Constable, Ian Hopkins, said Police learned of the explosion around 10:33 p.m. "Children were among those killed," he added, "and the wounded were taken to eight hospitals..."

曼彻斯特首席警官伊恩·霍普金斯 期二早些时候对记者说，警方在晚上10:33左右获悉了爆炸事件

PTPC
ТЕЛЕРАДИОСЕТЬ РОССИИ

Chief Constable Hopkins said that a man had detonated "an improvised explosive device" and had been killed in the blast. He said the Police believed that the man had acted alone, but that they were trying to determine whether he had been part of a wider network. "This is currently being treated as a terrorist incident until we know otherwise," he later added in a hastily-released statement…

Главный констебль Хопкинс сказал, что мужчина привел в действие «самодельное взрывное устройство» и погиб в результате взрыва.

INDIA TV

At least one explosion went off in the foyer of the Arena, according to the British Transport Police, the force that protects the Manchester Victoria train station next to the venue. The station was quickly evacuated…

ब्रिटिश परिवहन पुलिस के अनुसार, अखाड़ा के फ़ोयर में कम से कम एक विस्फोट हुआ, जो बल अखाड़े के बगल में मैनचेस्टर विक्टोरिया ट्रेन स्टेशन की सुरक्षा करता है। स्टेशन को खाली कराया गया।

TV TOKYO

We have just learned that a bomb disposal team has arrived on the scene as part of the ongoing investigation, and that the security cordon around the Arena has been widened...

捜査の一環として爆弾処理チームが現場に到着したばかりであり、アリーナ周辺の警備隊が拡大された。

sky NEWS LIVE

Sky News can now confirm that Ms. Grande herself was not hurt. TMZ, the entertainment news website, reported that she was 'in hysterics' over the deadly blast. She tweeted the following message to her 45 million followers world wide...

Ariana Grande
@ArianaGrande

broken.
from the bottom of my heart, i am so so sorry. i don't have words...'

3.51am 23 May 2017

BBC NORTH WEST TODAY

... after which she pledged to do everything that she could to help all those affected by the attack.

This is Chloe Chang for BBC North-West Tonight live from the Manchester Arena...

Day 2

As the next day dawns an atmosphere of disbelief hangs over the city. Nobody can fully grasp what has happened. That someone could have wreaked such terror and hate on innocent children is beyond comprehension. Commuters arriving in the centre on their way to work find themselves speaking in low whispers to complete strangers. Or simply stopping in the middle of the street, staring, not seeing...

Messages of sympathy and support pour in from around the world. The Queen holds a minute's silence inside Buckingham Palace. Prime Minister Theresa May condemns the attack from the front of Number 10 Downing Street. EU President Jean-Claude Juncker expresses his great sadness and profound shock. His colleague at the Council of Europe, Donald Tusk, declares that his heart is in Manchester this day. Kofi Annan calls the sickening attack an assault on humanity itself.

Monuments around the world are lit up in the colours of the Union Jack in an act of solidarity with the people of Great Britain. These include the Brandenburg Gate, the Eiffel Tower, the Colosseum, and the Empire State Building.

People begin to leave flowers everywhere across the city. Individuals of all ages, races and creeds pay private, silent tributes. But as the day wears on, the mood subtly starts to change, shifting from deep sorrow to a determination not to let the outrage defeat them.

Andy Burnham, Mayor for Greater Manchester, speaks for everyone, when he says in a simple statement, "We are grieving today, but we are strong. I know we'll help each other. That's who we are. That's what we do. They won't win."

A theme picked up by the Right Reverend David Walker, Bishop of Manchester, from outside Manchester Cathedral, where he stands flanked by the city's religious leaders from all the major faiths – Rabbi Reuben Silverman of the Manchester Reform Congregation; Irfan Muhammad Chishti, Imam of the Manchester Central Mosque; Raghbir Singh of the Sri Guru Gobind Singh Gurdwara; Suresh Mehta of the Jain Samaj, and Shastri Krishan Joshi, Pujari of the Radha Krishna Mandir Temple.

"We must not allow the terrorists to dictate the way we live," declares the Bishop, speaking on behalf of all. "Manchester is a wonderfully diverse city, and we can all of us pull together. We've done it before, and we'll do so again. We had another bomb here twenty-one years ago, so we're not unused to tragedy. But they didn't defeat us then, and they won't defeat us today."

This growing mood of defiance is echoed by tweets and statements from other high profile figures in the city throughout the day.

Lucy Powell, MP for Manchester Central, tells her followers, "People are coming together to support the families who've lost their children, and the children who've lost their friends. That is the spirit of our city, and that spirit will never, ever die."

Philip Neville, former Manchester United and England footballer, posts a photograph of the city with the sun rising above it. Over it he tweets the words, 'We will not be defeated. We will stand strong. We are Manchester.'

BBC
NORTH WEST
TODAY

Manchester Attack: Albert Square Vigil of Peace
BBC News Online

At the scene: Chloe Chang reporting:

CHLOE:

> Thousands of people have gathered this evening in Albert Square for a vigil in remembrance of those who fell during last night's terror attack at the Manchester Arena. What began as an outward sign of solidarity and support for the victims' families has grown to become a spontaneous show of love and defiance that Manchester will come through this together and survive even stronger than before.
>
> Members of the Sikh Community have set up stalls ringing the square, offering free refreshments to everyone attending the vigil, many of whom are holding up home-made banners with hand-made messages and drawings.
>
> Eddy Newman, Lord Mayor for the City of Manchester, has just called for a minute's silence, during which you could hear nothing but the occasional stifled sob above the cooing of pigeons and the distant hum of traffic.

Chloe speaks in barely a whisper.

> The crowds are so large that they completely fill the Square spilling over into the surrounding streets, reaching as far as the nearby St Peter's Square, which has witnessed more than enough suffering through Manchester's history.

She remains quiet for what remains of the tribute.

> But now that the minute's silence is over, these crowds, numbering at least fifty thousand, have erupted into huge

spontaneous applause, which you can hear reverberating all around the venerable statues that adorn this old Square, which still remains the city's beating heart today.

The applause continues unabated for more than a minute.

The Lord Mayor is trying to make himself heard but has realised he must not interrupt this genuine outpouring of love, but simply allow it to run its course, until it has subsided sufficiently for him to speak further. He looks deeply humbled, almost on the brink of tears himself, as he continues to wait...

Finally he speaks in a voice trembling with emotion.

LORD MAYOR:
We're not going to accept evil acts that threaten to divide us. That will never happen. For we are the many, they are the few. We'll get through this, because we're from Manchester. We always have, and we always will.

CHLOE:
The Lord Mayor now lights a candle in front of the Town Hall and invites all those who are standing alongside him to do the same – Amber Rudd, the Home Secretary; John Bercow, Speaker of the House of Commons, and Jeremy Corbyn, Leader of the Opposition.

A City United.

Tony Walsh, the popular Manchester poet, is now invited to come up to the microphone to read his much-loved poem *This is the Place*. Commissioned by the local charity 'Forever Manchester' to celebrate the city, never has there been a better time for its words to be heard, not just for the thousands gathered in Albert Square this evening, but for the millions of people listening right around the world.

When he reaches one particular verse, his words are taken up by the entire crowd.

CROWD:
> *If you're looking for history, then yeah, we've a wealth*
> *But the Manchester way is to make it yourself*
> *So make us a record, a new number one*
> *And make us a brew while you're up, love – go on...*

CHLOE:
> Following the inevitable, much-needed laughter, on this day of all days, he builds to a stirring climax.
>
> This is Chloe Chang reporting from Albert Square, Manchester, leaving the last words to the poet Tony Walsh...

TONY WALSH:
> *This is the place that has helped shape the world*
>
> *And this is the place with appliance of science*
> *We're on it, atomic, we strut with defiance*
> *In the face of a challenge we always stand tall*
> *Mancunians in union deliver it all*
>
> *Such as housing and libraries, health, education*
> *And Unions and Co-ops, the first railway station*
> *This is the place Henry Royce strolled with Rolls*
> *And we've rocked and we've rolled with our own Northern Soul*
>
> *And this is the place where we first played as kids*
> *And me Mam lived and died here, she loved it, she did*
> *And this is the place where our folks came to work*
> *Where they struggled in puddles and hurt in the dirt*

*And they built us a city, they built us these towns
And they coughed on the cobbles to the deafening sound
Of the steaming machines and the screaming of slaves
They were scheming for greatness, they dreamed to their graves*

*And they left us a spirit, they left us a vibe
The Mancunian Way to survive and to thrive
And to work and to build, to connect and create
Greater Manchester's greatness is keeping it great*

*And so this is the place now we've kids of our own
Some are born here, some drawn here, but all call it home
Because this is a place that's been through some hard times
Oppressions, recessions, depressions and dark times*

*And there's hard times again in these streets of our city
But we won't take defeat and we don't want your pity
Because this is a place where we stand strong together
With a smile on our face, Mancunians for ever..."*

*

Day 8

In the hours and days that follow, Chloe is run ragged. As well as conducting regular updates and interviews for local and national television, she provides material for the BBC's website, and hosts a series of Late Night phone-ins on Radio Manchester. The lines have never been busier…

CHLOE:
> Hi there to all you night owls listening right now. If you're finding it hard to sleep in the wake of what's happened, if you've a story you need to share, if you're feeling anxious or scared, or if you just want company and the comfort of hearing friendly voices, then please stay tuned. I'm here with you right through the night till six am. You can contact us in all the usual ways. We've also got a special guest with us tonight – Ruth Warner. Ruth's an experienced counsellor and psychotherapist, and so if you've got something particular that's worrying you, just call our hotline and you'll be put straight through to her.
>
> Ruth?

RUTH:
> Yes. Let me reassure anyone who's thinking of calling, anything you say to me will be treated in the strictest confidence. You won't need to go on air if you don't want to...

CHLOE:
> ... but if you think that what you have to say might help others of our listeners, then we're here waiting for your call. Right, Ruth?

RUTH:
> Right, Chloe.

CHLOE:
> So – we'll start taking your calls right after this...

Chloe cues in some music.

ARIANA GRANDE:
> *And we can deny it as much as we want*
> *But in time our feelings will show*

Cause sooner or later we'll wonder why
The truth is everyone knows...

The song fades.

CHLOE:
>All the tracks we'll be playing tonight will be by Ariana. That was *Almost Is Never Enough* from her first album, *Yours Truly*. Stay tuned for more from her later.
>
>And now our first caller tonight is... oh... I think it's someone I know. Can you repeat your name for me please?

CALLER:
>Lorrie. Lorrie Zlatan.

CHLOE:
>Wow – Lorrie and I were students together back at MMU. What are you doing with yourself these days?

LORRIE:
>I work at Islington Mill.

CHLOE:
>The Art Gallery in Salford?

LORRIE:
>That's right, yes.

CHLOE:
>And are you OK?

LORRIE:
>I am. I'm fine, thank God. But I might so easily not have been.

CHLOE:
>Why's that? Were you there at the Manchester Arena?

LORRIE:
No. But I should've been.

CHLOE:
Would you like to tell us what happened?

LORRIE: (*hesitantly, then gradually becoming more emotional*):
Like everybody listening, I'm a huge fan of Ariana. I bought a ticket for the concert as soon as they went on sale. I was really looking forward to it. But stupidly I'd got the dates mixed up. There was a big event on at the Gallery that night. A private view of a new show. There was no way I couldn't be there. And so I sold my ticket at a cut price to a friend. Someone I work with. Sunanda. She didn't have to be at the opening, and so she was able to go to the concert instead of me. When I first heard about the attack, I tried to call her, but I couldn't get through. I sent text after text, until...

CHLOE:
Yes...?

LORRIE:
Eventually I heard from her mum. She was alright. Just a few cuts and bruises. But she'd been taken to hospital just as a precaution, then discharged a few hours later.

CHLOE:
We're so glad to hear that, Lorrie.

LORRIE:
But the thing is, I feel so guilty. That should've been me, not Su. If I hadn't been so stupid as to buy the ticket in the first place, then I wouldn't have sold it to her, and she wouldn't have got hurt. I put her in danger.

CHLOE:
But not intentionally, Lorrie.

LORRIE:
No, but still. I can't stop thinking about it. She's not been back to work since. She's still too much in shock.

RUTH:
If I might interject here, Chloe?

CHLOE:
By all means.

RUTH:
Hi Lorrie. It's Ruth Warner here. What you're experiencing is not at all unusual. It's the kind of guilt that any of us in your position would feel. It's perfectly natural to blame ourselves for something we did, or didn't do, when someone we're close to gets hurt. But what you did in letting your friend have your ticket was a generous thing to do. You acted only out of kindness, nothing more. But you've touched on something here that many people listening will relate to, that feeling of helplessness, of wishing things might have been different. If only this, if only that. Like the song says that we just heard, 'almost is never enough', but we all of us do the best that we can. Like *you* did, Lorrie, in trying and trying to get hold of your friend, until at last you did.

CHLOE:
I think it's time for some more music. Thank you, Lorrie. We hope Sunanda feels better again soon. We'll be back with another caller right after this.

ARIANA GRANDE:
How soon do we forget how we felt
Dealing with emotions that never left

Playing with the hand that we were dealt in this game
Maybe I'm the sinner and you're the saint
Gotta stop pretending what we ain't
Why we pointing fingers anyway when we're the same?

The song fades.

CHLOE:
> That was *Best Mistake I Ever Made*, from Ariana's second album, *My Everything*.

RUTH:
> With lyrics we'd all do well to listen to.

CHLOE:
> No one's pointing any fingers here.
> Now – our next caller is… Iyesha Young? Is that right?

IYESHA:
> Yes.

CHLOE:
> Hi, Iyesha. How are you feeling?

IYESHA:
> Better, thanks.

CHLOE:
> That's great to hear. I feel I should point out to our listeners that you and I have met once before, haven't we?

IYESHA:
> That's right, yes.

CHLOE:
> Would you mind telling everyone where that was?

IYESHA:
> In St Mary's Hospital. I was being treated for injuries from

the attack.

CHLOE:
But you're home now?

IYESHA:
Yes.

CHLOE:
And recovering?

IYESHA:
Yes. I've been lucky.

CHLOE:
You might call it 'lucky', Iyesha. But I think everyone else would say you've been amazingly brave. Let's start from the beginning, shall we...?

*

Day 4

QUEEN VISITS MANCHESTER CHILDREN'S HOSPITAL

Today Her Majesty the Queen made a surprise visit to the city to meet some of the children injured in Monday's terror attack at the Manchester Arena, describing the event as 'wicked...'

Chloe Chang reporting...
25 May 2017 BBC Online News UK

Afterwards Chloe has to pinch herself. Four years earlier,

almost to the day, she had been presenting a paper for her Finals at MMU about the Queen's recent visit to the city to open the headquarters for the Co-op in Angel Square. It was part of a critique of the complexities and ambiguities surrounding public attitudes towards the monarchy. She had put together a casebook of cuttings from previous royal visits, including the Queen's presence at the Commonwealth Games in 2002, when Chloe, then just ten years old, had taken part in the opening ceremony, along with hundreds of other Manchester school children. And now, fifteen years later, the Queen was visiting school children once more. Only this time Chloe, no longer a bystander, was reporting on the visit.

The atmosphere is in stark contrast with the most recent Royal visit to the city, when, as part of her Diamond Jubilee celebrations in 2012, Queen Elizabeth arrived to open the new Media City at Salford Quays, a centre Chloe is now quite familiar with, it being the Manchester headquarters for the BBC. Then, while she was about it, Her Majesty decided to gatecrash a wedding taking place at Manchester Town Hall, much to the delight of the bride and the groom.

The same delight has greeted this latest surprise visit by her, to pay tribute to the courage of the surviving victims. Chloe has not of course been allowed to interview the Queen, but, after presenting a quick introductory direct-to-camera piece as she arrived outside St Mary's Hospital, she has been permitted to follow her, at a discreet distance, as she visits the various wards and speaks to several of the children, all of them wounded in Monday night's attack.

It is while following the entourage that she overhears the remark about it having been 'wicked', and how she asks them whether, before what happened, they had enjoyed the concert. All of them say that they did. Nothing – not even Salman Abedi – has been able to spoil that. She is wearing a royal blue coat and a vivid, orange hat in her favoured boater style. Chloe smiles. That's the kind of detail her grandmother, Xiu Mei, would always look for first. The colour of the Queen's hat. Chloe has not seen her grandmother now for four years. Not since she went back with Chloe's father to Shenzen. She wonders if she might see this brief item on the BBC website back in China. She hopes so…

Towards the end of the visit, Her Majesty lingers a little longer in conversation with one of the older children. Chloe just manages to catch her name. Iyesha. She appears to be telling the Queen a long, convoluted story about how she had been saved from serious injury because of a coin, which she now holds up for Her Majesty to inspect.

"Yes, I see," Chloe hears her say. "We have several fine examples of these among our Royal Collection. There's something quite remarkable about a simple thing like a coin, something one takes for granted, somehow surviving down the centuries to the present day. An unbroken line. How do you come to have it…?"

Chloe does not hear what Iyesha says next. But afterwards, when the Queen has left the Ward, she approaches her to ask her. When she hears her story, she invites her to come on her radio phone-in to share it with her listeners.

"But only if you feel strong enough," she says. "And only if you want to."

Iyesha says she'll think about it. Chloe has not expected to hear back from her so soon…

*

Day 8 [cont'd]

CHLOE:
> So, Iyesha, what is it you would like to share with us this evening?

IYESHA:
> It's a long story.

CHLOE:
> That's fine. We've got all night. Just take your time. Whenever you're ready...

IYESHA: (*taking a deep breath*):
> OK. Here goes...

*

Day 1 (minus 7)

It's the week before the concert. Iyesha is counting down the days, marking them off on the calendar, like a prisoner doing time, even though she hasn't got a ticket – yet. But she's hoping that might change. For today is her birthday, when she turns sixteen...

It's a Monday, a school day, so she has to be up early. Not that she minds that. She wants to make sure she gets to the bus stop early enough to meet up with Bethany and Joelle. They're her best friends. They all go to Parrs Wood High School in East Didsbury together. *They're* sixteen already, so she feels glad to be joining their club. They'll make her smoke a cigarette behind the shelter. Not that she wants to. Not that any of them want to. She thinks smoking's disgusting. But it's what you do on the day of your sixteenth birthday. It's a ritual, a rite of passage. Then they'll check out the latest postings on Ariana Grande's website, on her Facebook, Twitter, Instagram and Snapchat pages. With her concert coming up at the Manchester Arena a week today, there's bound to be lots more news and pics.

Bethany and Joelle have already got their tickets. They look at the app on their phones every five minutes, just to make sure they're still there. Iyesha is hoping that today, seeing as how it's her birthday, her parents might spring it on her before she leaves the house.

When she goes downstairs, the omens look promising.

"How's my birthday girl?" her Dad asks her.

"One day older, one day wiser," chips in her Mum.

"Just as annoying but twice as ugly," points out Luther, her younger brother.

She contemplates a cutting reply, but she can't be bothered. It's too early, and it would only be lost on him. Why waste the effort when a hard look will suffice? What is it about younger brothers, she thinks? Why are they such losers?

She makes herself a piece of toast, which she lathers with peanut butter, pours herself a yoghurt drink, then sits at the kitchen table, trying to keep as nonchalant as she can. She doesn't have long to wait before her Dad walks in, making the sound of a great fanfare as he carries a large parcel before him.

Smiling, Iyesha takes it from him. But before she can begin to unwrap it, her Mum drops a few cards on the table in front of her.

"Open these first," she says, smiling.

Iyesha nods happily.

The first, from her Mum and Dad, has a picture of Ariana on the front, the one with the bunny ears from the cover of the *Dangerous Woman* album. Inside there's a diagram with instructions on how to make her own.

"Please tell me you're not going to wear those?" groans her brother.

"I might do," she says.

"You'll look a complete and utter twat."

"Is that what you think? Maybe you'll find out the hard way just what it means to incur the wrath of a truly dangerous woman."

"Yeah, right."

"That's enough, Luther," says Mum.

Luther looks to his dad for support, but he simply holds up his hands in mock surrender.

Next Iyesha opens the home-made card from her brother.

"I didn't know you cared."

"I don't."

She reads the message inside.

'Being related to me is the only gift you need.'

"Oh, but didn't you know, Luther? We're *not* related. Mum found you under a gooseberry bush and took pity on you. Now she's wishing she hadn't."

The two chase each other round the kitchen table before Mum intervenes.

"Why don't you open this one last card, then you can unwrap your parcel?"

Iyesha looks down at the one remaining card – she hopes there'll be more as the day progresses – and recognises the writing at once.

"It's from Auntie Grace," she says, her eyes lighting up. She loves her Auntie Grace, who always remembers her birthday.

Inside is a ten pound note.

'Buy yourself something you'd like but don't really need.'

Brilliant, thinks Iyesha. That's typical of Auntie Grace. Then she notices another message at the bottom.

'I hope you enjoy your *special* present. Think of it as a kind of coming-of-age.'

"How mysterious," she says. "What's she talking about?"

"I think you might be about to find out," says her Mum, and indicates the parcel brought in by her Dad. "Open it."

Iyesha picks it up. It's about the size of a shoe box, but extremely light. Puzzled, she unties the string around it, then begins to remove an outer layer of wrapping paper, which does indeed reveal a shoe box.

"Curiouser and curiouser," she says out loud.

She takes off the lid. Inside is another parcel, wrapped in newspaper. Inside that is another, then another, then another. Even Luther is intrigued now, and edges closer to his sister.

"It's like 'pass-the-parcel'," he says.

"Only without the music," she replies.

"And without you having to pass it along to anyone else," he adds.

"Shh," she says, as she unwraps the final layer. In her hand she holds what resembles a jewellery box.

"It's not an engagement ring, I hope," jokes her Dad.

"No chance," says Luther, "no one'd have her."

"Quiet," says Mum, in that way that brooks no further argument.

Iyesha carefully opens the lid of the box. It can't be a ticket for the concert, but that is momentarily forgotten in her desire to know what lies inside.

It's something very old and round. She delicately lifts it out between the thumb and forefinger of her right hand and holds it up to the light.

It's a coin.

Everyone is silent.

Iyesha supposes it must be really significant, but what? She doesn't understand. Just as her puzzlement is beginning to give way to disappointment – what kind of sixteenth birthday present is a rusty old coin? – her Mum steps in.

"Let me explain," she says.

"Can't it wait?" says Iyesha. "I don't want to miss my bus."

"No," says Mum, "it can't. Don't worry. I shan't take long."

Iyesha lays the coin upon the table, folds her hands in her

lap and waits for her Mum to begin. Luther reaches out to pick it up, but before his fingers can get anywhere near, Iyesha swats him away.

"It's Roman," says Mum. "In 1953 your great-grandfather, Toby, Auntie Grace's older brother, was involved in an accident at Bradford Colliery. There was a rockfall, blocking his usual way back. At first he tried to climb by a series of ladders up an old ventilation shaft, but one of these ladders came away, and he was left dangling high and dry. While he was trying to figure out a way down, he put his hand into a crevice in the wall, in the place where the ladder had come away, to steady himself, and it was there where he found this coin. It was Gracie later who identified it as Roman. She used to be an archaeologist, remember? Well, Toby kept it. He put it in his pocket, and, together with three other blokes, he managed to find another way back to the surface. It took them the best part of two days to make it. All the while he held onto this coin, and he reckoned it brought him good luck. Sometimes, he said, as they were crawling on their hands and knees along old, long-abandoned tunnels, he felt there were ghosts of other miners watching over him, maybe even the one who had lost this coin in the first place. There were times when he thought he might never find his way out of there, but he kept thinking about his baby daughter, who was just a year old, and that kept him going. Eventually, like I said, he reached the surface. After he did, he vowed to keep that coin in the pocket of whatever trousers he was wearing, so that he always had it near him. And so he did. Then, quite a few years later, when that baby girl had just turned sixteen, the pit was shut down, and Toby retired. Consequently he felt he no longer needed the old coin, so he decided he would give it to his daughter as a birthday present. That was Milly. My mother, your grandmother. And he said to her, 'I reckon as how this coin were only lent to me. It were someone else's before, and now it's your turn. I hope perhaps that you might hand it on too, when you think the time is right.' And so she did. When it was *my* sixteenth birthday. It's become a sort of tradition now. We pass it on to our oldest child – if we have one, that is – whether it's a boy or girl. It just so happens it's always been a girl so far. So here…" She formally hands the coin across to Iyesha. "Happy Birthday."

When her Mum first started to tell the story, Iyesha had thought it sounded boring. Everything that she described had happened such a long time ago. More than half a century. But then, in the telling, the story had grown, and now she finds herself compelled by it. It has gripped her utterly. To think that so insignificant a thing as this coin has descended in a line through four generations to now become hers. She finds herself wondering how long it had lain buried in the mine before her great-grandfather Toby had accidentally found it. And how many hands before that it had passed through. Back and back through all the centuries to when the Romans were here in Manchester. It feels impossible to comprehend.

"Thank you," she says, her voice little more than a hoarse whisper. For once even her brother knows when to keep quiet, and he says nothing.

It's her Dad who speaks next.

"And here's another remarkable thing," he says. "When Toby was trying to find his way out of the mine, one of the other men with him was my own grandfather Lamarr, who you've never met. He died before you were born."

"The G.I.?" says Luther.

"Yeah, that's him. He was stationed over here during the War, before the D-Day landings. While he was here he met Pearl, and when the War was over they got married. He liked Manchester, so he decided to stay. He'd been a miner back in America before, so he got himself a job here, and together they had five kids…"

"One of whom was Grandma Kendra," says Luther,

gradually fitting all the pieces together.

"That's right."

"And she's coming for tea tonight for a certain young lady's birthday," smiles Mum.

"Will she be baking a cake?" asks Luther brightly.

"Who says you'll be getting a piece if she does?" teases Iyesha, putting the coin carefully back in its box. "Shit, is that the time? I really will be late if I don't go now."

"One last thing," says Dad. He takes an envelope out of his back pocket. "Might the birthday girl be interested to know what's in here?"

Iyesha stops in her tracks.

"Is it...?" She can barely breathe. "Really...?"

"You'd best open it to find out," laughs Dad, casually flipping it towards her.

She makes a dive for it, misses, but it is caught by Luther, who, for once does not try to keep it from her, but presents it to her with a mock bow. She gratefully ruffles the hair on the top of his head, then tears open the envelope.

"Yes, yes, yes!" she squeals, and the whole family finds themselves leaping round the kitchen in a mad dance.

```
Live Nation presents
Ariana Grande
Dangerous Woman Tour
Plus special guests
Doors Open 5.30pm
Manchester Arena
ay 22 May 2017
```

*

Day 8 (cont'd)

CHLOE:

Thank you, Iyesha. Now feels like a good time to take a

short break and play some more music. After what you've just said, the perfect choice must surely be *Dangerous Woman*.

RUTH: (*interjecting*):
Chloe, do you know why Ariana has chosen this for the title of her latest album?

CHLOE:
No, Ruth. I don't. But I've a feeling you're going to tell me.

RUTH:
I bet Iyesha knows, don't you, Iyesha?

IYESHA:
Yeah – she posted a photo on Instagram of Nawal El-Sadaawi, an Egyptian feminist writer, with a quote from one of her novels, *Woman at Point Zero*. It says, 'They told me I was a savage and dangerous woman. I am speaking the truth. And the truth is savage and dangerous.'

CHLOE:
In that case, we'd better take a listen. We'll be back with more of Iyesha's story directly after this...

ARIANA GRANDE:
Don't need permission
Made my decision
God as my witness
Start what I finished...

CHLOE:
That was Ariana Grande with the title track of her latest album, *Dangerous Woman*. You're listening to BBC Radio Manchester's Late Night Phone-In with me, Chloe Chang, and my guest, the eminent psychotherapist, Ruth Warner. Our latest caller, Iyesha Young, has been telling us about

her experience of meeting Her Majesty the Queen in St Mary's Children's Hospital four days after the attack and her excitement in the days leading up to the concert. And now, I believe, you're going to tell us about what actually happened to you on the night itself, is that right, Iyesha?

IYESHA:
Yes.

CHLOE:
So long as you're sure? Remember – you can stop any time.

IYESHA:
No, it's fine. I want to. My Mum and Dad both think it'll really help me.

CHLOE:
OK then. Whenever you're ready…

*

Day 1

Iyesha, Bethany and Joelle arrive at the Manchester Arena at exactly half-past five, just as the doors are opening. Iyesha's Dad drops them off.

"I'll pick you up just here," he says indicating the drop-off point at Victoria Station immediately adjacent to the Arena, "at exactly ten-thirty. Don't be late."

"But the show's not due to finish till then," argues Iyesha. "Can't we make it fifteen minutes later?"

"Ten-thirty," replies her Dad in a voice that declares the matter is not open for discussion or debate. "I want to try and beat the crowds."

"But Dad…" moans Iyesha.

"Don't worry," chips in Bethany brightly. "I'll make sure we're here on time."

"Thank you. I'm glad at least one of you understands what I'm talking about. Have a good time. Bye." He sticks a hand through the open window of his Honda Civic and waves cheerily as he drives off.

"Bye, Grant," Bethany calls after him.

As soon as the car is out of sight, Iyesha wheels on her friend.

"Are you flirting with my Dad? Eugh! That's disgusting."

"Why not? He's cool."

"You wouldn't say that if you had to live with him."

"Come on, you two," says Joelle. "We're wasting valuable shopping time."

They head for the foyer where already a crowd of excited fans is fluttering around the merchandise.

There's everything there they could hope for – and more. T-shirts, crews, hoodies, sweat pants. Mugs, caps, posters, bags. Ear rings, necklaces, lockets, bracelets. Lip gloss, eye shadow, nail polish, scrunches. They each decide on a *Dangerous Woman* T-Shirt, the one with Ariana in the mask and the ears, then troop off to the toilets to change into them. Iyesha and Bethany, who've both got long hair, twist it into Ariana's trademark high pony tail, while Joelle, who doesn't, sports a jaunty *Yours Truly* baseball cap.

By the time they come out, they're really buzzing. Dressed to kill with their hoodies hanging loosely down their backs to reveal their shoulders and upper arms, just like Ariana does, they step out with arms linked back towards the central staircase. More and more fans are arriving by the second. Nearly all of them are young girls, some so young they're with their Mums or their big sisters, but most, like Iyesha, Bethany and Joelle, just with their friends. The atmosphere is electric, the excitement intense, as the foyer is filled with the sound of several thousand high-pitched voices reverberating like fledgling parakeets in a rain forest.

"Listen," says Joelle, always the sensible one of the three. "We'd best go in and find our seats."

The other two agree. They're none of them sitting together, having bought their tickets separately. Iyesha is in the Lower Tier, Bethany and Joelle the Upper.

"We know what the set list is," continues Joelle. It's true. It's been all over Snapchat since the tour began in Phoenix back in February. "She'll begin with *Be Alright* and end with *Into You*. For her encore she'll perform *Dangerous Woman*, which ends with an extended play-out by the band."

"I can't wait," squeals Bethany, bouncing up and down.

"Me neither," shrieks Iyesha even more loudly

"What I suggest," says Joelle, trying to carry on as calmly as she can in the face of her friends' near-hysteria, "is this. In the pause before *Dangerous Woman* – which we know there is, right, cos she's got to change her costume..."

"Yeah," says Bethany, her eyes lighting up, "the black latex." And she begins to strut around her friends, hands in the small of her back, perched up on her toes as if on high stiletto heels, which instantly Iyesha copies and joins in.

"Just listen a minute, will you?" cries Joelle exasperatedly. "During the pause while she's changing, we each of us make our way up the steps to the back of our tier. We watch her sing the song from there. Then, as soon as the band starts the outro, we head back right here, where we are now, and meet beside *that*..." She points to the giant poster advertising the show. "Then we can dash out across the street towards the Station..."

"Where Grant will be waiting," winks Bethany.

"Shut it, B. Yeah, OK, J, that's a great plan. Sorted?"

"Sorted," the other two chime back, giving each other a series of complicated high-fives, before they make their way via the different staircases towards their respective seats, each girl clutching her ticket in her hot, sweaty hands, as if their lives depended on it.

Iyesha checks where she has to go – Block 114, Lower Tier, Row V, Seat 21 – before taking a last look back at their agreed rendezvous point, the larger-than-life image of their larger-than-life idol.

*

Day 8 (cont'd)

IYESHA: (*excitedly recalling it with Chloe on the phone-in*):
The concert was brilliant. Everything about it was just perfect. From beginning to end. She sang all the hits. *Honeymoon Avenue, Moonlight, Break Free, Focus.* Each one with different lighting and stage sets. Back projections, pyrotechnics, lasers, dancers. It was amazing. One moment it was like a gym, with Ariana riding a stationary bike and lifting weights while singing *Side By Side*. The next it was *I Don't Care*, with silhouettes of same-sex and opposite-sex couples making out, with Ariana posing in front of them, while various different words were projected onto the screen. 'Empowered'. 'Grounded'. 'Not Asking For It'. 'Female'. 'Human'. Then all too soon it was the last song, *Into You*...

In her mind's eye Iyesha can still see the stage, completely draped in blue light, with the dancers all carrying blue neon glow lamps, which they sway from side to side, while the lights from twenty thousand mobile phones wink back...

IYESHA:

As soon as the song finished I made my way towards the back of the Lower Tier, where I stood to watch the encore, as we'd arranged. When Ariana left the stage, I turned to go. I walked through the doors, out of the auditorium, towards the staircase leading down to the foyer. A few parents had begun to arrive and were chatting to each other while they waited for their daughters to meet them. More and more people were beginning to leave just that little bit early, to avoid the rush, the same as us. I looked around for Bethany and Joelle, but I couldn't see them. I started to make my way towards the giant poster, and that's when it happened. I saw a flash of red. Really bright. Then an enormous explosion. It lifted me right into the air...

That's the last thing I remember...

The next thing I know, I'm waking up in hospital. With a searing pain down the side of my leg...

*

Day 1 (cont'd)

Bethany doesn't want to leave when Ariana finishes singing *Into You*. It had felt like she was singing directly and only for her.

"But it's what we arranged," insists Joelle. "Come on – Iyesha'll be wondering where we've got to."

Reluctantly Bethany allows herself to be dragged towards the exit doors. *Dangerous Woman* is just finishing.

*"Nothing to prove and I'm bulletproof
Taking control of this kind of moment
I'm locked and I'm loaded
Completely focused..."*

As Ariana leaves the stage for the final time, thousands of pink balloons descend from the rafters of the Arena. It's the perfect end to a perfect evening. Bethany makes a grab for one of the balloons as they float around her.

Just as she lunges towards it, she overbalances and falls to the floor. At the exact same moment, she hears a loud bang. So does everyone in the auditorium.

"It's the balloons," says someone.

"It's a speaker blowing," says someone else.

"No," says a third. "It's an explosion."

Just the word itself sends shock waves surging through the crowd. There is an instant panic. A stampede as people try to force their way out. Screams and shouts as they vault over hand rails, trip and stumble down stairways. Bethany is trampled on many times before Joelle somehow manages to haul her to her feet. They dash towards the nearest exit. But now there is a bottle neck. They feel themselves being squeezed through the narrow gap like toothpaste out of a tube, before spilling out into the foyer, where the scene that greets them is one of chaos and carnage. There are bodies on the floor, children screaming for their parents, stewards yelling at everyone to get out as fast as they can, police and paramedics charging in the opposite direction, struggling to get through to reach those who need them most, which seems to be everyone, everywhere. Outside, through the plate-glass windows, many of which have been shattered by the blast, so that Bethany and Joelle can feel themselves running over a trail of broken shards, the blue lights of ambulances are flashing in a mockery of the glow lamps from the end of the concert, the wail of sirens keening already for the loss of life.

Joelle catches sight of Iyesha lying on the floor among the debris, a paramedic bending over her. Instinctively she hurries towards her, only to be turned back by a steward, insisting that she leaves.

Outside Bethany spies Grant dashing across the street. His wife, Louise, Iyesha's Mum, is running with him.

"In there," cries Joelle. "Iyesha…"

Louise puts her hand to her mouth, briefly, then assumes immediate control. She finds the paramedic treating her daughter, who reassures her that she's survived.

"She's going to be fine," he tells her, "but she'll need to be taken to hospital."

"Which one?"

"St Mary's."

Louise nods and thanks him.

"Grant," she says, "you take Bethany and Joelle back to their homes. Girls, phone your parents *now* to tell them you're OK. I'll go with Iyesha in the ambulance. Grant, you can join me there later. Thank God Grace has offered to sit with Luther…"

And then she's gone.

By the time Bethany and Joelle have reached the car, they have started to shake. They cannot stop. Grant covers them with blankets from the boot. Then he roars away from the scene like a bat out of hell…

*

Day 8 (cont'd)

IYESHA:

When I woke up, I had a tube stuck in my arm and a Doctor was standing beside me.

"Welcome back," she said. "How are you feeling?"
"Sore," I said. "What happened?"
"There was an explosion," she said. "After the concert. You've been lucky."

That was when it dawned on me that others mustn't have been.

"I'm talking about this," said the Doctor, holding up the Roman coin. "We found it in the pocket of your jeans."

"I don't understand."

"A piece of shrapnel from the blast struck it," she continued. "That's what I mean when I say you've been lucky. It took the full force of a rather nasty-looking bolt. If it hadn't, the piece of metal may well have cut right through the femoral artery, and I wouldn't be having this conversation with you now."

She held up the coin between her finger and thumb as if it was the most precious thing imaginable. Which it was. Is...

Iyesha has begun to cry. She can be heard quietly weeping on the other end of the phone.

CHLOE:
Would you like to take a break, Iyesha?

IYESHA:
No. I'll be all right.

CHLOE:
Is this the story you told Queen Elizabeth?

IYESHA:
A little bit, yeah. Not all of it, though.

The thing is, I only put the coin in my pocket at the last minute, just before Dad drove us to the concert. If I hadn't...

CHLOE:
Why don't you tell us about the coin, Iyesha?

IYESHA:

My Auntie Grace told me that it was made some time around 195 AD. More than eighteen hundred years ago. I can't get my head round that. She says she knows this because of the picture of the head on the front. It's Decius Clodius Albinus. 195 AD is known as the Year of the Five Emperors. Rome was divided. Clodius was proclaimed Emperor only in Britain. That's why there are coins of him here. But not many. Because he wasn't Emperor for long. He was called Albinus because he was an albino. People at the time thought this made him special, that it marked him out as different, that he was lucky. Well... he *was* lucky – for me...

CHLOE:

Have you still got it?

IYESHA:

Yes. I'll never part with it now. It's been bashed about a bit. But my Dad's cleaned it up, and, where the piece of metal almost pierced it, he's made a small hole, which he's threaded with a small chain, so that I can wear it like a necklace all the time.

CHLOE:

A lucky charm.

IYSEA:

Yes, but that's just it. I know I should be grateful – and I am – but it feels all wrong. Why have *I* been spared when so many others haven't? I heard that one of the girls who died was only eight. I feel so guilty...

She starts to break down again.

RUTH:

Iyesha? It's Ruth here. Please try to listen to me if you can.

What you are describing is completely understandable. Many people in your position would feel the same. It's called 'survivor syndrome'. It occurs when a person believes they have somehow done something wrong by surviving a disaster when others haven't. We see it where there have been epidemics, or natural disasters like floods or earthquakes, or in a terrorist attack as in your case. It's more common than you might think, and because of that, we've found a number of ways to cope with it. First of all, try to remember that it's not *you* who's responsible for what happened. You didn't cause the attack, Salman Abedi did. Luck is random. Just because you have experienced *good* luck, while others have experienced the reverse, does not make it your fault. Think about your family and friends who love you, and how they feel about the fact that you've survived. Remind yourself of how grateful they are – even that brother of yours...

Iyesha can be heard laughing weakly down the phone.

Practice seeing your survival as a gift and share it with all those who love you. Do something for someone else, something that makes an impact, as a way of honouring those who were less fortunate than you. Guilt can give us a sense of purpose and direction. But remember – you have nothing to feel guilty about. Lastly, make sure you look after yourself. Get plenty of sleep. Eat well, take regular exercise. Sharpen up those Ariana Grande routines. And if you do ever find yourself struggling, don't be shy about asking for help. Things will be all right...

CHLOE:
And that seems like the right moment for some more music. You've set it up for us perfectly, Ruth. Thank you again, Iyesha, for your courage and your strength, and for sharing

your story with us here tonight. You've been an inspiration to us all...

So here's Ariana playing us out with *Be Alright*.

ARIANA:
We're in slow motion
Can't seem to get where we're going
But the high times are golden
Cause they all lead to better days

But daylight is so close
So don't you worry 'bout a thing
We're gonna be alright
Hey yeah
Oh yeah
We're gonna be alright...

*

Day 11

Manchester EveningNews

2nd June 2017

SCHOOL CHILDREN TO PERFORM WITH POP SUPERSTAR

The children of Parrs Wood High School Harmony Group have been invited to perform with Pop Superstar Ariana Grande at this Sunday's *One Love* Benefit Concert at Old Trafford Cricket Ground.

The high school singing sensation captured the hearts of the nation when a YouTube video of their tribute version of Ariana's song *My Everything* went viral. Ms Grande was reportedly so moved when she first heard it that she immediately invited them to appear alongside her.

Mark McElwee, Head Teacher of Parrs Wood High School, told us:

"I feel honoured that we have been asked to take part. Our children came together to represent the community in Manchester at a difficult time. They are determined to raise as much money as possible for the victims of the horrific attack and to show that we are stronger when we come together. The Harmony Group have demonstrated all the positive characteristics we would hope for in our young people, exemplifying Manchester's strength and resilience. We all feel immensely proud of them."

The talented choir from Parrs Wood High School in East Didsbury appeared on ITV's *This Morning* today to talk about how they will take to the stage in front of tens of thousands of people in this Sunday's Benefit Concert.

Speaking to hosts Eamonn Holmes and Ruth Langford, the choir revealed that they still don't know what they'll be singing on the day.

"We're really, really excited to perform with Ariana Grande, but we also know that we need to raise funds for those people who were injured and who passed away, because it's just devastating what happened," said 12 year-old soloist Natasha Seth. "We want to do as much as we can for everyone who was a victim."

Three of the choristers were actually at the Arena on Monday the 22nd of May and escaped with their lives – Bethany Wood, Joelle LaGrange and Iyesha Young.

16 year-old Joelle told the presenters: "The concert had just ended, and then we heard a really loud explosion. The next thing we knew we were trying to get away."

The school group had hoped to raise £2,000 for the families of the bombing victims but beat their target within two days of their song going viral, with the total currently standing at £4,402.

The message on their *JustGiving* page reads as follows:

'*Sing for Manchester* is meant as a message of hope, reminding everyone how powerful music can be in bringing communities together in times of need,', adding: 'We hope this is a fitting tribute to all the victims, their friends and families, the people of Manchester and their spirit, which will never be broken.'

*

Day 14

ONE LOVE MANCHESTER
SUNDAY
4 JUNE · MANCHESTER, UK
EMIRATES OLD TRAFFORD
ALL PROCEEDS WILL BENEFIT THE VICTIMS AND
THE FAMILIES AFFECTED BY THE MANCHESTER
ATTACK ON MAY 22, 2017
TICKETMASTER.CO.UK/ARIANAGRANDEMANCHESTER

CHLOE: (*speaking directly to camera*):

Today Manchester becomes the centre of the world. The eye of a hurricane in which she somehow manages to occupy the still calm centre. She holds up a mirror to show all those who look at her a reflection of themselves not as they are, but as they would like to be.

Where the world expects revenge, she offers reconciliation. Where the world seeks division, she presents them with unity. Where the world wants victims, Manchester shows them survivors. Where the world anticipates weakness, she gives them only strength. Where the world looks for hatred, she showers them with love.

One Love.

The name of the concert that is shortly to start, just two weeks after the bombing, when Ariana Grande keeps her promise to return, redeems the pledge she made to the people of the city, to thank them, to join with them, to celebrate their heroism, to honour their spirit which cannot be vanquished, which refuses to yield, even in this, its darkest hour.

The concert's allocation of fifty thousand tickets sold out within six minutes. It could have been sold a dozen times over, and would have been, had it not been for the need to make sure the Old Trafford Cricket Ground, where the concert is about to take place, is safe and secure.

She begins to walk among the crowds making their way towards the stadium.

It's a warm sunny afternoon. People are dressed in their summer clothes. They're wearing all the colours of the rainbow. This is not a wake. But a 'City United' in their defiance not to be defeated. Crowds are walking towards the ground as if to a pilgrimage. Police have asked us, for the sake of security, not to carry bags, and few of us do. Unfortunately I have to, for my microphone and i-pad. Those who arrive by tram have been able to travel free. Those who have come by Uber have been promised their fares will be donated to the charities set up to support the victims and their families.

I feel incredibly safe. Safe and lucky. Lucky to be alive, and lucky to be here this Sunday afternoon. A helicopter hovers reassuringly overhead. It feels like we are being watched over. I take a picture of it with my phone. Two Policemen stop me and ask me who I am with. I show them my BBC credentials and they ask me whether I've written anything about the helicopter alongside the picture. They don't explain the technology of how they have already been able to read my Notes App. Nor do I challenge them about it. I'm actually relieved that they can. They ask us not to film them, which we don't, which is why I'm telling you all this, rather than showing you. After some friendly banter back and forth between us, they ask to search my bag and check my ID.

"You have to understand," says one of them, "tensions are running high." Then he shakes my hand and lets me through. Manchester feels secure today.

The stadium is filling up now, as you can see. There's a real air of excitement and anticipation in the air. Not fear, just pride. That Manchester is doing this. Lots of people are showing off their new bee tattoos they've had done, just like Ariana Grande herself has, the emblem of a city built on hard work and graft. I've got one too. See?

She turns and points to the delicately etched symbol in the nape of her neck. Then she looks directly back to camera as she continues to speak.

Whatever the terrorists had hoped to achieve here in Manchester, it certainly wasn't a party like this....

The camera pans along thousands of brave, smiling, painted faces, as the people wave defiantly to the rest of the world watching on.

I'll leave you to enjoy the concert now, which is being beamed live to more than forty different television networks around the globe, as well as over a hundred radio stations.

This is Chloe Chang for BBC North West Tonight and Radio Manchester on 95.1 FM reporting from what feels like the centre of the world. One Love...

She raises two fingers in a peace sign towards the camera as she signs off.

*

For the next three hours the world holds its breath. That this tiny, brave, charismatic young woman from Boca Raton, Florida, who, having found herself at the centre of a maelstrom not of her making, should then, without fuss or in any way seeking to deflect attention away from the real reason why the world has come together to pledge its solidarity with a city that has taken her so unquestioningly to their hearts, has somehow been able to put together this concert, uniting artists from both sides of the Atlantic in less than ten days, when she herself has been rocked with grief, is nothing short of miraculous.

Justin Bieber, Katy Perry, Miley Cyrus and The Black-Eyed Peas from America join hands with Marcus Mumford, Imogen Heap, Little Mix and Coldplay from Britain. Stevie Wonder, Paul McCartney and Bono from U2 appear by video link. As does David Beckham, who reads a poem, and the players of both City and United, who deliver a message together.

But the concert belongs to Manchester. After a minute's silence for the victims, Gary Barlow and Take That fittingly set the mood with *Giants, Shine* and *Rule the World*, followed by Robbie Williams with *Strong* and *Angels*. Then, as the concert reaches its end, Liam Gallagher puts in a surprise, unannounced appearance with *Live Forever*. This after Ariana Grande has sung a version of *Don't Look Back In Anger*.

The lyrics of every song seem freighted with significance. Highly charged atomic particles, more powerful than a terrorist's bomb, colliding at speed, forming billions of new connections that did not exist before, explode with a unified message of resistance and hope.

*"There are giants across the water
There are giants heading home
In the middle of the madness
There are giants being born..."*

"I'm loving angels instead..."

*"But don't look back in anger
I heard you say..."*

And at the heart of it all is Ariana Grande herself. Entering almost shyly, diminutively, not dressed in the glamorous outfits of her stage show, but just in a pair of sky-blue denim jeans with rips at the knees and an over-sized white sweater with the cuffs pulled over her wrists, she looks as if she has just stepped up from out of the audience, which she might well have, such is their acceptance of her as one of them, so that nothing could be more natural than when the Council Leader Sir Richard Leese bestows upon her the title of 'Honorary Citizen of Manchester', the first recipient of such an award, for, to all those there at Old Trafford that evening, that's what she already is.

Nowhere is this exemplified more strongly than in the moment she surrenders the stage, not to some global superstar, but to the pupils of the Parrs Wood High School Harmony Group, who, with quiet, unassuming self-possession, stand before the crowd of fifty thousand people, just as the sun is setting, plainly attired in their school uniforms of navy blue and silver, the crests on their blazers embroidered with the motto *Believe, Achieve, Succeed.*

The effect, when they open their mouths to sing, is heart-stopping. The entire audience holds up hand-written cards, proclaiming 'For Our Angels...'

Chloe, who is standing close to the side of the stage, catches Iyesha's eye. She is trembling.

"Remember this moment," mouths Chloe.

Iyesha, swallowing hard, nods. Her fingers reach up to just below her throat. Chloe understands. She is clenching them around the Roman coin to give her the strength she needs, so that she can begin to sing too.

*"I've cried enough tears to see my own reflection in them
And then it was clear
I can't deny I really miss it
To think that I was wrong
I guess you don't know what you got 'til it's gone..."*

Ariana waits until they are almost half way through before she joins them.

*"You are, you are, you are my everything
You are, you are, you are my everything..."*

*

When Ariana closes the concert with a simple, heartfelt rendition of Judy Garland's *Over the Rainbow*, Ruth, who has been working as a volunteer at the gig, offering counselling for anyone who has found the emotions of the past three hours might have awakened a response almost too powerful for them to deal with, is immediately transported back in time, to that first *Manchester Pride* event thirty years before, when she had first danced with Yasmin. She feels again the strong pull of that unbroken line stretching back through time, yoking the history of the city into a continuous thread, slowly unspooling as it leads people away, like Ariadne, from the beast at the centre of the labyrinth towards the safety of the upper air, a river emerging back into the light, after a lifetime underground...

*

She runs into Chloe, who has just finished her final to-camera piece for the evening. She is speaking to someone, who, for a moment, Ruth thinks is actually Ariana Grande herself, but it turns out to be a look-alike, one of many she has seen during the course of the evening, though this one looks far more realistic than any of the others. The attention to detail is eerily uncanny.

"This is my friend, Lorrie," says Chloe, introducing her.

"Oh yes," says Ruth. "We spoke on the phone-in. Are you feeling better now?"

"I am," says Lorrie. "I found what you said really helpful. It's so easy to focus on the negative. But just look what happens," she adds, gesturing towards the joyful crowds leaving the stadium in such a carefree, easy manner, in such marked contrast to the scenes just a fortnight earlier, "when we do the opposite."

"You're right," says Ruth. "I think we tell ourselves to expect the worst as a way of fending off disappointment. Just think what we might accomplish if we could harness all of this positive energy here tonight."

"I'll never forget it," says Lorrie.

"I don't think any of us who were here ever will," says a voice.

"This is Sunanda," says Lorrie. "Sorry – I should have introduced you earlier."

"That's OK."

"You're the person who Lorrie was worried for after the concert?" asks Ruth.

"Yes. But as you can see, I'm fine now. It's been really important to come here this evening and feel safe again."

"I've spoken to so many people who've said the same," says Chloe.

"Me too," says Ruth.

"Like this enormous weight has been lifted," says Lorrie, removing her mask and ears, and pulling her hair free from its pony tail. Suddenly she looks a completely different person.

"Do you mind if I ask you something?" says Ruth.

"Sure, go ahead."

"Have you always enjoyed dressing up as other people?"

Chloe rolls her eyes. "You should've seen her at Uni. She was amazing. She really kept us guessing."

"Less so than I did," says Lorrie. "I find I don't need to so much these days."

"Why tonight then?"

"Because tonight was a special occasion. This," she says, holding up the mask, "wasn't about me. It was just my way of saying thank you."

"Then let *me* thank *you* by buying you a beer," says Sunanda.

"I'll drink to that," grins Lorrie.

"Me too," adds Chloe. "Want to join us, Ruth?"

Ruth shakes her head. It's nice of you to ask, she thinks, but I'm twice your age. "No thanks," she says. "I think I'll head home…"

*

She watches them walk ahead of her towards the main gate, arms linked and singing, and her thoughts turn back to Yasmin once more. She sighs. She still misses her, but less so than she did. She wonders if she's been watching tonight's show on TV.

Probably. Hasn't the whole world been...?

By the time she reaches the exit, the ground is practically empty. Nearly everyone has gone. Only the technicians remain, taking down the stage and clearing away the cables.

The sun has completely set now, and a high waxing, gibbous moon shines down upon her. She steps out onto Warwick Road and walks towards the Metrolink tram stop. She's not gone more than a few yards when she hears a faint drone, like a musical instrument, and someone singing in a high, cracked voice. The sound appears to be coming from the underpass, which takes pedestrians beneath the railway tracks to the station on the other side. As Ruth gets closer to the entrance, the louder it grows. The moon is casting a monochrome light. All the colours of the night merge into one.

Ruth can now see the source of the music and the singing. A woman of indeterminate age and mixed ethnicity. Heavily pregnant, she is playing the *habbān*, a bagpipe-like instrument from Yemen, conjuring deserts and mountains, filled with yearning and pain, love and longing, echoing down the years. Every so often she pauses in her playing to sing. She slips in and out of different languages. Ruth catches some words she recognises.

> "*I never knew you could hold moonlight in your hands*
> *Till the night I held you*
> *You are my moonlight, moonlight...*"

They're from one of Ariane Grande's songs she heard at the concert this evening. Sung this way, released from the backing tracks and amplification and dancers and lights, they strike her with the simplicity of their message. They remind her of Yasmin...

But now the woman is singing in a different language once

more, one that is unfamiliar to Ruth, before she returns to furiously playing the *habbān*, as if, like Ariadne, she is in search of something she has lost.

Suddenly she stops. She grips Ruth's wrist and their eyes lock. Ruth is aware of fires burning in the darkness. Then the woman wrenches herself free. Her dress slips from her shoulder. Ruth becomes fleetingly aware of a tattoo inked into it. An impression of wings and feathers, a light pulsing through the skin. An angel. She has seen this woman before, years ago. The last time she saw Yasmin. She was old back then. How is it possible for her to be pregnant now?

But then she is gone, hurrying down the underpass. Ruth calls after her, but hears only the echo of her own voice bouncing back to her from the arched brick walls. She forces her feet to move, to follow her, but when she reaches the end of the tunnel, less than twenty yards away, and comes back up into the moonlit monochrome, the woman is nowhere to be seen. Ruth looks in every direction, but she has vanished completely, as if into the air.

Her eye is drawn to a street lamp on the corner, by the entrance to the tram stop. A moth is flying rapidly around it, banging its wings against the glass, desperately seeking to orientate itself towards the moon, to keep the source of light at a constant angle to its eye, so it can plot its escape from any sudden, unexpected attack. It will bend and twist and mould itself to the flame, doing whatever it must to keep evolving, to adapt, to survive, for it will not be deflected from pursuing its course, or reaching its goal.

11

2020 – 2011 – 2015 – 2016 – 2020 – 1995 – 1996 – 2020

CLIVE

2020

At precisely eight pm, Clive stands on the doorstep of his house applauding as loudly as he can, this house he shares with his partner, Florence, and their dog, Rafe, a Welsh collie, who accompanies Clive's clapping with a joyful barking of his own. Florence is not able to join them, having already left for work. Thursday used to be one of her regular evening slots at *The Band on the Wall* in the centre of the city. She tells Clive that they would applaud there, too, just before the start of her first set, which now she must perform without an audience, direct to camera, so that it can then be streamed live to whoever might tune in to watch her.

Clive edges towards the front gate so that he can see who else might be out. This week it's the entire street. Every house is represented by someone, banging a pan lid with a spoon, ringing a bell, cheering, whistling, singing, setting off party poppers, even fireworks, to mark the end of *Clap for Carers*, which has been such a celebratory weekly ritual for the past ten Thursdays.

Suggested quite casually by the Dutch yoga teacher, Annemarie Plas, to a group of friends via WhatsApp, the post went viral, appearing within two hours on Victoria Beckham's Facebook page, before being taken up by both the Prime Minister and the Queen as a symbol of the national spirit in the face of the pandemic.

Clive has come to look forward to this weekly coming-together of the street, the way it strengthens the bonds of neighbourhood and community at a time when it is needed most, especially now that the lockdown is being tightened even further. He hardly sees anyone these days, apart from the occasional wave through a window if he happens to be passing, or when he drops off shopping for those who might be shielding. As *he* should be too, except that he can't quite bring himself to do so. The thought of cutting himself off so completely from the rest of the world is inconceivable.

And so he has enjoyed these socially distanced parties each week, smiling ruefully across the street to his neighbours from behind his hand-made face mask, stitched for him by his sister, Anita, in Moss Side, who he hasn't now seen for more than three months. He likes the fact that this simple act, of clapping the carers and key workers, is being repeated at this precise moment, not just here, on the street where he lives, but right across the city and the country. He knows this because he will see it later on the TV news. Home and the world.

He likes as well the way the whole nation appears to have become creative, making rainbow 'thank you' signs to put up in their windows, to pursue new hobbies and crafts, rediscover old talents, taking up a musical instrument, learning to paint or draw, dressing up, dancing in the kitchen, joining Grayson Perry's Art Club. Clive himself, inspired by the photographer Nathan Whyburn, has created a collage of a nurse made up of more than two hundred separate digital images of the same person, Leanne, one of Florence's nieces, who works at St Mary's Hospital. The nurse as *Lady Madonna*, which is being sung now by all the people in the street.

But now it is all going to stop. Tonight will be the last *Clap for Carers*. Annemarie Plas has requested for it to be paused. She fears it's becoming routine, its true meaning in danger of being normalised – or worse, politicised. She's probably right, sighs Clive, as the applause begins to fade. He waits by the gate until everyone else has gone back inside their houses, behind their closed front doors.

Who knows when they'll be able to meet each other again? It's all so very different from when he and Florence first moved into Park Range nine years before...

*

2011

"It's the last Sunday in March," says Elaine, handing Clive the invitation. "Two weeks from today. We're hoping for fine weather."

Clive, struggling with boxes, looks down at the leaflet. "Yes, indeed," he says.

Park Range Residents' Association
Centenary Street Party

Sunday 27th March 2011 at 3pm

Refreshments Provided
Admission: Free.   Donations: Welcome.

"We do hope you'll come."

"Yes," says Clive, looking back up. "We'd love to."

"Splendid. I'm Elaine, by the way. Elaine Bishop."

"Clive Archer," he answers, trying to offer a hand to shake from beneath the pile of boxes he's juggling on his way from the hire van to the house.

"The Lecturer in Photography?" says Elaine.

"Yes, but how did you...?"

"Your reputation precedes you, Clive. Or rather, that of your wife. I'm quite a fan of the Florence Blundell Quintet. I have some of their CDs. Is she...?" Elaine strains to look beyond Clive.

"Sorry," says Clive. "She's at a gig."

"Ah, I see," she says, clearly disappointed. "Some other time then."

"Yes. No doubt."

"That's my partner-in-crime," says Elaine, pointing to a man of similar age posting leaflets further down the road. "Phil Barton. We're to blame for this knees-up and shindig, I'm afraid," she explains, pointing to the leaflet. "Though it's likely to be quite a sedate affair. Still, if it's cold we may have to resort to dancing to keep ourselves warm. Maybe Florence might play for us if we do...?"

"Maybe," smiles Clive.

"Sorry to hi-jack you like this, just as you're moving in." She indicates the boxes. "Do you want a hand?"

"I won't say no," replies Clive, handing one of the boxes to Elaine. "Sometimes I wonder why we need all this stuff. I've no idea where half of it's going to end up. In the skip probably."

"Oh, we've got excellent recycling facilities here if you need them. One of the Residents' Association's many innovative schemes."

"Right," says Clive, struggling awkwardly with the box. "Thanks. Well – I'd best be getting on."

"Yes, of course. See you in two weeks. Mustn't stand here chatting. I've leaflets to deliver."

Clive watches her scurry busily away from him. "What's the centenary we're celebrating?" he calls after her. "The street party," he adds, holding up the invite.

"Oh," says Elaine, beaming. "We've picked the date

deliberately. It coincides with the Census. It will be exactly one hundred years since the first-ever Census here on Park Range. Quite a milestone, I'm sure you agree."

Before he can answer she is half-way down the street and out of earshot.

He grins broadly. Already he can tell. He's going to enjoy living here. Somewhere with a strong sense of identity and place...

Clive has secretly always wanted to live in Victoria Park. Less than one and a half miles from where he grew up in Moss Side, separated by the great divide of Wilmslow Road, it is like entering a different country, even now. More prosperous, more affluent, more cushioned from hardship and privation. Initially a gated community for the burgeoning middle classes when it was first conceived in the middle of the 19th century, it quickly became a Bohemian enclave, for artists, musicians, writers and politicians, so that it became synonymous with radicalism and the espousal of liberal values. Richard Cobden, the Corn Law reformer, lived there. So, too, did Elizabeth Gaskell, Charles Hallé, the founder of the city's orchestra, Ford Madox Brown, the creator of the Manchester Murals, as well as, for a time, the Pankhursts. Now it is much more egalitarian. Many of the larger houses have been converted into flats. Students live there, and, just around the corner from where Clive and Florence move into, is the famous Curry Mile.

Park Range was built in 1911 on land that was formerly the 'fallow field', by which the local neighbourhood is still known, drained by the meandering Birch Brook. It linked a string of farms, which, although long disappeared, live on in many of the current street names. Rush Holme Grove, The Oaks, Old Hall Lane, Lady Barn, Hope Bank...

On the morning of the street party, the weather proves

mercifully kind. Clive joins his next-door neighbour, Harry Spooner, in posting up on gateposts photocopies of details of all the people who lived in each house back at the time of that first Census a hundred years before. It makes for revealing reading. The occupants are solicitors, merchants, engineers, teachers, accountants, or individuals of private means. Nearly all are from Manchester or Lancashire, with just a handful of recent arrivals from elsewhere in England – Stafford, Exeter, London. All are white and Christian. The majority are men, with many women having boycotted it. "If we're not entitled to vote," so their argument ran, "why should we add our names to the Census…?"

Now, in 2011, the demographic breakdown could hardly be more diverse, or more egalitarian. Philip Barton – Elaine's 'partner-in-crime', as she so playfully had described him, who Clive meets for the first time that morning – informs him that now the street has more women than men, with representatives from at least eighteen countries, four continents, and seven different faiths,. "Eight, if you include 'no faith'," he says. "In only forty households."

"We've got the whole world on our doorstep," declares Harry.

Clive agrees. "That would make a great title for a project," he says. "Park Range is a modern microcosm and should be celebrated as such."

Philip looks doubtful. "What do you mean? We don't want to draw attention to ourselves. We're simply a reflection of the way things are these days."

"That's what I'm saying. And isn't that wonderful? I can't remember ever feeling so welcomed. The spirit of Manchester encapsulated in a single street."

"I like the sound of that."

"How about we do a 21st century equivalent of what Harry's been doing this morning with his gatepost flyers? We could take a simple photograph of each house in the street, with whoever lives there now standing before their front door, with a caption underneath stating their names, where they're from originally, and what they do."

"Then place it alongside the photocopy of who lived there before in 1911," says Philip, now becoming excited by the idea. "Only those who want to, of course," he adds as a caveat.

"Of course," agrees Clive. "But it will stand as a snapshot for future generations – who knows, maybe in another hundred years – to compare with how life is for them here in Park Range then."

"If there still *is* a Park Range," chips in Elaine, who has now joined them with cups of tea.

"Oh, I think there will be," replies Philip. "Don't you?"

"There'll be something, I suppose," she concedes.

"Exactly," says Clive.

"Let's think about it some more, then put it to the Residents' Association," says Philip decisively.

"Hear, hear!" agrees Elaine. "So what next? Might Florence be going to play something for us?" she asks cheekily.

"I think she might," says Clive smiling. "In fact, I think she's already started."

Florence sashays towards them playing a version of Miles Davis's *So What?* Soon the whole street is dancing, Phil with his wife, Nicky; Elaine with her son, Max; Harry with his wife Katrina, and everyone.

*

2015

It takes two years for Phil and Nicky to get all of the various ducks in a row before they can get started on the project. Then it takes a further two years to interview everyone in the street, collect their stories, and take their photographs. They don't want these photographs to look 'professional', or be digitally enhanced in any way, just ordinary snapshots taken in natural light, with the members of each household posing in whatever way they choose beside their own individual front doors.

Clive respects this. Besides, he has his own major exhibition to curate at MMU – the George Wright Retrospective – and this takes up all of his available time. The following year he retires, after giving the introduction to the inaugural Arthur Lewis Lecture, and sets about what had been a long term goal of his, a book detailing George Wright's life and career, to be called *A Northern Gaze*. So that when Phil and Elaine inform him that the project is complete, he is quite taken by surprise, sorry not to have been more involved.

"Never mind," they reassure him, "you've taken part – that's the main thing."

Phil explains that they've been offered a fortnight's exhibition space in the *Ahmed Iqbah Ullah Education Centre* in the basement of Manchester Central Library, whose newly-reopened Local History section on the ground floor will host an interactive touch screen version, but that first there is to be a public Open Day at the magnificent Victoria Baths, winner of the BBC's Restoration series in 2003. Built at the same time as Park Range, just a quarter of a mile away on Hathersage Road, it is the perfect venue for the Exhibition, for it would have been used by many of the street's original inhabitants from the Census of 1911. Designed by Henry Price, Manchester's first-ever city architect, it was described when it was opened as 'the most splendid municipal bathing institution anywhere in the country, a Water Palace of which every Mancunian can be proud.' Not only did the building provide spacious and extensive facilities for swimming, bathing and leisure, it was built of the highest quality materials with many period decorative features – stained glass, terracotta tiles and mosaic floors. But by the late 1980s. along with much of Manchester, it was experiencing hard times. Forced to close because of government cuts, it fell into disrepair, was boarded up, suffered vandalism and looting, until eventually it was threatened with demolition. Only the dedicated commitment of a local action group managed to rescue it, until it won that prestigious BBC award and was so saved from the wrecker's ball. Now it has been restored to all of its original glory.

"Yes," agrees Clive, "it's the perfect venue. I shall look forward to it."

But on the morning of the Exhibition he feels unwell. In truth, he has been feeling under the weather for weeks. But on this particular day he wakes in considerable pain. He passes blood in his urine. Florence calls the doctor. Within two hours he is admitted to the Manchester Royal Infirmary. The next day he undergoes an emergency prostatectomy.

*

2020

Two years later Clive is given the all-clear, but given his age and his ethnicity, he is deemed medium to high risk of the cancer returning elsewhere, and is subject to regular tests and screening. So far it hasn't. But when, the following year, Covid hits, his doctor advises him to shield, but Clive is reluctant to do this. His neighbours on Park Range have been amazing in their support for him during his recovery, and now that he is at last feeling better, he wants to do something for them in return. Many are older than he is, while others are struggling with being furloughed, or home schooling, or being prevented from seeing elderly relatives, so he volunteers to collect shopping, or prescriptions, on their behalf. Then, inspired by the example of the footballer Marcus Rashford, he offers to help out at a local food bank. But he's careful. He's meticulous about wearing a face mask, maintaining social distancing, washing his hands.

It's Florence he worries about more than himself. No longer able to sing or play in her various jazz clubs, she's like a bear with a sore head. She's begun keeping unsociable, nocturnal hours, sleeping by day, prowling the house by night, or taking long, solitary walks with Rafe, their dog, who is disturbed by this sudden change to his routine.

"This won't do," Clive eventually tells her. "We're both of us artists," he says. "We should use this enforced time at home for more creative purposes."

Florence agrees. She can see the sense in what Clive is saying. She hauls herself back from the twilit nether world she's been inhabiting, and tentatively begins to compose new music. She takes to writing lyrics – a new venture for her – and then she starts to present a series of gigs from their living room via Facebook and YouTube.

Clive, meanwhile, takes out his notes and jottings for *A Northern Gaze* once more. He can glimpse a possible way forward at last. But he needs something else first. Something less daunting in its scale. Something he can see an end to. Something quick...

Then, on the last Thursday in May, the night when he claps for the carers and key workers from his front gate for the last time, the idea comes to him.

He will recreate those doorstep portraits from five years before, to capture this extraordinary moment they are all of them collectively living through, when the whole world closes its doors against the virus, keeping the world away. Here in Park Range, they will *open* their doors, albeit virtually, to let the rest of the world back in.

He knows all the residents by name now. He is on speaking terms with most, quite friendly with many, even the students in the shared house at Number 13, whose gallery of faces changes from year to year. Some of the houses have different people living in them from five years before, but not many, and most are keen to take part, once he has outlined his proposal to them, which he does through a series of Zoom chats and WhatsApp calls.

He will take the portraits in exactly the same configurations as before, honest and authentic, using natural light only, so that they might be placed alongside the ones from 2015 for direct comparison. The one crucial difference this time will be that everyone will be wearing face masks. The symbol of life under Covid, when we can no longer readily recognise just who we are any more, as if we are still discovering the answer...

By the summer he has completed taking all of the photographs. As the country begins to ease out of lockdown, he decides he will arrange a modest local exhibition for them, one that can be easily navigated within the current regulations, observing the rule of six.

He persuades the trustees of the Methodist International House at Hirstwood on Daisy Bank Road in Victoria Park to let him use their Common Room for the August Bank Holiday weekend. Once a private house, Hirstwood was purchased by the Methodists in the 1920s for conferences and retreats. In the 1970s a small hall of residence was built in the grounds to accommodate overseas students at the University. Having been forced to close since Easter due to the pandemic, they are now gearing themselves up for students to return for the new term in September. They see the Exhibition as the ideal opportunity for them to test out their new safety procedures and happily agree to act as hosts. It is decided that on the Saturday the Exhibition will be open only to residents of Park Range, who will attend within their own bubbles at regular, pre-arranged thirty-minute slots, while on the Sunday and Monday they will admit the wider general public, but that places will be strictly limited. Visitors must first go online to reserve a time, where they will be allocated a code, which they must present before being admitted.

Jamilah Mursal, the Warden at Hirstwood, inspires confidence, and Clive is more than happy to hand over the logistics of the arrangements to her.

"We are happy to help," she says. "Your Exhibition is in perfect keeping with what we try to do here." She points to a copy of their mission on the notice board in the entrance to the Common Room.

'*Methodist International House extends a warm greeting to International, European and Home students from wherever in the world they come. Successive teams of Wardens, Advisers and Tutors have remained true to the founding vision for a community-oriented, multi-cultural and multi-faith residence in the heart of modern Manchester. Welcome to your Home from Home.*'

Clive leaves her with some posters and flyers she has agreed to put up in advance of the weekend.

THE WORLD ON OUR DOORSTEP

Stories from a Manchester Street
A Photographic Portrait

Methodist International House
Hirstwood, Daisy Bank Road, Rusholme

August Bank Holiday 2020

View by Appointment: www.worldonourdoorstep.com

*

The day before the Exhibition is due to open, Tanya, Clive's former technician at MMU, arrives with Khav to help install the photographs. In addition to the portraits of each household,

Clive has taken images of the street as a whole. Tanya has scanned these, then enlarged them to cover the boards onto which the portraits will be hung, so that each grouping appears *in situ* in the digital street. She then proceeds to arrange these in two rows, so that the viewers, when they arrive, will be invited to follow a prescribed route, as if walking up one side of the street, then back down the other, with sufficient space in between to avoid any infringements of the two-metre rule. To accompany and enrich the experience, Tanya has created a soundtrack of people applauding, banging pans, cheering and whistling, from when they had clapped the carers and key workers, which had first suggested the idea to Clive to begin with. The finished effect is more than he could have hoped for.

"Brilliant," declares Khav. "This is exactly what people need right now. A proper affirmation. Tan, you're a genius, innit?"

Together she and Tanya walk up and down each row, nodding and smiling at each portrait they pass, almost as if they are saying, "Hello – pleased to meet you," to every single person.

The World On Our Doorstep: Catalogue
(Children & Pets in Brackets)

1. Judith & Ron
Lived in street since: 1975
Place of Origin: Manchester, via London & Goole
Occupation: Teachers (retired)

2. Rashid & Robena
Lived in street since: 1984
Place of Origin: Punjab, via Salford
Occupation: Restaurant Owners, Curry Mile

3. Farah & Abdul, (Sara, Irfaan, Saba)
Lived in street since: 2002
Place of Origin: Faisalabad, Pakistan
Occupation: Taxi Driver, Housewife

4. Claire & Andrew, (Jennie)
Lived in street since: 2004
Place of Origin: Ladysmith, South Africa, via Warwick
Occupation: Social Workers

5. Sabine & Graham, (Zara, Clarissa)
Lived in street since: 2009
Place of Origin: Lübeck, Germany; Oxford & Kent
Occupation: Charity Workers

6. Elaine, (Max)
Lived in street since: 1979
Place of Origin: Indiana, USA
Occupation: Infant teacher (retired)

7. Renata & Leo
Lived in street since: 2015
Place of Origin: Berlin, Germany & Darwen, Lancs
Occupation: Linguist & Rector

8. Tanmayee, Setor, Dave, Ovi
Lived in street since: 2016
Place of Origin: India, Ghana, China, Romania
Occupation: Students

9. Afzal & Rowshanara, (Mumeenul, Bulbis, Jasmin, Mueedul, Arefa)
Lived in street since: 1992
Place of Origin: Bangladesh, via Stockport
Occupation: Insurance Broker, Housewife

10. Dezi & Abigail, (Arthur the Dog)
Lived in street since: Dezi born there, Abi since 2011
Place of Origin: Manchester & Ireland via Australia
Occupation: Musician, Physiotherapist

11. Ralf & Lida, (Sasha, Gina)
Lived in street since: 1994
Place of Origin: Aalen, Germany & Tehran, Iran
Occupation: Systems Manager, Maths Lecturer

12. Halimo
Lived in street since: 1994
Place of Origin: Somalia, via Djibouti
Occupation: NHS Translator

13. Walaiti & Gurpurshad
Lived in street since: 1986
Place of Origin: India, via South Wales
Occupation: Car Salesman, Housewife

14. Anandi & Mehmood
Lived in street since: 1977
Place of Origin: Jhelum, Pakistan & Mumbai, India
Occupation: Lecturer in Media Studies, Professor of Creative Writing, University of Beirut

15. Phil & Helena, (Ollie the Cat)
Lived in street since: 1991
Place of Origin: Stoke-on-Trent & County Kerry
Occupation: Artists & Wandering Scholars

16. Harry & Katrina
Lived in street since: 1998
Place of Origin: Harpurhey & Dewsbury
Occupation: Trade Unionist, Nursery Teacher

17. Elisabet & Abassi, (Haroon, Sara)
Lived in street since: 2005
Place of Origin: Murcia, Spain & Karachi, Pakistan
Occupation: Data Analyst, Local Radio Presenter

18. Austin & Michaela
Lived in street since: 2013
Place of Origin: Amersham, via Italy, Austria, USA; & Germany, via Croatia
Occupation: Social Anthropologists

19. Cécile & Rob, (Ella, Maggie)
Lived in street since: 2009
Place of Origin: Angoulême, France & Manchester
Occupation: Teacher, Accountant

20. Amanda & Laura
Lived in street since: 2013
Place of Origin: Edmonton, Canada & Zaragoza, Spain
Occupation: Lab technicians

21. Clive & Florence, (Rafe, the Dog)
Lived in street since: 2011
Place of Origin: Ashton, via St Kitts & Nevis; Coal Miner's Daughter, Manchester
Occupation: Lecturer (retired), Jazz Musician

"This is bloody beamin', Clive," grins Khav, "Fulgent, candescent."

"I've no idea what you're talking about," laughs Clive, "but thank you anyway."

"It does exactly what it says on the tin, innit? The world on our doorstep. You could repeat this in every street, estate, block of flats in the land, and though every story would be different, unique, the impulse behind them would be exactly the same. Heroic journeys in search of a home."

"Perhaps we should do it in our street, babe?" says Tanya.

"Yeah, we could start right now." She links her arm through Tanya's and together they pose before Clive, who takes an instant picture of them with his phone.

"Khav and Tan," continues Tanya, playing along. "Arrived in street...?"

"At the start of July," fills in Khav. "Our own lockdown bubble."

"Originally from...?"

"Manchester via Amritsar," answers Khav.

"Jackson, Mississippi via the Bight of Benin," adds Tanya.

"Or maybe we should do it where my *Maa* lives," suggests Khav. "It's got the perfect name for it, innit? *Albion* Street."

Laughing, arms still linked, they wish Clive good luck.

"I'll be back Monday evening to help you take it down,"

says Tanya, and then they are gone, entwined in the close embrace of their bubble, rising effortlessly into the air, where they will bump and buffet against others, not knowing where the breeze will take them, or where they will next touch solid ground, but simply trusting that they will, confident they'll land safely without having burst...

*

RUTH

2020

Lockdown hits *Tulip House* hard.

Ruth can continue to treat her clients remotely, either by phone or by Zoom, but the other specialists – the acupuncturist, reflexologist, chiropractor and osteopath – all have to stop their practice immediately. This means they can no longer afford to pay the monthly rental for their spaces, so that Ruth must apply for a government loan to cover her loss of income, which is a much more complicated and long-drawn-out process being self-employed, while Meera, her formidable but indispensable receptionist, has had to be furloughed.

The hallway, where clients used to wait, is empty and silent. The music of Cam or Florence no longer conveys the atmosphere of sophisticated calm Ruth had contrived so carefully to create, and she finds herself rattling around in the house on Lapwing Lane all by herself again, as she has not done since she first converted it, more than twenty-five years before...

*

1995

Ruth surveys the transformation with quiet satisfaction.

The last of the builders have gone, the contracts have been signed by each of the tenants, the new receptionist has been hired, a highly impressive young woman called Meera, who is looking to return to work now that her children have all started school. She is frighteningly efficient, and Ruth feels certain that *Tulip House* is in safe hands.

She allows herself the pleasure of taking herself on a conducted tour of the now completely altered house that has been her home since she was born here in 1954, and in which she has lived entirely alone since 1974, after Lily had died. It was only the previous year, 1994, when she had passed the momentous landmark of turning forty, that she had at last been galvanised into action. Now, looking around at all the changes, she wonders why she allowed so much time to elapse before taking the plunge. Her friends had been encouraging her to take steps for years. Especially Yasmin.

"You're sitting on a potential gold mine," she had said...

Well – time will prove whether that is the case.

Actually she knows perfectly well why she delayed so long. It was the emotional weight of all that she had inherited. Not just from Lily, or Roland. But from their wider circle of friends, with whom their lives were so intricately bound. Annie and Hubert. Delphine, George, Francis.

She had kept everything, throwing nothing away, so that, in the end, there was no room for herself any more. Now, apart from George's papers, which she'd had to sort through after he died, and which she has now filed away in boxes in the attic, for she believes they constitute an archive of a working life too valuable to dispose of casually, she has restricted herself to just a single item per person, each of which she has placed in a separate room in the house, after which that room is now named, so that Meera, when *Tulip House* opens for business next week, will be able to direct their clients to the correct one accurately and efficiently. These new bespoke nomenclatures will provide privacy, discretion, reassurance, confidentiality and, above all, distinction.

Annie's sampler, Hubert's clock. Lily's collage, Roland's computer board. Delphine's bird's nest, Eve's comet. Francis's telescope and George's photograph.

And above all, giving the house its name, the model yacht, *The Tulip*, made by Ruth's great-grandfather, who she never knew, but whose legacy remains...

She walks slowly from room to room.

The yacht sits discreetly on a shelf behind what will be Meera's desk in the main entrance. This is where everyone who comes for an appointment must go first, to register their arrival, then afterwards to pay and arrange any future follow-ups, so everyone will see it. Ruth enjoys the idea that what had been old Mr Kaufmann's modest carving for his daughter, which she herself never got to see, and which was Lily's only tether to her past, which she somehow managed to hold on to throughout the traumas of her formative years, should at last have found itself a safe mooring, where it can be enjoyed and admired without risk or fear by all the strangers who will visit here.

On one wall of the hallway, where clients will wait to be called for their treatments, is a notice board providing details of all the services offered by *Tulip House*, as well as all of the required information regarding health and safety, plus fire regulations. On the wall opposite, Roland's original Computer Logic Board hangs framed, as it has done since the week after he died. It is perhaps the only thing not to have been altered during the house's conversion. For Ruth this not only provides her with a necessary link to her father, it stands on its own merits as an intriguing, but untroubling piece of abstract modern art, which is diverting and distracting, without being disturbing, for the clients while they wait. More significantly, it represents, for Ruth, a kind of universal portrait, free from all constraints of race, religion or gender, a random collision of chance and opportunity, like a promise of hope for the future, that *Tulip House*, in some broader, unspecified way, offers this for all who pass through her doors. It is, to Ruth's mind, a mirror.

There are two consulting rooms on the ground floor, which open directly off the hallway. What had previously been the dining room. has been renamed *Spindle*. It contains Lily's four collagraphs of the spindle tree she planted in the garden at the back of the house in memory of Annie, which this room looks out onto, in each of the different seasons. This is now where the acupuncturist, Mr Lao, has his couch, his anatomical charts, and his supply of needles. "Very appropriate," he pronounces to Ruth when finalising the tenant's agreement between them, "in a room called *Spindle*."

The former lounge is where Ruth herself will practise. It will also serve as her own private sitting room in the evenings, and is furnished accordingly, with a sofa and armchairs, a low table, where there is always a ready supply of tissues. On the mantelpiece above the still-working fireplace is Hubert's clock, which ticks softly and comfortably in the inevitable silences that will punctuate her psychotherapy sessions. In fact the whole domestic nature of the décor, Ruth knows from experience, her clients will find reassuring, and will put them at ease. As will the framed sampler stitched by Annie – completed on the very night that George first brought Lily here, when she was at her most wretched and desperate – which hangs on the wall facing the sofa, where all of her clients will sit, or lie, with its nostalgic reminders of childhoods of old, with their dreams of innocence. The embroidered text from Deuteronomy, outlined in, what to Ruth's eyes, is a pleasing running stitch, holds up a promise of recovery and renewal.

That which was lost has been found.

And so she names the room *Ariadne*, for she too used a spool of thread to help her find her way home.

Upstairs, on the first floor, are three former bedrooms, which have now been turned into clinics for the osteopath, chiropractor and reflexologist – respectively Vivienne, Surayya, Shawne. The staircase leading to these three rooms is wide enough to accommodate a stair lift for those who require it, and there are further chairs on the landing, should anyone need them. On a glass shelf on one wall, high enough to be unreachable by even the tallest client, is the fragile bird's nest that had been Delphine's, below which is hung the painting made with mosses and plant dyes by Delphine's mother, Eve, of Halley's Comet, while on a table positioned in a small niche next to a narrow, vertical window is Francis's telescope, trained towards the skies beyond, with instructions on how to use it printed on a small card beside it. The three rooms have been named, each in accordance with their size, after the three inner Galilean moons of Jupiter – *Io*, *Europa* and *Ganymede*, with *Io* being the smallest and *Ganymede* the largest – while a smaller, steeper staircase leads up to the private attic on the second floor, named for *Callisto*, the moon which follows a single, separate, outer orbit, and which serves as Ruth's own bedroom. Inside hangs the framed photograph by George of the sixteen-year-old Giulia swatting at a recalcitrant terrier with her 'Miss Manchester Ice Creams' tiara, which is always guaranteed to bring a smile to her lips, especially if it has been a trying day with testing clients...

Having completed her solitary tour of the converted house, she returns to the hallway with a feeling of immense satisfaction and pleasure. She can hardly wait for Monday to arrive and the first clients to walk through the front door with its stained glass panels of reds and greens and golds, which now, as the sun is starting to set, throw dappled patterns of light on the wooden parquet floor. She walks over to what she is already referring to as Meera's desk, where a CD player sits on one corner, into which she inserts a recently reissued recording of Cam singing live at *The Queen's Hotel*. *'Here I'll Stay.'*

"There's a far place I'm told
Where I'll find a field of gold
But here I'll stay with you..."

Ruth closes her eyes, allowing herself to be drawn into the web of Cam's voice, luxuriating in its silky, sultry tones. It is like wallowing in a deep, warm, bubble bath, scented with aromatic oils and surrounded by candles, which she wants to surrender herself to completely.

But just as she is on the point of running herself one, the doorbell rings. She is of a mind not to answer it, but it rings again, insistently. Reluctantly, she lifts herself out of her reverie and opens the door.

It's Yasmin. She is smiling mischievously, waving a bottle of wine seductively in one hand. The sun paints her hair in flecks of gold and red and green.

"I thought you might want to celebrate," she says with a grin.

"Actually," says Ruth, returning her smile, "I was just on the point of taking a bath."

"Even better," says Yasmin. "Care for some company?"

"Your timing, as always," says Ruth, closing the door behind her, "is perfect."

Yasmin loops her arms around the back of Ruth's neck and draws her towards her in a long and lingering kiss. Coming up for air several seconds later, Ruth takes Yasmin's hand in her own and leads her past *Ariadne* and *Spindle*, up the stairs past *Io, Europa* and *Ganymede*, towards the waiting, distant moon of *Callisto*. The bath will have to wait till later.

Cam's voice oozes through the narrowest of spaces between

them.

> "*Yes I know exactly where I belong*
> *And it's here I'll stay with you...*"

*

1996

But less than a year later Yasmin's timing is less than perfect.

It's the end of the financial year. Meera, who, as well as continuing to expertly manage the appointments for the entire team, has unilaterally expanded her remit to include book-keeping and accounts, announces to Ruth that *Tulip House* has exceeded all targets and forecasts for its first year of operations, and is already turning over a modest profit.

"That's wonderful, Meera," says Ruth. "But are you sure?"

Meera looks at Ruth with incredulity that she could possibly doubt such a thing.

"*Gambeerata se...?*"

"No, of course not," replies Ruth, who, like all of the practitioners, is rather frightened of Meera, as though *she* were the boss, and Ruth the employee. But all the clients adore her. They are always bringing in cakes and sweets for her, which Meera always admonishes them about, appearing to accept their gifts reluctantly, while secretly being delighted.

"You can give me a raise now, isn't it?" she says now, looking directly at Ruth.

"Yes, I suppose," stammers Ruth. "If you think we can afford it?"

"*Bilkul nahin.* Of course we can't. Are you foolish? One swallow doesn't make a summer."

"No, of course not," says Ruth a second time.

"*Shayad thoda sa...?* Well, maybe just a little, huh? I look into it."

"Yes. Thank you."

"Don't mention it…"

Later that evening Ruth calls Yasmin on her recently-acquired Nokia 1610, which Yasmin wears like a second skin.

"I feel like celebrating," says Ruth.

"Me too."

"Oh?"

"No – you go first."

"Where are you? It sounds noisy."

"She was a stranger in town," replies Yasmin, immediately adopting a Jack Kerouac accent, "a gypsy heart with no one to call. I must find somewhere warm, she thought, where the bright souls are. On and on through the rain she walked. Another bar, another café, each one the same. Finally she saw it, exactly what she'd been looking for. It beckoned to her from across the street, its neon light winking on and off in the night. She pressed her hand to the glass, then opened the door. Inside, beneath densely patterned walls, cocooned in the warm glow of chandeliers, she drank black coffee and red wine, and smoked French cigarettes. Old records turned. Gypsy, Coltrane, Leonard Cohen and Tom Waits. Soon she was dancing on creaky floorboards, lost in the sad and lonely eyes of a northern man – or woman…"

"OK," laughs Ruth. "I know exactly where you are. I'll be right over."

She skips out of the front door and heads straight for the *Folk Bar Café*, less than half a mile away, left on Burton Road, whose 'promo' chalked above the bar Yasmin has just been reading from…

By the time she arrives, both of them are flushed, Ruth from running, Yasmin from drinking.

"How many have you had?" says Ruth when she sees the state that Yasmin is in already.

"Who's counting?" replies Yasmin with a decided slur.

"Good job it's a Friday then," jokes Ruth. "You wouldn't want to be facing Year Eights with the hangover you're going to wake up with tomorrow."

"I'm not going to face Year Eights ever again."

"What do you mean?"

"I've quit, packed it in, flown the coop."

"But you can't. Teachers have to give a term's notice, don't they? Unless..." The truth begins to dawn on Ruth.

"I couldn't face the thought of another minute, let alone another term. My whole life seemed to be passing before my eyes in a never-ending roll-call of registers, assemblies, bus duties and detentions. All those stupid, pointless rules – tuck-your-shit-in, take-your-coat-off, tie-your-hair-back, put-your-tie-straight; remove-that-ear-ring, nose-ring, nail-polish, lipstick – and they were just the ones aimed at *me*. I thought – what am I doing? I don't believe in any of it. The dead hand of conformity is no way to bring the best out of young people. They need the freedom to say what they think, challenge the rules, express who they are, create something new. I know *I* do..."

Ruth lets her talk herself to a standstill. Then, as if speaking to one of her clients, asks her a simple question.

"So – what are you going to do instead?"

Yasmin looks Ruth directly in the eye. All the anger and rage leaves her face. She smiles, and it is an expression of such openness, such joy, such radiance, that it takes Ruth's breath away.

"Don't you know?" she says. "I'm going to travel. Before I get too old."

"You're not old. You only turned forty last month."

"I feel old. That's what teaching does for you. It makes you old before your time."

"Don't be ridiculous."

"Don't call me that. You're not my mum."

"No. Sorry."

"You're supposed to be my lover."

"I am, and have been for ten years, but…"

"What?"

"Lovers are meant to share things, discuss them, not just spring them on each other like this."

"And there was I thinking that love was supposed to make you reckless, carefree, impetuous, in the moment."

"Yes, but sensible too sometimes."

"That's an oxymoron."

"You can take the girl out of the teacher, but not the teacher out of the girl."

"Don't."

"I only meant looking out for each other."

"I know what you meant."

"I just don't want you to do something in haste now that you might regret later."

"Just fuck off with your 'sensible', will you? You've always known who I am, what I'm like. Stop trying to change me into…"

"What?"

"You!"

Ruth recoils. Yasmin's words are like nails. But she knows she must endure them, for she sees the truth in them.

Yasmin now begins to speak in a voice so low that Ruth can barely hear her. She leans closer to her to try and catch what she is saying. Yasmin grabs her wrist to make sure that she doesn't miss a single syllable. The words are so familiar that Ruth has forgotten what they mean. Now it is as if she is hearing them for the first time, fresh, new-minted, and they imprint themselves into her almost physically. One by one, slowly, like coins being posted in a tin through a slot, each one spinning on its axis till it noisily drops. Yasmin's eyes never leave Ruth's for an instant while she speaks them. They electrify her.

> *"Let us not to the marriage of true minds*
> *Admit impediments. Love is not love*
> *Which alters when it alteration finds,*
> *Or bends with the remover to remove..."*

Ruth tries to prise Yasmin's fingers from her wrist, but her grip is a vice.

> *"O no! it is an ever-fixèd mark*
> *That looks on tempests and is never shaken;*
> *It is the star to every wand'ring bark,*
> *Whose worth's unknown, although her height be taken..."*

She is reminded of the story Jenna told her of the benchmark incised into the sandstone of the tower of St Ann's Church, which she had used to try and regain her balance after the IRA bomb, but such is the ferocity of Yasmin's desire that Ruth cannot tear her gaze away from her. It is like looking at the Medusa, with eyes like whirlpools. She feels herself drowning inside them, losing her bearings, turning to stone with each flung, snake-hissed syllable.

> *"Love's not Time's fool, though rosy lips and cheeks*
> *Within her bending sickle's compass come;*
> *Love alters not with her brief hours and weeks,*
> *But bears it out even to the edge of doom..."*

Yasmin's voice is barely a whisper, but so sure in its conviction, that, even if she made no sound at all, Ruth would still hear her, like the hum of telegraph wires coursing through her veins, like ice, like fire, transcending language, almost as if she were speaking in tongues.

> *"If this be error and upon me prov'd,*

I never spoke, nor no one ever lov'd..."

Finally she stops. The rim of Yasmin's glass quivers and vibrates, emitting an eerie, high-pitched whine that stabs the space between them like a needle. It stretches and attenuates, an invisible thread, wound so tight and taut that eventually it must snap and break, which finally it does, the drawn-out, painful puncturing of a balloon, from which the air wheezes slowly out before evaporating into nothing.

Ruth stays silent for a long while. She has felt every word resonate and land, each one of them a painful blow to the heart. Eventually she exhales a long, slow breath. Yasmin releases her grip on her wrist, uncoiling her fingers slowly and separately, so that they leave a finely etched mark where each has been. Ruth massages it tentatively.

"I'm sorry if I hurt you," says Yasmin at last.

Ruth shakes her head. "I needed to be."

Yasmin sighs. "The curse of being an English teacher," she says, trying to lighten the mood. "All those bits of Shakespeare you had to learn stay with you. They're bound to come out in the end."

"I suppose."

"So..."

"So..." says Ruth, trying to force a thin smile, "where will you go?"

"Wherever the wind blows."

"How long for?"

"As long as it takes."

"And when will you go?"

"Tomorrow. Now. And I want you to come with me."

Ruth's stomach involuntarily tightens. A wave of nausea threatens to overwhelm her. "You're serious, aren't you?"

"Never more so."

Ruth shakes her head.

"I can't."

"Why?"

"You know why?"

"No I don't. You have to tell me."

"The business has only just started. We've only just begun to turn a profit."

"All the more reason to go now. It's a success. If Meera is as capable as you say she is, she could keep things ticking over for you."

"I'm certain she could."

"Well then…"

"What about my clients? I can't just abandon them."

"Don't you have colleagues you could send them on to?"

"Yes, I suppose I do. But…"

"What?"

"I don't want to."

Yasmin gasps audibly.

"There," says Ruth, "I've said it now. I love my work…"

"I thought you loved *me*?"

"I do. But…"

"What? You love your work *more*?"

"No, but it's taken me more than ten years to reach this point. I don't want to let it go just when it's starting to take off.

"We've been together for ten years too."

"Yes, I know…"

"Well?"

"I don't want to leave Manchester, that's the truth of it. It's my home. It's all I've ever known."

"Then it's time you spread your wings."

"No, I don't agree. This is where I feel I belong."

"Manchester?"

"Yes."

Yasmin starts to laugh, mirthlessly at first, but gradually becoming louder and shriller.

"What is it?"

"You've just given me an idea. I now know exactly where I'm going to travel to."

"Where?"

"To all the different Manchesters in the world."

"What are you talking about?"

"I looked it up once. There are nearly forty of them. Most are in America, but there are some in Canada, South America, Africa, Australia, even a couple in India. I'm going to visit them all. I'm going to buy myself a blow-up pillow with a map of the world on it, and put stickers on it each time I reach a new Manchester. Then I'm going to fall asleep on it every night and dream you were there with me. 'Wish you were here...' "

And she promptly does just that. She rests her head on Ruth's shoulder. Her mouth falls open. Flecks of spittle and drool gather at each corner. She starts to snore.

Ruth sadly disentangles herself from her, lays her head gently on the table top, then walks to the bar, where she hands the waiter a ten pound note.

"Can you call her a taxi please?" she asks sadly.

"Sure," he says. "Any message when I wake her?"

Ruth shakes her head, then changes her mind. "Just this. Tell her..."

"Yes...?"

"Just tell her I'm sorry, that's all..."

She walks slowly back along Lapwing Lane towards her house. A light rain has begun to fall. She finds it surprisingly soothing. She decides not to go straight home but instead extends her walk past her house and into Didsbury Village. The Rhodes Clock Tower, just outside where the old railway station used to be, is caught in the glow of a nearby street lamp, the rain illuminated as it falls across the clock face, which shows the time coming up to half-past ten. It's still quite early. The streets are so quiet that Ruth had thought it must be later. But the pubs have not yet shut, so that's why – everyone's indoors, the Village is practically deserted, and she has the whole place to herself. She realises that, although she has lived in Didsbury all her life and must have passed by the Clock Tower hundreds of time, she doesn't know anything about it. Why, for example, is it called the *Rhodes* Clock Tower? Remonstrating with herself for her lack of curiosity, she determines to read the bronze plaque set into the white Portland stone. She understands that this is merely an act of displacement, in order to distract and distance herself from the distressing scene with Yasmin just now, but she reads what it says anyway.

'In memory of Dr John Milson Rhodes 1847 – 1909
A Friend to Humanity'

A Friend to Humanity? That's quite a claim. She learns that he was born in Broughton and practised medicine here in Didsbury. He became a member of the Chorlton Board of Guardians with responsibility for administering the Poor Laws. Appalled by the conditions he routinely discovered in the workhouses, he set about a programme of vigorous reform, resulting in pioneering training for nurses, recognition of the special needs required by adults with a learning disability, the creation of the nearby Withington Hospital, as well as advocating greater support for the homeless. How could she not have known about him?

Just at that moment, the Clock above her strikes the three quarters. The sound of its mechanism whirring into life startles her, and she makes a small involuntary cry. She senses a sudden movement close by. A darker shape within the shadow cast by the tower. She approaches cautiously. She sees a woman leaning against it, clearly the worse for wear. An empty bottle falls from her hand, clattering noisily as it rolls off the kerb into the gutter. The sound it makes appears to rouse the woman from her stupor, and she starts, somewhat tunelessly, to sing. It's the same song that Ruth was listening to back in *Tulip House* before she went out to meet Yasmin.

> *"For that land is a sandy illusion*
> *It's the theme of a dream gone astray*
> *And the world others woo*
> *I can find loving you*
> *And here, I guess, I'll stay with you…"*

The woman is staring directly at Ruth without seeing her. She attempts to stand but lurches unsteadily, threatening to fall once more. Ruth catches hold of her arm to save her. The rank, threadbare coat she is wearing slips off her shoulder, revealing a tattoo in the unmistakable shape and pattern of an angel. But before Ruth can examine it more closely, the woman has wrenched herself free and staggered away, reeling down the road. A moth flutters erratically around the light illuminating the clock face.

Standing beneath it, her eyes alighting once more on the inscription to John Milson Rhodes, 'Friend to Humanity', Ruth feels even surer in her resolve to stay. She will miss Yasmin, but her work is here…

The following Monday morning she applies for a place on the part-time Post-Graduate MSc Diploma in Housing Policy & Practice at Salford University. Counselling and therapy are only part of the solution. She no longer wishes to be the one left to pick up the pieces. She wants, if she can, to try and prevent those pieces from being dropped to begin with. If she is to exert any sort of meaningful influence, if she wants to instigate lasting change at a sustainable level, she needs to be part of a bigger conversation. She will see her clients for three days a week and study the rest. She can do this, she knows. With a renewed sense of hope and purpose, she retraces her route back along Lapwing Lane towards where her home and work combine beneath the same roof.

The rain is falling harder now, but she no longer cares. She steps inside the stained glass front door of *Tulip House* and shuts it firmly behind her. Casting off her coat and kicking off her shoes, she stands in the hallway in front of the framed Computer Logic Board constructed by her father, its pareidolian valves and transistors primed and ready, waiting for her to throw the switch and let the random connections apophenically collide. She smiles. For an instant, she could swear, the abstract array of electronic circuitry, which has always reminded her of a face, right from when she was a child, smiles back.

*

2020

REFORM RADIO

CHLOE:

Hi. A warm welcome to *Sharp Talking*, Reform Radio's Live Chat Night, happening here every Friday from 7pm till 10pm with me, Chloe Chang. For those regular listeners among you, it's great to be sharing the cyber-sphere with you once more, and for those of you joining us for the first time – hey, what took you so long? Starting life in a South Manchester basement in 2013, Reform Radio moved to the Old Granada studios in 2015 and, at 7pm on the 3rd of October of that year, began 24/7 online broadcasting of the best in music, arts and culture to the world. And we're still doing it today. We're a not-for-profit company that supports young adults into employment. Our *radio* community supports the *wider* community, and so it goes around. It's never been needed more than now, has it, folks, during the current pandemic? So please feel free to join in the conversation in all the usual ways – Twitter, Facebook, Instagram – you know the drill. We'd love to hear from you.

My guest this evening is Ruth Warner, Deputy Lead on Housing and Homelessness for the Greater Manchester Combined Authority, with specific responsibility for coordinating *'A Bed Every Night'*, an initiative introduced when Covid first hit. Hi, Ruth. Thanks for joining us.

RUTH:

Thank you for having me.

It's been three years since Ruth and Chloe last met, in the aftermath of the Manchester Arena attack, during another late-night phone-in.

"I thought you worked for the BBC," says Ruth, perplexed, when Chloe invites her to do this interview.

"I do. But I don't have a fixed contract with anyone. I'm freelance. I go where the work is. Reform Radio gave me my first job, shortly after I graduated, so I feel a certain loyalty. Besides, I think they do really important work. No one else is talking about what you and I are about to this evening, except in the briefest of sound bites..."

CHLOE:

This must be an incredibly busy time for you right now, especially during lockdown, so let's begin straight away with *'A Bed Every Night'*. Can you tell our listeners what the scheme is?

RUTH:

Nobody should have to sleep rough on the streets of Greater Manchester. Not in the 21st century. *'A Bed Every Night'* tries to do what it says on the tin. It provides a comfortable bed, a warm welcome, and personal support for anyone who is sleeping rough, or at imminent risk of sleeping rough, anywhere in Greater Manchester. This is the North. We do things differently here. We live by a different set of values. We don't walk on by.

CHLOE:

So what do you do?

RUTH:

With politicians, sports stars, charities, businesses, the public and private sector, faith and community groups, and the public all coming together, a crisis which has escalated so catastrophically in this current time of austerity can be tackled and, eventually, removed from our social landscape once and for all.

CHLOE:

Fine words, Ruth. Stirring sentiments, no doubt. But what do they mean in practice? Forgive me if I appear cynical, but haven't we heard politicians from all sides trotting out this kind of empty rhetoric before? What makes this initiative different from any of the others?

RUTH:

To begin with, I'm not a politician. I'm a trained psychotherapist with a post-graduate diploma in Social Housing. My sole remit is to help as many people as I can, first by trying to house them, next by exploring what it was that drove them on the streets to begin with, finally by supporting them to make whatever long-term changes they need to keep off them in the future. But the pandemic has brought its own additional challenges. I've helped run hostels for years, but those models aren't appropriate now. We can't risk a further transmission of the virus by putting people together into shared accommodation. They need safe, sustainable, self-contained units. And that's where *'A Bed Every Night'* comes into its own.

CHLOE:
How?

RUTH:
Already more than two thousand rough sleepers have been placed into hotels, many of which would otherwise have had to close. Their generosity has been overwhelming. We put out the call and hundreds of establishments have answered it.

CHLOE:
That's marvellous, Ruth, but you've already said that one of your priorities is to provide accommodation that's sustainable. As soon as the lockdown is over, hotels are going to want to go back to business as usual as quickly as they can, aren't they, with guests who can pay?

RUTH:
That's where the voluntary sector comes in. The response from faith and community groups has been fantastic, and we want to build on that for the future. But I take your point. That's why our Mayor, Andy Burnham, has written to Robert Jenrick, Secretary of State for Housing, Communities & Local Government, to request an additional five million pounds from their recently introduced *'Everyone In'* scheme, which is intended to replace *'A Bed Every Night'* in the longer term. The problem, Chloe, as I'm certain your listeners can appreciate, is that the economic hardships brought about by Covid have seen a worrying rise

in homelessness as a consequence, and yet this new Government *'Everyone In'* scheme offers support only for those who were homeless *before* the start of the pandemic, and none whatsoever for people who have become so *during* it. In addition it's asking us to move people on from those short-term placements in hotels into more permanent accommodation, without providing the necessary resources to render such accommodation, even if it existed to begin with, Covid-safe.

CHLOE:

What has Andy Burnham written in his letter?

RUTH:

It's a long letter. I won't read it all now. He makes many important points. The whole text is available on the Greater Manchester Council website. But his essential message is a simple one. 'Dear Robert', he writes, 'I don't doubt your personal commitment to making progress on homelessness, but I urge you to honour the spirit of *'Everyone In'*. Let those words mean exactly what they say, and let – everyone – in.' Like I said at the top, Chloe, we do things differently here in Manchester. We don't just walk on by.

CHLOE:

Thank you, Ruth. I hope everyone out there tonight can hear the passion in my guest's voice coming through whatever device you might be listening to us on here at reformradio.co.uk, because even speaking to her via Zoom, like I'm doing right now, that passion is palpable.

RUTH:

Can I just add that if anyone listening feels they might want to volunteer, or donate, if they go to our website – bedeverynight.co.uk – they can follow the links. They can also check on how many people we're helping at any given time, for we update our figures daily. Right now, I can tell you, as of today, we have supported three thousand, one hundred and seventy-nine rough sleepers across Manchester since the beginning of the pandemic, of which one thousand, one hundred and thirty-one have been able to transfer already into safe, long-term accommodation, and last night four hundred and seventy people received a bed for the night for the first time.

CHLOE:
That's an impressive set of stats, Ruth.

RUTH:
But just imagine what more we could achieve if we had the right resources.

CHLOE:
OK. Thanks, Ruth. So – if any of you have any questions you'd like to put to our guest this evening, now's the time to get in touch via all the usual digital platforms. But first, we'll take a short break with Manchester's own, Yemi Bolatiwa, and her follow-up to *Word of Mouth – Takin' Over*. The word on the streets is that's exactly what she's doing...

Music begins...

While they are off air, Chloe thanks Ruth again.

"No," says Ruth. "Thank *you*. The more people we can reach with our message, the better chance we have of making things happen."

Just as she is about to disconnect from Zoom, a flyer pinned to a notice board behind where Chloe is sitting catches her eye.

"What's that?" she asks.

"What? This?" answers Chloe, taking it down. She holds it up to the screen so that Ruth might read it.

THE WORLD ON OUR DOORSTEP

Stories from a Manchester Street

A Photographic Portrait

Methodist International House
Hirstwood, Daisy Bank Road, Rusholme

August Bank Holiday 2020

View by Appointment: www.worldonourdoorstep.com

"Thanks," says Ruth. "What's your connection with it?"

"The person putting it together – Clive Archer – used to be my tutor. He's a great guy. I wouldn't be here today if it hadn't been for him. Do you know him?"

Ruth shakes her head, still studying the flyer.

"Why the interest, if you don't mind me asking?"

"The venue," says Ruth. "Hirstwood."

"Yes?"

"A family connection, that's all." She wonders whether to say more. Chloe's open demeanour naturally invites the sharing of confidences, so she decides that she will. "Do you know the work of the photographer George Wright?" she asks. "He was my uncle, sort of. He lived there for a while as a boy."

"In which case, you should definitely go," urges Chloe. "Clive is absolutely nuts about George Wright. He would love to meet you."

And then, without missing a beat, she flips on her headphones and is back live on air once more.

CHLOE:

That was Yemi Bolatiwa and *Takin' Over*. Thanks, Yemi. We'll be hearing more from her later in the programme. My next guest is…

*

CLIVE & RUTH

2020

Ruth arrives in good time for her pre-booked slot at the Exhibition. She stands at the end of the drive leading up to Hirstwood. Then she takes from her bag an old black-and-white photograph she has brought with her and holds it up for comparison. Yes, it is definitely the same house, with its half-timbered frontage. Outwardly very little appears to have changed. It's in what must have been the garden where she notices the changes.

In the photograph in her hand a ten-year-old George is standing next to his mother, Annie, on the porch outside the front door, in an uncanny foreshadowing of the Exhibition she is about to see inside. He is proudly holding a box, on which Ruth can make out the letters *'How To Build Your Own Crystal Radio Set'*. She can picture a different scene, in which George, tongue protruding from the corner of his mouth in concentration, is assisting his father to put it together – Hubert – who, Ruth imagines, must have taken this photograph she is now holding. She can detect the faint shadow of a man, holding a camera, silhouetted on the forecourt across which she now strides.

Once inside, aware that she has only a limited window in which she can view the Exhibition, Ruth walks up and down the two rows of images, set out as if they are the houses on either side of Park Range. Immediately she finds herself caught up in wanting to know more about the stories of the people posing so proudly beside their front doors, the countries they came from, and the journeys they must have had to make, or their parents or grandparents before them, in order for them to be standing there so purposefully. She thinks of the journey her own mother had to make to reach the leafy suburbs of Lapwing Lane. Lily. Not so far in miles – less than ten – but light years in terms of what she had had to overcome. And who knows if she ever would have, if it had not been for George, finding her by chance one rain-sodden night in Angel Meadow?

George. That is her main reason for coming here this afternoon. She looks around her. Sitting at a small table, wearing a face mask and latex gloves, greeting people as they arrive and handing them a copy of the easy-to-wipe laminated catalogue, is a man of a similar age to herself, perhaps slightly older. From what she can see of his face above the mask, he would appear to be smiling. His eyes radiate joy at seeing the pleasure on other people's faces as they are faced by the cast of residents from Park Range awaiting them, like the chorus from *Our Town*, with Park Range as a kind of Every Street.

She pauses. Every Street. That was where Yasmin had a flat in Ancoats, close to where the old 1824 Round Church used to be, where now there's just a circular brick wall and a few gravestones. At the opposite end is the new ziggurat building, housing flats for young professionals, very much the kind that Yasmin would have liked back then. Sleek and contemporary. Like her. Yasmin. Even after more than twenty years, she will pop into her head unbidden...

She approaches the man with the mask.

"Are you Clive?" she says.

"I am."

"I'm Ruth. I'd offer to shake your hand except that we're not allowed to these days."

"No."

"And elbow bumps feel faintly ridiculous."

"They do. How can I help you, Ruth?"

"Chloe Chang suggested I talk to you."

"Chloe Chang," echoes Clive, leaning back in his chair. Even with his mask, Ruth can now tell for certain that he is smiling.

"She thought you might be interested in this." She holds out the photograph she has brought with her towards him. He takes off his glasses and brings it close up to his face to study it more carefully. After a few moments he returns it to her with a puzzled frown.

"Chloe tells me you're trying to write a book about George Wright?"

"Trying being the operative word."

"He was my Uncle."

Clive's eyes nearly pop from their sockets.

"And this," she says, handing back the photo once more and pointing to the small boy with the box radio set, "is him aged ten."

The significance dawns on Clive at last. "Then that means this," he gestures to the building in which they sit, "was his home?"

"For a short time, yes. After here the family moved to Manley Park, and from there to Lapwing Lane. Which is where I still live today."

Clive is speechless.

"He was your Uncle?" he manages to say at last.

"Adoptive."

Clive's eyebrows shoot up above his mask.

"A long story, which I'm happy to tell you at some point, but maybe not today, not here. You have people coming to the Exhibition who'll be wanting to speak to you."

"Can you wait? I finish in about half an hour. Perhaps we could speak then?"

Clive's eagerness reminds Ruth of the young George in the photograph, who can hardly wait for his father to help him build the radio set.

"All right," she smiles. "I can wait."

"Better still. Go round to our house. We only live five minutes from here."

"In the real Park Range?"

"As opposed to this simulation. Exactly. We're allowed to sit outside in the garden, I believe?"

"So long as we remain 'socially distanced'," Ruth replies, raising the fingers of each hand like speech marks.

Clive chuckles. "Quite so. I'll text Florence to let her know you're on the way."

"Florence, as in the jazz trumpeter and singer?"

"Yes. Do you know her?"

"Not personally, no. But I love her music. I've heard her play any number of times. When I saw your photos back in there," she says, indicating the Exhibition, "I thought I recognised her. I just didn't join the dots."

Clive shrugs, as if he's used to this reaction, of people recognising his wife, but not him. He's clearly very proud of her.

"See you in half an hour," he says.

"Half an hour," she echoes...

Three hours – and two bottles of wine – later, Clive and Ruth are still talking. Florence has left them to it, retreating through the French windows back into the house, where she can be heard improvising a version of Miles Davis's *Moon Dreams*.

"You've really been through the mill," says Ruth, after hearing about Clive's surgery.

"But I'm better now," he says. "I'm clear."

"But you're still struggling with the book?"

"I'm stuck." He leans back and spreads his hands. He's removed his mask now. His face is an open book. Ruth can see that here is a man who wears his heart on his sleeve.

"Perhaps I can help you. You clearly love George as a photographer, but you don't know him as a man. How could you? You never met him. His pictures only tell you so much."

"They show someone who loved his fellow human beings. That much is clear."

"It's true. He did. But he was a quiet man. A private man. With few friends. Apart from Francis, of course." She pours herself another glass. "You know about Francis, I presume?"

"Not really. I met him once – Francis. Not long after George had died. At that funny little gallery of his. That's where I first saw George's work. It blew me away. There was one photograph in particular…"

"Which one?"

"It was of me, actually. With Christopher. My brother. We were both kids. Chris was sky-diving from the top of a rusty old container at the back of the Hulme Crescents. George had captured us perfectly. Chris in rapturous free fall, me wishing I was somewhere else." He laughs quietly at the memory.

"I know the picture," says Ruth.

"You do?"

She pauses before answering. The particular image Clive has been describing makes her think of herself and Yasmin, the fundamental difference between them, she so cautious, Yasmin casting caution to the wind.

"And I think I know why his photographs move people so much," she continues. "It's because he captures moments that are timeless. Deeply personal, yet at the same time universal, so that we instantly recognise ourselves in them, even if we were never actually there. Somehow he *puts* us there."

"You're right."

"And that's why I think you're stuck. Because what else is there to say?"

"Plenty. There's the contextual and compositional analysis of each separate image for a start."

"I suppose. But that's all rather dry and academic. George would not have been interested in a book like that. He'd have wanted something much more down to earth."

"Nuts and Bolts."

"I beg your pardon?"

"The title of his first exhibition."

"Yes. I'd forgotten. That's it exactly. And the only way you're going to do that is if you write a book that's more about George the man and the times he grew up in, using the photographs as a kind of running commentary alongside. And that's where I think *I* can help you. Celebrate his work as a sign writer and his hours at the speedway track as equal companions to his skills with a camera, which he carried around with him like it was an extension of his right arm, which to all intents and purposes it was. But what you need to focus on more, if you'll pardon the pun, are the real loves of his life – his motor bikes, his tinkering, his parents, Lily, his students – he was a wonderful teacher, don't forget, which I'm sure will resonate strongly with *you*, Clive – but at the heart of everything, front and centre, lies Francis. Always it comes back to Francis. Even though they were apart for far longer than they were together. Everything they did was a sort of unfinished love letter to the other…"

She pauses again. She had not known she would say quite so much, and how it would touch her so profoundly.

"These things have a way of repeating themselves, don't they?"

Ruth looks up. Florence has wandered back out into the garden. It is she who has spoken these words to her just now, words that seem to have risen up from deep within Ruth herself.

"Like a phrase of music, the same few notes, playing over and over, round and round, till they land, and finally make their mark…"

She drifts away again, caught up in a new train of thought. *Moon Dreams* shifts into *Time after Time*…

"So," says Ruth, collecting herself once more, "I ought to

be getting back. But before I go, I've brought with me two other photographs that I want to leave with you."

She pulls a large A4 Manila envelope out from her bag and lays it on the table between herself and Clive.

"When George died," she continues, "it was left to me to clear out his flat. The amount of stuff he had you wouldn't believe. He never threw a thing away evidently. He kept everything. Sketch books, contact sheets, strips of negatives, prints. Most of which have never seen the light of day. He left no instructions with them, and I've just kept them in an attic all this time. They're the most extraordinary archive, Clive, and they deserve to be properly curated, then made available, not just in some dusty academic institute, but somewhere they can be readily accessible and seen by anyone who wants to. They tell a story, Clive, an important one, about the unsung lives of ordinary people, children mostly, trying to make sense of the world they're growing up in, wondering just who they'll be. George was on hand to witness all this, over half a century of tumultuous change, and his photographs are a chronicle of those times, a testament to his love for the people he lived and worked and walked among. I think that this is the story you've got to try and tell with your book, Clive. But only if you think you're up to it. If you decide that you think you are, then I'll let you have the whole archive, every last scrap of it, but first – here's a taster. These are two photographs that have never been exhibited in public. They're from his private collection, I suppose you could say, except that George would never have used such a high-flown phrase. He'd have just shaken his head and lit that pipe of his that he was never without."

She slides the envelope towards Clive.

"Go on. Open it. Inside are the first and last photographs George ever took. The first was in 1930, with his beloved *Foth Derby*, his first-ever camera, sold to him by Francis, which he called 'Future Perfect', for it captured a moment in time that had yet to take place, but that would soon be consigned to the past, using technology that wasn't yet available, and the last, taken with the same camera, on the day he died, more than half a century later, just before his accident."

Swallowing hard, Clive opens the envelope. Hardly daring to breathe, he slowly withdraws the two prints.

The first shows Francis, caught off-guard, smiling through a crowd at Barton Aerodrome, on the edge of Chat Moss, on the day of the Kings Cup Air Race, a look of pure joy on his face, as if he cannot believe his good fortune.

The last is a portrait of a motor bike, George's beloved DOT RS. It gleams in the sunlight. Looking more closely, Clive perceives George's reflection caught in the shiny chrome surface, where a moth is casually basking. The expression on George's face is calm, contented, relaxed. Yes, it seems to say, it's been a good life, all things considered...

*

Afterwards Ruth knows exactly what she will do.

Until today, it had been more than twenty years since she was last in Victoria Park. Not since Delphine died. She decides therefore she will take a look at where she used to live. From Park Range she walks up Kent Road West until she reaches Conyngham Road, where she takes a left, following it to where it joins Oxford Place, then right into Daisy Bank Road.

She stands in front of Newbury House. All traces of Delphine are long gone, which is fine, for Delphine would not have wanted it any differently. She has left her mark in other ways. Now the house is a shelter for young men, a home for recovering addicts. Ruth regards it with satisfaction. She can't think why it has taken her so long to reach a decision that, had she been one of her own clients, she'd have been advising her to take quite some time ago.

She turns quickly on her heels. She will grasp the nettle and act the moment she gets back home. She catches the 43 bus from Upper Brook Street to Lapwing Lane, which takes her less than half an hour.

As she opens the front door to *Tulip House*, she is bathed in flecks of red and green and gold from the last of the evening sun filtering through the stained glass panels. She immediately sits behind her desk and fires off two emails.

To: Mr Lao, Vivienne, Surayya, Shawne
From: Ruth

Subject: Proposed Changes to Tulip House

Hi,

This email may come as something of a surprise to you but what it contains is something I have been considering for quite some time. The situation brought about by Covid has focused my thinking more sharply.

I have decided to repurpose Tulip House as a homeless shelter for women and small children. There is urgent need for such provision, as I am sure you are well aware, especially since the pandemic, and it is a matter of great personal importance to me also.

Let me reassure you that I do not envisage this happening for at least two years, for there will be a great deal of work to be done to implement all of the changes that will be necessary. Consequently I hereby give you each twelve months' notice to find yourselves alternative space where you can continue your practice. It goes without saying that you will be free to take with you all of your own individual clients, who you have built up over the years.

If you have any questions – which I'm sure you will – please arrange to call me at your convenience next week. I would like to take this opportunity of thanking you for your loyalty, especially in these current challenging times, which I have always deeply appreciated.

With warmest wishes
Ruth

She saves the email in 'drafts'. She feels no qualms about the decision she has made. A year is ample time for them to make new arrangements for themselves.

The second email is to Meera.

Hi Meera,

I trust you have enjoyed the August Bank Holiday?

I have a proposition I would like to put to you concerning your future employment here at Tulip House. I have attached a copy of the email I have sent to Mr Lao, Vivienne, Surayya and Shawne, in which I outline my plans for a change of use here.

I will not beat about the bush. I would like to offer you the position of Manager of the new shelter. This will mean a significant increase in your salary, the exact details of which we can discuss when we next meet. There will be much to do in making Tulip House suitable for accommodating six mothers and their children, which is the kind of number I am envisaging, particularly in terms of all the alterations that will be needed to be made to the internal structure of the building – additional toilet, shower, cooking and laundry facilities, for example, not to mention the countless legal and planning hoops that will have to be jumped through – and I should like to put you in charge of supervising these changes, again with appropriate financial remuneration.

I hope that you will look favourably on my proposal, and I look forward to hearing your response. Perhaps we might speak via Zoom at some point in the coming week.

Best wishes
Ruth

She knows that Meera will initially tut and disapprove and pour instant cold water on the entire scheme, but she feels equally certain that she will relish the challenge and that she will accept. Builders, electricians, plasterers and plumbers will cross swords with Meera at their peril. They will none of them be any match for her indomitable resolve once her mind is made up.

As Ruth's is now.

She is about to save this email, too, in 'drafts', but then she pauses. Why is she not sending them both right now, before she has a chance to change her mind? Her finger hangs suspended over the keyboard, ready and poised, curved like the talon of a kestrel as it hovers on the wind. Then it pounces and presses 'send'.

*

At the same moment, Clive's hands, too, rest above his laptop, pondering whether to make a beginning. Meeting Ruth has galvanised him. The gift of George's complete archive is like manna from heaven. He has no excuses now. He must put it off no longer. Nor does he want to. His recent brush with mortality has confirmed that time is no longer limitless, and the re-imagining of *The World On Our Doorstep* has rekindled his desire to make something of his own again.

Downstairs he can hear Florence at work on the beginnings of a new song. Snatches of notes on a piano, fragments of lyrics, something about tracing a line, making marks on the land, drift up towards him where he sits in his study at the top of the house, a house which still bears traces of its former occupants, a layer of paint, a creaking floorboard, a pair of initials scratched on a piece of skirting, traces Clive treasures especially.

He lets his fingers type.

'A northern gaze...'

What does he mean by this phrase? It had seemed so right when he first thought of it as the title for his book, something that everyone would know and recognise. But now he's not so sure. Is he just tapping into stereotypes? That gritty, no-nonsense, in-your-face, take-no-prisoners kind of attitude that's supposed to be synonymous with the North? Along with the dry, laconic, self-deprecating wit? Or the hard, unyielding northern light that painters seek out for its unchanging truthfulness of tone? So that people unfamiliar with it can dismiss it with a helpless shrug, as if they just don't get it – which they don't. "Oh, I went to Manchester once," they declare, "but it rained." As if that's all there is to say. Clive had wanted to trade on all of those received misconceptions and fling them back in the reader's face. "Is that what you really think? Well, look again…"

But now he feels quite differently. He picks up the two photographs that Ruth has left with him, the first and last that George ever took, miraculously bookending his life. He now knows exactly what he means by 'a northern gaze'.

It's love.

The same love that's now reflected in the expressions on the faces of those people standing outside their front doors here on Park Range. The world on our doorstep. Fellow travellers in search of a home. Even those who've yet to find one still recognise that look. Because everyone, everywhere, is making that journey.

He knows now what he will write. He hears Florence singing up to him from below. Outside his window the starlings begin their nightly murmuration.

He begins…

*

Ruth, too, sees the starlings swooping, as the sky darkens outside her own window.

And then, suddenly, they descend as one, to roost on ledges and rooftops. The silence which follows is unsettling. She shivers. She is reminded of those days before she started *Tulip House*, after Lily and Roland had died, how she would rattle around by herself in this big, empty house. What she's doing now, by turning it into a safe haven for those who find themselves in need of one, springs from the same impulse which drove Lily to open it up for orphaned children at the end of the War. *Blossoms in the Dust.* Ruth had not consciously realised the connection before, but there it undoubtedly is, and the thought of it pleases her. This is the right thing to do. The house will not be quiet much longer. Already she can hear the echoes of those voices filling the emptiness, the different languages combining to create their own unique symphony.

But they are not here just yet, and Ruth feels the need for company right now. She switches on the internet radio beside her bed. She randomly tunes to all the different stations transmitting simultaneously from right around the world, another kind of murmuration, and one she finds immensely comforting.

Finally the murmuration alights. The radio settles on one station, on one voice. Chloe's. She is just wrapping up her weekend chat show on Reform Radio. *Sharp Talking.*

CHLOE:
> It's been a difficult year, hasn't it, folks? We've never felt so isolated, so cut off from each other, as we try to keep at bay this mysterious foe that we never see, but that we know is in the air, around us all the time, like a fog rising from one of the three rivers in whose confluence this great city of ours was born. A fog that curls around our ankles and wraps itself about us, like a cocoon. It covers our faces, even our eyes sometimes, so that we forget to see what's right in front of us. That we're all in this together, and that, together, we're going to make it through. Whatever our background, whatever our faith, whatever language we speak – and there are more than two hundred spoken here in Manchester – there are more things that unite us than divide us. I'm struck by this every day, as I'm sure you are too, in

the simple acts of kindness that we witness all around us, collecting someone's shopping, putting up signs in our windows, saying 'help', or 'thank you', or simply 'hello', waving from our doorways to neighbours across the streets, stopping to check that a person sleeping rough in a shop doorway is OK, all these and more, these are what will see us through. I've just time before I sign off for the night to tell you about just such an act of simple kindness that's taking place in Victoria Park this weekend. 'The World On Our Doorstep'. An exhibition celebrating the basic human need we all of us have to find a place to call home, and to welcome others to share that home with us. And nowhere offers a finer welcome to the strangers at her gates than Manchester. The show runs for one more day. Try and catch it if you can. It was first curated five years ago by the people of Park Range and has been re-imagined in response to the times we find ourselves in by my old Media Studies tutor from MMU – Clive Archer. Inspired, he says, by the way we all of us came together to clap our carers and key workers. So – what I say to you tonight is this. Wherever you are right now, whatever it is that you're doing, stop. Go outside. Don't worry if you're in your pyjamas – nobody cares. Stand on your doorsteps, or throw open your windows of whichever floor you're on, and start clapping. For yourselves, for each other, and for everyone. We're all in this together, and together we'll see this through. Go. Now. All of you. Let's reconnect. *I've* started. Listen. Have *you*? Come on – I can't hear you. Let's break free from the shackles of this virus. Let's burst out of those cocoons. Let's flex our wings. Like Manchester moths, let's fly to the moon.

Ruth finds herself caught up in the exuberance of Chloe's rallying cry. She flings open the front door of *Tulip House* and begins to applaud. The whole street, she sees, has joined her. The whole city. The whole world. The sound of their clapping pulsates like the beating of thousands of pairs of wings...

Back in Park Range Florence has finished the new song. She joyously segues into the Sinatra classic.

"Fly me to the moon and let me play among the stars
Let me see what spring is like on Jupiter and Mars..."

Clive finds himself joining in. He is typing freely. The tapping of his fingers on the keyboard provides a driving, percussive underscore that grows and swells with the rhythm of the applause sweeping across the city.

"In other words, please be true
In other words, I love you..."

When the clapping finally stops, Ruth returns indoors. She lets her hand linger on the door handles of *Spindle* and *Ariadne*. She climbs the stairs, passing *Io, Europa* and *Gannymede*, up towards the outer moon of *Callisto*, where she has her bedroom. Callisto, a Greek nymph, secret lover of Artemis – Diana – goddess of the hunt, the wilderness, chastity, and the Moon. A satellite composed equally of fire and ice. A surface of scarps and ridges, chains of impact craters, underground oceans and a silicate core.

Like Yasmin.

Ruth has not heard from her in a long while. When first she went away, she was as good as her word. She would send Ruth postcards from each of the Manchesters she visited. With a photo of a prominent landmark on the front, and the same repeated message on the back.

'Wish You Were Here...'

But never a forwarding address, so Ruth could never reply.

Manchester, Ontario.
Manchester, Wisconsin.
Manchester, Seattle.
Manchester, New Hampshire.
Manchester, Montana.
Manchester, Missouri.
Manchester, Georgia.
Manchester, Alabama.

Then further afield – Manchester, Pando, a rubber plantation in Bolivia. Manchester, Nickerie, a coffee farm in Suriname, next to a village called Paradise. Manchester, Jamaica, in Middlesex County, close by Spanish Town, the island's original capital.

Then to Australia – overlooking the Eyre Peninsula not far from Adelaide. Next to Manchester Square, in the Southern Highlands of New South Wales.

All of these and more.

And after she had visited all of the Manchesters, she took herself to all the cities she is twinned with – St Petersburg in Russia, Chemnitz in Germany, Wuhan in China – before that name resounded like a death knell.

Then silence.
Not a word. Not for years.

Ruth climbs into bed in the heart of *Callisto*, the oldest surviving surface in the entire solar system, its rotation locked, to be synchronous with its orbit around Jupiter, sixteen earth days each, always with a dark side, for ever secret and hidden.

She picks up her mobile phone. Chloe's words on the radio come back to her.

"We're all in this together. Together we'll see this through.

Reconnect."

They reverberate around her brain. Reconnect. Reconnect...

She opens Facebook. Into the search box she types Yasmin's name. It takes no time at all to find her. Just over a tenth of a second for the mobile signal in her phone to connect with the satellite orbiting the earth at seven thousand miles an hour, at a height of more than twenty-two miles up into space, and then just over another tenth of a second to bounce back.

And there she is. As large as life. Ruth recognises her instantly. The years have been kind to her. Her smile is a mile wide – quite literally – for that is the distance covered by the satellite in those two tenths of a second. Yet somehow it has been compressed into just three hundred pixels per inch on the screen of her phone.

Ruth is feeling completely overwhelmed. Her brain simply cannot compute these juxtapositions of time and space. Breathing in deeply, she selects the Message option. Her fingers tremble. Slowly she types, using just her thumb, carefully and deliberately.

'Hello...'

She waits.

She waits one minute, five minutes, ten.

Nothing.

Sighing, she lays the phone beside her on the pillow and waits some more.

She closes her eyes.

The second she does so, she hears a loud, insistent ping. She opens her eyes immediately, picks up the phone, and there it is, waiting for her.

Yasmin's reply.

Just a single word.

Yet it contains all that needs to be said.

'Hello...'

12

2021

It begins with a series of phone calls.

1. Lance to Lorrie

"Good morning. Islington Mill. Sunanda speaking. How may I help you...? I'm sorry, Caller. Would you mind repeating that please...? You wish to speak to Ms Zlatan...? I'll just see if she is available. One moment please..."

Sunanda holds the phone to her chest and whispers to Lorrie, who is busy disinfecting all the surfaces of the foyer with anti-bacterial wipes.

"It's for you," she mouths.

Lorrie frowns.

"Can't you deal with it?"

"He's most insistent."

"What's his name?"

"I'm sorry. I didn't catch it."

Lorrie frowns even harder.

"I couldn't understand half of what he was saying."

"Why? Is it a bad line?"

"No, it's not that."

"What then?"

"It's just the words he was using. I think perhaps he's a poet."

"If he's looking to hire the space for a reading, surely he knows we're not allowed to open for public events until May 17th."

"Will you speak to him" asks Sunanda, holding the phone towards her, "please?"

Lorrie wrinkles her nose in disgust at the thought of taking the phone directly from Sunanda's hand, even though she is wearing hygienist's gloves. She signals instead for Sunanda to transfer the call to the switchboard on the desk, which she scrupulously re-wipes before cautiously picking up the receiver.

"Yes?"

"Mi wantin' to speak wid Miss Lorelei Zlatan."

"This is she."

"Ah, mi heart it leap wid joy at di sound. A salmon yuh mek of I."

Lorrie is at a loss for words.

A low chuckle purrs down the phone. Then a voice like warm honey oozes into her ear.

"Mi can just picture yuh, Miss Lorelei. Yuh mouth openin' an' a-closin' like a goldfish. So while yuh swim once more around dat bowl yuh in, let mi introduce I. Lance King, Miss Lorelei, at yuh service. Though mi tink yuh already know who mi am."

Lorrie is flailing. "I'm sorry, Lance, you're not ringing any bells. I'm sure I'd remember…"

"Wah gwaan, gyal…?"

"Er…"

"Dat OK, Miss Lorelei. Mi de yah, mi de yah. Did mi dawta no' tell yuh mi call?"

"Molly…?"

"Dat right. Mi dawta. Mi sweet Carib grackle. She show I yuh photos on di Facebook page. Dancin' on di high wire, spinnin' di flame…"

Lorrie is beginning to understand.

"Fire poi," she explains.

"Dat wah mi sayin', gyal. Mi think it amazin'. Just wah di world need right now."

"Thank you. But is that why you called? Only I…"

"Let mi start from di beginnin', gyal. Yuh sittin' comfortable? Sum time mi live here in di city, but most time yuh find I back on St Kitts, di land o' mi forefathers. Mi organise di festivals, music an' dancin', Capisterre, Molineaux, Green Valley... Den like di rest o' di Carib nations, dat coronavirus it strike we. But no' too badly. Now wi got she on di run. Jus' forty-four cases, zero deaths, twenty percent o' di people get di vaccine already. BA start resumin' di flights cum May..."

"I'm not following you, Lance. Where's this all leading?"

"St Kitts, gyal – weh else? Mi askin' if yuh cum wid mi to walk di high wire at di Green Valley Festival?"

"Oh!" Lorrie holds the phone away from her briefly and mimes an ecstatic celebration, before returning calmly. "When is that, Lance?"

"Whit Monday. In Cayon."

"Let me check my diary. I won't be a moment."

She holds the phone away from her once more, bouncing excitedly on the balls of her feet, while counting slowly from one to ten.

"Yes," she says, trying to maintain a smooth professionalism of tone, "I appear to have a window around then."

"Raz. Den everytin' cool. Di rules say it safe now tuh meet outside. Text I wen a waah gud time fi yuh be. Irie."

And then he is gone.

Lorrie has to pinch herself hard.

Immediately she makes another call.

2. Lorrie to Molly

"Did you send photos of me to your Dad?"

"I can't remember. I might've done. But they're on my Facebook page, where anyone can see them. Why?"

"He just called me."

"Really? When?"

"Now. I've just put the phone down."

"Oh. What did he want?"

"He's offered me a job."

"But you've got a job."

"No, not that kind of job. Just a one-off. A festival in May."

"Aerial work?"

"I think so."

"You *think* so? Don't you *know*?"

"He was a bit vague about the details.

"That's my Dad for you."

"And I couldn't understand what he said half the time."

"The patois stuff?"

"Yes, I suppose."

"Pay no attention to it. It's all an affectation."

"An attractive one, though, don't you think? I love the sound of it. It's like music."

"That's exactly what he wants you to think."

"Oh. I was feeling all excited. Now you've punctured my balloon a little."

"Sorry. I didn't mean to. He's genuine enough. Just make sure you get a contract, that's all."

"Don't worry, I will. I'm good with contracts, they're meat and drink to me, as you well know."

"So is he in Manchester at the moment?"

"I think he must be. He wants to meet up. Has he not called you?"

"No, but that's not unusual. It depends how long he's over for. He's been better since Blessing was born. But then Covid came and, well…"

Lorrie allows a short pause while they both of them silently acknowledge the continuing disruption to their daily lives brought on by the virus. There's such a marked contrast between the *laissez-faire* attitude her friend has towards her family – rarely seeing either of her parents – compared to the almost claustrophobic relationship she has with her own wide extended Polish family. She smiles. She knows which type she prefers. They may all live on top of one another in the mobile home in Cheetham Hill, so that she has little in the way of privacy or space, but she wouldn't want it any other way.

"So when in May will you be going?" asks Molly eventually.

"I'm not sure. Your Dad said something about Whitsun."

"Right. That'll be Green Valley. So long as you're back by the end of July."

"Oh?" responds Lorrie, her antennae immediately quivering. "Why's that then?"

"I don't think I'm quite ready to reveal that yet."

"Ever the enigmatic artist."

"Let's just say I have the beginnings of an idea."

"For M.I.F?" News of Molly's commission for this summer's Manchester International Festival has spread round Islington Mill like wild fire.

"I'd very much like you to be involved – so long as you're back from gallivanting with my Dad by then."

"Don't worry. I will be. I expect I'll only be there a couple of days."

"Not forgetting the two weeks' isolation when you get back. I need you fit and ready for July."

Lorrie can hardly believe what she's hearing. Two festival gigs in the space of half an hour.

"Tell me how it goes," says Molly. "And next time you speak to my father, remind him that he has a granddaughter itching to see him again. We could meet up in the park, tell him. That's if he can remember where it is."

Lorrie laughs. "Sure," she says. She knows her friend is joking.

"Oh," says Molly. "One last thing before I go. Ask him about the Mongoose Play."

"What?"

But Molly has already hung up.

3. Molly to Apichu

Six months earlier Molly had heard Chloe's call to arms on Reform Radio and responded with an enormous smile. Trust Chloe, she had thought. She herself had not gone out into the street to join the wave of applause rolling across the city – Blessing had been having a disturbed night, which she was prone to from time to time, "I've got grow-y legs," she had tearfully complained – but she had heard it coming through the open window, and had silently joined in by miming.

But it was something else that Chloe had said in that magnificent rant of hers, something just casually lobbed in as an aside, which had stayed with her. That remark about more than two hundred languages currently being spoken in Manchester…

The next morning she took her sketch book outside, perched on the brick wall by the gate at the front, and started to draw.

"Uh-oh," said Michael half an hour later, as he brought her a coffee, along with a chocolate chip cookie made that morning by Nadia – "with my help," insisted Blessing, who proudly held it in front of her on a plate, rather like a page carrying a crown for a queen, as she offered it to her mother, taking great care not to stumble or trip.

"Uh-oh," said Michael again.

"Uh-oh," repeated Blessing.

"Your mother's drawing birds again."

Molly instinctively closed the sketch pad.

"Let me see, let me see," demanded Blessing, jumping up and down.

Molly opened the pad once more to reveal dozens and

dozens of drawings of birds, all of them in flight, wheeling about the sky, looking for a place to land. Blessing traced their flight with her chocolatey fingers, which she then proceeded to lick with immense pleasure and satisfaction.

"We know what that means, don't we, Blessing?" said Michael, beaming.

Blessing shook her head amiably.

"It means," said Michael, "that something big is on its way."

"Like an elephant?" asked Blessing.

"Elephants don't fly," teased Michael.

"Dumbo does," said Blessing seriously. "Doesn't he, Mummy?"

"Yes," she said, "but what about Blessing? Can *she* fly?" And she had swept her up in her arms and wheeled her round and about, high above her head.

"Look at me, Daddy," giggled Blessing. "I'm flying. Just like one of Mummy's birds…"

It was true, what Michael said. She always drew birds whenever a new idea was forming. Obsessively, repeatedly. It was the *idea* that was looking for a place to land, not the actual birds.

Now, six months later, she has it. But she has not voiced it out loud yet. Not even tentatively to Michael, who knows not to press her, but to be patient. She'll tell him when she's ready, and he senses that the time is coming soon. Molly senses it too. Dropping that hint to Lorrie is a sure sign of it. But Lorrie's participation is just one part of the jigsaw. There are other pieces to be identified yet, before she can think about trying to articulate just what it is – which she knows she'll have to do soon, if she's to be ready for the Festival. She will need to speak to Khav at the Arts Council about match funding. But first she must check in with Apichu…

"Hi."

"Hi. What a nice surprise. Let me switch to video."

"Me too."

"There. That's better. I'm just hanging out washing, as you can see."

"Have you moved into the cottage yet?"

"Sadly not. We're still in the caravan. There – see? Be careful, Samancha. That girl – honestly, she's fearless. Look who's here, Sam. It's Molly. Don't you want to come and say hello? Apparently not. She's too busy looking for worms."

"Don't worry. Blessing's not here with me either just now. She's with Nadia, which means I've got a whole morning to myself."

"Lucky you. I'd call Tom, only he's on a deadline. Since Covid he's been in much demand for articles on the geopolitical nature of the disease, the way different countries are handling it, mostly from left wing radical online journals, who want to show just how badly the government here's messed up."

"They're not wrong."

"Maybe not, but it's completely unprecedented. Nobody's been prepared for anything quite on this scale before. I think the way each country has dealt with it, or tried to, says more about their national identity, rather than anything else. Even here in Britain we can't agree on what's best, can we? England, Wales, Scotland, Northern Ireland – all of us doing things slightly differently. Who's to say which way's best? Local or global? It's impossible to know. All we can do is to carefully monitor, try not to judge, then learn from each other. That's what Tom thinks anyway, which is why he's in such demand, collating all the different approaches from around the world. Just look at what's been going on back in my old country of Peru. When the pandemic first hit, the government was widely praised for imposing really strict lockdown measures almost before anyone else. Now it has the highest *per capita* death rate from the virus of any country in the world."

"What happened?"

"It's what we've been talking about. Local-v-global, and the tensions between them. When the lockdown really began to bite, especially in the cities, thousands of families fled the capital of Lima for their rural hometowns. With small children and possessions strapped to their backs, they trekked the hundreds of miles through the Andes to return to their families for shelter and support. My family would probably have done the same, leaving the *pueblos jóvenos* of Medalla Milagrosa for their ancestral village in the mountains. I wish they had…" She tails off.

"Are they OK?"

Apichu shakes her head. "They died. My mother, grandmother…"

"I'm so sorry."

"But that came after."

"After what?"

"By April nearly two hundred thousand had requested support from their local districts to return home to the countryside. Many had lost their jobs after businesses were closed and people were ordered to stay indoors from the 16th of March. Some of those who decided it was better to walk home than stay in the capital were repelled by the Army or Police, who fired tear gas in an attempt to stop them. The Government hoped that the pain suffered by its citizens would be short-term and eventually justified by a victory over the virus. Instead, the mass migration of my country's families became symbolic of its failure to understand its people. Back in the *pueblos* the people tried to live as they'd always done, shopping for food every day in the markets – people like my *madre* and *abuela*. If you knew those shanties like I do, Molly, you'd soon see just how rapidly a virus could spread there. Tom says that if the

Government had only paid for all those who wanted to return to the countryside to stay somewhere safe and secure for fourteen days in quarantine, then tens of thousands of lives might have been saved. I think he's probably right."

"So why didn't they?"

"There've been four presidents in Peru in less than a year. I guess they were distracted..."

The two young women remain silent for a while.

"So," continues Apichu, "the cottage has had to take a bit of a back seat for a while. But there's not much left to do. We'll be in there before the year's end, won't we, *chiquita*?" she adds. Samancha has toddled across to her, delightedly dangling a worm from her fingers. Apichu hoists her onto her hip. "Do you want to help me peg out some more washing? That's a good girl. "She puts her down again and hands her a peg, which Samancha promptly pops into her mouth. "*Aiee, mi pequeña burbujita,*" says Apichu, hastily taking it away.

"But we can't, though, can we, live in this... *burbujita*...?"

"*Burbujita, sí* – bubble..."

"... permanently? Sooner or later, it's going to burst."

"Pop, *sí*." Apichu puts her finger into the corner of her mouth and makes a crisp, hollow popping sound. Samancha claps her hands.

"Again," she says. Apichu obliges, and Samancha tries to make the sound herself. She wanders contentedly back towards the caravan, making repeated, unsuccessful attempts, giggling each time.

"Apparently," says Molly, "I adored bubbles as a child. One of the very few memories I have of being with my mum when I was tiny was going into Manchester on the bus to see the Bubble Man in Piccadilly Gardens. He used to blow bubbles so big that I thought I could step right inside them... He's not there now, of course. Another casualty of Covid."

"Did you not see your *madre* very much as a little girl?"

"No," says Molly simply. "I was what you call a Granny Reardun."

"What's that?"

"I was brought up by Nadia – my grandmother, my *abuela*."

"Ah. Your mother was not married?"

"No. But that wasn't the reason. Nadia was just better at it. Michael, Blessing and I still live with her now."

Apichu looks down. "I wish my *madre* could have joined us here. Tom was all in favour. I asked her. But she said no. Now... it's too late."

Molly pauses a moment before continuing.

"Do you still have the piece of cotton I gave you last summer?"

"The sampler, *si*. Look. There it is, hanging on the line." Apichu turns the camera on her phone towards where it flutters in the wind.

Molly smiles. "It was the first piece I ever made on the loom we bought from you."

"Yes, I remember..."

"Me too..."

Both recall an afternoon from the previous year, the day after the summer solstice, when Molly had first seen Lorrie walking the tightrope the previous evening, a rare oasis during that brief interlude between the first and second waves of the pandemic, when everyone had thought it had gone away for good, when Michael and Molly and Blessing had driven in Nadia's sister Farida's car the twelve miles north from Barton Bridge to the Cockey Moor, and Samancha and Blessing had happily cavorted with Tom's dog, Ralph, and Molly had presented Apichu with the sampler. There was washing blowing on the line that day, too. Molly imagines there always is. She's reminded of the Philip Larkin poem, *Wedding Wind*. She pictures Apichu, like the woman in the poem, carrying the chipped pail to the chicken-run, while her husband, Tom, has gone to look at the floods, or repair the slates that have fallen from the roof, then setting it down to simply sit and stare, the wind hunting through clouds, thrashing her apron and sheets on the line, wondering whether so much joy can ever be borne, in this perpetual bodying-forth by the wind, like a thread carrying all her hopes and dreams...

She had asked Apichu then what the sampler made her think of...

Apichu looks at it minutely. It is a small, seemingly abstract design of blue thread meandering between irregularly-shaped patches of greens and browns and greys. Some of the lines picked out in blue disappear from time to time, under a sleeve of dark grey. Molly appears to have followed no pattern to achieve this effect, leaving what has randomly emerged in the fibre apparently to happenstance or chance, with the prospect of any of it ever being repeatable distantly remote. But this is not the case. The algorithm she has used to produce the sample is deliberately complex and has been carefully worked out. Over time, and with a sufficiently long enough piece of cloth – covering several hundred feet or more – the observant eye would be able to detect a pattern, albeit an unpredictable one.

"Did you really make this up as you went along?" Apichu asks.

"To begin with," says Molly, "but I always had an idea in mind."

"Which was...?"

Molly shakes her head and playfully taps the side of her nose with her finger. "Tell me what you see in it first."

"The land," says Apichu. "The sky. Green fields. Rivers."

"And the patches of grey?"

"Buildings, people?"

Molly smiles. "You see it all so instinctively. I wish

everyone saw my work that way."

"Now it's your turn," says Apichu. "Tell me what I'm missing."

"Nothing. That's exactly what I was trying for. Except perhaps…"

"Yes?"

"Do you see where the blue threads disappear beneath the heavy squares of grey?"

"Yes."

"I was thinking of the way the city has tried to force the rivers underground, to bury them, so that we don't see just how filthy and polluted they've become, so that we might forget about them."

"But they keep reappearing, don't they? Here… and here… and here. Water will always find a way."

"Yes. It will."

"Just like we will."

"I hope so…"

"Bubbles are not illusions," she says now, as Apichu hangs the last of her washing on the line. "We know perfectly well they burst. But still we chase them. Like dreams."

Samancha totters back excitedly from the caravan. "Listen, Mummy!" Then she proceeds to place her finger into the corner of her mouth and makes three consecutive perfect popping sounds.

That's what we do, thinks Molly, applauding Samancha. We chase them, we pop them. Then we blow some more. When she was tiny, chasing these dreams with Jenna, she didn't only like those very large ones, which she wanted to climb inside. She liked those that would cluster together, lots and lots of them, each of them quite tiny in themselves, like *she* was, but which could grow to be quite enormous. These, she remembers, were harder to burst.

"You've got an idea for a new piece, haven't you?" says Apichu, grinning broadly.

"Maybe," says Molly. "Maybe. I'll keep you posted…"

4. Khav to Molly

"Yo, Moll!"

"Yo, Khav!"

"Hey!"

"Hey!"

"Just got word your application for match funding for the Festival commission's been approved."

Molly breathes an enormous sigh of relief. "Thanks, Khav. That's brilliant."

"Brilliant? It's fuckin' awesome."

Molly laughs.

"You'll be getting official confirmation from the Arts Council tomorrow by email. So make sure you check your inbox, innit?"

5. Lorrie to Sunanda

"Lorrie? I thought you'd gone?"

"Almost. I'm at the airport, just going through the endless security."

"Good luck. Did you settle on a name finally?"

This has been the topic of much conversation between them since Lance first offered Lorrie the gig.

"I did."

"Well?"

"It was my family's idea. It's what they call me here at home. 'What else should you be known by?' my Uncle Pavel said…"

"What is it?"

"Oh – sorry. I was distracted by having to juggle hand sanitiser, face mask, mobile phone and my carry-on."

"If anyone can manage that, you can."

"Lorelenka," she says at last. "Lorelenka."

"Perfect. What does Lance think?"

"Oh, you know? He's very laid back about it. 'Whateva rocks yuh boat, gyal'. But that's not why I'm calling."

"No, I didn't suppose it was."

"I need you to make some calls for me. For Molly."

"Sure. Shoot."

Sunanda picks up her pen and a pad, primed and ready, then listens as Lorrie outlines what she needs her to do.

"OK. Got that. Will do. Have a great trip. See you after you come out of quarantine…"

6. Sunanda to Tracy

BBC
NORTH WEST
TODAY

UK COTTON BACK IN PRODUCTION IN MANCHESTER

Chloe Chang reporting online, 17th May 2021

Long before Manchester had football, it had cotton.

The city and surrounding region was built on the success of spinning and sewing during the industrial revolution, giving rise to its catchy nickname, Cottonopolis. But as production slowed, moved off-shore and we began to import more and more of our textiles, those beautiful red brick mills in the North-West fell silent. Like Tower Mill (*pictured below*) in Dukinfield, close to the Ashton Canal.

Now, ending a 40-year hiatus, cotton is once again back on the production line in this, and other mills like it, throughout the county.

After a £6m investment, textile manufacturer *Lancashire Fine Cottons* has started spinning cotton imported from the sunny fields of southern California to here in Greater Manchester, producing yarn that's being used right across the region in a newly reopened supply chain spanning different former mill towns.

"It's really re-engaged the weavers, finishers and dyers to pull together and forge those chains back again," says Tracy Hawkins, Managing Director of Tower Mill. "There's an enormous appetite for provenance and quality, especially if it's Manchester-made. That's what we provide."

I decided to follow this supply chain – from bale to rail – challenging businesses in the North-West to make a garment from cotton in its rawest form, all the way through to the finished article.

To Dye For

So, with a bobbin of freshly spun Manchester cotton in hand from Tower Mill, I headed 45 miles north to the town of Blackburn.

We arrive and hand across our yarn. Colour is the next stage of the process.

"We're going to take this into our dye house," says Anthony Green, CEO of *Blackburn Yarn Dyers*. "We're going to load it onto a dye stand, we're going to bleach it, we're going to dye it, then we're going to dry it."

The whole process should take about eight hours, I'm told...

Good Yarn

Our bobbin then joins scores of others, submerged into a huge boiling kettle of dye. A short while later, it reappears from behind clouds of steam as newly-dyed bright yellow cotton yarn. Then, after a trip through a huge dryer, our bobbin is fresh and dry.

I'm now back in the car and heading up the road to Burnley.

Spin Cycle

Debbie Catterall is the current boss of *John Spencer & Sons*, a sixth-generation family weaving business owned by the great-great-great grandson of the original founders. The mill is the last remaining traditional cotton weaver in Burnley.

"Our order book is really healthy," she says. "The number of developments that we're doing have huge potential, so the next six months' forecast is looking great. So much so that we're having to put on extra shifts and recruit additional staff to fulfil that need."

This is just one of many good news stories for Manchester's renaissance textile manufacturers.

Stitched Up

I hand over my yellow bobbin and it's mounted on to the loom. Within moments, the loom gets to work, and at rapid speed! The yarn is interlaced and a woven sun-bright fabric begins to appear. I'm beginning to see the emergence of a garment I could soon be wearing!

Another 25 miles back down the M66, and I'm back in Manchester for the last stage of this reconnected supply chain. With yellow cloth in hand I arrive at *Private White VC*, another factory that has survived the turbulent changes of clothing manufacture.

At the peak of the industry, 90 years ago in 1911, an

estimated 8 billion yards of cloth were produced. Today we're making this yellow shirt from little more than 2 yards. But it is Manchester-spun, Lancashire-dyed, Lancashire-woven – and now Manchester-stitched.

James Eden is the Supervisor at *Private White VC*: "I don't think we'll ever see a return to the halcyon days of Cottonopolis," he says. "But on a local, national and global scale, there are huge opportunities for businesses and brands like ours to create sustainable, viable and ultimately very profitable businesses by making things here again in Manchester, and selling to an international marketplace."

Sewn Up

After a 100-mile round trip across Lancashire, I've seen the rawest of materials become the finest of garments, cutting out the need for cheap imports from other countries.

In an area rooted in centuries of textile history, expertise and resounding pride, the cotton process is slowly being sewn back together.

*

"Am I speaking to Tracy Hawkins?"

"Yes. And you are…?"

"Sunanda Biswas. Islington Mill. We're an Art Gallery in Salford. I'm calling on behalf of one of our artists, Molly Wahid."

"Yes – I've heard of her."

"She was wondering if you might be able to assist her in the production of a specially-designed piece of textile for an installation she's been commissioned to present for this summer's Manchester International Festival...?"

"Tell me more..."

Sunanda briefly summarises the idea for Molly's design. Listening on the other end, Tracy's jaw drops at the sheer scale of the ambition.

"Wow," she says, when Sunanda has finished. The vision it evokes is irresistible. "I have to be honest. We've never attempted anything quite like this before. I won't pretend it's not going to be a challenge. But please tell Molly that we're definitely up for it."

"That's great to hear, Tracy. I'll let Molly know at once, and I'm sure she'll be in touch with you directly to finalise the details..."

7. Sunanda to Dmitiri

MANCHESTER MUSEUM

Entomology

Manchester Museum's worldwide collection of bugs is estimated to house some two and a half million specimens and is thought to represent the third largest entomological depository in the UK. The origin of Manchester's insect collections dates back to the foundation of the Museum by the 'Manchester Society for Promotion of Natural History' following the demise of Major Leigh Philips, who donated on his death in 1814, his illustrious *Cabinet of Curiosities*, containing hundreds of *diptera*, different types of fly found in Manchester at the time, as well as his groundbreaking early observations on the emergence of the melanic version of the peppered moth – *biston betularia carbonaria* – better known as the Manchester Moth.

"Dmitri Logunov, Entomology Department, Manchester Museum. How may I be of assistance?"

"Good morning, Mr Logunov. My name's Sunanda Biswas and I'm calling on behalf of the artist Molly Wahid. As part of her research for a new outdoor art installation she is preparing, she is hoping she might visit your collection of Manchester Moth specimens and see them for herself at first hand. She understands that the Museum is temporarily closed just now, due to coronavirus, but she is wondering whether it might be possible to arrange a private visit, in which you could show her round – socially distanced of course, having taken a lateral flow test first – and give her the benefit of your renowned expertise?"

Dmitri is both intrigued and flattered.

"Well, Ms Biswas, I'm sure we should be able to find a way to make that happen. Leave it with me. I'll call you back in a few days…"

8. Sunanda to Jackie

"Sure, Sunanda," says Jackie Wells, CEO of *Rope & Rigging*, "we could do that. What's the span again between the two buildings?"

"Four hundred and fifty feet."

"That's quite a walk."

"But doable?"

"Oh yeah. No problem. You've got the necessary permissions?"

"We have."

"And you want a safety net beneath, I assume?"

"Definitely."

"That's good. We wouldn't go ahead otherwise. Right – we'll send someone to do a site visit next week, OK?"

"Can you make it the week after? That's when the artist will be available. She's currently in St Kitts."

"Lucky girl. Call us when she gets back, and we'll fix a time to fit in with her."

"Great. Will do. Thanks, Jackie…"

9. Sunanda to Richard

The last of the calls Sunanda has been tasked by Lorrie to make proves the most difficult. Not the phone call itself, which could not go better, but in finding out just who it is she needs to speak to in the first place.

When Lorrie first adds it to the list, Sunanda thinks it will be relatively straightforward, simply a matter of sourcing, then hiring what Molly has requested, But it proves the opposite. They're all either unavailable, too expensive, or still not Covid-compliant. She has to go directly back to Molly to find out precisely what she needs, and how she imagines it being used. Once Molly has explained her vision to her, Sunanda is blown away. She now understands exactly what is required, and she makes it her number one priority. It's like following a series of clues in a treasure hunt, but eventually she stumbles upon gold in the unlikely form of Richard and Austin.

BALLOON RETIREMENT HOME

Welcome to the Balloon Retirement Home, which was set up in 2011 by Richard Gahan and Austin Heginbottom to preserve those "once-loved-but-not-forgotten" hot-air balloons from disposal or scrapping for the future benefit of pilots, spotters, photographers & enthusiasts, anyone, in fact, with a general interest in ballooning…

"Yeah," says Richard, when Sunanda finally tracks him down, "we'd be up for that. It sounds amazing."

"Great. Would you mind telling me a bit about yourself, so I can then run this all past Molly?"

"Sure. No problem. I live in Tottington, near Bury. I was born just a couple of miles away in Holcombe Brook. I remember first getting excited by balloons when I heard about the Zeppelin Airship raid on my local primary school during the 1st World War, and that this was on the exact same spot that James Sadler landed after he became the first Englishman ever to take to the skies in a hot air balloon in 1775. It just seemed amazing to me that you could take off from a field on Angel Meadow in Manchester, drift for hours up in the blue, then come down to land right beside where I went to school. It still does. I started piloting balloons myself fifteen years ago. That's when I met Austin. We're both financial consultants by day, but ballooning is our passion. We go all over Europe, flying to festivals, giving people rides, spreading the word. We both noticed just how short-lived an actual balloon's life appeared to be, with many ending up on the scrap heap, including some real vintage models. So – ten years ago we decided to start rescuing any we came across that were on the point of being chucked out. That's how the Retirement Home came into being. We've dozens of balloons now, all shapes and sizes – you'd be surprised. We might even have the exact one Molly is looking for. Or something like it. I'll get back to you."

"Would you? That'd be great. Molly'll be thrilled…"

10. Tanya to Molly

"Molly?"

"Hi, Tan. Thanks for getting back to me."

"You're welcome. Khav said you had some queries?"

"I do. Actually, I'm hoping you might be able to do more

than just answer questions."

"OK. Fire away."

"Khav's told you about the commission?"

"Not really. She said it'd be better if I heard it first from you."

"Fair enough. I'll do my best. It's really a very simple idea, but as is so often the case, that simplicity masks a whole bunch of complex stuff, combining lots of different elements – set, costumes, props, performers. Most of these are pretty much sorted now – or they will be – but I'm still struggling with the music. Actually, it's not really music I'm thinking about so much, as creating some kind of soundscape."

"Right. What do you have in mind?"

"That's just it. I'm not sure. But what I do know is this. The sound lies at the very heart of the whole concept behind the event."

"No pressure then," says Tanya.

Molly smiles. She's always liked Tan. Ever since she first met her at MMU. Nothing phases her.

"Here's what I think," she begins. "Forgive me if it kind of meanders."

"No worries."

"I want some people to be able to speak some text – actually, lots of people, about two hundred, live and amplified – and I want this speaking to be somehow converted into singing. I'm not talking some crappy, jingly Songify app here. I'm looking for something that's more... I don't know... epic... monumental."

"OK. I could do that."

"Really?"

"Sure."

"Brilliant. But here's the thing. They're not all going to be speaking the same text at the same time, or at the same tempo – some'll be quick, some'll be slow, and some'll be in between –

and they'll all be overlapping, interweaving, joining as one. And I want it, like I said, to be *live*, in the moment, unpredictable, and *random*. The random nature of it is crucial to me. It's kind of the point. Aleatory, you know? Like the throwing of a dice? There *is* a pattern underlying it, but it's not immediately detectable, so that when, in the end, everything does all come together, which it will, you've no idea how it happened." She pauses. "Sorry, Tan. I guess I'm not making much sense."

"No, you are. I get what you're after, and I reckon I know how to achieve it."

"You do?"

"It'll require a special type of creative coding."

"Creative coding? What's that?"

"It's just a different approach to the way you use computer code, with an emphasis on the aesthetic as much as the functional. There's already quite a lot of software programmes out there – Cinder, Jungulator, Max MSP – but I'll probably make my own."

"And you can do that?"

"I can try."

"You're a genius, Tan."

"Wait till you hear what I come up with first."

"I have complete faith in you. I'm also wondering if you can do something similar with the visuals…?"

"Let's not run before we can walk, eh Moll?"

"OK. Point taken. When do you think you might have something I can listen to?

"Give me a week…"

11. Molly to Lorrie

"Hi, Lorrie. I just thought I'd check in now that you're back."

"Thanks, Molly. Yes – I flew back from St Kitts ten days ago. I've just another four days of self-isolating to go – which is easier said than done here in Collingham Street."

Molly knows what she means. She's visited Lorrie where she lives a couple of times, a collection of adjoining mobile homes, which house all of her large extended family. Molly remembers being introduced to aunts and uncles and grandparents and cousins, as well as Lorrie's father, all of whom were constantly trooping in and out of each other's caravans. It was noisy, chaotic, but hugely enjoyable. She had been made to feel immediately welcome. Nobody seemed to mind at all that she would confuse Pavel with Krysztof, Lena with Agniewska. "Don't worry about it," Lorrie's father Milosz had told her. "We're never sure ourselves." But if anyone can manage to self-isolate there, thinks Molly, it will be Lorrie, whose meticulous and obsessive attention to detail has become something of a legend to everyone at Islington Mill.

"So how was it? The Festival, I mean?"

"Oh," says Lorrie, somewhat evasively, "it was fine."

"Fine? Is that all?"

"No – it was great."

"Was it Green Valley?"

"St Mary Cayon, yes. I did three shows in the end on successive nights. Lance had rigged a wire for me slung above the stage, from where I'd do poi in between the different acts."

"How was he?"

"Who?"

"My Dad – who do you think?"

"Oh," says Lorrie, somewhat distractedly. "Fine." That word again. "Why?"

"Well," says Molly, "not to put too fine a point on it, he's always been a bit of a ladies' man. Or, as my Mum would say, 'He can't keep his dick in his pants'."

"Oh, I see what you mean. I didn't see that much of him, to

be honest, he was really busy, but whenever I did, he couldn't have been nicer. The perfect gentleman in fact."

"Really?" What's Lorrie not telling me, wonders Molly...?

Actually, she'd found him curiously old-fashioned. The epitome of old world chivalry and charm. He behaved with impeccable taste and good manners throughout her stay, maintaining a discreet distance at all times, not so much, she felt, because of Covid, but more out of respect for her. He met her at Golden Rock Airport, then put her into a cab, which took her to a hotel in Basseterre. She was puzzled. She had expected to stay with him. Molly had told her that he had a large, ramshackle apartment in the old French quarter of Capisterre. "He'll probably put you up there," she had said, "there's plenty of room." But no. The cab took her the eight miles along the Kim Collins Highway to a hotel in Cayon.

"Mi call round lata," he said. "Mi show yuh di stage."

The hotel turned out to be rather splendid. *Ottley's*. A converted plantation house from when the island grew sugar, surrounded by lush forest, overlooking the black sandy beach of Hermitage Bay. But she felt wrong-footed. She'd been hoping that Lance would show her the sights of the island – which he did, though not until a couple of days later...

In the meantime, she decided to make the most out of this unexpected turn of events. She had never before stayed in any kind of hotel anywhere, let alone one as grand as this, and she quickly realised she could very easily acquire a taste for it. *Ottley's* had a private pool and a cocktail lounge with rattan furniture. Her room had a shower and a Jacuzzi, a balcony overlooking tropical gardens. She immediately made herself at home there, taking advantage of every amenity on offer. A girl could get used to this, she thought...

Extract from Lorrie's Journal:

Later that evening Lance was as good as his word. He showed up just as the sun was setting in what I later learned was a 1956 Pontiac convertible, decked out in the island's colours of red, green and gold. He insisted I sat in the back, while he drove us to Basseterre. He headed straight for Port Zante, to Timo's Bar, where everyone knew him. They showed us to a table overlooking the ocean. We had shrimp and squid. He talked to me about the island, the festivals, his life there. He also talked a lot about you, Molly, how proud he is of what you've accomplished, his delight in having a grandchild...

The next day was mainly taken up with rehearsals at Green Valley. He was around, but we didn't get to hang out. Everyone was too busy. After he'd dropped me back at Ottley's the previous night, he'd said a cab would arrive to take me to Molineux, where the stage was set up, even though it was less than a mile and a half away, which it duly did. That evening, before the show started, he sent me a bouquet of red poincianas to the small tent that served as my dressing room, the island's national flower.

I didn't see him after the show, but the same cab took me back to Ottley's, where a message was waiting for me at reception.

"Raz, gyal," it read, "yuh di talk o' di town."

The following morning, just as I was finishing my breakfast out on the terrace, he called to say he'd pick me up in an hour. "Mi wanna show yuh di sights..."

Once again he acted with great courtesy and politesse, almost as if he was my chauffeur. He would open the car door for me before I got in or out. We drove close to the volcanic crater of Mount Liamuiga, we drank rum at Clay Villa, he showed me the petroglyphs carved into the rocks at Palmetto

Point, we watched brown pelicans taking off from Great Salt Pond...

That night there were flowers once more waiting for me before the performance...

Afterwards, when the show was over, Lance invited everyone who'd been involved in the Festival in any way to join him for a party at The Mongoose Beach Bar in Basseterre, including me. Once again he picked me up in his 1956 Pontiac, but with several others this time, so we didn't get a chance for further talk...

The party was good. Lance DJ'd it, and he was in his element. We danced till dawn. Then, as the sun was rising over Nevis Peak, just as some of us were thinking about starting to drift away, we were halted in our tracks...

They came out of the forest on the slopes of the Conaree Hills, a whole barrel of them...

We heard them before we saw them, the rhythm of their feet, stamping in the earth to the accompaniment of steel drums, the skittering of stones down the mountainside, like the start of an avalanche. Then we saw the clouds of dust, kicked up by their coming, out of which the entire rag-tag army of them finally emerged. The players, the actors, the mummers. The performers of the Mongoose Play, after whom the beach bar had been named. They were wearing animal masks with feathered head-dresses, walking on stilts, clashing pan lids with wooden sticks, bellowing like bulls, as they crashed into the square to present their pageant...

More of a dance than a drama, chanted in Creole, it told the story of how, long ago, St Kitts became overrun with snakes and rats. Actors personifying these roles darted in and out among us, with slithering coils of rope and six-inch nails hammered into planks of wood for snapping jaws with barbed wire teeth. To rid themselves of this pestilence, the islanders imported an army of mongi. These creatures of nightmare leapt upon the snakes and rats, tossing them high into their air. They seized them in their mouths and shook them till they were dead.

A great celebration ensued, a party not unlike the one we'd all been enjoying ourselves just a few hours before, but the mongi were not satisfied. Having rid the island of the rats and snakes, they now set about sating their voracious appetites instead upon the native chickens. They devoured these in a matter of minutes, leaving nothing but the bones and feathers, which they spat out contemptuously into the dust. Next they turned their attention towards us, and slowly they began to advance...

We knew it was all a pretence, a game of make-believe, an ancient folk tradition, but against the backdrop of a global pandemic, a deadly invisible virus, it exerted a powerful hold over all of us who'd stayed to watch it unfold, so that none of us could avert our gaze, least of all me.

Just as the mongi threatened to overwhelm us, Lance was at my side.

"Some time di cure," he said, "worse dan di disease..."

At which point actors operating giant puppets representing the Red-Tailed Hawk of the Caribbean swooped out of the sky, the sun at their backs, their feathered wings glinting in the light, to pluck the mongi out of the air...

And then they were gone. Vanished. Like the witches in Macbeth.

"Di earth ave bubbles as di wata ave," whipered Lance, as if reading my thoughts. "An' dem yah a o' dem"

"Where?"

"Inna air, inna tin air. Dem melt as breath inna di wind..."

In spite of the sun's warmth, I felt a shiver down my spine.

"It only a story," said Lance.
"Is it?"
"Live an' let live."
"If only..."
"It a tricky balance," he said.
"It is," I replied. "Like walking a tightrope..."
He looked at me then and smiled. "Yuh got it in one, gyal."
I smiled back.
"Time wi did pan wi way – yuh no' wa fi miss yuh flight..."
"No. I don't..."
Laughing, he escorted me back to his red, green and gold Pontiac, and dropped me back at Ottley's...

I didn't see him again till it was time for me to leave. He was at the airport the next morning, having come to say goodbye. His behaviour remained irreproachable. Even so, I had the distinct impression I was being gently wooed, courted almost, as if by some medieval troubadour...

Just as my flight was called, he placed a red poinciana behind my ear and kissed my hand, nothing more, and I laughed. I confess to feeling quite a frisson. I think I might have blushed. If I did, he said nothing that might have drawn attention to it. He merely waved his hand.
"Bi gaan, gyal," he said. "Lata. Mi see yuh lickle more..."

"The perfect gentleman," says Lorrie again.

If Molly is surprised by Lorrie's account of the way her father has acted, she gives no indication of it. In fact nothing about her father surprises her. Instead she moves immediately into talk about her idea.

"So," she says, "here's what I want you to do as part of my installation."

Lorrie's eyes widen in astonishment as Molly explains.

"Yes," she says. "Oh yes. Most definitely, yes..."

12. Chloe to Molly

"Hi, Molly. Congratulations on the commission."

"Thanks, Chloe."

"Would you care to comment?"

"What? Are you interviewing me now?"

"Sorry. Old Habits. I could do, though, if you like?"

"Who for?"

"*Reform Radio* probably. We're doing a series of features on the Festival coming up."

"Hmm. Maybe. I'm not sure. I know it's a cliché, but I prefer to let my work speak for itself."

"Why do artists always say that?"

"Because it's true."

"Sounds like a get-out-of-jail-free card to me."

"You're probably right. It's easier, I suppose. Michael's always saying I should cultivate a less stand-offish approach with the media."

"He might have a point."

"He does. I'm just nervous, I guess."

"About what?"

"Sounding pretentious?"

"You wouldn't Molly. That just isn't you."

"Pigeon-holing it, then. Limiting the way people see it. Words can do that sometimes."

"Try me."

"OK... Here goes..."

"Take your time."

"And this is just between you and me? You're not sitting there with notebook in hand?"

"I promise."

"I try to resist definitions. But I suppose what I am is a conceptual artist. I draw, I make short films, recently I've taught myself to weave. But really these are all different versions of the same thing. A kind of sketch book testing out random thoughts until a new idea presents itself."

"So what's the idea this time?"

"That's just it, Chloe. I'm realising that, whatever medium I might choose, my ideas are cut from the same cloth."

"And what cloth is that?"

"Here. This city. Where you and I both live. Where we grew up. Even though our families came from somewhere else. Manchester. It's both my muse and my subject. And also my canvas. I want to show work that couldn't be made anywhere else. But at the same time I want it to connect and resonate everywhere."

"A tall order."

"Do you think so? I happen to believe that the themes I'm interested in are universal."

"Which are...?"

"Home. Belonging. Hope."

"OK. So in that case couldn't you make the work anywhere too?"

"I don't think so, no."

"Why's that?"

"For one thing, Manchester's who I am. I think the artist has to have a genuine connection with the work she makes, and the place she makes it. She has to inhabit it. To breathe the same air. At least *I* do. For me, it has to be personal. Otherwise it's in danger of not ringing true, of not being authentic, and the public soon see through that. If they can feel that what you're making matters – *really* matters – to you, deep down, in a way that's truly fundamental, then they're willing to come on the journey with you, to see if it has meaning for them too."

"Like with your *Thin Blue Line* installation three years ago?"

"Exactly. I couldn't have made that piece if I hadn't been trying to make sense out of the journeys made across this city by my grandfather, and *his* father before him. I was trying to make my own journey as a kind of homage. The public may only have seen long lines of thin blue tape, criss-crossing the city, all joining up at *The Etihad*. Some of them may simply have thought it was all just some kind of tribute to a football team. But that's OK. It was a kind of pilgrimage, and I was tapping into those yearnings and longings we all of us have to be part of such journeys. Others may have thought it was some reference to police tape at a crime scene. The fact that *The Etihad* is built on the site of a former coalfield, which was closed before it needed to be, might have made them think I was making some kind of political statement."

"And were you?"

"Not specifically, no. But if that's how some people want to respond, I'm fine with it. That's why I'm nervous about talking about the work. I don't want to tell people what to think before they see it."

"What *do* you want then?"

"For them just to experience it, I guess. Then find their own personal connection with it."

"So what did the thin blue line mean for you?"

"All of those things, I think, and more. I chose blue specifically because my grandfather and great-grandfather were both draughtsmen. They each used a blue pencil to make their own marks, on maps and plans, architects' drawings and the like. I could have used any colour, but I chose blue because it was personal to *me*. In the end, people followed its trail from wherever they started their journey. I'm attracted to the random nature of that, how every day, on our way to work, or prayer, or recreation, or family, we find ourselves cheek by jowl with thousands of people we neither know nor recognise, yet here we all are, united by a common purpose, sharing the same space, inhabiting the same city, breathing the same air like I said, all of us making journeys, all of us alighting together, in search of somewhere we can call home."

"Home, belonging, hope."

"Yes. Sorry. Once I start, I find it hard to stop. Another reason why I prefer not to talk about my work, but just let people experience it for themselves."

"Fair enough. But is there anything at all you can say about the new work?"

"Are you *sure* you're not recording this?"

"No. Honestly. I'm just genuinely interested, that's all."

"Will you be coming along?"

"You bet."

"Well, in that case, I'll just say this. For the last year we've all been shut away from each other, locked down in our own individual bubbles, and I wanted to make something that could only be experienced by people being *together*, coming out of those bubbles and being back on the streets again, shoulder to shoulder, side by side. I was inspired partly by something *you* said on the radio, Chloe, some six months ago…"

"Really? I'm intrigued…"

"Partly by something Clive said on the day of that George Wright Exhibition…"

"The day Petros, Lorrie, Khav and I graduated…"

"And the day I started…"

"Something about 'the principal thing…' "

"Written on the domed ceiling of Central Library…"

"Painted by George Wright…"

"But mostly to celebrate Manchester. And St Peter's Square seemed the perfect place to do it."

"Because of the Library?"

"Partly."

"Because of Peterloo then?"

"Not specifically. But it's a symbol, isn't it, that resonates? Manchester's had a fair amount of shit flung at it down the years. There've been earthquakes, hurricanes, firestorms, terror attacks and suicide bombs. But nothing breaks us, does it? The city was built on three Cs – Cotton, Coal and Canals – and when those three collapsed, there was a fourth C – a Conflagration. And out of that conflagration the city has re-imagined itself – through another C – Culture. Art heals, Chloe. I really believe that. It transforms, it regenerates, it creates. Another C. And here are two more – Crucible and Communion. That's what I'm aiming for."

"And its title?"

"Ornaments of Grace?"

"Yes. Exactly."

"I believe that applies to all of us. We're all ornaments of grace…"

*

Manchester EveningNews

15th June 2021

BRADFORD PIT MEMORIAL

Latest Plans Revealed

Chloe Chang reporting…

I first interviewed Lauren Murphy three years ago, while I was working for the much-missed local radio station *MCR Live*. A Design Graduate from Manchester Metropolitan University, and the granddaughter of a miner who had worked at Bradford Colliery, Lauren had set up the Bradford Pit Project, in her words, to "ensure that the people and places that contributed to the development of Manchester will be marked and celebrated."

Set up in 2013, the project has been on a long journey. As well as collecting stories, photographs and other memorabilia, the long-term goal has always been to put in place a permanent Memorial in the form of a statue on the site of the former mine, which is now occupied by *SportCity* and *The Etihad*, home of Manchester City, who have been keen supporters of Lauren's ambitions.

In order to realise the Memorial Lauren carried out an extensive community engagement programme and archive project, over a three-year period from 2014 to 2017, in order to evidence the need to permanently mark the area's rich heritage. Following this, a successful proposal to develop the Memorial was then put forward to Manchester City Council, who, after a lengthy period of concept design development, finally, six months ago, gave their approval for the project to go ahead Now, this week, work has begun at last to install the statue, which is in the form of an etched glass engraving, housed in a cast-iron frame.

"I am beyond thrilled," said Lauren yesterday, when a crane began lowering the Memorial, designed by long-term partners in the project, Broadbent Studios, into its final resting place.

The Memorial depicts photographs of miners superimposed onto a map of the former colliery. The site it is to occupy is the same as that used by the Salford-born conceptual artist, Molly Wahid, three years ago for her thrilling *Thin Blue Line* installation, in which lines of blue thread led crowds to this exact spot, where she rose, winged like an angel, from a cairn of coal. Molly has been commissioned to present her latest commission,

Ornaments of Grace, at next month's Manchester International Festival.

Meanwhile work will continue on the remaining elements of the Bradford Pit Memorial and surrounding landscape over the next few weeks, and, under current restriction and limitations, plans are being reviewed for an official small-scale unveiling event for the miners and their families.

But later this year, as early as August perhaps, when fans are once more permitted to return to *The Etihad* to watch live football for the start of the new season, it will be seen by more than fifty thousand people every time that Manchester City play their games there.

"When they pulled the mine down they cleared away everything," recalls former miner, Michael Doherty. "It was a wasteland for years until they started developing, which was a brilliant thing to do. But there was nothing to remind the community, the people passing, of what used to be here. Now everyone will be able to see this Memorial and say, 'There was a pit here once. What a great job they did...'"

Hear, hear!

*

On the same day less than half a mile away from where the Bradford Pit Memorial is being lowered into place, another, even smaller ceremony is taking place. It involves just a single person. Petros. He is planting a tree in Philips Park Cemetery. This, too, is a kind of memorial. He is commemorating not someone who has died, so much as someone who is starting again. Himself. He has chosen the spot where he is planting the tree with particular care, and for a particular reason. Or two, to be more precise. The type of tree he is planting has also been chosen for a particular purpose.

It is close to a statue of an angel, as near to the bank of the River Medlock as he can reach at this remote stage in its journey towards its confluence with the Irwell...

It is exactly ten months to the day since he first decided to embark upon this pilgrimage – which is what he now understands this journey he is making to be – after what had been something of an epiphany for him. That, too, had occurred while looking down upon the Medlock – Manchester's forgotten river – from a bridge on Baring Street, close by Piccadilly Station. He had that morning just closed on a deal to sell four apartments he'd converted in the former Co-op Tobacco Factory in Angel Meadow for a cool quarter million each. At the last minute the deal had almost been scuppered by a shuffling old bag lady trying to hustle him for some change. Fortunately he had managed to palm her off with a ten pound note just seconds before his clients arrived, who appeared not to see her, as she vanished down some convenient rat-hole, almost as if she had never been, leaving nothing behind but the memory of the angel tattoo inked into her unwashed shoulder, which Petros had caught a fleeting glimpse of as she thrust out a gnarled hand towards him, and her threadbare coat had momentarily slipped from her arm...

Afterwards he had met up with Chloe at a trendy artisan coffee shop she knew in Ancoats called *The Colony*. Chloe, as she invariably did, had given him a hard time, making him question the morality of what he was doing, but with such a light, almost playful touch that he could never take offence. The opposite, in fact. He found himself agreeing with her.

His feet had automatically taken him there. The bridge at Baring Street. He was on his way to look at a new development nearby, one of many planned for the regeneration of the Mayfield area behind the station, what the investors were referring to as 'Piccadilly East', the next hot spot for young entrepreneurs. Until recently it had been a complete no-go area, the seediest of red-light districts, where business was carried out hurriedly and squalidly in bricked-up railway arches surrounded by dirty needles, discarded syringes, and foraging rats.

Now, already, squares have been cleared, coffee shops are springing up alongside the gentrified Rochdale Canal, a mere stone's throw away from the city's bustling gay quarter, with its bars and night clubs, its drag queens and comics, its murals and window-boxes. Even the Medlock, too, is ripe for restoration, it would seem.

It's certainly ripe, thinks Petros, as the stench of rank and foetid sewage rises up from beneath the bridge. But it will not be so easily reclaimed as the canals around the city have been. So much of it has been culverted, blocked up, filled in and abandoned, hidden away from the millions who walk, drive or ride across it in the trams each day, like a dirty secret. It has, Petros realises, been a constant thread stitched throughout his life…

When his Great-great-great-grandfather Konstantin first arrived here from Chios in the 1830s, he crossed the Medlock near Ardwick, which was at that time the southern boundary of the city. He settled in Salford, not far from where the Medlock still joins the Irwell today, at Potato Wharf in the Castlefield Basin. Konstantin's son, Vassily, set up the family Mastic Works in Ducie Street Warehouse less than a half a mile away at the Irwell's confluence with the Irk, and Petros's father, Alexis, still has an office next to Peter House on Oxford Road, beneath which the Medlock flows via one of it many culverts. A muddy stretch of it is still visible at the back of MMU, where Petros was a student, and now, in this moment of self-examination, he stands on the Baring Bridge looking down into another tiny outflow of it. If it were not so murky, after more than a century of pollution at the hands of the tanneries, dyers and chemical works that have poured their effluent into it, he might just be able to make out his reflection in it, even on this cloudy, overcast day, but he cannot. No clues come to him from its impervious, stagnant waters.

But when he looks more closely, he can see that the river is not in fact as putrid as it is widely held to be. It doesn't exactly flow, but it does trickle – just. Signs of life returning to it have been noted by enthusiastic birdwatchers, who have left a record of their sightings on a temporary hoarding on the bridge, which Petros looks at now. Canada geese have been spotted, as have finches, robins and thrushes, along with dunnocks, wagtails and dippers – even a kingfisher and a sparrowhawk. As if to demonstrate the fact, a moorhen casually cruises from between the rusting iron grille that marks the point where the Medlock emerges from the culvert, which carries it from what was once an old Gas Works, beneath a car park at *The Etihad*, before it disappears once more less than a hundred yards further on beneath the Science Institute on London Road. Petros watches the moorhen glide casually by, its unseen webbed feet paddling determinedly ahead of the current.

The river was once navigable for a considerable portion of its lower reaches, back in the 18th century, when James Brindley was constructing the country's first ever industrial canal for the Duke of Bridgewater, which finished at the point where the Irwell and the Medlock joined, allowing cargoes to continue their journeys further up each river. Petros knows that the Council has a long-term vision to open it up completely again in the future – he knows this because he gave evidence to the Environment Agency responsible for compiling what became known as *A Ten Year Green & Blue Infrastructure Strategy for the City* as to how such a scheme might benefit potential future property development – but as yet there are no plans, or, crucially, funds, to implement it. Just pie-in-the-sky, as far as Petros was concerned at the time, but it suited him well to speak in its favour during the consultation process, good to have his voice heard, his face seen, his profile raised.

But now he's not so sure. Yes, he would love to see the Medlock released from its underground prison, to flow freely and unfettered once again, but not merely as a backdrop for yet more desirable penthouse apartments for young professionals. Now he thinks it would be better to open up a green space right in the heart of the city. Manchester has no real parks to speak of, not in its centre. Those that survive still are all on the perimeter, in the outer boroughs – ironic really, when Manchester was the first city in the country to put aside land for public parks, for the benefit of its working people, as havens to breathe cleaner air, open spaces away from the factories, well-tended with flowers and fountains, plus added amenities such as tennis courts, bowling greens and ornamental ponds. Then they went out of favour. Many were neglected, or worse, becoming no-go areas, the last refuges of gangs and addicts, locked up, closed down, abandoned, concreted over, built on. But now they are valued again. Friends' Associations are springing up to reclaim them. Tow paths are being reopened along the canals. Trees have been planted. Tiny oases of handkerchief-sized pockets of green have begun to sprout in the city. Like Sackville Gardens, where the statue of Alan Turing sits on his bronze bench, just across the bridge from where Petros now stands, looking down into the slowly reawakening Medlock, like a slumbering serpent, which one day might rise up like a Chinese dragon, garlanded and bedecked with colour, spitting fire, which the city, if it can ever shake off the shackles of lockdown, might once more dance and party beside.

Petros looks back towards the giant hulk of Mayfield, which was formerly a mighty railway sidings, goods yard and engineering works, where welders worked through the night repairing locomotives, the night sky filled with their sparks arcing above the station's glass cathedral dome, which, having laid silent for a generation, now resounds to the incessant roar of wrecking balls, pneumatic drills and jackhammers, biting into brick, cleaving into concrete, watched over by the towering cranes that look down over the city like gods from Olympus, as they strive to build their new Jerusalem, their Elysian palaces of glass and steel, from which Petros will make his next quarter-million, then party the nights away in *The Warehouse Project*, voted the UK's coolest, hottest night club complex, deep within the as yet undeveloped belly of Mayfield.

He stops. He turns away. He is breathing heavily, panting hard. He looks back down to the thickly oozing Medlock gurgling below him like a drain, gulping for air, just in time to catch a final glimpse of the moorhen as it disappears from sight beneath the next culverted tunnel.

Enough.

He recalls those lines of Prospero's from *The Tempest*, after he has finally quelled the storm. Petros had studied and loved the play for 'A' level, and its vision of a brave new world had first set the fires of ambition burning within him. But now he feels those flames might just be starting to die down.

'*Our revels now are ended. These, our actors, as I foretold you, were all spirits and are melted into air, into thin air...*'

Is that what is happening to him now, he wonders?

'*And, like the baseless fabric of this vision, the cloud-capp'd towers, the gorgeous palaces... shall dissolve...*'

Surely not, he thinks, surely not...?

'*And, like this insubstantial pageant faded, leave not a wrack behind...*'

He reels away. Is this what people mean by a Damascene moment?

He looks back at the river, seeping out of the shadow of the past, trickling towards an unseen future, but flowing still. It was here before we came, he thinks. it will survive us after we've gone. The marks we make upon it are what we leave behind.

A wedge of egrets skewers out of the tunnel, white against the black waters of the river. An ancestral memory stirs within him.

He knows exactly what he is going to do. He knows it with a certainty that is ferocious in its intensity.

A sense of certainty, yes.

He will follow the course of the Medlock from its source in the Strinesdale Hills to the east of Oldham to where it enters the old city boundary, near Ardwick, where it plunges underground into the culverts, tunnels and drains that underpin the city, retracing the route of those that went before him, until it empties into the Irwell, just half a mile or so from where the River Irk also joins this confluence, where Manchester first began.

He will pursue this task alone, as a challenge to his resolve, to prove to himself that he can, to fly in the face of those who would say it is foolhardy. He will do this as a way of reeling himself in, of bringing himself back to a sense of who he really is, what he really wants from his life. Money may make the world go round, but it's not what makes it tick, or chime, or resonate with meaning.

Below him, underneath the bridge, crouching beside the muddy Medlock, he sees a figure. Although he cannot see the face, the form seems familiar, the way the body shuffles, doggedly, like a caterpillar trying to cross a road, a suicide mission, but somehow making it to the other side. Now he remembers. This is the same woman from earlier, outside the Tobacco Factory, who Petros had had to buy off with a ten pound note, to shoo her away, so that she wouldn't tarnish the frontage of his investment, lower the tone of the neighbourhood, or cause a scene or embarrassment.

The woman with the angel tattoo.

Now it is *his* turn to feel embarrassed. He watches her squat beside the water's edge and sprinkle some bread crumbs at her feet. At once she is surrounded by the ever-present starlings, who strut fearlessly towards her, their beaks pecking straight from her hand. Undeterred she starts to sing, a guttural drone from the back of her throat, simultaneously overlaid with ancient wordless melodies, which swoop and soar and plunge, with squeezed vowels and clicked consonants, producing sounds that are as ageless as the running of water over stones, the spitting and crackling of flames in a fire, the roaring of wind through the trees, the marching of feet underground. But it is a song of the city as much as it is a song of the earth. Petros understands this, as does a colony of rats emerging from the culvert to scent the rise and fall of its notes on the air. Another ancestral memory stirs in Petros. He sees the tears of Chios hang in their attenuated clusters from the branches of the mastic trees. He knows he needs to harvest them before they stretch too far and break, before they fall to the ground and are lost and trampled on in the stampede. He will become an embroiderer. Like his great-grandfather Konstantin had been, back on the island of Chios, harvesting the mastic. He will stitch himself back together, where he has become so unravelled of late…

But first he will need to thread himself through the needle of the Medlock's tunnels, pass through their pupa of concrete and brick, until he can emerge at last on the other side, fully imagined, face to face with who he has become, in the fierce glare of recognition.

He reels away from the bridge. The city reels along with him. He looks down at his feet. Which way will they take him? He begins to understand. This is not the road to Damascus after all, but to Delphi, where his father waits for him at the crossroads. Alexis. The father from whom he has been estranged for almost a decade…

"You are no son of mine," he had raged, when Petros had informed him that he did not wish to follow him into the family business, but to branch out on his own, to try his luck in the shark-infested waters of the property market, without compass or life-raft. They had barely spoken since...

The woman has stopped singing. She is nowhere to be seen. The rats have retreated back into the sewer. The starlings have scattered to all corners of the city. The egrets fly across the face of the sun.

Without pausing to consider why, the action outpacing any thought, he picks up his phone and rapidly punches out a text.

"Are you ready?" it reads.

Chloe, picking it up, smiles and texts back.

"I've been ready all my life."
"So am I," he replies.
"Are you sure? Are you certain?"
"Yes," he texts. "I'm certain. I'm ready."
"Hold on to that thought. We go into Tier 3 from tomorrow..."

Another tightening of restrictions...

And so his grand scheme has had to be put on hold, at least in part, while the second wave of the virus surges through the city, and lockdown exerts its unyielding vice-like grip.

"You will just have to learn the quiet art of patience," says Chloe, when next they speak via Zoom. "The river will still be there when this is all over."

"I suppose," he says.

"Lockdown can't last for ever."

"Can't it?"

"When the first Queen Elizabeth was on the throne, they were always having plagues and pandemics. They were forever shutting down the Playhouses. Only they didn't call it 'lockdown'. Instead, the people were 'sequestered'. That's a much gentler word, isn't it? Less externally enforced, more self-imposed. There's a kind of cloistered monasticism about it that sounds more reassuring somehow. Don't you agree?"

Petros says nothing but continues to listen carefully.

"It's also quite ascetic, quite self-disciplined, which is kind of appropriate for the task that lies ahead of you, don't you think?"

"Possibly."

"I can just see you in a monk's cell, can't you, stripped bare of all but the essentials, as you get ready to go on your pilgrimage?"

"Are you teasing me?" he says, but without a hint of rancour.

"Only a little," she says.

He closes his eyes and smiles. He rolls the word around his tongue, savouring the sound of it. "Sequestration."

"That's better," she says. "Think of it as meditation."

"Ommm," he chants, and they both laugh.

"In France," she continues, "they call it *'le confinement'*. Like the old-fashioned word for pregnancy. I prefer that best of all. It's more hopeful. It makes you think that something bright and new will be born because of it."

He opens his eyes and looks directly at her. "Yes," he says. "Yes."

They are silent for a while.

"What's that word your sister used?" asks Chloe some time later. "After I met her at the Zorba flash mob?" Callista. Chloe had interviewed her for *MCR Live* as the whole of Market Street had been irresistibly drawn to join her in a mass Greek dance for charity. The mood had been infectious and Callista had presided over it all.

"*Philotimo*," he says, smiling.

"That's right," says Chloe.

Petros shakes his head in admiration. "The things you remember. That was five years ago."

"*Do* good, *be* good?" asks Chloe, ignoring him.

"That's right."

"*Philotimo*," she repeats.

"*Philotimo*," he echoes after her...

In the months that followed life has indeed felt monastic for Petros. He has conducted his work entirely from home. But though the construction business has, like everything else, suffered due to Covid, it has fared better than most – there has even been an unexpected upturn in the property market, with people desperately seeking the kind of excitement and escape that moving somewhere new invariably elicits – but most are looking to move *out* of the city, rather than into it, and so, inevitably, transactions have slowed, the number of deals has diminished, and he has found himself with more time on his hands than he has been used to.

And so Petros has filled these additional hours with meticulous planning. He has sourced every possible map he can find that depicts the sinuous, meandering course of the Medlock as it flows through the city, going right back to Roper's map of 1803, Adshead's map half a century later, then a series of overhead maps taken in the 1950s by the RAF for the Ministry of Works, right through to the latest satellite images from Google Earth. He pins them all up on noticeboards around his home office and studies them minutely. He peppers them with drawing pins of different colours, linking them with lengths of cotton. It is becoming a military operation. He makes a number of reconnaissance trips to particular places. He takes photographs. He keeps detailed notes.

But then he hits a brick wall. Literally.

It quickly becomes apparent to him that it will be

impossible for him to carry out his original plan. From where the river leaves the cemetery at Philips Park, it then plunges into a labyrinth of culverts, tunnels, pipes and drains that he now realises are, to all intents and purposes, impassable. At least for him. Especially if he is to undertake this journey alone – which it has become increasingly vital for him to do, this is a solo mission – but to try and follow the river underground by himself would be foolish. Worse, it would be dangerous. And what would it achieve? Some of these culverts are less than two feet in height in places and are filled with the flow of the river, a flow that is frequently rank and foetid. In other places the tunnels stretch for hundreds of yards in total darkness, cut through with countless in-flows and side-channels constructed over the years that it would be far too easy to get lost among them and never find a way out. Even where the Medlock remains above ground in the city, it is, for the most part, quite inaccessible, hemmed in by high walls, with no possibility of a path alongside to follow. He contemplates wading through the centre of the channel, but this too, he discovers to his cost after a somewhat humiliating test run, is equally impractical, for in places the river bed is too deep, more than twice his own height, where in others it has become so silted up with the years of detritus dumped in it, that he all too quickly becomes stuck in the layers of encrusted sludge, several feet thick, which threaten to suck him down.

He needs a Plan B…

After further Zoom chats with Chloe, he has it.

In the middle of the morning of the 15th of June, which happens to coincide with his twenty-ninth birthday, he will leave his one-bedroom apartment on the eleventh floor of the four-hundred-and-seventy-feet-tall Deansgate West Tower, then walk the five hundred yards to St Peter's Square, where he will catch a Pink Line tram to Oldham Mumps, which he will reach forty minutes later. From there he will catch the Number 84 bus that will take him the final one and a half miles to Lees Post Office, on the edge of the Strinedale Hills, where the Medlock has its source. From here it is seven and a half miles to Philips Park Cemetery. If he were walking along roads, he reckons it would take him two and a half hours. But because he will be following the river, allowing for the bends and the terrain, he will allow for four...

He reaches the source just before midday and texts Chloe, who has arranged to meet him at the Cemetery with the tree.

Her reply pings back instantly.

> "Great. I have the unveiling of the Bradford Pit Memorial first. But I should be through by five at the latest. Let's keep checking in."

Taking a deep breath, with a deliberately exaggerated first step, he sets off. He has begun...

It's a fine midsummer's morning, with high white clouds in a Constable sky. He passes the Sunny Bank Cemetery. It feels appropriate to be bookending this first part of his pilgrimage with a tribute to those who've travelled this way before him.

From there he drops to Nether Lees, passes the weir at Pitses Mill, down to Alt Fold and Lower Bottoms, below Fitton Hill to Bankfield Clough and Bardsey. Then on through Limehurst and Boodle Wood, overlooking Waterloo, before entering Daisy Nook Country Park, where the river runs parallel to the aqueduct carrying the disused Hollinwood Branch Canal that once linked Ashton with Oldham. The river swings west now, with more sweeping twists and bends, under Ash Bridge, by the golf course at Brookdale, through Bell Clough, into the Medlock Vale, with a steeper weir at Clayton Bridge, where the railway line passes overhead, conveying trains from Manchester to Leeds. To his left, between the trees bordering a small park, Petros can just make out the 15th century moated manor house, Clayton Hall, which once belonged to Lord Byron, and later to Humphrey Chetham, who had a dream of founding a school for local children, which ultimately he did, as depicted by Ford Madox Brown in one of his Manchester Murals. After passing the Hall, the river disappears briefly beneath Bank Bridge Road, only to reappear almost immediately on the edge of Philips Park Cemetery. Petros checks his phone. It's half-past four.

"Almost there," he texts.
"Me too," replies Chloe.

They arrive at the statue of the angel at exactly the same time. She props the tree and the spade against the back of it, while he scrapes off the mud from his boots against the granite headstone. She is wearing, Petros notices, a face mask which proclaims, 'Reclaim the Streets'. He remembers to put on his own wordless mask just in time. Perhaps he should consider wearing one the same as Chloe? For, in a way, isn't that what he's also trying to do? No. That would be just another male appropriation. If he is to wear such a mask, it should be for the right reasons. She would be sure to call him out, and be right to do so. But she wrong-foots him again. As she always does.

"You need to commit," she says. "If you're serious about something, why deny it? Here. Wear this." She tosses him a mask, which he unwraps, reads, then smiles.

Laughing, he puts it on.

"That's better," she says, then throws him the spade. "Now – get digging…"

Petros has fully accepted the reality that his initial idea – to walk the entire length of the Medlock – is impractical. The alternative that, with Chloe's help, he has managed to devise in its place is, he now firmly believes, a better course of action to take. She has reminded him just exactly why he felt compelled to undertake this journey in the first place. It is a homage to the one made by his ancestors when they first arrived in Manchester, a recognition of their courage and self-sacrifice, as well as an opportunity to finally end the feud with his father and bring about a lasting reconciliation. At the same time, by doing what he is now about to commence, he hopes to make many more people aware of the lost river that flows beneath their feet as they travel across the city, and not just the Medlock, but Manchester's other lost rivers, the Tib, the Gore, Shooter's, Crowcroft and Dog Kennel Brook, all of which and more lie buried and forgotten, out of sight, out of mind, as well as all the cargo of hidden stories they carry with them, of the heroic voyages made along them by those seeking to find shelter and refuge here in this city, which has always been a haven for the homeless and the dispossessed, right from its earliest beginnings, when the Huguenots first arrived here, and before them the Flemish weavers, and before them the displaced Celtic tribes, who sought to build a new settlement here, after the Romans had abandoned it. And how this same impulse continues to the present day, the migration of people from the trouble spots of the world, all alighting here, like birds from less protected climes.

Petros will plant a tree at the beginning and end of this walk across the city – a mastic tree – in honour of his ancestors' homeland. It may not be the perfect climate for it, or the best soil conditions, but it will adapt. It will learn to, in order to survive. Just as his ancestors did. Petros will become an embroiderer, like his Great-Grandfather Konstantin before him, graft the cutting he has taken, and tend it in this new earth.

Along the way, he will follow the course of the Medlock as close to it as he can. Whenever it surfaces from beneath its culverted tunnel, he will leave a sign, like one of those blue plaques that are put up to commemorate where somebody famous once lived, informing people that this stretch of murky water that they can now see, grateful once more to be back in the light, back in the air, is part of the River Medlock, one of the three great rivers of Manchester. Then, every two metres along the concrete pavements that he walks, tracing its route 'under his feet', as the words on his mask defiantly proclaim, he will make the mark of a blue circle, echoing the 'Keep Your Distance' signs that are to be found everywhere across the city. He will do this with a tennis ball, which he will dip into a tin of biodegradable, environmentally-friendly, clay-based, paint that is free from chemicals.

He will begin immediately after he has planted the first tree in Philips Park Cemetery. He will paint the blue way-markers this very night. He takes a pair of disposable latex gloves from the small rucksack he carries on his back and stretches them over his fingers. He puts on a hooded top, pulling the hood firmly over his head, readjusts the mask that Chloe has given him, then holds aloft the first of the tennis balls.

"Eco Warrior," declares Chloe, raising her right fist with a mischievous grin. "Guerilla Painter. Like Banksy."

She and Petros do a fist-pump together. They have agreed that she will follow the route he has made at first light the following morning, filming the route with her phone, then uploading the images to her own Twitter, Snapchat and Instagram sites, where she has hundreds of followers, in order to spread the word, using an array of different hash-tags.

#undergroundoverground
#whatslostisfound
#blueisthecolour
#jointhedots
#keepitsafe
#sharethesecret
#underyourfeet
#plantatreebuildahome
#followthebouncingball

In the meantime Chloe will drive to the end point, where she will place the second tree at an agreed spot, to be ready for him to plant once he gets there.

He watches her walk away from him and waits. He waits, with his back leaning against the statue of the angel at the edge of the cemetery. He waits until he hears, from across the far side of the Cemetery, a mile away in Beswick, the Church of the Resurrection and St Barnabas – St Barnabas the peacemaker, the renouncer of property, the protector of crops, the vanquisher of storms – tolling the hour. It is time. He ceremonially lifts the lid from the tin of thick, glutinous, non-splash paint, dips the tennis ball into it, revolves it until it is evenly coated in blue, then raises it into the air. He is ready to continue. It is eight o' clock, still light, but dusk is beginning to tincture the sky. It will take him approximately three hours to walk the final part of the Medlock's journey to its confluence with the Irwell, allowing for all of its ox-bow bends and meanders, its clove-hitch, bow-line, overhand and reef-knot doubling-back on itself. It will be dark by the time he completes his journey, which is what he will need it to be, in order to carry out the final act undisturbed.

From the Cemetery he walks towards the iconic Grade II-listed gasometers on *The Etihad* car park, bouncing the blue ball every two metres. From the Gas Works, he skirts the recently installed drive-through Covid Testing Site on New Viaduct Street, crosses into Ashton Canal Park, where the river re-emerges once more, taking him underneath Cambrian Street into Holt Town, swinging back east towards Clayton, past the Church of All Souls, where it disappears by Limekiln Lane, only to surface briefly again at Pin Mill Brow, before dropping deep into a subterranean chasm at the junction of the Mancunian Way with London Road behind Piccadilly Goods Station.

Here he leaves the first of his blue plaques.

'At this very spot, right under your feet, flows the River Medlock, one of the three great rives of Manchester. Stop and think about it. Follow the bouncing ball. Join the dots...'

The river remains hidden for a considerable distance now. Petros makes his way above ground via Travis Street towards the heart of Mayfield, deep in the throes of its massive gentrification, still bouncing the ball as he goes, to Baring Street, the site of his original epiphany, where, from its bridge in the centre, he had first looked down upon the river and noticed it for the first time, the moorhen paddling against the current away from the culvert, the wedge of egrets skewering out of the tunnel, the woman with the angel tattoo squatting on the shingle at the water's edge, feeding breadcrumbs to the starlings, the colony of rats scenting the air.

Tonight, Petros sees none of these. Instead he is surrounded by the twenty-four hour workings of Mayfield and Piccadilly East. Welders in their iron shields and face visors send fountains of sparks from their blow torches cascading into the night sky. The city is a crucible of fire, being forged anew all around him as he walks.

The river plunges back underground once more, beneath the old Courbusier-styled UMIST Buildings, through whose concrete canyons Petros now walks, still depositing his blue dots every two metres. Between Altrincham Street and Princess Street it reappears triumphantly. Two hundred years ago this stretch of the river was still navigable, but no longer. Petros may be able to see it once more, but he cannot follow it, for it is held captive, trapped in the ravines between India House and the magnificent former Refuge Assurance Building, now *The Kimpton Clocktower Hotel*. Looking down, Petros can just make out the opening from the river into what was once the old Duke's Tunnel, which was used for carrying coal by starvationers to the depot up at Store Street. The roof was so low that the boatmen were forced to propel their way along it by lying on their backs, using their feet against its arched brick roof, like upturned beetles.

The closest Petros can get to the Medlock through this part of the city is to proceed straight down Sackville Street, in sight of the Alan Turing statue, right along Princess Street, then, after first passing Asia House, left into Charles Street, until he reaches Oxford Road, where it briefly reappears at Hulme Street. He leaves a blue plaque on each corner.

Observe below the River Medlock, from the Old English 'Medlac' or 'Medelok', meaning 'the stream that flows through the meadow...' Look and imagine... See and remember...

He is back on his old stomping ground here, close to where he was a student at MMU, but even in the eight years since he graduated, there have been significant changes. He can still find his way about, but Friedrich Engels, who visited here many times while writing *The Condition of the Working Class in England*, when this part of Manchester was known as 'Little Ireland', would find it utterly unrecognisable. He would be even more surprised to bump into a statue of himself erected four years ago in front of a theatre called *Home*, opposite where once *The Haçienda* had stood. Petros places another blue plaque at the statue's feet.

Coming up for air...
Reaching for the light...
Water finds a way...

Engels observed how the river would frequently flood, especially here in the summer rains, at Little Ireland, which he nicknamed the Augean stable of Manchester. It would be so completely submerged by the overflowing of the foul and pestilential effluents routinely disgorged into it, that many of the houses would fill with raw sewage right to the ceilings, and the inhabitants be forced to make their escape through the rooftops, before seeking a new home somewhere close by...

The Medlock too is now close to finding its home, as is Petros, but not before it twists and turns its tortuous way through Gaythorn, Knott Mill, Potato Wharf and the Giant's Basin. He's fully found his rhythm now, walking, bouncing, walking, bouncing. Leaving a trail for others to follow after him, just as he has walked in the footsteps of those who went before. A trail of tears. The tears of Chios. Stepping stones to help them find their way.

From First Street, he crosses the aptly named Medlock Street onto City Road, which follows the river, uncovered at last, providing the perfect setting for the towers of glass and steel, with their luxury penthouse apartments, which have sprung up alongside both banks here, their glittering lights reflected and twinkling on the water's coal black surface, a sheer opaque obsidian.

Petros has come full circle. He places the last of his blue plaques.

What was lost is found...
Share the secret...

He is standing directly outside the Deansgate West Tower,

the place he himself now calls home, from where he stepped out earlier this day to begin the journey he is now at last completing some thirteen hours later – though in truth he began it more than a decade ago, the day he decided not to join his father's business, but pursue his own path instead.

The river now disappears for the final time, underneath Deansgate, to empty into the Irwell, at the Cloverleaf Weir, the place where the Romans had made their first camp, Castlefield, from where Petros's great grand-father had then sailed the half mile to Ducie Bridge, where the Irwell meets the Irk, where he had then developed the city's first mastic factory, within the confluence of Manchester's three main rivers.

Petros crosses Deansgate into Castlefield now. The Basin has been greatly renovated in recent years, in contrast to the dereliction that has choked much of the rest of the Medlock's journey through the city. It is a prime visitor attraction. There are bars lining the junction of the canals and rivers here. Normally this part of Manchester is buzzing. But not since Covid. For now the bars lie silent. Though one or two are doing a modest take-out trade before they are permitted to reopen fully in the next few weeks. Petros can see a distanced queue of five or six people standing in front of one of them just before it closes for the night.

The hard industrial landscaping has been softened by the addition of some patches of grass, with shrubs in planters, flowers in hanging baskets, a few sapling trees, close to where the ground falls away towards the river. It is at this spot where Chloe has said she will leave the second small tree for him to plant when he gets here, together with a spade. He looks around, but he cannot see them anywhere. Perhaps he's mistaken, and they're somewhere else? Perhaps she's been delayed, and is on another story? Perhaps she's not coming…?

He takes out his phone to text her that he's arrived, to ask again where she's hidden them, but first he pauses. He sits on one of the repainted iron capstans beside the water's edge and reflects on the journey he has just completed. His arms and shoulders are stiff from the constant repetition of bouncing the various tennis balls as he walked. But it's a good pain, one that comes with immense satisfaction from having accomplished what he set out to do. The nine months of planning have paid off. Those nine months of sequestration and confinement, out of which perhaps something new is emerging. But he knows he could not have done it without Chloe's constant prompting and encouraging, understanding intuitively just why it was so important for him to undertake such a task, and he wants to tell her so, to thank her, and to… what? He's not quite sure. He only hopes that when he sees her the right words will present themselves.

In the distance he hears the Town Hall clock strike eleven. He is just about to begin his text when he hears her voice speaking softly behind him, just as the last chime finishes and fades..

"You made it then?"

He turns as she steps out of the shadows into the light cast from an old wrought-iron street lamp set into the cobbled street. She is carrying the tree and the spade. A pair of moths dance around the flame.

"Yes," he says. "I did."

"I never doubted you would."

"I didn't think to see you here."

"Didn't you?"

"It's not what we arranged."

"Isn't it?"

"I just…"

"What…?"

Now that she is standing here in front of him, he feels that any words he thought he might say are quite unnecessary.

She hands him the spade, and he silently starts to dig. When the hole is ready, she passes him the tree, which he carefully plants, before patting back all the soil he had previously unearthed.

When it is complete, he stands back, regarding it.

"Yes," he says, "it's finished."

"Really?" she says, raising an eyebrow. "I'd say it's hardly begun." She languorously raises both arms above her head and stretches them luxuriously.

It is a signal.

The people Petros had spotted queuing near one of the bars now surge towards him, clapping and whistling, and singing *Happy Birthday*.

Petros cannot believe what he is seeing. Hurrying towards him are his father, Alexis, his mother, Sophia, his sister, Callista, her husband, Andreas, and Yannis, their son.

"Chloe told us what you were doing," says Callista, "so we just had to come."

Petros turns sharply to remonstrate with Chloe, but she has already slipped away.

"Don't be cross with her," says Sophia. "She has a good heart."

Petros softens immediately. He knows this to be true.

"When she first told us what you were planning," says Andreas, "I didn't understand it. Not at first."

"It was Chloe who explained it. It's not *what* you were doing, but *why*."

"Yes," says Petros, as if only understanding it for the first time himself.

"Won't you get into trouble for painting all those blue dots?" asks Yannis anxiously.

"I don't think so," smiles Petros. "How's anyone going to know it was me?"

"You'll have been caught on CCTV," he answers seriously.

"Why do you think I've been wearing a mask and a

hoodie?"

Everyone laughs.

Only Alexis, his father, has not yet spoken. He is looking at the tree. His eyes are shining. Father and son regard one another from a distance for a long time.

"To hell with the virus," he says at last. "Besides, I've had the vaccination." The others look at him strangely. Then he lunges towards Petros and fiercely embraces him. "My son," he cries. "My son..."

*

Half an hour later, after the family have all departed, with promises on all sides to see each other again very soon – "You are part of our bubble now," they tell him – Petros takes a last look around at where the Medlock empties into the Irwell, and breathes deeply.

He becomes aware of someone standing quite close to him. Less than two metres. He turns round. It's Chloe. They look at each other a long time.

"That was a good thing you did," he says to her at last. "Thank you."

"It was worth it to see the look on your father's face," she says.

"Yes," he says. "It was."

Another silence falls between them.

"So," says Petros, "what now?"

Chloe smiles. "I reckon it's about time you and I formed our own bubble, don't you?"

Petros looks at her in wonder. She has always been that one step ahead of him.

Arm in arm, they walk slowly back towards Deansgate's West Tower, from where, in Petros's apartment on the eleventh floor, they will be able to look out across the whole city, *their* city, together...

As they do so, a voice begins to sing in the shadow of the conjoined rivers. It is the woman with the angel tattoo. She is singing a love song, or maybe it's a lullaby, to a small child sleeping beside her...

"Koimísou kai ótan sikotheís, tha filíso apalá ta cheíli sou
Tha sas káno dóro tis Chíou, me óla ta ómorfa ploía tis
Kai tha eíste diásimoi stin Anatolí kai ti Dýsi
Kai vretheíte epitélous éna spíti..."

"Sleep, and when you rise, I will gently kiss your lips
I will make you a present of Chios, with all of its beautiful ships
And you will be famous in the East and the West
And find yourself a home at last..."

*

"Ladies and gentlemen," booms the voice on the PA, "will you please give a real Manchester welcome to one of her most celebrated sons, who tonight headlines the Legends Stage right here in Albert Square in the heart of the city – Graham Nash!"

To a huge roar the former Hollies and Crosby, Stills & Nash superstar walks onto the stage in front of the Town Hall with the rest of his band. The crowd numbers ten thousand, less than a fifth of what might have been expected in pre-Covid times, but substantial nevertheless.

"Wow," says Nash. "Thank you. It's incredible to be here tonight, and to see so many happy, healthy people back in the centre of Manchester again."

More cheers greet this remark. The pervading mood is one of joy, relief, gratitude and celebration – sheer delight that this year's International Festival is actually able to be taking place, and that one of their own should be appearing as part of it.

"I'm going to begin," he continues, "with a song from my most recent album that could almost have been written for the times we currently find ourselves in."

"Where are we going...?
Where are we going...?

This path tonight – where will it lead me?
Crumbling rock and stones on fire
This path tonight – you'd better believe me
I'm stumbling to my heart's desire
On this path tonight...

Where are we going...?
Where are we going...?"

Threaded through the crowd are all of Molly's supporters for her installation, which will follow on immediately after Graham Nash has finished his set.

Jenna, Séydou, Awa and Omar are there, with Maleek too, who is excitedly jumping up and down between them. A little further on, Michael and Nadia are juggling a fidgety Blessing, who insists on being carried by Lance, who patiently lets her tug gently on his dreads.

"Would you believe it if I told you that Graham Nash was playing almost fifty years ago at *The Majestic* in Eccles the night Sol and I got married?" smiles Nadia, shaking her head incredulously.

"No," laughs Jenna, "I wouldn't."

Michael catches sight of Tom and Apichu, arriving at the last minute, with Samancha on Tom's shoulders, and waves. Apichu, Michael notices, is wearing the piece of cloth Molly wove and gave to her as a gift a year ago.

Elsewhere are members of Lorrie's extended fairground and circus family – Pavel, and Krizstof, amicably bickering as usual, Agniewska fussing from one to the other of them, while further apart Lena and Milosz scan the skies, hoping and praying that the weather remains fine – and most importantly calm – for Lorrie's walk in less than an hour's time.

Also anxiously checking the skies is Clive. Rain has been forecast for tomorrow. He fervently hopes that it doesn't come early. Florence, too, is due to be playing outdoors soon.

"Don't worry," whispers a voice beside him. He turns. It's Ruth. The weather couldn't be more perfect.

She's right. The stars arch bright and clear overhead. A giant waxing gibbous moon hangs high to the east. Clive visibly relaxes his shoulders. Ruth returns her attention back to the Legends Stage, where Graham Nash, whose music formed the backdrop to her own teenage years, has started on a new song, which once more feels freighted with meaning.

"Through the cracks in the city I can see the sad traces
Of yesterday's empires and tomorrow's bad dreams
They'll come back to haunt us like the gaze in a mirror
Reflecting mistakes that we took to extremes..."

In another part of the Square, Chloe and Petros stand with their arms around one another. Alexis, Sophia, Callista and Andreas look on happily, while eight-year-old Yannis weaves in and out between them all.

"The cracks in the city will trap us and trip us
Making us fall to the ground that we love
And through the cracks in the city I can hear voices calling
Taking us all from below to above..."

Agniewska unwraps a picnic she has brought with her and starts handing out their favourite sausage, *kielbasa starowiejska* – "From the old country," she declares – washed down with bottles of *Żywiec* beer.

In a clear space just in front of the stage, the children have all gathered – Samancha, Blessing, Yannis – watched with curiosity by Maleek, who, after encouragement from Awa, joins with them as they dance together to the music.

Nash, noticing them, naturally leads his set to a conclusion, ending with one of his most well-known songs, which the audience joyfully sing for him.

"You, who are on the road
Must have a code that you can live by
And so, become yourself
Because the past is just a goodbye

Nash steps away from the microphone, watching in wide-eyed wonder as fifty thousand smiling faces sing the words he first wrote half a century ago on the other side of the world back to him now in the city where he grew up as a boy. It is a homecoming for all of them.

Teach your children well
Their fathers' hell did slowly go by
And feed them on your dreams
The one they pick's the one you'll know by

Don't you ever ask them why
If they told you, you would cry
So just look at them and sigh
And know they love you..."

*

After the encores – *Our House* and *Just A Song Before I Go* – the PA announcer proceeds with the following request:

"We warmly invite you all now to make your way to St Peter's Square, just a four minute walk away on this deliciously warm and balmy summer's evening, to witness the new installation by Salford-born artist Molly Wahid, specially commissioned for this year's Festival. Could I remind you, please, to maintain social distancing between you and your fellow spectators at all times, and follow the directions of the stewards, who will guide you safely round? We're most grateful for your cooperation. Thank you..."

A frisson of anticipation runs through the crowd as the street lights along Mount Street and Peter Street are suddenly dimmed, then replaced with lit braziers, whose flames cast dancing shadows on the walls of the buildings. It is exactly the same route Ruth took thirty-five years earlier as part of that very first Manchester Pride. She smiles at the memory. The path they must all follow tonight is lined with blue tape, strung above head height, a signature flourish by Molly, linking this new installation directly back to her previous one...

Fifteen minutes later, when all the crowds have finally converged on St Peter's Square, the street lights there too are momentarily blacked out. In the darkness that follows, the electric hum of the approaching trams seems preternaturally loud. Suddenly they cut abruptly to silence. None will be running through the Square for the next half-hour. The stage is now set. The installation is about to begin...

MIF Manchester International Festival

Ornaments of Grace
A Public Art Performance Installation by Molly Wahid

A Scene in Ten Acts

1:

The lights return. A follow spot picks out a lone figure, who stands on top of the two-storey portico, marking the entrance to Manchester Central Library. It is Florence.

She picks up her trumpet and starts to play the opening bars of Aaron Copland's *Fanfare for the Common Man*. Its thrilling clarion call reverberates through the Square.

2:

As she begins it a second time, another light picks out Lorrie – Lorelenka – on the opposite side of Peter Street, towards the top of *The Midland Hotel*.

From the third floor balcony of its corner turret, she steps out onto a high wire, which stretches the four hundred and fifty feet to where it joins the Library, like an umbilical cord.

The crowd, looking up, gasps.

Lorelenka is dressed entirely in white. On her head she

wears the white cotton cloth, the *qurqash* that Molly has inherited, from Nadia, Ishtar and Rose, then back through the centuries to when it was first made, on the loom that now sits in Molly's studio in Islington Mill, having been rescued from the old stone weaver's cottage being renovated by Tom and Apichu, with its repeating pattern of moths caught in a web of laurel leaves, ready to take wing, white on white on white, first woven two hundred and sixty years before, almost to the day, by the handloom weaver Edwin Stone on the edge of Cockey Moor. She wears it in the same fashion that Molly wore it for her *Thin Blue Line* installation three years before, draped around her head and falling down her back. Similarly, just as Molly did then, Lorrie – Lorelenka – has a pair of white angel's wings rising from between her shoulders.

She places one foot confidently in front of the other, slowly edging her way across the wire, erected the previous day by Jackie and her team from Rope & Rigging Ltd, a specially customised cable, coated in blue – another thin blue line, slicing the night sky. Florence continues to play, improvising now around the theme, as Lorelenka advances towards the middle of the span. She dances, rather than walks, lifting each leg high into the air, arching her foot, pointing her toe. She flexes her shoulders so that the muscles in her back ripple, opening, then closing the pair of wings. Now she has become a moth, as well as an angel, a white peppered moth, dappled by the follow spot with flecks of light and shadow. It is as if she is evolving right before the people's eyes. The emergence of a melanic pigmentation.

The crowd holds its collective breath. Maleek watches it all through the gaps between her fingers, which she has placed in front of her eyes.

After five agonising minutes, Lorelenka reaches the other side. She steps off the wire to enormous, relieved applause, onto the flat, metre-wide, leaded rim above the Library's Tuscan rotunda, just below its central domed roof, at exactly the same moment that Florence finishes playing.

Immediately the mood changes.

3:

Lorelenka runs around the leaded rim. At the same instant Tanya begins her randomly coded soundscape.

Tanya is installed in an office on the fifth floor of Number Two St Peter's Square, directly opposite the Library's Corinthian Portico, from where, through the latticed tracery screen of Portland stone, cantilevered above the block's entrance, she can see the entire Square below her.

Matching her own feet, which she drums on the concrete floor beneath her like a Foley artist, in time to the rhythm of Lorelenka's running, she records, loops and instantly replays the echo of each step and stride, so that it sounds like Lorrie is leading an advancing army of thousands of feet, all of them marching towards the city.

As Lorelenka runs, following in her wake, the curved rotunda of the Library's exterior is simultaneously wrapped in the enormous length of cotton manufactured for Molly by Tower Mill. It falls from just below the leaded rim, where Lorelenka runs, right down to street level. Based on the first thing she ever constructed using the loom from Tom and Apichu's cottage, its seemingly abstract design of blue thread meandering between irregularly shaped patches of greens and browns and greys, is now re-imagined on a vast scale, four hundred feet in length by sixty feet in height. As it encircles the Library's walls, it ripples in the light, like water.

Apichu, looking at it now, is stunned. She runs her fingers through the sampler for this design, which Molly had given to her the day they first met. Now she can see what Molly envisaged. Writ large like this, it appears to encompass the entire city.

"You've done it," she whispers out loud. *It's just as Molly had hoped it would be. Water finds a way. It always does. The rivers will not be buried. They seek what light they can.*

Elsewhere in the crowd Chloe holds Petros closer to her.

"See," she says. "Look. It's you."

"It's all of us," *he answers back, and kisses her.*

4:

Now, several things begin to happen at once. Tanya, speaking to Sunanda via a mobile phone, gives her the signal to cue the next section of the installation. Sunanda is in the Glass-Covered Walkway, linking the Library with the Town Hall.

Designed by Sampson & Haugh, as is the building across the Square where Tanya sits, its air-tight seal made possible by the mastic produced by Petros's father, it currently contains two hundred excited young people.

Holding up her hand where they can all see her, Sunanda counts down with her fingers from five to one, then points towards the exit.

The doors slide open and the two hundred young people run out into the Square with seemingly spontaneous, but carefully rehearsed precision, lining themselves in rows upon the Portico steps, slotted between each of the Corinthian columns. They are dressed, as per Molly's instruction, however they wish, so long as it is in some combination of reds, greens and yellows – the colours of the Flag of St Kitts, the National Emblem of Yemen, and the Manchester Coat of Arms – and so long as there are no words or logos to interrupt the pattern. The effect is a blur of speed and movement, all of them distinct, unique, individual, yet at the same time connected, as part of a unified whole.

They each wear a separate headset, complete with ear-piece and microphone. Into those headsets, Tanya now programmes the sound of a shruti box, the portable harmonium Khav had used for her Final Presentation at MMU several years before, which she now plays live, sitting next to Tanya in Number Two St Peter's Square. Tuned to a series of different chords, she opens, then closes the bellows, opens, then closes. Tanya records, amplifies, then replays the different notes and pitches.

The young people have been asked, as soon as they hear the drone in their ears, to sing, a wordless 'aah', to any of the notes that fit with that chord. Tanya instantly loops and records these also, replicating each note several times over. Two hundred voices quickly become a thousand, five thousand, ten thousand. She fades the sound of the running feet, so that now the whole of St Peter's Square is filled instead with this chorus of human voices, washing over the crowds, rising up towards the sky.

By this time Lorelenka has climbed down from the Tuscan Rotunda via a ladder onto the roof of the Portico, replacing Florence there. She at once launches into a spectacular fire poi routine. Her wrists rapidly revolve. They spin an invisible, three-dimensional web around her, as though an entourage of fire-flies accompanies her in a glittering figure of eight, wrapping her head, arms and body in filaments of light, a moth dancing to reach her own flame.

Just as she did a year ago, back at Islington Mill, when the city was emerging from its first lockdown, which Molly had captured on her phone, and posted on her Facebook page, where Lance had first seen it and been captivated, but now magnified many-fold. He watches her again from within the entranced crowd, even more mesmerised by her than he was before. "Mi sweet Carib grackle," he murmurs softly. "Mi golden oriole..."

5:

Tanya now feeds into the headsets of the young people the text Molly has prepared for them. This text has been broken down into a series of ten shorter pre-recorded phrases, which Tanya delivers to them randomly, in any order.

This is the beating heart of the installation, its pulse, its life-blood.

Each of the young people has been specially chosen. Ranging in age from nine to nineteen, they individually represent one of the two hundred languages spoken in the city today. From Europe to Asia. Africa to the Americas. The World on our Doorstep. French, German, Spanish, Portuguese. Italian, Greek, Polish, Russian. Arabic, Turkish, Persian, Pashto. Hindi, Marathi, Gujurati, Tamil. Cantonese, Thai, Korean, Uyghar. Xhosa, Yoruba, Wolof, Swahili. And dozens more besides.

Tanya feeds in each section of text in the appropriate language. Each young person at once proceeds to speak it back, phrase by phrase, out loud into their microphones. Tanya then creatively codes these words, so that each is instantaneously converted from spoken to sung. She randomly selects, from the menu of notes available within the pentatonic scale of each droned chord, a separate melody for every single voice, which she then mixes and layers, building them into an unexpected, unpredicted harmony. What starts off as a complete cacophony of disconnected, discordant sounds, all of them competing in their own separate languages, gradually conjoins, merging from their different streams into a single river of song.

Jenna is astonished. This, she now realises, is what her daughter was searching for in those drawings of birds she had first seen five years ago at Molly's final show as a student. They had filled the gallery. Jenna was surrounded by them. They spiralled above, around and through her, screeching in a wild but unified chorus, demanding to be heard. Just as they do now, in the soaring voices of these brightly hopeful young people. Jenna looks up. It is as if, merely by thinking of them, she has willed them into existence. Starlings, thousands of them, begin their nightly murmuration above the rooftops of the city at exactly this moment, almost as if Molly has choreographed them, in a wheeling clamorous ballet.

6:

At the same time Tanya projects a series of animations onto a transparent black mesh behind which the young people are standing. This mesh acts in a similar way to a gauze, so that the young people, lit from behind, remain visible to the crowd, while the front of the mesh serves as a screen for the animations, which are based on a series of paper cut-outs made by Molly following her visit to Dmitri at the Museum. Each cut-out depicts a Manchester Moth, in various stages of opening and closing its wings, with each pair being uniquely patterned to represent the gradual stages in their evolution from *biston betularia typica* through *medianigra* to the final *carbonaria*. stage. Tanya has transferred Molly's cut-outs onto a continuous roll of paper, outlining each of the moths with punch-holes, in a kind of binary morse code, as if for a music box or pianola. Khav feeds these through a home-made mechanism, which she operates live by simply turning a handle. Tanya, using the programme she has created specifically for the purpose, converts these patterns into video, rather than audio files. She projects them onto the mesh screen in front of the young people, so that, as they open their mouths to speak, the individual words of their text, which have been transformed by Tanya into song, are now made manifest as moths. They appear to pour out of their mouths, then fly up towards Lorelenka, irresistibly drawn to her continually spinning flames of poi, messages of hope being transmitted along a never-ending line of telegraph wires across the land, like the cable Lorelenka has walked across, summoning all the peoples of the world to come to Manchester, in a dare of moth imagines.

The crowd is entranced beyond words. Maleek spreads her fingers in front of her face as widely as she can. She is no longer afraid.

7:

At that moment, as the singing and the animation continue to eddy and flow, rise and surge, high above the Beetham Tower at the farthest end of Deansgate, the highest point in the city, visible above the rooftops of St Peter's Square, lit by its own light, Richard Gahan pilots his rescued balloon towards them. In a slow and graceful, elegant glide it arrives at its destination just as the music is reaching its climax. It hovers directly above the domed roof of the Library.

Maleek points to the sky and claps her hands.

Immediately Richard, with his co-pilot Austin, lowers four

guy ropes. These are caught by four technicians, dressed in black and positioned north, south, east and west around the leaded rim of the rotunda. They then proceed to tether each one securely, so that the balloon can remain in place above the central dome.

The crowd is transfixed. The rescued balloon is exactly the one that Molly had hoped it would be. Painted as a globe, illuminated from within, it is the one which had been used for the opening ceremony of the Commonwealth Games here in Manchester nearly twenty years before, the one which had soared above what is now The Etihad Stadium, and from which the aerial artist Lindsay Butcher had performed such death-defying feats, rescued by Richard, here, now.

Chloe, looking up now from below as this same balloon once more hovers above the city, recalls meeting Lindsay after that opening ceremony, in which she had taken part when still only ten years old. The words Lindsay had said to her, in answer to her artless, star-struck question, come back to her now.

"Aren't you frightened," Chloe had asked her, "when performing at such a height?" Up close Chloe could see that Lindsay's leotard was covered in lightly-coloured wing patterns.

"You get used to it," Lindsay had said. "Like everything. It becomes quite normal after a while. You see things so much clearer from up there. The city looks so different. Like a sleeping giant. A cocoon."

Before the adult moth breaks free and flies, thinks Chloe now. She must have mentioned this memory to Molly at some point, and Molly had remembered, and now repurposed it. Isn't that what artists do?

8:

While everyone has been distracted by the arrival of the

world in the form of a balloon, the young people have completed the speaking of all ten phrases of their individual text. Tanya has managed to combine them all into a concerted and unified close. The animated moths have all flown up towards Lorelenka's fire.

Following the briefest of pauses, the young people now speak in chorus, as one, all the words in English. Tanya converts this into a simple, harmonised melody, which rings out across the whole city. Simultaneously the words are projected onto the mesh screen above the Portico Roof, behind which the flames from the poi have now been doused.

> *"Wisdom is the principal thing*
> *Therefore get wisdom*
> *And within all thy getting*
> *Get understanding*
>
> *Exalt her and she shall promote thee*
> *She shall bring thee to honour*
> *When thou dost embrace her*
> *She shall give to thine head*
> *An Ornament of Grace*
>
> *A Crown of Glory shall she deliver to thee…"*

9:

The projection fades, leaving the words to linger a moment longer, palimpsests retained at the back of the retina, before finally evaporating, to reveal a different Lorelenka. Where before she was white, now she is entirely clad in a glittering black. The transformation of the Manchester Moth is complete.

A cable is lowered from the gondola of the balloon, which she clips with a carabiner to a loop around her waist. She is then raised into the air, while the four technicians untether the ropes securing the balloon. Immediately it soars into the night sky above the city. A whole world of light and wonder. Lorelenka performs a spectacular choreographed sequence of aerobatics, one that she has been rehearsing in her imagination ever since she first saw it, on a strip of silent, scratchy super 8 millimetre film in the caravan on Collingham Street.

Lena, looking up at her from St Peter's Square below with tears in her eyes, whispers hoarsely. "A Rhine Maiden at last. Just like her grandmother, her namesake, Lorelei..."

10:
The moment the balloon is directly over the main body of the Square, the four technicians on the roof of the Tuscan Rotunda fire four confetti cannons, just as Florence reprises the opening bars from the *Fanfare for the Common Man*, releasing tens of thousands of paper moths into the night sky, from where they gracefully descend upon the waiting crowds below. Each one is different, unique, yet each belongs to the same family.

The crowds look up in wonder, stretching their arms out wide to gather them safely in, as they flutter and fall silently towards the many-layered land...

*

Slowly the crowds disperse. The trams start running again. The technicians begin taking down the equipment.

Molly gathers everyone together who took part inside the Glass Walkway and thanks them all profusely.

"You are all of you," she says, "ornaments of grace, and you have truly delivered a crown of glory to everyone who came here this evening. I'm sure they'll never forget it. I know

I shan't. Thank you, from the bottom of my heart."

They all respond by giving her a prolonged round of applause. Because of Covid, nobody hugs each other, as they might otherwise have done, but she feels their love just the same. She tries to make sure she says goodbye to each and every one of them, saving her most especial thanks for Tanya, who has helped her stitch the entire installation together.

"No worries," she says. "I enjoyed it."

Khav looks proudly on. "So long as you're happy, innit?"

"Ecstatic," says Molly...

Afterwards, when everyone has finally gone, she heads back out into St Peter's Square and sits on the steps in front of the Library. She is emotionally drained. She has no real sense of how it has all been received. While it was taking place, she positioned herself as anonymously as she could among the crowd to try and gauge their reaction, but she was too focused on the technical aspects of it all, wondering whether they would all actually work, to take in people's responses, then worrying that Lorrie might fall from the wire, or the balloon would not arrive in time...

She quickly sends a text to Lorrie and to Richard to thank and congratulate them, hoping that they have landed safely somewhere, and promising to see them as soon as she can.

Almost immediately a reply pings in from Lorrie.

"Touch down executed perfectly. Am in the middle of Heaton Park. Do you remember seeing The Stone Roses here? Xxx"

Molly instantly texts back.

"Yes. Of course I remember.
*'On the edge of something shattering
We're coming through...'*

BTW you were truly awesome. Xxx"

"Crowns of Glory all round then? Must dash. Richard & Austin need help in packing away the world. See U L8R? Xxx"

"Tell them thanks again from me – they've been absolute heroes..."

She sits back on the Library steps as the Town Hall clock strikes eleven. She closes her eyes and exhales deeply, trying to savour the moment. She becomes aware of someone standing over her. She feels a shadow fall across her. She opens her eyes and looks up.

It's her mother.

Jenna says nothing. She simply stands there, looking at her daughter with a deep, immense pride. Molly looks up. Her face is illuminated by the light cast from the street lamp overhead. Jenna is briefly aware of the merest hint of the scar left by the sliver of glass in her cheek from the IRA bomb twenty five years before. Mostly it is invisible. Molly herself never thinks of it. Nor does Jenna. She is only aware of it in certain lights, like tonight, when it shows like the faintest of shadows from the past, especially when she smiles, as she does now. Jenna brushes her daughter's cheek tenderly with the tip of her thumb. Molly smiles. The mark is part of who she is, of who they both are. Jenna smiles back. Slowly she leans forward. She places a kiss gently upon Molly's brow, before letting her head rest against her daughter's. The two of them stay like that a long while.

Finally, Jenna says, "We're going to listen to Florence play at Swan Street. Want to come?"

She holds out her hand towards her. Molly takes it and rises to her feet.

"Yes," she says. "I'd love to..."

Jenna nods.

"Good. I'll see you later then."

"Yes," says Molly. "I shan't be long..."

She watches her mother walk away from her, knowing,

perhaps for the first time in her life, exactly when she will be seeing her next...

Jenna crosses to the other side of St Peter's Square. As she reaches its junction with Mosley Street, she stops and waves. Molly waves back. They both of them smile once more. Then Jenna turns on her heel and immediately quickens her pace. She doesn't hesitate. She knows precisely which road she will take...

She is reminded of a night forty years ago, when she had furiously stormed away from Lance, along the Linear Walkway of Chorlton Fold, the former Loop Line from The Delph, linking the collieries from Linneyshaw Common to the Boothstown Basin, as she sought the refuge of Farida's house. Cursing all the way, she had stumbled upon the old Unitarian Chapel that still stood beside the disused railway track and read the plaque about John Henry Poynting, the son of the vicar there a hundred years before. He had been the first person accurately to measure the weight of the earth – thirteen billion trillion tons – which has now lifted completely from Jenna's shoulders at last, as light and free and full of air as the balloon that had risen up into the night sky at the end of Molly's installation. Now, as she continues to walk, she recalls what else was written on that blue plaque about John Henry Poynting.

'*When we examine Nature's garment,*' he suggested, '*we discover just how many, or rather how few, threads of which it is woven. We try to detect a pattern. We observe how each separate thread enters the pattern, and then, from our understanding of these patterns from the past, we try to predict the pattern yet to come.*'

Back when she first read this, Jenna was not satisfied by it. She still isn't today. Poynting's theory implies laws of immutability, resistant to the possibility of change, change she feels she has implemented many times in the years that have followed.

But Poynting is not yet finished.

'We stand in front of Nature's Loom as we watch the weaving of the garment. While we follow one particular thread in the pattern, it suddenly disappears, and a thread of a different colour takes its place. Is this a new thread? Or is it merely the old thread turning a new and unfamiliar face to us? How can we tell? So, as we watch the weaving of Nature's garment, we resolve it in our imagination into threads of ether spangled over with beads of matter. But should we, or should we not, therefore, conclude from this reasoning a single, irrefutable Law, which can be applied to every case in all instances? Or should we rather regard a Law of Nature as nothing but a formulation of observed correspondences?'

Jenna found this much more acceptable. It offered the possibility of new correspondences not yet observed. It still does.

She stops in her tracks. Immediately she turns around and retraces her steps back to Molly, who is still standing in front of the entrance to the Library, running over in her mind not just the events of the last hour, the details of the installation, but everything that has led to its creation. When she sees Jenna striding purposefully back towards her, she smiles. Her mother can still retain the capacity to surprise her.

"Let's walk to Swan Street together, shall we?" says Jenna, holding out her hand.

Molly takes it in her own. "I'd rather get a taxi," she quips.

Laughing, arm in arm, the two of them hail the nearest cab, the possibility of a new correspondence floating between them.

*

An hour earlier, just as the thousands of paper moths are falling from the night sky, Ruth is holding out both her hands, like a child, desperate to try and catch one of them. Tears are streaming down her face. They began when the young people started to sing the words that are inscribed around the dome of the Great Hall Reading Room inside Central Library, and they have not stopped since.

She is thinking of the day the Library was first opened, by King George V and his wife, Queen Mary of Tek, on a warm afternoon nearly ninety years ago. Not that she was there of course, but George and Francis were, and they had both told her about it. How Francis had filmed it with his hand-held *Kinamo* movie camera, assisted by his good friend Winifred, and how it had been George who had written those words around the perimeter of the dome's ceiling in the first place.

She wonders what they would each have made of tonight's event. She believes they would have loved every aspect of it. Francis would have relished the digital technology that had made such effects as the animated moths possible, and he would have been astounded by the sight of the hot air balloon soaring above the city. It would have reminded him, surely, of the stories told to him by the hundred-year-old Laurel Stone, who he had recorded onto those early wax discs, light years away from the creative coding required to produce the sound worlds which swept over everyone tonight, while George, she is certain, would have been captivated by the expressions of awe and wonder on the faces of the people in the crowd, especially the children, and would have wanted to photograph them. Both of them would have loved Florence's soulful interpretation of the Copland.

That is where she's now headed. To hear Florence play again. She has a late-night slot at *The Band on the Wall* on Swan Street as part of the Festival. Ruth will have to hurry if she is not to be late. Just then she hears the rumble of a tram approaching behind her and she hops aboard. She loves the trams. They've transformed the city. This one takes her up Mosley Street, past the City Art Gallery, where the Grayson Perry Art Club Exhibition has finally opened at last, with so many people wanting to see it that she herself has had to pre-book a slot more than two weeks into the future. The tram then follows the route taken by the Manchester Yeomanry Cavalry as they harried and hounded the innocent men, women and children away from St Peter's Field on the day of the infamous Peterloo Massacre, slashing at them with their sabres as they rode through and over them, kettling them into this narrow thoroughfare. How far the city has come in two hundred years, thinks Ruth. The tram now skirts the edge of Piccadilly Gardens, once the lair of the Daub Holes, a waste land of lime pits, and the site of Manchester's first hospital, on the far side of which stood the late, lamented, much-missed *Queen's Hotel*. Then it turns left into Market Street, home of *The Clarion Café*, where Delphine, Ruth learned once, was proposed to by a doctor from that same – now Royal – Infirmary. Next the tram swings right into High Street, alongside the Arndale Shopping Centre, where the IRA Bomb exploded in 1996, before climbing up Shudehill, from where, if she cranes her neck as far as she can to the left, she can just make out the back of the Manchester Arena, where Ariana Grande had sung on the night of the terrorist attack, just behind Victoria Station, under whose arches Lily had sought shelter in her days of sleeping rough, before the tram pulls into the Interchange, from where it is less than a five-minute walk down Rochdale Road into Swan Street, where *The Band on the Wall* awaits at New Cross.

Ruth attends quite regularly, but not on her own. Usually she goes with a group. So this is a first for her, and she is feeling quite nervous. But once she steps inside, she is quickly reassured by the familiarity of the surroundings, the photos of bands and singers who've played here in the past, from the trad jazz days of Acker Bilk and Chris Barber, through the seventies when many of the city's punk bands played their first gigs here – The Buzzcocks, The Fall, Joy Division – to the likes of Mica Paris and Florence Blundell more recently.

She's early, which is what she wanted. She chooses a table in the far corner, from where she can see people arrive. A photo of Roy Beauregard King hangs on the wall beside her. Clive is standing at the bar. He waves and mimes, asking if she would like a drink. She shakes her head. Not yet, she mouths.

In no time at all it starts to fill up. She's lucky to have found a seat, for people are standing now between the tables. She's growing anxious. She's finding it more and more difficult to keep track of who's coming in. She sees Jenna arrive, with her daughter, Molly. Her husband, Séydou, is waiting to greet her, along with a whole crowd of Molly's supporters, who give her a great cheer the moment she walks in. Ruth recognises the girl who was walking the tightrope. She's talking to an older man with dreadlocks, who, she realises, from the way Jenna has described him in their sessions of old, must be Molly's father. She can immediately see the attraction, for he's still roguishly handsome. Then she sees two other women – a small girl with a turban and a tall girl with an Afro. Finally she sees Chloe, who sees Ruth at once and waves, smiling. She appears to have a young man in tow. Perhaps he's quite recent? The way they keep exchanging covert looks and glances with one another suggests that he must be.

She's beginning to feel hot and flustered. She should have accepted Clive's offer of a drink earlier. She's so thirsty. The back of her throat burns and aches. But it's too late now. There's too much of a crush at the bar, and if she were to get up now, she'd lose her seat for sure. I'll give it five more minutes, she thinks, then I'll go. She tries to steady her breathing. She's no longer used to crowds. But then nobody is. Not after twelve months of lockdown. She looks at the clock on the wall. Four minutes have passed already. It's no use. She might as well go now. She scrapes back her chair and gets to her feet, then...

"Hello," says a voice from behind her.

It stops Ruth in her tracks. She slowly looks round. It's her. She's come after all.

"Hello," she replies, her face stretching into a wide smile. She can't help herself.

"Hello," she says again.

"Hello," says the first voice once more.

Yasmin.

And then suddenly both of them are speaking together.

"I couldn't find you."

"I've saved you a space."

"I got stuck at the bar."

"I nearly didn't come."

"I'm glad you did."

"So am I."

"Do you still drink red wine?"

"Yes."

"Yes."

Then a pause, during which they look at each a long time.

"Yes?" asks Yasmin.

"Yes," answers Ruth. "Yes..."

Now someone is speaking into the microphone on the tiny pocket handkerchief of a stage. He's trying to get the people's attention.

"Ladies and gentlemen," he is saying. "Did you see the *Ornaments of Grace* installation?"

Another huge cheer goes up from Molly's friends and supporters.

"Wasn't it amazing? We're delighted to have the artist, Molly Wahid, with us in the audience here tonight." The MC holds up his hands in mock surrender as he tries to quell the prolonged applause that follows. Eventually he succeeds. "Those of you who were there would have seen our next guest performing as part of that incredible event. Well – she's hot-footed it back from St Peter's Square to play this special late-night slot for us now. Will you please welcome to the stage one of The *Band on the Wall*'s resident favourites, the Florence Blundell Quintet?"

Florence makes her way through the crowded bar, glass in hand, to thunderous cheers.

"Thank you," she says, then pauses to take a sip of wine. She's in no kind of hurry, allowing the audience time to settle and grow quiet. Eventually she speaks. "I thought I'd begin with a new song, one that's...."

An immediate smattering of applause interrupts her.

"Thanks. Yeah." She smiles. "Like I said, it's one that's been lingering in the shadows for a while, waiting for the right time to be brought out into the light. Well, I reckon that right time might just have come tonight."

She takes another sip of wine

"Yeah. I started it almost a year ago, when my partner – Mr Clive Archer..."

She indicates Clive, still standing sheepishly at the bar. He shyly acknowledges the murmurs of recognition that run around the room as Florence mentions his name, especially from Chloe and Petros, Tanya and Khav, Molly and Lorrie, who whistle loudly and enthusiastically. Florence raises her glass towards them, before carrying on.

"... was mounting an Exhibition of photographs he'd taken of the street where we live..."

Her pianist playfully inserts a few bars from the Lerner & Loewe classic as Florence takes another sip of wine. Listening at the back, Ruth feels herself starting to blush.

Florence continues.

"One of the people who went to that Exhibition got talking

to Clive afterwards, and he brought her over to meet me. I believe she's here tonight." She quickly scans the room. "Ruth – are you still around…?"

Yasmin encourages Ruth to stand up. Normally such a thing would make her wish the ground would simply swallow her up, but tonight is different. She is suffused with such happiness that she takes it in her stride, even managing a tiny wave.

"Yeah – there she is," continues Florence. "Our good friend, Ruth Warner. Well – something Ruth said that night got me thinking. I don't think even she knew the effect her words had on me. But they led to this song, which – with your permission – I shall now sing in public for the very first time. Thank you, Ruth."

She raises her glass.

"But before I do, I'd like to dedicate it to a relative of mine, a Great-Great-Great Aunt." She laughs. "I'm not sure how many 'greats…'"

The audience smile along with her as she wryly shakes her head.

"Her name was Esther. Later she called herself Ishtar, and she always dressed in white. Like the tightrope walker in Molly's installation tonight. It was she who first encouraged my great-grandfather, Harold, to pick up the trumpet as a small boy. He passed it on to his son, Alan, who passed it on to his son, Derek, my Dad, who passed it on to me. Yeah…"

She pauses to take another sip of wine.

"The line stretches down the years, more than a hundred and twenty of them, so that when I play, it feels like I can hear them too, tapping me on the shoulder, passing it on, saying, 'Go on, girl. It's your turn now…'"

She remembers when she was just sixteen years old, playing in the Glossop High School Brass Band, at what turned out to be the very last concert in the old Kings Hall at Belle Vue, before they knocked it down.

She steps onto the stage and at once looks out into the auditorium, to see if she can see her Dad, Derek. She spots him immediately, nodding his head towards her from the front row and smiling. She smiles back. She feels no nerves, just excitement, as she always does before a performance.

Their teacher gently raps his lectern with his baton. Then, when he's certain every single pair of eyes is focused on him, he raises his hands and brings them in to start.

They are note-perfect. Derek watches Florence from his front row seat, sees her stand to take her solo, hears her hold that line...

They take their bows as the audience rises to its feet, shouting for more. The conductor seizes the moment. He turns back to the band, says something inaudible to them, they smile and he raises his arms once more, signalling they are about to begin again. The audience sits back down in hushed anticipation.

And so The Glossop High School Band begins the last ever tune to be played in the old Kings Hall. As soon as the first notes descend from the stage, the audience sighs and spontaneously applauds. The conductor turns to face them and with his baton invites them to sing along.

"Should auld acquaintance be forgot
And never brought to mind
We'll take a cup of kindness yet
For Auld Lang Syne..."

Florence chuckles at the memory, a deep, warm sound that rises from the back of her throat like a run of notes she might play when she's jamming with the band, and the music's really taking off.

"But the line stretches deeper and further," she says. "My Dad was a miner. He worked at Bradford Pit until it was closed.

So when I play, I hear it in his hammer as it rang against the coal face. I feel it in the air, humming with the singing wires of colliery wheel at the pithead, the earth shaking in the rumble of falling rocks deep underground. I watch it forge a river of fire in the blacksmith's yard, weave a thousand threads in the clattering looms of the mill, weld together sparks of light in the overhead tram cables, see it crackle as rail tracks bend and buckle, feel it as a low vibration coming through the soles of my feet, a wild elephant storming out of the forest, hooves trampling the spine of the country, a storm cloud of dust pursuing it, escaping the cruelties of a harsh empire, scouring the land for a new home."

She's riffing now, and the audience is responding as if she was playing, not speaking, vocalising their appreciation, punctuated with rounds of applause, like drum rolls and cymbal crashes.

She looks across to Molly, who is hanging on her every word.

"It's a fine line we walk, isn't it?"

Molly nods seriously.

"You may not know this," continues Florence, "but Molly and I are related."

A murmur of surprise ripples through the audience..

"That's right. You remember that Great-Great-Great Aunt I mentioned? Esther? Ishtar?"

"Yeah," they call back.

"Well, *she* was Molly's great-grandmother. Which makes us... what?"

"Third cousins," replies Molly.

"Yeah. Something like that. I reckon, somewhere along the line, we're all of us related, aren't we?"

"Right," agree the audience, smiling warmly.

"So," says Florence, turning to the rest of her band. "Are we ready, guys?"

She picks up her muted trumpet and begins to play. She plays it so softly that the audience has to lean forward as one to hear her. When she starts at last to sing, they are on the edge of their seats.

"We make marks on the land...
dig up the years...
draw lines in the sand...
leave a trail of tears...

With each relic and bone...
we're unearthing the past...
with each root and each stone
the days lengthen and last...

And what will remain...
when our work is all done...
when we've washed every stain...
from the face of the sun...

Though we stumble and fall...
through the dark as we roam...
we still answer the call...
that is drawing us home..."

Florence plays a second trumpet solo, the notes stretched and attenuated so thinly they resemble finely spun cloth, drawing the listeners into their web, holding them there, hardly daring to breathe, lest they break the spell. Seamlessly she resumes the song.

"Making marks on the land...
unspooling the reel
outline of a hand...
imprint of a heel

We've been here before...
and we'll pass by again...
the stone has its flaw...
the wood has its grain...

So we draw on the earth...
carve in the air...
measure our worth...
record we were here...

The value of work...
when our labour is done...
its memory will lurk...
long after we are gone..."

Florence plays a third trumpet solo. At last she releases a cascade of different notes, allowing them to tumble into the air, so that they might take wing and soar. She traces the notes' effortless rise and fall, like the cadence of telegraph wires, looped and laced above the city, the twisted stitch of lives across the years, raining out of the sky, catching each note as she releases it, gathering them all together, thistledown on the wind, trapped infinitesimally between her lips, through which she blows, to let the notes dance and fall, back into the earth, like tiny seeds, which might lie dormant for centuries, or poke through the soil tomorrow, before singing the final verse *a capella*, allowing each word to hang suspended.

"So these lines in the sand...
leave their shadow and trace...
and our marks on the land...
time will never erase..."

She closes with a final muted trumpet note, which diminishes imperceptibly into an Aeolian silence. It hovers in the air, quivering, vibrating the rims of the audience's glasses.

Each of them listening knows that it will never completely fade. They will carry it with them always, before passing it on to those who will follow...

*

Jenna has been awake all night. She has been turning many things over in her mind. Now she has come to a decision. There is something she must do.

She sits on the edge of Maleek's bed, waiting for her to wake.

Maleek is sleeping better these days. She no longer has the nightmares. Or rarely. And when she does, they don't consume her with the same terror as they once did, when the effects of them would linger for days, burying her somewhere so deep that nobody could reach her.

But she's not had such an episode for months now. Only the occasional tremor, when she will murmur and moan in Arabic, but then settle and return to sleep again.

As she is doing now. Her face is serene and clear. As a child's should be.

Maleek's English is improving each week. She speaks it with growing fluency and confidence, especially when she's at school, where she has made friends, and which she trots to happily each morning. But not this morning. Today, when it eventually dawns, is a Saturday, and Jenna has other plans...

Theirs is a multi-lingual house, here in Fairfield Square, in the heart of the Moravian Settlement. As well as English, three other languages are spoken. When Séydou, Omar and Awa are all there, they mostly converse in French together. Sometimes Omar and Awa will fall back into Wolof, the language of their childhood in Senegal, while Séydou and Awa can both get by in Arabic, especially Awa, following her time in the camps and hospitals of Amman. This has proved invaluable in helping Maleek to settle in. Now, as is so often the way with children, Maleek can slip comfortably between all four languages, shifting from one to another mid-sentence, depending on who she is speaking to.

Jenna continues to wait.

Outside the sky is starting to lighten. The birds have begun their raucous chorus, clamouring to tell the world of their existence, that mixture of nest-building, staking their claim to a territory, attracting a mate, or simply singing for the sheer pleasure of it.

Maleek begins to stir too. She opens her eyes and immediately smiles.

"Good morning, Mamma," she says sleepily, then adds:

"*Bonjour, Maman.*"

"*Sabah alkhyr, Mama.*"

"*Jaam nga fananë, Yaay.*"

Jenna's heart turns over.

"Wake up, sleepy-head," she says. "We're going on an outing."

"OK, Mamma," says Maleek unquestioningly, turning back the quilt and getting out of bed.

"You get dressed, while I make you some breakfast."

Maleek rubs her eyes. "Can I have French toast please?"

"Yes, Maleekah, you can have French toast."

"Where are we going?"

"It's a surprise."

"Is Papa coming too?"

"No. It's just you and me."

Maleek pads off towards the bathroom. "Can we go by tram?" she asks.

"Yes," says Jenna. "We can go by tram…"

Half an hour later they are standing on the platform of

Droylsden's tram stop. Maleek adores the trams, the way they glide almost silently along the rails, with just the slightest hum from the overhead power cables, and the polite way they quietly beep as they approach a stop or junction.

"Which stop do we need?" she asks.

"Pomona," says Jenna, knowing that Maleek will want to look at the Metro map and work out the best route for them to take.

There are currently eight lines, which radiate from St Peter's Square in the centre of the city to different termini at Altrincham, Ashton, Bury, East Didsbury, Eccles, the Airport, Rochdale and the Trafford Centre, serving ninety-nine stations between them. Each line is indicated by a different colour. It takes Maleek less than thirty seconds to work out which way they must go.

"It's easy," she says. "We take the blue line all the way. We don't even need to change trams. Pomona is twelve stops from here."

She skips happily back to Jenna just as a tram arrives. It will take them just under thirty minutes to reach their destination. Maleek counts the stations off as they pass through them.

Droylsden, Cemetery Road, Edge Lane, Clayton Hall, Velopark, The Etihad, Holt Town, New Islington, Piccadilly, Piccadilly Gardens, St Peter's Square, Deansgate-Castlefield, Cornbrook, and finally Pomona.

"Here we are, Mamma. Quickly now, this is our stop…"

They walk along the tow-path beside the Bridgewater Canal. Maleek keeps up a constant running commentary, pointing out the different things that catch her eye – a barge painted with crowns and roses, a heron perching motionless on one leg, the redbrick warehouses and factory chimneys now turned into loft apartments, the bridges, walkways, the forest of skyscrapers mushrooming behind them into the sky, a supermarket trolley that has been thrown into the canal – while Jenna keeps her eyes peeled for a way into Pomona Island itself, which is screened off from them by the temporary construction hoardings scrawled with graffiti and topped with barbed wire. Every few yards there are signs ordering people to 'Keep Out'. 'Danger'. 'Warning'. 'Private Property'. 'Trespassers Will Be Prosecuted'.

Eventually she sees what she's been looking for. Just before Castlefield, where the original Roman settlement used to be, is St George's Island, the industrial wasteland where she and Lance first had sex when she was a student. There's a white footbridge beside a block of flats called Pomona Wharf.

"This way," she says, indicating a metal fence close to the water's edge.

They shimmy around it, then follow what is part of the Irwell back in the direction of Cornbrook, where the Romans built the very first bridge to cross the river. Jenna keeps a tight hold of Maleek's hand at all times, as they manoeuvre their way carefully under the bridge, before they immediately double-back on themselves, to climb a flight of old, worn, slimy stone steps. At the top Jenna pauses. She scans the metal fence. There used to be a gap somewhere near here, she's sure of it, but perhaps it's been boarded up? No – there it is. She and Maleek scurry towards it, trying not to slip.

"Where are we going?" asks Maleek doubtfully.

"Through this gap," says Jenna, sounding brighter than she feels. Maybe this wasn't such a good idea after all.

"I don't think I want to."

"Come along," urges Jenna. It's too late to turn back now. "You can squeeze through there. It'll be an adventure."

Reluctantly Maleek complies.

But once they're through, her fears are forgotten in an instant. Stretching before her is a slice of wilderness, caught between the canal and the river, a forgotten wasteland suspended between the past and the future, abandoned while the three different local authorities of Trafford, Salford and Manchester, under whose combined jurisdiction the island slips between, argue over how it should be developed, with planning still withheld, so that now this unlikely urban oasis has emerged, a haven for unexpected flora and fauna.

Maleek's first impulse is to run off and explore. But Jenna remains cautious. The place looks like a war zone, with the bombed-out ruins of half-demolished former buildings. Those few that have not been flattened by the diggers or the wrecking ball poke through decades of ivy, weeds and nettles. She supposes Maleek must have witnessed her fair share of ravaged landscapes in her time, but who knows what dangers lurk unseen beneath the undergrowth – rusty metal, broken glass, jagged concrete.

"Be careful," she warns. "No running. Watch where you put your feet."

"Yes, Mamma."

Jenna looks around. Molly told her about this place when she came here three years ago and found that fragment of all that remained of Sol's mural, the bleached skirting board, with those faded flakes of paint, which nevertheless clearly showed the traces of a girl handing her father an umbrella, marks that she, Jenna, had made herself. The words of Florence's song the night before at *The Band on the Wall* reminded her strongly of those marks, and she wanted to show Maleek something of her own story, of where she had come from, and its connection to Maleek too.

She looks around her. Maleek is absorbed in exploration, picking things up, examining them for a while, then putting them back. Jenna finds it almost impossible to believe that once, not so very long ago, this had been the third largest port in England, despite being more than forty miles inland, where huge cargo ships from all around the world had docked and been unloaded, by men from the same country that Maleek has been forced to flee, Yasser, Jenna's father's grandfather among them.

Now it is just as Molly had described it to her...

New saplings push through the concrete, gradually being covered by mosses and lichens, which clog generations of dumped rubbish. Swathes of meadowsweet grow through and around a burnt-out motor cycle. Beetles writhe in the innards of an old mattress. Convolvulus binds round a rusting capstan.

Jenna squats low by the water's edge to watch hundreds of tiny fish, their gleaming backs giving way to the deep expanse of the dark canal beneath them. Birds scud through the grasses. Larks, finches, she even sees an egret, perched like a ballet dancer *en pointe*, a pale statue poised above the surface of the black water.

She sits in this well-thumbed fold in the map, this cracked crease in the page, trying to get her bearings, to uncover its special geometry of man-made canals and railway bridges, forging a spine through the city, and her own place within it. She watches a lone rat pick its way delicately and sure-footedly along the remnant of an old sewage pipe before dropping out of sight...

She is roused from her reverie by Maleek suddenly calling to her. She has been constructing an elaborate system of dams and bridges over the narrow rills and channels of murky water that ooze up beneath her feet. She wants to help the smaller animals, she says, which she is sure must live here in great abundance, to be able to cross safely from one patch of dry land to another.

"Mamma," she cries, "come and see the bridge I've built."

Smiling, Jenna joins her. "Very good," she says. "I think you have the makings of becoming a fine engineer one day."

Maleek laughs. "I don't want to be an engineer."

"Oh, don't you? What *would* you like to do then?"

"I'd like to be tightrope walker," she says quite seriously, "like that lady last night."

Jenna raises an eyebrow and ruffles Maleek's hair. She is about to move on, when something about the bridge that Maleek has constructed catches her eye. She stoops to inspect it more closely.

"Where did you find this piece of wood?" she asks her.

"Over there." Maleek points to a jumble of planks.

"Were there any others like this one?"

"No," she says. "This was definitely the best. That's why I chose it. The rest were just bits of rubbish."

"There's something painted on it. Can you see?"

"What?"

Jenna lifts it away from where Maleek has so carefully placed it and lifts it closer to her. She finds that suddenly she can scarcely breathe. She can feel her pulse beating wildly. The skin on the back of her neck begins to prickle. She is forced to sit down on the nearby capstan.

"What is it, Mamma? You look like you've seen a ghost."

Jenna looks back at Maleek.

"I think I have…"

She is remembering a time more than forty years ago, the last time she was here, the afternoon her father unveiled his mural, which had taken him more than a decade to make, and she, Jenna, had not even wanted to be there…

"Come," she says to Maleek. "Sit beside me. I want to tell you a story…

"On Tuesday 28th March 1978, exactly fifty years to the day since my grandfather Hejaz made his night-time journey by narrow boat from Barton Dock to Bradford Pit to meet King

Amanullah, my father was ready at last. A small group of family and friends had gathered. Nadia was there, your Grandma, having taken a day off from work; so, too, were Ishtar, *my* grandmother, now eighty, dressed in white from head to toe as usual; Auntie Far, Grandma's sister; Salwa and Jamal, Farida and Grandma's parents, and me, at the start of my Easter holidays from school, fifteen years old and cross."

Maleek giggles. Jenna wraps an arm around her shoulder, then carries on with the story.

"George was there too, my father's teacher, standing to one side, smoking his pipe, his camera slung over his shoulder, with his friend Francis, having roared in at the last minute on his classic 1958 DOT Villiers – 'made right here in Manchester, on Ellesmere Street,' as he never tired of telling people – as well as Mr Tunstall, Grandma's former boss from Turner's with his wife Mrs Tunstall, and Eric and Ray, Susan and Brenda, my parents' friends from school.

"Once everyone had arrived, George stood on a beer crate and called for attention, then handed over to Sol – my father.

" 'I'm not going to make a speech,' said Sol.

" 'Good,' called out Ray, only to be shushed at once by Brenda and Susan.

" 'I just thought I'd better show you what it is I've been up to all this time, and to thank you all for putting up with me while I squirreled myself away in the evenings and weekends these past few months.'

" 'Years, more like,' laughed George.

" 'For ever,' I added, rolling my eyes.

" 'But most of all, I want to thank *you*, Nadia, for believing in me, for encouraging me, for giving me a good talking to when I've needed it, and for loving me. Thank you.' At which point I stuck two fingers down my throat.

" 'I also want to dedicate this mural to Ishtar, my mother, for more than anyone's, this is *her* story.'

"He pulled on a piece of rope and the tarpaulins fell away to reveal the entire mural.

"Everyone applauded, gasping with delight and amazement. The day was cold and crisp. The sky was cloudless and a brilliant, clear blue. The sun shone down directly, illuminating the colours with a fierce brightness, and everyone surged forward, keen to examine every detail, exclaiming over each new discovery.

" 'Oh,' they said. 'Look.' And 'See,' they pointed. 'Do you recognise this?' they wondered. 'And that?' they asked. 'And isn't this…?'

"Ishtar clung to Grandma with such pride and joy. 'He's done it,' she said, her eyes shining. 'He's captured it all. Every last detail.'

"Grandma linked her arm through hers and led her gently towards the centre of the mural. 'Isn't that you,' she asked, 'standing at the top of the colliery steps, about to go and speak to Hejaz for the very first time?'

"Ishtar brought her eyes right up to the painting. 'Was I really so certain he would turn round when I called?'

"Grandma laughed warmly. 'I'm so glad that he did…' "

Jenna wipes her eyes. She has finished telling the story. She holds up the piece of wood for Maleek to see,

"I do believe that this is the very piece of wood that shows that moment, when my grandmother met my grandfather for the very first time."

Maleek pores over the painting.

"Yes," she says excitedly. "I can see them. Two people." Then she adds, "Is your grandfather the one named after the mountains near where I used to live?"

"Hejaz, yes. That's right."

"What was he like?"

"I don't know," says Jenna sadly. "I never knew him. He

died before I was born."

"I think he must have been nice, don't you?"

"Yes," says Jenna. "I think he must have been..."

"Shall we go and see Grandma?" says Jenna a few moments later. She is conscious of using the exact same words that she used with Molly after the IRA bomb. Maleek responds just as Molly had done all those years before. Her face beams with delight. History continues to repeat itself, as Jenna says next, "Let's go and see when the next bus leaves for Eccles then, shall we."

But this is the point where the present takes over from the past.

Maleek wrinkles her nose.

"Can't we get the tram instead?"

Jenna grins. "Come on then," she says, holding out her hand. "Let's show her the piece of wood you found."

"Just a minute," says Maleek. "I need to find another piece for my bridge first."

Jenna watches as Maleek scrabbles among the pile of what she calls 'rubbish' for a replacement. Expertly she rummages through various bits and scraps, quickly dismissing them, until finally she extracts a rusty metal grating panel about a yard long.

"What do you think?" she says, dragging it triumphantly.

"Perfect," says Jenna.

Maleek lays it carefully across the water channel, then skips back to Jenna, just as a light rain begins to fall.

"Uh-oh," she says. "We'd better hurry."

The two hold hands as they quickly retrace their steps back towards Cornbrook.

"From there we'll need to get the red line to the Trafford Centre," says Maleek.

"Will we?" smiles Jenna.

"Yes," says Maleek seriously. "Then probably a bus. But I don't know which one."

"I expect we'll find out," says Jenna.

"Yes, Mamma, I expect we will."

"I think it's time you learned the special Manchester rain song," says Jenna. "By The Beautiful South. It was one of Molly's favourites when she was your age."

"Molly's my step-sister, isn't she?" asks Maleek artlessly.

"Yes," laughs Jenna. "I suppose she must be…"

"From Northenden to Partington, it's rain
From Altrincham to Chadderton, it's rain
From Moss Side to Swinton, hardly Spain
It's a picture postcard of 'Wish they never came'

So dry your clothes once again
Upon the radiator
What makes Britain great
Makes Manchester yet greater

From Cheetham Hill to Wythenshawe, it's rain
Gorton, Salford, Sale, pretty much the same
I'm caught without my jacket once again
The raindrops on my face, they play a sweet refrain…"

Maleek now joins in the chorus with great gusto, as together she and Jenna splash through the puddles.

"What makes Britain great
Makes Manchester yet greater…"

*

Epilogue

The light was fading in the western sky. Dru could just make out the curve of low hills, shaped like suckling breasts, which gave the settlement its name. Mamucium. Skirting the wooded rise, he saw the ring of fires smouldering in the valley of the three rivers. He had been marching hard all day, ever since he left the Oak River Fort at first light. There'd been times when he doubted he'd ever reach Redstones. But there it was, and as he drew nearer, he began to make out the shapes of men and horses. Dru was planning to rest a few days there, before continuing to stake out the road further north, beyond the Ribble, towards the Wall.

It felt like he'd been on the move for the last three years, ever since his capture by the Imperial Army when they cut their way through the villages of Galicia. A soldier had pinned him to the ground, a spear at his throat, and offered him a simple choice. Either march with us, or end up like your father, whose severed head was hoisted on a burning palisade. Since then he'd crossed the Weeping Mountains, wrestling with lynx and bear. He'd plodded through the wet marshlands of Southern Gaul. He'd endured a stormy crossing through the channel that separated Breizh from The Fleet. They'd marched in testudo as local tribes rained down sharpened sticks and stones from their hill forts. For the last year they'd sliced their way north, slashing and burning in broad, straight lines through field and forest, carving out the wide marches for the larger forces to follow on behind them. And now he was in desperate need of rest.

He sent on ahead a dozen men to scout the last mile and to warn the Camp Commander of their approach. A hunter's moon rose in the night sky. He waited till the last man had safely arrived before finding a place to sleep for himself – a small hollow in the base of a dead tree close to one of the fires.

Within moments of settling himself, he was asleep...

He awoke early to the smell of wood smoke. A raven croaked in the chill air. His bones ached. He heard the snort and stamp of tethered horses nearby, their hooves delicately balanced, their breath forming statues. He could hear the sound of water. Just beyond the circle of camp fires, which had all but gone out, the ground dropped away. He let his eyes accustom to the grey light. A pale sun was painting the sky. He wandered down the slope, following the sound of the water. A young woman was lowering a bucket at the river's edge. She heard a twig crack as he approached and froze. She was kneeling, her back towards him. Dru carried on walking until he was right behind her. It was her reflection he saw first, slowly rippling in the water. Briefly their eyes met. He expected her to look frightened, or to bolt, like a hare startled from the thickets, but she held his gaze, before dipping the bucket into the water to fill it, obscuring both their faces as she did so.

He caught her by the wrist. He had a little of the native language, enough to ask her name and where she lived. "Bron," she said, and pointed. Her arm stretched away towards where the three rivers met. In their confluence was a small huddle of low huts with makeshift roofs of earth...

Three days passed. The men were getting restless. They'd drunk themselves into a stupor the first night, gambling with the soldiers who were garrisoned there. On the second night they'd sampled most of the local women. But not Bron. Dru made it clear that she was off limits. By the third night fights had started to break out. Many of the men were itching to be on the move again, while some of those stationed there were keen to join them. It was a small Camp, barely meriting the name. The quarters were basic. There were no baths, no temple, no villa. The whole place felt impermanent, a way station only, towards the bigger settlements of Ebor and Vinovia, and it was clear the soldiers posted there felt forgotten by Rome.

But Dru looked around and saw nuts growing on the trees. He saw fruit being picked from orchards in the valley. He saw pigs rooting for acorns in the copses. He saw deer stripping bark from the saplings. He saw eels coiled and wallowing in the ditches. He saw fish gathering in shoals where the rivers met. He saw food. He saw water. And he saw Bron. When he held her close under the blood red moon at night, and when he watched the sparks from the fires dancing with the stars in the sky, he looked in her eyes and saw more than just himself reflected back, more than the sureness of her gaze. He saw a future.

They reared and bucked beside the stamping horses, and the next morning, while the camp still snored, Dru took his knife and cut the rope that tethered one of them. He climbed astride it and lifted Bron before him. She whispered something in the horse's ear and, lacing her fingers through its mane, together she and Dru rode away towards the confluence of the three rivers, where a small family of rats foraged among the still glowing embers...

A month passed. Then another.

The moon completed a third elliptical orbit of the earth. Dru watched as it waxed and waned, and wondered.

Nobody had been to look for him. He felt the shackle of Rome loosening with each new day that passed. Bron had introduced him to the others in the camp. Children and women mostly. A few older men, frail and toothless. It was clear they looked to him to lead them. But where? Bron explained that they'd always been nomads, wandering in search of the next bend in the river, where there might be another small thicket of trees to coppice, where they might make camp till another Hunter's Moon had risen and set.

"Not this time," warned Dru. He could see movement in the fort at Redstones, below the breast-shaped hills. The Camp was being disbanded. Some men were marching north, he noticed, but not many. Most were scattering south. Back to Rome, or, if Dru's instincts were correct, to melt away into the wilderness of Mercia and take their chances, to go native, as he had chosen to do.

"Wait," he counselled the old men. "Let the fort empty first. Then let me take Bron to scout the river," the one he had learned they called the Erewell, the widest of the three whose confluence they nestled in. The other two, the smaller ones, the Irk and the Medeloc, drained into the Erewell, the Irk by a hanging ditch, which, to Dru's trained eyes, had the makings of a rampart to defend themselves behind, and the Medeloc just below the fort at Redstones. He would follow the Erewell to its source. Bron had told him of another fort three leagues to the north, at a place called Coccium. The Witch Queen Cartimandua held sway there. A Brigantes stronghold. It was said she garotted her enemies and buried them deep in the peat bogs below the surface of the earth.

"We should be careful," she said. "She is a vassal to Rome. She is protected by her."

"But look around you," said Dru. "Rome is leaving. This Witch Queen you speak of will not now feel safe. She will be looking to leave herself..."

They ride from the camp at first light. The course of the Erewell acts as their guide. After two leagues a tributary joins them. "The Croal," says Bron. "The Mykel Brok." A thousand strides further, they are joined by another. "The Roch," says Bron. "The Rac Ceto. Opposite the wood. See?" She points to a carr of alders in a bog close by. Dru has cause to be grateful to the horse, who understands the terrain, who knows where he can tread, and where he cannot. Carefully he guides them through the dead marshes. Gradually the land dries. The channel of the river narrows as it climbs.

"We're close," says Bron, and Dru slows the horse to a walk. "This is the moor at Coccium," she adds. "Look," she points. Her outstretched arm traces the course of a smaller brook, trickling down to join the Erewell from across the moor. Jackdaws circle noisily above a steep mound to the east. Black smoke rises in coils behind it. They approach with care. The fort is deserted. Not two days since. It has been put to the torch. Fires are still smouldering. The birds feast on the corpses.

"Some will have fled," says Bron. "They will be hiding in the hills. We must take care."

"They will not trouble us," says Dru. "They will be too frightened. If we find any, we'll take them with us."

"As slaves?" asks Bron.

"No," says Dru. "That will not be our way. We will make a welcome for all."

Bron nods. Then turns. She puts a finger to her lips, tiptoes silently towards one of the fires that is still burning. She circles around it. She passes briefly from Dru's sight. He grows anxious and calls her name. When she returns, she is carrying a small child. A boy. Naked and hungry, he has not seen two summers. "I shall call him Med," she says. "One who has survived. We shall take him with us."

Dru agrees. Though he doubts this boy will live through another winter. But he will help him try. They will have other sons. And daughters. They will need to. If they are to make their mark in this land.

"Come," he says. "We should be going. If we are to be back before nightfall."

Just as they are leaving the fort, something shiny catches Dru's eye. It glints in the last of the sun's hard light. He stoops to pick it up. It's a coin. Roman. The head of Decimus Clodius Albinus adorns one side. Dru bites its rim to test it.

"The Year of the Five Emperors," he says.

Bron says nothing. She doesn't understand what he means. She attends instead to the boy, Med, who is fussing.

Dru looks down. He sees a second coin, then another, then several. He tries to scoop them up.

"No," says Bron. "The time of Rome is over. What do we need their coins for? Leave them here. As tribute."

Dru nods. There is wisdom in Bron's words. He gathers all the coins into his fist, then hurls them as far as he can. He watches them arc like fish leaping, then hears the splash as they land in the small brook that flows into the Erewell across the moor at Coccium. Let the waters take them...

*

In the wilderness of Pomona, close to the edge of the Irwell, a rat noses from her most recent refuge within a broken pipe. She cautiously scents the air. Tentatively she takes a step outside. It feels safe. For now. The signs are hopeful, the prospects good.

She scuttles back to the pipe to collect her litter of twelve pups. They have been hiding there for the last seven days. They've not yet opened their eyes, but they are beginning to perceive the light through their still-sealed lids. The mother needs to move them to higher ground, for the pipe has started to fill with water. Although they still cannot see, nor hear yet, their sense of smell is already finely tuned. The mother knows they will be able to follow where she leads them.

She picks her way through the detritus of the wasteland until she reaches another channel of water. She could easily swim across it, but her pups would drown. She explores along the bank of the channel, until she discovers a narrow bridge. Someone has laid a piece of metal over the water to the other side. It is just wide enough for her and her pups to cross. The mother tests it to see whether it will take her weight. It does.

She hurries back to where she has left her twelve babies waiting for her. They huddle around her for protection and warmth. She leads them to the bridge. One by one they cross, all of them, safely to the other side...

*

It is dusk by the time Dru and Bron return to the camp. Look-outs have been posted to watch for their coming. They sing songs of joy to welcome them back. Dru looks about him. Med is asleep in Bron's arms. Yes, he thinks. This is a good place to settle. A good place to call home. Here in the confluence of the three rivers...

Postscript

2022

Jenna and Séydou now live full time in Fairfield Square. Séydou has retired from *Médecins Sans Frontières,* but is still called on occasionally to give operational advice when the organisation is planning to enter a new war zone.

His daughter, Awa, remains at the Royal Manchester Children's Hospital, where she is now a Speciality Registrar in Paediatrics. His son, Omar, is continuing with his Research Fellowship at the Manchester Institute of Biotechnology, as part of Dr Konstantina Drocou's team investigating the evolution of new diseases, with a particular focus on the emergence of new coronavirus variants.

Zafirah has been transferred from Yemen to Djibouti to be closer to her parents, where she coordinates the supplies of food and medicines by air and sea whenever a temporary cease-fire permits. Dr Nina Müller of the International Red Cross has left the Za'atari Camp in Jordan to head up a new team in Tigray, Ethiopia, while Zainab is now a psychiatric nurse at the Priory Hospital, Cheadle, near Manchester.

Jenna still works for the Refugee Council but in a more strategic capacity now. She no longer undertakes as many overseas field trips, so that she can be around more for Maleek.

Maleek has just begun her first year at Fairfield High School for Girls. She has settled in well and made many friends. Her wounds are healed. She has no more nightmares. She speaks fluent English with a strong Manchester accent.

*

Chloe has been invited to join the team of guest presenters for

BBC's *Newsnight*. She continues to host her phone-in and talk-show programmes on Radio Manchester, presents occasional special reports still for *North-West Tonight*, as well as writing online feature articles for *The Guardian* and *The Independent*.

Petros has formed a new company – *Philotimo*, which literally translates from the Greek as 'being good by doing good'. Its mission is to persuade property developers to include affordable units in any new build, and to convert existing derelict buildings into shelters and hostels to support the homeless and assist rough sleepers in coming off the streets. His first success has been the purchase of Ashton House, the former women's hostel built towards the end of the 19th century, where the glass artist Caitlin Mallone lived for several years. This is now a women's and children's home. Ruth is one of its Trustees.

Tulip House is soon to reopen as a smaller Women's Refuge, to be managed by Meera. Ruth and Yasmin have cautiously agreed to keep seeing each other.

Chloe and Petros decide to launch a joint blog. Their first posting is to announce their engagement. Petros promises Chloe that, for their first dance after they get married, he will learn the Kyoko routine from the film *Ex Machina*.

*

Clive's book *A Northern Gaze* is to be turned into a documentary series for BBC 4. Florence will compose the theme music. The couple still live in Park Range with their dog, Rafe.

*

Tom has completed the renovation of the old weaver's cottage on Cockey Moor near Bury. He and Apichu finally moved in earlier this year. Samancha, who was three last Christmas, is expecting a baby brother or sister before the next one.

*

Khav and Tanya continue to live in Fallowfield. Tanya still works in the Media Department of MMU, but no longer as a technician. She has recently been appointed as a Lecturer in Creative Coding for SODA, the School of Digital Arts. Khav still juggles her time between the Arts Council and the Manchester Festival, and she has now been invited to become an Artistic Advisor to the Board of Z-Arts, having worked there as a Community Arts practitioner for the last ten years.

Her sister Priya still lives with her husband Duleep and their children Dilsher and Rukmini in her mother Geetha's home on Albion Road near Platt Fields. Priya has been able to re-launch her mobile hairdressing business, *The Salon in your Living Room*, and is her former ebullient self again. Dilsher, now aged thirteen, has just become the North-West Under 18's Chess Champion, while Rukmini wants to be a break dancer like her Auntie Khav.

Khav and Tanya have registered to become a civil partnership. The ceremony will take place at Manchester's Contact Theatre on Oxford Road next summer.

*

Lorrie continues to perform internationally at festivals under the stage name *Lorelenka* as a tightrope walker, fire poi and aerial artist. She has recently set up her own YouTube channel, which has picked up more than 35,000 followers world-wide in its first three months.

Just last month she live-streamed her wedding to the Promoter and DJ Lance King on the stage of the St Kitts Music Festival at Bird Rock, Basseterre, during the headline act by The Ting Tings. They plan to return to Manchester in the autumn.

*

Molly, Michael and Blessing continue to live in Patricroft, with Nadia, who is now 82 years young, in the house first lived in by Yasser and Rose, then later Ishtar and Hejaz, and where Sol was born. In the Queen's Birthday Honours List Nadia is awarded an MBE for 'services to adult literacy'. After the success of her *Ornaments of Grace* installation, Molly is planning her next large outdoor event, but as yet is giving no clues as to what it will be.

Michael continues to lecture in the History Department of the University of Manchester. Last month he posted the following on Facebook:

Michael Adebayo added 8 new photos.

Molly, Blessing and I would like to introduce you to our newest addition, Pomona Hope Wahid Adebayo, to be known as Hope, born yesterday at 13:50 weighing 7lbs 11oz at home as planned. We are over the moon.

Hope is the light that shines on the water. Hope is the harbour we all of us sail towards. There is an old Yoruba proverb my mother taught me. The shortest way is the way to home. But the longest way is to reach the first bend. Hope is the hand that guides us on our way...

*

Here ends the final book of *Ornaments of Grace*

'Where no wood is, the fire goeth out; so where there is no tale-bearer, the strife ceaseth...'

Proverbs 26: 20

The Story of a Coin

195 AD:
Following the death of Pertinax, Decius Clodius Albinus is appointed Governor of the Roman province of Britannia and declares himself Emperor. Unfortunately for Clodius, so do four other generals. This becomes known as the Year of the Five Emperors. In order to consolidate his somewhat weak position, Clodius hastily orders coins bearing his portrait to be struck at the Roman Fort of Ribchester, thirty-eight miles north of Manchester, but his bid to become sole Emperor fails with his death four years later.

368 AD:
The Romans are beginning to withdraw from Britain. Dru, a conscripted centurion from Galicia, posted to Mamucium (the Latin name for Manchester), deserts and decides to remain. He meets Bron, a local Setanti tribeswoman, and the two ride away together to make a new camp. They follow the course of the River Irwell towards its source. At the abandoned hill fort at Coccium, (also known as Castlesteads), near Bury, they come across a cache of Roman coins left behind by the departing soldiers. Dru takes as many as he can carry, but Bron persuades him to leave them behind. As tribute. He agrees. He and Bron return to Manchester and decide to settle in the confluence of the three rivers – the Irwell, the Irk and the Medlock.

1785:
Caroline Lees and her eight-year-old daughter, Agnes, are living temporarily at the home of her Cousin Silas, a weaver, in a cottage close to the Elton Brook on the edge of Cockey Moor. One day Agnes, while playing with her brother James and Silas's sons, Ham and Shem, finds one of the coins dropped by Dru fourteen hundred years before. James tragically dies in the Elton Brook. Agnes blames herself. Shortly afterwards her

father, John, returns to take his wife and daughter to the Moravian Settlement in Fairfield, which he has helped to build. On their way they get caught up in enormous crowds clamouring to see a Balloon Flight in Angel Meadow. While waiting to get through, Agnes sees a young boy fall into the River Irwell. Instinctively she plunges in and rescues him. The boy's name is Amos. He is an orphan, and John and Caroline decide to adopt him and take him with them to Fairfield.

1798:

Agnes and Amos turn twenty-one. During their time at the Moravian Settlement, where, since the age of fourteen, they have lived separately in the Single Sisters' and Single Brethren's houses respectively, they have fallen in love and desire to marry. Everyone is in favour, but first they must submit their request to the Lot, a draw of chance, leaving the decision to Fate, or God, who is deemed infallible. The Lot decides against them, so they flee the Settlement in the middle of the night and escape back to the cottage of Cousin Silas. There, they perform their own secret marriage ceremony under the stars. Amos gives Agnes a ring he has forged from iron, while Agnes gives Amos the Roman coin as a token of her love.

1808:

Ten years later Amos and Agnes have fallen on hard times. Amos is forced to work away, in the coal mines of Bradford Pit, close to the Ashton Canal. While working the newly-excavated Charlotte seam, there is a gas explosion and Amos is badly injured. It takes the other workers three days to dig him out. He survives, but he has lost the coin in the accident.

1953:

The Bradford Pit is now a much-extended, fully modernised mine, employing three thousand men. An electrical fault causes a fire to break out, which damages the winding gear used to bring the men back to the surface at the end of their shift. Three hundred and fifty men are stranded more than half a mile underground. In order to get back to the surface, they must climb a series of ladders up a narrow ventilation shaft. One of the men, Toby Chadwick, takes it on himself to supervise the men's safe return. In relays of five at a time they painstakingly make their way up. Toby, with four other men, is the last to make the ascent. But the ladders in the ventilation shaft have not been constructed to carry such sustained weight, and as he steps onto the first of them, it comes away from the rock face, leaving him dangling in mid-air. In order to save himself, he plunges his hand into the hole where the ladder once held. As he does so, he finds the Roman coin. Eventually he and the other four remaining men make their way back to the surface by following older, long-abandoned shafts, and Toby decides he will keep the coin with him at all times, since it has brought him such good luck.

1968:
Bradford Colliery is shut down. Although there is reckoned to be at least another century's worth of coal to be mined, it is considered uneconomical to do so. Toby retires. No longer needing the coin to bring him luck, he decides he will pass it on to his oldest child, his daughter Milly, who is sixteen. Between them, they decide that this will now become a family tradition.

1975:
Milly gets married.

1980:
Milly has a daughter. Louise.

1996:
Louise turns sixteen. Milly duly passes the coin on to her.

2001:

Aged twenty-one, Louise has a child with Grant, who shortly afterwards she marries. Grant is the grandson of one of the other four men who escaped from the fire in Bradford Colliery by following the old abandoned mine shafts with Toby. His name was Lamarr Young, a former GI from the southern state of Georgia, where, before the War, he had been a miner. He was stationed at Melland Camp, near Gorton, while awaiting embarkation for D-Day, where he met and courted Pearl. After the War they married and had five children – Lamarr Jr, Candice, Dwight, and the twins, Kendra and LaShawne. Kendra has a son, and this is Grant, who marries Louise. They name their child, also a daughter, Iyesha.

2017:

Iyesha turns sixteen. On the day of her birthday she is given the coin with great ceremony. She is also given, almost as an afterthought, a ticket to see Ariana Grande at the Manchester Arena. Just before she leaves for the concert, Iyesha puts the coin into her jeans pocket. After the show has ended, she is badly injured in the terror attack. But her life is saved by the coin in her pocket, which takes the full force of a piece of shrapnel, thus preventing it from possibly severing her femoral artery. She tells part of her story to the Queen when she is visited by her in hospital, then fully to Chloe on a Radio Manchester phone-in after she has gone back home. Iyesha is a pupil at the Parrs Wood High School, East Didsbury, where she is a member of a choir. This choir records a version of the Ariana Grande song *My Everything* to raise money for the victims. Its success is such that Ariana invites them to perform with her at the *One Love Benefit Concert* just two weeks after the attack. Iyesha, who has sufficiently recovered to be able to take part, clutches the coin in her hand, which Grant has now had made into a necklace for her, to give her the strength to sing.

Languages Currently Spoken in Manchester

Acholi - spoken in Uganda and South Sudan
Afrikaans – spoken in South Africa
Akan (Asante) - spoken in Ghana and the Ivory Coast
Albanian
Amharic - spoken in Ethiopia
Arabic
Armenian
Assyrian (Aramaic) - spoken in Iran and Syria
Azeri - spoken in Azerbaijan
Balochi - spoken in Iran
Beja (Bedawi)- spoken in Sudan
Bemba - spoken in NE Zambia
Bengali – spoken in India
Bengali (Sylheti) - spoken in North Eastern Bangladesh
Berber/Tamazight – spoken in Morocco
Bikol - spoken in the Philippines
British Sign Language
Bulgarian
Caribbean Creole English
Caribbean Creole French
Chechen
Chichewa (Nyanja) - spoken in Zambia
Chinese (Cantonese) - spoken in China
Chinese (Hakka) - spoken in Southern China and Taiwan
Chinese (Hokkien/ Fujianese) - spoken in China, SE Asia
Chinese (Mandarin/ Putonghua) - spoken in China
Chitonga - spoken in Zambia
Chitrali/Khowar - spoken in North Western Pakistan
Czech
Dagaare - spoken in Ghana and Burkina Faso
Danish
Dari - spoken in Afghanistan
Dutch/Flemish
Ebira - spoken in Nigeria
Edo/Bini - spoken in Nigeria
Efik-Ibibio - spoken in Nigeria
Eleme - spoken in Nigeria
English
Esan - spoken in Nigeria

Estonian
Ewe – south-eastern Ghana and southern Togo
Fang Farsi - spoken in Iran and Afghanistan
Filipino
Finnish
French
Fula - spoken in Guinea, Cameroon and Sudan
Ga - spoken in Ghana
Gaelic – spoken in Ireland
Gallic – spoken in Scotland
Georgian
German
Gorani - spoken in Kosovo, Albania and Macedonia
Greek
Greek (Cypriot)
Guarani - spoken in Paraguay
Gujarati - spoken in India
Hausa - spoken in Chad
Hebrew
Hindi
Hungarian
Icelandic
Idoma - spoken in Nigeria
Igala - spoken in Nigeria
Igbo - spoken in Nigeria
Indonesian
Italian
Japanese
Kannada - spoken in India
Katchi - spoken in India and Pakistan
Kikuyu - spoken in Kenya
Kinyarwanda - spoken in Rwanda
Kirghiz - spoken in Kyrgyzstan
Kirundi - spoken in Rwanda
Konkani - spoken on the Western coast of India
Korean
Krio - spoken in Sierra Leone
Kurdish (Kurmanji) - spoken in Iran
Kurdish (Bahdini) - spoken in Iran
Kurdish (Sorani) - spoken in Iran
Latvian

Lingala - spoken in the Democratic Republic of Congo
Lithuanian
Lozi - spoken in Zambia
Luganda - spoken in Uganda
Lugbara - spoken in Uganda
Macedonian
Malay
Malayalam - spoken in India
Maldivian - spoken in the Maldive Islands
Malinke - spoken in West Africa
Maltese
Marathi - spoken in India
Mende - spoken in Sierra Leone
Mongolian (Khalkha)
Myanma – spoken in Burma
Nahuatl – spoken in Mexico
Ndebele - spoken in South Africa and Zimbabwe
Nigerian
Nepali
Pahari - spoken in Nepal and India
Pangasinan - spoken in the Philippines
Panjabi - spoken in Pakistan & India
Panjabi (Gurmukhi)
Panjabi (Mirpuri)
Panjabi (Pothwari)
Pashto - spoken in Afghanistan and Pakistan
Persian – spoken in Iran
Pidgin English
Polish
Portuguese
Quecha (Peru)
Romani (Kelderash) spoken in Romania & Ukraine
Romani (East Slovak)
Romani (Baltic)
Romanian
Romany (English Romanes)
Russian
Samoan
Serbian/Croatian/Bosnian
Sesotho - spoken in South Africa
Setswana - spoken in Southern Africa

Shona - spoken in Zimbabwe and Zambia
Shelta - spoken in Ireland
Sindhi - spoken in Pakistan
Sinhala - spoken in Sri Lanka
Slovak
Slovenian
Somali
Spanish
Swahili (Bajuni/Tikuu) - spoken widely in East Africa
Swahili (Brava/ Mwiini) - spoken widely in East Africa
Swahili (Kiswahili) - spoken widely in East Africa
Swazi (Siswati) - spoken in Swaziland
Swedish
Tagalog – spoken in the Philippines
Tamil - spoken in India and Sri Lanka
Telugu - spoken in India
Temne - spoken in Sierra Leone
Thai
Tigre - spoken in Sudan
Tigrinya - spoken in Eritrea
Tiv - spoken in Nigeria
Tumbuka - spoken in Malawi, Zambia and Tanzania
Turkish
Turkmen
Ukrainian
Umbundu - spoken in Angola
Urdu - spoken in Pakistan and India
Urhobo-Isoko - spoken in Nigeria
Uyghur – spoken in China
Vietnamese
Welsh
Wolof - spoken in Senegal
Xhosa - spoken in South Africa
Yiddish
Yoruba - spoken in Western Africa
Zulu - spoken in South Africa

[supplied by the Multilingual Manchester Project, University of Manchester]

Other Manchesters

Canada:
Manchester, Durham County, Ontario (pop.9395)
Manchester, Guysborough County, Novia Scotia (pop. 4670)

USA:
Manchester, Jackson County, Wisconsin (pop. 848)
Manchester, Kitsap County, Washington (pop. 5413)
Manchester, Chesterfield County, Richmond, Virginia (pop. 18,804)
Manchester, Bennington County, Vermont (pop. 4258)
Manchester, Houston, Texas (pop. 4000 approx.)
Manchester, Coffee County, Tennessee (pop. 10,102)
Manchester, Kingsbury County, South Dakota (now a ghost town)
Manchester, York County, Pennsylvania (pop. 2763)
Manchester, Grant County, Oklahoma (pop. 103)
Manchester, Adams County, Ohio (pop. 2023)
Manchester, Ontario County, New York (pop. 1728)
Manchester, Cumberland County, North Carolina (pop. 24,643)
Manchester, Hillsborough County, New Hampshire (pop. 112,109)
Manchester, St. Louis County, Missouri (pop. 18,110)
Manchester, Cascade County, Montana (pop. 1720)
Manchester, Freeborn County, Minnesota (pop. 57)
Manchester, Washtenaw County, Michigan (pop. 1993)
Manchester-by-the-Sea, Essex County, Massachusetts (pop. 5429)
Manchester, Kennebec County, Maine (pop. 2580)
Manchester, Carroll County, Maryland (pop. 4832)
Manchester, Calcasieu Parish, Louisiana (pop. 354)
Manchester, Dickenson County, Kansas (pop. 130)
Manchester, Clay County, Kentucky (pop. 1779)
Manchester, Delaware County, Iowa (pop. 5019)
Manchester, Dearborn County, Indiana (pop. 3215)
Manchester, Montgomery County, Indiana (pop. 38)
Manchester, Scott County, Illinois (pop. 258)
Manchester, Meriwether County, Georgia (pop. 3961)
Manchester, Hartford County, Connecticut (pop. 29,972)
Manchester, Mendocino County, California (pop. 218)
Manchester, Walker County, Alabama (pop. 91)
Manchester, Ocean County, New Jersey (pop. 43,416)
Manchester, Custer County, Nebraska (pop. 1650)

South America:
Manchester, Nickerie, Suriname (pop. 748)
Manchester, Pando, Bolivia (pop. 195)

Caribbean:
Manchester, Middlesex County, Jamaica (pop. 190,812)

Australia:
Manchester, Iron Knob, Eyre Peninsula, South Australia (pop. 199)
Manchester Square, New South Wales, Australia (pop. 19)

Africa:
Additionally there is a township in Kenya, which was originally named for the 6th Duke of Manchester, but which has subsequently been redesignated as:

Moi's Bridge, Trans-Nzoia County, Kenya (pop. 16,395)

India
Two cities in India have been nicknamed 'the Manchester of India':

Ahmedabad, Gujurat (pop. 5.57 million)
Kanpur, Uttar Pradesh (pop. 2.92 million)

Variants of the Manchester Moth

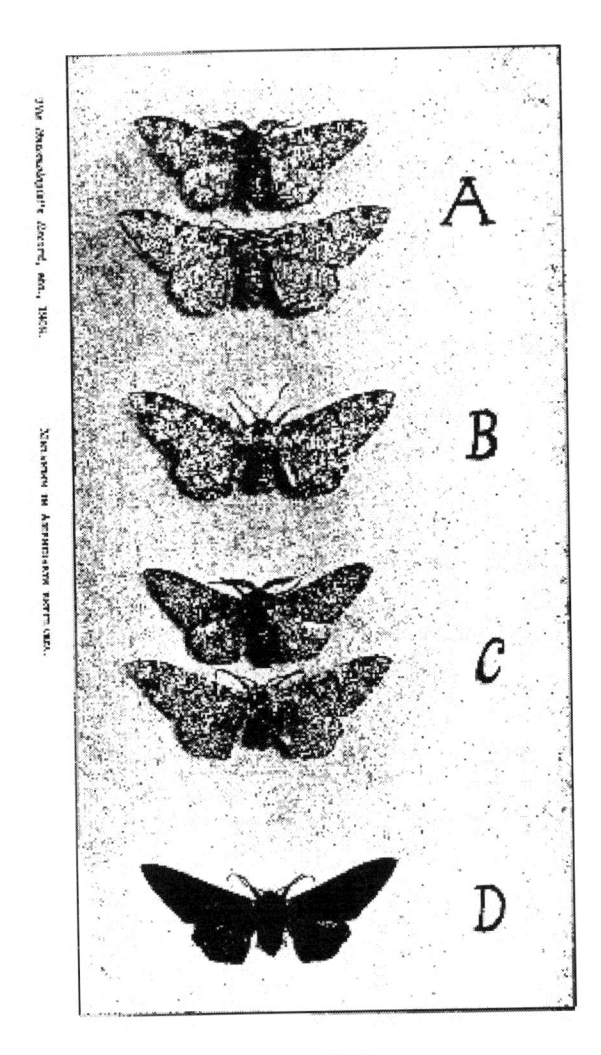

Peppered Moth
Manchester Museum
Illustration: Philips, Leigh, 1804
Euclemensia woodiella: Cosmopterigidae: Lepidoptera: Insecta:

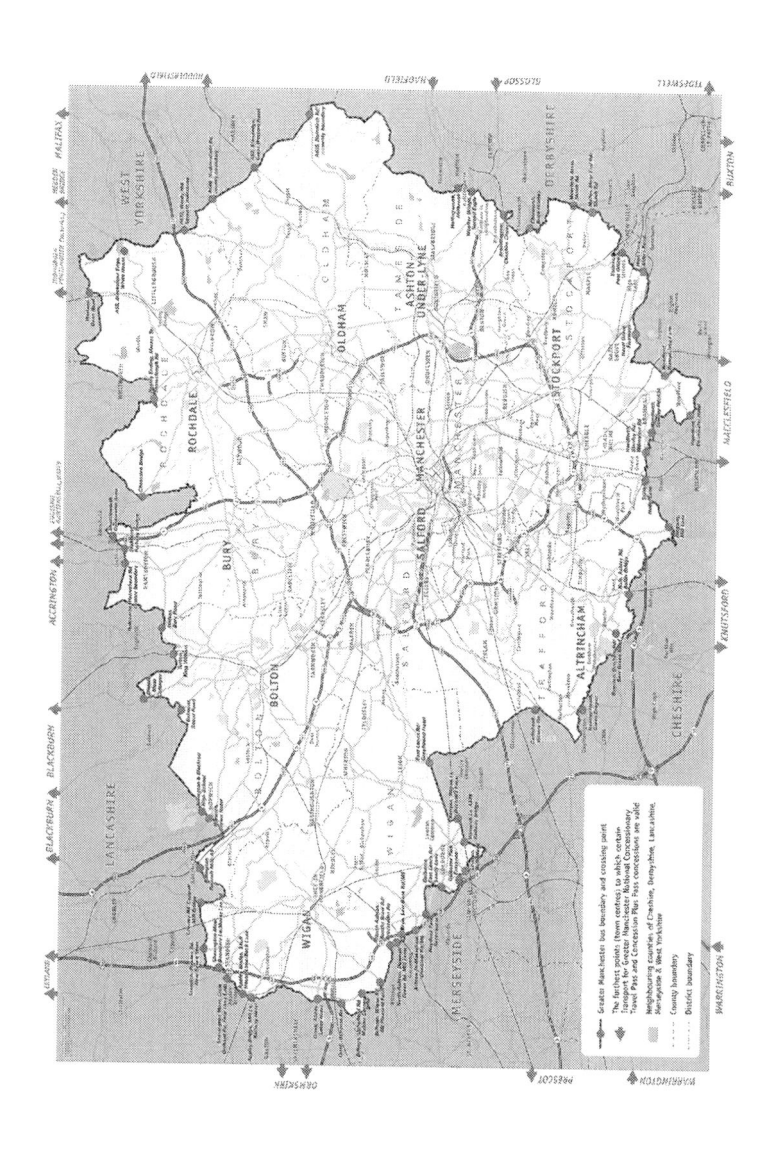

Current Map of Greater Manchester

Dramatis Personae

(in order of appearance)

CAPITALS = Main Characters; **Bold** = Significant Characters;
Plain = Characters (who appear once or twice only)

JENNA, daughter of Sol & Nadia, mother of Molly
Sol, Nadia's husband, Jenna's father, Molly's grandfather
Hejaz, Sol's father, Yasser's son
Yasser, Hejaz's father
Rose, Yasser's wife
MOLLY, Jenna's daughter, an artist
Séydou, Médecins Sans Frontières, Jenna's partner
Nadia, Jenna's mother
GEORGE, a photographer and teacher
LANCE, Anita's son, Jenna's boyfriend & Molly's father
Esther/Ishtar, Hejaz's wife, Sol's mother
Anita, Lance's mother, Community Worker, Moss Side
Bex, friend of Jenna in Squat
Zafirah, Yemeni Aid Worker
Viraj Mendis, asylum & sanctuary seeker
Karen Roberts, campaigner in support of Viraj, later his wife
Father John Methuen, Rector of the Church of the Ascension, Hulme, where Viraj Mendis seeks sanctuary
Spike, friend of Jenna in Squat
Dougie, friend of Jenna in Squat
Caroline, friend of Jenna in Squat, Dougie's girl friend
Amani Yayha, female Yemeni rapper
Farida, Nadia's sister, Jenna's aunt
Tawakkol Karwan, Yemeni Nobel Peace Laureate
DJ Persian, The Reno Club
PC Nigel Taylor, police officer who helps Jenna during Moss Side Riots
Nigel Taylor's father
MALEEK, orphaned child in Yemen
Saba El-Harazy, Maleek's mother, cleaner at Hodeidah Airport

Vice-Chancellor MMU, 1984
Amreen Qureshi, Jenna's job-share at IPPR
Salwa, Nadia & Farida's mother
Jamal, Nadia & Farida's father
'The Aunties', Salwa's widowed friends
Barbara, teacher at Fairfield High School, Moravian Settlement, friend of Ruth
RUTH, Lily and Roland's daughter, a psychotherapist
Grace, a retired archaeologist, Iyesha's Great Aunt
Mishal Hussain, BBC News Presenter
Michael, Molly's husband, Lecturer in History at University of Manchester
Aid Worker, Mishqafa Camp, Yemen
Meera, receptionist and book-keeper at Tulip House
Angelina Jolie, actor & political campaigner
Florence Blundell, jazz singer and trumpeter, Clive's partner
Major Naveed Khan, UN Delegation, Yemen
Dr Nina Müller, Mishqafa Camp
Zainab, aid worker in Yemen, later mental health nurse at Cheadle Royal Hospital
Tony Walsh, Manchester poet
Sybil, Marriage Registrar, Heron House, Manchester
Ndeyou, Séydou's ex-wife
Awa, Seydou's daughter
Omar, Seydou's son
Lily, George's adoptive sister, Roland's wife, Ruth's mother
Roland, Lily's husband, former German POW, early computer worker
Mary Chadwick, wife of Jabez, mother of Grace, friend of Lily
Ruth Kaufmann, Lily's mother, Ruth's grandmother
Ngonzia, Michael's mother from Nigeria
Nnenne & Ndidi, Ngonzia's sisters
Kirsty Young, former presenter of Desert Island Discs
Blessing, Molly & Michael's daughter
Cam, aka Chamomile Catch, the Manchester Songbird
FRANCIS, former audio-visual specialist, now a gallery owner
DELPHINE, retired Audiology Professor

Lester Sleigh, solicitor in Denton
Lorna Woods, Mr Sleigh's secretary
Giulia Lockhart, fashion designer
Annie Wright, George's mother & Hubert's wife
Friedrich Kaufmann, Ruth Kaufmann's father
Hubert Wright, George's father & Annie's husband
Cancer Doctor, Christie's Hospital
Luigi, former Head Porter at The Queen's Hotel
Giancarlo, Luigi's nephew
Arnold Murray, former lover of Alan Turing
Leroy Beauregard King, a jazz trumpeter, Lance's father
Christopher, Clive's brother
CLIVE ARCHER, retired Lecturer in Media Studies MMU, Florence's partner
Pearl, Lily's friend from St Bridget's, wife of Lamarr
Lamarr Young, former GI, ex-miner, husband of Pearl
Lamarr Jr, Pearl & Lamarr's son
Candice, Pearl & Lamarr's daughter
Dwight, Pearl & Lamarr's second son
Kendra, Pearl & Lamarr's younger daughter, grandmother of Iyesha
LaShawne, Kendra's twin sister
Jenny, Lily's friend from St Bridget's
Gertrude Riall, retired singing teacher, Jenny's companion
Sammy, a Native American, Delphine's father
Eve, a deaf mute, Delphine's mother
Charles Trevelyan, retired surgeon, Manchester Royal Infirmary
Leonard Gorodkin, Coroner for Bob's Lane Ferry disaster
Bernard Carroll, ferryman & victim of disaster
Albert Wimbleton, victim of disaster
Brian Hillier, victim of disaster
Roy Platt, victim of disaster
Alan Cliff, victim of disaster
Daniel MacAlister, injured survivor
George Morrell, injured survivor
Robert Kilgour, injured survivor

Stephen Hunter, injured survivor
Jim Fogarty, temporary ferryman successor to Bernard Carroll
Dorothy Fogarty, Jim's wife
Caitlin Mallone, glass artist, Francis's mother
Winifred, Francis's 'passepartout' in Denton shop
Saoirse Kineen, aspiring glass artist exhibiting at Francis's gallery
Tommy Thunder, a Native American
Old Moon, a Native American
Linda Billings, mother of toddler at Ishtar's accident
Alan Rees, florist's delivery van driver
Alan Carmichael LLB, Coroner at Delphine's inquest
Dr Hamid, Delphine's GP
Nancy Cotton, a librarian
Laurel Stone, a 100 year-old suffragist
Mr Vogts, George's Anglo-German English teacher at William Hulme's Grammar School
Mrs Tiffin, George's piano teacher
Archie Rowe, a sign writer
L.S. Lowry, the painter
Catch, a Native American blacksmith, father of Cam
Clem, freed Louisana slave, wife of Catch, mother of Cam
Craig, owner of Buile Hill Motors
Paul Turner, Gay Men's Officer, Manchester City Council 1986
Maggie Fairweather, Lesbian Officer, Manchester City Council 1986
Michael Fish, BBC Weather Man
Julie Goodyear, actress portraying Bet Lynch in Coronation Street
Shirley, Jacqui, Bez, friends of Barbara who dress up as Village People
Yasmin, an English teacher, a friend of Ruth
Ariana Grande, pop superstar
CHLOE CHANG, journalist and TV news reporter
Eddy Newman, Lord Mayor of City of Manchester
Andy Burnham, Mayor of Greater Manchester
Right Reverend David Walker, Bishop of Manchester

Xie Mei, Chloe's grandmother
Bao, Chloe's father
LORELEI ZLATAN, aka Lorrie, aka Lorelenka, Gallery Manager at Islington Mill, a tightrope walker & aerial artist
Iyesha Young, teenage fan of Ariana Grande
Bethany Wood, friend of Iyesha
Joelle LaGrange, friend of Iyesha
Louise, Iyesha's mother
Grant, Iyesha's father
Luther, Iyesha's brother
Toby, Iyesha's great-grandfather, Grace's brother
Milly, Iyesha's grandmother, Toby's daughter
Doctor treating Iyesha at St Mary's Children's Hospital
Mark McElwee, Head of Parrs Wood Comprehensive School
Homeless Woman with Angel Tattoo
Elaine Bishop, Park Range Residents' Association
Phil Barton, Park Range Residents' Association
Jamilah Mursal, Warden at Hirstwood, Methodist International Centre
Tanya, media technician at MMU
Khavita Kaur, aka Khav, arts administrator for Arts Council & Manchester International Festival
Sunanda Biswas, Lorrie's assistant at Islington Mill
Apichu, originally from Peru, Tom's wife, friend of Molly
Tom, freelance journalist, Apichu's husband, building a house
Samancha, Tom & Apichu's daughter
Tracy Hawkins, Manager at Tower Mill
Anthony Green, Manager at Blackburn Yarn Dyers
Debbie Catterall, boss of John Spencer Weavers
James Eden, boss of Private White VC
Dmitri Logunov, Head of Entomology, Manchester Museum
Richard Gahan, Balloonist
Austin Heginbottom, Balloonist
Jackie Wells, Manager Rope & Rigging Ltd
Krysztof, Lorrie's great uncle
Pavel, Lorrie's great uncle
Lena, Lorrie's grandmother

Lorelei, Lorrie's late grandmother
Agniewska, Lorrie's great aunt
Milosz, Lorrie's father
Lauren Murphy, Bradford Pit Project
Michael Doherty, ex-miner, Bradford Colliery
PETROS, a property developer, friend of Chloe
Konstantin, Petros' great-great-grandfather
Vassily, Petros' great-grandfather
Alexis, Petros' father
Sophia, Petros' mother
Callista, Petros' sister
Andreas, Callista's husband
Yannis, Andres & Callista's son
Small child sleeping beside woman with angel tattoo
Graham Nash, a musician
Young People in Molly's installation
Dru, a Roman conscript, initially from Galicia
Bron, a Setanti tribeswoman
Med, a foundling boy
Female rat and her twelve pups

The following are mentioned by name:

[The Stone Roses]
[Child Rebels in Aden]
[Johnny Ray, a singer]
[Captain on Flight to Yemen]
[MMU Student Accommodation Officer]
[Abi Abdullah Saleh, former President of Yemen]
[Abd Rabbuh Mansoor Hadi, Deputy President of Yemen]
[Al-Qaeda Militants]
[Houthi Insurgents]
[Ahmed, Saleh's son]
[Sunni & Shia factions in Yemen]
[Militant Tendency, Manchester Labour Party]
[Blairites]
[Bennites]

[Graham Stringer, Leader of Manchester City Council 1980s]
[John Nicholson, Deputy Leader]
[Pat Karney, Senior Labour Party Councillor, Manchester 1980s]
[Arnold Spencer, ditto]
[Bernard Sutton, ditto]
[Richard Lees, ditto]
[Yemeni refugees]
[Protestors in support of Viraj Mendis]
[Police Officers arresting Viraj]
[Douglas Hurd, Home Secretary 1989]
[Amnesty International Officials]
[UN Officials]
[Meryam, Yemeni victim for refusing to be a child bride]
[Yemeni Students in empty building next to Hotel Al-Mer, Aden]
[Ian Curtis, vocalist Joy Division]
[Gillian Gilbert, keyboard player New Order]
[Bernard Sumner, guitarist & vocalist New order]
[Crowds at The Haçienda]
[Tony Wilson, founder of Factory Records & The Haçienda]
[Patrick Geddes, Scottish Town Planner]
[A.A. Milne, writer]
[Joni Mitchell, singer-songwriter]
[Malcolm X, Black Power Leader]
[Neil Armstrong, astronaut]
[Thomas Paine, 18th century Radical]
[Bertolt Brecht, dramatist]
[Mary Shelley, author]
[Voltaire, writer & philosopher]
[Pierre-Joseph Roudon, philosopher]
[Girls with Lance in Squat]
[John Henry Poynting, 19th century physicist]
[Leila Mourad, Egyptian pop singer]
[Naghat al-Saghira, ditto]
[Mounira al-Madeyha, ditto]
[Tawakkol Karwan's father, a poet]
[Tawwakol Karwan's mother, a lawyer]
[William Cobbett, 19th century Radical]
[Manchester's Magistrates, early 19th century]
[Soldiers marching through Aden streets]
[Army Commander, Aden]
[Police at Squat, Moss Side]

[Policewoman with torch]
[Crowd in Moss Lane East haranguing Police]
[Police Officer with bag of cannabis]
[White Desk Sergeant at Platt Lane Police Station]
[Yemeni Govt. Officials in Crater, Ma'alla, Tawahi]
[Goatherd near Taiz]
[Children asking for dollars & pens near Taiz]
[Muhammad Ali, world champion boxer]
[Bob Marley, musician]
[Crowds at The Reno & The Nile]
[Rikki Rogers, vocalist Harlem Shuffle]
[Max Thompson, sax player Harlem Shuffle]
[The Valentine Brothers, soul singers]
[Gang of black youths outside The Reno]
[Off-duty white policemen outside The Reno]
[Soldiers at road-blocks outside Taiz]
[Families fleeing Taiz]
[General of Coalition Forces at Checkpoint outside Taiz]
[Houthi Soldiers near Mosques in Taiz]
[Mrs Martin, Head of Reprographics at Jenna's school]
[Staff & Pupils arriving at Jenna's school]
[Steel Pulse, a reggae band]
[The Buzzcocks, a punk band]
[Deputy Head, Jenna's school]
[Harassed Officials & Office Workers at The Citadel, Taiz]
[Frightened Civilians in Taiz]
[Houthi Troops entering Taiz]
[Major, Houthi Troops, Taiz]
[Local Taiz Youths hurling stones at soldiers]
[Moss Side Community Leaders, Moss Side 1981]
[James Anderton, Chief Constable of Greater Manchester 1981]
[Rioters in Moss Side]
[Police & Riot Squad in Moss Side]
[John Carpenter, film director]
[Kurt Russell, actor]
[14 Police Officers trapped inside Platt Lane Police Station]
[Police with batons emerging from Black Marias]
[Mother of PC Nigel Taylor]
[Children playing on slag heaps at Bradford Pit]
[Women collecting coal in baskets on their backs]
[Old men collecting coal in prams]

[Paramedics treating PC Nigel Taylor]
[Gang of black & white youths who throw a brick at Jenna]
[Soldiers at Airport Terminal, Hodeidah]
[Waiting Passengers, Hodeidah Airport]
[Passengers on flight from Taiz to Hodeidah]
[Graduating students & families, Whitworth Hall 1984]
[Edward Lorenz, US meteorologist]
[Margaret Thatcher, former Prime Minister of UK]
[Cronies of Council Leader Graham Stringer]
[Douglas Mason, Policy Chief Adam Smith Institute]
[Tony Blair, former Prime Minister of UK]
[Eric Cantona, Man Utd footballer]
[Xenophobic fan abusing Cantona]
[Journalists at Press Conference by Cantona]
[Soldier emerging from beneath jeep, Hodeidah Airport]
[Soldier intercepting Maleek on runway]
[Midwife with Jenna after birth of Molly]
[Jenna's GP]
[Homeless people on UK streets]
[Yuppie Traders on Stock Exchange]
[Captain on Paris to Manchester flight]
[Cardboard Citizens Theatre Company]
[Man accusing IRA of Manchester bomb]
[Young paramedic treating Grace after bomb attack]
[Bubble Man in Piccadilly Gardens]
[Donald Trump, former US President]
[Barack Obama, former US President]
[Lily Allen, pop singer]
[Benedict Cumberbatch, actor]
[Liam & Noel Gallagher, Oasis]
[David Hepworth, former TV Presenter 1980s]
[Elvis Costello, musician]
[Marcus Rashford, footballer & charity worker]
[Boris Johnson, UK Prime Minister]
[BBC Newsreader]
[Amber Rudd, Home Secretary, 2017]
[John Flavin, 17th century Dissenting Preacher]
[Soldiers at Mishqafa Camp, Aden]
[Children in Refugee Camp]
[Sabaa Tahir, author]
[Eleanor Rathbone, President of NUWSS after Millicent Fawcett]

[Zafirah's parents in Djibouti]
[Somalis in Ali-Addeh Camp, Djibouti]
[Ethiopians in Holl-Holl Camp, Djibouti]
[Yemenis in Murkhazi Camp, Djibouti]
[World War 1 Soldiers in Whitworth Park]
[The Sex Pistols, punk band]
[Bill Grundy, former Granada TV presenter]
[John Cooper Clarke, Bard of Salford, Poet Laureate of Punk]
[The Smiths, indie rock band]
[John Nash, 18th century architect]
[William Kent, ditto]
[Robert Adam, ditto]
[Charles Barry, ditto]
[Johnny Marr, guitarist The Smiths]
[Morrissey, vocalist The Smiths]
[Audience at G-Mex]
[Rita Tushingham, film actor 1960s]
[Female fans of Morrissey]
[Kind Security Guard, G-Mex]
[Crazed, red-eyed homeless person, Knott Mill]
[Bill Nighy, actor]
[Simon Pegg, actor]
[Ian McKewan, writer]
[Chris Martin, vocalist Coldplay]
[William Hague, former Leader of Conservative Party]
[13 year-old Iraqi girl war victim]
[Ruth's female friends she goes to plays & concerts with]
[Andrew Carnegie, philanthropist]
[Elizabeth Taylor, author]
[Rosamund Lehmann, author]
[Dorothy Whipple, author]
[Lettice Cooper, author]
[Delegates from UN, MSF, Save the Children, Oxfam, International Red Cross at Mishqafa Camp]
[Doctors & Aid Workers in Mishqafa Camp]
[Syrian Refugees, Za'atari Camp, Jordan]
[Matt, Barbara's husband]
[Year 7 & Year 11 Students, Fairfield Girls' School]
[Annie Horniman, owner of Gaiety Theatre]
[Stanley Houghton, playwright, author of 'Hindle Wakes']
[Ruth Kaufmann's fiancé]

[Ruth Kaufmann's fiancé's parents]
[James Sauer, archaeologist]
[Malnourished woman in surgical gown with daughter]
[Wounded Man hooked up to catheter]
[Doctors & Patients, Al-Thawra Hospital Hodeidah]
[Friday Worshippers, Badr & Al-Hashoosh Mosques Sana'a]
[Bride & Wedding Guests, Al-Raqa village]
[Khaled al-Nadhri, Provincial health Offical North-West Yemen]
[Hana Abri, wounded 12 year-old girl Hodeidah]
[Walaa Abzi, Hana's mother]
[Hana Absi's Father, teacher in Hodeidah]
[Guests at Molly & Michael's Wedding]
[Laurence Olivier, actor]
[Audience at Royal Exchange Theatre]
[Military Guard from Southern Transitional Council]
[Qasim al-Raymi, Yemeni Al-Qaeda Leader]
[Sandi Tostvig, President of Women of the Year]
[Lady Antonella Lothian, journalist & founder of Women of the Year]
[George Eliot, writer]
[Camilla, Duchess of Cornwall]
[Lauren Laverne, radio presenter, current host of Desert Island Discs]
[Trustees on Board of CARE UK]
[Patti Smith, poet & singer]
[Dr Konstantina Drosou, Manchester Institute of Biotechnology]
[Danny Boyle, film & theatre director]
[Julie Hesmondhalgh, actor portraying Mother Courage]
[Elders at Fairfield Moravian Settlement]
[Stewards on flight to Amman]
[Representatives of Active Care Solutions, a foster agency]
[Sleigh, Son & Booth, solicitors]
[Henry Wood, conductor & founder of Promenade Concerts]
[Ludwig van Beethoven, composer]
[Prometheus, the bringer of fire]
[Passers-by, Heaton Park]
[August Halsinger, Francis's father]
[Winsome Winnie Brown, aviatrix 1930s]
[King George V]
[Sefton Delmer, originator of Radio Aspidistra]
[Sir Bernard Lovell, radio astronomer, Jodrell Bank]
[Village People, gay pop group]
[Pair of Gladiators, men in fancy dress pulling chariot at M/cr Pride]

[Paramedics who find Francis]
[Elkie Brooks, Salford-born jazz singer]
[Fatalities from The Lusitania]
[Angry Mob in Denton]
[Robin Peacock, Chief Constable of Manchester 1915]
[Queen Victoria]
[Onslow Ford, sculptor of statue of Queen Victoria, Piccadilly Gardens]
[Small Crowd bidding farewell to The Queen's Hotel]
[King of Belgium]
[King of Portugal]
[King of Romania]
[Emperor of Brazil]
[Prince Louis Napoleon]
[President Ulysses S. Grant]
[General Gordon of Khartoum]
[Charles Dickens, author]
[William Makepeace Thackeray, author]
[William Houldsworth, textile tycoon, original owner of The Queen's Hotel]
[Thomas Houldsworth, William's son, a racehorse breeder]
[Louis Mitchell & The Dixie Kings, jazz musicians]
[Lamarr Jr's wife & children]
[Mourners at Lily's funeral]
[Henry Hill Vale, architect of St Paul's Methodist Church, Didsbury]
[Factory Workers, Cadishead]
[Ferry Passengers, Bob's Lane]
[Eye-witnesses, Bob's Lane Ferry Disaster]
[Emergency services attending aftermath of disaster]
[Police frogmen in Manchester Ship Canal]
[Sir Henry Platt, early 20th century orthopaedic surgeon Manchester Royal Infirmary]
[Retired colleagues of Delphine]
[Speeding Cyclist who almost knocks down Delphine]
[Warden at Newbury House]
[Alastair Hetherington, Editor of The Guardian, 1971]
[Les Gibbard, Guardian cartoonist 1970s & 80s]
[Technicians, North West Forensics Laboratory]
[Workers, Partington Coal Basin]
[Manager, Shell Chemicals]
[Victor Collins, a retired boxer, later married to Winifred]

[Winifred's grandchildren]
[Achilles, a Greek hero]
[Patroclus, Achilles' lover]
[Scarlett O'Hara, Gone with the Wind]
[Rhett Butler, ditto]
[Lerner & Loewe, composer & lyricist of My Fair Lady]
[Sandy Powell, 1930s Manchester comic actor]
[Diana Dors, film star]
[Honor Blackman, actor & Bond Girl]
[Stanley Baker, actor]
[Christopher Lee, actor]
[The Bee Gees, singers & musicians, born in Chorlton, Manchester]
[Jackson & Newport, cinema chain owners]]
[Henry Elder, cinema architect]
[Nova Pilbeam, British actor, 1930s]
[Alfred Hitchcock, film director]
[Peter Lorre, actor]
[Joan Fontaine, actor]
[Barbara Shelley, actor, aka Queen of Hammer]
[Solomon Sheckman, impresario]
[Esther Sheckman, wife of Solomon]
[Dorothy Sheckman, daughter of Solomon & Esther]
[Frederick Nietzsche, philosopher]
[Richard Strauss, composer]
[Mary Thornley, Manchester 'danseuse']
[Winnie & Hilda, The Lido Singers, aka A Song, A Smile & A See-Saw]
[Mickey Mouse, a cartoon character]
[Menander, a Roman playwright]
[Dr Beeching, Chair of British Railways]
[Geoffrey Chaucer, writer]
[Ship's Captain, boat from Isle of Man 1919]
[Guards at Intern Camp, Isle of Man]
[Guglielmo Marconi, inventor of the radio telegraph]
[1st Earl of Ellesmere]
[Edward Heath, former Prime Minister UK}
{Gatekeeper, Irlam Locks]
[Christopher Columbus, explorer]
[Vasco de Gama, explorer]
[Amerigo Vespucci, explorer]
[Ambulance Driver, Chat Moss]
[Schoolchildren, Godfrey Ermen School, Patricroft]

[Anxious Mother, Busy Bees Nursery]
[Derek, of Bridge Motors, Didsbury]
[Joe Gormley, National Union of Miners President, 1970s]
[Michael Thompsett, NASA Engineer]
[Nasir Ahmed, pioneer of digital cameras]
[Doctor treating Lily at Withington Hospital]
[Reverend A.E. Walker, Christ Church Patricroft]
[Mr al-Haideri, leader of Salford's first mosque]
[Ambulancemen, Liverpool Road, Eccles]
[Michael Wooton, Manager Sanctuary Housing]
[Bargemen assisting Yasser]
[Asif, a cart driver]
[Stevedores at Pomona Dock from around the world]
[Confucius, a philosopher]
[Francis Bacon, essayist]
[Sister Basil, Headmistress St Philip's RC School, Broughton]
[Clerk, Coroner's Court]
[Police Officer at Delphine's flat]
[Ambulanceman, ditto]
[Doctor, ditto]
[Pathologist submitting report to Coroner]
[Neighbour of Delphine]
[James Jepson, architect Levenshulme Library]
[Leos Janacek, composer]
[Charles Ives, composer]
[Burgess & Gaitt, building contractors]
[Sir Charles Alfred Cropps MP, 1st Baron of Parmoor]
[Librarian, Levenshulme Library]
[Adult students at George's Night School classes at The Mechanics' Institute]
[Gerard Manley Hopkins, a poet]
[William Wordsworth, a poet]
[Peter Craven speedway rider Belle Vue]
[Ivan Mauger, ditto]
[Ove Fundin, ditto]
[Jason Crump, ditto]
[Peter Collins]
[Workmen inside Manchester Central Library]
[Rudolf Koch, designer of Wallau font]
[William Morris, artist & writer]
[Paul Renner, font designer]

[Otto Beckmann, ditto]
[Peter Behrens, ditto]
[Giorgio Vasari, artist & critic]
[Michaelangelo, artist]
[Sir Edwin Lutyens, designer of Cenotaphs]
[Jake, the German Shepherd dog]
[Aaron, brother of Craig, owner of Buile Hill Motors]
[St Chad, Anglo-Saxon saint]
[King Penda, of Mercia]
[Daniel Defoe, writer & chronicler]
['Worsley Man', body found preserved in peat bog]
['Lindow Man', ditto]
['Lindow Woman', ditto]
[John Leland, Tudor chronicler of the realm]
[King Henry VIII]
[Mother Ann Lee, founder of the Shakers]
[George Stephenson, engineer of first steam railway locomotive]
[Mary Whitehouse, campaigner against permissive society]
[Malcolm Muggeridge, ditto]
[Bishop Huddleston, ditto]
[Lord Longford, ditto]
[Cliff Richard, pop singer, ditto]
[Tom Robinson, 80s musician]
[Abel Heywood, twice Mayor of Manchester during Victoria's reign]
[Crowds at Manchester Pride]
[Barbra Streisand, singing superstar]
[Donna Summer, disco singer]
[Gloria Gaynor, disco singer]
[Chaka Khan, disco singer]
[Soft Cell, pop duo]
[The Weather Girls, pop group]
[Decimus Clodius Albinus, Emperor of Rome 195 AD]
[Felipe Rose, founder member of Village People]
[Grace Jones, diva]
[Dead or Alive, 80s pop group]
[Sister Sledge, disco group]
[Madonna, pop superstar]
[David Bowie, musician & actor]
[Queen, rock group]
[Frankie Goes To Hollywood, 80s pop group]
[Kylie Minogue, pop superstar]

[Sylvester, disco singer]
[Cast from La Cage Aux Folles, drag queens]
[Whitney Houston, pop superstar]
[Abba, Swedish pop group]
[Dusty Springfield, 60s pop singer]
[Nina Simone, jazz singer & musician]
[Judy Garland, film star]
[Friends of Francis in Bookbinder's]
[George Frederick Handel, composer]
[Florence Blundell Quintet, jazz musicians]
[Mae West, film star]
[Hiawatha, legendary Native American]
[Old Nokomis, Daughter of the Moon]
[Wenonah, the West Wind]
[Minnehaha, Hiawatha's mother]
[Fans of Ariana Grande]
[Chief Constable Ian Hopkins, Greater Manchester 2017]
[British Transport Police]
[Bomb Disposal Squad, Manchester Arena]
[Early Morning Commuters in Manchester, day after terror attack]
[Queen Elizabeth II]
[Theresa May, former Prime Minister of UK]
[Jean-Claude Juncker, EU President]
[Donald Tusk, President of Council of Europe]
['Kofi Annan, former Head of UN]
[Rabbi Reuben Silverman, Manchester Reform Synagogue]
[Irfan Muhammad Chishti, Chief Imam Manchester Central Mosque]
[Ragbir Singh, Sri Guru Gobind Singh Gurdwara]
[Shastri Krishnan Joshi, Pujari Radha Krishna Mandir Temple]
[Lucy Powell MP, Manchester Central]
[Phil Neville, former Man Utd & England footballer]
[John Bercow, former Speaker of House of Commons]
[Jeremy Corbyn, former Leader of Labour Party]
[Salman Abedi, terrorist responsible for Manchester Arena attack]
[Nawal El-Sadaawi, Egyptian feminist writer]
[Crowds at Ariana Grande concert]
[Stewards at Ariana Grande concert]
[Emergency Services at Ariana Grande concert]
[Eamon Holmes, presenter of ITV's This Morning]
[Ruth Langford, ditto]
[Natasha Seth, soloist with Parrs Wood School Harmony Group]

[Crowds at One Love Concert]
[Security Guards at One Love Concert]
[Justin Bieber, pop star]
[Katy Perry, pop star]
[Miley Cyrus, pop star]
[The Black-Eyed Peas, US rappers]
[Marcus Muford, vocalist with Mumford & Sons]
[Imogen Heap, singer-songwriter]
[Little Mix, female R&B singers]
[Coldplay, indie rock group]
[Stevie Wonder, musician]
[Paul McCartney, musician]
[Bono, vocalist with U2 & political campaigner]
[David Beckham, former Man Utd & England footballer]
[Members of Man City & Man Utd football teams 2017]
[Gary Barlow, singer & composer]
[Take That, Manchester boy band]
[Robbie Williams, pop star]
[Sir Richard Leese, Leader of City Council 2017]
[Rafe, a dog]
[Annemarie Plas, Dutch yoga teacher, originator of Clap for Carers]
[Victoria Beckham, fashion designer]
[Clive's neighbours in Park Range]
[Grayson Perry, artist]
[Nathan Whyburn, photographer]
[Leanne, Florence's niece]
[Richard Cobden, Corn Law Reformer]
[Charles Hallé, founder of orchestra]
[Ford Madox Brown, pre-Raphaelite artist]
[Richard & Emmeline Pankhurst, campaigners for Women's Suffrage]
[Nicky Barton, Phil's wife]
[Max Bishop, Elaine's son]
[Katrina Spooner, Harry's wife]
[Arthur Lewis, Noble Laureate in Economics]
[Henry Price, Manchester first City Architect]
[Trustees of Hirstwood]
[Park Range Residents appearing in The World on our Doorstep:
(children in brackets)
    Judith & Ron, retired teachers
    Rashid & Robena, restaurant owners
    Farah & Abdul, taxi driver & housewife (Sara, Irfan, Saba)

Claire & Andrew, social workers (Jennie)
Sabine & Graham, charity workers (Zara, Clarissa)
Elaine, retired infant teacher (Max)
Renata & Leo, linguist & rector
Tamanyee, Setor, Dave, Ovi, students
Afzal & Rowshanara, insurance broker & housewife (Mumeenul, Bulbis, Jasmin, Mueedul, Arefa)
Dezi & Abigail, musician & physiotherapist (Arthur, a dog)
Ralf & Lida, systems manager & maths lecturer (Sacha, Gina)
Halimo, NHS translator
Walaati & Gurpurshad, car salesman & housewife
Ananda & Mehmood, Media Studies Lecturer & Professor of Creative Writing, Beirut
Phil & Helena, artists & wandering scholars (Ollie, a cat)
Harry & Katrina, trade unionist & nursery teacher (retired)
Elisabet & Abassi, data analyst & local radio presenter (Haroon, Sara)
Austin & Michaela, social anthropologists
Cécile & Rob, teacher & accountant (Ella, Maggie)
Amanda & Laura, lab technicians]
[Builders at Tulip House]
[Meera's children]
[Mr Lao, acupuncturist]
[Ariadne, daughter of King Minos of Crete]
[Vivienne, osteopath]
[Surayya, chiropractor]
[Shawne, reflexologist]
[Clients at Tulip House]
[Jack Kerouak, writer]
[Yasmin's Year 8 pupils]
[Waiter, Folk Bar Café]
[Dr John Milson Rhodes, Poor Law Reformer, Friend to Humanity]
[Robert Jenrick, Secretary of State for Housing, Community & Local Government 2020]
[Yemi Bolatiwa, Manchester singer]
[People clapping across Manchester]
[Apichu's parents, Medalla Milagrosa, Lima]
[Peruvians trekking to the Andes during Covid]
[Peruvian Police]
[4 Peruvian Presidents in a single year]
[Kim Collins, athlete from St Kitts & Nevis]

[Performers of Mongoose Play]
[James Brindley, engineer of Bridgewater Canal]
[Duke of Bridgewater]
[Alan Turing, early computer pioneer]
[Prospero, character in The Tempest]
[John Constable, painter]
[Lord Byron, poet]
[Humphrey Chetham, founder of Chetham's School, Manchester]
[Welders in Mayfield at night]
[PA Announcer, Albert Square]
[Graham Nash's Band]
[Crowds for Molly's installation]
[Edwin Stone, handloom weaver who first made the piece of cloth]
[4 Technicians on roof of Central Library]
[Queen Mary of Tek]
[Audience at The Band on the Wall]
[MC at The Band on the Wall]
[The Beautiful South, Manchester pop group]
[Roman soldier in Galicia]
[Roman troops under Dru's command]
[Camp Commander, Redstones Fort, Mamucium]
[Celtic tribes in confluence of three rivers]
[Cartimandua, local Brigantes 'Witch Queen']
[Priya, Khav's older sister]
[Duleep, Priya's husband]
[Dilsher, Priya & Duleep's son]
[Rukmini, Dilsher's sister]
[Geetha, Priya & Khav's mother]
[Pertinax, Roman Governor of Britannia]

Acknowledgements
(for *Ornaments of Grace* as a whole)

Writing is usually considered to be a solitary practice, but I have always found the act of creativity to be a collaborative one, and that has again been true for me in putting together the sequence of novels which comprise *Ornaments of Grace*. I have been fortunate to have been supported by so many people along the way, and I would like to take this opportunity of thanking them all, with apologies for any I may have unwittingly omitted.

First of all I would like to thank Ian Hopkinson, Larysa Bolton, Tony Lees and other staff members of Manchester's Central Reference Library, who could not have been more helpful and encouraging. That is where the original spark for the novels was lit and it has been such a treasure trove of fascinating information ever since. I would especially like to thank Jenny Marsden and Jane Parry, the Archives and Neighbourhood Engagement & Delivery Officers respectively for the Local History Dept of Manchester Library Services – Jenny for introducing me to the inspiring *Stories of a Manchester Street* project coordinated by Phil Barton and Elaine Bishop of the Park Range Residents Association, and Jane for her support in enabling me to use individual reproductions of the remarkable Manchester Murals by Ford Madox Brown, which can be viewed in the Great Hall of Manchester Town Hall. They are exceptional images and I recommend you going to see them if you are ever in the vicinity. I would also like to thank the staff of other libraries and museums in Manchester, namely the John Rylands Library, Manchester University Library, the Manchester Museum, the People's History Museum and also Salford's Working Class Movement Library, where Lynette Cawthra was especially helpful, as was Aude Nguyen Duc at The Manchester Literary & Philosophical Society, the much-loved Lit & Phil, the first and oldest such society anywhere in the world, 238 years young and still going strong.

In addition to these wonderful institutions, I have many individuals to thank also. Barbara Derbyshire from the Moravian Settlement in Fairfield has been particularly patient and generous with her time in telling me so much of the community's inspiring history. No less inspiring has been Lauren Murphy, founder of the Bradford Pit Project, which is a most moving collection of anecdotes, memories, reminiscences, artefacts and original art works dedicated to the lives of people connected with Bradford Colliery. You can find out more about their work at: www.bradfordpit.com. Martin Gittins freely shared some of his encyclopaedic knowledge of the part the River Irwell has played in Manchester's story, for which I have been especially grateful.

I should also like to thank John and Anne Horne for insights into historical medical practice; their daughter, Ella, for inducting me into the mysteries of chemical titration, which, if I have subsequently got it wrong, is my fault not hers; Tony Smith for his deep first hand understanding of spinning and weaving; Sarah Lawrie for her in-depth and enthusiastic knowledge of the Manchester music scene of the 1980s, which happened just after I left the city so I missed it; Sylvia Tiffin for her previous research into Manchester's lost theatres; the sonic artists Kathy Hinde and Matthew 'I-am-the-Mighty-Jungulator' Olden for their skills, expertise and generosity in helping me to envision aspects of Molly's final installation, and Brian Hesketh for his specialist knowledge in a range of such diverse topics as hot air balloons, how to make a crystal radio set, old maps, the intricacies of a police constable's notebook and preparing reports for a coroner's inquest.

Throughout this intensive period of writing and research, I have been greatly buoyed up by the keen support and interest of many friends, most notably Theresa Beattie, Laïla Diallo, Chris Dumigan, Viv Gordon, Phil King, Rowena Price, Gavin Stride, Chris Waters, and Irene Willis. Thank you to you all. In addition, Sue & Rob Yockney have been extraordinarily helpful in more ways than I can mention. Their advice on so many matters, both artistic and practical, has been beyond measure.

A number of individuals have very kindly – and bravely – offered to read early drafts of the novels: Rachel Burn, Lucy Cash, Chris & Julie Phillips. Their responses have been positive, constructive, illuminating and encouraging, particularly when highlighting those passages which needed closer attention from me, which I have tried my best to address. Thank you.

There are many references to particular songs, occurring throughout the twelve books. These are all available to listen to on various platforms, as are the jazz and classical pieces also mentioned. Two songs, however, have been written specifically for *Ornaments of Grace*. The first, *The Song of Weights & Measures*, with music by Chris Dumigan, appears in both Books 4 and 12, while the second, *Marks on the Land*, with music by Phil King, features in Book 12. This latter is available to listen to by going to: vimeo.com/165425043. I am extremely grateful for both Chris's and Phil's contributions.

I would also like to pay a special tribute to my friend Andrew Pastor, who has endured months and months of fortnightly coffee sessions during which he has listened so keenly and with such forbearance to the various difficulties I may have been experiencing at the time. He invariably came up with the perfect comment or idea, which then enabled me to see more clearly a way out of whatever tangle I happened to have found myself in. He also suggested several avenues of further research I might undertake to navigate towards the next bend in one of the three rivers, all of which have been just what were needed. These books could not have finally seen the light of day without his irreplaceable input.

Finally I would like to thank my wife, Amanda, for her endless patience, encouragement and love. These books are dedicated to her and to our son, Tim.

Biography

Chris grew up in Manchester and currently lives in West Dorset, after brief periods in Nottinghamshire, Devon and Brighton. Over the years he has managed to reinvent himself several times – from florist's delivery van driver to Punch & Judy man, drama teacher, theatre director, community arts co-ordinator, creative producer, to his recent role as writer and dramaturg for choreographers and dance companies.

Between 2003 and 2009 Chris was Director of Dance and Theatre for *Take Art*, the arts development agency for Somerset, and between 2009 and 2013 he enjoyed two stints as Creative Producer with South East Dance leading on their Associate Artists programme, followed by a year similarly supporting South Asian dance artists for *Akademi* in London. From 2011 to 2017 he was Creative Producer for the Bonnie Bird Choreography Fund.

Chris has worked for many years as a writer and theatre director, most notably with New Perspectives in Nottinghamshire and Farnham Maltings in Surrey under the artistic direction of Gavin Stride, with whom Chris has been a frequent collaborator.

Directing credits include: three Community Plays for the Colway Theatre Trust – *The Western Women* (co-director with Ann Jellicoe), *Crackling Angels* (co-director with Jon Oram), and *The King's Shilling*; for New Perspectives – *It's A Wonderful Life* (co-director with Gavin Stride), *The Railway Children* (both adapted by Mary Elliott Nelson); for Farnham Maltings – *The Titfield Thunderbolt, Miracle on 34th Street* and *How To Build A Rocket* (all co-directed with Gavin Stride); for Oxfordshire Touring Theatre Company – *Bowled A Googly* by Kevin Dyer; for Flax 303 – *The Rain Has Voices* by Shiona Morton, and for Strike A Light – *I Am Joan* and *Prescribed*, both written by Viv Gordon and co-directed with Tom Roden, and *The Book of Jo* as dramaturg.

Theatre writing credits include: *Firestarter, Trying To Get Back Home, Heroes* – a trilogy of plays for young people in partnership with Nottinghamshire & Northamptonshire Fire Services; *You Are Harry Kipper & I Claim My Five Pounds, It's Not Just The Jewels, Bogus* and *One of Us* (the last co-written with Gavin Stride) all for New Perspectives; *The Birdman* for Blunderbus; for Farnham Maltings *How To Build A Rocket* (as assistant to Gavin Stride), and *Time to Remember* (an outdoor commemoration of the centenary of the first ever Two Minutes Silence); *When King Gogo Met The Chameleon* and *Africarmen* for Tavaziva Dance, and most recently *All the Ghosts Walk with Us* (conceived and performed with Laïla Diallo and Phil King) for ICIA, Bath University and Bristol Old Vic Ferment Festival, (2016-17); *Posting to Iraq* (performed by Sarah Lawrie with music by Tom Johnson for the inaugural Women & War Festival in London 2016), and *Tree House* (with music by Sarah Moody, which toured southern England in autumn 2016). In 2018 Chris was commissioned to write the text for *In Our Time*, a film to celebrate the 40th Anniversary of the opening of The Brewhouse Theatre in Taunton, Somerset.

Between 2016 and 2019 Chris collaborated with fellow poet Chris Waters and jazz saxophonist Rob Yockney to develop two touring programmes of poetry, music, photography and film: *Home Movies* and *Que Pasa?* In 2020 Chris was invited by Wassail Theatre Company to be part of a collaborative project with 6 other writers to create the play *The Time of Our Lives* in response to Covid 19 as part of the *Alternative Endings* project.

Chris regularly works with choreographers and dance

artists, offering dramaturgical support, creative and business advice. These have included among others: Alex Whitley, All Play, Ankur Bahl, Antonia Grove, Anusha Subramanyam, Archana Ballal, Ballet Boyz, Ben Duke, Ben Wright, Charlie Morrissey, Crystal Zillwood, Darkin Ensemble, Divya Kasturi, Dog Kennel Hill, f.a.b. the detonators, Fionn Barr Factory, Heather Walrond, Hetain Patel, Influx, Jane Mason, Joan Clevillé, Kali Chandrasegaram, Kamala Devam, Karla Shacklock, Khavita Kaur, Krishna Zivraj-Nair, Laïla Diallo, Lîla Dance, Lisa May Thomas, Liz Lea, Lost Dog, Lucy Cash, Luke Brown, Marisa Zanotti, Mark Bruce, Mean Feet Dance, Nicola Conibère, Niki McCretton, Nilima Devi, Pretty Good Girl, Probe, Rachael Mossom, Richard Chappell, Rosemary Lee, Sadhana Dance, Seeta Patel, Shane Shambhu, Shobana Jeyasingh, Showmi Das, State of Emergency, Stop Gap, Subathra Subramaniam, Tavaziva Dance, Tom Sapsford, Theo Clinkard, Urja Desai Thakore, Vidya Thirunarayan, Viv Gordon, Yael Flexer, Yorke Dance Project (including the Cohan Collective) and Zoielogic.

Chris is married to Amanda Fogg, a former dance practitioner working principally with people with Parkinson's.

Ornaments of Grace: Previous Titles

- Pomona
- Enclave
- Nymphs & Shepherds
- The Spindle Tree
- Return
- Kettle
- Victor
- A Grain of Mustard Seed
- The Waxing of a Great Tree
- All the Fowls of the Air
- The Principal Thing

All Cover Designs by Kama Glover

Printed in Great Britain
by Amazon